MW00777422

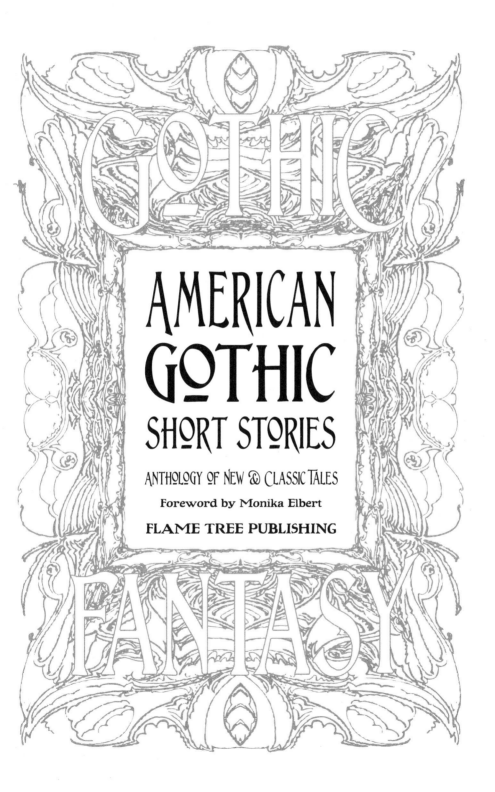

AMERICAN GOTHIC
SHORT STORIES

ANTHOLOGY OF NEW & CLASSIC TALES

Foreword by Monika Elbert

FLAME TREE PUBLISHING

This is a FLAME TREE Book

Publisher & Creative Director: Nick Wells
Project Editor: Gillian Whitaker
Editorial Board: Josie Mitchell, Taylor Bentley, Catherine Taylor

Publisher's Note: Due to the historical nature of the classic text, we're aware that there may be some language used which has the potential to cause offence to the modern reader. However, wishing overall to preserve the integrity of the text, rather than imposing contemporary sensibilities, we have left it unaltered.

FLAME TREE PUBLISHING
6 Melbray Mews, Fulham,
London SW6 3NS, United Kingdom
www.flametreepublishing.com

First published 2019

19 21 23 22 20
1 3 5 7 9 10 8 6 4 2

ISBN: 978-1-78755-295-1

The cover image is created by Flame Tree Studio based on artwork by Slava Gerj and Gabor Ruszkai.

A copy of the CIP data for this book is available from the British Library.

Printed and bound in China

See our new fiction imprint
FLAME TREE PRESS | FICTION WITHOUT FRONTIERS
New and original writing in Horror, Crime, SF and Fantasy
flametreepress.com

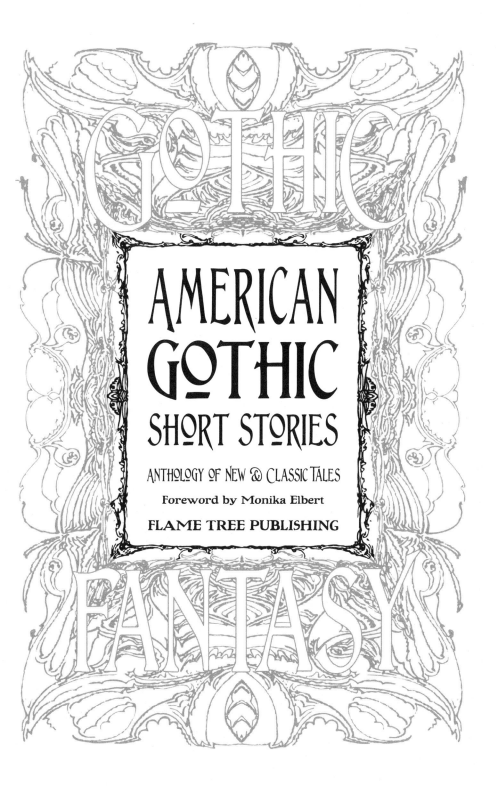

GOTHIC

AMERICAN GOTHIC

SHORT STORIES

ANTHOLOGY OF NEW & CLASSIC TALES

Foreword by Monika Elbert

FLAME TREE PUBLISHING

FANTASY

Contents

Foreword: American Gothic Short Stories

CAN THERE BE a haunting without having a sufficient history, or an appreciation of a national past? Can one simply accept the past of the British (or other immigrant) ancestors? Can America, with its mobility and rootlessness, have its own version of Gothic? Poe, arguably the most famous American Gothic writer, is known for his declaration, 'I maintain that terror is not of Germany, but of the soul', in an effort to dispel the influence of German Gothic writers. His comment is somewhat disingenuous as he tries to distance himself from any connection to his predecessors. Gothic terror is very much of the Americas. The sense of an evil past began the moment Puritans stepped on American ground and began proselytizing and colonizing. Puritan leader John Winthrop would promulgate the idea of American exceptionalism with his arrogant vision of the Puritan settlement as a 'city on the hill', a sense of entitlement that ultimately promoted an intolerance of outsiders and a perverse sense of self-righteousness. Such ideas would haunt Hawthorne in his Gothic stories and his New England romances, with their re-enactment of or reference to the Salem Witch Trials of 1692.

The 'sins of the fathers' motif that is the mainstay of English Gothic, as revealed in the Ur-gothic novel *The Castle of Otranto* (1764), by Horace Walpole, is transmuted from British to American soil; whereas the British Gothic focused on the abuse of power by a privileged feudal aristocracy, American Gothic evolved from fears of the unknown territory as well as of class distinctions based on religion or wealth. In Irving's 'The Devil and Tom Walker', the greed of the colonial and pioneering American stealing land from the Native American and then wresting power from the local poor farmer is highlighted in Tom Walker's pact with the devil. Nathaniel Hawthorne's 'The Minister's Black Veil' introduces us to a Puritan divine who cannot hide his sin any longer and hides behind the black veil, the allegorical message to his townspeople being that they all suffer from the effects of original sin. Hawthorne would analyze another type of hubris in 'The Birthmark', in which the scientist figure, Aylmer, competes with nature in an effort to improve upon his already perfect wife. The Gothic genre embodies the human impulse to oppress and subdue, as there is a constant battle between the empowered and disempowered.

Within the Gothic cadre, there is a misogynistic obsession on the male's part with the perfect wife or mate. In Poe's 'Berenice', the narrator finds himself obsessed with his wife's teeth and hangs onto them fetishistically after her death. Charlotte Perkins Gilman would use the marital Gothic to attack the domineering physician husband in 'The Yellow Wallpaper' and the scientific establishment that would condone the rest cure (promoted by S. Weir Mitchell). 'The Little Room' by Madeline Yale Wynne shows the loss of creativity and enthusiasm when women are denied a room of their own after marriage. Freeman's 'Luella Miller' shows the upshot of a woman who has been babied all her life and who consumes friends, husband, and relatives with her neediness. Edith Wharton's 'Kerfol' examines how legally and psychologically women are locked into the turret of their oppressive husbands' domicile. The Gothic theme of marital imprisonment sometimes converges with the idea of racial intolerance or fears of 'the other'. In Kate Chopin's 'Désirée's Baby', a Creole wife forfeits her marriage and the welfare of her child in order to placate her husband who accuses her of being black; the irony of the ending is horrifying.

Southern or Civil War Gothic shows the lasting ill effects of the plantation system as well as the horrors of war and its aftermath – the Gothic idea of home and homelessness emerges most emphatically. American Gothic writers like Bierce, Stowe, Chesnutt, and Cable all focus on the displacement of the African American and the Gothic horrors associated with the institution of slavery. Flannery O'Connor and William Faulkner are Southern Gothic writers for whom the blight of the Southern past could not be obliterated. A mixed Gothic story, like the Northern writer Crane's 'The Monster', would transport Southern racism to the North, so that the black protagonist in the story is monstrously different even before the accident that disfigured him.

The nineteenth-century American Gothic became ever more tied to the dehumanization associated with industrialization and commercialism in such urban Gothic stories as Melville's 'Bartleby the Scrivener' (1853), in which Bartleby becomes increasingly more cadaver-like from the stress of working on Wall Street. Other authors, like Jewett, Bierce, Lovecraft, Cram, and Jackson would focus on the other curse of capitalistic Gothic – the increasing alienation from Nature and the destruction of the ecosystem. But all these Gothic writers offer a cautionary tale to humanity and the promise of redemption if we focus on rationality over irrationality, brotherhood over isolation, and generosity over greed. Gothic, seemingly a literature of oppression, repression, and depression, can ultimately liberate us from the morass of self.

Monika Elbert

Publisher's Note

AMERICAN GOTHIC literature is difficult to define, yet its identity is guided by many of the concerns of the society for which it's written. Its stories engage with that curious combination of fascination and repulsion, toying with the tantalizing nature of the obscure and the uncanny emergence of the hidden. We've attempted to bring together its many strands in this collection, with atmospheric stories exploring everything from the female gothic to frontier fiction and the wild swamplands of the deep South. Here you'll find familiar ground from the European Gothic transformed for new territory: expect a fair share of monsters and monstrous behavior, whether bred from complex society attitudes or mad science experiments. And that's not to mention unquiet graves, mysterious characters, gothic marriages, fearful desires, speculating neighbors, cursed bloodlines and an abundance of decaying mansions and family estates…

Alongside classic authors that helped shape the genre we're pleased to publish talented modern writers whose stories give contemporary voicing to the themes of the older works. For example, the unraveling of the rational mind seen in Edgar Allan Poe and Charlotte Perkins Gilman sees its parallels in modern day, as does the strong Southern setting of Flannery O'Connor's works. We've tried to include a real mix of tales, from Clark Ashton Smith's 'The Devotee of Evil', which details a character's obsessive desire to understand and manifest 'absolute evil', to Shirley Jackson's 'My Uncle in the Garden' and an early piece of Lovecraftian cosmic horror by Ramsey Campbell. We hope this results in an absorbing collection in which just the slightest ripple of uncertainty can be felt as the American Gothic – in equal parts intriguing and terrifying – uncoils its tendrils.

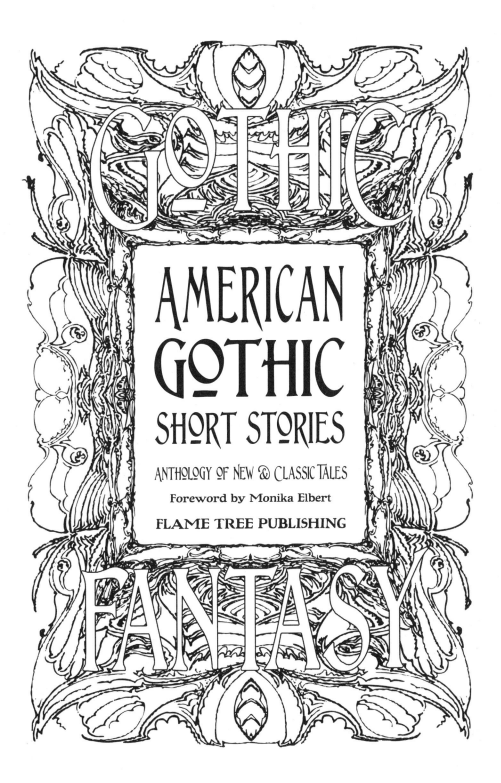

GOTHIC

AMERICAN GOTHIC

SHORT STORIES

ANTHOLOGY OF NEW & CLASSIC TALES

Foreword by Monika Elbert

FLAME TREE PUBLISHING

FANTASY

The Bell in the Fog

Gertrude Atherton

Chapter I

THE GREAT AUTHOR had realized one of the dreams of his ambitious youth, the possession of an ancestral hall in England. It was not so much the good American's reverence for ancestors that inspired the longing to consort with the ghosts of an ancient line, as artistic appreciation of the mellowness, the dignity, the aristocratic aloofness of walls that have sheltered, and furniture that has embraced, generations and generations of the dead. To mere wealth, only his astute and incomparably modern brain yielded respect; his ego raised its goose-flesh at the sight of rooms furnished with a single check, conciliatory as the taste might be. The dumping of the old interiors of Europe into the glistening shells of the United States not only roused him almost to passionate protest, but offended his patriotism – which he classified among his unworked ideals. The average American was not an artist, therefore he had no excuse for even the affectation of cosmopolitanism. Heaven knew he was national enough in everything else, from his accent to his lack of repose; let his surroundings be in keeping.

Orth had left the United States soon after his first successes, and, his art being too great to be confounded with locality, he had long since ceased to be spoken of as an American author. All civilized Europe furnished stages for his puppets, and, if never picturesque nor impassioned, his originality was as overwhelming as his style. His subtleties might not always be understood – indeed, as a rule, they were not – but the musical mystery of his language and the penetrating charm of his lofty and cultivated mind induced raptures in the initiated, forever denied to those who failed to appreciate him.

His following was not a large one, but it was very distinguished. The aristocracies of the earth gave to it; and not to understand and admire Ralph Orth was deliberately to relegate one's self to the ranks. But the elect are few, and they frequently subscribe to the circulating libraries; on the Continent, they buy the Tauchnitz edition; and had not Mr. Orth inherited a sufficiency of ancestral dollars to enable him to keep rooms in Jermyn Street, and the wardrobe of an Englishman of leisure, he might have been forced to consider the tastes of the middle-class at a desk in Hampstead. But, as it mercifully was, the fashionable and exclusive sets of London knew and sought him. He was too wary to become a fad, and too sophisticated to grate or bore; consequently, his popularity continued evenly from year to year, and long since he had come to be regarded as one of them. He was not keenly addicted to sport, but he could handle a gun, and all men respected his dignity and breeding. They cared less for his books than women did, perhaps because patience is not a characteristic of their sex. I am alluding, however, in this instance, to men-of-the-world. A group of young literary men – and one or two women – put him on a pedestal and kissed the earth before it. Naturally, they imitated him, and as this flattered him, and he had a kindly heart deep among the cere-cloths of his formalities, he sooner or later wrote 'appreciations' of them all, which nobody living could understand, but which owing to the subtitle and signature answered every purpose.

With all this, however, he was not utterly content. From the twelfth of August until late in the winter – when he did not go to Homburg and the Riviera – he visited the best houses in England, slept in state chambers, and meditated in historic parks; but the country was his one passion, and he longed for his own acres.

He was turning fifty when his great-aunt died and made him her heir: 'as a poor reward for his immortal services to literature', read the will of this phenomenally appreciative relative. The estate was a large one. There was a rush for his books; new editions were announced. He smiled with cynicism, not unmixed with sadness; but he was very grateful for the money, and as soon as his fastidious taste would permit he bought him a country-seat.

The place gratified all his ideals and dreams – for he had romanced about his sometime English possession as he had never dreamed of woman. It had once been the property of the Church, and the ruin of cloister and chapel above the ancient wood was sharp against the low pale sky. Even the house itself was Tudor, but wealth from generation to generation had kept it in repair; and the lawns were as velvety, the hedges as rigid, the trees as aged as any in his own works. It was not a castle nor a great property, but it was quite perfect; and for a long while he felt like a bridegroom on a succession of honeymoons. He often laid his hand against the rough ivied walls in a lingering caress.

After a time, he returned the hospitalities of his friends, and his invitations, given with the exclusiveness of his great distinction, were never refused. Americans visiting England eagerly sought for letters to him; and if they were sometimes benumbed by that cold and formal presence, and awed by the silences of Chillingsworth – the few who entered there – they thrilled in anticipation of verbal triumphs, and forthwith bought an entire set of his books. It was characteristic that they dared not ask him for his autograph.

Although women invariably described him as 'brilliant', a few men affirmed that he was gentle and lovable, and any one of them was well content to spend weeks at Chillingsworth with no other companion. But, on the whole, he was rather a lonely man.

It occurred to him how lonely he was one gay June morning when the sunlight was streaming through his narrow windows, illuminating tapestries and armor, the family portraits of the young profligate from whom he had made this splendid purchase, dusting its gold on the black wood of wainscot and floor. He was in the gallery at the moment, studying one of his two favorite portraits, a gallant little lad in the green costume of Robin Hood. The boy's expression was imperious and radiant, and he had that perfect beauty which in any disposition appealed so powerfully to the author. But as Orth stared today at the brilliant youth, of whose life he knew nothing, he suddenly became aware of a human stirring at the foundations of his aesthetic pleasure.

"I wish he were alive and here," he thought, with a sigh. "What a jolly little companion he would be! And this fine old mansion would make a far more complementary setting for him than for me."

He turned away abruptly, only to find himself face to face with the portrait of a little girl who was quite unlike the boy, yet so perfect in her own way, and so unmistakably painted by the same hand, that he had long since concluded they had been brother and sister. She was angelically fair, and, young as she was – she could not have been more than six years old – her dark-blue eyes had a beauty of mind which must have been remarkable twenty years later. Her pouting mouth was like a little scarlet serpent, her skin almost transparent, her pale hair fell waving – not curled with the orthodoxy of childhood – about her tender bare shoulders. She wore a long white frock, and clasped tightly against her breast a doll far more gorgeously arrayed than herself. Behind her were the ruins and the woods of Chillingsworth.

Orth had studied this portrait many times, for the sake of an art which he understood almost as well as his own; but today he saw only the lovely child. He forgot even the boy in the intensity of this new and personal absorption.

"Did she live to grow up, I wonder?" he thought. "She should have made a remarkable, even a famous woman, with those eyes and that brow, but – could the spirit within that ethereal frame stand the enlightenments of maturity? Would not that mind – purged, perhaps, in a long probation from the dross of other existences – flee in disgust from the commonplace problems of a woman's life? Such perfect beings should die while they are still perfect. Still, it is possible that this little girl, whoever she was, was idealized by the artist, who painted into her his own dream of exquisite childhood."

Again he turned away impatiently. "I believe I am rather fond of children," he admitted. "I catch myself watching them on the street when they are pretty enough. Well, who does not like them?" he added, with some defiance.

He went back to his work; he was chiselling a story which was to be the foremost excuse of a magazine as yet unborn. At the end of half an hour he threw down his wondrous instrument – which looked not unlike an ordinary pen – and making no attempt to disobey the desire that possessed him, went back to the gallery. The dark splendid boy, the angelic little girl were all he saw – even of the several children in that roll-call of the past – and they seemed to look straight down his eyes into depths where the fragmentary ghosts of unrecorded ancestors gave faint musical response.

"The dead's kindly recognition of the dead," he thought. "But I wish these children were alive."

For a week he haunted the gallery, and the children haunted him. Then he became impatient and angry. "I am mooning like a barren woman," he exclaimed. "I must take the briefest way of getting those youngsters off my mind."

With the help of his secretary, he ransacked the library, and finally brought to light the gallery catalogue which had been named in the inventory. He discovered that his children were the Viscount Tancred and the Lady Blanche Mortlake, son and daughter of the second Earl of Teignmouth. Little wiser than before, he sat down at once and wrote to the present earl, asking for some account of the lives of the children. He awaited the answer with more restlessness than he usually permitted himself, and took long walks, ostentatiously avoiding the gallery.

"I believe those youngsters have obsessed me," he thought, more than once. "They certainly are beautiful enough, and the last time I looked at them in that waning light they were fairly alive. Would that they were, and scampering about this park."

Lord Teignmouth, who was intensely grateful to him, answered promptly.

"I am afraid," he wrote, "that I don't know much about my ancestors – those who didn't do something or other; but I have a vague remembrance of having been told by an aunt of mine, who lives on the family traditions – she isn't married – that the little chap was drowned in the river, and that the little girl died too – I mean when she was a little girl – wasted away, or something – I'm such a beastly idiot about expressing myself, that I wouldn't dare to write to you at all if you weren't really great. That is actually all I can tell you, and I am afraid the painter was their only biographer."

The author was gratified that the girl had died young, but grieved for the boy. Although he had avoided the gallery of late, his practiced imagination had evoked from the throngs of history the high-handed and brilliant, surely adventurous career of the third Earl of Teignmouth. He had pondered upon the deep delights of directing such a mind and character, and had caught himself envying the dust that was older still. When he read of the lad's early death, in spite of his regret that such promise should have come to naught, he admitted to a secret thrill of satisfaction that the boy had so soon ceased to belong to anyone. Then he smiled with both sadness and humor.

"What an old fool I am!" he admitted. "I believe I not only wish those children were alive, but that they were my own."

The frank admission proved fatal. He made straight for the gallery. The boy, after the interval of separation, seemed more spiritedly alive than ever, the little girl to suggest, with her faint appealing smile, that she would like to be taken up and cuddled.

"I must try another way," he thought, desperately, after that long communion. "I must write them out of me."

He went back to the library and locked up the *tour de force* which had ceased to command his classic faculty. At once, he began to write the story of the brief lives of the children, much to the amazement of that faculty, which was little accustomed to the simplicities. Nevertheless, before he had written three chapters, he knew that he was at work upon a masterpiece – and more: he was experiencing a pleasure so keen that once and again his hand trembled, and he saw the page through a mist. Although his characters had always been objective to himself and his more patient readers, none knew better than he – a man of no delusions – that they were so remote and exclusive as barely to escape being mere mentalities; they were never the pulsing living creations of the more full-blooded genius. But he had been content to have it so. His creations might find and leave him cold, but he had known his highest satisfaction in chiselling the statuettes, extracting subtle and elevating harmonies, while combining words as no man of his tongue had combined them before.

But the children were not statuettes. He had loved and brooded over them long ere he had thought to tuck them into his pen, and on its first stroke they danced out alive. The old mansion echoed with their laughter, with their delightful and original pranks. Mr. Orth knew nothing of children, therefore all the pranks he invented were as original as his faculty. The little girl clung to his hand or knee as they both followed the adventurous course of their common idol, the boy. When Orth realized how alive they were, he opened each room of his home to them in turn, that evermore he might have sacred and poignant memories with all parts of the stately mansion where he must dwell alone to the end. He selected their bedrooms, and hovered over them – not through infantile disorders, which were beyond even his imagination – but through those painful intervals incident upon the enterprising spirit of the boy and the devoted obedience of the girl to fraternal command. He ignored the second Lord Teignmouth; he was himself their father, and he admired himself extravagantly for the first time; art had chastened him long since. Oddly enough, the children had no mother, not even the memory of one.

He wrote the book more slowly than was his wont, and spent delightful hours pondering upon the chapter of the morrow. He looked forward to the conclusion with a sort of terror, and made up his mind that when the inevitable last word was written he should start at once for Homburg. Incalculable times a day he went to the gallery, for he no longer had any desire to write the children out of his mind, and his eyes hungered for them. They were his now. It was with an effort that he sometimes humorously reminded himself that another man had fathered them, and that their little skeletons were under the choir of the chapel. Not even for peace of mind would he have descended into the vaults of the lords of Chillingsworth and looked upon the marble effigies of his children. Nevertheless, when in a superhumorous mood, he dwelt upon his high satisfaction in having been enabled by his great-aunt to purchase all that was left of them.

For two months he lived in his fool's paradise, and then he knew that the book must end. He nerved himself to nurse the little girl through her wasting illness, and when he clasped her hands, his own shook, his knees trembled. Desolation settled upon the house, and he wished he had left one corner of it to which he could retreat unhaunted by the child's presence. He took long tramps, avoiding the river with a sensation next to panic. It was two days before he got back to his table, and then he had made up his mind to let the boy live. To kill him off, too, was more than his augmented stock of human nature could endure. After all, the lad's death had been purely accidental, wanton. It was just that he should live – with one of the author's inimitable suggestions of future greatness; but, at the end, the parting was almost as bitter as the other. Orth knew then how men feel when their sons go forth to encounter the world and ask no more of the old companionship.

The author's boxes were packed. He sent the manuscript to his publisher an hour after it was finished – he could not have given it a final reading to have saved it from failure – directed his secretary to examine the proof under a microscope, and left the next morning for Homburg. There, in inmost circles, he forgot his children. He visited in several of the great houses of the Continent until November; then returned to London to find his book the literary topic of the day. His secretary handed him the reviews; and for once in a way he read the finalities of the nameless. He found himself hailed as a genius, and compared in astonished phrases to the prodigiously clever talent which the world for twenty years had isolated under the name of Ralph Orth. This pleased him, for every writer is human enough to wish to be hailed as a genius, and immediately. Many are, and many wait; it depends upon the fashion of the moment, and the needs and bias of those who write of writers. Orth had waited twenty years; but his past was bedecked with the headstones of geniuses long since forgotten. He was gratified to come thus publicly into his estate, but soon reminded himself that all the adulation of which a belated world was capable could not give him one thrill of the pleasure which the companionship of that book had given him, while creating. It was the keenest pleasure in his memory, and when a man is fifty and has written many books, that is saying a great deal.

He allowed what society was in town to lavish honors upon him for something over a month, then cancelled all his engagements and went down to Chillingsworth.

His estate was in Hertfordshire, that county of gentle hills and tangled lanes, of ancient oaks and wide wild heaths, of historic houses, and dark woods, and green fields innumerable – a Wordsworthian shire, steeped in the deepest peace of England. As Orth drove towards his own gates he had the typical English sunset to gaze upon, a red streak with a church spire against it. His woods were silent. In the fields, the cows stood as if conscious of their part. The ivy on his old gray towers had been young with his children.

He spent a haunted night, but the next day stranger happenings began.

Chapter II

HE ROSE EARLY, and went for one of his long walks. England seems to cry out to be walked upon, and Orth, like others of the transplanted, experienced to the full the country's gift of foot-restlessness and mental calm. Calm flees, however, when the ego is rampant, and today, as upon others too recent, Orth's soul was as restless as his feet. He had walked for two hours when he entered the wood of his neighbor's estate, a domain seldom honored by him, as it, too, had been bought by an American – a flighty hunting widow, who displeased the fastidious taste of the author. He heard children's voices, and turned with the quick prompting of retreat.

As he did so, he came face to face, on the narrow path, with a little girl. For the moment he was possessed by the most hideous sensation which can visit a man's being – abject terror. He believed that body and soul were disintegrating. The child before him was his child, the original of a portrait in which the artist, dead two centuries ago, had missed exact fidelity, after all. The difference, even his rolling vision took note, lay in the warm pure living whiteness and the deeper spiritual suggestion of the child in his path. Fortunately for his self-respect, the surrender lasted but a moment. The little girl spoke.

"You look real sick," she said. "Shall I lead you home?"

The voice was soft and sweet, but the intonation, the vernacular, were American, and not of the highest class. The shock was, if possible, more agonizing than the other, but this time Orth rose to the occasion.

"Who are you?" he demanded, with asperity. "What is your name? Where do you live?"

The child smiled, an angelic smile, although she was evidently amused. "I never had so many questions asked me all at once," she said. "But I don't mind, and I'm glad you're not sick. I'm Mrs. Jennie Root's little girl – my father's dead. My name is Blanche – you *are* sick! No? – and I live in Rome, New York State. We've come over here to visit Pa's relations."

Orth took the child's hand in his. It was very warm and soft.

"Take me to your mother," he said, firmly; "now, at once. You can return and play afterwards. And as I wouldn't have you disappointed for the world, I'll send to town today for a beautiful doll."

The little girl, whose face had fallen, flashed her delight, but walked with great dignity beside him. He groaned in his depths as he saw they were pointing for the widow's house, but made up his mind that he would know the history of the child and of all her ancestors, if he had to sit down at table with his obnoxious neighbor. To his surprise, however, the child did not lead him into the park, but towards one of the old stone houses of the tenantry.

"Pa's great-great-great-grandfather lived there," she remarked, with all the American's pride of ancestry. Orth did not smile, however. Only the warm clasp of the hand in his, the soft thrilling voice of his still mysterious companion, prevented him from feeling as if moving through the mazes of one of his own famous ghost stories.

The child ushered him into the dining room, where an old man was seated at the table reading his Bible. The room was at least eight hundred years old. The ceiling was supported by the trunk of a tree, black, and probably petrified. The windows had still their diamond panes, separated, no doubt, by the original lead. Beyond was a large kitchen in which were several women. The old man, who looked patriarchal enough to have laid the foundations of his dwelling, glanced up and regarded the visitor without hospitality. His expression softened as his eyes moved to the child.

"Who 'ave ye brought?" he asked. He removed his spectacles. "Ah!" He rose, and offered the author a chair. At the same moment, the women entered the room.

"Of course you've fallen in love with Blanche, sir," said one of them. "Everybody does."

"Yes, that is it. Quite so." Confusion still prevailing among his faculties, he clung to the naked truth. "This little girl has interested and startled me because she bears a precise resemblance to one of the portraits in Chillingsworth – painted about two hundred years ago. Such extraordinary likenesses do not occur without reason, as a rule, and, as I admired my portrait so deeply that I have written a story about it, you will not think it unnatural if I am more than curious to discover the reason for this resemblance. The little girl tells me that her ancestors lived in this very house, and as my little girl lived next door, so to speak, there undoubtedly is a natural reason for the resemblance."

His host closed the Bible, put his spectacles in his pocket, and hobbled out of the house.

"He'll never talk of family secrets," said an elderly woman, who introduced herself as the old man's daughter, and had placed bread and milk before the guest. "There are secrets in every family, and we have ours, but he'll never tell those old tales. All I can tell you is that an ancestor of little Blanche went to wreck and ruin because of some fine lady's doings, and killed himself. The story is that his boys turned out bad. One of them saw his crime, and never got over the shock; he was foolish like, after. The mother was a poor scared sort of creature, and hadn't much influence over the other boy. There seemed to be a blight on all the man's descendants, until one of them went to America. Since then, they haven't prospered, exactly, but they've done better, and they don't drink so heavy."

"They haven't done so well," remarked a worn patient-looking woman. Orth typed her as belonging to the small middle-class of an interior town of the eastern United States.

"You are not the child's mother?"

"Yes, sir. Everybody is surprised; you needn't apologize. She doesn't look like any of us, although her brothers and sisters are good enough for anybody to be proud of. But we all think she strayed in by mistake, for she looks like any lady's child, and, of course, we're only middle-class."

Orth gasped. It was the first time he had ever heard a native American use the term middle-class with a personal application. For the moment, he forgot the child. His analytical mind raked in the new specimen. He questioned, and learned that the woman's husband had kept a hat store in Rome, New York; that her boys were clerks, her girls in stores, or type-writing. They kept her and little Blanche – who had come after her other children were well grown – in comfort; and they were all very happy together. The boys broke out, occasionally; but, on the whole, were the best in the world, and her girls were worthy of far better than they had. All were robust, except Blanche. "She coming so late, when I was no longer young, makes her delicate," she remarked, with a slight blush, the signal of her chaste Americanism; "but I guess she'll get along all right. She couldn't have better care if she was a queen's child."

Orth, who had gratefully consumed the bread and milk, rose. "Is that really all you can tell me?" he asked.

"That's all," replied the daughter of the house. "And you couldn't pry open father's mouth."

Orth shook hands cordially with all of them, for he could be charming when he chose. He offered to escort the little girl back to her playmates in the wood, and she took prompt possession of his hand. As he was leaving, he turned suddenly to Mrs. Root. "Why did you call her Blanche?" he asked.

"She was so white and dainty, she just looked it."

Orth took the next train for London, and from Lord Teignmouth obtained the address of the aunt who lived on the family traditions, and a cordial note of introduction to her. He then spent an hour anticipating, in a toy shop, the whims and pleasures of a child – an incident of paternity which his book-children had not inspired. He bought the finest doll, piano, French dishes, cooking apparatus, and playhouse in the shop, and signed a check for thirty pounds with a sensation of positive rapture. Then he took the train for Lancashire, where the Lady Mildred Mortlake lived in another ancestral home.

Possibly there are few imaginative writers who have not a leaning, secret or avowed, to the occult. The creative gift is in very close relationship with the Great Force behind the universe; for aught we know, may be an atom thereof. It is not strange, therefore, that the lesser and closer of the unseen forces should send their vibrations to it occasionally; or, at all events, that the imagination should incline its ear to the most mysterious and picturesque of all beliefs. Orth frankly dallied with the old dogma. He formulated no personal faith of any sort, but his creative faculty, that ego within an ego, had made more than one excursion into the invisible and brought back literary treasure.

The Lady Mildred received with sweetness and warmth the generous contributor to the family sieve, and listened with fluttering interest to all he had not told the world – she had read the book – and to the strange, Americanized sequel.

"I am all at sea," concluded Orth. "What had my little girl to do with the tragedy? What relation was she to the lady who drove the young man to destruction—?"

"The closest," interrupted Lady Mildred. "She was herself!"

Orth stared at her. Again he had a confused sense of disintegration. Lady Mildred, gratified by the success of her bolt, proceeded less dramatically:

"Wally was up here just after I read your book, and I discovered he had given you the wrong history of the picture. Not that he knew it. It is a story we have left untold as often as possible, and I tell it to you only because you would probably become a monomaniac if I didn't. Blanche Mortlake – that Blanche – there had been several of her name, but there has not been one since – did not die in childhood, but lived to be twenty-four. She was an angelic child, but little angels sometimes grow up into very naughty girls. I believe she was delicate as a child, which probably gave her that spiritual look. Perhaps she was spoiled and flattered, until her poor little soul was stifled, which is likely. At all events, she was the coquette of her day – she seemed to care for nothing but breaking hearts; and she did not stop when she married, either. She hated her husband, and became reckless. She had no children. So far, the tale is not an uncommon one; but the worst, and what makes the ugliest stain in our annals, is to come.

"She was alone one summer at Chillingsworth – where she had taken temporary refuge from her husband – and she amused herself – some say, fell in love – with a young man of the yeomanry, a tenant of the next estate. His name was Root. He, so it comes down to us, was a magnificent specimen of his kind, and in those days the yeomanry gave us our great soldiers. His beauty of face was quite as remarkable as his physique; he led all the rural youth in sport, and was a bit above his class in every way. He had a wife in no way remarkable, and two little boys, but was always more with his friends than his family. Where he and Blanche Mortlake met I don't know – in the woods, probably, although it has been said that he had the run of the house. But, at all events, he was wild about her, and she pretended to be about him. Perhaps she was, for women have stooped before and since. Some women can be stormed by a fine man in any circumstances; but, although I am a woman of the world, and not easy to shock, there are some things I tolerate so hardly that it is all I can do to bring myself to believe in them; and stooping is one. Well, they were the scandal of the county for months, and then, either because she had tired of her new toy, or his grammar grated after the first glamor, or because she feared her husband, who was returning from the Continent, she broke off with him and returned to town. He followed her, and forced his way into her house. It is said she melted, but made him swear never to attempt to see her again. He returned to his home, and killed himself. A few months later she took her own life. That is all I know."

"It is quite enough for me," said Orth.

The next night, as his train travelled over the great wastes of Lancashire, a thousand chimneys were spouting forth columns of fire. Where the sky was not red it was black. The place looked like hell. Another time Orth's imagination would have gathered immediate inspiration from this wildest region of England. The fair and peaceful counties of the south had nothing to compare in infernal grandeur with these acres of flaming columns. The chimneys were invisible in the lower darkness of the night; the fires might have leaped straight from the angry cauldron of the earth.

But Orth was in a subjective world, searching for all he had ever heard of occultism. He recalled that the sinful dead are doomed, according to this belief, to linger for vast reaches of time in that borderland which is close to earth, eventually sent back to work out their final salvation; that they work it out among the descendants of the people they have wronged; that suicide is held by the devotees of occultism to be a cardinal sin, abhorred and execrated.

Authors are far closer to the truths enfolded in mystery than ordinary people, because of that very audacity of imagination which irritates their plodding critics. As only those who dare to make mistakes succeed greatly, only those who shake free the wings of their imagination brush, once in a way, the secrets of the great pale world. If such writers go wrong, it is not for the mere brains to tell them so.

Upon Orth's return to Chillingsworth, he called at once upon the child, and found her happy among his gifts. She put her arms about his neck, and covered his serene unlined face with soft kisses. This completed the conquest. Orth from that moment adored her as a child, irrespective of the psychological problem.

Gradually he managed to monopolize her. From long walks it was but a step to take her home for luncheon. The hours of her visits lengthened. He had a room fitted up as a nursery and filled with the wonders of toyland. He took her to London to see the pantomimes; two days before Christmas, to buy presents for her relatives; and together they strung them upon the most wonderful Christmas tree that the old hall of Chillingsworth had ever embraced. She had a donkey-cart, and a trained nurse, disguised as a maid, to wait upon her. Before a month had passed she was living in state at Chillingsworth and paying daily visits to her mother. Mrs. Root was deeply flattered, and apparently well content. Orth told her plainly that he should make the child independent, and educate her, meanwhile. Mrs. Root intended to spend six months in England, and Orth was in no hurry to alarm her by broaching his ultimate design.

He reformed Blanche's accent and vocabulary, and read to her out of books which would have addled the brains of most little maids of six; but she seemed to enjoy them, although she seldom made a comment. He was always ready to play games with her, but she was a gentle little thing, and, moreover, tired easily. She preferred to sit in the depths of a big chair, toasting her bare toes at the log-fire in the hall, while her friend read or talked to her. Although she was thoughtful, and, when left to herself, given to dreaming, his patient observation could detect nothing uncanny about her. Moreover, she had a quick sense of humor, she was easily amused, and could laugh as merrily as any child in the world. He was resigning all hope of further development on the shadowy side when one day he took her to the picture-gallery.

It was the first warm day of summer. The gallery was not heated, and he had not dared to take his frail visitor into its chilly spaces during the winter and spring. Although he had wished to see the effect of the picture on the child, he had shrunk from the bare possibility of the very developments the mental part of him craved; the other was warmed and satisfied for the first time, and held itself aloof from disturbance. But one day the sun streamed through the old windows, and, obeying a sudden impulse, he led Blanche to the gallery.

It was some time before he approached the child of his earlier love. Again he hesitated. He pointed out many other fine pictures, and Blanche smiled appreciatively at his remarks, that were wise in criticism and interesting in matter. He never knew just how much she understood, but the very fact that there were depths in the child beyond his probing riveted his chains.

Suddenly he wheeled about and waved his hand to her prototype. "What do you think of that?" he asked. "You remember, I told you of the likeness the day I met you."

She looked indifferently at the picture, but he noticed that her color changed oddly; its pure white tone gave place to an equally delicate gray.

"I have seen it before," she said. "I came in here one day to look at it. And I have been quite often since. You never forbade me," she added, looking at him appealingly, but dropping her eyes quickly. "And I like the little girl – and the boy – very much."

"Do you? Why?"

"I don't know" – a formula in which she had taken refuge before. Still her candid eyes were lowered; but she was quite calm. Orth, instead of questioning, merely fixed his eyes upon her, and waited. In a moment she stirred uneasily, but she did not laugh nervously, as another child would have done. He had never seen her self-possession ruffled, and he had begun to doubt he ever should. She was full of human warmth and affection. She seemed made for love, and every creature who came within her ken adored her, from the author himself down to the litter of puppies presented to her by the stable-boy a few weeks since; but her serenity would hardly be enhanced by death.

She raised her eyes finally, but not to his. She looked at the portrait.

"Did you know that there was another picture behind?" she asked.

"No," replied Orth, turning cold. "How did you know it?"

"One day I touched a spring in the frame, and this picture came forward. Shall I show you?"

"Yes!" And crossing curiosity and the involuntary shrinking from impending phenomena was a sensation of aesthetic disgust that *he* should be treated to a secret spring.

The little girl touched hers, and that other Blanche sprang aside so quickly that she might have been impelled by a sharp blow from behind. Orth narrowed his eyes and stared at what she revealed. He felt that his own Blanche was watching him, and set his features, although his breath was short.

There was the Lady Blanche Mortlake in the splendor of her young womanhood, beyond a doubt. Gone were all traces of her spiritual childhood, except, perhaps, in the shadows of the mouth; but more than fulfilled were the promises of her mind. Assuredly, the woman had been as brilliant and gifted as she had been restless and passionate. She wore her very pearls with arrogance, her very hands were tense with eager life, her whole being breathed mutiny.

Orth turned abruptly to Blanche, who had transferred her attention to the picture.

"What a tragedy is there!" he exclaimed, with a fierce attempt at lightness. "Think of a woman having all that pent up within her two centuries ago! And at the mercy of a stupid family, no doubt, and a still stupider husband. No wonder – today, a woman like that might not be a model for all the virtues, but she certainly would use her gifts and become famous, the while living her life too fully to have any place in it for yeomen and such, or even for the trivial business of breaking hearts." He put his finger under Blanche's chin, and raised her face, but he could not compel her gaze. "You are the exact image of that little girl," he said, "except that you are even purer and finer. She had no chance, none whatever. You live in the woman's age. Your opportunities will be infinite. I shall see to it that they are. What you wish to be you shall be. There will be no pent-up energies here to burst out into disaster for yourself and others. You shall be trained to self-control – that is, if you ever develop self-will, dear child – every faculty shall be educated, every school of life you desire knowledge through shall be opened to you. You shall become that finest flower of civilization, a woman who knows how to use her independence."

She raised her eyes slowly, and gave him a look which stirred the roots of sensation – a long look of unspeakable melancholy. Her chest rose once; then she set her lips tightly, and dropped her eyes.

"What do you mean?" he cried, roughly, for his soul was chattering. "Is – it – do you—?" He dared not go too far, and concluded lamely, "You mean you fear that your mother will not give you to me when she goes – you have divined that I wish to adopt you? Answer me, will you?"

But she only lowered her head and turned away, and he, fearing to frighten or repel her, apologized for his abruptness, restored the outer picture to its place, and led her from the gallery.

He sent her at once to the nursery, and when she came down to luncheon and took her place at his right hand, she was as natural and childlike as ever. For some days he restrained his curiosity, but one evening, as they were sitting before the fire in the hall listening to the storm, and just after he had told her the story of the erl-king, he took her on his knee and asked her gently if she would not tell him what had been in her thoughts when he had drawn her brilliant future. Again her face turned gray, and she dropped her eyes.

"I cannot," she said. "I – perhaps – I don't know."

"Was it what I suggested?"

She shook her head, then looked at him with a shrinking appeal which forced him to drop the subject.

He went the next day alone to the gallery, and looked long at the portrait of the woman. She stirred no response in him. Nor could he feel that the woman of Blanche's future would stir the man in him. The paternal was all he had to give, but that was hers forever.

He went out into the park and found Blanche digging in her garden, very dirty and absorbed. The next afternoon, however, entering the hall noiselessly, he saw her sitting in her big chair, gazing out into nothing visible, her whole face settled in melancholy. He asked her if she were ill, and she recalled herself at once, but confessed to feeling tired. Soon after this he noticed that she lingered longer in the comfortable depths of her chair, and seldom went out, except with himself. She insisted that she was quite well, but after he had surprised her again looking as sad as if she had renounced every joy of childhood, he summoned from London a doctor renowned for his success with children.

The scientist questioned and examined her. When she had left the room he shrugged his shoulders.

"She might have been born with ten years of life in her, or she might grow up into a buxom woman," he said. "I confess I cannot tell. She appears to be sound enough, but I have no X-rays in my eyes, and for all I know she may be on the verge of decay. She certainly has the look of those who die young. I have never seen so spiritual a child. But I can put my finger on nothing. Keep her out-of-doors, don't give her sweets, and don't let her catch anything if you can help it."

Orth and the child spent the long warm days of summer under the trees of the park, or driving in the quiet lanes. Guests were unbidden, and his pen was idle. All that was human in him had gone out to Blanche. He loved her, and she was a perpetual delight to him. The rest of the world received the large measure of his indifference. There was no further change in her, and apprehension slept and let him sleep. He had persuaded Mrs. Root to remain in England for a year. He sent her theatre tickets every week, and placed a horse and phaeton at her disposal. She was enjoying herself and seeing less and less of Blanche. He took the child to Bournemouth for a fortnight, and again to Scotland, both of which outings benefited as much as they pleased her. She had begun to tyrannize over him amiably, and she carried herself quite royally. But she was always sweet and truthful, and these qualities, combined with that something in the depths of her mind which defied his explorations, held him captive. She was devoted to him, and cared for no other companion, although she was demonstrative to her mother when they met.

It was in the tenth month of this idyl of the lonely man and the lonely child that Mrs. Root flurriedly entered the library of Chillingsworth, where Orth happened to be alone.

"Oh, sir," she exclaimed, "I must go home. My daughter Grace writes me – she should have done it before – that the boys are not behaving as well as they should – she didn't tell me, as I was having such a good time she just hated to worry me – Heaven knows I've had enough worry – but now I must go – I just couldn't stay – boys are an awful responsibility – girls ain't a circumstance to them, although mine are a handful sometimes."

Orth had written about too many women to interrupt the flow. He let her talk until she paused to recuperate her forces. Then he said quietly:

"I am sorry this has come so suddenly, for it forces me to broach a subject at once which I would rather have postponed until the idea had taken possession of you by degrees—"

"I know what it is you want to say, sir," she broke in, "and I've reproached myself that I haven't warned you before, but I didn't like to be the one to speak first. You want Blanche – of course, I couldn't help seeing that; but I can't let her go, sir, indeed, I can't."

"Yes," he said, firmly, "I want to adopt Blanche, and I hardly think you can refuse, for you must know how greatly it will be to her advantage. She is a wonderful child; you have never been blind to that; she should have every opportunity, not only of money, but of association. If I adopt her legally, I shall, of course, make her my heir, and – there is no reason why she should not grow up as great a lady as any in England."

The poor woman turned white, and burst into tears. "I've sat up nights and nights, struggling," she said, when she could speak. "That, and missing her. I couldn't stand in her light, and I let her stay. I know I oughtn't to, now – I mean, stand in her light – but, sir, she is dearer than all the others put together."

"Then live here in England – at least, for some years longer. I will gladly relieve your children of your support, and you can see Blanche as often as you choose."

"I can't do that, sir. After all, she is only one, and there are six others. I can't desert them. They all need me, if only to keep them together – three girls unmarried and out in the world, and three boys just a little inclined to be wild. There is another point, sir – I don't exactly know how to say it."

"Well?" asked Orth, kindly. This American woman thought him the ideal gentleman, although the mistress of the estate on which she visited called him a boor and a snob.

"It is – well – you must know – you can imagine – that her brothers and sisters just worship Blanche. They save their dimes to buy her everything she wants – or used to want. Heaven knows what will satisfy her now, although I can't see that she's one bit spoiled. But she's just like a religion to them; they're not much on church. I'll tell you, sir, what I couldn't say to anyone else, not even to these relations who've been so kind to me – but there's wildness, just a streak, in all my children, and I believe, I know, it's Blanche that keeps them straight. My girls get bitter, sometimes; work all the week and little fun, not caring for common men and no chance to marry gentlemen; and sometimes they break out and talk dreadful; then, when they're over it, they say they'll live for Blanche – they've said it over and over, and they mean it. Every sacrifice they've made for her – and they've made many – has done them good. It isn't that Blanche ever says a word of the preachy sort, or has anything of the Sunday-school child about her, or even tries to smooth them down when they're excited. It's just herself. The only thing she ever does is sometimes to draw herself up and look scornful, and that nearly kills them. Little as she is, they're crazy about having her respect. I've grown superstitious about her. Until she came I used to get frightened, terribly, sometimes, and I believe she came for that. So – you see! I know Blanche is too fine for us and ought to have the best; but, then, they are to be considered, too. They have their rights, and they've got much more good than bad in them. I don't know! I don't know! It's kept me awake many nights."

Orth rose abruptly. "Perhaps you will take some further time to think it over," he said. "You can stay a few weeks longer – the matter cannot be so pressing as that."

The woman rose. "I've thought this," she said; "let Blanche decide. I believe she knows more than any of us. I believe that whichever way she decided would be right. I won't say anything to her, so you won't think I'm working on her feelings; and I can trust you. But she'll know."

"Why do you think that?" asked Orth, sharply. "There is nothing uncanny about the child. She is not yet seven years old. Why should you place such a responsibility upon her?"

"Do you think she's like other children?"

"I know nothing of other children."

"I do, sir. I've raised six. And I've seen hundreds of others. I never was one to be a fool about my own, but Blanche isn't like any other child living – I'm certain of it."

"What *do* you think?"

And the woman answered, according to her lights: "I think she's an angel, and came to us because we needed her."

"And I think she is Blanche Mortlake working out the last of her salvation," thought the author; but he made no reply, and was alone in a moment.

It was several days before he spoke to Blanche, and then, one morning, when she was sitting on her mat on the lawn with the light full upon her, he told her abruptly that her mother must return home.

To his surprise, but unutterable delight, she burst into tears and flung herself into his arms.

"You need not leave me," he said, when he could find his own voice. "You can stay here always and be my little girl. It all rests with you."

"I can't stay," she sobbed. "I can't!"

"And that is what made you so sad once or twice?" he asked, with a double eagerness.

She made no reply.

"Oh!" he said, passionately, "Give me your confidence, Blanche. You are the only breathing thing that I love."

"If I could I would," she said. "But I don't know – not quite."

"How much do you know?"

But she sobbed again and would not answer. He dared not risk too much. After all, the physical barrier between the past and the present was very young.

"Well, well, then, we will talk about the other matter. I will not pretend to disguise the fact that your mother is distressed at the idea of parting from you, and thinks it would be as sad for your brothers and sisters, whom she says you influence for their good. Do you think that you do?"

"Yes."

"How do you know this?"

"Do you know why you know everything?"

"No, my dear, and I have great respect for your instincts. But your sisters and brothers are now old enough to take care of themselves. They must be of poor stuff if they cannot live properly without the aid of a child. Moreover, they will be marrying soon. That will also mean that your mother will have many little grandchildren to console her for your loss. I will be the one bereft, if you leave me. I am the only one who really needs you. I don't say I will go to the bad, as you may have very foolishly persuaded yourself your family will do without you, but I trust to your instincts to make you realize how unhappy, how inconsolable I shall be. I shall be the loneliest man on earth!"

She rubbed her face deeper into his flannels, and tightened her embrace. "Can't you come, too?" she asked.

"No; you must live with me wholly or not at all. Your people are not my people, their ways are not my ways. We should not get along. And if you lived with me over there you might as well stay here, for your influence over them would be quite as removed. Moreover, if they are of the right stuff, the memory of you will be quite as potent for good as your actual presence."

"Not unless I died."

Again something within him trembled. "Do you believe you are going to die young?" he blurted out.

But she would not answer.

He entered the nursery abruptly the next day and found her packing her dolls. When she saw him, she sat down and began to weep hopelessly. He knew then that his fate was sealed. And when, a year later, he received her last little scrawl, he was almost glad that she went when she did.

An Occurrence at Owl Creek Bridge

Ambrose Bierce

Chapter I

A MAN STOOD upon a railroad bridge in northern Alabama, looking down into the swift water twenty feet below. The man's hands were behind his back, the wrists bound with a cord. A rope closely encircled his neck. It was attached to a stout cross-timber above his head and the slack fell to the level of his knees. Some loose boards laid upon the ties supporting the rails of the railway supplied a footing for him and his executioners – two private soldiers of the Federal army, directed by a sergeant who in civil life may have been a deputy sheriff. At a short remove upon the same temporary platform was an officer in the uniform of his rank, armed. He was a captain. A sentinel at each end of the bridge stood with his rifle in the position known as 'support', that is to say, vertical in front of the left shoulder, the hammer resting on the forearm thrown straight across the chest – a formal and unnatural position, enforcing an erect carriage of the body. It did not appear to be the duty of these two men to know what was occurring at the center of the bridge; they merely blockaded the two ends of the foot planking that traversed it.

Beyond one of the sentinels nobody was in sight; the railroad ran straight away into a forest for a hundred yards, then, curving, was lost to view. Doubtless there was an outpost farther along. The other bank of the stream was open ground – a gentle slope topped with a stockade of vertical tree trunks, loopholed for rifles, with a single embrasure through which protruded the muzzle of a brass cannon commanding the bridge. Midway up the slope between the bridge and fort were the spectators – a single company of infantry in line, at 'parade rest', the butts of their rifles on the ground, the barrels inclining slightly backward against the right shoulder, the hands crossed upon the stock. A lieutenant stood at the right of the line, the point of his sword upon the ground, his left hand resting upon his right. Excepting the group of four at the center of the bridge, not a man moved. The company faced the bridge, staring stonily, motionless. The sentinels, facing the banks of the stream, might have been statues to adorn the bridge. The captain stood with folded arms, silent, observing the work of his subordinates, but making no sign. Death is a dignitary who when he comes announced is to be received with formal manifestations of respect, even by those most familiar with him. In the code of military etiquette silence and fixity are forms of deference.

The man who was engaged in being hanged was apparently about thirty-five years of age. He was a civilian, if one might judge from his habit, which was that of a planter. His features were good – a straight nose, firm mouth, broad forehead, from which his long, dark hair was combed straight back, falling behind his ears to the collar of his well-fitting frock coat. He wore a moustache and pointed beard, but no whiskers; his eyes were large and dark gray, and had a kindly expression which one would hardly have expected in one whose neck was in the hemp. Evidently this was no vulgar assassin. The liberal military code makes provision for hanging many kinds of persons, and gentlemen are not excluded.

The preparations being complete, the two private soldiers stepped aside and each drew away the plank upon which he had been standing. The sergeant turned to the captain, saluted and placed himself immediately behind that officer, who in turn moved apart one pace. These movements left the condemned man and the sergeant standing on the two ends of the same plank, which spanned three of the cross-ties of the bridge. The end upon which the civilian stood almost, but not quite, reached a fourth. This plank had been held in place by the weight of the captain; it was now held by that of the sergeant. At a signal from the former the latter would step aside, the plank would tilt and the condemned man go down between two ties. The arrangement commended itself to his judgment as simple and effective. His face had not been covered nor his eyes bandaged. He looked a moment at his 'unsteadfast footing', then let his gaze wander to the swirling water of the stream racing madly beneath his feet. A piece of dancing driftwood caught his attention and his eyes followed it down the current. How slowly it appeared to move! What a sluggish stream!

He closed his eyes in order to fix his last thoughts upon his wife and children. The water, touched to gold by the early sun, the brooding mists under the banks at some distance down the stream, the fort, the soldiers, the piece of drift – all had distracted him. And now he became conscious of a new disturbance. Striking through the thought of his dear ones was sound which he could neither ignore nor understand, a sharp, distinct, metallic percussion like the stroke of a blacksmith's hammer upon the anvil; it had the same ringing quality. He wondered what it was, and whether immeasurably distant or nearby – it seemed both. Its recurrence was regular, but as slow as the tolling of a death knell. He awaited each new stroke with impatience and – he knew not why – apprehension. The intervals of silence grew progressively longer; the delays became maddening. With their greater infrequency the sounds increased in strength and sharpness. They hurt his ear like the thrust of a knife; he feared he would shriek. What he heard was the ticking of his watch.

He unclosed his eyes and saw again the water below him. "If I could free my hands," he thought, "I might throw off the noose and spring into the stream. By diving I could evade the bullets and, swimming vigorously, reach the bank, take to the woods and get away home. My home, thank God, is as yet outside their lines; my wife and little ones are still beyond the invader's farthest advance."

As these thoughts, which have here to be set down in words, were flashed into the doomed man's brain rather than evolved from it the captain nodded to the sergeant. The sergeant stepped aside.

Chapter II

PEYTON FARQUHAR was a well-to-do planter, of an old and highly respected Alabama family. Being a slave owner and like other slave owners a politician, he was naturally an original secessionist and ardently devoted to the Southern cause. Circumstances of an imperious nature, which it is unnecessary to relate here, had prevented him from taking service with that gallant army which had fought the disastrous campaigns ending with the fall of Corinth, and he chafed under the inglorious restraint, longing for the release of his energies, the larger life of the soldier, the opportunity for distinction. That opportunity, he felt, would come, as it comes to all in wartime. Meanwhile he did what he could. No service was too humble for him to perform in the aid of the South, no adventure too perilous for him to undertake if consistent with the character of a civilian who was at heart a soldier, and who in good faith and without too much qualification assented to at least a part of the frankly villainous dictum that all is fair in love and war.

One evening while Farquhar and his wife were sitting on a rustic bench near the entrance to his grounds, a gray-clad soldier rode up to the gate and asked for a drink of water. Mrs. Farquhar was only too happy to serve him with her own white hands. While she was fetching the water her husband approached the dusty horseman and inquired eagerly for news from the front.

"The Yanks are repairing the railroads," said the man, "and are getting ready for another advance. They have reached the Owl Creek bridge, put it in order and built a stockade on the north bank. The commandant has issued an order, which is posted everywhere, declaring that any civilian caught interfering with the railroad, its bridges, tunnels, or trains will be summarily hanged. I saw the order."

"How far is it to the Owl Creek bridge?" Farquhar asked.

"About thirty miles."

"Is there no force on this side of the creek?"

"Only a picket post half a mile out, on the railroad, and a single sentinel at this end of the bridge."

"Suppose a man – a civilian and student of hanging – should elude the picket post and perhaps get the better of the sentinel," said Farquhar, smiling, "what could he accomplish?"

The soldier reflected. "I was there a month ago," he replied. "I observed that the flood of last winter had lodged a great quantity of driftwood against the wooden pier at this end of the bridge. It is now dry and would burn like tinder."

The lady had now brought the water, which the soldier drank. He thanked her ceremoniously, bowed to her husband and rode away. An hour later, after nightfall, he repassed the plantation, going northward in the direction from which he had come. He was a Federal scout.

Chapter III

AS PEYTON FARQUHAR fell straight downward through the bridge he lost consciousness and was as one already dead. From this state he was awakened – ages later, it seemed to him – by the pain of a sharp pressure upon his throat, followed by a sense of suffocation. Keen, poignant agonies seemed to shoot from his neck downward through every fiber of his body and limbs. These pains appeared to flash along well defined lines of ramification and to beat with an inconceivably rapid periodicity. They seemed like streams of pulsating fire heating him to an intolerable temperature. As to his head, he was conscious of nothing but a feeling of fullness – of congestion. These sensations were unaccompanied by thought. The intellectual part of his nature was already effaced; he had power only to feel, and feeling was torment. He was conscious of motion. Encompassed in a luminous cloud, of which he was now merely the fiery heart, without material substance, he swung through unthinkable arcs of oscillation, like a vast pendulum. Then all at once, with terrible suddenness, the light about him shot upward with the noise of a loud splash; a frightful roaring was in his ears, and all was cold and dark. The power of thought was restored; he knew that the rope had broken and he had fallen into the stream. There was no additional strangulation; the noose about his neck was already suffocating him and kept the water from his lungs. To die of hanging at the bottom of a river! The idea seemed to him ludicrous. He opened his eyes in the darkness and saw above him a gleam of light, but how distant, how inaccessible! He was still sinking, for the light became fainter and fainter until it was a mere glimmer. Then it began to grow and brighten, and he knew that he was rising toward the surface – knew it with reluctance, for he was now very comfortable. "To be hanged and drowned," he thought, "that is not so bad; but I do not wish to be shot. No; I will not be shot; that is not fair."

He was not conscious of an effort, but a sharp pain in his wrist apprised him that he was trying to free his hands. He gave the struggle his attention, as an idler might observe the feat of a juggler, without interest in the outcome. What splendid effort! – what magnificent, what superhuman strength! Ah, that was a fine endeavor! Bravo! The cord fell away; his arms parted and floated upward, the hands dimly seen on each side in the growing light. He watched them with a new interest as first one and then the other pounced upon the noose at his neck. They tore it away and thrust it fiercely aside, its undulations resembling those of a water snake. "Put it back, put it back!" He thought he shouted these words to his hands, for the undoing of the noose had been succeeded by the direst pang that he had yet experienced. His neck ached horribly; his brain was on fire, his heart, which had been fluttering faintly, gave a great leap, trying to force itself out at his mouth. His whole body was racked and wrenched with an insupportable anguish! But his disobedient hands gave no heed to the command. They beat the water vigorously with quick, downward strokes, forcing him to the surface. He felt his head emerge; his eyes were blinded by the sunlight; his chest expanded convulsively, and with a supreme and crowning agony his lungs engulfed a great draught of air, which instantly he expelled in a shriek!

He was now in full possession of his physical senses. They were, indeed, preternaturally keen and alert. Something in the awful disturbance of his organic system had so exalted and refined them that they made record of things never before perceived. He felt the ripples upon his face and heard their separate sounds as they struck. He looked at the forest on the bank of the stream, saw the individual trees, the leaves and the veining of each leaf – he saw the very insects upon them: the locusts, the brilliant bodied flies, the gray spiders stretching their webs from twig to twig. He noted the prismatic colors in all the dewdrops upon a million blades of grass. The humming of the gnats that danced above the eddies of the stream, the beating of the dragonflies' wings, the strokes of the water spiders' legs, like oars which had lifted their boat – all these made audible music. A fish slid along beneath his eyes and he heard the rush of its body parting the water.

He had come to the surface facing down the stream; in a moment the visible world seemed to wheel slowly round, himself the pivotal point, and he saw the bridge, the fort, the soldiers upon the bridge, the captain, the sergeant, the two privates, his executioners. They were in silhouette against the blue sky. They shouted and gesticulated, pointing at him. The captain had drawn his pistol, but did not fire; the others were unarmed. Their movements were grotesque and horrible, their forms gigantic.

Suddenly he heard a sharp report and something struck the water smartly within a few inches of his head, spattering his face with spray. He heard a second report, and saw one of the sentinels with his rifle at his shoulder, a light cloud of blue smoke rising from the muzzle. The man in the water saw the eye of the man on the bridge gazing into his own through the sights of the rifle. He observed that it was a gray eye and remembered having read that gray eyes were keenest, and that all famous marksmen had them. Nevertheless, this one had missed.

A counter-swirl had caught Farquhar and turned him half round; he was again looking at the forest on the bank opposite the fort. The sound of a clear, high voice in a monotonous singsong now rang out behind him and came across the water with a distinctness that pierced and subdued all other sounds, even the beating of the ripples in his ears. Although no soldier, he had frequented camps enough to know the dread significance of that deliberate, drawling, aspirated chant; the lieutenant on shore was taking a part in the morning's work. How coldly and pitilessly – with what an even, calm intonation, presaging, and enforcing tranquility in the men – with what accurately measured interval fell those cruel words:

"Company!…Attention!…Shoulder arms!…Ready!…Aim!…Fire!"

Farquhar dived – dived as deeply as he could. The water roared in his ears like the voice of Niagara, yet he heard the dull thunder of the volley and, rising again toward the surface, met shining bits of metal, singularly flattened, oscillating slowly downward. Some of them touched him on the face and hands, then fell away, continuing their descent. One lodged between his collar and neck; it was uncomfortably warm and he snatched it out.

As he rose to the surface, gasping for breath, he saw that he had been a long time under water; he was perceptibly farther downstream – nearer to safety. The soldiers had almost finished reloading; the metal ramrods flashed all at once in the sunshine as they were drawn from the barrels, turned in the air, and thrust into their sockets. The two sentinels fired again, independently and ineffectually.

The hunted man saw all this over his shoulder; he was now swimming vigorously with the current. His brain was as energetic as his arms and legs; he thought with the rapidity of lightning:

"The officer," he reasoned, "will not make that martinet's error a second time. It is as easy to dodge a volley as a single shot. He has probably already given the command to fire at will. God help me, I cannot dodge them all!"

An appalling splash within two yards of him was followed by a loud, rushing sound, *diminuendo*, which seemed to travel back through the air to the fort and died in an explosion which stirred the very river to its deeps! A rising sheet of water curved over him, fell down upon him, blinded him, strangled him! The cannon had taken an hand in the game. As he shook his head free from the commotion of the smitten water he heard the deflected shot humming through the air ahead, and in an instant it was cracking and smashing the branches in the forest beyond.

"They will not do that again," he thought; "the next time they will use a charge of grape. I must keep my eye upon the gun; the smoke will apprise me – the report arrives too late; it lags behind the missile. That is a good gun."

Suddenly he felt himself whirled round and round – spinning like a top. The water, the banks, the forests, the now distant bridge, fort and men, all were commingled and blurred. Objects were represented by their colors only; circular horizontal streaks of color – that was all he saw. He had been caught in a vortex and was being whirled on with a velocity of advance and gyration that made him giddy and sick. In a few moments he was flung upon the gravel at the foot of the left bank of the stream – the southern bank – and behind a projecting point which concealed him from his enemies. The sudden arrest of his motion, the abrasion of one of his hands on the gravel, restored him, and he wept with delight. He dug his fingers into the sand, threw it over himself in handfuls and audibly blessed it. It looked like diamonds, rubies, emeralds; he could think of nothing beautiful which it did not resemble. The trees upon the bank were giant garden plants; he noted a definite order in their arrangement, inhaled the fragrance of their blooms. A strange roseate light shone through the spaces among their trunks and the wind made in their branches the music of Aeolian harps. He had not wish to perfect his escape – he was content to remain in that enchanting spot until retaken.

A whiz and a rattle of grapeshot among the branches high above his head roused him from his dream. The baffled cannoneer had fired him a random farewell. He sprang to his feet, rushed up the sloping bank, and plunged into the forest.

All that day he traveled, laying his course by the rounding sun. The forest seemed interminable; nowhere did he discover a break in it, not even a woodman's road. He had not known that he lived in so wild a region. There was something uncanny in the revelation.

By nightfall he was fatigued, footsore, famished. The thought of his wife and children urged him on. At last he found a road which led him in what he knew to be the right direction. It was as wide and straight as a city street, yet it seemed untraveled. No fields bordered it, no dwelling anywhere. Not so much as the barking of a dog suggested human habitation. The black bodies of the trees formed a straight wall on both sides, terminating on the horizon in a point, like a diagram in a lesson in perspective. Overhead, as he looked up through this rift in the wood, shone great golden stars looking unfamiliar and grouped in strange constellations. He was sure they were arranged in some order which had a secret and malign significance. The wood on either side was full of singular noises, among which – once, twice, and again – he distinctly heard whispers in an unknown tongue.

His neck was in pain and lifting his hand to it found it horribly swollen. He knew that it had a circle of black where the rope had bruised it. His eyes felt congested; he could no longer close them. His tongue was swollen with thirst; he relieved its fever by thrusting it forward from between his teeth into the cold air. How softly the turf had carpeted the untraveled avenue – he could no longer feel the roadway beneath his feet!

Doubtless, despite his suffering, he had fallen asleep while walking, for now he sees another scene – perhaps he has merely recovered from a delirium. He stands at the gate of his own home. All is as he left it, and all bright and beautiful in the morning sunshine. He must have traveled the entire night. As he pushes open the gate and passes up the wide white walk, he sees a flutter of female garments; his wife, looking fresh and cool and sweet, steps down from the veranda to meet him. At the bottom of the steps she stands waiting, with a smile of ineffable joy, an attitude of matchless grace and dignity. Ah, how beautiful she is! He springs forwards with extended arms. As he is about to clasp her he feels a stunning blow upon the back of the neck; a blinding white light blazes all about him with a sound like the shock of a cannon – then all is darkness and silence!

Peyton Farquhar was dead; his body, with a broken neck, swung gently from side to side beneath the timbers of the Owl Creek bridge.

A Vine on a House

Ambrose Bierce

ABOUT THREE MILES from the little town of Norton, in Missouri, on the road leading to Maysville, stands an old house that was last occupied by a family named Harding. Since 1886 no one has lived in it, nor is anyone likely to live in it again. Time and the disfavor of persons dwelling thereabout are converting it into a rather picturesque ruin. An observer unacquainted with its history would hardly put it into the category of 'haunted houses', yet in all the region round such is its evil reputation. Its windows are without glass, its doorways without doors; there are wide breaches in the shingle roof, and for lack of paint the weatherboarding is a dun gray. But these unfailing signs of the supernatural are partly concealed and greatly softened by the abundant foliage of a large vine overrunning the entire structure. This vine of a species which no botanist has ever been able to name has an important part in the story of the house.

The Harding family consisted of Robert Harding, his wife Matilda, Miss Julia Went, who was her sister, and two young children. Robert Harding was a silent, cold-mannered man who made no friends in the neighborhood and apparently cared to make none. He was about forty years old, frugal and industrious, and made a living from the little farm which is now overgrown with brush and brambles. He and his sister-in-law were rather tabooed by their neighbors, who seemed to think that they were seen too frequently together not entirely their fault, for at these times they evidently did not challenge observation. The moral code of rural Missouri is stern and exacting.

Mrs. Harding was a gentle, sad-eyed woman, lacking a left foot.

At some time in 1884 it became known that she had gone to visit her mother in Iowa. That was what her husband said in reply to inquiries, and his manner of saying it did not encourage further questioning. She never came back, and two years later, without selling his farm or anything that was his, or appointing an agent to look after his interests, or removing his household goods, Harding, with the rest of the family, left the country. Nobody knew whither he went; nobody at that time cared. Naturally, whatever was movable about the place soon disappeared and the deserted house became 'haunted' in the manner of its kind.

One summer evening, four or five years later, the Rev. J. Gruber, of Norton, and a Maysville attorney named Hyatt met on horseback in front of the Harding place. Having business matters to discuss, they hitched their animals and going to the house sat on the porch to talk. Some humorous reference to the somber reputation of the place was made and forgotten as soon as uttered, and they talked of their business affairs until it grew almost dark. The evening was oppressively warm, the air stagnant.

Presently both men started from their seats in surprise: a long vine that covered half the front of the house and dangled its branches from the edge of the porch above them was visibly and audibly agitated, shaking violently in every stem and leaf.

"We shall have a storm," Hyatt exclaimed.

Gruber said nothing, but silently directed the other's attention to the foliage of adjacent trees, which showed no movement; even the delicate tips of the boughs silhouetted against the clear sky were motionless. They hastily passed down the steps to what had been a lawn and looked upward at the vine, whose entire length was now visible. It continued in violent agitation, yet they could discern no disturbing cause.

"Let us leave," said the minister.

And leave they did. Forgetting that they had been traveling in opposite directions, they rode away together. They went to Norton, where they related their strange experience to several discreet friends. The next evening, at about the same hour, accompanied by two others whose names are not recalled, they were again on the porch of the Harding house, and again the mysterious phenomenon occurred: the vine was violently agitated while under the closest scrutiny from root to tip, nor did their combined strength applied to the trunk serve to still it. After an hour's observation they retreated, no less wise, it is thought, than when they had come.

No great time was required for these singular facts to rouse the curiosity of the entire neighborhood. By day and by night crowds of persons assembled at the Harding house 'seeking a sign'. It does not appear that any found it, yet so credible were the witnesses mentioned that none doubted the reality of the 'manifestations' to which they testified.

By either a happy inspiration or some destructive design, it was one day proposed – nobody appeared to know from whom – the suggestion came to dig up the vine, and after a good deal of debate this was done. Nothing was found but the root, yet nothing could have been more strange!

For five or six feet from the trunk, which had at the surface of the ground a diameter of several inches, it ran downward, single and straight, into a loose, friable earth; then it divided and subdivided into rootlets, fibers and filaments, most curiously interwoven. When carefully freed from soil they showed a singular formation. In their ramifications and doublings back upon themselves they made a compact network, having in size and shape an amazing resemblance to the human figure. Head, trunk and limbs were there; even the fingers and toes were distinctly defined; and many professed to see in the distribution and arrangement of the fibers in the globular mass representing the head a grotesque suggestion of a face. The figure was horizontal; the smaller roots had begun to unite at the breast.

In point of resemblance to the human form this image was imperfect. At about ten inches from one of the knees, the *cilia* forming that leg had abruptly doubled backward and inward upon their course of growth. The figure lacked the left foot.

There was but one inference – the obvious one; but in the ensuing excitement as many courses of action were proposed as there were incapable counselors. The matter was settled by the sheriff of the county, who as the lawful custodian of the abandoned estate ordered the root replaced and the excavation filled with the earth that had been removed.

Later inquiry brought out only one fact of relevancy and significance: Mrs. Harding had never visited her relatives in Iowa, nor did they know that she was supposed to have done so.

Of Robert Harding and the rest of his family nothing is known. The house retains its evil reputation, but the replanted vine is as orderly and well-behaved a vegetable as a nervous person could wish to sit under of a pleasant night, when the katydids grate out their immemorial revelation and the distant whippoorwill signifies his notion of what ought to be done about it.

Somnambulism: A Fragment

Charles Brockden Brown

[The following fragment will require no other preface or commentary than an extract from the Vienna Gazette of June 14, 1784:

"At Great Glogau, in Silesia, the attention of physicians, and of the people, has been excited by the case of a young man, whose behavior indicates perfect health in all respects but one. He has a habit of rising in his sleep, and performing a great many actions with as much order and exactness as when awake. This habit for a long time showed itself in freaks and achievements merely innocent, or, at least, only troublesome and inconvenient, till about six weeks ago. A that period a shocking event took place about three leagues from the town, and in the neighborhood where the youth's family resides. At young lady, traveling with her father by night, was shot dead upon the road, by some person unknown. The officers of justice took a good deal of pains to trace the author of the crime, and at length, by carefully comparing circumstances, a suspicion was fixed upon this youth. After an accurate scrutiny, by the tribunal of the circle, he has been declared author of the murder: but what renders the case truly extraordinary is, that there are good reasons for believing that the deed was perpetrated by the youth while asleep, and was entirely unknown to himself. The young woman was the object of his affection, and the journey in which she had engaged had given him the utmost anxiety for her safety."]

OUR GUESTS were preparing to retire for the night, when somebody knocked loudly at the gate. The person was immediately admitted, and presented a letter to Mr. Davis. This letter was from a friend, in which he informed our guest of certain concerns of great importance, on which the letter-writer was extremely anxious to have a personal conference with his friend; but knowing that he intended to set out from —— four days previous to his writing, he was hindered from setting out by the apprehension of missing him upon the way. Meanwhile, he had deemed it best to send a special message to quicken his motions, should he be able to find him.

The importance of this interview was such, that Mr. Davis declared his intention of setting out immediately. No solicitations could induce him to delay a moment. His daughter, convinced of the urgency of his motives, readily consented to brave the perils and discomforts of a nocturnal journey.

This event had not been anticipated by me. The shock that it produced in me was, to my own apprehension, a subject of surprise. I could not help perceiving that it was greater than the occasion would justify. The pleasures of this intercourse were, in a moment, to be ravished from me. I was to part from my new friend, and when we should again meet it was impossible to foresee. It was then that I recollected her expressions that assured me that her choice was fixed upon another. If I saw her again, it would probably be as a wife. The claims of friendship, as well as those of love, would then be swallowed up by a superior and hateful obligation.

But, though betrothed, she was not wedded. That was yet to come; but why should it be considered as inevitable? Our dispositions and views must change with circumstances. Who was he that Constantia Davis had chosen? Was he born to outstrip all competitors in ardor and fidelity? We cannot fail of choosing that which appears to us most worthy of choice. He had hitherto been unrivaled; but was not this day destined to introduce to her one, to whose merits every competitor must yield? He that would resign this prize, without an arduous struggle, would, indeed, be of all wretches the most pusillanimous and feeble.

Why, said I, do I cavil at her present choice? I will maintain that it does honor to her discernment. She would not be that accomplished being which she seems, if she had acted otherwise. It would be sacrilege to question the rectitude of her conduct. The object of her choice was worthy. The engagement of her heart in his favor was unavoidable, because her experience had not hitherto produced one deserving to be placed in competition with him. As soon as his superior is found, his claims will be annihilated. Has not this propitious accident supplied the defects of her former observation? But soft! Is she not betrothed? If she be, what have I to dread? The engagement is accompanied with certain conditions. Whether they be openly expressed or not, they necessarily limit it. Her vows are binding on condition that the present situation continues, and that another does not arise, previously to marriage, by whose claims those of the present lover will be justly superseded.

But how shall I contend with this unknown admirer? She is going whither it will not be possible for me to follow her. An interview of a few hours is not sufficient to accomplish the important purpose that I meditate; but even this is now at an end. I shall speedily be forgotten by her. I have done nothing that entitles me to a place in her remembrance. While my rival will be left at liberty to prosecute his suit, I shall be abandoned to solitude, and have no other employment than to ruminate on the bliss that has eluded my grasp. If scope were allowed to my exertions, I might hope that they would ultimately be crowned with success; but, as it is, I am manacled and powerless. The good would easily be reached, if my hands were at freedom: now that they are fettered, the attainment is impossible.

But is it true that such is my forlorn condition? What is it that irrecoverably binds me to this spot? There are seasons of respite from my present occupations, in which I commonly indulge myself in journeys. This lady's habitation is not at an immeasurable distance from mine. It may be easily comprised within the sphere of my excursions. Shall I want a motive or excuse for paying her a visit? Her father has claimed to be better acquainted with my uncle. The lady has intimated that the sight of me, at any future period, will give her pleasure. This will furnish ample apology for visiting their house. But why should I delay my visit? Why not immediately attend them on their way? If not on their whole journey, at least for a part of it? A journey in darkness is not unaccompanied with peril. Whatever be the caution or knowledge of their guide, they cannot be supposed to surpass mine, who have trodden this part of the way so often that my chamber floor is scarcely more familiar to me. Besides, there is danger, from which, I am persuaded, my attendance would be sufficient, an indispensable safeguard.

I am unable to explain why I conceived this journey to be attended with uncommon danger. My mind was, at first, occupied with the remoter consequences of this untimely departure, but my thoughts gradually returned to the contemplation of its immediate effects. There were twenty miles to a ferry, by which the travelers designed to cross the river, and at which they expected to arrive at sunrise the next morning. I have said that the intermediate way was plain and direct. Their guide professed to be thoroughly acquainted with it. From what quarter, then, could danger be expected to arise? It was easy to enumerate and magnify possibilities; that a tree, or ridge, or stone unobserved might overturn the carriage; that their horse might fail, or be urged, by some accident, to flight, were far from being impossible. Still they were such as justified caution. My vigilance would, at least, contribute to their security. But I could not for a moment divest myself of the belief that my aid was indispensable. As I pondered on this image my emotions arose to terror.

All men are, at times, influenced by inexplicable sentiments. Ideas haunt them in spite of all their efforts to discard them. Prepossessions are entertained, for which their reason is unable to discover any adequate cause. The strength of a belief, when it is destitute of any rational foundation, seems, of itself, to furnish a new ground for credulity. We first admit a powerful persuasion, and then, from reflecting on the insufficiency of the ground on which it is built, instead of being prompted to dismiss it, we become more forcibly attached to it.

I had received little of the education of design. I owed the formation of my character chiefly to accident. I shall not pretend to determine in what degree I was credulous or superstitious. A belief, for which I could not rationally account, I was sufficiently prone to consider as the work of some invisible agent; as an intimation from the great source of existence and knowledge. My imagination was vivid. My passions, when I allowed them sway, were uncontrollable. My conduct, as my feelings, was characterized by precipitation and headlong energy.

On this occasion I was eloquent in my remonstrances. I could not suppress my opinion that unseen danger lurked in their way. When called upon to state the reasons of my apprehensions, I could only enumerate the possibilities of which they were already apprised, but which they regarded in their true light. I made bold enquiries into the importance of the motives that should induce them to expose themselves to the least hazard. They could not urge their horse beyond his real strength. They would be compelled to suspend their journey for some time the next day. A few hours were all that they could hope to save by their utmost expedition. Were a few hours of such infinite moment?

In these representations I was sensible that I had over-leaped the bounds of rigid decorum. It was not my place to weigh his motives and inducements. My age and situation, in this family, rendered silence and submission my peculiar province. I had hitherto confined myself within bounds of scrupulous propriety, but now I had suddenly lost sight of all regards but those which related to the safety of the travelers.

Mr. Davis regarded my vehemence with suspicion. He eyed me with more attention than I had hitherto received from him. The impression which this unexpected interference made upon him, I was, at the time, too much absorbed in other considerations to notice. It was afterwards plain that he suspected my zeal to originate in a passion for his daughter, which it was by no means proper for him to encourage. If this idea occurred to him, his humanity would not suffer it to generate indignation or resentment in his bosom. On the contrary, he treated my arguments with mildness, and assured me that I had over-rated the inconveniences and perils of the journey. Some regard was to be paid to his daughter's ease and health. He did not believe them to be materially endangered. They should make suitable provision of cloaks and caps against the inclemency of the air. Had not the occasion been extremely urgent, and of that urgency he alone could be the proper judge, he should certainly not consent to endure even these trivial inconveniences. "But you seem," continued he, "chiefly anxious for my daughter's sake. There is, without doubt, a large portion of gallantry in your fears. It is natural and venial in a young man to take infinite pains for the service of the ladies; but, my dear, what say you? I will refer this important question to your decision. Shall we go, or wait till the morning?"

"Go, by all means," replied she. "I confess the fears that have been expressed appear to be groundless. I am bound to our young friend for the concern he takes in our welfare, but certainly his imagination misleads him. I am not so much a girl as to be scared merely because it is dark."

I might have foreseen this decision; but what could I say? My fears and my repugnance were strong as ever.

The evil that was menaced was terrible. By remaining where they were till the next day they would escape it. Was no other method sufficient for their preservation? My attendance would effectually obviate the danger.

This scheme possessed irresistible attractions. I was thankful to the danger for suggesting it. In the fervor of my conceptions, I was willing to run to the world's end to show my devotion to the lady. I could sustain, with alacrity, the fatigue of many nights of traveling and watchfulness. I should unspeakably prefer them to warmth and ease, if I could thereby extort from this lady a single phrase of gratitude or approbation.

I proposed to them to bear them company, at least till the morning light. They would not listen to it. Half my purpose was indeed answered by the glistening eyes and affectionate looks of Miss Davis, but the remainder I was pertinaciously bent on likewise accomplishing. If Mr. Davis had not suspected my motives, he would probably have been less indisposed to compliance. As it was, however, his objections were insuperable. They earnestly insisted on my relinquishing my design. My uncle, also, not seeing anything that justified extraordinary precautions, added his injunctions. I was conscious of my inability to show any sufficient grounds for my fears. As long as their representations rung in my ears, I allowed myself to be ashamed of my weakness, and conjured up a temporary persuasion that my attendance was, indeed, superfluous, and that I should show most wisdom in suffering them to depart alone.

But this persuasion was transient. They had no sooner placed themselves in their carriage, and exchanged the parting adieus, but my apprehensions returned upon me as forcibly as ever. No doubt, part of my despondency flowed from the idea of separation, which, however auspicious it might prove to the lady, portended unspeakable discomforts to me. But this was not all. I was breathless with fear of some unknown and terrible disaster that awaited them. A hundred times I resolved to disregard their remonstrances, and hover near them till the morning. This might be done without exciting their displeasure. It was easy to keep aloof and be unseen by them. I should doubtless have pursued this method if my fears has assumed any definite and consistent form; if, in reality, I had been able distinctly to tell what it was that I feared. My guardianship would be of no use against the obvious sources of danger in the ruggedness and obscurity of the way. For that end I must have tendered them my services, which I knew would be refused, and, if pertinaciously obtruded on them, might justly excite displeasure. I was not insensible, too, of the obedience that was due to my uncle. My absence would be remarked. Some anger and much disquietude would have been the consequences with respect to him. And after all, what was this groundless and ridiculous persuasion that governed me? Had I profited nothing by experience of the effects of similar follies? Was I never to attend to the lessons of sobriety and truth? How ignominious to be thus the slave of a fortuitous and inexplicable impulse! To be the victim of terrors more chimerical than those which haunt the dreams of idiots and children! They can describe clearly, and attribute a real existence to the object of their terrors. Not so can I.

Influenced by these considerations, I shut the gate at which I had been standing, and turned towards the house. After a few steps I paused, turned, and listened to the distant sounds of the carriage. My courage was again on the point of yielding, and new efforts were requisite before I could resume my first resolutions.

I spent a drooping and melancholy evening. My imagination continually hovered over our departed guests. I recalled every circumstance of the road. I reflected by what means they were to pass that bridge, or extricate themselves from this slough. I imagined the possibility of their guide's forgetting the position of a certain oak that grew in the road. It was an ancient tree, whose boughs extended, on all sides, to an extraordinary distance. They seemed disposed by nature in that way in which they would produce the most ample circumference of shade. I could not recollect any other obstruction from which much was to be feared. This indeed was several miles distant, and its appearance was too remarkable not to have excited attention.

The family retired to sleep. My mind had been too powerfully excited to permit me to imitate their example. The incidents of the last two days passed over my fancy like a vision. The revolution was almost incredible which my mind had undergone, in consequence of these incidents. It was so abrupt and entire that my soul seemed to have passed into a new form. I pondered on every incident till the surrounding scenes disappeared, and I forgot my real situation. I mused upon the image of Miss Davis till my whole soul was dissolved in tenderness, and my eyes overflowed with tears. There insensibly arose a sort of persuasion that destiny had irreversably decreed that I should never see her more.

While engaged in this melancholy occupation, of which I cannot say how long it lasted, sleep overtook me as I sat. Scarcely a minute had elapsed during this period without conceiving the design, more or less strenuously, of sallying forth, with a view to overtake and guard the travelers; but this design was embarrassed with invincible objections, and was alternately formed and laid aside. At length, as I have said, I sunk into profound slumber, if that slumber can be termed profound, in which my fancy was incessantly employed in calling up the forms, into new combinations, which had constituted my waking reveries. The images were fleeting and transient, but the events of the morrow recalled them to my remembrance with sufficient distinctness. The terrors which I had so deeply and unaccountably imbibed could not fail of retaining some portion of their influence, in spite of sleep.

In my dreams, the design which I could not bring myself to execute while awake I embraced without hesitation. I was summoned, methought, to defend this lady from the attacks of an assassin. My ideas were full of confusion and inaccuracy. All that I can recollect is that my efforts had been unsuccessful to avert the stroke of the murderer. This, however, was not accomplished without drawing on his head a bloody retribution. I imagined myself engaged, for a long time, in pursuit of the guilty, and, at last, to have detected him in an artful disguise. I did not employ the usual preliminaries which honor by a mortal wound.

I should not have described these phantoms had there not been a remarkable coincidence between them and the real events of that night. In the morning, my uncle, whose custom it was to rise first in the family, found me quietly reposing in the chair in which I had fallen asleep. His summons roused and startled me. This posture was so unusual that I did not readily recover my recollection, and perceive in what circumstances I was placed.

I shook off the dreams of the night. Sleep had refreshed and invigorated my frame, as well as tranquilized my thoughts. I still mused on yesterday's adventures, but my reveries were more cheerful and benign. My fears and bodements were dispersed with the dark, and I went into the fields, not merely to perform the duties of the day, but to ruminate on plans for the future.

My golden visions, however, were soon converted into visions of despair. A messenger arrived before noon, intreating my presence, and that of my uncle, at the house of Dr. Inglefield, a gentleman who resided at the distance of three miles from our house. The messenger explained the intention of this request. It appeared that the terrors of the preceding evening had some mysterious connection with truth. By some deplorable accident, Miss Davis had been shot on the road, and was still lingering in dreadful agonies at the house of this physician. I was in a field near the road when the messenger approached the house. On observing me, he called me. His tale was meagre and imperfect, but the substance of it was easy to gather. I stood for a moment motionless and aghast. As soon as I recovered my thoughts I set off full speed, and made not a moment's pause till I reached the house of Inglefield.

The circumstances of this mournful event, as I was able to collect them at different times, from the witnesses, were these. After they had parted from us, they proceeded on their way for some time without molestation. The clouds disappearing, the starlight enabled them with less difficulty to discern their path. They met not a human being till they came within less than three miles of the oak which I have before described. Here Miss Davis looked forward with some curiosity and said to her father, "Do you not see someone in the road before us? I saw him this moment move across from the fence on the right and stand still in the middle of the road."

"I see nothing, I must confess," said the father: "but that is no subject of wonder; your young eyes will of course see farther than my old ones."

"I see him clearly at this moment," rejoined the lady. "If he remain a short time where he is, or seems to be, we shall be able to ascertain his properties. Our horse's head will determine whether his substance be impassive or not."

The carriage slowly advancing and the form remaining in the same spot, Mr. Davis at length perceived it, but was not allowed a clearer examination, for the person, having, as it seemed, ascertained the nature of the cavalcade, shot across the road, and disappeared. The behavior of this unknown person furnished the travelers with a topic of abundant speculation.

Few possessed a firmer mind than Miss Davis; but whether she was assailed, on this occasion, with a mysterious foreboding of her destiny; whether the eloquence of my fears had not, in spite of resolution, infected her; or whether she imagined evils that my incautious temper might draw upon me, and which might originate in our late interview, certain it was that her spirits were visibly depressed. This accident made no sensible alteration in her. She was still disconsolate and incommunicative. All the efforts of her father were insufficient to inspire her with cheerfulness. He repeatedly questioned her as to the cause of this unwonted despondency. Her answer was, that her spirits were indeed depressed, but she believed that the circumstance was casual. She knew of nothing that could justify despondency. But such is humanity. Cheerfulness and dejection will take their turns in the best regulated bosoms, and come and go when they will, and not at the command of reason. This observation was succeeded by a pause. At length Mr. Davis said, "A thought has just occurred to me. The person whom we just now saw is young Althorpe."

Miss Davis was startled: "Why, my dear father, should you think so? It is too dark to judge, at this distance, by resemblance of figure. Ardent and rash as he appears to be, I should scarcely suspect him on this occasion. With all the fiery qualities of youth, unchastised by experience, untamed by adversity, he is capable no doubt of extravagant adventures, but what could induce him to act in this manner?"

"You know the fears that he expressed concerning the issue of this night's journey. We know not what foundation he might have had for these fears. He told us of no danger that ought to deter us, but it is hard to conceive that he should have been thus vehement without cause. We know not what motives might have induced him to conceal from us the sources of his terror. And since he could not obtain our consent to his attending us, he has taken these means, perhaps, of effecting his purpose. The darkness might easily conceal him from our observation. He might have passed us without our noticing him, or he might have made a circuit in the woods we have just passed, and come out before us."

"That I own," replied the daughter, "is not improbable. If it be true, I shall be sorry for his own sake, but if there be any danger from which his attendance can secure us, I shall be well pleased for all our sakes. He will reflect with some satisfaction, perhaps, that he has done or intended us a service. It would be cruel to deny him a satisfaction so innocent."

"Pray, my dear, what think you of this young man? Does his ardor to serve us flow from a right source?"

"It flows, I have no doubt, from a double source. He has a kind heart, and delights to oblige others: but this is not all. He is likewise in love, and imagines that he cannot do too much for the object of his passion."

"Indeed!" exclaimed Mr. Davis, in some surprise. "You speak very positively. That is no more than I suspected; but how came you to know it with so much certainty?"

"The information came to me in the directest manner. He told me so himself."

"So ho! Why, the impertinent young rogue!"

"Nay, my dear father, his behavior did not merit that epithet. He is rash and inconsiderate. That is the utmost amount of his guilt. A short absence will show him the true state of his feelings. It was unavoidable, in one of his character, to fall in love with the first woman whose appearance was in any degree specious. But attachments like these will be extinguished as easily as they are formed. I do not fear for him on this account."

"Have you reason to fear for him on any account?"

"Yes. The period of youth will soon pass away. Overweening and fickle, he will go on committing one mistake after another, incapable of repairing his errors, or of profiting by the daily lessons of experience. His genius will be merely an implement of mischief. His greater capacity will be evinced merely by the greater portion of unhappiness that, by means of it, will accrue to others or rebound upon himself."

"I see, my dear, that your spirits are low. Nothing else, surely, could suggest such melancholy presages. For my part, I question not, but he will one day be a fine fellow and a happy one. I like him exceedingly. I shall take pains to be acquainted with his future adventures, and do him all the good that I can."

"That intention," said his daughter, "is worthy of the goodness of your heart. He is no less an object of regard to me than to you. I trust I shall want neither the power nor inclination to contribute to his welfare. At present, however, his welfare will be best promoted by forgetting me. Hereafter, I shall solicit a renewal of intercourse."

"Speak lower," said the father. "If I mistake not, there is the same person again." He pointed to the field that skirted the road on the left hand. The young lady's better eyes enabled her to detect his mistake. It was the trunk of a cherry-tree that he had observed.

They proceeded in silence. Contrary to custom, the lady was buried in musing. Her father, whose temper and inclinations were molded by those of his child, insensibly subsided into the same state.

The re-appearance of the same figure that had already excited their attention diverted them anew from their contemplations. "As I live," exclaimed Mr. Davis, "that thing, whatever it be, haunts us. I do not like it. This is strange conduct for young Althorpe to adopt. Instead of being our protector, the danger, against which he so pathetically warned us, may be, in some inscrutable way, connected with this personage. It is best to be upon our guard."

"Nay, my father," said the lady, "be not disturbed. What danger can be dreaded by two persons from one? This thing, I dare say, means us no harm. What is at present inexplicable might be obvious enough if we were better acquainted with this neighborhood. It is not worth a thought. You see it is now gone." Mr. Davis looked again, but it was no longer discernible.

They were now approaching a wood. Mr. Davis called to the guide to stop. His daughter enquired the reason of this command. She found it arose from his uncertainty as to the propriety of proceeding.

"I know not how it is," said he, "but I begin to be affected with the fears of young Althorpe. I am half resolved not to enter this wood. That light yonder informs that a house is near. It may not be inadvisable to stop. I cannot think of delaying our journey till morning; but, by stopping a few minutes, we may possibly collect some useful information. Perhaps it will be expedient and practicable to procure the attendance of another person. I am not well pleased with myself for declining our young friend's offer."

To this proposal Miss Davis objected the inconveniences that calling at a farmer's house, at this time of night, when all were retired to rest, would probably occasion. "Besides," continued she, "the light which you saw is gone: a sufficient proof that it was nothing but a meteor."

At this moment they heard a noise, at a small distance behind them, as of shutting a gate. They called. Speedily an answer was returned in a tone of mildness. The person approached the chaise, and enquired who they were, whence they came, whither they were going, and, lastly, what they wanted.

Mr. Davis explained to this inquisitive person, in a few words, the nature of their situation, mentioned the appearance on the road, and questioned him, in his turn, as to what inconveniences were to be feared from prosecuting his journey. Satisfactory answers were returned to these enquiries.

"As to what you seed in the road," continued he, "I reckon it was nothing but a sheep or a cow. I am not more scary than some folks, but I never goes out a' nights without I sees some sich thing as that, that I takes for a man or woman, and am scared a little oftentimes, but not much. I'm sure after to find that it's nothing but a cow, or hog, or tree, or something. If it wasn't some sich thing you seed, I reckon it was Nick Handyside."

"Nick Handyside! Who was he?"

"It was a fellow that went about the country a' nights. A shocking fool to be sure, that loved to plague and frighten people. Yes. Yes. It couldn't be nobody, he reckoned, but Nick. Nick was a droll thing. He wondered they'd never heard of Nick. He reckoned they were strangers in these here parts."

"Very true, my friend. But who is Nick? Is he a reptile to be shunned, or trampled on?"

"Why I don't know how as that. Nick is an odd soul to be sure; but he don't do nobody no harm, as ever I heard, except by scaring them. He is easily skeart though, for that matter, himself. He loves to frighten folks, but he's shocking apt to be frightened himself. I reckon you took Nick for a ghost. That's a shocking good story, I declare. Yet it's happened hundreds and hundreds of times, I guess, and more."

When this circumstance was mentioned, my uncle, as well as myself, was astonished at our own negligence. While enumerating, on the preceding evening, the obstacles and inconveniences which the travelers were likely to encounter, we entirely and unaccountably overlooked one circumstance, from which inquietude might reasonable have been expected. Near the spot where they now were lived a Mr. Handyside, whose only son was an idiot. He also merited the name of monster, if a projecting breast, a misshapen head, features horrid and distorted, and a voice that resembled nothing that was ever heard before, could entitle him to that appellation. This being, besides the natural deformity of his frame, wore looks and practiced gesticulations that were, in an inconceivable degree, uncouth and hideous. He was mischievous, but his freaks were subjects of little apprehension to those who were accustomed to them, though they were frequently occasions of alarm to strangers. He particularly delighted in imposing on the ignorance of strangers and the timidity of women. He was a perpetual rover. Entirely bereft of reason, his sole employment consisted in sleeping, and eating, and roaming. He would frequently escape at night, and a thousand anecdotes could have been detailed respecting the tricks which Nick Handyside had played upon wayfarers.

Other considerations, however, had, in this instance, so much engrossed our minds, that Nick Handyside had never been once thought of or mentioned. This was the more remarkable, as there had very lately happened an adventure, in which this person had acted a principal part. He had wandered from home, and got bewildered in a desolate tract, known by the name of Norwood. It was a region, rude, sterile, and lonely, bestrewn with rocks, and embarrassed with bushes.

He had remained for some days in this wilderness. Unable to extricate himself, and, at length, tormented with hunger, he manifested his distress by the most doleful shrieks. These were uttered with most vehemence, and heard at greatest distance, by night. At first, those who heard them were panic-struck; but, at length, they furnished a clue by which those who were in search of him were guided to the spot. Notwithstanding the recentness and singularity of this adventure, and the probability that our guests would suffer molestation from this cause, so strangely forgetful had we been, that no caution on this head had been given. This caution, indeed, as the event testified, would have been superfluous, and yet I cannot enough wonder that in hunting for some reason, by which I might justify my fears to them or to myself, I had totally overlooked this mischief-loving idiot.

After listening to an ample description of Nick, being warned to proceed with particular caution in a part of the road that was near at hand, and being assured that they had nothing to dread from human interference, they resumed their journey with new confidence.

Their attention was frequently excited by rustling leaves or stumbling footsteps, and the figure which they doubted not to belong to Nick Handyside, occasionally hovered in their sight. This appearance no longer inspired them with apprehension. They had been assured that a stern voice was sufficient to repulse him, when most importunate. This antic being treated all others as children. He took pleasure in the effects which the sight of his own deformity produced, and betokened his satisfaction by a laugh, which might have served as a model to the poet who has depicted the ghastly risibilities of Death. On this occasion, however, the monster behaved with unusual moderation. He never came near enough for his peculiarities to be distinguished by starlight. There was nothing fantastic in his motions, nor anything surprising, but the celerity of his transitions. They were unaccompanied by those howls, which reminded you at one time of a troop of hungry wolves, and had, at another, something in them inexpressibly wild and melancholy. This monster possessed a certain species of dexterity. His talents, differently applied, would have excited rational admiration. He was fleet as a deer. He was patient, to an incredible degree, of watchfulness, and cold, and hunger. He had improved the flexibility of his voice, till his cries, always loud and rueful, were capable of being diversified without end. Instances had been known, in which the stoutest heart was appalled by them; and some, particularly in the case of women, in which they had been productive of consequences truly deplorable.

When the travelers had arrived at that part of the wood where, as they had been informed, it was needful to be particularly cautious, Mr. Davis, for their greater security, proposed to his daughter to alight. The exercise of walking, he thought, after so much time spent in a close carriage, would be salutary and pleasant. The young lady readily embraced the proposal. They forthwith alighted, and walked at a small distance before the chaise, which was now conducted by the servant. From this moment the spectre, which, till now, had been occasionally visible, entirely disappeared. This incident naturally led the conversation to this topic. So singular a specimen of the forms which human nature is found to assume could not fail of suggesting a variety of remarks.

They pictured to themselves many combinations of circumstances in which Handyside might be the agent, and in which the most momentous effects might flow from his agency, without its being possible for others to conjecture the true nature of the agent. The propensities of this being might contribute to realize, on an American road, many of those imaginary tokens and perils which abound in the wildest romance. He would be an admirable machine, in a plan whose purpose was to generate or foster, in a given subject, the frenzy of quixotism. No theatre was better adapted than Norwood to such an exhibition. This part of the country had long been deserted by beasts of prey. Bears might still, perhaps, be found during a very rigorous season, but wolves which, when the country was a desert, were extremely numerous, had now, in consequence of increasing population, withdrawn to more savage haunts. Yet the voice of Handyside, varied with the force and skill of which he was known to be capable, would fill these shades with outcries as ferocious as those which are to be heard in Siamese or Abyssinian forests. The tale of his recent elopement had been told by the man with whom they had just parted, in a rustic but picturesque style.

"But why," said the lady, "did not our kind host inform us of this circumstance? He must surely have been well acquainted with the existence and habits of this Handyside. He must have perceived to how many groundless alarms our ignorance, in this respect, was likely to expose us. It is strange that he did not afford us the slightest intimation of it."

Mr. Davis was no less surprised at this omission. He was at a loss to conceive how this should be forgotten in the midst of those minute directions, in which every cause had been laboriously recollected from which he might incur danger or suffer obstruction.

This person, being no longer an object of terror, began to be regarded with a very lively curiosity. They even wished for his appearance and near approach, that they might carry away with them more definite conceptions of his figure. The lady declared she should be highly pleased by hearing his outcries, and consoled herself with the belief that he would not allow them to pass the limits which he had prescribed to his wanderings, without greeting them with a strain or two. This wish had scarcely been uttered, when it was completely gratified.

The lady involuntarily started, and caught hold of her father's arm. Mr. Davis himself was disconcerted. A scream, dismally loud, and piercingly shrill, was uttered by one at less than twenty paces from them.

The monster had shown some skill in the choice of a spot suitable to his design. Neighboring precipices, and a thick umbrage of oaks, on either side, contributed to prolong and to heighten his terrible notes. They were rendered more awful by the profound stillness that preceded and followed them. They were able speedily to quiet the trepidations which this hideous outcry, in spite of preparation and foresight, had produced, but they had not foreseen one of its unhappy consequences.

In a moment Mr. Davis was alarmed by the rapid sound of footsteps behind him. His presence of mind, on this occasion, probably saved himself and his daughter from instant destruction. He leaped out of the path, and, by a sudden exertion, at the same moment, threw the lady to some distance from the tract. The horse that drew the chaise rushed by them with the celerity of lightning. Affrighted at the sounds which had been uttered at a still less distance from the horse than from Mr. Davis, possibly with a malicious design to produce this very effect, he jerked the bridal from the hands, that held it, and rushed forward with headlong speed. The man, before he could provide for his own safety, was beaten to the earth. He was considerably bruised by the fall, but presently recovered his feet, and went in pursuit of the horse.

This accident happened at about a hundred yards from the oak, against which so many cautions had been given. It was not possible, at any time, without considerable caution, to avoid it. It was not to be wondered at, therefore, that, in a few seconds, the carriage was shocked against the trunk, overturned, and dashed into a thousand fragments. The noise of the crash sufficiently informed them of this event. Had the horse been inclined to stop, a repetition, for the space of some minutes, of the same savage and terrible shrieks would have added tenfold to his consternation and to the speed of his flight. After this dismal strain had ended, Mr. Davis raised his daughter from the ground. She had suffered no material injury. As soon as they recovered from the confusion into which this accident had thrown them, they began to consult upon the measures proper to be taken upon this emergency. They were left alone. The servant had gone in pursuit of the flying horse. Whether he would be able to retake him was extremely dubious. Meanwhile they were surrounded by darkness. What was the distance of the next house could not be known. At that hour of the night they could not hope to be directed, by the far-seen taper, to any hospitable roof. The only alternative, therefore, was to remain where they were, uncertain of the fate of their companion, or to go forward with the utmost expedition.

They could not hesitate to embrace the latter. In a few minutes they arrived at the oak. The chaise appeared to have been dashed against a knotty projecture of the trunk, which was large enough for a person to be conveniently seated on it. Here again they paused. Miss Davis desired to remain here a few minutes to recruit her exhausted strength. She proposed to her father to leave her here, and go forward in quest of the horse and the servant. He might return as speedily as he thought proper. She did not fear to be alone. The voice was still. Having accomplished his malicious purposes, the spectre had probably taken his final leave of them. At all events, if the report of the rustic was true, she had no personal injury to fear from him.

Through some deplorable infatuation, as he afterwards deemed it, Mr. Davis complied with her entreaties, and went in search of the missing. He had engaged in a most unpromising undertaking. The man and horse were by this time at a considerable distance. The former would, no doubt, shortly return. Whether his pursuit succeeded or miscarried, he would surely see the propriety of hastening his return with what tidings he could obtain, and to ascertain his master's situation. Add to this, the impropriety of leaving a woman, single and unarmed, to the machinations of this demoniac. He had scarcely parted with her when these reflections occurred to him. His resolution was changed. He turned back with the intention of immediately seeking her. At the same moment, he saw the flash and heard the discharge of a pistol. The light proceeded from the foot of the oak. His imagination was filled with horrible forebodings. He ran with all his speed to the spot. He called aloud upon the name of his daughter, but, alas! she was unable to answer him. He found her stretched at the foot of the tree, senseless, and weltering in her blood. He lifted her in his arms, and seated her against the trunk. He found himself stained with blood, flowing from a wound, which either the darkness of the night, or the confusion of his thoughts, hindered him from tracing. Overwhelmed with a catastrophe so dreadful and unexpected, he was divested of all presence of mind. The author of his calamity had vanished. No human being was at hand to succor him in his uttermost distress. He beat his head against the ground, tore away his venerable locks, and rent the air with his cries.

Fortunately there was a dwelling at no great distance from this scene. The discharge of a pistol produces a sound too loud not to be heard far and wide in this lonely region. This house belonged to a physician. He was a man noted for his humanity and sympathy. He was roused, as well as most of his family, by a sound so uncommon. He rose instantly, and calling up his people, proceeded with lights to the road. The lamentations of Mr. Davis directed them to the place. To the physician the scene was inexplicable. Who was the author of this distress; by whom the pistol was discharged; whether through some untoward chance or with design, he was as yet uninformed, nor could he gain any information from the incoherent despair of Mr. Davis.

Every measure that humanity and professional skill could suggest were employed on this occasion. The dying lady was removed to the house. The ball had lodged in her brain, and to extract it was impossible. Why should I dwell on the remaining incidents of this tale? She languished till the next morning, and then expired.

Stone Baby

Terri Bruce

LITHOPEDION, the doctor had said.

Stone baby.

Lynne's hands reflexively clenched in her lap as she stared unseeing out the passenger-side window, replaying the conversation. The words echoed hollowly in her head, dull and meaningless.

Gary took one hand off the wheel long enough to squeeze her knee. "Honey? Are you okay?" In the same moment, he slammed on the brakes and leaned on the horn. "Asshole!" he shouted, then turned to Lynne. "Did you see that? That guy just cut in front of us, almost caused an accident?"

No, she hadn't seen it.

Dimly, she registered the busy, midday city traffic – pedestrians, bike messengers, delivery trucks. So much fruitless noise and hurry. It hammered at her, and she squeezed her eyes shut so she wouldn't have to see it.

They had been trying for so long to have a child. And, at some point, there had been one, growing inside her – and then it had turned to stone.

The landscape – strip malls, office parks, cars, pedestrians – blurred as the tears she'd been struggling to hold back since the doctor's office trembled on her lashes and then spilled over, tracking silently down her cheeks.

"It will have to come out," the doctor had said.

He hadn't used the word miscarriage – but that's what it was. Only, instead of breaking down and being absorbed by the body or expelled in the usual rush of blood, the baby had stayed inside her. Stayed inside her and calcified – the body's defense mechanism against blood poisoning.

Their perfect, precious infant – dead.

"Hey, are you hungry?" Gary asked.

The tears continued to slide down her cheeks.

* * *

Lynne lay in bed and stared up at the ceiling. Beside her, Gary snored away peacefully, the sweltering night air not bothering him one bit. She splayed her fingers on her abdomen.

Would she be able to feel the egg-sized lump within her if she pressed hard enough?

Her fingers flexed against the rough blue cotton of her camisole, but she didn't press down; somehow, the certainty would be worse. Just the thought of feeling the fossilized fetus inside her made her skin crawl.

It was unusual, the doctor had said, but not abnormal. It happened. Heck, the doctor had casually reported, a Chinese woman had had one in her for sixty years.

Sixty years.

The tears had stopped as soon as they reached home; no, sooner than that – when Gary had pulled up to the speaker at the drive-thru and then, when she had shook her head no that she didn't want anything, ordered her a hamburger, anyway.

After that, she'd just felt empty and tired. Now, though, as she lay in the sweltering heat, her skin sticky with a thin film of sweat, she just felt…detached. Like a scientist examining an interesting problem.

Part of her wondered at how calm – how devoid of feeling – she was.

Maybe this was what shock felt like.

Or maybe she was a bad person.

It was as if the surgical gauze neatly lining the doctor's shelves had been wound around her, mummy-style; she kept turning the same thoughts over: she had been pregnant at some point – the thing she had wanted so desperately had happened – and she'd been completely unaware.

How could she have not known?

Shouldn't she have known?

She was a woman – weren't women, *real* women, supposed to know things instinctively about babies, about *their* baby?

She thought she should feel some way about that – shame, sorrow, maybe even fear – but she felt…nothing.

What kind of mother did that make her? Was that why the baby had died – because she wasn't fit to be a mother? Maybe her lack of notice and love in those first, precious months had doomed the small life inside her. Left unnourished with human affection, it had shriveled and died.

As she replayed the conversation in the doctor's office over and over and over in her head, some of the numbness wore off. She expected grief to replace it, thought maybe, like the calcification of her baby's remains, the numbness had been a protective shell expelled over her emotions to stave off the overwhelming grief that would follow on the heels of losing a baby.

Instead, as she ran a hand over her abdomen again, gently so she wouldn't feel the lump inside of her, she felt a scalding stab of disgust and then a simmering of resentment; for three years this *thing* had hunkered inside her, taking up the space meant for a child – a living child – and preventing her from having others. It was as if the child had decided if it couldn't be born, it wouldn't let any others be, either. This thing inside her was sabotaging her, trying to stop her from having children.

No, she wasn't sad – she was angry. This thing inside her was sickening – and she wanted it out. The sooner, the better.

She moved her hand away from her abdomen with a shudder of revulsion. She reached down and pulled the sheet up to her chin like a protective shield. The humid, smothering night air deadened all sound, leaving only the noise of Gary's snuffling snores to lull her to sleep.

The doctor had said once it was removed, there might be a chance she could still conceive.

That thought should give her hope, even joy, but instead, unease passed over her.

What if the next one turned to stone, too?

Her eyes drifted closed, sleep overtaking her. Just before she lost consciousness, a small voice inside her said, "There won't be a next one. This is the only baby you'll have."

And then the hard lump inside her moved.

* * *

Lynne leaned against the counter, still in her camisole and sweat pants, nursing a lukewarm cup of sludgy coffee – her third. Christ, she was tired. So God-damned tired.

She'd been exhausted for so long now she couldn't remember when it had started – certainly long before the meeting with the doctor. And there were pains, on occasion, deep in her belly that she had assumed had to do with getting older. But now, now she knew – it was the stone baby.

The doctor had said it was dead, that it was stone, that her body no longer nourished it, as it would a real child, but now, now Lynne knew better.

It was feeding off her.

It was the only explanation that made sense.

When she'd dragged herself, bone-tired, from bed this morning and looked in the mirror, she'd hardly recognized her face. Her cheek bones and chin stuck out at sharp angles, her cheeks sunken and hollow. Dark circles rimmed her eyes. Looking at her twig-like arms, thin enough to be snapped by a strong breeze, she'd been horrified. When had she grown so thin and frail? It was as if overnight all the vitality had been sucked from her. And then she knew – it was the lump of rock in her belly. Discovered, threatened, it was fighting back. It was tenacious, dug in, and wouldn't go without a fight.

"Honey?" said Gary, as he entered the kitchen, straightening his tie.

Lynne jumped, startled by the sudden intrusion.

Gary smiled at her wanly, sympathetically. He came closer, smelling of spicy aftershave and medicated shampoo. The cotton of his dress shirt was soft as he pulled her head to his shoulder and stroked her hair sympathetically.

"Still sad?" he asked.

A stab of anger sliced through her. What did he mean 'still'? They had only just found out yesterday that she'd been pregnant – almost three months along – and that their baby had *died*.

But was it really dead if it fed off her?

Revulsion shuddered through her, and she pushed Gary away. She straightened up, feeling the three cups of coffee heave in her stomach like a giant water balloon, and she clamped her jaw shut to keep the gorge from rising.

"You okay?" Gary asked, seeming to note more the 'green about the gills' look on her face than the sudden need for air, for space, to not to be touched.

"Yeah, fine." She quickly glanced around the antiseptic kitchen – white basket-weave tile, grey-veined white marble counters, stainless steel appliances, white tile floor – searching for crackers, for mints, for a glass of water to settle her stomach, to distract her from the feeling of her life force being sucked from her into the putrescent, decaying thing inside her. Because she could feel it now – could feel the energy flowing from her to it like a giant, gaping wound. The thing inside her was greedy, hungry. It would suck her dry if it could. Well, the doctor could suck it out of her with one of those liposuction tubes for all she cared. Suck on her would it? Let's see how it liked it.

"You going to call the doctor today?" Gary asked absently, already turning away to finish tying his tie as he searched for his keys and briefcase.

And then she felt it again, the same as the night before – the flutter, deep and low, like a tiny bird shaking its wings.

One hand went to her abdomen – instinct – to lay there gently, soothingly as a soft gasp of surprise escaped her lips.

"What was that?" Gary asked, half turning back to her.

"Yes," she said softly. "I'll call the doctor."

* * *

Lynne lay on her back in bed, her hand absently on her abdomen, drifting somewhere between asleep and awake.

It had been three days, and she still hadn't called the doctor.

A soft noise caught her attention, pulled her slowly toward wakefulness. She lay still in the deep, thick dark of the suffocating summer night, straining her ears. She held her breath, waiting to see if the noise repeated.

There. Up high – near the ceiling. Over by the window.

Her brain worked hard, trying to identify the soft rustling sound. Wings? Was there a bat in the room?

It was too dark to see – it was a new moon and the thick, dense leaves of the giant oak outside the window blocked whatever feeble illumination might filter in from the house across the street or the stars above.

The rustling grew louder as whatever it was drew closer. She heard a flutter beside her, in the vicinity of the nightstand. She barely had time to catch her breath and hold it, torn between annoyance and fear, before the next sound came: a soft, sad sigh.

Lynne tensed. Was she awake? Dreaming?

Did it matter?

She strained her eyes, trying to see in to the velvet dark to no avail. The darkness was absolute.

"How's the baby?" asked a quiet voice, male if she had to put a gender to it. The speaker seemed to be standing off to the side of the bed.

Lynne relaxed, irritation replacing the uncertainty of a moment ago. This was a dream.

The question annoyed her. Dreaming about her dead child annoyed her. The fact that she hadn't called the doctor yet annoyed her.

"Dead," she said, flatly, perversely. Her fingers resting lightly on her abdomen flexed automatically – a combination of protectiveness and anger – and she hated herself for that small movement, which betrayed so much.

"No, it's not," said the voice, a hint of amusement in its soft, gentle tone.

Torrid emotion – some combination of rage and grief – silenced her. She fumed, wanting to smash her fist into the smug face – and she was sure it was smug – of whoever was speaking.

"See for yourself," the voice said.

Against her will, as if she couldn't stop herself, she complied – some perverse desire to prove the voice wrong, to say, "See? I told you so," moved her to burrow her fingers below the hem of her top to splay her hand firmly on the naked flesh where her shirt and her sweatpants met.

Nothing.

She bit her lip, holding back a wave of revulsion as she pressed harder, searching, for the first time, for the egg-sized lump within her. She moved her hand slowly across her stomach, the skin soft, the light muscling below that taut, pressing lightly at first and then harder. Nausea and fear rose inside her. She bit down, forcing herself to do this. The baby was dead. It was beyond dead – it was a rock. There was no hope – none. She needed to accept that.

Still nothing.

She couldn't feel the lump. She couldn't feel anything.

A shattering wave of grief washed over her, bringing the pricking of tears to her eyes. Her searching hand stilled, and she let it fall onto the bed beside her, relieving it from the light grip it had held on her abdomen for the last three days.

She stared vacantly up into the dark, feeling nothing inside her – not breath, not gnawing hunger, not draining energy. She was fully alone inside her body once more.

"Fuck off," she whispered softly to the dream/hallucination/wishful thinking plaguing her.

And then…

Something.

A soft flutter like a hummingbird, deep and low inside. And then another, quicker, one. *I'm here*, the baby seemed to be saying. *You're not alone.*

"See?" said the voice – and it wasn't smug, but reassuring. A gentle rustle followed – bat wings? – and then silence.

* * *

"The doctor called again," Gary said as he entered the kitchen behind her.

Lynne made a non-committal noise as she stood at the stove, weight on one foot, and stirred the risotto for dinner.

"Haven't you called yet?"

Reflexively, her free hand went to her abdomen. The pulse was still there – strong and steady beneath her hand now instead of the faint flutter she'd first felt. There was definitely something alive inside her. And it was growing. She could feel it, leaden and heavy within her, pushing her insides apart, rearranging them to make room for itself.

She kept her back to Gary, avoiding his eyes, as he came up behind her. He slid an arm around her, and she half turned away so his hand wouldn't fall on her belly, so he wouldn't feel the motion there.

"What's going on, babe? Why haven't you scheduled the procedure yet?"

He tried to nuzzle her hair. She shrugged and made a show of needing to get to the spice cabinet as an excuse to slip out of his suffocating embrace and smothering concern.

She felt his eyes on her, studying her. It felt like an invasion, a condescension. She fought the urge to cover her abdomen with a protective hand.

"I know this is hard for you," Gary said softly. "You won't have to go alone, you know. I'll be there with you the entire time."

She busied herself at the stove, nodding absently, as if agreeing, as if everything he said made sense. As if everything was just that easy.

"Listen, I'll call and make the appointment, okay? I can at least do that much for you. How about for next week?"

"Okay," she said, knowing she wouldn't go.

* * *

That night, she lay in bed, feeling the steady pulse beneath her splayed fingers. The rhythm soothed her.

I'm here. I'm here. I'm here, it seemed to chant. It was the background noise to her life now, always with her. She breathed in and out in time with it, walked in step with it, found herself swaying to it when she came to and found she'd been staring off into space, her thoughts God only knew where.

In the dark, she heard the familiar rustle that she'd come to associate with her nocturnal visitor, followed by the smell of moss and cool, dark earth. The visitor landed lightly, but solidly, slipping in like a whisper and then settling into a steady and comforting silence.

She never turned on the light; she didn't want to know what he looked like. Or maybe it was that she was afraid there wasn't really anyone there.

"How's the baby?" asked the voice.

Lithopedion, the doctor had said.

Stone baby.

She didn't doubt that the doctor spoke the truth. Doubt nibbled at her, fraying the edges of her certainty. She pressed her hand into her abdomen harder, reassuring herself the steady thrumming was still there, that she wasn't imagining it.

"It's stone," she said, unable to keep a mournful wail from tinging the words, unshed fears turning to tears in the back of her throat. "They said it's made of stone."

The voice laughed – a light and happy sound of genuine amusement. "Of course it is. What else are babies made of?"

The words dispelled her unease. Of course it was made of stone. Why had she thought the doctor's diagnosis was incompatible with life? Babies didn't have to be flesh and blood and didn't have to have a beating heart to be real, to be alive.

Lynne relaxed.

The flutter in her belly quickened, seeming a little bit frantic, she thought. She rubbed her growing belly soothingly, warmly. *I'm here, little one. Everything is okay.*

The baby kicked in response.

The voice laughed again. "He likes you."

"Is it a he?" Warmth – pride, maybe – washed through her. *He.* She liked that.

"Maybe," said the voice with a teasing lilt.

Lynne contemplated the darkness for a moment, embarrassed to say what she wanted to say. "Thank you," she said softly.

"For what?"

"For making things easier. For helping me to understand." Lynne hesitated again, afraid her question would upset the visitor – or perhaps more afraid of the answer.

"Are you…are you an angel?" she asked.

"Maybe," the voice answered, again with that teasing note as if he knew a joke she didn't. Then with a fluttering rustle that didn't disturb the stifling night air, he was gone.

* * *

Did she speak or only think she spoke? Was there a voice or did she only dream it? She wasn't sure the answers mattered.

"Did you call the doctor yet?" Gary asked, walking into the kitchen, tying his necktie as he walked. "He's called three times to confirm the new appointment."

She made a non-committal noise.

Gary paused, halfway to reaching for the coffee pot, and shot her a quizzical look. "Hon, I thought you wanted to have a baby? You can't get pregnant with that thing blocking the way."

Her hand went to her abdomen.

"It's not a thing," she said defiant, protective. "It's a baby."

Gary softened. He abandoned the coffeepot and strode across the room to her. He reached for her shoulders, rubbing them comfortingly. "I'm sorry. I misspoke. I know that thing…that it was a baby – a life. And I don't mean to be dismissive or act like it doesn't matter."

It *is* a life, she said, or maybe only thought, but it didn't matter because Gary was hugging her, and she was turning away so he couldn't feel her swelling stomach.

"Would it help if we…if we had a memorial service?" Gary asked tentatively, his face creased in the puzzled frown it permanently wore when contemplating her these days. "We could bury the…remains. Get a headstone. Would that help?"

Lynne made a disgruntled noise and turned away in disgust. *Bury our baby alive?* she wanted to shout at him. *What kind of monster are you?*

"Lynne?" Gary called as she retreated from the room. "Honey, wait…"

But she had no patience for Gary and his detachment, Gary and his inane suggestions, Gary and his complete obliviousness to the reality that their baby would soon be born. What was it going to eat? Where would it sleep? A stone baby was special, different. She didn't know what to expect, what to ask. And Gary…Gary just wouldn't understand.

She stomped upstairs to the bedroom. She turned the lock behind her, so she could be alone. She lay down on the bed, on her side, curled in a fetal position, mimicking how she imagined the baby lay inside her, and placed a hand on her abdomen, stroking it soothingly. The baby kicked hard.

"Hush, little one," she said softly. "It'll be okay. I'll keep you safe. I won't let them hurt you."

* * *

"How's the baby?"

"It's not moving." The words rushed out in a torrent of self-loathing and fear. Tears leaked down her cheeks, and she covered her face in shame. The baby hadn't moved in two weeks. She'd stroked it, talked to it, but nothing – no reaction. She'd even begged: *Just one sign you're in there. Please. Please don't be dead. Please don't be just a hunk of stone. Just give me a sign.*

Had she killed it after all? Worse now, now that she had known it was there and had had time to fall in love with it, than before when it had lurked unseen inside her.

The visitor laughed, simultaneously dismissing and soothing her fears. "Of course not. Do you want it to kick? It's made of stone – you would be injured. It doesn't want to hurt you."

Lynne didn't dare hope that the voice spoke the truth. "How do I know it's still alive if I can't feel it?"

"Can't you tell?"

She thought maybe she could; there was something lurking in her mind – thoughts and feelings not quite her own. Nothing concrete – just a presence, growing ever so slightly, day by day. All Id and unfocused need.

Lynne rubbed a hand across her abdomen, flushing with relief – and excitement. She could talk to it – and it to her.

"I can hear him," she said softly. "But I don't understand what he's saying. What does he want?"

"What everyone wants – to live."

Something wild and ecstatic fluttered inside her, and she wasn't sure if the feeling belonged to her or the baby.

"Be patient," the voice said. "Have faith. If anything were wrong, I would tell you. The baby is doing well. You are doing well. We know this has been difficult for you."

Lynne didn't know what he meant by 'we' – was he referring to God? She supposed so – after all, this baby was a miracle. It had died and been resurrected – metaphorically speaking, because, of course, it had never actually been dead. The doctor had been mistaken on that point. He himself had admitted that stone babies were rare – she could hardly blame him for lacking experience in these matters.

A tremor of happiness washed through her – when she'd thought she'd unknowingly carried a dead child for three years she had wondered at her fitness to be a mother. But now, now, she knew: her avoidance of the doctor had been a mother's natural instinct. She had simply been protecting her baby, before she'd even understood it was a baby. Stone babies took a little longer to gestate than regular babies, it seemed, and in those three years, she had carried it and nourished it. And now, now it was so big and so strong – one had only to look at her belly, the bulge clearly visible, to see just how big and strong he was going to be.

She was going to be a wonderful mother.

* * *

Her fingers splayed across her abdomen. Her stomach was bloated, distorted. Gary had called the doctor.

"He says it has to come out."

The voice said different.

She'd run to her room – her room now; Gary was forbidden. His snoring made it hard to hear the baby's murmurings, and he complained that she talked in her sleep, only, of course, she wasn't sleeping, and she wasn't talking to herself – and locked the door. Gary had had a stubborn, angry look in his eyes she had never seen before.

She curled on the bed, the velvety dark encapsulating her like a cocoon. Her stomach was so large she had to cradle it with both hands to try and keep the weight from pulling at her. She was tired all the time now – not the gnawing, used-up tired of before, but rather like she had been walking uphill for a very long time.

She tried to focus on what the visitor was saying, listening hard to the soft voice above the sound of Gary hammering on the door and the thrumming of the baby's voice in her mind.

"Of course your stomach is big. The baby is growing. It won't be long now." The voice hesitated. "But, perhaps you are sorry now that we gave you this baby to carry."

"No!" she said quickly.

"You understand it will claw its way out of you? It will hurt."

"I don't care."

"The wings are the tricky part. So easy to cause a breach."

Her voice faltered. "Wings? Why does it have wings?"

The voice laughed. "How's it supposed to fly without wings?"

And that made perfect sense.

* * *

"I can't do this anymore," Gary said. "That thing inside you is killing you, and you refuse to do anything about it. I won't stand here and watch you die. Either that thing goes or I do."

"It's not a thing," she said reflexively. There was no point in being angry – he never listened. He didn't understand.

She sat on the couch. He stood over her. Typical. As if he could dominate her, as if he could order her about like she were a child.

"Listen to yourself. You need help. Please…if you ever loved me—"

She jumped to her feet. "I'll what? Murder our child?" Except, that wasn't quite right because she wasn't even sure it was his. How could he, a mere flesh and blood man, have made a baby with wings, a baby made of stone? He couldn't have. It was impossible.

"Lynne, please—" The break in Gary's voice – close to a sob – upset her more than anything he said. It was the weakness of it, the lack of understanding.

"Get out," she said coldly, hand protectively – defiantly – on her distended stomach. "The baby and I want to be alone."

* * *

The labor pains started around midnight – clutching, grasping pains clawing at her insides. She gasped awake, jerking upright to clutch at her stomach.

Wings rustled in the dark; she wasn't alone.

"It's time," the voice said gently.

The pains were coming closer together now, twisting and tearing at her insides, and she wailed in agony as she doubled over.

"We're here," the voice said. "We won't leave you until it is over."

She was nearly insensate from the pain so the sound of many pairs of wings rustling was nearly lost on her, but she felt them, a thickness to the dark that indicated the presence of many bodies. She flopped back against the bed, her back arching in pain as another spasm wracked her and she groaned.

"The baby…something is wrong…"

"No," said the voice. "This is how it is supposed to be. The baby is stone – it has to claw its way down the birth channel. We are sorry for the pain."

She understood then, as she hadn't before, that she wasn't going to survive. To bring the baby to life, she had to die.

And, like everything else the voice had told her, that made sense.

She'd felt she'd died when the doctor had given her the news that the baby was dead. And now she realized, she had. The numbness she had felt – in that moment, she had turned to stone – which had allowed the baby to turn to flesh.

Through the agony, she felt a pang of fear for the parentless child's future, but this was quickly pushed aside. The baby wouldn't be alone – it would go with the voice. With the angels. It was theirs, after all. She knew that – had known that from the beginning. And that was okay. At least she had been a mother, even if for a short time. She had carried it and nourished it and loved it. That was enough. It would remember her – always.

Lynne writhed against the bed. The pain repeatedly drove her to the brink of blacking out and then cruelly receded before rendering her blissfully unconscious, leaving her to fully experience the next wave of wrenching agony.

She screamed and panted throughout the long night. The baby made its way inch by agonizing inch down the birth canal, its stone head pushing aside her hips, her cervix, and everything else in its path. At some point, blood began to flow from between her legs.

By the time the faintest brushstrokes of dawn etched the night sky, the bed was soaked through with blood and sweat. Lynne lay tangled in the sodden sheets, too weak to move as she felt the sharp little claws gain purchase at the exit of the birth canal and begin to pull itself out.

"Almost there," said the voice. "Just a little longer, and it will all be over."

There was a sudden, sharp contraction and her body pushed hard against the baby, expelling it in a rush of fluid. Dimly, Lynne heard it squish wetly onto the bed.

She lay panting as contractions continued to wrack her, expelling the afterbirth. She whimpered weakly, a vague protest.

"You did well," the voice said.

Still the blood flowed out between her legs – blood that seemed to ebb from everywhere inside her with every beat of her heart. Something was wrong – she was bleeding uncontrollably.

She struggled to sit up. She wanted to see the baby – wanted to see it before she died.

She reached down and pulled the tiny, squirming body from the pool of blood and gore, wiped the tiny face with its hard, marble-like eyes and snout-like nose. She carefully folded back the wildly fluttering wings and wrapped the snarling bundle in her arms, cuddling it to her.

It snapped and growled as she held it close.

Hush, little one, hush.

A small, fierce tremor of pride ran through her, briefly cutting through the pain and exhaustion. She had done it. Despite the odds, despite the early self-doubt and fears, she had carried – and delivered – this baby safely. The baby hadn't died. She hadn't killed it.

She was a good mother.

There was a rustle of wings as dawn washed over the assembled witnesses to the birth. The one she took for the speaker – tall, crudely shaped, with skin like weathered gray granite and wide, leathery wings – held out its clawed hands, waiting for her to turn over the precious bundle. Lynne shivered and hugged the baby tighter, sorry to let go. But she couldn't keep it – it had to go with its own kind. She knew that, had always known she was only a temporary guardian. With the last of her strength, she stretched out and placed the baby in the gargoyle's arms.

Jean-ah Poquelin

George Washington Cable

IN THE FIRST DECADE of the present century, when the newly established American Government was the most hateful thing in Louisiana – when the Creoles were still kicking at such vile innovations as the trial by jury, American dances, anti-smuggling laws, and the printing of the Governor's proclamation in English – when the Anglo-American flood that was presently to burst in a crevasse of immigration upon the delta had thus far been felt only as slippery seepage which made the Creole tremble for his footing – there stood, a short distance above what is now Canal Street, and considerably back from the line of villas which fringed the river-bank on Tchoupitoulas Road, an old colonial plantation-house half in ruin.

It stood aloof from civilization, the tracts that had once been its indigo fields given over to their first noxious wildness, and grown up into one of the horridest marshes within a circuit of fifty miles.

The house was of heavy cypress, lifted up on pillars, grim, solid, and spiritless, its massive build a strong reminder of days still earlier, when every man had been his own peace officer and the insurrection of the blacks a daily contingency. Its dark, weatherbeaten roof and sides were hoisted up above the jungly plain in a distracted way, like a gigantic ammunition-wagon stuck in the mud and abandoned by some retreating army. Around it was a dense growth of low water willows, with half a hundred sorts of thorny or fetid bushes, savage strangers alike to the 'language of flowers' and to the botanist's Greek. They were hung with countless strands of discolored and prickly smilax, and the impassable mud below bristled with *chevaux de frise* of the dwarf palmetto. Two lone forest-trees, dead cypresses, stood in the center of the marsh, dotted with roosting vultures. The shallow strips of water were hid by myriads of aquatic plants, under whose coarse and spiritless flowers, could one have seen it, was a harbor of reptiles, great and small, to make one shudder to the end of his days.

The house was on a slightly raised spot, the levee of a draining canal. The waters of this canal did not run; they crawled, and were full of big, ravening fish and alligators, that held it against all comers.

Such was the home of old Jean Marie Poquelin, once an opulent indigo planter, standing high in the esteem of his small, proud circle of exclusively male acquaintances in the old city; now a hermit, alike shunned by and shunning all who had ever known him. "The last of his line," said the gossips. His father lies under the floor of the St. Louis Cathedral, with the wife of his youth on one side, and the wife of his old age on the other. Old Jean visits the spot daily. His half-brother – alas! there was a mystery; no one knew what had become of the gentle, young half-brother, more than thirty years his junior, whom once he seemed so fondly to love, but who, seven years ago, had disappeared suddenly, once for all, and left no clue of his fate.

They had seemed to live so happily in each other's love. No father, mother, wife to either, no kindred upon earth. The elder a bold, frank, impetuous, chivalric adventurer; the younger a gentle, studious, book-loving recluse; they lived upon the ancestral estate like mated birds, one always on the wing, the other always in the nest.

There was no trait in Jean Marie Poquelin, said the old gossips, for which he was so well known among his few friends as his apparent fondness for his 'little brother'.

"Jacques said this", and "Jacques said that"; he "would leave this or that, or anything to Jacques", for "Jacques was a scholar", and "Jacques was good", or "wise", or "just", or "far-sighted", as the nature of the case required; and "he should ask Jacques as soon as he got home", since Jacques was never elsewhere to be seen.

It was between the roving character of the one brother, and the bookishness of the other, that the estate fell into decay. Jean Marie, generous gentleman, gambled the slaves away one by one, until none was left, man or woman, but one old African mute.

The indigo-fields and vats of Louisiana had been generally abandoned as unremunerative. Certain enterprising men had substituted the culture of sugar; but while the recluse was too apathetic to take so active a course, the other saw larger, and, at times, equally respectable profits, first in smuggling, and later in the African slave-trade. What harm could he see in it? The whole people said it was vitally necessary, and to minister to a vital public necessity – good enough, certainly, and so he laid up many a doubloon that made him none the worse in the public regard.

One day old Jean Marie was about to start upon a voyage that was to be longer, much longer, than any that he had yet made. Jacques had begged him hard for many days not to go, but he laughed him off, and finally said, kissing him:

"*Adieu, 'tit frère.*"

"No," said Jacques, "I shall go with you."

They left the old hulk of a house in the sole care of the African mute, and went away to the Guinea coast together.

Two years after, old Poquelin came home without his vessel. He must have arrived at his house by night. No one saw him come. No one saw 'his little brother'; rumor whispered that he, too, had returned, but he had never been seen again.

A dark suspicion fell upon the old slave-trader. No matter that the few kept the many reminded of the tenderness that had ever marked his bearing to the missing man. The many shook their heads. "You know he has a quick and fearful temper"; and "why does he cover his loss with mystery?"

"Grief would out with the truth."

"But," said the charitable few, "look in his face; see that expression of true humanity." The many did look in his face, and, as he looked in theirs, he read the silent question: "Where is thy brother Abel?" The few were silenced, his former friends died off, and the name of Jean Marie Poquelin became a symbol of witchery, devilish crime, and hideous nursery fictions.

The man and his house were alike shunned. The snipe and duck hunters forsook the marsh, and the wood-cutters abandoned the canal. Sometimes the hardier boys who ventured out there snake-shooting heard a slow thumping of oar-locks on the canal. They would look at each other for a moment half in consternation, half in glee, then rush from their sport in wanton haste to assail with their gibes the unoffending, withered old man who, in rusty attire, sat in the stern of a skiff, rowed homeward by his white-headed African mute.

"O Jean-ah Poquelin! O Jean-ah! Jean-ah Poquelin!"

It was not necessary to utter more than that. No hint of wickedness, deformity, or any physical or moral demerit; merely the name and tone of mockery: "Oh, Jean-ah Poquelin!" and while they tumbled one over another in their needless haste to fly, he would rise carefully from his seat, while the aged mute, with downcast face, went on rowing, and rolling up his brown fist and extending it toward the urchins, would pour forth such an unholy broadside of French imprecation and invective as would all but craze them with delight.

Among both blacks and whites the house was the object of a thousand superstitions. Every midnight they affirmed, the *feu follet* came out of the marsh and ran in and out of the rooms, flashing from window to window. The story of some lads, whose words in ordinary statements were worthless, was generally credited, that the night they camped in the woods, rather than pass the place after dark, they saw, about sunset, every window blood-red, and on each of the four chimneys an owl sitting, which turned his head three times round, and moaned and laughed with a human voice. There was a bottomless well, everybody professed to know, beneath the sill of the big front door under the rotten veranda; whoever set his foot upon that threshold disappeared forever in the depth below.

What wonder the marsh grew as wild as Africa! Take all the Faubourg Ste. Marie, and half the ancient city, you would not find one graceless dare-devil reckless enough to pass within a hundred yards of the house after nightfall.

* * *

The alien races pouring into old New Orleans began to find the few streets named for the Bourbon princes too strait for them. The wheel of fortune, beginning to whirl, threw them off beyond the ancient corporation lines, and sowed civilization and even trade upon the lands of the Graviers and Girods. Fields became roads, roads streets. Everywhere the leveller was peering through his glass, rodsmen were whacking their way through willow-brakes and rose-hedges, and the sweating Irishmen tossed the blue clay up with their long-handled shovels.

"Ha! That is all very well," quoth the Jean-Baptistes, fueling the reproach of an enterprise that asked neither co-operation nor advice of them, "but wait till they come yonder to Jean Poquelin's marsh; ha! ha! ha!" The supposed predicament so delighted them, that they put on a mock terror and whirled about in an assumed stampede, then caught their clasped hands between their knees in excess of mirth, and laughed till the tears ran; for whether the street-makers mired in the marsh, or contrived to cut through old 'Jean-ah's' property, either event would be joyful. Meantime a line of tiny rods, with bits of white paper in their split tops, gradually extended its way straight through the haunted ground, and across the canal diagonally.

"We shall fill that ditch," said the men in mud-boots, and brushed close along the chained and padlocked gate of the haunted mansion. Ah, Jean-ah Poquelin, those were not Creole boys, to be stampeded with a little hard swearing.

He went to the Governor. That official scanned the odd figure with no slight interest. Jean Poquelin was of short, broad frame, with a bronzed leonine face. His brow was ample and deeply furrowed. His eye, large and black, was bold and open like that of a war-horse, and his jaws shut together with the firmness of iron. He was dressed in a suit of Attakapas cottonade, and his shirt unbuttoned and thrown back from the throat and bosom, sailor-wise, showed a herculean breast; hard and grizzled. There was no fierceness or defiance in his look, no harsh ungentleness, no symptom of his unlawful life or violent temper; but rather a peaceful and peaceable fearlessness. Across the whole face, not marked in one or another feature, but as it were laid softly upon the countenance like an almost imperceptible veil, was the imprint of some great grief. A careless eye might easily overlook it, but, once seen, there it hung – faint, but unmistakable.

The Governor bowed.

"*Parlez-vous français?*" asked the figure.

"I would rather talk English, if you can do so," said the Governor.

"My name, Jean Poquelin."

"How can I serve you, Mr. Poquelin?"

"My 'ouse is yond'; *dans le marais là-bas.*"

The Governor bowed.

"Dat *marais* billong to me."

"Yes, sir."

"To me; Jean Poquelin; I hown 'im meself."

"Well, sir?"

"He don't billong to you; I get him from me father."

"That is perfectly true, Mr. Poquelin, as far as I am aware."

"You want to make strit pass yond'?"

"I do not know, sir; it is quite probable; but the city will indemnify you for any loss you may suffer – you will get paid, you understand."

"Strit can't pass dare."

"You will have to see the municipal authorities about that, Mr. Poquelin."

A bitter smile came upon the old man's face:

"*Pardon, Monsieur,* you is not *le Gouverneur?*"

"Yes."

"*Mais,* yes. You har *le Gouverneur* – yes. Veh-well. I come to you. I tell you, strit can't pass at me 'ouse."

"But you will have to see—"

"I come to you. You is *le Gouverneur.* I know not the new laws. I ham a Fr-r-rench-a-man! Fr-rench-a-man have something *aller au contraire* – he come at his *Gouverneur.* I come at you. If me not had been bought from me king like *bossals* in the hold time, ze king gof France would-a-show *Monsieur le Gouverneur* to take care his men to make strit in right places. *Mais,* I know; we billong to *Monsieur le Président.* I want you do somesin for me, eh?"

"What is it?" asked the patient Governor.

"I want you tell *Monsieur le Président,* strit – can't – pass – at – me – 'ouse."

"Have a chair, Mr. Poquelin"; but the old man did not stir. The Governor took a quill and wrote a line to a city official, introducing Mr. Poquelin, and asking for him every possible courtesy. He handed it to him, instructing him where to present it.

"Mr. Poquelin," he said with a conciliatory smile, "tell me, is it your house that our Creole citizens tell such odd stories about?"

The old man glared sternly upon the speaker, and with immovable features said:

"You don't see me trade some Guinea nigga?"

"Oh, no."

"You don't see me make some smuggling?"

"No, sir; not at all."

"But, I am Jean Marie Poquelin. I mine me hown bizniss. Dat all right? Adieu."

He put his hat on and withdrew. By and by he stood, letter in hand, before the person to whom it was addressed. This person employed an interpreter.

"He says," said the interpreter to the officer, "he come to make you the fair warning how you muz not make the street pas' at his 'ouse."

The officer remarked that "such impudence was refreshing"; but the experienced interpreter translated freely.

"He says: 'Why you don't want?'" said the interpreter.

The old slave-trader answered at some length.

"He says," said the interpreter, again turning to the officer, "the marass is a too unhealth' for peopl' to live."

"But we expect to drain his old marsh; it's not going to be a marsh."

"*Il dit*—" The interpreter explained in French.

The old man answered tersely.

"He says the canal is a private," said the interpreter.

"Oh! *That* old ditch; that's to be filled up. Tell the old man we're going to fix him up nicely."

Translation being duly made, the man in power was amused to see a thunder-cloud gathering on the old man's face.

"Tell him," he added, "by the time we finish, there'll not be a ghost left in his shanty."

The interpreter began to translate, but—

"*J' comprends, J' comprends*," said the old man, with an impatient gesture, and burst forth, pouring curses upon the United States, the President, the Territory of Orleans, Congress, the Governor and all his subordinates, striding out of the apartment as he cursed, while the object of his maledictions roared with merriment and rammed the floor with his foot.

"Why, it will make his old place worth ten dollars to one," said the official to the interpreter.

"'Tis not for de worse of de property," said the interpreter.

"I should guess not," said the other, whittling his chair – "seems to me as if some of these old Creoles would liever live in a crawfish hole than to have a neighbor."

"You know what make old Jean Poquelin make like that? I will tell you. You know—"

The interpreter was rolling a cigarette, and paused to light his tinder; then, as the smoke poured in a thick double stream from his nostrils, he said, in a solemn whisper: "He is a witch."

"Ho, ho, ho!" laughed the other.

"You don't believe it? What you want to bet?" cried the interpreter, jerking himself half up and thrusting out one arm while he bared it of its coat-sleeve with the hand of the other. "What you want to bet?"

"How do you know?" asked the official.

"Dass what I goin' to tell you. You know, one evening I was shooting some *grosbec*. I killed three, but I had trouble to fine them, it was becoming so dark. When I have them I start' to come home; then I got to pas' at Jean Poquelin's house."

"Ho, ho, ho!" laughed the other, throwing his leg over the arm of his chair.

"Wait," said the interpreter. "I come along slow, not making some noises; still, still—"

"And scared," said the smiling one.

"*Mais*, wait. I get all pas' the 'ouse. 'Ah!' I say; 'All right!' Then I see two thing' before! Hah! I get as cold and humide, and shake like a leaf. You think it was nothing? There I see, so plain as can be (though it was making nearly dark), I see Jean Marie Poquelin walkin' right in front, and right there beside of him was something like a man – but not a man – white like paint! – I dropp' on the grass from scared – they pass'; so sure as I live 'twas the ghos' of Jacques Poquelin, his brother!"

"Pooh!" said the listener.

"I'll put my han' in the fire," said the interpreter.

"But did you never think," asked the other, "that that might be Jack Poquelin, as you call him, alive and well, and for some cause hid away by his brother?"

"But there har' no cause!" said the other, and the entrance of third parties changed the subject.

Some months passed and the street was opened. A canal was first dug through the marsh, the small one which passed so close to Jean Poquelin's house was filled, and the street, or rather a sunny road, just touched a corner of the old mansion's dooryard. The morass ran dry. Its venomous denizens slipped away through the bulrushes; the cattle roaming freely upon its hardened surface trampled the superabundant undergrowth. The bellowing frogs croaked to westward. Lilies and the flower-de-luce sprang up in the place of reeds; smilax and poison-oak gave way to the purple-plumed iron-weed and pink spiderwort; the bindweeds ran everywhere blooming as they ran, and on one of the dead cypresses a giant creeper hung its green burden of foliage and lifted its scarlet trumpets. Sparrows and red-birds flitted through the bushes, and dewberries grew ripe beneath. Over all these came a sweet, dry smell of salubrity which the place had not known since the sediments of the Mississippi first lifted it from the sea.

But its owner did not build. Over the willow-brakes, and down the vista of the open street, bright new houses, some singly, some by ranks, were prying in upon the old man's privacy. They even settled down toward his southern side. First a wood-cutter's hut or two, then a market gardener's shanty, then a painted cottage, and all at once the faubourg had flanked and half surrounded him and his dried-up marsh.

Ah! Then the common people began to hate him. "The old tyrant!"

"You don't mean an old *tyrant*?"

"Well, then, why don't he build when the public need demands it? What does he live in that unneighborly way for?"

"The old pirate!"

"The old kidnapper!" How easily even the most ultra Louisianians put on the imported virtues of the North when they could be brought to bear against the hermit. "There he goes, with the boys after him! Ah! Ha! Ha! Jean-ah Poquelin! Ah! Jean-ah! Aha! Aha! Jean-ah Marie! Jean-ah Poquelin! The old villain!" How merrily the swarming Américains echo the spirit of persecution! "The old fraud," they say – "pretends to live in a haunted house, does he? We'll tar and feather him some day. Guess we can fix him."

He cannot be rowed home along the old canal now; he walks. He has broken sadly of late, and the street urchins are ever at his heels. It is like the days when they cried: "Go up, thou bald-head," and the old man now and then turns and delivers ineffectual curses.

To the Creoles – to the incoming lower class of superstitious Germans, Irish, Sicilians, and others – he became an omen and embodiment of public and private ill-fortune. Upon him all the vagaries of their superstitions gathered and grew. If a house caught fire, it was imputed to his machinations. Did a woman go off in a fit, he had bewitched her. Did a child stray off for an hour, the mother shivered with the apprehension that Jean Poquelin had offered him to strange gods. The house was the subject of every bad boy's invention who loved to contrive ghostly lies. "As long as that house stands we shall have bad luck. Do you not see our pease and beans dying, our cabbages and lettuce going to seed and our gardens turning to dust, while every day you can see it raining in the woods? The rain will never pass old Poquelin's house. He keeps a fetich. He has conjured the whole Faubourg St. Marie. And why, the old wretch? Simply because our playful and innocent children call after him as he passes."

A 'Building and Improvement Company', which had not yet got its charter, 'but was going to', and which had not, indeed, any tangible capital yet, but 'was going to have some', joined the 'Jean-ah Poquelin' war. The haunted property would be such a capital site for a market-house! They sent a deputation to the old mansion to ask its occupant to sell. The deputation never got beyond the chained gate and a very barren interview with the African mute. The President of the Board was then empowered (for he had studied French in Pennsylvania and was considered qualified) to call and persuade M. Poquelin to subscribe to the company's stock; but—

"Fact is, gentlemen," he said at the next meeting, "it would take us at least twelve months to make Mr. Pokaleen understand the rather original features of our system, and he wouldn't subscribe when we'd done; besides, the only way to see him is to stop him on the street."

There was a great laugh from the Board; they couldn't help it. "Better meet a bear robbed of her whelps," said one.

"You're mistaken as to that," said the President. "I did meet him, and stopped him, and found him quite polite. But I could get no satisfaction from him; the fellow wouldn't talk in French, and when I spoke in English he hoisted his old shoulders up, and gave the same answer to everything I said."

"And that was—?" asked one or two, impatient of the pause.

"That it 'don't worse w'ile?'"

One of the Board said: "Mr. President, this market-house project, as I take it, is not altogether a selfish one; the community is to be benefited by it. We may feel that we are working in the public interest [the Board smiled knowingly], if we employ all possible means to oust this old nuisance from among us. You may know that at the time the street was cut through, this old Poquelann did all he could to prevent it. It was owing to a certain connection which I had with that affair that I heard a ghost story [smiles, followed by a sudden dignified check] – ghost story, which, of course, I am not going to relate; but I *may* say that my profound conviction, arising from a prolonged study of that story, is, that this old villain, John Poquelann, has his brother locked up in that old house. Now, if this is so, and we can fix it on him, I merely *suggest* that we can make the matter highly useful. I don't know," he added, beginning to sit down, "but that it is an action we owe to the community – hem!"

"How do you propose to handle the subject?" asked the President.

"I was thinking," said the speaker, "that, as a Board of Directors, it would be unadvisable for us to authorize any action involving trespass; but if you, for instance, Mr. President, should, as it were, for mere curiosity, *request* someone, as, for instance, our excellent Secretary, simply as a personal favor, to look into the matter – this is merely a suggestion."

The Secretary smiled sufficiently to be understood that, while he certainly did not consider such preposterous service a part of his duties as secretary, he might, notwithstanding, accede to the President's request; and the Board adjourned.

Little White, as the Secretary was called, was a mild, kind-hearted little man, who, nevertheless, had no fear of anything, unless it was the fear of being unkind.

"I tell you frankly," he privately said to the President, "I go into this purely for reasons of my own."

The next day, a little after nightfall, one might have descried this little man slipping along the rear fence of the Poquelin place, preparatory to vaulting over into the rank, grass-grown yard, and bearing himself altogether more after the manner of a collector of rare chickens than according to the usage of secretaries.

The picture presented to his eye was not calculated to enliven his mind. The old mansion stood out against the western sky, black and silent. One long, lurid pencil-stroke along a sky of slate was all that was left of daylight. No sign of life was apparent; no light at any window, unless it might have been on the side of the house hidden from view. No owls were on the chimneys, no dogs were in the yard.

He entered the place, and ventured up behind a small cabin which stood apart from the house. Through one of its many crannies he easily detected the African mute crouched before a flickering pine-knot, his head on his knees, fast asleep.

He concluded to enter the mansion, and, with that view, stood and scanned it. The broad rear steps of the veranda would not serve him; he might meet someone midway. He was measuring, with his eye, the proportions of one of the pillars which supported it, and estimating the practicability of climbing it, when he heard a footstep. Someone dragged a chair out toward the railing, then seemed to change his mind and began to pace the veranda, his footfalls resounding on the dry boards with singular loudness. Little White drew a step backward, got the figure between himself and the sky, and at once recognized the short, broad-shouldered form of old Jean Poquelin.

He sat down upon a billet of wood, and, to escape the stings of a whining cloud of mosquitoes, shrouded his face and neck in his handkerchief, leaving his eyes uncovered.

He had sat there but a moment when he noticed a strange, sickening odor, faint, as if coming from a distance, but loathsome and horrid.

Whence could it come? Not from the cabin; not from the marsh, for it was as dry as powder. It was not in the air; it seemed to come from the ground.

Rising up, he noticed, for the first time, a few steps before him a narrow footpath leading toward the house. He glanced down it – ha! right there was someone coming – ghostly white!

Quick as thought, and as noiselessly, he lay down at full length against the cabin. It was bold strategy, and yet, there was no denying it, Little White felt that he was frightened. "It is not a ghost," he said to himself. "I *know* it cannot be a ghost"; but the perspiration burst out at every pore, and the air seemed to thicken with heat. "It is a living man," he said in his thoughts. "I hear his footstep, and I hear old Poquelin's footsteps, too, separately, over on the veranda. I am not discovered; the thing has passed; there is that odor again; what a smell of death! Is it coming back? Yes. It stops at the door of the cabin. Is it peering in at the sleeping mute? It moves away. It is in the path again. Now it is gone." He shuddered. "Now, if I dare venture, the mystery is solved." He rose cautiously, close against the cabin, and peered along the path.

The figure of a man, a presence if not a body – but whether clad in some white stuff or naked the darkness would not allow him to determine – had turned, and now, with a seeming painful gait, moved slowly from him. "Great Heaven! Can it be that the dead do walk?" He withdrew again the hands which had gone to his eyes. The dreadful object passed between two pillars and under the house. He listened. There was a faint sound as of feet upon a staircase; then all was still except the measured tread of Jean Poquelin walking on the veranda, and the heavy respirations of the mute slumbering in the cabin.

The little Secretary was about to retreat; but as he looked once more toward the haunted house a dim light appeared in the crack of a closed window, and presently old Jean Poquelin came, dragging his chair, and sat down close against the shining cranny. He spoke in a low, tender tone in the French tongue, making some inquiry. An answer came from within. Was it the voice of a human? So unnatural was it – so hollow, so discordant, so unearthly – that the stealthy listener shuddered again from head to foot, and when something stirred in some bushes nearby – though it may have been nothing more than a rat – and came scuttling through the grass, the little Secretary actually turned and fled. As he left the enclosure he moved with bolder leisure through the bushes; yet now and then he spoke aloud: "Oh, oh! I see, I understand!" and shut his eyes in his hands.

How strange that henceforth Little White was the champion of Jean Poquelin! In season and out of season – wherever a word was uttered against him – the Secretary, with a quiet, aggressive force that instantly arrested gossip, demanded upon what authority the statement or conjecture was made; but as he did not condescend to explain his own remarkable attitude, it was not long before the disrelish and suspicion which had followed Jean Poquelin so many years fell also upon him.

It was only the next evening but one after his adventure that he made himself a source of sullen amazement to one hundred and fifty boys, by ordering them to desist from their wanton hallooing. Old Jean Poquelin, standing and shaking his cane, rolling out his long-drawn maledictions, paused and stared, then gave the Secretary a courteous bow and started on. The boys, save one, from pure astonishment, ceased, but a ruffianly little Irish lad, more daring than any had yet been, threw a big hurtling clod, that struck old Poquelin between the shoulders and burst like a shell. The enraged old man wheeled with uplifted staff to give chase to the scampering vagabond; and – he may have tripped, or he may not, but he fell full length. Little White hastened to help him up, but he waved him off with a fierce imprecation and staggering to his feet resumed his way homeward. His lips were reddened with blood.

Little White was on his way to the meeting of the Board. He would have given all he dared spend to have stayed away, for he felt both too fierce and too tremulous to brook the criticisms that were likely to be made.

"I can't help it, gentlemen; I can't help you to make a case against the old man, and I'm not going to."

"We did not expect this disappointment, Mr. White."

"I can't help that, sir. No, sir; you had better not appoint any more investigations. Somebody'll investigate himself into trouble. No, sir; it isn't a threat, it is only my advice, but I warn you that whoever takes the task in hand will rue it to his dying day – which may be hastened, too."

The President expressed himself 'surprised'.

"I don't care a rush," answered Little White, wildly and foolishly. "I don't care a rush if you are, sir. No, my nerves are not disordered; my head's as clear as a bell. No, I'm *not* excited." A Director remarked that the Secretary looked as though he had waked from a nightmare.

"Well, sir, if you want to know the fact, I have; and if you choose to cultivate old Poquelin's society you can have one, too."

"White," called a facetious member, but White did not notice. "White," he called again.

"What?" demanded White, with a scowl.

"Did you see the ghost?"

"Yes, sir; I did," cried White, hitting the table, and handing the President a paper which brought the Board to other business.

The story got among the gossips that somebody (they were afraid to say Little White) had been to the Poquelin mansion by night and beheld something appalling. The rumor was but a shadow of the truth, magnified and distorted as is the manner of shadows. He had seen skeletons walking, and had barely escaped the clutches of one by making the sign of the cross.

Some madcap boys with an appetite for the horrible plucked up courage to venture through the dried marsh by the cattle-path, and come before the house at a spectral hour when the air was full of bats. Something which they but half saw – half a sight was enough – sent them tearing back through the willow-brakes and acacia bushes to their homes, where they fairly dropped down, and cried:

"Was it white?"

"No – yes – nearly so – we can't tell – but we saw it." And one could hardly doubt, to look at their ashen faces, that they had, whatever it was.

"If that old rascal lived in the country we come from," said certain Américains, "he'd have been tarred and feathered before now, wouldn't he, Sanders?"

"Well, now he just would."

"And we'd have rid him on a rail, wouldn't we?"

"That's what I allow."

"Tell you what you *could* do." They were talking to some rollicking Creoles who had assumed an absolute necessity for doing *something*.

"What is it you call this thing where an old man marries a young girl, and you come out with horns and—"

"*Charivari?*" asked the Creoles.

"Yes, that's it. Why don't you shivaree him?" Felicitous suggestion.

Little White, with his wife beside him, was sitting on their doorsteps on the sidewalk, as Creole custom had taught them, looking toward the sunset. They had moved into the lately-opened street. The view was not attractive on the score of beauty. The houses were small and scattered, and across the flat commons, spite of the lofty tangle of weeds and bushes, and spite of the thickets of acacia, they needs must see the dismal old Poquelin mansion, tilted awry and shutting out the declining sun. The moon, white and slender, was hanging the tip of its horn over one of the chimneys.

"And you say," said the Secretary, "the old black man has been going by here alone? Patty, suppose old Poquelin should be concocting some mischief; he don't lack provocation; the way that clod hit him the other day was enough to have killed him. Why, Patty, he dropped as quick as *that*! No wonder you haven't seen him. I wonder if they haven't heard something about him up at the drug-store. Suppose I go and see."

"Do," said his wife.

She sat alone for half an hour, watching that sudden going out of the day peculiar to the latitude.

"That moon is ghost enough for one house," she said, as her husband returned. "It has gone right down the chimney."

"Patty," said Little White, "the drug-clerk says the boys are going to shivaree old Poquelin tonight. I'm going to try to stop it."

"Why, White," said his wife, "you'd better not. You'll get hurt."

"No, I'll not."

"Yes, you will."

"I'm going to sit out here until they come along. They're compelled to pass right by here."

"Why, White, it may be midnight before they start; you're not going to sit out here till then."

"Yes, I am."

"Well, you're very foolish," said Mrs. White in an undertone, looking anxious, and tapping one of the steps with her foot.

They sat a very long time talking over little family matters.

"What's that?" at last said Mrs. White.

"That's the nine-o'clock gun," said White, and they relapsed into a long-sustained, drowsy silence.

"Patty, you'd better go in and go to bed," said he at last.

"I'm not sleepy."

"Well, you're very foolish," quietly remarked Little White, and again silence fell upon them.

"Patty, suppose I walk out to the old house and see if I can find out anything."

"Suppose," said she, "you don't do any such – listen!"

Down the street arose a great hubbub. Dogs and boys were howling and barking; men were laughing, shouting, groaning, and blowing horns, whooping, and clanking cow-bells, whinnying, and howling, and rattling pots and pans.

"They are coming this way," said Little White. "You had better go into the house, Patty."

"So had you."

"No. I'm going to see if I can't stop them."

"Why, White!"

"I'll be back in a minute," said White, and went toward the noise.

In a few moments the little Secretary met the mob. The pen hesitates on the word, for there is a respectable difference, measurable only on the scale of the half century, between a mob and a *charivari*. Little White lifted his ineffectual voice. He faced the head of the disorderly column, and cast himself about as if he were made of wood and moved by the jerk of a string. He rushed to one who seemed, from the size and clatter of his tin pan, to be a leader. "*Stop these fellows, Bienvenu, stop them just a minute, till I tell them something.*" Bienvenu turned and brandished his instruments of discord in an imploring way to the crowd. They slackened their pace, two or three hushed their horns and joined the prayer of Little White and Bienvenu for silence. The throng halted. The hush was delicious.

"Bienvenu," said Little White, "don't shivaree old Poquelin tonight; he's—"

"My fwang," said the swaying Bienvenu, "who tail you I goin' to chahivahi somebody, eh? Yon sink bickause I make a little playfool wiz zis tin pan zat I am *dhonk*?"

"Oh, no, Bienvenu, old fellow, you're all right. I was afraid you might not know that old Poquelin was sick, you know, but you're not going there, are you?"

"My fwang, I vay soy to tail you zat you ah dhonk as de dev'. I am *shem* of you. I ham ze servan' of ze *publique*. Zese *citoyens* goin' to wickwest Jean Poquelin to give to the Ursuline' two hondred fifty dolla'—"

"*Hé quoi!*" cried a listener, "*Cinq cent piastres, oui!*"

"*Oui!*" said Bienvenu, "and if he wiffuse we make him some lit' *musique*; ta-ra ta!" He hoisted a merry hand and foot, then frowning, added: "Old Poquelin got no bizniz dhink s'much w'isky."

"But, gentlemen," said Little White, around whom a circle had gathered, "the old man is very sick."

"My faith!" cried a tiny Creole, "we did not make him to be sick. W'en we have say we going make *le charivari*, do you want that we hall tell a lie? My faith! 'sfools!"

"But you can shivaree somebody else," said desperate Little White.

"*Oui*" cried Bienvenu, "*et chahivahi* Jean-ah Poquelin tomo'w!"

"Let us go to Madame Schneider!" cried two or three, and amid huzzas and confused cries, among which was heard a stentorian Celtic call for drinks, the crowd again began to move.

"*Cent piastres pour l'hôpital de charité!*"

"Hurrah!"

"One hongred dolla' for Charity Hospital!"

"Hurrah!"

"Whang!" went a tin pan, the crowd yelled, and Pandemonium gaped again.

They were off at a right angle.

Nodding, Mrs. White looked at the mantle-clock.

"Well, if it isn't away after midnight."

The hideous noise downstreet was passing beyond earshot. She raised a sash and listened. For a moment there was silence. Someone came to the door.

"Is that you, White?"

"Yes." He entered. "I succeeded, Patty."

"Did you?" said Patty, joyfully.

"Yes. They've gone down to shivaree the old Dutchwoman who married her step-daughter's sweetheart. They say she has got to pay a hundred dollars to the hospital before they stop."

The couple retired, and Mrs. White slumbered. She was awakened by her husband snapping the lid of his watch.

"What time?" she asked.

"Half-past three. Patty, I haven't slept a wink. Those fellows are out yet. Don't you hear them?"

"Why, White, they're coming this way!"

"I know they are," said White, sliding out of bed and drawing on his clothes, "and they're coming fast. You'd better go away from that window, Patty. My! What a clatter!"

"Here they are," said Mrs. White, but her husband was gone. Two or three hundred men and boys pass the place at a rapid walk straight down the broad, new street, toward the hated house of ghosts. The din was terrific. She saw Little White at the head of the rabble brandishing his arms and trying in vain to make himself heard; but they only shook their heads laughing and hooting the louder, and so passed, bearing him on before them.

Swiftly they pass out from among the houses, away from the dim oil lamps of the street, out into the broad starlit commons, and enter the willowy jungles of the haunted ground. Some hearts fail and their owners lag behind and turn back, suddenly remembering how near morning it is. But the most part push on, tearing the air with their clamor.

Down ahead of them in the long, thicket-darkened way there is – singularly enough – a faint, dancing light. It must be very near the old house; it is. It has stopped now. It is a lantern, and is under a well-known sapling which has grown up on the wayside since the canal was filled. Now it swings mysteriously to and fro. A goodly number of the more ghost-fearing give up the sport; but a full hundred move forward at a run, doubling their devilish howling and banging.

Yes; it is a lantern, and there are two persons under the tree. The crowd draws near – drops into a walk; one of the two is the old African mute; he lifts the lantern up so that it shines on the other; the crowd recoils; there is a hush of all clangor, and all at once, with a cry of mingled fright and horror from every throat, the whole throng rushes back, dropping every thing, sweeping past Little White and hurrying on, never stopping until the jungle is left behind, and then to find that not one in ten has seen the cause of the stampede, and not one of the tenth is certain what it was.

There is one huge fellow among them who looks capable of any villany. He finds something to mount on, and, in the Creole *patois*, calls a general halt. Bienvenu sinks down, and, vainly trying to recline gracefully, resigns the leadership. The herd gather round the speaker; he assures them that they have been outraged. Their right peaceably to traverse the public streets has been trampled upon. Shall such encroachments be endured? It is now daybreak. Let them go now by the open light of day and force a free passage of the public highway!

A scattering consent was the response, and the crowd, thinned now and drowsy, straggled quietly down toward the old house. Some drifted ahead, others sauntered behind, but everyone, as he again neared the tree, came to a stand-still. Little White sat upon a bank of turf on the opposite side of the way looking very stern and sad. To each newcomer he put the same question:

"Did you come here to go to old Poquelin's?"

"Yes."

"He's dead." And if the shocked hearer started away he would say: "Don't go away."

"Why not?"

"I want you to go to the funeral presently."

If some Louisianian, too loyal to dear France or Spain to understand English, looked bewildered, someone would interpret for him; and presently they went. Little White led the van, the crowd trooping after him down the middle of the way. The gate, that had never been seen before unchained, was open. Stern Little White stopped a short distance from it; the rabble stopped behind him. Something was moving out from under the veranda. The many whisperers stretched upward to see. The African mute came very slowly toward the gate, leading by a cord in the nose a small brown bull, which was harnessed to a rude cart. On the flat body of the cart, under a black cloth, were seen the outlines of a long box.

"Hats off, gentlemen," said Little White, as the box came in view, and the crowd silently uncovered.

"Gentlemen," said Little White, "here come the last remains of Jean Marie Poquelin, a better man, I'm afraid, with all his sins – yes a better – a kinder man to his blood – a man of more self-forgetful goodness – than all of you put together will ever dare to be."

There was a profound hush as the vehicle came creaking through the gate; but when it turned away from them toward the forest, those in front started suddenly. There was a backward rush, then all stood still again staring one way; for there, behind the bier, with eyes cast down and labored step, walked the living remains – all that was left – of little Jacques Poquelin, the long-hidden brother – a leper, as white as snow.

Dumb with horror, the cringing crowd gazed upon the walking death. They watched, in silent awe, the slow *cortége* creep down the long, straight road and lessen on the view, until by and by it stopped where a wild, unfrequented path branched off into the undergrowth toward the rear of the ancient city.

"They are going to the *Terre aux Lépreux*," said one in the crowd. The rest watched them in silence.

The little bull was set free; the mute, with the strength of an ape, lifted the long box to his shoulder. For a moment more the mute and the leper stood in sight, while the former adjusted his heavy burden; then, without one backward glance upon the unkind human world, turning their faces toward the ridge in the depths of the swamp known as the Leper's Land, they stepped into the jungle, disappeared, and were never seen again.

The Tomb-Herd

Ramsey Campbell

*...the Herd that standeth watch at the secret portal each tomb is known to have, and
that thrive on that which groweth out of the inhabitants thereof...*
Alhazred's Necronomicon

THERE ARE MYRIAD unspeakable terrors in the cosmos in which our universe is but an
atom; and the two gates of agony, life and death, gape to pour forth infinities of abominations.
And the other gates which spew forth their broods are, thank God, little known to most of us.
Few can have seen the spawn of ultimate corruption, or known that centre of insane chaos
where Azathoth, the blind idiot god, bubbles mindlessly; I myself have never seen these things –
but God knows that what I saw in those cataclysmic moments in the church at Kingsport
transcends the ultimate earthly knowledge.

If I had not been the victim of circumstances, I know that I would never have come near
rotted, ancient Kingsport. But I had little money in those days, and when I recollected the
invitation of a friend, made long past, who resided in Kingsport, to become his secretary, I
wondered with scant hope if this post might yet be in need of a tenant. I knew that my friend
would not easily acquire any person who would stay with him for long; not many would relish a
stay of any length in that place of ill repute.

Thinking thus, I gathered what few belongings I yet possessed into a trunk, loaded them
into a small sports car, and set out for Massachusetts. Before I reached my destination I became
disquieted by the general tenor of the surroundings – grim, brooding country, sparse of
habitation and densely wooded. There were certain places which filled me with a stronger
unease: the path the macadam took beside the rushing Miskatonic, for instance, so that the
reflection of the passing vehicle was distorted oddly by the black scum-covered water; the
diversion which caused my conveyance to take a path straight through the middle of a marsh,
where the trees closed overhead so that the ooze around me could barely be seen; and the
densely-wooded hillsides, which caused me to recall certain things hinted about the outposts
of cosmic forces in Wilbraham country. It was not that I was terrified by anything I beheld, for
I am not – or was not in those days – particularly superstitious; it was simply a vague unease,
stemming from the strangely primeval appearance of the surroundings.

Bear this in mind – my nature was not superstitious, and because of this I was not frightened,
as some might have been, by certain hints and intimations of my friend's communications with
me. He had spoken increasingly of certain things he had learned from readings of various
antiquated volumes; he talked of "a forgotten cycle of superstitious lore which would have
been better unknown"; and he mentioned strange and alien names, and even towards the
last hinted of actual worship of trans-spatial beings still practiced in such towns as Dunwich,
Arkham, Innsmouth and that in which he resided. In his last letter he had spoken wildly of a
temple to Yog-Sothoth, which existed conterminously with an actual church in Kingsport, in

which monstrous rituals had been performed, and where 'gates', if opened by forgotten alien incantations, would gape to let elder daemons pass from other spheres. There was a particularly hideous legend, so he said, concerning the errand on which these daemons came; but even he forbore to recount this, at least until he had visited the alien temple's earthly location. Since this letter, some three weeks ago, I had heard nothing from him; and I could only conjecture that, in such a highly nervous state, he might be willing to pay for any companionship. Thus I might yet acquire a post as secretary. Had I realised what monstrous abominations waited in reality upon my journey to Kingsport, I would assuredly have returned to my former mode of existence.

Upon my entrance into the first of Kingsport's archaic, mossy streets, I began to feel a lurking sense of blasphemous terrors ahead. Supposing my friend had already acquired a secretary, at any rate, what would I then do? Supposing he had taken up residence in some other state? A journey made back to my own city now would be made at least partially at night, and I did not find the thought pleasant of taking the hill roads in darkness, when they so often fell sheerly away upon one side into an abyss. But the thought of possible work made me press on.

I turned up Aubray Street, and at once became aware with certainty that something had gone wrong. The house which I knew as my friend's, set well back from the road, overgrown with ivy that twisted in myriad grotesque shapes, was locked and shuttered. No sign of life was discernible inside it, and outside the garden was filled with a brooding quiet, while my shadow on the fungus-overgrown lawn appeared eldritch and distorted, like that of some ghoul-born being from nether pits.

Upon inquiring of this anomaly from the strangely reticent neighbours, I learned that my friend had visited the deserted church in the centre of Kingsport after dark, and that this must have called the vengeance of those from outside upon him. The church was merely a gate through to undreamable dimensions, and those that passed through the gate were in a form that none could look upon. The likeness may be seen carved, so one venerable rustic whispered, in certain vaults on Yuggoth and ancient statues in Zothique. And the house of my friend, too, had become a haven to the ones from beyond, which was the reason why all shunned it.

Even then, I began to wonder at these hideous and abnormal legends which pervaded Kingsport and the neighbouring towns. There was almost a tangible air of lurking alien horror in the place, which might have given rise to these abominable tales. But I disliked the fungoid-white trees which grew in the garden of the house on Aubray Street, and also a certain shape which I seemed to glimpse at an upper window, which gave an amount of credibility to the horrors.

I did not wish to ask whether the old recluse could tell me of the monstrous legend of the church which my friend had refused to recount. So I left the old man to his rambling house and mouldering books, and retraced my path across the lichen-grown lawn to the eldritch building on Aubray Street.

I became aware of the strength of the tales when I saw the open front door, and realised that nobody would dare to enter. As I entered the curiously-shadowed hall, I seemed to perceive something at the top of the staircase; a shadow passed across the crimson-lit wall on the landing. But the shadow was of something so blasphemous and terrible that I can only be thankful that I did not perceive it more clearly. A monstrous sound, as of some fearful and moist body lumbering across the floorboards above, was borne to my ears; and it was some minutes before I could overcome the cosmic horror that gripped me sufficiently to ascend the creaking, slime-exuding stairs and search for that which I suspected. But nothing could be seen in the oak-beamed, twilit upper rooms; and I descended, finally, to explore the lower regions of the storied old building.

It was in the lower regions, I remembered, that my friend had been wont to peruse certain archaic and terrible volumes, to write notes concerning his findings, and to pursue sundry other pastimes in his rumoured searches. The room which had been his study I discovered without much difficulty; the desk, covered with sheets of notepaper, the bookcases filled with leather-bound and skin-bound volumes, the desk-lamp, seeming incongruous in the room full of volumes centuries old – all these bespoke the room's one-time use. I entered, noting the dust which lay over the room and all its contents. The light was dim, and that circumstance alone accounted for my not observing certain bizarre evidence in the room.

I approached the desk, brushing the dust from its surface and that of the seat, and turned on the light. The beams of electricity, streaming out across the room, were very reassuring; but there was something not quite pleasant, even so, about the manner in which certain shadows clustered in one or two corners of the room. But I would not allow such things to disturb me, and I turned to the first of the papers.

This bore the heading 'Corroborative Evidence', and was clipped to a thick assortment of such papers. The paper which first presented itself to my eye dealt with the Maya tribe of Central America. But what was to be gathered from such annotations as 'Rain gods (water elementals?) have strange trunk-proboscis (as have many of the Great Old Ones) as may be seen in statues. Major Maya deity was Kukulkan (Cthulhu?)'

It appeared that my friend had been attempting to unify various cycles of legend and superstition with one central cycle, which was, if recurrent references were to be believed, far older than the human race. Whence all his information had been gathered, I did not need to ask, seeing the numerous antiquated volumes around the walls of the room. If, I considered, I was to read the notes with a degree of understanding, it would be best if I could find some set of notes regarding this hideous legend-cycle.

This I soon discovered, in a rack below the desk. I opened the large set of notes, and immediately I gave a gasp of horror. The page upon which the set had opened had a photograph gummed to the page. But how, if the gates of the nethermost gulf had not been opened on Earth, could this abomination have been produced? It showed a reef out in the middle of some oily black expanse of water; in the background were the faint lights of a far-off coastal city. Above the moon swung in the vaults of space, strangely distorted by mist. But how could what that gibbous moon revealed exist? – those slimy things which cavorted in the pitchy water and crawled on the reef, those things with their scaly bodies and webbed fingers, their huge staring eyes and wide mouths and frog-like gills? – those blasphemies which still had a revoltingly half-human appearance, from which came a dread suspicion of the hideous truth?

In that stomach-wrenching moment of horrible knowledge, realisation of the abnormal ghastlinesses after which my friend had been searching and which, perhaps, he had stirred out of aeon-long sleep in the Kingsport church, I closed the book. But I soon opened it again, for even such shockingly conclusive evidence could not quite convince me. And after all, the strangely absent man had been my friend; I could only attempt to warn others, if I could procure evidence that beings – though perhaps not even from this universe – had absconded with him.

For long hours I pored over my friend's synopsis of this monstrous and alien myth-cycle: the legends of how Cthulhu came down from an indescribable sphere beyond the furthest bounds of this universe, of the monstrous polar civilisations and abominably unhuman races from black Yuggoth on the rim, of hideous Leng and its monastery-prisoned high priest which must needs cover what should be its face, and of multifarious blasphemies whose existence is only rumoured, except in certain legendary places of the world. I read of what Azathoth had resembled before that monstrous nuclear chaos had been bereft of mind and will. I read of many-featured Nyarlathotep, and learned of the shapes which the crawling chaos could assume which men have never before dared to relate. I became aware of the full shape, and the source, of the unspeakable Hounds of Tindalos, and I learned how one may glimpse a dhole fully, and what one would then see.

But these secret and unwholesome revelations, and even the sketches, reproductions and photographs which accompanied them, were not so shocking as the notes I discovered at the back of the desk. These notes consisted of my friend's personal research into this ghastly cycle, and the strange personages and, at times, beings which he had met. I would not dare to quote much of these notes, with their threats to sanity and order; but I will reveal certain which bear monstrously on my later experiences.

The entries began the winter before, and the relevant details continued thereafter chronologically.

December 17. Today [began the notes] *I unearthed an eldritch legend concerning more than one church in Kingsport and the surrounding countryside. My informant spoke of past days, when certain churches were meeting-places for those practicing the worship of morbid and alien gods. Subterranean tunnels were burrowed to hideous onyx temples, and there are rumours that all those that crawled down the tunnels to worship were not human. Other tales mention that the church in Asquith Place, in the centre of Kingsport, was the hub of this ghastly movement, and there are references to passages to other spheres connected with the building, now long disused.*

December 23. The subject of Christmas brought certain legends to my informant's mind today. A Yule rite practiced in the Asquith Place church was long rumoured to occur, and, as far as the informant can relate, may still occur. It had to do with something evoked in the buried necropolis below the church, where a great number of Kingsport's dead were laid. The rite would be performed tomorrow evening, if such things exist.

December 24. I went down to Asquith Place tonight. A great crowd had already gathered there; they carried no lights, but the whole scene was illuminated by strange floating globular objects, which gave off an eldritch corpse-light and flitted away at my approach. When the crowd realised that I had not come to join them, they made as if to pursue, and I fled. I believe I was followed, but I did not see what pursued. Whatever it was, it possessed more than four legs. Will I ever dare to leave my house after dark again?

January 13. My informant has not revealed anything further. It seems that he had been drawn into that ghastly gathering on the eve of Yuletide, and he now only offers me the warning that I should leave Kingsport completely. If I visit the church in the daytime, I will find nothing; if I go after dark, I will awaken the lurkers in that abominable buried necropolis. After that, I would be visited; but it would not be by the people of Kingsport. Apparently, once the cosmic lunacies which reside below the church have been awakened on Yuletide, it may be many years before they return to their own sphere.

(Here occurs what is either a hiatus in the notes or a period where none were written. At any rate, the next is dated several months later.)

September 30. I am about to visit Asquith Place's church before I leave Kingsport – tonight seems the best night, or possibly tomorrow night. I must know if that abominable tale is true! Surely the abominations of those nether regions will not harm me – they feed on other things.

October 1. Tomorrow I will leave, never to return. I went to that haunted and ghoulish building tonight. My God, that abnormality – that cosmic perversion – that I saw – almost too monstrous for the sake of sanity! I descended those onyx stairs to the subterranean vault, and saw that herd of horrors in full view, and realised their occupation. I tried to flee the town before returning here. But why did all the streets turn back to the church? Has the monstrous thing I saw and guessed indeed unhinged my mind?

October 2. The greatest horror of all has happened. I cannot leave Kingsport. All the roads returned to this house today – I should have realised the power of those from Outside. And now I am prisoned in this house, terrified by those things pressed whitely against the panes, staring in with their lich-like eyes. Where can I turn? A telegram to the one person I can trust may gain results.

(Now followed the section which horrified me more than anything else. My friend must have been preparing the telegram by writing it on the page while outside unspeakable shamblers made their way towards him – as became hideously evident as the writing progressed.)

To Richard Dexter. Come at once to Kingsport. You are needed urgently by me here for protection from agencies which may kill me – or worse – if you do not come immediately. Will explain as soon as you reach me...But what is this thing that flops unspeakably down the passage towards this room? It cannot be that abomination which I met in the nitrous vaults below Asquith Place...IA! YOG-SOTHOTH! CTHULHU FHTAGN!

But that ended the notes in this stack of my friend's. Whatever he had seen slithering through the doorway in that last moment of horror had carried him away without trace. And I was left with an unexplained affair of half-revealed hideousness.

Ultimately, of course, I realised there was but one course, if I were to rend this cloaking mass of monstrous hints. I would be forced to visit the antique church on the hill. Even from the Aubray Street residence the black steeple on the hill could be seen, its tip a corpse-white from the pallid light of the peering gibbous moon. The tower, rearing up from the mound in the centre of the town, resembled some cosmic statue or hideous gravestone of an alien titan race.

It was a little time before I could persuade myself to leave that haunted building on Aubray Street. What if my visit to the subterranean vaults stirred whatever lurking down there out of its merciful coma? However horrific might have been my friend's fate, however imperative might it be that others should be warned away from this place of hideousness, it would be futile if I, too, was unable to leave Kingsport. But, again, of what use would the simple notes of my friend be in persuading outsiders to destroy the horror? So, finally, I rose from my chair to leave – and saw.

At the movement of the desk caused by my rising, the desk had shifted, so that the position of the desk lamp was changed. It now shone on a path leading from the desk to the door – and there were traces in the dust along that path. How can I attempt to describe the appearance of those traces? – they were so unlike footprints that I did not realise that they were, indeed, the tracks of feet; did not realise what had made them until I saw those in the vault below the church. If you can visualise the marks which a sea-anemone would make, dropped regularly along a path, perhaps you may see why I did not guess the real nature of the marks.

As I paused at the front entrance to the house, I peered back down the passage for a last glimpse of the place – for I would not return there, but leave Kingsport immediately after I had seen whatever might lurk below the church. A ray of moonlight from a staircase window illuminated the hall. Did I glimpse something staring through the banisters, something corpse-pale which resembled nothing of this earth? I did not pause to be sure, but slammed the door on that house and all its nighted secrets, and stood staring shudderingly towards that legendary building at Kingsport's centre.

When I reached it the church was lit by the gibbous moon which swung high in the gulfs of space, and the tottering gravestones, overgrown with repulsively decaying vegetation, cast curious shadows over the fungus-strewn grass. I made my way through that nightmare landscape and finally reached and closed behind me the rotting portal.

As soon as I closed the door I knew that something was amiss. Had not my friend spoken of the place as 'long disused'? If so, who – or what – had ignited the torches in the verdigris-encrusted wall-brackets? As I stared affrightedly at these, I perceived a yawning aperture in the floor which could be nothing but the gate to those unsuspected tunnels to monstrous elder regions deep in the earth.

I remember a hideous scramble down tunnels which seemed at one minute to be carved through solid rock and the next through charnel earth. I can remember the vast space, entered by other tunnels, into which I finally plunged. I recollect those twelve monstrous statues which crouched, six on each side, at the entrance to the fabled necropolis – statues which depicted things of which I dare not think. I recollect the half-sentient look of those images, as if they but slept in waiting for some abominable awakening. I remember those slabs on the floor, stretching off into blackness, each with its hideously dead once-human tenant. Worst of all, I remember – recalling also certain morbid and whispered words of Abdul Alhazred – the hideous, nauseating fungi which grew inches high from each corpse and swayed hideously from some charnel breeze.

This is where the doctors do not believe me. They do not believe that I saw that gate on some other fabulous sphere open – open, not in the wall, but in the centre of empty space. They cannot credit what I saw rolling, plopping, surging monstrously through that portal with its angles which could not exist inside three sane dimensions. But I saw the glistening, gelatinous, amorphous tide which surged over the nitrous floor; I saw them as they flowed towards the inhuman crouching statues. Thirteen ghastly cosmic blights had burst upon the world down in the fungoid vaults under Kingsport. I did not lose consciousness when the things merged with the statues, nor when those statues moved of their own accord towards the slabs of terror. I did not even faint when the titan things began to claw at the fungus growing on the corpses, and tear it off to swallow the nauseating, obscenely-fed vegetation. It was only when the last of the unspeakably shapeless beings started to flop towards me that I finally fell to the slimy stone, unconscious.

Of my flight through the tottering streets, while hideous shapes gibbered above me, I remember little. If a doctor from Arkham had not accosted me, I shudder to think upon my possible end. But I was taken to St Mary's hospital in Arkham, whence after I learned to keep silent regarding my monstrous experiences, I was discharged as sane. My fearful questionings elicited that no papers or books were found in the house on Aubray Street in Kingsport. But why do I have certain unspeakable urges on the sight of a corpse or graveyard?

I know of the evidence of the stains of fungi upon the faces and claws of the statues in the vault. If only this, my mind might yet rest at night. But afterwards I began to conjecture what the thirteenth abomination had done after I became unconscious. I think again of those desires which remain with me, and which I dare not relate.

And I think of those stains of fungi which I found at the last – those stains on my own face and hands.

Po' Sandy

Charles W. Chesnutt

ON THE NORTHEAST CORNER of my vineyard in central North Carolina, and fronting on the Lumberton plank-road, there stood a small frame house, of the simplest construction. It was built of pine lumber, and contained but one room, to which one window gave light and one door admission. Its weatherbeaten sides revealed a virgin innocence of paint. Against one end of the house, and occupying half its width, there stood a huge brick chimney: the crumbling mortar had left large cracks between the bricks; the bricks themselves had begun to scale off in large flakes, leaving the chimney sprinkled with unsightly blotches. These evidences of decay were but partially concealed by a creeping vine, which extended its slender branches hither and thither in an ambitious but futile attempt to cover the whole chimney. The wooden shutter, which had once protected the unglazed window, had fallen from its hinges, and lay rotting in the rank grass and jimson-weeds beneath. This building, I learned when I bought the place, had been used as a schoolhouse for several years prior to the breaking out of the war, since which time it had remained unoccupied, save when some stray cow or vagrant hog had sought shelter within its walls from the chill rains and nipping winds of winter.

One day my wife requested me to build her a new kitchen. The house erected by us, when we first came to live upon the vineyard, contained a very conveniently arranged kitchen; but for some occult reason my wife wanted a kitchen in the back yard, apart from the dwelling-house, after the usual Southern fashion. Of course I had to build it.

To save expense, I decided to tear down the old schoolhouse, and use the lumber, which was in a good state of preservation, in the construction of the new kitchen. Before demolishing the old house, however, I made an estimate of the amount of material contained in it, and found that I would have to buy several hundred feet of lumber additional, in order to build the new kitchen according to my wife's plan.

One morning old Julius McAdoo, our colored coachman, harnessed the gray mare to the rockaway, and drove my wife and me over to the sawmill from which I meant to order the new lumber. We drove down the long lane which led from our house to the plank-road; following the plank-road for about a mile, we turned into a road running through the forest and across the swamp to the sawmill beyond. Our carriage jolted over the half-rotted corduroy road which traversed the swamp, and then climbed the long hill leading to the sawmill. When we reached the mill, the foreman had gone over to a neighboring farmhouse, probably to smoke or gossip, and we were compelled to await his return before we could transact our business. We remained seated in the carriage, a few rods from the mill, and watched the leisurely movements of the mill-hands. We had not waited long before a huge pine log was placed in position, the machinery of the mill was set in motion, and the circular saw began to eat its way through the log, with a loud whir which resounded throughout the vicinity of the mill. The sound rose and fell in a sort of rhythmic cadence, which, heard from where we sat, was not unpleasing, and not loud enough to prevent conversation. When the saw started on its second journey through the log, Julius observed, in a lugubrious tone, and with a perceptible shudder:

"Ugh! But dat des do cuddle my blood!"

"What's the matter, Uncle Julius?" inquired my wife, who is of a very sympathetic turn of mind. "Does the noise affect your nerves?"

"No, Mis' Annie," replied the old man, with emotion, "I ain' narvous; but dat saw, a-cuttin' en grindin' thoo dat stick er timber, en moanin', en groanin', en sweekin', kyars my 'memb'ance back ter ole times, en 'min's me er po' Sandy." The pathetic intonation with which he lengthened out the 'po' Sandy' touched a responsive chord in our own hearts.

"And who was poor Sandy?" asked my wife, who takes a deep interest in the stories of plantation life which she hears from the lips of the older colored people. Some of these stories are quaintly humorous; others wildly extravagant, revealing the Oriental cast of the negro's imagination; while others, poured freely into the sympathetic ear of a Northern-bred woman, disclose many a tragic incident of the darker side of slavery.

"Sandy," said Julius, in reply to my wife's question, "was a nigger w'at useter b'long ter ole Mars Marrabo McSwayne. Mars Marrabo's place wuz on de yuther side'n de swamp, right nex' ter yo' place. Sandy wuz a monst'us good nigger, en could do so many things erbout a plantation, en alluz 'ten' ter his wuk so well, dat w'en Mars Marrabo's chilluns growed up en married off, dey all un 'em wanted dey daddy fer ter gin 'em Sandy fer a weddin' present. But Mars Marrabo knowed de res' would n' be satisfied ef he gin Sandy ter a'er one un 'em; so w'en dey wuz all done married, he fix it by 'lowin' one er his chilluns ter take Sandy fer a mont' er so, en den ernudder for a mont' er so, en so on dat erway tel dey had all had 'im de same lenk er time; en den dey would all take him roun' ag'in, 'cep'n' oncet in a w'ile w'en Mars Marrabo would len' 'im ter some er his yuther kinfolks 'roun' de country, w'en dey wuz short er han's; tel bimeby it got so Sandy did n' hardly knowed whar he wuz gwine ter stay fum one week's een' ter de yuther.

"One time w'en Sandy wuz lent out ez yushal, a spekilater come erlong wid a lot er niggers, en Mars Marrabo swap' Sandy's wife off fer a noo 'oman. W'en Sandy come back, Mars Marrabo gin 'im a dollar, en 'lowed he wuz monst'us sorry fer ter break up de fambly, but de spekilater had gin 'im big boot, en times wuz hard en money skase, en so he wuz bleedst ter make de trade. Sandy tuk on some 'bout losin' his wife, but he soon seed dey want no use cryin' ober spilt merlasses; en bein' ez he lacked de looks er de noo 'oman, he tuk up wid her atter she'd be'n on de plantation a mont' er so.

"Sandy en his noo wife got on mighty well tergedder, en de niggers all 'mence' ter talk about how lovin' dey wuz. Wen Tenie wuz tuk sick oncet, Sandy useter set up all night wid 'er, en den go ter wuk in de mawnin' des lack he had his reg'lar sleep; en Tenie would 'a' done anythin' in de worl' for her Sandy.

"Sandy en Tenie had n' be'n libbin' tergedder fer mo' d'n two mont's befo' Mars Marrabo's old uncle, w'at libbed down in Robeson County, sent up ter fin' out ef Mars Marrabo could n' len' 'im er hire 'im a good ban' fer a mont' er so. Sandy's marster wuz one er dese yer easy-gwine folks w'at wanter please eve'ybody, en he says yas, he could len' 'im Sandy. En Mars Marrabo tol' Sandy fer ter git ready ter go down ter Robeson nex' day, fer ter stay a mont' er so.

"It wuz monst'us hard on Sandy fer ter take 'im 'way fum Tenie. It wuz so fur down ter Robeson dat he did n' hab no chance er comin' back ter see her tel de time wuz up; he would n' 'a' mine comin' ten er fifteen mile at night ter see Tenie, but Mars Marrabo's uncle's plantation wuz mo' d'n forty mile off. Sandy wuz mighty sad en cas' down atter w'at Mars Marrabo tol' 'im, en he says ter Tenie, sezee:

"'I'm gittin' monst'us ti'ed er dish yer gwine roun' so much. Here I is lent ter Mars Jeems dis mont', en I got ter do so-en-so; en ter Mars Archie de nex' mont', en I got ter do so-en-so; den I got ter go ter Miss Jinnie's: en hit's Sandy dis en Sandy dat, en Sandy yer en Sandy dere, tel it 'pears ter me I ain' got no home, ner no marster, ner no mistiss, ner no nuffin. I can't eben keep a wife: my yuther ole 'oman wuz sol' away widout my gittin' a chance fer ter tell her goodbye; en now I got ter go off en leab you, Tenie, en I dunno whe'r I'm eber gwine ter see you ag'in er no. I wisht I wuz a tree, er a stump, er a rock, er sump'n w'at could stay on de plantation fer a w'ile.'

"Atter Sandy got thoo talkin', Tenie didn' say naer word, but des sot dere by de fier, studyin' en studyin'. Bimeby she up 'n' says:

"'Sandy, is I eber tol' you I wuz a cunjuh 'oman?'

"Co'se Sandy had n' nebber dremp' er nuffin lack dat, en he made a great 'miration w'en he hear w'at Tenie say. Bimeby Tenie went on:

"'I ain' goophered nobody, ner done no cunjuh wuk, fer fifteen year er mo'; en w'en I got religion I made up my mine I would n' wuk no mo' goophèr. But dey is some things I doan b'lieve it's no sin fer ter do; en ef you doan wanter be sent roun' fum pillar ter pos', en ef you doan wanter go down ter Robeson, I kin fix things so you won't haf ter. Ef you'll des say de word, I kin turn you ter w'ateber you wanter be, en you kin stay right whar you wanter, ez long ez you mineter.'

"Sandy say he doan keer; he's will-in' fer ter do anythin' fer ter stay close ter Tenie. Den Tenie ax 'im ef he doan wanter be turnt inter a rabbit.

"Sandy say, 'No, de dogs mought git atter me.'

"'Shill I turn you ter a wolf?' sez Tenie.

"'No, eve'ybody 's skeered er a wolf, en I doan want nobody ter be skeered er me.'

"'Shill I turn you ter a mawkin'-bird?'

"'No, a hawk mought ketch me. I wanter be turnt inter sump'n w'at'll stay in one place.'

"'I kin turn you ter a tree,' sez Tenie. 'You won't hab no mouf ner years, but I kin turn you back oncet in a w'ile, so you kin git sump'n ter eat, en hear w'at 's gwine on.'

"Well, Sandy say dat'll do. En so Tenie tuk 'im down by de aidge er de swamp, not fur fum de quarters, en turnt 'im inter a big pine-tree, en sot 'im out 'mongs' some yuther trees. En de nex' mawnin', ez some er de fiel' han's wuz gwine long dere, dey seed a tree w'at dey did n' 'member er habbin' seed befo'; it wuz monst'us quare, en dey wuz bleedst ter 'low dat dey had n' 'membered right, er e'se one er de saplin's had be'n growin' monst'us fas'.

"W'en Mars Marrabo 'skiver' dat Sandy wuz gone, he 'lowed Sandy had runned away. He got de dogs out, but de las' place dey could track Sandy ter wuz de foot er dat pine-tree. En dere de dogs stood en barked, en bayed, en pawed at de tree, en tried ter climb up on it; en w'en dey wuz tuk roun' thoo de swamp ter look fer de scent, dey broke loose en made fer dat tree ag'in. It wuz de beatenis' thing de w'ite folks eber hearn of, en Mars Marrabo 'lowed dat Sandy must 'a' clim' up on de tree en jump' off on a mule er sump'n, en rid fur ernuff fer ter spile de scent. Mars Marrabo wanted ter 'cuse some er de yuther niggers er heppin' Sandy off, but dey all 'nied it ter de las'; en eve'ybody knowed Tenie sot too much sto' by Sandy fer ter he'p 'im run away whar she could n' nebber see 'im no mo'.

"W'en Sandy had be'n gone long ernuff fer folks ter think he done got clean away, Tenie useter go down ter de woods at night en turn 'im back, en den dey 'd slip up ter de cabin en set by de fire en talk. But dey ha' ter be monst'us keerful, er e'se somebody would 'a' seed 'em, en dat would 'a' spile' de whole thing; so Tenie alluz turnt Sandy back in de mawnin' early, befo' anybody wuz a-stirrin'.

"But Sandy did n' git erlong widout his trials en tribberlations. One day a woodpecker come erlong en 'mence' ter peck at de tree; en de nex' time Sandy wuz turnt back he had a little roun' hole in his arm, des lack a sharp stick be'n stuck in it. Atter dat Tenie sot a sparrer-hawk fer ter watch de tree; en w'en de woodpecker come erlong nex' mawnin' fer ter finish his nes', he got gobble' up mos' 'fo' he stuck his bill in de bark.

"Nudder time, Mars Marrabo sent a nigger out in de woods fer ter chop tuppentime boxes. De man chop a box in dish yer tree, en hack' de bark up two er th'ee feet, fer ter let de tuppentime run. De nex' time Sandy wuz turnt back he had a big skyar on his lef' leg, des lack it be'n skunt; en it tuk Tenie nigh 'bout all night fer ter fix a mixtry ter kyo it up. Atter dat, Tenie sot a hawnet fer ter watch de tree; en w'en de nigger come back ag'in fer ter cut ernudder box on de yuther side'n de tree, de hawnet stung 'im so hard dat de ax slip en cut his foot nigh 'bout off.

"W'en Tenie see so many things happenin' ter de tree, she 'eluded she 'd ha' ter turn Sandy ter sump'n e'se; en atter studyin' de matter ober, en talkin' wid Sandy one ebenin', she made up her mine fer ter fix up a goopher mixtry w'at would turn herse'f en Sandy ter foxes, er sump'n, so dey could run away en go some'rs whar dey could be free en lib lack w'ite folks.

"But dey ain' no tellin' w'at's gwine ter happen in dis worl'. Tenie had got de night sot fer her en Sandy ter run away, w'en dat ve'y day one er Mars Marrabo's sons rid up ter de big house in his buggy, en say his wife wuz monst'us sick, en he want his mammy ter len' 'im a 'oman fer ter nuss his wife. Tenie's mistiss say sen' Tenie; she wuz a good nuss. Young mars wuz in a tarrible hurry fer ter git back home. Tenie wuz washin' at de big house dat day, en her mistiss say she should go right 'long wid her young marster. Tenie tried ter make some 'scuse fer ter git away en hide 'tel night, w'en she would have eve'ything fix' up fer her en Sandy; she say she wanter go ter her cabin fer ter git her bonnet. Her mistiss say it doan matter 'bout de bonnet; her head-hank-cher wuz good ernuff. Den Tenie say she wanter git her bes' frock; her mistiss say no, she doan need no mo' frock, en w'en dat one got dirty she could git a clean one whar she wuz gwine. So Tenie had ter git in de buggy en go 'long wid young Mars Dunkin ter his plantation, w'ich wuz mo' d'n twenty mile away; en dey wa'n't no chance er her seein' Sandy no mo' 'tel she come back home. De po' gal felt monst'us bad 'bout de way things wuz gwine on, en she knowed Sandy mus' be a wond'rin' why she didn' come en turn 'im back no mo'.

"Wiles Tenie wuz away nussin' young Mars Dunkin's wife, Mars Marrabo tuk a notion fer ter buil' 'im a noo kitchen; en bein' ez he had lots er timber on his place, he begun ter look 'roun' fer a tree ter hab de lumber sawed out'n. En I dunno how it come to be so, but he happen fer ter hit on de ve'y tree w'at Sandy wuz turnt inter. Tenie wuz gone, en dey wa'n't nobody ner nuffin fer ter watch de tree.

"De two men w'at cut de tree down say dey nebber had sech a time wid a tree befo': dey axes would glansh off, en did n' 'pear ter make no progress thoo de wood; en of all de creakin', en shakin', en wobblin' you eber see, dat tree done it w'en it commence' ter fall. It wuz de beatenis' thing!

"W'en dey got de tree all trim' up, dey chain it up ter a timber waggin, en start fer de sawmill. But dey had a hard time gittin' de log dere: fus' dey got stuck in de mud w'en dey wuz gwine crosst de swamp, en it wuz two er th'ee hours befo' dey could git out. W'en dey start' on ag'in, de chain kep' a-comin' loose, en dey had ter keep a-stoppin' en a-stoppin' fer ter hitch de log up ag'in. W'en dey commence' ter climb de hill ter de sawmill, de log broke loose, en roll down de hill en in 'mongs' de trees, en hit tuk nigh 'bout half a day mo' ter git it haul' up ter de sawmill.

"De nex' mawnin' atter de day de tree wuz haul' ter de sawmill, Tenie come home. W'en she got back ter her cabin, de fus' thing she done wuz ter run down ter de woods en see how Sandy wuz gittin' on. Wen she seed de stump standin' dere, wid de sap runnin' out'n it, en de limbs layin' scattered roun', she nigh 'bout went out'n her min'. She run ter her cabin, en got her goopher mixtry, en den follered de track er de timber waggin ter de sawmill. She knowed Sandy could n' lib mo' d'n a minute er so ef she turnt him back, fer he wuz all chop' up so he 'd 'a' be'n bleedst ter die. But she wanted ter turn 'im back long ernuff fer ter 'splain ter 'im dat she had n' went off a-purpose, en lef 'im ter be chop' down en sawed up. She did n' want Sandy ter die wid no hard feelin's to'ds her.

"De han's at de sawmill had des got de big log on de kerridge, en wuz start-in' up de saw, w'en dey seed a 'oman runnin' up de hill, all out er bref, cryin' en gwine on des lack she wuz plumb 'stracted. It wuz Tenie; she come right inter de mill, en th'owed herse'f on de log, right in front er de saw, a-hollerin' en cryin' ter her Sandy ter fergib her, en not ter think hard er her, fer it wa'n't no fault er hern. Den Tenie 'membered de tree did n' hab no years, en she wuz gittin' ready fer ter wuk her goopher mixtry so ez ter turn Sandy back, w'en de mill-hands kotch holt er her en tied her arms wid a rope, en fasten' her to one er de posts in de sawmill; en den dey started de saw up ag'in, en cut de log up inter bo'ds en scantlin's right befo' her eyes. But it wuz mighty hard wuk; fer of all de sweekin', en moanin', en groanin', dat log done it w'iles de saw wuz a-cuttin' thoo it. De saw wuz one er dese yer ole-timey, up-en-down saws, en hit tuk longer dem days ter saw a log 'en it do now. Dey greased de saw, but dat did n' stop de fuss; hit kep' right on, tel fin'ly dey got de log all sawed up.

"W'en de oberseah w'at run de sawmill come fum breakfas', de han's up en tell him 'bout de crazy 'oman – ez dey s'posed she wuz – w'at had come runnin' in de sawmill, a-hollerin' en gwine on, en tried ter th'ow herse'f befo' de saw. En de oberseah sent two er th'ee er de han's fer ter take Tenie back ter her marster's plantation.

"Tenie 'peared ter be out'n her min' fer a long time, en her marster ha' ter lock her up in de smoke-'ouse 'tel she got ober her spells. Mars Marrabo wuz monst'us mad, en hit would 'a' made yo' flesh crawl fer ter hear him cuss, 'caze he say de spekilater w'at he got Tenie fum had fooled 'im by wukkin' a crazy 'oman off on him. Wiles Tenie wuz lock up in de smoke-'ouse, Mars Marrabo tuk 'n' haul de lumber fum de sawmill, en put up his noo kitchen.

"Wen Tenie got quiet' down, so she could be 'lowed ter go 'roun' de plantation, she up'n' tole her marster all erbout Sandy en de pine-tree; en w'en Mars Marrabo hearn it, he 'lowed she wuz de wuss 'stracted nigger he eber hearn of. He did n' know w'at ter do wid Tenie: fus' he thought he 'd put her in de po'house; but fin'ly, seein' ez she did n' do no harm ter nobody ner nuffin, but des went 'roun' moanin', en groanin', en shakin' her head, he 'cluded ter let her stay on de plantation en nuss de little nigger chilluns w'en dey mammies wuz ter wuk in de cotton-fiel'.

"De noo kitchen Mars Marrabo buil' wuz n' much use, fer it had n' be'n put up long befo' de niggers 'mence' ter notice quare things erbout it. Dey could hear sump'n moanin' en groanin' 'bout de kitchen in de night-time, en w'en de win' would blow dey could hear sump'n a-hollerin' en sweekin' lack it wuz in great pain en sufferin'. En it got so atter a w'ile dat it wuz all Mars Marrabo's wife could do ter git a 'oman ter stay in de kitchen in de daytime long ernuff ter do de cookin'; en dey wa'n't naer nigger on de plantation w'at would n' rudder take forty dan ter go 'bout dat kitchen atter dark – dat is, 'cep'n' Tenie; she did n' 'pear ter min' de ha'nts. She useter slip 'roun' at night, en set on de kitchen steps, en lean up agin de do'-jamb, en run on ter herse'f wid some kine er foolishness w'at nobody could n' make out; fer Mars Marrabo had th'eaten' ter sen' her off'n de plantation ef she say anything ter any er de yuther niggers 'bout de pine-tree. But somehow er 'nudder de niggers foun' out all erbout it, en dey all knowed de kitchen wuz ha'nted by Sandy's sperrit. En bimeby hit got so Mars Marrabo's wife herse'f wuz skeered ter go out in de yard atter dark.

"Wen it come ter dat, Mars Marrabo tuk en to' de kitchen down, en use' de lumber fer ter buil' dat ole school'ouse w'at you er talkin' 'bout pullin' down. De school'ouse wuz n' use' 'cep'n' in de daytime, en on dark nights folks gwine 'long de road would hear quare soun's en see quare things. Po' ole Tenie useter go down dere at night, en wander 'roun' de school'ouse; en de niggers all 'lowed she went fer ter talk wid Sandy's sperrit. En one winter mawnin', w'en one er de boys went ter school early fer ter start de fire, w'at should he fin' but po' ole Tenie, layin' on de flo', stiff, en col', en dead. Dere did n' 'pear ter be nuffin pertickler de matter wid her – she had des grieve' herse'f ter def fer her Sandy. Mars Marrabo didn' shed no tears. He thought Tenie wuz crazy, en dey wa'n't no tellin' w'at she mought do nex'; en dey ain' much room in dis worl' fer crazy w'ite folks, let 'lone a crazy nigger.

"Hit wa'n't long atter dat befo' Mars Marrabo sol' a piece er his track er lan' ter Mars Dugal' McAdoo – *my* ole marster – en dat 's how de ole school'ouse happen to be on yo' place. Wen de wah broke out, de school stop', en de ole school'ouse be'n stannin' empty ever sence – dat is, 'cep'n' fer de ha'nts. En folks sez dat de ole school'ouse, er any yuther house w'at got any er dat lumber in it w'at wuz sawed out'n de tree w'at Sandy wuz turnt inter, is gwine ter be ha'nted tel de las' piece er plank is rotted en crumble' inter dus'."

Annie had listened to this gruesome narrative with strained attention.

"What a system it was," she exclaimed, when Julius had finished, "under which such things were possible!"

"What things?" I asked, in amazement. "Are you seriously considering the possibility of a man's being turned into a tree?"

"Oh, no," she replied quickly, "not that"; and then she murmured absently, and with a dim look in her fine eyes, "Poor Tenie!"

We ordered the lumber, and returned home. That night, after we had gone to bed, and my wife had to all appearances been sound asleep for half an hour, she startled me out of an incipient doze by exclaiming suddenly—

"John, I don't believe I want my new kitchen built out of the lumber in that old schoolhouse."

"You wouldn't for a moment allow yourself," I replied, with some asperity, "to be influenced by that absurdly impossible yarn which Julius was spinning today?"

"I know the story is absurd," she replied dreamily, "and I am not so silly as to believe it. But I don't think I should ever be able to take any pleasure in that kitchen if it were built out of that lumber. Besides, I think the kitchen would look better and last longer if the lumber were all new."

Of course she had her way. I bought the new lumber, though not without grumbling. A week or two later I was called away from home on business. On my return, after an absence of several days, my wife remarked to me:

"John, there has been a split in the Sandy Run Colored Baptist Church, on the temperance question. About half the members have come out from the main body, and set up for themselves. Uncle Julius is one of the seceders, and he came to me yesterday and asked if they might not hold their meetings in the old schoolhouse for the present."

"I hope you didn't let the old rascal have it," I returned, with some warmth. I had just received a bill for the new lumber I had bought.

"Well," she replied, "I couldn't refuse him the use of the house for so good a purpose."

"And I'll venture to say," I continued, "that you subscribed something toward the support of the new church?"

She did not attempt to deny it.

"What are they going to do about the ghost?" I asked, somewhat curious to know how Julius would get around this obstacle.

"Oh," replied Annie, "Uncle Julius says that ghosts never disturb religious worship, but that if Sandy's spirit *should* happen to stray into meeting by mistake, no doubt the preaching would do it good."

Désirée's Baby

Kate Chopin

AS THE DAY was pleasant, Madame Valmonde drove over to L'Abri to see Désirée and the baby.

It made her laugh to think of Désirée with a baby. Why, it seemed but yesterday that Désirée was little more than a baby herself; when Monsieur in riding through the gateway of Valmonde had found her lying asleep in the shadow of the big stone pillar.

The little one awoke in his arms and began to cry for "Dada". That was as much as she could do or say. Some people thought she might have strayed there of her own accord, for she was of the toddling age. The prevailing belief was that she had been purposely left by a party of Texans, whose canvas-covered wagon, late in the day, had crossed the ferry that Coton Mais kept, just below the plantation. In time Madame Valmonde abandoned every speculation but the one that Désirée had been sent to her by a beneficent Providence to be the child of her affection, seeing that she was without child of the flesh. For the girl grew to be beautiful and gentle, affectionate and sincere, – the idol of Valmonde.

It was no wonder, when she stood one day against the stone pillar in whose shadow she had lain asleep, eighteen years before, that Armand Aubigny riding by and seeing her there, had fallen in love with her. That was the way all the Aubignys fell in love, as if struck by a pistol shot. The wonder was that he had not loved her before; for he had known her since his father brought him home from Paris, a boy of eight, after his mother died there. The passion that awoke in him that day, when he saw her at the gate, swept along like an avalanche, or like a prairie fire, or like anything that drives headlong over all obstacles.

Monsieur Valmonde grew practical and wanted things well considered: that is, the girl's obscure origin. Armand looked into her eyes and did not care. He was reminded that she was nameless. What did it matter about a name when he could give her one of the oldest and proudest in Louisiana? He ordered the corbeille from Paris, and contained himself with what patience he could until it arrived; then they were married.

Madame Valmonde had not seen Désirée and the baby for four weeks. When she reached L'Abri she shuddered at the first sight of it, as she always did. It was a sad-looking place, which for many years had not known the gentle presence of a mistress, old Monsieur Aubigny having married and buried his wife in France, and she having loved her own land too well ever to leave it. The roof came down steep and black like a cowl, reaching out beyond the wide galleries that encircled the yellow stuccoed house. Big, solemn oaks grew close to it, and their thick-leaved, far-reaching branches shadowed it like a pall. Young Aubigny's rule was a strict one, too, and under it his negroes had forgotten how to be gay, as they had been during the old master's easy-going and indulgent lifetime.

The young mother was recovering slowly, and lay full length, in her soft white muslins and laces, upon a couch. The baby was beside her, upon her arm, where he had fallen asleep, at her breast. The yellow nurse woman sat beside a window fanning herself.

Madame Valmonde bent her portly figure over Désirée and kissed her, holding her an instant tenderly in her arms. Then she turned to the child.

"This is not the baby!" she exclaimed, in startled tones. French was the language spoken at Valmonde in those days.

"I knew you would be astonished," laughed Désirée, "at the way he has grown. The little cochon de lait! Look at his legs, mamma, and his hands and fingernails – real fingernails. Zandrine had to cut them this morning. Isn't it true, Zandrine?"

The woman bowed her turbaned head majestically, "Mais si, Madame."

"And the way he cries," went on Désirée, "is deafening. Armand heard him the other day as far away as La Blanche's cabin."

Madame Valmonde had never removed her eyes from the child. She lifted it and walked with it over to the window that was lightest. She scanned the baby narrowly, then looked as searchingly at Zandrine, whose face was turned to gaze across the fields.

"Yes, the child has grown, has changed," said Madame Valmonde, slowly, as she replaced it beside its mother. "What does Armand say?"

Désirée's face became suffused with a glow that was happiness itself.

"Oh, Armand is the proudest father in the parish, I believe, chiefly because it is a boy, to bear his name; though he says not – that he would have loved a girl as well. But I know it isn't true. I know he says that to please me. And mamma," she added, drawing Madame Valmonde's head down to her, and speaking in a whisper, "he hasn't punished one of them – not one of them – since baby is born. Even Negrillon, who pretended to have burnt his leg that he might rest from work – he only laughed, and said Negrillon was a great scamp. Oh, mamma, I'm so happy; it frightens me."

What Désirée said was true. Marriage, and later the birth of his son, had softened Armand Aubigny's imperious and exacting nature greatly. This was what made the gentle Désirée so happy, for she loved him desperately. When he frowned she trembled, but loved him. When he smiled, she asked no greater blessing of God. But Armand's dark, handsome face had not often been disfigured by frowns since the day he fell in love with her.

When the baby was about three months old, Désirée awoke one day to the conviction that there was something in the air menacing her peace. It was at first too subtle to grasp. It had only been a disquieting suggestion; an air of mystery among the blacks; unexpected visits from far-off neighbors who could hardly account for their coming. Then a strange, an awful change in her husband's manner, which she dared not ask him to explain. When he spoke to her, it was with averted eyes, from which the old love-light seemed to have gone out. He absented himself from home; and when there, avoided her presence and that of her child, without excuse. And the very spirit of Satan seemed suddenly to take hold of him in his dealings with the slaves. Désirée was miserable enough to die.

She sat in her room, one hot afternoon, in her peignoir, listlessly drawing through her fingers the strands of her long, silky brown hair that hung about her shoulders. The baby, half naked, lay asleep upon her own great mahogany bed, that was like a sumptuous throne, with its satin-lined half-canopy. One of La Blanche's little quadroon boys – half naked too – stood fanning the child slowly with a fan of peacock feathers. Désirée's eyes had been fixed absently and sadly upon the baby, while she was striving to penetrate the threatening mist that she felt closing about her. She looked from her child to the boy who stood beside him, and back again; over and over. "Ah!" It was a cry that she could not help; which she was not conscious of having uttered. The blood turned like ice in her veins, and a clammy moisture gathered upon her face.

She tried to speak to the little quadroon boy; but no sound would come, at first. When he heard his name uttered, he looked up, and his mistress was pointing to the door. He laid aside the great, soft fan, and obediently stole away, over the polished floor, on his bare tiptoes.

She stayed motionless, with gaze riveted upon her child, and her face the picture of fright.

Presently her husband entered the room, and without noticing her, went to a table and began to search among some papers which covered it.

"Armand," she called to him, in a voice which must have stabbed him, if he was human. But he did not notice. "Armand," she said again. Then she rose and tottered towards him. "Armand," she panted once more, clutching his arm, "look at our child. What does it mean? Tell me."

He coldly but gently loosened her fingers from about his arm and thrust the hand away from him. "Tell me what it means!" she cried despairingly.

"It means," he answered lightly, "that the child is not white; it means that you are not white."

A quick conception of all that this accusation meant for her nerved her with unwonted courage to deny it. "It is a lie; it is not true, I am white! Look at my hair, it is brown; and my eyes are gray, Armand, you know they are gray. And my skin is fair," seizing his wrist. "Look at my hand; whiter than yours, Armand," she laughed hysterically.

"As white as La Blanche's," he returned cruelly; and went away leaving her alone with their child.

When she could hold a pen in her hand, she sent a despairing letter to Madame Valmondé.

"My mother, they tell me I am not white. Armand has told me I am not white. For God's sake tell them it is not true. You must know it is not true. I shall die. I must die. I cannot be so unhappy, and live."

The answer that came was brief:

"My own Désirée: Come home to Valmondé; back to your mother who loves you. Come with your child."

When the letter reached Désirée she went with it to her husband's study, and laid it open upon the desk before which he sat. She was like a stone image: silent, white, motionless after she placed it there.

In silence he ran his cold eyes over the written words.

He said nothing. "Shall I go, Armand?" she asked in tones sharp with agonized suspense.

"Yes, go."

"Do you want me to go?"

"Yes, I want you to go."

He thought Almighty God had dealt cruelly and unjustly with him; and felt, somehow, that he was paying Him back in kind when he stabbed thus into his wife's soul. Moreover he no longer loved her, because of the unconscious injury she had brought upon his home and his name.

She turned away like one stunned by a blow, and walked slowly towards the door, hoping he would call her back.

"Goodbye, Armand," she moaned.

He did not answer her. That was his last blow at fate.

Désirée went in search of her child. Zandrine was pacing the sombre gallery with it. She took the little one from the nurse's arms with no word of explanation, and descending the steps, walked away, under the live-oak branches.

It was an October afternoon; the sun was just sinking. Out in the still fields the negroes were picking cotton.

Désirée had not changed the thin white garment nor the slippers which she wore. Her hair was uncovered and the sun's rays brought a golden gleam from its brown meshes. She did not take the broad, beaten road which led to the far-off plantation of Valmonde. She walked across a deserted field, where the stubble bruised her tender feet, so delicately shod, and tore her thin gown to shreds.

She disappeared among the reeds and willows that grew thick along the banks of the deep, sluggish bayou; and she did not come back again.

Some weeks later there was a curious scene enacted at L'Abri. In the center of the smoothly swept back yard was a great bonfire. Armand Aubigny sat in the wide hallway that commanded a view of the spectacle; and it was he who dealt out to a half dozen negroes the material which kept this fire ablaze.

A graceful cradle of willow, with all its dainty furbishings, was laid upon the pyre, which had already been fed with the richness of a priceless layette. Then there were silk gowns, and velvet and satin ones added to these; laces, too, and embroideries; bonnets and gloves; for the corbeille had been of rare quality.

The last thing to go was a tiny bundle of letters; innocent little scribblings that Désirée had sent to him during the days of their espousal. There was the remnant of one back in the drawer from which he took them. But it was not Désirée's; it was part of an old letter from his mother to his father. He read it. She was thanking God for the blessing of her husband's love:

"But above all," she wrote, "night and day, I thank the good God for having so arranged our lives that our dear Armand will never know that his mother, who adores him, belongs to the race that is cursed with the brand of slavery."

The Dark Presser

E.E.W. Christman

THERE'S *something wrong with my house.*

Margo thought this – not for the first time – as she was roused from a fitful sleep full of unremembered dark dreams. Her house used to be such a quiet, comfortable place. It was about as unusual as a reliable sedan or a packed lunch. Now, it seemed to quake and tremble in the night, whimpering from dusk until dawn. Margo rubbed the sleep from her eyes. What had she heard? A creaking floorboard? A water pipe? As she flicked on the bedside lamp, there was a moment, half dream and half waking world, where the light shined on one of the shadows and failed to banish it.

Someone in the doorway, Margo's sleep-addled brain thought. But when she blinked, there was just an empty doorway. Her heart still faltered. Just a beat or two, but her breath caught in her throat and she carefully watched the door, making sure it was a trick of the light. As nothing happened and the seconds creeped by, she relaxed. Then there it was: the now-frequent creaking. It sounded like it was coming from downstairs.

There's nothing to be scared of, Margo told herself. *Just a house starting to show its age. Maybe squirrels in the crawlspace.* Still, she threw the covers off and went downstairs, her feet padding quietly across the wooden floor. There was nothing to see, like always. Just the living room, the kitchen with the dinner dishes she hadn't finished, the half bath. Margo turned on the lights as she investigated. Just to see better. Not to keep her breath even or her heart from pounding.

She noted the floor didn't creak when she walked down here, and immediately dismissed the thought. It made her anxious, and she needed to fall back asleep when she confirmed nothing was here. Which, of course, there wasn't. The first floor was vacant save for herself. She ran through the rooms again, switching all the lights off. She got to the stairs and turned off the last downstairs light. As she did, a shadow appeared on the stairs, illuminated by the upstairs hall. Arms hanging to the knees. No, not entirely arms. *Claws.* And the glint of fangs in a mouth that was much too big.

When Margo blinked, the apparition was gone. Her scream lasted a little longer.

There's something wrong with my house, she thought again as she crawled back into bed, leaving the lights on. *Or with me.*

* * *

What did someone do when they started to see things? She still had to go to work, clean her house, and pay her bills. Margo needed sleep. Her life couldn't just go on hold while her imagination ran wild.

But the creaking. The incessant, earnest *creaking* of the boards. Now Margo could only sink into her blankets as she was awakened. Even with her eyes closed, she could see that dark figure waiting for her in the doorway.

Margo woke up around three and never went back to sleep. When her alarm went off at six, she told herself she could do this, and she tried to believe it. She blasted the exhaustion from her bones with a hot shower. She made coffee and drank a big cup before pouring the rest of the pot in a giant tumbler. How long could someone replace a good night's sleep with caffeine? A week? Had she slept at all during exam week? Margo felt like she hadn't. Still, she was running out of days before she had to admit she had a real problem.

Margo took the train into the city and stared at a computer blankly for approximately eight hours. She didn't accomplish anything, and she tried not to talk to anyone. Whenever she felt herself dozing off, the creature pried her eyelids back open and she pretended to work furiously.

The workday passed slowly. She spent lunch outside with another cup of coffee and a salad that she mostly just picked at, trying to stay awake. When it was finally over and she could drag her tired body onto the train back home, she began to doze off in her seat. She didn't mean to; too many handsy men and amateur pickpockets. But she couldn't stop herself as the exhaustion took over and forced her eyes to close and her head to lull forward. When Margo looked up again blearily, there was no one else aboard. The car had been so packed moments before; where had everyone gone? And outside, there should be the city in the distance and the industrial district ahead. There was only black. Were they passing through a tunnel? Lights zoomed by. The train rattled along the tracks. Should it be going so fast?

Outside, there was a flash. Like something blocking one of the lights. Something enormous, she realized, was clinging to the window like a fly. Something with oily skin and long, sharp claws. It was watching her with emerald eyes. Margo blinked, and the creature was inside. Inches away from her face. It was slimy, like ink oozed from its flesh, and its eyes were less like emeralds and more like toxic waste. It reached for her with grotesque white claws –

Margo jerked awake, flailing at the woman sitting next to her. She must've yelled; a few people were staring. Someone with a lot of piercings and pink hair had their phone out and was recording her.

I'm a mess, she thought as she hurried from the train, her cheeks burning. Her nightmares were beginning to follow her around. *This is what losing your mind feels like.*

Her house was a short walk from the train station. The crisp autumn air revived her a little after the ride from downtown; she felt a little more alert.

Outside of her duplex, she saw Jason grabbing his mail. He was young and worked from home. Or she assumed he worked from home. He never seemed to go anywhere. He'd lived there almost three months, and his car was always in the drive. As she came up the walk, Jason smiled and waved.

"Hi, Margo!" He called.

"Hi, Jason."

"You coming down with something? You look a little…" He fumbled for an inoffensive word and failed.

"Awful?"

"You said it."

"I'm not sleeping. House makes noise."

"Uh, ok. Can you be more specific? What kind of noise?"

"House noises," she shrugged. She didn't want to tell him about her disappearing/reappearing visage of a monstrous shadow creature. It was hard enough to focus on using real words. She was just so tired.

"Could it be me? I'm sorry, I'm kind of a night owl."

"No, it's coming from my side. You never bother me."

"Well, if you need anything, call me. I'm usually up super late, so you won't bother me at all. I mean it!" He called as she unlocked her door.

"Ok, thanks Jason. See you later."

Margo made it to the couch. Her whole body ached with the need to sleep. She didn't even get her coat or shoes off.

When she opened her eyes again, Margo's head felt like it was being split open, and the room was dark. There was a moment of sheer panic as she groggily reached for the lamp. *Can't be dark can't be dark can't see...*

The living room was empty. Margo hated the relief she felt. It was childish.

Nightmares. Just nightmares.

Then, the creaking. Margo turned to stone as the wood groaned somewhere above her. She glanced up as if she could see through the ceiling. Every muscle tensed.

Something pounded across the floor. Heavy feet, moving too quickly toward the stairs. Margo didn't wait.

"Shitshitshitshit*shit!*"

She bolted from the couch like a shot. She headed for the front door, not daring to glance up the stairs to see what might be descending them. The pounding was in her ears now, following her as she hit the grass on the lawn. Margo didn't turn until she was across the street, standing in her neighbor's yard.

Her front door was wide open. Every window was dark save for the living room's. And no one followed her outside.

The pounding slowed as her heart stopped racing and the blood stopped rushing to her ears. And as she calmed, she thought:

Either someone is in my house, or I'm crazy.

I need to know which.

Yet when she tried to walk back across the street, her feet felt like lead. It defied every instinct she had to go back inside, because even if it was her imagination or some fever dream, her body still screamed *danger.*

There were lights on in the other half of the house. Jason. He'd said he'd wanted to help. Margo wondered how far that help would go.

Can't hurt to ask.

When Jason opened the door, his eyes widened. Margo didn't know how most people looked after they'd just been chased out of their home by phantom trespassers in the night, but *deranged* came to mind.

"Hi, Jason."

"House makes noise?" He asked.

"House makes noise. I think...I think someone might be in my house. Or I had a nightmare. This is so embarrassing."

"No, no, please! I want to help." He smiled, and it made Margo feel a little less absurd. "Do you want me to come over?"

She did. She imagined walking through those dark rooms, flicking the lights on as dread filled her belly with each lightswitch. "Thanks. I know it's stupid."

"Should I bring something to like, defend ourselves with?"

When Jason produced a baseball bat from the hall closet and armed Margo with it, she immediately felt a small bit of the weight that had been dragging her down for days lift. They started upstairs, since that was where she'd heard the footsteps. They meticulously checked each closet and cranny, anywhere someone could hide. Jason also checked all the windows to ensure they were locked. They left all the lights on.

Downstairs was easy work. The back door was still locked, and the kitchen and living room were totally vacant. No one had been here. That meant the problem was internal. Margo's heart sank.

"What's wrong with me?" She muttered, not really intending Jason to hear her.

"Absolutely nothing. You're perfect." He smiled. Margo smiled back, a little hesitantly. Did neighbors call each other perfect?

"Perfect people can sleep through the night without hearing weird noises and—" she cut herself off.

"And?"

She took a deep breath. Maybe it would feel good to say it. "And...see things."

"What kind of things?"

Margo looked at her feet.

"How about this: I'll make us some tea, and you can tell me what's going on. Zero judgment," he held up his hands as if in surrender. "Promise."

"Ok," Margo agreed after a moment. They weren't friends, but they'd always been friendly. And she did need someone to talk to. Even if it was to just feel like a normal human for five minutes.

In the kitchen, Jason turned on the stove and Margo fished out a couple of peppermint tea bags and some mugs. Jason made her sit down while they waited for the pot to boil and she told him about the dreams; the noises in the night that kept her awake; the emerald-eyed monster in her house, then on the train.

"No wonder you can't sleep. Something that scary would keep me up, too."

"It's nerve-wracking. Like I'm constantly looking over my shoulder, waiting for something to *get* me. It makes me feel like a little kid."

"You had nightmares like that when you were a little kid?"

"Well, no. Not like *this*. Just being so scared of nothing, you know?"

"Yeah, I know what you mean." The pot began to hiss behind him. He handed her a steaming mug. The warmth felt good in her hands.

"Thanks again, Jason. I know this is totally bananas. But it means a lot that you came over."

"Stop thanking me. You're literally steps away. It was nothing."

Margo got up to get some milk for her tea. As she swiveled from her stool, she saw their reflections in the sliding glass door that led to the back yard. Her mug hit the floor and shattered, splattering minty tea everywhere.

There, in front of the stove, holding an identical brown mug, was the sable monster with flashing eyes, its claws clutching the tea. It turned to look where Margo was looking, and their eyes locked in the glass. She turned quickly, and across the counter from her was Jason. She'd never noticed his green eyes...

He said nothing. He only smiled again. A grim, wicked smile.

Margo ran for the front door. She didn't care if she was hallucinating. She just wanted out of this house, wanted away from her green-eyed neighbor.

"I guess the game is over!" Jason called after her cheerily. Margo grabbed the door and screamed. The doorknob grew red hot in her hand, leaving an imprint on her palm. She whirled, clutching her burned hand to her chest. Jason was waiting in the living room. Still wearing that horrible smile.

"Leaving? But you didn't finish your tea."

"Stay away!" She darted up the stairs. Lightbulbs burst around her as Margo reached the second floor and ran to the bedroom. Glass rained down on her, and she could hear Jason behind her.

She slammed the bedroom door and held the handle tightly. There was no lock, but at least she was on one side and he was on the other. "Leave me alone, Jason! Just leave!"

The lights had shattered in here as well. The only light came from the streetlight outside, and the only sound now was the sound of Margo's panicked, gulping breaths.

"Margo." The voice called her name, letting the 'o' hang in the air almost playfully. Like they were playing hide and seek. Her blood froze; the voice hadn't come from the hall.

When she turned, she could see it. The creature from her nightmares, standing in the shadowy corner of her room, more alive than such a thing should have been. In the half-waking world of her dreams, it had been a vague animal, a horror movie prop. Here, where she was definitely awake, she could see the rise and fall of its chest, she could hear its raspy breathing. Margo thought she could even smell it. Something rancid. Like old meat left in the sun. The monster walked slowly out of the corner. It stepped into the shafts of pale light from the window, and Jason stood in one spot, while the creature stood in the shadows. Half neighbor, half horror.

"I'm not going to let you go, Margo. I've been watching you." Jason's voice was all wrong. It was his, but there was another voice underneath now. Something inhuman. Something growling and guttural. He took another step. Margo flung the bedroom door open and tried to run. But as she opened the door, there was something in the dark hall. The beast stood before her, dark arms wide, its verdant eyes hungry. Margo screamed. She kicked and hit as those terrible, long arms wrapped around her. The claws pressed into her back. She felt them dig into her skin. The dripping maw opened wide. Almost like it was smiling at her. It growled:

"You're perfect."

The Dead Valley

Ralph Adams Cram

I HAVE A FRIEND, Olof Ehrensvärd, a Swede by birth, who yet, by reason of a strange and melancholy mischance of his early boyhood, has thrown his lot with that of the New World. It is a curious story of a headstrong boy and a proud and relentless family: the details do not matter here, but they are sufficient to weave a web of romance around the tall yellow-bearded man with the sad eyes and the voice that gives itself perfectly to plaintive little Swedish songs remembered out of childhood. In the winter evenings we play chess together, he and I, and after some close, fierce battle has been fought to a finish – usually with my own defeat – we fill our pipes again, and Ehrensvärd tells me stories of the far, half-remembered days in the fatherland, before he went to sea: stories that grow very strange and incredible as the night deepens and the fire falls together, but stories that, nevertheless, I fully believe.

One of them made a strong impression on me, so I set it down here, only regretting that I cannot reproduce the curiously perfect English and the delicate accent which to me increased the fascination of the tale. Yet, as best I can remember it, here it is.

"I never told you how Nils and I went over the hills to Hallsberg, and how we found the Dead Valley, did I? Well, this is the way it happened. I must have been about twelve years old, and Nils Sjöberg, whose father's estate joined ours, was a few months younger. We were inseparable just at that time, and whatever we did, we did together.

"Once a week it was market day in Engelholm, and Nils and I went always there to see the strange sights that the market gathered from all the surrounding country. One day we quite lost our hearts, for an old man from across the Elfborg had brought a little dog to sell, that seemed to us the most beautiful dog in all the world. He was a round, woolly puppy, so funny that Nils and I sat down on the ground and laughed at him, until he came and played with us in so jolly a way that we felt that there was only one really desirable thing in life, and that was the little dog of the old man from across the hills. But alas! We had not half money enough wherewith to buy him, so we were forced to beg the old man not to sell him before the next market day, promising that we would bring the money for him then. He gave us his word, and we ran home very fast and implored our mothers to give us money for the little dog.

"We got the money, but we could not wait for the next market day. Suppose the puppy should be sold! The thought frightened us so that we begged and implored that we might be allowed to go over the hills to Hallsberg where the old man lived, and get the little dog ourselves, and at last they told us we might go. By starting early in the morning we should reach Hallsberg by three o'clock, and it was arranged that we should stay there that night with Nils's aunt, and, leaving by noon the next day, be home again by sunset.

"Soon after sunrise we were on our way, after having received minute instructions as to just what we should do in all possible and impossible circumstances, and finally a repeated injunction that we should start for home at the same hour the next day, so that we might get safely back before nightfall.

"For us, it was magnificent sport, and we started off with our rifles, full of the sense of our very great importance: yet the journey was simple enough, along a good road, across the big hills we knew so well, for Nils and I had shot over half the territory this side of the dividing ridge of the Elfborg. Back of Engelholm lay a long valley, from which rose the low mountains, and we had to cross this, and then follow the road along the side of the hills for three or four miles, before a narrow path branched off to the left, leading up through the pass.

"Nothing occurred of interest on the way over, and we reached Hallsberg in due season, found to our inexpressible joy that the little dog was not sold, secured him, and so went to the house of Nils's aunt to spend the night.

"Why we did not leave early on the following day, I can't quite remember; at all events, I know we stopped at a shooting range just outside of the town, where most attractive pasteboard pigs were sliding slowly through painted foliage, serving so as beautiful marks. The result was that we did not get fairly started for home until afternoon, and as we found ourselves at last pushing up the side of the mountain with the sun dangerously near their summits, I think we were a little scared at the prospect of the examination and possible punishment that awaited us when we got home at midnight.

"Therefore we hurried as fast as possible up the mountain side, while the blue dusk closed in about us, and the light died in the purple sky. At first we had talked hilariously, and the little dog had leaped ahead of us with the utmost joy. Latterly, however, a curious oppression came on us; we did not speak or even whistle, while the dog fell behind, following us with hesitation in every muscle.

"We had passed through the foothills and the low spurs of the mountains, and were almost at the top of the main range, when life seemed to go out of everything, leaving the world dead, so suddenly silent the forest became, so stagnant the air. Instinctively we halted to listen.

"Perfect silence – the crushing silence of deep forests at night; and more, for always, even in the most impenetrable fastnesses of the wooded mountains, is the multitudinous murmur of little lives, awakened by the darkness, exaggerated and intensified by the stillness of the air and the great dark: but here and now the silence seemed unbroken even by the turn of a leaf, the movement of a twig, the note of night bird or insect. I could hear the blood beat through my veins; and the crushing of the grass under our feet as we advanced with hesitating steps sounded like the falling of trees.

"And the air was stagnant – dead. The atmosphere seemed to lie upon the body like the weight of sea on a diver who has ventured too far into its awful depths. What we usually call silence seems so only in relation to the din of ordinary experience. This was silence in the absolute, and it crushed the mind while it intensified the senses, bringing down the awful weight of inextinguishable fear.

"I know that Nils and I stared towards each other in abject terror, listening to our quick, heavy breathing, that sounded to our acute senses like the fitful rush of waters. And the poor little dog we were leading justified our terror. The black oppression seemed to crush him even as it did us. He lay close on the ground, moaning feebly, and dragging himself painfully and slowly closer to Nils's feet. I think this exhibition of utter animal fear was the last touch, and must inevitably have blasted our reason – mine anyway; but just then, as we stood quaking on the bounds of madness, came a sound, so awful, so ghastly, so horrible, that it seemed to rouse us from the dead spell that was on us.

"In the depth of the silence came a cry, beginning as a low, sorrowful moan, rising to a tremulous shriek, culminating in a yell that seemed to tear the night in sunder and rend the world as by a cataclysm. So fearful was it that I could not believe it had actual existence: it passed previous experience, the powers of belief, and for a moment I thought it the result of my own animal terror, a hallucination born of tottering reason.

"A glance at Nils dispelled this thought in a flash. In the pale light of the high stars he was the embodiment of all possible human fear, quaking with an ague, his jaw fallen, his tongue out, his eyes protruding like those of a hanged man. Without a word we fled, the panic of fear giving us strength, and together, the little dog caught close in Nils's arms, we sped down the side of the cursed mountains – anywhere, goal was of no account: we had but one impulse – to get away from that place.

"So under the black trees and the far white stars that flashed through the still leaves overhead, we leaped down the mountain side, regardless of path or landmark, straight through the tangled underbrush, across mountain streams, through fens and copses, anywhere, so only that our course was downward.

"How long we ran thus, I have no idea, but by and by the forest fell behind, and we found ourselves among the foothills, and fell exhausted on the dry short grass, panting like tired dogs.

"It was lighter here in the open, and presently we looked around to see where we were, and how we were to strike out in order to find the path that would lead us home. We looked in vain for a familiar sign. Behind us rose the great wall of black forest on the flank of the mountain: before us lay the undulating mounds of low foothills, unbroken by trees or rocks, and beyond, only the fall of black sky bright with multitudinous stars that turned its velvet depth to a luminous gray.

"As I remember, we did not speak to each other once: the terror was too heavy on us for that, but by and by we rose simultaneously and started out across the hills.

"Still the same silence, the same dead, motionless air – air that was at once sultry and chilling: a heavy heat struck through with an icy chill that felt almost like the burning of frozen steel. Still carrying the helpless dog, Nils pressed on through the hills, and I followed close behind. At last, in front of us, rose a slope of moor touching the white stars. We climbed it wearily, reached the top, and found ourselves gazing down into a great, smooth valley, filled half way to the brim with – what?

"As far as the eye could see stretched a level plain of ashy white, faintly phosphorescent, a sea of velvet fog that lay like motionless water, or rather like a floor of alabaster, so dense did it appear, so seemingly capable of sustaining weight. If it were possible, I think that sea of dead white mist struck even greater terror into my soul than the heavy silence or the deadly cry – so ominous was it, so utterly unreal, so phantasmal, so impossible, as it lay there like a dead ocean under the steady stars. Yet through that mist *we must go*! There seemed no other way home, and, shattered with abject fear, mad with the one desire to get back, we started down the slope to where the sea of milky mist ceased, sharp and distinct around the stems of the rough grass.

"I put one foot into the ghostly fog. A chill as of death struck through me, stopping my heart, and I threw myself backward on the slope. At that instant came again the shriek, close, close, right in our ears, in ourselves, and far out across that damnable sea I saw the cold fog lift like a water-spout and toss itself high in writhing convolutions towards the sky. The stars began to grow dim as thick vapor swept across them, and in the growing dark I saw a great, watery moon lift itself slowly above the palpitating sea, vast and vague in the gathering mist.

"This was enough: we turned and fled along the margin of the white sea that throbbed now with fitful motion below us, rising, rising, slowly and steadily, driving us higher and higher up the side of the foothills.

"It was a race for life; that we knew. How we kept it up I cannot understand, but we did, and at last we saw the white sea fall behind us as we staggered up the end of the valley, and then down into a region that we knew, and so into the old path. The last thing I remember was hearing a strange voice, that of Nils, but horribly changed, stammer brokenly, 'The dog is dead!' and then the whole world turned around twice, slowly and resistlessly, and consciousness went out with a crash.

"It was some three weeks later, as I remember, that I awoke in my own room, and found my mother sitting beside the bed. I could not think very well at first, but as I slowly grew strong again, vague flashes of recollection began to come to me, and little by little the whole sequence of events of that awful night in the Dead Valley came back. All that I could gain from what was told me was that three weeks before I had been found in my own bed, raging sick, and that my illness grew fast into brain fever. I tried to speak of the dread things that had happened to me, but I saw at once that no one looked on them save as the hauntings of a dying frenzy, and so I closed my mouth and kept my own counsel.

"I must see Nils, however, and so I asked for him. My mother told me that he also had been ill with a strange fever, but that he was now quite well again. Presently they brought him in, and when we were alone I began to speak to him of the night on the mountain. I shall never forget the shock that struck me down on my pillow when the boy denied everything: denied having gone with me, ever having heard the cry, having seen the valley, or feeling the deadly chill of the ghostly fog. Nothing would shake his determined ignorance, and in spite of myself I was forced to admit that his denials came from no policy of concealment, but from blank oblivion.

"My weakened brain was in a turmoil. Was it all but the floating phantasm of delirium? Or had the horror of the real thing blotted Nils's mind into blankness so far as the events of the night in the Dead Valley were concerned? The latter explanation seemed the only one, else how explain the sudden illness which in a night had struck us both down? I said nothing more, either to Nils or to my own people, but waited, with a growing determination that, once well again, I would find that valley if it really existed.

"It was some weeks before I was really well enough to go, but finally, late in September, I chose a bright, warm, still day, the last smile of the dying summer, and started early in the morning along the path that led to Hallsberg. I was sure I knew where the trail struck off to the right, down which we had come from the valley of dead water, for a great tree grew by the Hallsberg path at the point where, with a sense of salvation, we had found the home road. Presently I saw it to the right, a little distance ahead.

"I think the bright sunlight and the clear air had worked as a tonic to me, for by the time I came to the foot of the great pine, I had quite lost faith in the verity of the vision that haunted me, believing at last that it was indeed but the nightmare of madness Nevertheless, I turned sharply to the right, at the base of the tree, into a narrow path that led through a dense thicket. As I did so I tripped over something. A swarm of flies sung into the air around me, and looking down I saw the matted fleece, with the poor little bones thrusting through, of the dog we had bought in Hallsberg.

"Then my courage went out with a puff, and I knew that it all was true, and that now I was frightened. Pride and the desire for adventure urged me on, however, and I pressed into the close thicket that barred my way. The path was hardly visible: merely the worn road of some small beasts, for, though it showed in the crisp grass, the bushes above grew thick and hardly penetrable. The land rose slowly, and rising grew clearer, until at last I came out on a great slope of hill, unbroken by trees or shrubs, very like my memory of that rise of land we had topped in order that we might find the dead valley and the icy fog. I looked at the sun; it was bright and clear, and all around insects were humming in the autumn air, and birds were darting to and fro. Surely there was no danger, not until nightfall at least; so I began to whistle, and with a rush mounted the last crest of brown hill.

"There lay the Dead Valley! A great oval basin, almost as smooth and regular as though made by man. On all sides the grass crept over the brink of the encircling hills, dusty green on the crests, then fading into ashy brown, and so to a deadly white, this last color forming a thin ring, running in a long line around the slope. And then? Nothing. Bare, brown, hard earth, glittering with grains of alkali, but otherwise dead and barren. Not a tuft of grass, not a stick of brushwood, not even a stone, but only the vast expanse of beaten clay.

"In the midst of the basin, perhaps a mile and a half away, the level expanse was broken by a great dead tree, rising leafless and gaunt into the air. Without a moment's hesitation I started down into the valley and made for this goal. Every particle of fear seemed to have left me, and even the valley itself did not look so very terrifying. At all events, I was driven by an overwhelming curiosity, and there seemed to be but one thing in the world to do – to get to that Tree! As I trudged along over the hard earth, I noticed that the multitudinous voices of birds and insects had died away. No bee or butterfly hovered through the air, no insects leaped or crept over the dull earth. The very air itself was stagnant.

"As I drew near the skeleton tree, I noticed the glint of sunlight on a kind of white mound around its roots, and I wondered curiously. It was not until I had come close that I saw its nature.

"All around the roots and barkless trunk was heaped a wilderness of little bones. Tiny skulls of rodents and of birds, thousands of them, rising about the dead tree and streaming off for several yards in all directions, until the dreadful pile ended in isolated skulls and scattered skeletons. Here and there a larger bone appeared – the thigh of a sheep, the hoofs of a horse, and to one side, grinning slowly, a human skull.

"I stood quite still, staring with all my eyes, when suddenly the dense silence was broken by a faint, forlorn cry high over my head. I looked up and saw a great falcon turning and sailing downward just over the tree. In a moment more she fell motionless on the bleaching bones.

"Horror struck me, and I rushed for home, my brain whirling, a strange numbness growing in me. I ran steadily, on and on. At last I glanced up. Where was the rise of hill? I looked around wildly. Close before me was the dead tree with its pile of bones. I had circled it round and round, and the valley wall was still a mile and a half away.

"I stood dazed and frozen. The sun was sinking, red and dull, towards the line of hills. In the east the dark was growing fast. Was there still time? *Time!* It was not *that* I wanted, it was *will*! My feet seemed clogged as in a nightmare. I could hardly drag them over the barren earth. And then I felt the slow chill creeping through me. I looked down. Out of the earth a thin mist was rising, collecting in little pools that grew ever larger until they joined here and there, their currents swirling slowly like thin blue smoke. The western hills halved the copper sun. When it was dark I should hear that shriek again, and then I should die. I knew that, and with every remaining atom of will I staggered towards the red west through the writhing mist that crept clammily around my ankles, retarding my steps.

"And as I fought my way off from the Tree, the horror grew, until at last I thought I was going to die. The silence pursued me like dumb ghosts, the still air held my breath, the hellish fog caught at my feet like cold hands.

"But I won! Though not a moment too soon. As I crawled on my hands and knees up the brown slope, I heard, far away and high in the air, the cry that already had almost bereft me of reason. It was faint and vague, but unmistakable in its horrible intensity. I glanced behind. The fog was dense and pallid, heaving undulously up the brown slope. The sky was gold under the setting sun, but below was the ashy gray of death. I stood for a moment on the brink of this sea of hell, and then leaped down the slope. The sunset opened before me, the night closed behind, and as I crawled home weak and tired, darkness shut down on the Dead Valley."

The Monster

Stephen Crane

Chapter I

LITTLE JIM was, for the time, engine Number 36, and he was making the run between Syracuse and Rochester. He was fourteen minutes behind time, and the throttle was wide open. In consequence, when he swung around the curve at the flowerbed, a wheel of his cart destroyed a peony. Number 36 slowed down at once and looked guiltily at his father, who was mowing the lawn. The doctor had his back to this accident, and he continued to pace slowly to and fro, pushing the mower.

Jim dropped the tongue of the cart. He looked at his father and at the broken flower. Finally he went to the peony and tried to stand it on its pins, resuscitated, but the spine of it was hurt, and it would only hang limply from his hand. Jim could do no reparation. He looked again towards his father.

He went on to the lawn, very slowly, and kicking wretchedly at the turf. Presently his father came along with the whirring machine, while the sweet, new grass blades spun from the knives. In a low voice, Jim said, "Pa!"

The doctor was shaving this lawn as if it were a priest's chin. All during the season he had worked at it in the coolness and peace of the evenings after supper. Even in the shadow of the cherry-trees the grass was strong and healthy. Jim raised his voice a trifle. "Pa!"

The doctor paused, and with the howl of the machine no longer occupying the sense, one could hear the robins in the cherry-trees arranging their affairs. Jim's hands were behind his back, and sometimes his fingers clasped and unclasped. Again he said, "Pa!" The child's fresh and rosy lip was lowered.

The doctor stared down at his son, thrusting his head forward and frowning attentively. "What is it, Jimmie?"

"Pa!" repeated the child at length. Then he raised his finger and pointed at the flowerbed. "There!"

"What?" said the doctor, frowning more. "What is it, Jim?"

After a period of silence, during which the child may have undergone a severe mental tumult, he raised his finger and repeated his former word – "There!" The father had respected this silence with perfect courtesy. Afterwards his glance carefully followed the direction indicated by the child's finger, but he could see nothing which explained to him. "I don't understand what you mean, Jimmie," he said.

It seemed that the importance of the whole thing had taken away the boy's vocabulary, He could only reiterate, "There!"

The doctor mused upon the situation, but he could make nothing of it. At last he said, "Come, show me."

Together they crossed the lawn towards the flowerbed. At some yards from the broken peony Jimmie began to lag. "There!" The word came almost breathlessly.

"Where?" said the doctor.

Jimmie kicked at the grass. "There!" he replied.

The doctor was obliged to go forward alone. After some trouble he found the subject of the incident, the broken flower. Turning then, he saw the child lurking at the rear and scanning his countenance.

The father reflected. After a time he said, "Jimmie, come here." With an infinite modesty of demeanor the child came forward. "Jimmie, how did this happen?"

The child answered, "Now – I was playin' train – and – now – I runned over it."

"You were doing what?"

"I was playin' train."

The father reflected again. "Well, Jimmie," he said, slowly, "I guess you had better not play train any more today. Do you think you had better?"

"No, sir," said Jimmie.

During the delivery of the judgment the child had not faced his father, and afterwards he went away, with his head lowered, shuffling his feet.

Chapter II

IT WAS APPARENT from Jimmie's manner that he felt some kind of desire to efface himself. He went down to the stable. Henry Johnson, the negro who cared for the doctor's horses, was sponging the buggy. He grinned fraternally when he saw Jimmie coming. These two were pals. In regard to almost everything in life they seemed to have minds precisely alike. Of course there were points of emphatic divergence. For instance, it was plain from Henry's talk that he was a very handsome negro, and he was known to be a light, a weight, and an eminence in the suburb of the town, where lived the larger number of the negroes, and obviously this glory was over Jimmie's horizon; but he vaguely appreciated it and paid deference to Henry for it mainly because Henry appreciated it and deferred to himself. However, on all points of conduct as related to the doctor, who was the moon, they were in complete but unexpressed understanding. Whenever Jimmie became the victim of an eclipse he went to the stable to solace himself with Henry's crimes. Henry, with the elasticity of his race, could usually provide a sin to place himself on a footing with the disgraced one. Perhaps he would remember that he had forgotten to put the hitching-strap in the back of the buggy on some recent occasion, and had been reprimanded by the doctor. Then these two would commune subtly and without words concerning their moon, holding themselves sympathetically as people who had committed similar treasons. On the other hand, Henry would sometimes choose to absolutely repudiate this idea, and when Jimmie appeared in his shame would bully him most virtuously, preaching with assurance the precepts of the doctor's creed, and pointing out to Jimmie all his abominations. Jimmie did not discover that this was odious in his comrade. He accepted it and lived in its shadow with humility, merely trying to conciliate the saintly Henry with acts of deference. Won by this attitude, Henry would sometimes allow the child to enjoy the felicity of squeezing the sponge over a buggy-wheel, even when Jimmie was still gory from unspeakable deeds.

Whenever Henry dwelt for a time in sackcloth, Jimmie did not patronize him at all. This was a justice of his age, his condition. He did not know. Besides, Henry could drive a horse, and Jimmie had a full sense of this sublimity. Henry personally conducted the moon during the splendid journeys through the country roads, where farms spread on all sides, with sheep, cows, and other marvels abounding.

"Hello, Jim!" said Henry, poising his sponge. Water was dripping from the buggy. Sometimes the horses in the stalls stamped thunderingly on the pine floor. There was an atmosphere of hay and of harness.

For a minute Jimmie refused to take an interest in anything. He was very downcast. He could not even feel the wonders of wagon-washing. Henry, while at his work, narrowly observed him.

"Your pop done wallop yer, didn't he?" he said at last.

"No," said Jimmie, defensively; "he didn't."

After this casual remark Henry continued his labor, with a scowl of occupation. Presently he said: "I done tol' yer many's th' time not to go a-foolin' an' a-projjeckin' with them flowers. Yer pop don' like it nohow." As a matter of fact, Henry had never mentioned flowers to the boy.

Jimmie preserved a gloomy silence, so Henry began to use seductive wiles in this affair of washing a wagon. It was not until he began to spin a wheel on the tree, and the sprinkling water flew everywhere, that the boy was visibly moved. He had been seated on the sill of the carriage-house door, but at the beginning of this ceremony he arose and circled towards the buggy, with an interest that slowly consumed the remembrance of a late disgrace.

Johnson could then display all the dignity of a man whose duty it was to protect Jimmie from a splashing. "Look out, boy! Look out! You done gwi' spile yer pants. I raikon your mommer don't 'low this foolishness, she know it. I ain't gwi' have you round yere spilin' yer pants, an' have Mis' Trescott light on me pressen'ly. 'Deed I ain't." He spoke with an air of great irritation, but he was not annoyed at all. This tone was merely a part of his importance. In reality he was always delighted to have the child there to witness the business of the stable. For one thing, Jimmie was invariably overcome with reverence when he was told how beautifully a harness was polished or a horse groomed. Henry explained each detail of this kind with unction, procuring great joy from the child's admiration.

Chapter III

AFTER JOHNSON had taken his supper in the kitchen, he went to his loft in the carriage house and dressed himself with much care. No belle of a court circle could bestow more mind on a toilet than did Johnson. On second thought, he was more like a priest arraying himself for some parade of the church. As he emerged from his room and sauntered down the carriage-drive, no one would have suspected him of ever having washed a buggy.

It was not altogether a matter of the lavender trousers, nor yet the straw hat with its bright silk band. The change was somewhere, far in the interior of Henry. But there was no cake-walk hyperbole in it. He was simply a quiet, well-bred gentleman of position, wealth, and other necessary achievements out for an evening stroll, and he had never washed a wagon in his life.

In the morning, when in his working-clothes, he had met a friend – "Hello, Pete!" "Hello, Henry!" Now, in his effulgence, he encountered this same friend. His bow was not at all haughty. If it expressed anything, it expressed consummate generosity – "Good-evenin', Misteh Washington." Pete, who was very dirty, being at work in a potato-patch, responded in a mixture of abasement and appreciation – "Good-evenin', Misteh Johnsing."

The shimmering blue of the electric arc lamps was strong in the main street of the town. At numerous points it was conquered by the orange glare of the outnumbering gaslights in the windows of shops. Through this radiant lane moved a crowd, which culminated in a throng before the post-office, awaiting the distribution of the evening mails. Occasionally there came into it a shrill electric street-car, the motor singing like a cageful of grasshoppers, and possessing a great gong that clanged forth both warnings and simple noise. At the little theatre, which was a varnish and red plush miniature of one of the famous New York theatres, a company of strollers was to play 'East Lynne'. The young men of the town were mainly gathered at the corners, in distinctive groups, which expressed various shades and lines of chumship, and had little to do with any social gradations. There they discussed everything with critical insight, passing the whole town in review as it swarmed in the street. When the gongs of the electric cars ceased for a moment to harry the ears, there could be heard the sound of the feet of the leisurely crowd on the bluestone pavement, and it was like the peaceful evening lashing at the shore of a lake. At the foot of the hill, where two lines of maples sentinelled the way, an electric lamp glowed high among the embowering branches, and made most wonderful shadow-etchings on the road below it.

When Johnson appeared amid the throng a member of one of the profane groups at a corner instantly telegraphed news of this extraordinary arrival to his companions. They hailed him. "Hello, Henry! Going to walk for a cake tonight?"

"Ain't he smooth?"

"Why, you've got that cake right in your pocket, Henry!"

"Throw out your chest a little more."

Henry was not ruffled in any way by these quiet admonitions and compliments. In reply he laughed a supremely good-natured, chuckling laugh, which nevertheless expressed an underground complacency of superior metal.

Young Griscom, the lawyer, was just emerging from Reifsnyder's barber shop, rubbing his chin contentedly. On the steps he dropped his hand and looked with wide eyes into the crowd. Suddenly he bolted back into the shop. "Wow!" he cried to the parliament; "You ought to see the coon that's coming!"

Reifsnyder and his assistant instantly poised their razors high and turned towards the window. Two belathered heads reared from the chairs. The electric shine in the street caused an effect like water to them who looked through the glass from the yellow glamor of Reifsnyder's shop. In fact, the people without resembled the inhabitants of a great aquarium that here had a square pane in it. Presently into this frame swam the graceful form of Henry Johnson.

"Chee!" said Reifsnyder. He and his assistant with one accord threw their obligations to the winds, and leaving their lathered victims helpless, advanced to the window. "Ain't he a taisy?" said Reifsnyder, marvelling.

But the man in the first chair, with a grievance in his mind, had found a weapon. "Why, that's only Henry Johnson, you blamed idiots! Come on now, Reif, and shave me. What do you think I am – a mummy?"

Reifsnyder turned, in a great excitement. "I bait you any money that vas not Henry Johnson! Henry Johnson! Rats!" The scorn put into this last word made it an explosion. "That man was a Pullman-car porter or someding. How could that be Henry Johnson?" he demanded, turbulently. "You vas crazy."

The man in the first chair faced the barber in a storm of indignation. "Didn't I give him those lavender trousers?" he roared.

And young Griscom, who had remained attentively at the window, said: "Yes, I guess that was Henry. It looked like him."

"Oh, vell," said Reifsnyder, returning to his business, "if you think so! Oh, vell!" He implied that he was submitting for the sake of amiability.

Finally the man in the second chair, mumbling from a mouth made timid by adjacent lather, said: "That was Henry Johnson all right. Why, he always dresses like that when he wants to make a front! He's the biggest dude in town – anybody knows that."

"Chinger!" said Reifsnyder.

Henry was not at all oblivious of the wake of wondering ejaculation that streamed out behind him. On other occasions he had reaped this same joy, and he always had an eye for the demonstration. With a face beaming with happiness he turned away from the scene of his victories into a narrow side street, where the electric light still hung high, but only to exhibit a row of tumble-down houses leaning together like paralytics.

The saffron Miss Bella Farragut, in a calico frock, had been crouched on the front stoop, gossiping at long range, but she espied her approaching caller at a distance. She dashed around the corner of the house, galloping like a horse. Henry saw it all, but he preserved the polite demeanor of a guest when a waiter spills claret down his cuff. In this awkward situation he was simply perfect.

The duty of receiving Mr. Johnson fell upon Mrs. Farragut, because Bella, in another room, was scrambling wildly into her best gown. The fat old woman met him with a great ivory smile, sweeping back with the door, and bowing low. "Walk in, Misteh Johnson, walk in. How is you dis ebenin', Misteh Johnson – how is you?"

Henry's face showed like a reflector as he bowed and bowed, bending almost from his head to his ankles, "Good-evenin', Mis' Fa'gut; good-evenin'. How is you dis evenin'? Is all you' folks well, Mis' Fa'gut?"

After a great deal of kowtow, they were planted in two chairs opposite each other in the living room. Here they exchanged the most tremendous civilities, until Miss Bella swept into the room, when there was more kowtow on all sides, and a smiling show of teeth that was like an illumination.

The cooking-stove was of course in this drawing room, and on the fire was some kind of a long-winded stew. Mrs. Farragut was obliged to arise and attend to it from time to time. Also young Sim came in and went to bed on his pallet in the corner. But to all these domesticities the three maintained an absolute dumbness. They bowed and smiled and ignored and imitated until a late hour, and if they had been the occupants of the most gorgeous salon in the world they could not have been more like three monkeys.

After Henry had gone, Bella, who encouraged herself in the appropriation of phrases, said, "Oh, ma, isn't he divine?"

Chapter IV

A SATURDAY EVENING was a sign always for a larger crowd to parade the thoroughfare. In summer the band played until ten o'clock in the little park. Most of the young men of the town affected to be superior to this band, even to despise it; but in the still and fragrant evenings they invariably turned out in force, because the girls were sure to attend this concert, strolling slowly over the grass, linked closely in pairs, or preferably in threes, in the curious public dependence upon one another which was their inheritance. There was no particular social aspect to this gathering, save that group regarded group with interest, but mainly in silence. Perhaps one girl would nudge another girl and suddenly say, "Look! There goes Gertie Hodgson and her sister!" And they would appear to regard this as an event of importance.

On a particular evening a rather large company of young men were gathered on the sidewalk that edged the park. They remained thus beyond the borders of the festivities because of their dignity, which would not exactly allow them to appear in anything which was so much fun for the younger lads. These latter were careering madly through the crowd, precipitating minor accidents from time to time, but usually fleeing like mist swept by the wind before retribution could lay hands upon them.

The band played a waltz which involved a gift of prominence to the bass horn, and one of the young men on the sidewalk said that the music reminded him of the new engines on the hill pumping water into the reservoir. A similarity of this kind was not inconceivable, but the young man did not say it because he disliked the band's playing. He said it because it was fashionable to say that manner of thing concerning the band. However, over in the stand, Billie Harris, who played the snare-drum, was always surrounded by a throng of boys, who adored his every whack.

After the mails from New York and Rochester had been finally distributed, the crowd from the post-office added to the mass already in the park. The wind waved the leaves of the maples, and, high in the air, the blue-burning globes of the arc lamps caused the wonderful traceries of leaf shadows on the ground. When the light fell upon the upturned face of a girl, it caused it to glow with a wonderful pallor. A policeman came suddenly from the darkness and chased a gang of obstreperous little boys. They hooted him from a distance. The leader of the band had some of the mannerisms of the great musicians, and during a period of silence the crowd smiled when they saw him raise his hand to his brow, stroke it sentimentally, and glance upward with a look of poetic anguish. In the shivering light, which gave to the park an effect like a great vaulted hall, the throng swarmed, with a gentle murmur of dresses switching the turf, and with a steady hum of voices.

Suddenly, without preliminary bars, there arose from afar the great hoarse roar of a factory whistle. It raised and swelled to a sinister note, and then it sang on the night wind one long call that held the crowd in the park immovable, speechless. The band-master had been about to vehemently let fall his hand to start the band on a thundering career through a popular march, but, smitten by this giant voice from the night, his hand dropped slowly to his knee, and, his mouth agape, he looked at his men in silence. The cry died away to a wail and then to stillness. It released the muscles of the company of young men on the sidewalk, who had been like statues, posed eagerly, lithely, their ears turned. And then they wheeled upon each other simultaneously, and, in a single explosion, they shouted, "One!"

Again the sound swelled in the night and roared its long ominous cry, and as it died away the crowd of young men wheeled upon each other and, in chorus, yelled, "Two!"

There was a moment of breathless waiting. Then they bawled, "Second district!" In a flash the company of indolent and cynical young men had vanished like a snowball disrupted by dynamite.

Chapter V

JAKE ROGERS was the first man to reach the home of Tuscarora Hose Company Number Six. He had wrenched his key from his pocket as he tore down the street, and he jumped at the spring-lock like a demon. As the doors flew back before his hands he leaped and kicked the wedges from a pair of wheels, loosened a tongue from its clasp, and in the glare of the electric light which the town placed before each of its hose-houses the next comers beheld the spectacle of Jake Rogers bent like hickory in the manfulness of his pulling, and the heavy cart was moving slowly towards the doors. Four men joined him at the time, and as they swung with the cart out into the street, dark figures sped towards them from the ponderous shadows back of the electric lamps. Some set up the inevitable question, "What district?"

"Second," was replied to them in a compact howl. Tuscarora Hose Company Number Six swept on a perilous wheel into Niagara Avenue, and as the men, attached to the cart by the rope which had been paid out from the windlass under the tongue, pulled madly in their fervor and abandon, the gong under the axle clanged incitingly. And sometimes the same cry was heard, "What district?"

"Second."

On a grade Johnnie Thorpe fell, and exercising a singular muscular ability, rolled out in time from the track of the oncoming wheel, and arose, dishevelled and aggrieved, casting a look of mournful disenchantment upon the black crowd that poured after the machine. The cart seemed to be the apex of a dark wave that was whirling as if it had been a broken dam. Back of the lad were stretches of lawn, and in that direction front-doors were banged by men who hoarsely shouted out into the clamorous avenue, "What district?"

At one of these houses a woman came to the door bearing a lamp, shielding her face from its rays with her hands. Across the cropped grass the avenue represented to her a kind of black torrent, upon which, nevertheless, fled numerous miraculous figures upon bicycles. She did not know that the towering light at the corner was continuing its nightly whine.

Suddenly a little boy somersaulted around the corner of the house as if he had been projected down a flight of stairs by a catapultian boot. He halted himself in front of the house by dint of a rather extraordinary evolution with his legs. "Oh, ma," he gasped, "can I go? Can I, ma?"

She straightened with the coldness of the exterior mother-judgment, although the hand that held the lamp trembled slightly. "No, Willie; you had better come to bed."

Instantly he began to buck and fume like a mustang. "Oh, ma," he cried, contorting himself – "oh, ma, can't I go? Please, ma, can't I go? Can't I go, ma?"

"It's half-past nine now, Willie."

He ended by wailing out a compromise: "Well, just down to the corner, ma? Just down to the corner?"

From the avenue came the sound of rushing men who wildly shouted. Somebody had grappled the bell-rope in the Methodist church, and now over the town rang this solemn and terrible voice, speaking from the clouds. Moved from its peaceful business, this bell gained a new spirit in the portentous night, and it swung the heart to and fro, up and down, with each peal of it.

"Just down to the corner, ma?"

"Willie, it's half-past nine now."

Chapter VI

THE OUTLINES of the house of Dr. Trescott had faded quietly into the evening, hiding a shape such as we call Queen Anne against the pall of the blackened sky. The neighborhood was at this time so quiet, and seemed so devoid of obstructions, that Hannigan's dog thought it a good opportunity to prowl in forbidden precincts, and so came and pawed Trescott's lawn, growling, and considering himself a formidable beast. Later, Peter Washington strolled past the house and whistled, but there was no dim light shining from Henry's loft, and presently Peter went his way. The rays from the street, creeping in silvery waves over the grass, caused the row of shrubs along the drive to throw a clear, bold shade.

A wisp of smoke came from one of the windows at the end of the house and drifted quietly into the branches of a cherry-tree. Its companions followed it in slowly increasing numbers, and finally there was a current controlled by invisible banks which poured into the fruit-laden boughs of the cherry-tree. It was no more to be noted than if a troop of dim and silent gray monkeys had been climbing a grapevine into the clouds.

After a moment the window brightened as if the four panes of it had been stained with blood, and a quick ear might have been led to imagine the fire-imps calling and calling, clan joining clan, gathering to the colors. From the street, however, the house maintained its dark quiet, insisting to a passer-by that it was the safe dwelling of people who chose to retire early to tranquil dreams. No one could have heard this low droning of the gathering clans.

Suddenly the panes of the red window tinkled and crashed to the ground, and at other windows there suddenly reared other flames, like bloody spectres at the apertures of a haunted house. This outbreak had been well planned, as if by professional revolutionists.

A man's voice suddenly shouted: "Fire! Fire! Fire!" Hannigan had flung his pipe frenziedly from him because his lungs demanded room. He tumbled down from his perch, swung over the fence, and ran shouting towards the front-door of the Trescotts'. Then he hammered on the door, using his fists as if they were mallets. Mrs. Trescott instantly came to one of the windows on the second floor. Afterwards she knew she had been about to say, "The doctor is not at home, but if you will leave your name, I will let him know as soon as he comes."

Hannigan's bawling was for a minute incoherent, but she understood that it was not about croup.

"What?" she said, raising the window swiftly.

"Your house is on fire! You're all ablaze! Move quick if—" His cries were resounding in the street as if it were a cave of echoes. Many feet pattered swiftly on the stones. There was one man who ran with an almost fabulous speed. He wore lavender trousers. A straw hat with a bright silk band was held half crumpled in his hand.

As Henry reached the front-door, Hannigan had just broken the lock with a kick. A thick cloud of smoke poured over them, and Henry, ducking his head, rushed into it. From Hannigan's clamor he knew only one thing, but it turned him blue with horror. In the hall a lick of flame had found the cord that supported 'Signing the Declaration'. The engraving slumped suddenly down at one end, and then dropped to the floor, where it burst with the sound of a bomb. The fire was already roaring like a winter wind among the pines.

At the head of the stairs Mrs. Trescott was waving her arms as if they were two reeds.

"Jimmie! Save Jimmie!" she screamed in Henry's face. He plunged past her and disappeared, taking the long-familiar routes among these upper chambers, where he had once held office as a sort of second assistant house-maid.

Hannigan had followed him up the stairs, and grappled the arm of the maniacal woman there. His face was black with rage. "You must come down," he bellowed.

She would only scream at him in reply: "Jimmie! Jimmie! Save Jimmie!" But he dragged her forth while she babbled at him.

As they swung out into the open air a man ran across the lawn, and seizing a shutter, pulled it from its hinges and flung it far out upon the grass. Then he frantically attacked the other shutters one by one. It was a kind of temporary insanity.

"Here, you," howled Hannigan, "hold Mrs. Trescott – and stop—"

The news had been telegraphed by a twist of the wrist of a neighbor who had gone to the fire-box at the corner, and the time when Hannigan and his charge struggled out of the house was the time when the whistle roared its hoarse night call, smiting the crowd in the park, causing the leader of the band, who was about to order the first triumphal clang of a military march, to let his hand drop slowly to his knees.

Chapter VII

HENRY PAWED awkwardly through the smoke in the upper halls. He had attempted to guide himself by the walls, but they were too hot. The paper was crimpling, and he expected at any moment to have a flame burst from under his hands.

"Jimmie!"

He did not call very loud, as if in fear that the humming flames below would overhear him.

"Jimmie! Oh, Jimmie!"

Stumbling and panting, he speedily reached the entrance to Jimmie's room and flung open the door. The little chamber had no smoke in it at all. It was faintly illuminated by a beautiful rosy light reflected circuitously from the flames that were consuming the house. The boy had apparently just been aroused by the noise. He sat in his bed, his lips apart, his eyes wide, while upon his little white-robed figure played caressingly the light from the fire. As the door flew open he had before him this apparition of his pal, a terror-stricken negro, all tousled and with wool scorching, who leaped upon him and bore him up in a blanket as if the whole affair were a case of kidnapping by a dreadful robber chief. Without waiting to go through the usual short but complete process of wrinkling up his face, Jimmie let out a gorgeous bawl, which resembled the expression of a calf's deepest terror. As Johnson, bearing him, reeled into the smoke of the hall, he flung his arms about his neck and buried his face in the blanket. He called twice in muffled tones: "Mam-ma! Mam-ma!" When Johnson came to the top of the stairs with his burden, he took a quick step backward. Through the smoke that rolled to him he could see that the lower hall was all ablaze. He cried out then in a howl that resembled Jimmie's former achievement. His legs gained a frightful faculty of bending sideways. Swinging about precariously on these reedy legs, he made his way back slowly, back along the upper hall. From the way of him then, he had given up almost all idea of escaping from the burning house, and with it the desire. He was submitting, submitting because of his fathers, bending his mind in a most perfect slavery to this conflagration.

He now clutched Jimmie as unconsciously as when, running toward the house, he had clutched the hat with the bright silk band.

Suddenly he remembered a little private staircase which led from a bedroom to an apartment which the doctor had fitted up as a laboratory and work-house, where he used some of his leisure, and also hours when he might have been sleeping, in devoting himself to experiments which came in the way of his study and interest.

When Johnson recalled this stairway the submission to the blaze departed instantly. He had been perfectly familiar with it, but his confusion had destroyed the memory of it.

In his sudden momentary apathy there had been little that resembled fear, but now, as a way of safety came to him, the old frantic terror caught him. He was no longer creature to the flames, and he was afraid of the battle with them. It was a singular and swift set of alternations in which he feared twice without submission, and submitted once without fear.

"Jimmie!" he wailed, as he staggered on his way. He wished this little inanimate body at his breast to participate in his tremblings. But the child had lain limp and still during these headlong charges and countercharges, and no sign came from him.

Johnson passed through two rooms and came to the head of the stairs. As he opened the door great billows of smoke poured out, but gripping Jimmie closer, he plunged down through them. All manner of odors assailed him during this flight. They seemed to be alive with envy, hatred, and malice. At the entrance to the laboratory he confronted a strange spectacle. The room was like a garden in the region where might be burning flowers. Flames of violet, crimson, green, blue, orange, and purple were blooming everywhere. There was one blaze that was precisely the hue of a delicate coral. In another place was a mass that lay merely in phosphorescent inaction like a pile of emeralds. But all these marvels were to be seen dimly through clouds of heaving, turning, deadly smoke.

Johnson halted for a moment on the threshold. He cried out again in the negro wail that had in it the sadness of the swamps. Then he rushed across the room. An orange-colored flame leaped like a panther at the lavender trousers. This animal bit deeply into Johnson. There was an explosion at one side, and suddenly before him there reared a delicate, trembling sapphire shape like a fairy lady. With a quiet smile she blocked his path and doomed him and Jimmie. Johnson shrieked, and then ducked in the manner of his race in fights. He aimed to pass under the left guard of the sapphire lady. But she was swifter than eagles, and her talons caught in him as he plunged past her. Bowing his head as if his neck had been struck, Johnson lurched forward, twisting this way and that way. He fell on his back. The still form in the blanket flung from his arms, rolled to the edge of the floor and beneath the window.

Johnson had fallen with his head at the base of an old-fashioned desk. There was a row of jars upon the top of this desk. For the most part, they were silent amid this rioting, but there was one which seemed to hold a scintillant and writhing serpent.

Suddenly the glass splintered, and a ruby-red snakelike thing poured its thick length out upon the top of the old desk. It coiled and hesitated, and then began to swim a languorous way down the mahogany slant. At the angle it waved its sizzling molten head to and fro over the closed eyes of the man beneath it. Then, in a moment, with a mystic impulse, it moved again, and the red snake flowed directly down into Johnson's upturned face.

Afterwards the trail of this creature seemed to reek, and amid flames and low explosions drops like red-hot jewels pattered softly down it at leisurely intervals.

Chapter VIII

SUDDENLY all roads led to Dr. Trescott's. The whole town flowed towards one point. Chippeway Hose Company Number One toiled desperately up Bridge Street Hill even as the Tuscaroras came in an impetuous sweep down Niagara Avenue. Meanwhile the machine of the hook-and-ladder experts from across the creek was spinning on its way. The chief of the fire department had been playing poker in the rear room of Whiteley's cigar-store, but at the first breath of the alarm he sprang through the door like a man escaping with the kitty.

In Whilomville, on these occasions, there was always a number of people who instantly turned their attention to the bells in the churches and school-houses. The bells not only emphasized the alarm, but it was the habit to send these sounds rolling across the sky in a stirring brazen uproar until the flames were practically vanquished. There was also a kind of rivalry as to which bell should be made to produce the greatest din. Even the Valley Church, four miles away among the farms, had heard the voices of its brethren, and immediately added a quaint little yelp.

Dr. Trescott had been driving homeward, slowly smoking a cigar, and feeling glad that this last case was now in complete obedience to him, like a wild animal that he had subdued, when he heard the long whistle, and chirped to his horse under the unlicensed but perfectly distinct impression that a fire had broken out in Oakhurst, a new and rather high-flying suburb of the town which was at least two miles from his own home. But in the second blast and in the ensuing silence he read the designation of his own district. He was then only a few blocks from his house. He took out the whip and laid it lightly on the mare. Surprised and frightened at this extraordinary action, she leaped forward, and as the reins straightened like steel bands, the doctor leaned backward a trifle. When the mare whirled him up to the closed gate he was wondering whose house could be afire. The man who had rung the signal-box yelled something at him, but he already knew. He left the mare to her will.

In front of his door was a maniacal woman in a wrapper. "Ned!" she screamed at sight of him. "Jimmie! Save Jimmie!"

Trescott had grown hard and chill. "Where?" he said. "Where?"

Mrs. Trescott's voice began to bubble. "Up – up – up—" She pointed at the second-story windows.

Hannigan was already shouting: "Don't go in that way! You can't go in that way!"

Trescott ran around the corner of the house and disappeared from them. He knew from the view he had taken of the main hall that it would be impossible to ascend from there. His hopes were fastened now to the stairway which led from the laboratory. The door which opened from this room out upon the lawn was fastened with a bolt and lock, but he kicked close to the lock and then close to the bolt. The door with a loud crash flew back. The doctor recoiled from the roll of smoke, and then bending low, he stepped into the garden of burning flowers. On the floor his stinging eyes could make out a form in a smoldering blanket near the window. Then, as he carried his son towards the door, he saw that the whole lawn seemed now alive with men and boys, the leaders in the great charge that the whole town was making. They seized him and his burden, and overpowered him in wet blankets and water.

But Hannigan was howling: "Johnson is in there yet! Henry Johnson is in there yet! He went in after the kid! Johnson is in there yet!"

These cries penetrated to the sleepy senses of Trescott, and he struggled with his captors, swearing, unknown to him and to them, all the deep blasphemies of his medical-student days. He rose to his feet and went again towards the door of the laboratory. They endeavored to restrain him, although they were much affrighted at him.

But a young man who was a brakeman on the railway, and lived in one of the rear streets near the Trescotts, had gone into the laboratory and brought forth a thing which he laid on the grass.

Chapter IX

THERE WERE hoarse commands from in front of the house. "Turn on your water, Five!" "Let 'er go, One!" The gathering crowd swayed this way and that way. The flames, towering high, cast a wild red light on their faces. There came the clangor of a gong from along some adjacent street. The crowd exclaimed at it. "Here comes Number Three!" "That's Three a-comin'!" A panting and irregular mob dashed into view, dragging a hose-cart. A cry of exultation arose from the little boys. "Here's Three!" The lads welcomed Never-Die Hose Company Number Three as if it was composed of a chariot dragged by a band of gods. The perspiring citizens flung themselves into the fray. The boys danced in impish joy at the displays of prowess. They acclaimed the approach of Number Two. They welcomed Number Four with cheers. They were so deeply moved by this whole affair that they bitterly guyed the late appearance of the hook and ladder company, whose heavy apparatus had almost stalled them on the Bridge Street hill. The lads hated and feared a fire, of course. They did not particularly want to have anybody's house burn, but still it was fine to see the gathering of the companies, and amid a great noise to watch their heroes perform all manner of prodigies.

They were divided into parties over the worth of different companies, and supported their creeds with no small violence. For instance, in that part of the little city where Number Four had its home it would be most daring for a boy to contend the superiority of any other company. Likewise, in another quarter, where a strange boy was asked which fire company was the best in Whilomville, he was expected to answer "Number One." Feuds, which the boys forgot and remembered according to chance or the importance of some recent event, existed all through the town.

They did not care much for John Shipley, the chief of the department. It was true that he went to a fire with the speed of a falling angel, but when there he invariably lapsed into a certain still mood, which was almost a preoccupation, moving leisurely around the burning structure and surveying it, putting meanwhile at a cigar. This quiet man, who even when life was in danger seldom raised his voice, was not much to their fancy. Now old Sykes Huntington, when he was chief, used to bellow continually like a bull and gesticulate in a sort of delirium. He was much finer as a spectacle than this Shipley, who viewed a fire with the same steadiness that he viewed a raise in a large jack-pot. The greater number of the boys could never understand why the members of these companies persisted in re-electing Shipley, although they often pretended to understand it, because "My father says" was a very formidable phrase in argument, and the fathers seemed almost unanimous in advocating Shipley.

At this time there was considerable discussion as to which company had gotten the first stream of water on the fire. Most of the boys claimed that Number Five owned that distinction, but there was a determined minority who contended for Number One. Boys who were the blood adherents of other companies were obliged to choose between the two on this occasion, and the talk waxed warm.

But a great rumor went among the crowds. It was told with hushed voices. Afterwards a reverent silence fell even upon the boys. Jimmie Trescott and Henry Johnson had been burned to death, and Dr. Trescott himself had been most savagely hurt. The crowd did not even feel the police pushing at them. They raised their eyes, shining now with awe, towards the high flames.

The man who had information was at his best. In low tones he described the whole affair. "That was the kid's room – in the corner there. He had measles or somethin', and this coon – Johnson – was a-settin' up with 'im, and Johnson got sleepy or somethin' and upset the lamp, and the doctor he was down in his office, and he came running up, and they all got burned together till they dragged 'em out."

Another man, always preserved for the deliverance of the final judgment, was saying: "Oh, they'll die sure. Burned to flinders. No chance. Hull lot of 'em. Anybody can see." The crowd concentrated its gaze still more closely upon these flags of fire which waved joyfully against the black sky. The bells of the town were clashing unceasingly.

A little procession moved across the lawn and towards the street. There were three cots, borne by twelve of the firemen. The police moved sternly, but it needed no effort of theirs to open a lane for this slow cortege. The men who bore the cots were well known to the crowd, but in this solemn parade during the ringing of the bells and the shouting, and with the red glare upon the sky, they seemed utterly foreign, and Whilomville paid them a deep respect. Each man in this stretcher party had gained a reflected majesty. They were footmen to death, and the crowd made subtle obeisance to this august dignity derived from three prospective graves. One woman turned away with a shriek at sight of the covered body on the first stretcher, and people faced her suddenly in silent and mournful indignation. Otherwise there was barely a sound as these twelve important men with measured tread carried their burdens through the throng.

The little boys no longer discussed the merits of the different fire companies. For the greater part they had been routed. Only the more courageous viewed closely the three figures veiled in yellow blankets.

Chapter X

OLD JUDGE Denning Hagenthorpe, who lived nearly opposite the Trescotts, had thrown his door wide open to receive the afflicted family. When it was publicly learned that the doctor and his son and the negro were still alive, it required a specially detailed policeman to prevent people from scaling the front porch and interviewing these sorely wounded. One old lady appeared with a miraculous poultice, and she quoted most damning Scripture to the officer when he said that she could not pass him. Throughout the night some lads old enough to be given privileges or to compel them from their mothers remained vigilantly upon the kerb in anticipation of a death or some such event. The reporter of the Morning Tribune rode thither on his bicycle every hour until three o'clock.

Six of the ten doctors in Whilomville attended at Judge Hagenthorpe's house.

Almost at once they were able to know that Trescott's burns were not vitally important. The child would possibly be scarred badly, but his life was undoubtedly safe. As for the negro Henry Johnson, he could not live. His body was frightfully seared, but more than that, he now had no face. His face had simply been burned away.

Trescott was always asking news of the two other patients. In the morning he seemed fresh and strong, so they told him that Johnson was doomed. They then saw him stir on the bed, and sprang quickly to see if the bandages needed readjusting. In the sudden glance he threw from one to another he impressed them as being both leonine and impracticable.

The morning paper announced the death of Henry Johnson. It contained a long interview with Edward J. Hannigan, in which the latter described in full the performance of Johnson at the fire. There was also an editorial built from all the best words in the vocabulary of the staff. The town halted in its accustomed road of thought, and turned a reverent attention to the memory of this hostler. In the breasts of many people was the regret that they had not known enough to give him a hand and a lift when he was alive, and they judged themselves stupid and ungenerous for this failure.

The name of Henry Johnson became suddenly the title of a saint to the little boys. The one who thought of it first could, by quoting it in an argument, at once overthrow his antagonist, whether it applied to the subject or whether it did not.

"Nigger, nigger, never die.
Black face and shiny eye."

Boys who had called this odious couplet in the rear of Johnson's march buried the fact at the bottom of their hearts.

Later in the day Miss Bella Farragut, of No. 7 Watermelon Alley, announced that she had been engaged to marry Mr. Henry Johnson.

Chapter XI

THE OLD JUDGE had a cane with an ivory head. He could never think at his best until he was leaning slightly on this stick and smoothing the white top with slow movements of his hands. It was also to him a kind of narcotic. If by any chance he mislaid it, he grew at once very irritable, and was likely to speak sharply to his sister, whose mental incapacity he had patiently endured for thirty years in the old mansion on Ontario Street. She was not at all aware of her brother's opinion of her endowments, and so it might be said that the judge had successfully dissembled for more than a quarter of a century, only risking the truth at the times when his cane was lost.

On a particular day the judge sat in his armchair on the porch. The sunshine sprinkled through the lilac-bushes and poured great coins on the boards. The sparrows disputed in the trees that lined the pavements. The judge mused deeply, while his hands gently caressed the ivory head of his cane.

Finally he arose and entered the house, his brow still furrowed in a thoughtful frown. His stick thumped solemnly in regular beats. On the second floor he entered a room where Dr. Trescott was working about the bedside of Henry Johnson. The bandages on the negro's head allowed only one thing to appear, an eye, which unwinkingly stared at the judge. The latter spoke to Trescott on the condition of the patient. Afterward he evidently had something further to say, but he seemed to be kept from it by the scrutiny of the unwinking eye, at which he furtively glanced from time to time.

When Jimmie Trescott was sufficiently recovered, his mother had taken him to pay a visit to his grandparents in Connecticut. The doctor had remained to take care of his patients, but as a matter of truth he spent most of his time at Judge Hagenthorpe's house, where lay Henry Johnson. Here he slept and ate almost every meal in the long nights and days of his vigil.

At dinner, and away from the magic of the unwinking eye, the judge said, suddenly, "Trescott, do you think it is—" As Trescott paused expectantly, the judge fingered his knife. He said, thoughtfully, "No one wants to advance such ideas, but somehow I think that that poor fellow ought to die."

There was in Trescott's face at once a look of recognition, as if in this tangent of the judge he saw an old problem. He merely sighed and answered, "Who knows?" The words were spoken in a deep tone that gave them an elusive kind of significance.

The judge retreated to the cold manner of the bench. "Perhaps we may not talk with propriety of this kind of action, but I am induced to say that you are performing a questionable charity in preserving this negro's life. As near as I can understand, he will hereafter be a monster, a perfect monster, and probably with an affected brain. No man can observe you as I have observed you and not know that it was a matter of conscience with you, but I am afraid, my friend, that it is one of the blunders of virtue." The judge had delivered his views with his habitual oratory. The last three words he spoke with a particular emphasis, as if the phrase was his discovery.

The doctor made a weary gesture. "He saved my boy's life."

"Yes," said the judge, swiftly – "yes, I know!"

"And what am I to do?" said Trescott, his eyes suddenly lighting like an outburst from smoldering peat. "What am I to do? He gave himself for – for Jimmie. What am I to do for him?"

The judge abased himself completely before these words. He lowered his eyes for a moment. He picked at his cucumbers.

Presently he braced himself straightly in his chair. "He will be your creation, you understand. He is purely your creation. Nature has very evidently given him up. He is dead. You are restoring him to life. You are making him, and he will be a monster, and with no mind."

"He will be what you like, judge," cried Trescott, in sudden, polite fury. "He will be anything, but, by God! He saved my boy."

The judge interrupted in a voice trembling with emotion: "Trescott! Trescott! Don't I know?"

Trescott had subsided to a sullen mood. "Yes, you know," he answered, acidly; "but you don't know all about your own boy being saved from death." This was a perfectly childish allusion to the judge's bachelorhood. Trescott knew that the remark was infantile, but he seemed to take desperate delight in it.

But it passed the judge completely. It was not his spot.

"I am puzzled," said he, in profound thought. "I don't know what to say."

Trescott had become repentant. "Don't think I don't appreciate what you say, judge. But—"

"Of course!" responded the judge, quickly. "Of course."

"It—" began Trescott.

"Of course," said the judge.

In silence they resumed their dinner.

"Well," said the judge, ultimately, "it is hard for a man to know what to do."

"It is," said the doctor, fervidly.

There was another silence. It was broken by the judge:

"Look here, Trescott; I don't want you to think—"

"No, certainly not," answered the doctor, earnestly.

"Well, I don't want you to think I would say anything to – it was only that I thought that I might be able to suggest to you that – perhaps – the affair was a little dubious."

With an appearance of suddenly disclosing his real mental perturbation, the doctor said: "Well, what would you do? Would you kill him?" he asked, abruptly and sternly.

"Trescott, you fool," said the old man, gently.

"Oh, well, I know, judge, but then—" He turned red, and spoke with new violence: "Say, he saved my boy – do you see? He saved my boy."

"You bet he did," cried the judge, with enthusiasm. "You bet he did." And they remained for a time gazing at each other, their faces illuminated with memories of a certain deed.

After another silence, the judge said, "It is hard for a man to know what to do."

Chapter XII

LATE ONE EVENING Trescott, returning from a professional call, paused his buggy at the Hagenthorpe gate. He tied the mare to the old tin-covered post, and entered the house. Ultimately he appeared with a companion – a man who walked slowly and carefully, as if he were learning. He was wrapped to the heels in an old-fashioned ulster. They entered the buggy and drove away.

After a silence only broken by the swift and musical humming of the wheels on the smooth road, Trescott spoke. "Henry," he said, "I've got you a home here with old Alek Williams. You will have everything you want to eat and a good place to sleep, and I hope you will get along there all right. I will pay all your expenses, and come to see you as often as I can. If you don't get along, I want you to let me know as soon as possible, and then we will do what we can to make it better."

The dark figure at the doctor's side answered with a cheerful laugh. "These buggy wheels don' look like I washed 'em yesterday, docteh," he said.

Trescott hesitated for a moment, and then went on insistently, "I am taking you to Alek Williams, Henry, and I—"

The figure chuckled again. "No, 'deed! No, seh! Alek Williams don' know a hoss! 'Deed he don't. He don' know a hoss from a pig." The laugh that followed was like the rattle of pebbles.

Trescott turned and looked sternly and coldly at the dim form in the gloom from the buggy-top. "Henry," he said, "I didn't say anything about horses. I was saying—"

"Hoss? Hoss?" said the quavering voice from these near shadows. "Hoss? 'Deed I don' know all erbout a boss! 'Deed I don't." There was a satirical chuckle.

At the end of three miles the mare slackened and the doctor leaned forward, peering, while holding tight reins. The wheels of the buggy bumped often over out-cropping boulders. A window shone forth, a simple square of topaz on a great black hillside. Four dogs charged the buggy with ferocity, and when it did not promptly retreat, they circled courageously around the flanks, baying. A door opened near the window in the hillside, and a man came and stood on a beach of yellow light.

"Yah! Yah! You Roveh! You Susie! Come yah! Come yah this minit!"

Trescott called across the dark sea of grass, "Hello, Alek!"

"Hello!"

"Come down here and show me where to drive."

The man plunged from the beach into the surf, and Trescott could then only trace his course by the fervid and polite ejaculations of a host who was somewhere approaching. Presently Williams took the mare by the head, and uttering cries of welcome and scolding the swarming dogs, led the equipage towards the lights. When they halted at the door and Trescott was climbing out, Williams cried, "Will she stand, docteh?"

"She'll stand all right, but you better hold her for a minute. Now, Henry." The doctor turned and held both arms to the dark figure. It crawled to him painfully like a man going down a ladder. Williams took the mare away to be tied to a little tree, and when he returned he found them awaiting him in the gloom beyond the rays from the door.

He burst out then like a siphon pressed by a nervous thumb. "Hennery! Hennery, ma ol' frien'. Well, if I ain' glade. If I ain' glade!"

Trescott had taken the silent shape by the arm and led it forward into the full revelation of the light. "Well, now, Alek, you can take Henry and put him to bed, and in the morning I will—"

Near the end of this sentence old Williams had come front to front with Johnson. He gasped for a second, and then yelled the yell of a man stabbed in the heart.

For a fraction of a moment Trescott seemed to be looking for epithets. Then he roared: "You old black chump! You old black – Shut up! Shut up! Do you hear?"

Williams obeyed instantly in the matter of his screams, but he continued in a lowered voice: "Ma Lode amassy! Who'd ever think? Ma Lode amassy!"

Trescott spoke again in the manner of a commander of a battalion. "Alek!"

The old negro again surrendered, but to himself he repeated in a whisper, "Ma Lode!" He was aghast and trembling.

As these three points of widening shadows approached the golden doorway a hale old negress appeared there, bowing. "Good-evenin', docteh! Good-evenin'! Come in! Come in!" She had evidently just retired from a tempestuous struggle to place the room in order, but she was now bowing rapidly. She made the effort of a person swimming.

"Don't trouble yourself, Mary," said Trescott, entering. "I've brought Henry for you to take care of, and all you've got to do is to carry out what I tell you." Learning that he was not followed, he faced the door, and said, "Come in, Henry."

Johnson entered. "Whee!" shrieked Mrs. Williams. She almost achieved a back somersault. Six young members of the tribe of Williams made a simultaneous plunge for a position behind the stove, and formed a wailing heap.

Chapter XIII

"YOU KNOW very well that you and your family lived usually on less than three dollars a week, and now that Dr. Trescott pays you five dollars a week for Johnson's board, you live like millionaires. You haven't done a stroke of work since Johnson began to board with you – everybody knows that – and so what are you kicking about?"

The judge sat in his chair on the porch, fondling his cane, and gazing down at old Williams, who stood under the lilac-bushes. "Yes, I know, jedge," said the negro, wagging his head in a puzzled manner. "'Tain't like as if I didn't 'preciate what the docteh done, but – but – well, yeh see, jedge," he added, gaining a new impetus, "it's – it's hard wuk. This ol' man nev' did wuk so hard. Lode, no."

"Don't talk such nonsense, Alek," spoke the judge, sharply. "You have never really worked in your life – anyhow, enough to support a family of sparrows, and now when you are in a more prosperous condition than ever before, you come around talking like an old fool."

The negro began to scratch his head. "Yeh see, jedge," he said at last, "my ol' 'ooman she cain't 'ceive no lady callahs, nohow."

"Hang lady callers" said the judge, irascibly. "If you have flour in the barrel and meat in the pot, your wife can get along without receiving lady callers, can't she?"

"But they won't come ainyhow, jedge," replied Williams, with an air of still deeper stupefaction. "Noner ma wife's frien's ner noner ma frien's 'll come near ma res'dence."

"Well, let them stay home if they are such silly people."

The old negro seemed to be seeking a way to elude this argument, but evidently finding none, he was about to shuffle meekly off. He halted, however. "Jedge," said he, "ma ol' 'ooman's near driv' abstracted."

"Your old woman is an idiot," responded the judge.

Williams came very close and peered solemnly through a branch of lilac. "Judge," he whispered, "the chillens."

"What about them?"

Dropping his voice to funereal depths, Williams said, "They – they cain't eat."

"Can't eat!" scoffed the judge, loudly. "Can't eat! You must think I am as big an old fool as you are. Can't eat – the little rascals! What's to prevent them from eating?"

In answer, Williams said, with mournful emphasis, "Hennery." Moved with a kind of satisfaction at his tragic use of the name, he remained staring at the judge for a sign of its effect.

The judge made a gesture of irritation. "Come, now, you old scoundrel, don't beat around the bush any more. What are you up to? What do you want? Speak out like a man, and don't give me any more of this tiresome rigamarole."

"I ain't er-beatin' round 'bout nuffin, jedge," replied Williams, indignantly. "No, seh; I say whatter got to say right out. 'Deed I do."

"Well, say it, then."

"Jedge," began the negro, taking off his hat and switching his knee with it, "Lode knows I'd do jes 'bout as much fer five dollehs er week as ainy cul'd man, but – but this yere business is awful, jedge. I raikon 'ain't been no sleep in – in my house sence docteh done fetch 'im."

"Well, what do you propose to do about it?"

Williams lifted his eyes from the ground and gazed off through the trees. "Raikon I got good appetite, an' sleep jes like er dog, but he – he's done broke me all up. 'Tain't no good, nohow. I wake up in the night; I hear 'im, mebbe, er-whimperin' an' er-whimperin', an' I sneak an' I sneak until I try th' do' to see if he locked in. An' he keep me er-puzzlin' an' er-quakin' all night long. Don't know how'll do in th' winter. Can't let 'im out where th' chillen is. He'll done freeze where he is now." Williams spoke these sentences as if he were talking to himself. After a silence of deep reflection he continued: "Folks go round sayin' he ain't Hennery Johnson at all. They say he's er devil!"

"What?" cried the judge.

"Yesseh," repeated Williams, in tones of injury, as if his veracity had been challenged. "Yesseh. I'm er-tellin' it to yeh straight, jedge. Plenty cul'd people folks up my way say it is a devil."

"Well, you don't think so yourself, do you?"

"No. 'Tain't no devil. It's Hennery Johnson."

"Well, then, what is the matter with you? You don't care what a lot of foolish people say. Go on 'tending to your business, and pay no attention to such idle nonsense."

"'Tis nonsense, jedge; but he *looks* like er devil."

"What do you care what he looks like?" demanded the judge.

"Ma rent is two dollehs and er half er month," said Williams, slowly.

"It might just as well be ten thousand dollars a month," responded the judge. "You never pay it, anyhow."

"Then, anoth' thing," continued Williams, in his reflective tone. "If he was all right in his haid I could stan' it; but, jedge, he's crazier 'n er loon. Then when he looks like er devil, an' done skears all ma frien's away, an' ma chillens cain't eat, an' ma ole 'ooman jes raisin' Cain all the time, an' ma rent two dollehs an' er half er month, an' him not right in his haid, it seems like five dollehs er week—"

The judge's stick came down sharply and suddenly upon the floor of the porch. "There," he said, "I thought that was what you were driving at."

Williams began swinging his head from side to side in the strange racial mannerism. "Now hol' on a minnet, jedge," he said, defensively. "'Tain't like as if I didn't 'preciate what the docteh done. 'Tain't that. Docteh Trescott is er kind man, an' 'tain't like as if I didn't 'preciate what he done; but – but—"

"But what? You are getting painful, Alek. Now tell me this: did you ever have five dollars a week regularly before in your life?"

Williams at once drew himself up with great dignity, but in the pause after that question he drooped gradually to another attitude. In the end he answered, heroically: "No, jedge, I 'ain't. An' 'tain't like as if I was er-sayin' five dollehs wasn't er lot er money for a man like me. But, jedge, what er man oughter git fer this kinder wuk is er salary. Yesseh, jedge," he repeated, with a great impressive gesture; "fer this kinder wuk er man oughter git er Salary." He laid a terrible emphasis upon the final word.

The judge laughed. "I know Dr. Trescott's mind concerning this affair, Alek; and if you are dissatisfied with your boarder, he is quite ready to move him to some other place; so, if you care to leave word with me that you are tired of the arrangement and wish it changed, he will come and take Johnson away."

Williams scratched his head again in deep perplexity. "Five dollehs is er big price fer bo'd, but 'tain't no big price fer the bo'd of er crazy man," he said, finally.

"What do you think you ought to get?" asked the judge.

"Well," answered Alek, in the manner of one deep in a balancing of the scales, "he looks like er devil, an' done skears e'rybody, an' ma chillens cain't eat, an' I cain't sleep, an' he ain't right in his haid, an'—"

"You told me all those things."

After scratching his wool, and beating his knee with his hat, and gazing off through the trees and down at the ground, Williams said, as he kicked nervously at the gravel, "Well, jedge, I think it is wuth—" He stuttered.

"Worth what?"

"Six dollehs," answered Williams, in a desperate outburst.

The judge lay back in his great armchair and went through all the motions of a man laughing heartily, but he made no sound save a slight cough. Williams had been watching him with apprehension.

"Well," said the judge, "do you call six dollars a salary?"

"No, seh," promptly responded Williams. "'Tain't a salary. No, 'deed! 'Tain't a salary." He looked with some anger upon the man who questioned his intelligence in this way.

"Well, supposing your children can't eat?"

"I—"

"And supposing he looks like a devil? And supposing all those things continue? Would you be satisfied with six dollars a week?"

Recollections seemed to throng in Williams's mind at these interrogations, and he answered dubiously. "Of co'se a man who ain't right in his haid, an' looks like er devil – but six dollehs—" After these two attempts at a sentence Williams suddenly appeared as an orator, with a great shiny palm waving in the air. "I tell yeh, jedge, six dollehs is six dollehs, but if I git six dollehs for bo'ding Hennery Johnson, I uhns it! I uhns it!"

"I don't doubt that you earn six dollars for every week's work you do," said the judge.

"Well, if I bo'd Hennery Johnson fer six dollehs er week, I uhns it! I uhns it!" cried Williams, wildly.

Chapter XIV

REIFSNYDER'S ASSISTANT had gone to his supper, and the owner of the shop was trying to placate four men who wished to be shaved at once. Reifsnyder was very garrulous – a fact which made him rather remarkable among barbers, who, as a class, are austerely speechless, having been taught silence by the hammering reiteration of a tradition. It is the customers who talk in the ordinary event.

As Reifsnyder waved his razor down the cheek of a man in the chair, he turned often to cool the impatience of the others with pleasant talk, which they did not particularly heed.

"Oh, he should have let him die," said Bainbridge, a railway engineer, finally replying to one of the barber's orations. "Shut up, Reif, and go on with your business!"

Instead, Reifsnyder paused shaving entirely, and turned to front the speaker. "Let him die?" he demanded. "How vas that? How can you let a man die?"

"By letting him die, you chump," said the engineer. The others laughed a little, and Reifsnyder turned at once to his work, sullenly, as a man overwhelmed by the derision of numbers.

"How vas that?" he grumbled later. "How can you let a man die when he vas done so much for you?"

"'When he vas done so much for you?'" repeated Bainbridge. "You better shave some people. How vas that? Maybe this ain't a barber shop?"

A man hitherto silent now said, "If I had been the doctor, I would have done the same thing."

"Of course," said Reifsnyder. "Any man vould do it. Any man that vas not like you, you – old – flint-hearted – fish." He had sought the final words with painful care, and he delivered the collection triumphantly at Bainbridge. The engineer laughed.

The man in the chair now lifted himself higher, while Reifsnyder began an elaborate ceremony of anointing and combing his hair. Now free to join comfortably in the talk, the man said: "They say he is the most terrible thing in the world. Young Johnnie Bernard – that drives the grocery wagon – saw him up at Alek Williams's shanty, and he says he couldn't eat anything for two days."

"Chee!" said Reifsnyder.

"Well, what makes him so terrible?" asked another.

"Because he hasn't got any face," replied the barber and the engineer in duct.

"Hasn't got any face!" repeated the man. "How can he do without any face?"

"He has no face in the front of his head.
In the place where his face ought to grow."

Bainbridge sang these lines pathetically as he arose and hung his hat on a hook. The man in the chair was about to abdicate in his favor. "Get a gait on you now," he said to Reifsnyder. "I go out at 7.31."

As the barber foamed the lather on the cheeks of the engineer he seemed to be thinking heavily. Then suddenly he burst out. "How would you like to be with no face?" he cried to the assemblage.

"Oh, if I had to have a face like yours—" answered one customer.

Bainbridge's voice came from a sea of lather. "You're kicking because if losing faces became popular, you'd have to go out of business."

"I don't think it will become so much popular," said Reifsnyder.

"Not if it's got to be taken off in the way his was taken off," said another man. "I'd rather keep mine, if you don't mind."

"I guess so!" cried the barber. "Just think!"

The shaving of Bainbridge had arrived at a time of comparative liberty for him. "I wonder what the doctor says to himself?" he observed. "He may be sorry he made him live."

"It was the only thing he could do," replied a man. The others seemed to agree with him.

"Supposing you were in his place," said one, "and Johnson had saved your kid. What would you do?"

"Certainly!"

"Of course! You would do anything on earth for him. You'd take all the trouble in the world for him. And spend your last dollar on him. Well, then?"

"I wonder how it feels to be without any face?" said Reifsnyder, musingly.

The man who had previously spoken, feeling that he had expressed himself well, repeated the whole thing. "You would do anything on earth for him. You'd take all the trouble in the world for him. And spend your last dollar on him. Well, then?"

"No, but look," said Reifsnyder; "supposing you don't got a face!"

Chapter XV

AS SOON AS Williams was hidden from the view of the old judge he began to gesture and talk to himself. An elation had evidently penetrated to his vitals, and caused him to dilate as if he had been filled with gas. He snapped his fingers in the air, and whistled fragments of triumphal music. At times, in his progress towards his shanty, he indulged in a shuffling movement that was really a dance. It was to be learned from the intermediate monologue that he had emerged from his trials laurelled and proud. He was the unconquerable Alexander Williams. Nothing could exceed the bold self-reliance of his manner. His kingly stride, his heroic song, the derisive flourish of his hands – all betokened a man who had successfully defied the world.

On his way he saw Zeke Paterson coming to town. They hailed each other at a distance of fifty yards.

"How do, Broth' Paterson?"

"How do, Broth' Williams?"

They were both deacons.

"Is you' folks well, Broth' Paterson?"

"Middlin', middlin'. How's you' folks, Broth' Williams?"

Neither of them had slowed his pace in the smallest degree. They had simply begun this talk when a considerable space separated them, continued it as they passed, and added polite questions as they drifted steadily apart. Williams's mind seemed to be a balloon. He had been so inflated that he had not noticed that Paterson had definitely shied into the dry ditch as they came to the point of ordinary contact.

Afterwards, as he went a lonely way, he burst out again in song and pantomimic celebration of his estate. His feet moved in prancing steps.

When he came in sight of his cabin, the fields were bathed in a blue dusk, and the light in the window was pale. Cavorting and gesticulating, he gazed joyfully for some moments upon this light. Then suddenly another idea seemed to attack his mind, and he stopped, with an air of being suddenly dampened. In the end he approached his home as if it were the fortress of an enemy.

Some dogs disputed his advance for a loud moment, and then discovering their lord, slunk away embarrassed. His reproaches were addressed to them in muffled tones.

Arriving at the door, he pushed it open with the timidity of a new thief. He thrust his head cautiously sideways, and his eyes met the eyes of his wife, who sat by the table, the lamplight defining a half of her face. "'Sh!" he said, uselessly. His glance travelled swiftly to the inner door which shielded the one bed-chamber. The pickaninnies, strewn upon the floor of the living room, were softly snoring. After a hearty meal they had promptly dispersed themselves about the place and gone to sleep. "'Sh!" said Williams again to his motionless and silent wife.

He had allowed only his head to appear. His wife, with one hand upon the edge of the table and the other at her knee, was regarding him with wide eyes and parted lips as if he were a spectre. She looked to be one who was living in terror, and even the familiar face at the door had thrilled her because it had come suddenly.

Williams broke the tense silence. "Is he all right?" he whispered, waving his eyes towards the inner door. Following his glance timorously, his wife nodded, and in a low tone answered:

"I raikon he's done gone t' sleep."

Williams then slunk noiselessly across his threshold.

He lifted a chair, and with infinite care placed it so that it faced the dreaded inner door. His wife moved slightly, so as to also squarely face it. A silence came upon them in which they seemed to be waiting for a calamity, pealing and deadly.

Williams finally coughed behind his hand. His wife started, and looked upon him in alarm. "'Pears like he done gwine keep quiet ternight," he breathed. They continually pointed their speech and their looks at the inner door, paying it the homage due to a corpse or a phantom. Another long stillness followed this sentence. Their eyes shone white and wide. A wagon rattled down the distant road. From their chairs they looked at the window, and the effect of the light in the cabin was a presentation of an intensely black and solemn night. The old woman adopted the attitude used always in church at funerals. At times she seemed to be upon the point of breaking out in prayer.

"He mighty quiet ter-night," whispered Williams. "Was he good ter-day?" For answer his wife raised her eyes to the ceiling in the supplication of Job. Williams moved restlessly. Finally he tiptoed to the door. He knelt slowly and without a sound, and placed his ear near the keyhole. Hearing a noise behind him, he turned quickly. His wife was staring at him aghast. She stood in front of the stove, and her arms were spread out in the natural movement to protect all her sleeping ducklings.

But Williams arose without having touched the door. "I raikon he er-sleep," he said, fingering his wool. He debated with himself for some time. During this interval his wife remained, a great fat statue of a mother shielding her children.

It was plain that his mind was swept suddenly by a wave of temerity. With a sounding step he moved towards the door. His fingers were almost upon the knob when he swiftly ducked and dodged away, clapping his hands to the back of his head. It was as if the portal had threatened him. There was a little tumult near the stove, where Mrs. Williams's desperate retreat had involved her feet with the prostrate children.

After the panic Williams bore traces of a feeling of shame. He returned to the charge. He firmly grasped the knob with his left hand, and with his other hand turned the key in the lock. He pushed the door, and as it swung portentously open he sprang nimbly to one side like the fearful slave liberating the lion. Near the stove a group had formed, the terror-stricken mother, with her arms stretched, and the aroused children clinging frenziedly to her skirts.

The light streamed after the swinging door, and disclosed a room six feet one way and six feet the other way. It was small enough to enable the radiance to lay it plain. Williams peered warily around the corner made by the door-post.

Suddenly he advanced, retired, and advanced again with a howl. His palsied family had expected him to spring backward, and at his howl they heaped themselves wondrously. But Williams simply stood in the little room emitting his howls before an open window. "He's gone! He's gone! He's gone!" His eye and his hand had speedily proved the fact. He had even thrown open a little cupboard.

Presently he came flying out. He grabbed his hat, and hurled the outer door back upon its hinges. Then he tumbled headlong into the night. He was yelling: "Docteh Trescott! Docteh Trescott!" He ran wildly through the fields, and galloped in the direction of town. He continued to call to Trescott, as if the latter was within easy hearing. It was as if Trescott was poised in the contemplative sky over the running negro, and could heed this reaching voice – "Docteh Trescott!"

In the cabin, Mrs. Williams, supported by relays from the battalion of children, stood quaking watch until the truth of daylight came as a reinforcement and made the arrogant, strutting, swashbuckler children, and a mother who proclaimed her illimitable courage.

Chapter XVI

THERESA PAGE was giving a party. It was the outcome of a long series of arguments addressed to her mother, which had been overheard in part by her father. He had at last said five words, "Oh, let her have it." The mother had then gladly capitulated.

Theresa had written nineteen invitations, and distributed them at recess to her schoolmates. Later her mother had composed five large cakes, and still later a vast amount of lemonade.

So the nine little girls and the ten little boys sat quite primly in the dining room, while Theresa and her mother plied them with cake and lemonade, and also with ice-cream. This primness sat now quite strangely upon them. It was owing to the presence of Mrs. Page. Previously in the parlor alone with their games they had overturned a chair; the boys had let more or less of their hoodlum spirit shine forth. But when circumstances could be possibly magnified to warrant it, the girls made the boys victims of an insufferable pride, snubbing them mercilessly. So in the dining room they resembled a class at Sunday-school, if it were not for the subterranean smiles, gestures, rebuffs, and poutings which stamped the affair as a children's party.

Two little girls of this subdued gathering were planted in a settle with their backs to the broad window. They were beaming lovingly upon each other with an effect of scorning the boys.

Hearing a noise behind her at the window, one little girl turned to face it. Instantly she screamed and sprang away, covering her face with her hands. "What was it? What was it?" cried everyone in a roar. Some slight movement of the eyes of the weeping and shuddering child informed the company that she had been frightened by an appearance at the window. At once they all faced the imperturbable window, and for a moment there was a silence. An astute lad made an immediate census of the other lads. The prank of slipping out and looming spectrally at a window was too venerable. But the little boys were all present and astonished.

As they recovered their minds they uttered warlike cries, and through a side door sallied rapidly out against the terror. They vied with each other in daring.

None wished particularly to encounter a dragon in the darkness of the garden, but there could be no faltering when the fair ones in the dining room were present. Calling to each other in stern voices, they went dragooning over the lawn, attacking the shadows with ferocity, but still with the caution of reasonable beings. They found, however, nothing new to the peace of the night. Of course there was a lad who told a great lie. He described a grim figure, bending low and slinking off along the fence. He gave a number of details, rendering his lie more splendid by a repetition of certain forms which he recalled from romances. For instance, he insisted that he had heard the creature emit a hollow laugh.

Inside the house the little girl who had raised the alarm was still shuddering and weeping. With the utmost difficulty was she brought to a state approximating calmness by Mrs. Page. Then she wanted to go home at once.

Page entered the house at this time. He had exiled himself until he concluded that this children's party was finished and gone. He was obliged to escort the little girl home because she screamed again when they opened the door and she saw the night.

She was not coherent even to her mother. Was it a man? She didn't know. It was simply a thing, a dreadful thing.

Chapter XVII

IN WATERMELON ALLEY the Farraguts were spending their evening as usual on the little rickety porch. Sometimes they howled gossip to other people on other rickety porches. The thin wail of a baby arose from a near house. A man had a terrific altercation with his wife, to which the alley paid no attention at all.

There appeared suddenly before the Farraguts a monster making a low and sweeping bow. There was an instant's pause, and then occurred something that resembled the effect of an upheaval of the earth's surface. The old woman hurled herself backward with a dreadful cry. Young Sim had been perched gracefully on a railing. At sight of the monster he simply fell over it to the ground. He made no sound, his eyes stuck out, his nerveless hands tried to grapple the rail to prevent a tumble, and then he vanished. Bella, blubbering, and with her hair suddenly and mysteriously dishevelled, was crawling on her hands and knees fearsomely up the steps.

Standing before this wreck of a family gathering, the monster continued to bow. It even raised a deprecatory claw. "Doh' make no botheration 'bout me, Miss Fa'gut," it said, politely. "No, 'deed. I jes drap in ter ax if yer well this evenin', Miss Fa'gut. Don' make no botheration. No, 'deed. I gwine ax you to go to er daince with me, Miss Fa'gut. I ax you if I can have the magnifercent gratitude of you' company on that 'casion, Miss Fa'gut."

The girl cast a miserable glance behind her. She was still crawling away. On the ground beside the porch young Sim raised a strange bleat, which expressed both his fright and his lack of wind. Presently the monster, with a fashionable amble, ascended the steps after the girl.

She grovelled in a corner of the room as the creature took a chair. It seated itself very elegantly on the edge. It held an old cap in both hands. "Don' make no botheration, Miss Fa'gut. Don' make no botherations. No, 'deed. I jes drap in ter ax you if you won' do me the proud of acceptin' ma humble invitation to er daince, Miss Fa'gut."

She shielded her eyes with her arms and tried to crawl past it, but the genial monster blocked the way. "I jes drap in ter ax you 'bout er daince, Miss Fa'gut. I ax you if I kin have the magnifercent gratitude of you' company on that 'casion, Miss Fa'gut."

In a last outbreak of despair, the girl, shuddering and wailing, threw herself face downward on the floor, while the monster sat on the edge of the chair gabbling courteous invitations, and holding the old hat daintily to his stomach.

At the back of the house, Mrs. Farragut, who was of enormous weight, and who for eight years had done little more than sit in an armchair and describe her various ailments, had with speed and agility scaled a high board fence.

Chapter XVIII

THE BLACK MASS in the middle of Trescott's property was hardly allowed to cool before the builders were at work on another house. It had sprung upward at a fabulous rate. It was like a magical composition born of the ashes. The doctor's office was the first part to be completed, and he had already moved in his new books and instruments and medicines.

Trescott sat before his desk when the chief of police arrived. "Well, we found him," said the latter.

"Did you?" cried the doctor. "Where?"

"Shambling around the streets at daylight this morning. I'll be blamed if I can figure on where he passed the night."

"Where is he now?"

"Oh, we jugged him. I didn't know what else to do with him. That's what I want you to tell me. Of course we can't keep him. No charge could be made, you know."

"I'll come down and get him."

The official grinned retrospectively. "Must say he had a fine career while he was out. First thing he did was to break up a children's party at Page's. Then he went to Watermelon Alley. Whoo! He stampeded the whole outfit. Men, women, and children running pell-mell, and yelling. They say one old woman broke her leg, or something, shinning over a fence. Then he went right out on the main street, and an Irish girl threw a fit, and there was a sort of a riot. He began to run, and a big crowd chased him, firing rocks. But he gave them the slip somehow down there by the foundry and in the railroad yard. We looked for him all night, but couldn't find him."

"Was he hurt any? Did anybody hit him with a stone?"

"Guess there isn't much of him to hurt anymore, is there? Guess he's been hurt up to the limit. No. They never touched him. Of course nobody really wanted to hit him, but you know how a crowd gets. It's like – it's like—"

"Yes, I know."

For a moment the chief of the police looked reflectively at the floor. Then he spoke hesitatingly. "You know Jake Winter's little girl was the one that he scared at the party. She is pretty sick, they say."

"Is she? Why, they didn't call me. I always attend the Winter family."

"No? Didn't they?" asked the chief, slowly. "Well – you know – Winter is – well, Winter has gone clean crazy over this business. He wanted – he wanted to have you arrested."

"Have me arrested? The idiot! What in the name of wonder could he have me arrested for?"

"Of course. He is a fool. I told him to keep his trap shut. But then you know how he'll go all over town yapping about the thing. I thought I'd better tip you."

"Oh, he is of no consequence; but then, of course, I'm obliged to you, Sam."

"That's all right. Well, you'll be down tonight and take him out, eh? You'll get a good welcome from the jailer. He don't like his job for a cent. He says you can have your man whenever you want him. He's got no use for him."

"But what is this business of Winter's about having me arrested?"

"Oh, it's a lot of chin about your having no right to allow this – this – this man to be at large. But I told him to tend to his own business. Only I thought I'd better let you know. And I might as well say right now, doctor, that there is a good deal of talk about this thing. If I were you, I'd come to the jail pretty late at night, because there is likely to be a crowd around the door, and I'd bring a – er – mask, or some kind of a veil, anyhow."

Chapter XIX

MARTHA GOODWIN was single, and well along into the thin years. She lived with her married sister in Whilomville. She performed nearly all the house-work in exchange for the privilege of existence. Everyone tacitly recognized her labor as a form of penance for the early end of her betrothed, who had died of small-pox, which he had not caught from her.

But despite the strenuous and unceasing workaday of her life, she was a woman of great mind. She had adamantine opinions upon the situation in Armenia, the condition of women in China, the flirtation between Mrs. Minster of Niagara Avenue and young Griscom, the conflict in the Bible class of the Baptist Sunday-school, the duty of the United States towards the Cuban insurgents, and many other colossal matters. Her fullest experience of violence was gained on an occasion when she had seen a hound clubbed, but in the plan which she had made for the reform of the world she advocated drastic measures. For instance, she contended that all the Turks should be pushed into the sea and drowned, and that Mrs. Minster and young Griscom should be hanged side by side on twin gallows. In fact, this woman of peace, who had seen only peace, argued constantly for a creed of illimitable ferocity. She was invulnerable on these questions, because eventually she overrode all opponents with a sniff. This sniff was an active force. It was to her antagonists like a bang over the head, and none was known to recover from this expression of exalted contempt. It left them windless and conquered. They never again came forward as candidates for suppression. And Martha walked her kitchen with a stern brow, an invincible being like Napoleon.

Nevertheless her acquaintances, from the pain of their defeats, had been long in secret revolt. It was in no wise a conspiracy, because they did not care to state their open rebellion, but nevertheless it was understood that any woman who could not coincide with one of Martha's contentions was entitled to the support of others in the small circle. It amounted to an arrangement by which all were required to disbelieve any theory for which Martha fought. This, however, did not prevent them from speaking of her mind with profound respect.

Two people bore the brunt of her ability. Her sister Kate was visibly afraid of her, while Carrie Dungen sailed across from her kitchen to sit respectfully at Martha's feet and learn the business of the world. To be sure, afterwards, under another sun, she always laughed at Martha and pretended to deride her ideas, but in the presence of the sovereign she always remained silent or admiring. Kate, the sister, was of no consequence at all. Her principal delusion was that she did all the work in the upstairs rooms of the house, while Martha did it downstairs. The truth was seen only by the husband, who treated Martha with a kindness that was half banter, half deference. Martha herself had no suspicion that she was the only pillar of the domestic edifice. The situation was without definitions. Martha made definitions, but she devoted them entirely to the Armenians and Griscom and the Chinese and other subjects. Her dreams, which in early days had been of love of meadows and the shade of trees, of the face of a man, were now involved otherwise, and they were companioned in the kitchen curiously, Cuba, the hot-water kettle, Armenia, the washing of the dishes, and the whole thing being jumbled. In regard to social misdemeanors, she who was simply the mausoleum of a dead passion was probably the most savage critic in town. This unknown woman, hidden in a kitchen as in a well, was sure to have a considerable effect of the one kind or the other in the life of the town. Every time it moved a yard, she had personally contributed an inch. She could hammer so stoutly upon the door of a proposition that it would break from its hinges and fall upon her, but at any rate it moved. She was an engine, and the fact that she did not know that she was an engine contributed largely to the effect. One reason that she was formidable was that she did not even imagine that she was formidable. She remained a weak, innocent, and pig-headed creature, who alone would defy the universe if she thought the universe merited this proceeding.

One day Carrie Dungen came across from her kitchen with speed. She had a great deal of grist. "Oh," she cried, "Henry Johnson got away from where they was keeping him, and came to town last night, and scared everybody almost to death."

Martha was shining a dish-pan, polishing madly. No reasonable person could see cause for this operation, because the pan already glistened like silver. "Well!" she ejaculated. She imparted to the word a deep meaning. "This, my prophecy, has come to pass." It was a habit.

The overplus of information was choking Carrie. Before she could go on she was obliged to struggle for a moment. "And, oh, little Sadie Winter is awful sick, and they say Jake Winter was around this morning trying to get Doctor Trescott arrested. And poor old Mrs. Farragut sprained her ankle in trying to climb a fence. And there's a crowd around the jail all the time. They put Henry in jail because they didn't know what else to do with him, I guess. They say he is perfectly terrible."

Martha finally released the dish-pan and confronted the headlong speaker. "Well!" she said again, poising a great brown rag. Kate had heard the excited newcomer, and drifted down from the novel in her room. She was a shivery little woman. Her shoulder-blades seemed to be two panes of ice, for she was constantly shrugging and shrugging. "Serves him right if he was to lose all his patients," she said suddenly, in blood-thirsty tones. She snipped her words out as if her lips were scissors.

"Well, he's likely to," shouted Carrie Dungen. "Don't a lot of people say that they won't have him an more? If you're sick and nervous, Doctor Trescott would scare the life out of you, wouldn't he? He would me. I'd keep thinking."

Martha, stalking to and fro, sometimes surveyed the two other women with a contemplative frown.

Chapter XX

AFTER THE RETURN from Connecticut, little Jimmie was at first much afraid of the monster who lived in the room over the carriage-house. He could not identify it in any way. Gradually, however, his fear dwindled under the influence of a weird fascination. He sidled into closer and closer relations with it.

One time the monster was seated on a box behind the stable basking in the rays of the afternoon sun. A heavy crepe veil was swathed about its head.

Little Jimmie and many companions came around the corner of the stable. They were all in what was popularly known as the baby class, and consequently escaped from school a half-hour before the other children. They halted abruptly at sight of the figure on the box. Jimmie waved his hand with the air of a proprietor.

"There he is," he said.

"O-o-o!" murmured all the little boys – "O-o-o!" They shrank back, and grouped according to courage or experience, as at the sound the monster slowly turned its head. Jimmie had remained in the van alone. "Don't be afraid! I won't let him hurt you," he said, delighted.

"Huh!" they replied, contemptuously. "We ain't afraid."

Jimmie seemed to reap all the joys of the owner and exhibitor of one of the world's marvels, while his audience remained at a distance – awed and entranced, fearful and envious.

One of them addressed Jimmie gloomily. "Bet you dassent walk right up to him." He was an older boy than Jimmie, and habitually oppressed him to a small degree. This new social elevation of the smaller lad probably seemed revolutionary to him.

"Huh!" said Jimmie, with deep scorn. "Dassent I? Dassent I, hey? Dassent I?"

The group was immensely excited. It turned its eyes upon the boy that Jimmie addressed. "No, you dassent," he said, stolidly, facing a moral defeat. He could see that Jimmie was resolved. "No, you dassent," he repeated, doggedly.

"Ho?" cried Jimmie. "You just watch! – You just watch!"

Amid a silence he turned and marched towards the monster. But possibly the palpable wariness of his companions had an effect upon him that weighed more than his previous experience, for suddenly, when near to the monster, he halted dubiously. But his playmates immediately uttered a derisive shout, and it seemed to force him forward. He went to the monster and laid his hand delicately on its shoulder. "Hello, Henry," he said, in a voice that trembled a trifle. The monster was crooning a weird line of negro melody that was scarcely more than a thread of sound, and it paid no heed to the boy.

Jimmie strutted back to his companions. They acclaimed him and hooted his opponent. Amid this clamor the larger boy with difficulty preserved a dignified attitude.

"I dassent, dassent I?" said Jimmie to him.

"Now, you're so smart, let's see you do it!"

This challenge brought forth renewed taunts from the others. The larger boy puffed out his checks. "Well, I ain't afraid," he explained, sullenly. He had made a mistake in diplomacy, and now his small enemies were tumbling his prestige all about his ears. They crowed like roosters and bleated like lambs, and made many other noises which were supposed to bury him in ridicule and dishonor. "Well, I ain't afraid," he continued to explain through the din.

Jimmie, the hero of the mob, was pitiless. "You ain't afraid, hey?" he sneered. "If you ain't afraid, go do it, then."

"Well, I would if I wanted to," the other retorted. His eyes wore an expression of profound misery, but he preserved steadily other portions of a pot-valiant air. He suddenly faced one of his persecutors. "If you're so smart, why don't you go do it?" This persecutor sank promptly through the group to the rear. The incident gave the badgered one a breathing-spell, and for a moment even turned the derision in another direction. He took advantage of his interval. "I'll do it if anybody else will," he announced, swaggering to and fro.

Candidates for the adventure did not come forward. To defend themselves from this counter-charge, the other boys again set up their crowing and bleating. For a while they would hear nothing from him. Each time he opened his lips their chorus of noises made oratory impossible. But at last he was able to repeat that he would volunteer to dare as much in the affair as any other boy.

"Well, you go first," they shouted.

But Jimmie intervened to once more lead the populace against the large boy. "You're mighty brave, ain't you?" he said to him. "You dared me to do it, and I did – didn't I? Now who's afraid?" The others cheered this view loudly, and they instantly resumed the baiting of the large boy.

He shamefacedly scratched his left shin with his right foot. "Well, I ain't afraid." He cast an eye at the monster. "Well, I ain't afraid." With a glare of hatred at his squalling tormentors, he finally announced a grim intention. "Well, I'll do it, then, since you're so fresh. Now!"

The mob subsided as with a formidable countenance he turned towards the impassive figure on the box. The advance was also a regular progression from high daring to craven hesitation. At last, when some yards from the monster, the lad came to a full halt, as if he had encountered a stone wall. The observant little boys in the distance promptly hooted. Stung again by these cries, the lad sneaked two yards forward. He was crouched like a young cat ready for a backward spring. The crowd at the rear, beginning to respect this display, uttered some encouraging cries. Suddenly the lad gathered himself together, made a white and desperate rush forward, touched the monster's shoulder with a far-outstretched finger, and sped away, while his laughter rang out wild, shrill, and exultant.

The crowd of boys reverenced him at once, and began to throng into his camp, and look at him, and be his admirers. Jimmie was discomfited for a moment, but he and the larger boy, without agreement or word of any kind, seemed to recognize a truce, and they swiftly combined and began to parade before the others.

"Why, it's just as easy as nothing," puffed the larger boy. "Ain't it, Jim?"

"Course," blew Jimmie. "Why, it's as e-e-easy."

They were people of another class. If they had been decorated for courage on twelve battle-fields, they could not have made the other boys more ashamed of the situation.

Meanwhile they condescended to explain the emotions of the excursion, expressing unqualified contempt for any one who could hang back. "Why, it ain't nothin'. He won't do nothin' to you," they told the others, in tones of exasperation.

One of the very smallest boys in the party showed signs of a wistful desire to distinguish himself, and they turned their attention to him, pushing at his shoulders while he swung away from them, and hesitated dreamily. He was eventually induced to make furtive expedition, but it was only for a few yards. Then he paused, motionless, gazing with open mouth. The vociferous entreaties of Jimmie and the large boy had no power over him.

Mrs. Hannigan had come out on her back porch with a pail of water. From this coign she had a view of the secluded portion of the Trescott grounds that was behind the stable. She perceived the group of boys, and the monster on the box. She shaded her eyes with her hand to benefit her vision. She screeched then as if she was being murdered. "Eddie! Eddie! You come home this minute!"

Her son querulously demanded, "Aw, what for?"

"You come home this minute. Do you hear?"

The other boys seemed to think this visitation upon one of their number required them to preserve for a time the hang-dog air of a collection of culprits, and they remained in guilty silence until the little Hannigan, wrathfully protesting, was pushed through the door of his home. Mrs. Hannigan cast a piercing glance over the group, stared with a bitter face at the Trescott house, as if this new and handsome edifice was insulting her, and then followed her son.

There was wavering in the party. An inroad by one mother always caused them to carefully sweep the horizon to see if there were more coming. "This is my yard," said Jimmie, proudly. "We don't have to go home."

The monster on the box had turned its black crepe countenance towards the sky, and was waving its arms in time to a religious chant. "Look at him now," cried a little boy. They turned, and were transfixed by the solemnity and mystery of the indefinable gestures. The wail of the melody was mournful and slow. They drew back. It seemed to spellbind them with the power of a funeral. They were so absorbed that they did not hear the doctor's buggy drive up to the stable. Trescott got out, tied his horse, and approached the group. Jimmie saw him first, and at his look of dismay the others wheeled.

"What's all this, Jimmie?" asked Trescott, in surprise.

The lad advanced to the front of his companions, halted, and said nothing. Trescott's face gloomed slightly as he scanned the scene.

"What were you doing, Jimmie?"

"We was playin'," answered Jimmie, huskily.

"Playing at what?"

"Just playin'."

Trescott looked gravely at the other boys, and asked them to please go home. They proceeded to the street much in the manner of frustrated and revealed assassins. The crime of trespass on another boy's place was still a crime when they had only accepted the other boy's cordial invitation, and they were used to being sent out of all manner of gardens upon the sudden appearance of a father or a mother. Jimmie had wretchedly watched the departure of his companions. It involved the loss of his position as a lad who controlled the privileges of his father's grounds, but then he knew that in the beginning he had no right to ask so many boys to be his guests.

Once on the sidewalk, however, they speedily forgot their shame as trespassers, and the large boy launched forth in a description of his success in the late trial of courage. As they went rapidly up the street, the little boy who had made the furtive expedition cried out confidently from the rear, "Yes, and I went almost up to him, didn't I, Willie?"

The large boy crushed him in a few words. "Huh!" he scoffed. "You only went a little way. I went clear up to him."

The pace of the other boys was so manly that the tiny thing had to trot, and he remained at the rear, getting entangled in their legs in his attempts to reach the front rank and become of some importance, dodging this way and that way, and always piping out his little claim to glory.

Chapter XXI

"BY-THE-WAY, Grace," said Trescott, looking into the dining room from his office door, "I wish you would send Jimmie to me before school-time."

When Jimmie came, he advanced so quietly that Trescott did not at first note him. "Oh," he said, wheeling from a cabinet, "here you are, young man."

"Yes, sir."

Trescott dropped into his chair and tapped the desk with a thoughtful finger. "Jimmie, what were you doing in the back garden yesterday – you and the other boys – to Henry?"

"We weren't doing anything, pa."

Trescott looked sternly into the raised eyes of his son. "Are you sure you were not annoying him in any way? Now what were you doing, exactly?"

"Why, we – why, we – now – Willie Dalzel said I dassent go right up to him, and I did; and then he did; and then – the other boys were 'fraid; and then – you comed."

Trescott groaned deeply. His countenance was so clouded in sorrow that the lad, bewildered by the mystery of it, burst suddenly forth in dismal lamentations. "There, there. Don't cry, Jim," said Trescott, going round the desk. "Only—" He sat in a great leather reading-chair, and took the boy on his knee. "Only I want to explain to you—"

After Jimmie had gone to school, and as Trescott was about to start on his round of morning calls, a message arrived from Doctor Moser. It set forth that the latter's sister was dying in the old homestead, twenty miles away up the valley, and asked Trescott to care for his patients for the day at least. There was also in the envelope a little history of each case and of what had already been done. Trescott replied to the messenger that he would gladly assent to the arrangement.

He noted that the first name on Moser's list was Winter, but this did not seem to strike him as an important fact. When its turn came, he rang the Winter bell. "Good-morning, Mrs. Winter," he said, cheerfully, as the door was opened. "Doctor Moser has been obliged to leave town today, and he has asked me to come in his stead. How is the little girl this morning?"

Mrs. Winter had regarded him in stony surprise. At last she said: "Come in! I'll see my husband." She bolted into the house. Trescott entered the hall, and turned to the left into the sitting room.

Presently Winter shuffled through the door. His eyes flashed towards Trescott. He did not betray any desire to advance far into the room. "What do you want?" he said.

"What do I want? What do I want?" repeated Trescott, lifting his head suddenly. He had heard an utterly new challenge in the night of the jungle.

"Yes, that's what I want to know," snapped Winter. "What do you want?"

Trescott was silent for a moment. He consulted Moser's memoranda. "I see that your little girl's case is a trifle serious," he remarked. "I would advise you to call a physician soon. I will leave you a copy of Dr. Moser's record to give to anyone you may call." He paused to transcribe the record on a page of his notebook. Tearing out the leaf, he extended it to Winter as he moved towards the door. The latter shrunk against the wall. His head was hanging as he reached for the paper. This caused him to grasp air, and so Trescott simply let the paper flutter to the feet of the other man.

"Good-morning," said Trescott from the hall. This placid retreat seemed to suddenly arouse Winter to ferocity. It was as if he had then recalled all the truths which he had formulated to hurl at Trescott. So he followed him into the hall, and down the hall to the door, and through the door to the porch, barking in fiery rage from a respectful distance. As Trescott imperturbably turned the mare's head down the road, Winter stood on the porch, still yelping. He was like a little dog.

Chapter XXII

"HAVE YOU HEARD the news?" cried Carrie Dungen as she sped towards Martha's kitchen. "Have you heard the news?" Her eyes were shining with delight.

"No," answered Martha's sister Kate, bending forward eagerly. "What was it? What was it?"

Carrie appeared triumphantly in the open door. "Oh, there's been an awful scene between Doctor Trescott and Jake Winter. I never thought that Jake Winter had any pluck at all, but this morning he told the doctor just what he thought of him."

"Well, what did he think of him?" asked Martha.

"Oh, he called him everything. Mrs. Howarth heard it through her front blinds. It was terrible, she says. It's all over town now. Everybody knows it."

"Didn't the doctor answer back?"

"No! Mrs. Howarth – she says he never said a word. He just walked down to his buggy and got in, and drove off as co-o-o-l. But Jake gave him jinks, by all accounts."

"But what did he say?" cried Kate, shrill and excited. She was evidently at some kind of a feast.

"Oh, he told him that Sadie had never been well since that night Henry Johnson frightened her at Theresa Page's party, and he held him responsible, and how dared he cross his threshold – and – and – and—"

"And what?" said Martha.

"Did he swear at him?" said Kate, in fearsome glee.

"No – not much. He did swear at him a little, but not more than a man does anyhow when he is real mad, Mrs. Howarth says."

"O-oh!" breathed Kate. "And did he call him any names?"

Martha, at her work, had been for a time in deep thought. She now interrupted the others. "It don't seem as if Sadie Winter had been sick since that time Henry Johnson got loose. She's been to school almost the whole time since then, hasn't she?"

They combined upon her in immediate indignation. "School? School? I should say not. Don't think for a moment. School!"

Martha wheeled from the sink. She held an iron spoon, and it seemed as if she was going to attack them. "Sadie Winter has passed here many a morning since then carrying her schoolbag. Where was she going? To a wedding?"

The others, long accustomed to a mental tyranny, speedily surrendered.

"Did she?" stammered Kate. "I never saw her."

Carrie Dungen made a weak gesture.

"If I had been Doctor Trescott," exclaimed Martha, loudly, "I'd have knocked that miserable Jake Winter's head off."

Kate and Carrie, exchanging glances, made an alliance in the air. "I don't see why you say that, Martha," replied Carrie, with considerable boldness, gaining support and sympathy from Kate's smile. "I don't see how anybody can be blamed for getting angry when their little girl gets almost scared to death and gets sick from it, and all that. Besides, everybody says—"

"Oh, I don't care what everybody says," said Martha.

"Well, you can't go against the whole town," answered Carrie, in sudden sharp defiance.

"No, Martha, you can't go against the whole town," piped Kate, following her leader rapidly.

"'The whole town,'" cried Martha. "I'd like to know what you call 'the whole town'. Do you call these silly people who are scared of Henry Johnson 'the whole town'?"

"Why, Martha," said Carrie, in a reasoning tone, "you talk as if you wouldn't be scared of him!"

"No more would I," retorted Martha.

"O-oh, Martha, how you talk!" said Kate. "Why, the idea! Everybody's afraid of him."

Carrie was grinning. "You've never seen him, have you?" she asked, seductively.

"No," admitted Martha.

"Well, then, how do you know that you wouldn't be scared?"

Martha confronted her. "Have you ever seen him? No? Well, then, how do you know you *would* be scared?"

The allied forces broke out in chorus: "But, Martha, everybody says so. Everybody says so."

"Everybody says what?"

"Everybody that's seen him say they were frightened almost to death. 'Tisn't only women, but it's men too. It's awful."

Martha wagged her head solemnly. "I'd try not to be afraid of him."

"But supposing you could not help it?" said Kate.

"Yes, and look here," cried Carrie. "I'll tell you another thing. The Hannigans are going to move out of the house next door."

"On account of him?" demanded Martha.

Carrie nodded. "Mrs. Hannigan says so herself."

"Well, of all things!" ejaculated Martha. "Going to move, eh? You don't say so! Where they going to move to?"

"Down on Orchard Avenue."

"Well, of all things! Nice house?"

"I don't know about that. I haven't heard. But there's lots of nice houses on Orchard."

"Yes, but they're all taken," said Kate. "There isn't a vacant house on Orchard Avenue."

"Oh yes, there is," said Martha. "The old Hampstead house is vacant."

"Oh, of course," said Kate. "But then I don't believe Mrs. Hannigan would like it there. I wonder where they can be going to move to?"

"I'm sure I don't know," sighed Martha. "It must be to some place we don't know about."

"Well," said Carrie Dungen, after a general reflective silence, "It's easy enough to find out, anyhow."

"Who knows – around here?" asked Kate.

"Why, Mrs. Smith, and there she is in her garden," said Carrie, jumping to her feet. As she dashed out of the door, Kate and Martha crowded at the window. Carrie's voice rang out from near the steps. "Mrs. Smith! Mrs. Smith! Do you know where the Hannigans are going to move to?"

Chapter XXIII

THE AUTUMN smote the leaves, and the trees of Whilomville were panoplied in crimson and yellow. The winds grew stronger, and in the melancholy purple of the nights the home shine of a window became a finer thing. The little boys, watching the sear and sorrowful leaves drifting down from the maples, dreamed of the near time when they could heap bushels in the streets and burn them during the abrupt evenings.

Three men walked down the Niagara Avenue. As they approached Judge Hagenthorpe's house he came down his walk to meet them in the manner of one who has been waiting.

"Are you ready, judge?" one said.

"All ready," he answered.

The four then walked to Trescott's house. He received them in his office, where he had been reading. He seemed surprised at this visit of four very active and influential citizens, but he had nothing to say of it.

After they were all seated, Trescott looked expectantly from one face to another. There was a little silence. It was broken by John Twelve, the wholesale grocer, who was worth $400,000, and reported to be worth over a million.

"Well, doctor," he said, with a short laugh, "I suppose we might as well admit at once that we've come to interfere in something which is none of our business."

"Why, what is it?" asked Trescott, again looking from one face to another. He seemed to appeal particularly to Judge Hagenthorpe, but the old man had his chin lowered musingly to his cane, and would not look at him.

"It's about what nobody talks of – much," said Twelve. "It's about Henry Johnson."

Trescott squared himself in his chair. "Yes?" he said.

Having delivered himself of the title, Twelve seemed to become more easy. "Yes," he answered, blandly, "we wanted to talk to you about it."

"Yes?" said Trescott.

Twelve abruptly advanced on the main attack. "Now see here, Trescott, we like you, and we have come to talk right out about this business. It may be none of our affairs and all that, and as for me, I don't mind if you tell me so; but I am not going to keep quiet and see you ruin yourself. And that's how we all feel."

"I am not ruining myself," answered Trescott.

"No, maybe you are not exactly ruining yourself," said Twelve, slowly, "but you are doing yourself a great deal of harm. You have changed from being the leading doctor in town to about the last one. It is mainly because there are always a large number of people who are very thoughtless fools, of course, but then that doesn't change the condition."

A man who had not heretofore spoken said, solemnly, "It's the women."

"Well, what I want to say is this," resumed Twelve: "Even if there are a lot of fools in the world, we can't see any reason why you should ruin yourself by opposing them. You can't teach them anything, you know."

"I am not trying to teach them anything." Trescott smiled wearily. "I – It is a matter of – well—"

"And there are a good many of us that admire you for it immensely," interrupted Twelve; "but that isn't going to change the minds of all those ninnies."

"It's the women," stated the advocate of this view again.

"Well, what I want to say is this," said Twelve. "We want you to get out of this trouble and strike your old gait again. You are simply killing your practice through your infernal pigheadedness. Now this thing is out of the ordinary, but there must be ways to – to beat the game somehow, you see. So we've talked it over – about a dozen of us – and, as I say, if you want to tell us to mind our own business, why, go ahead; but we've talked it over, and we've come to the conclusion that the only way to do is to get Johnson a place somewhere off up the valley, and—"

Trescott wearily gestured. "You don't know, my friend. Everybody is so afraid of him, they can't even give him good care. Nobody can attend to him as I do myself."

"But I have a little no-good farm up beyond Clarence Mountain that I was going to give to Henry," cried Twelve, aggrieved. "And if you – and if you – if you – through your house burning down, or anything – why, all the boys were prepared to take him right off your hands, and – and—"

Trescott arose and went to the window. He turned his back upon them. They sat waiting in silence. When he returned he kept his face in the shadow. "No, John Twelve," he said, "it can't be done."

There was another stillness. Suddenly a man stirred on his chair.

"Well, then, a public institution—" he began.

"No," said Trescott; "public institutions are all very good, but he is not going to one."

In the background of the group old Judge Hagenthorpe was thoughtfully smoothing the polished ivory head of his cane.

Chapter XXIV

TRESCOTT loudly stamped the snow from his feet and shook the flakes from his shoulders. When he entered the house he went at once to the dining room, and then to the sitting room. Jimmie was there, reading painfully in a large book concerning giraffes and tigers and crocodiles.

"Where is your mother, Jimmie?" asked Trescott.

"I don't know, pa," answered the boy. "I think she is upstairs."

Trescott went to the foot of the stairs and called, but there came no answer. Seeing that the door of the little drawing room was open, he entered. The room was bathed in the half-light that came from the four dull panes of mica in the front of the great stove. As his eyes grew used to the shadows he saw his wife curled in an armchair. He went to her. "Why, Grace." he said, "didn't you hear me calling you?"

She made no answer, and as he bent over the chair he heard her trying to smother a sob in the cushion.

"Grace!" he cried. "You're crying!"

She raised her face. "I've got a headache, a dreadful headache, Ned."

"A headache?" he repeated, in surprise and incredulity.

He pulled a chair close to hers. Later, as he cast his eye over the zone of light shed by the dull red panes, he saw that a low table had been drawn close to the stove, and that it was burdened with many small cups and plates of uncut tea-cake. He remembered that the day was Wednesday, and that his wife received on Wednesdays.

"Who was here today, Gracie?" he asked.

From his shoulder there came a mumble, "Mrs. Twelve."

"Was she – um," he said. "Why – didn't Anna Hagenthorpe come over?"

The mumble from his shoulder continued, "She wasn't well enough."

Glancing down at the cups, Trescott mechanically counted them. There were fifteen of them. "There, there," he said. "Don't cry, Grace. Don't cry."

The wind was whining round the house, and the snow beat aslant upon the windows. Sometimes the coal in the stove settled with a crumbling sound, and the four panes of mica flashed a sudden new crimson. As he sat holding her head on his shoulder, Trescott found himself occasionally trying to count the cups. There were fifteen of them.

Singed Moths

Emma Dawson

In Yorkshire, England, night-moths are called souls.

* * *

Poor moth! thy fate my own resembles – [...]
What gained we, little moth? Thy ashes
Thy one brief parting pang may show,
And withering thoughts for soul that dashes
From deep to deep are but a death more slow.
Carlyle's 'Tragedy of the Night-Moth'

Katharine's Diary

JUNE 21

WAITING for Elizabeth tonight, Charlotte and I sat in silence, unbroken save by the slight sounds of our work.

"While I pay court to a new 'one-eyed despot', I want to ask if you have thought that this is Midsummer Eve?" I asked at last, with a scornful laugh, but feeling more like crying, as I stopped the sewing-machine for a new needle.

"No, is it?" Charlotte answered, with a long sigh, and soon looking up from her desk to add: "Now I have spoiled that sheet of legal-cap! You made me think of our lawn with colored lanterns, our lace dresses, wide Roman sashes, diamonds and whole pearls, the kind men and fond women, and instead of 'City and County of San Francisco, ss.', I wrote Strauss waltzes and strawberry-ices. How could you?"

"Well," said I, "I had been thinking all day of the change our gloves and boots too shabby for daylight, hats years old, black silks that knew some of our old 'tea-fights' and have to be court-plastered like beaten pugilists, our dread to see things wear out or break because not sure of new ones, even what should pay car-fare kept for a loaf of bread."

"Our only caller," said Charlotte, "the landlady for her rent. Neither time nor money for books or papers. Theatre, concert, sail, and drive, joys for us no more than if we were ghosts."

"Shunned," said I, "except for insult, by those in our old rank of life, as if with our money went our culture, wit, sense, and purity."

"Innocent souls," said Charlotte, "forced to toil fourteen or sixteen hours a day, while the vile wretch at San Quentin works eight or ten, and sleeps with no care for food or rent."

"A steady grind of small economies," I went on, "that are both comic and cruel – a struggle for ten cents' worth of flour, one candle, five cents' worth of sugar, seventy-five-cent boots, and twenty-five-cent gloves."

"Forced to think," said Charlotte, "of claims due the unyielding body, and forget there can be joys the spirit needs; that we ever knew sunrise parties on horseback, garden-shaded hammocks at noon, sea-sands at sunset, or serenades by moonlight."

"In San Francisco," said I, "we know neither the fire-side glow thrown on our old silver-laden side-board in winter, nor the foreign travel of our summers, nor the red and yellow woods of fall we saw from the marble-terrace overlooking our landscape garden, with its lake and Swiss cottage – where the trees looked as if seen through the stained windows of our great library."

"Outdoors," said she, "we see only wind-blown dust or rain; indoors, we know our work, and a hysterical sort of good spirits."

"Our past in the East," I said, "is gone like a dream; folks treat us as though with our lost money went our brains."

"Not all," said she.

"Only exceptions that prove the rule," I answered.

After another hour of quiet, Charlotte lighted a fire, filled the tea-kettle, and spread the cloth.

"*We* will have a party supper," she said. "Elizabeth will be tired and hungry. If we had flour and a bit of suet (I have nearly forgotten what butter is), we could have some griddle cakes. If we had this or that, we could have the other. What will you have? – Broiled chicken, custard pie, and citron cake?"

"Oyster soup, quail on toast, and an omelette soufitee," I replied –

> "*If wishes were horses, beggers might ride;*
> *If wishes were fishes, we'd have some fried.*"

"Perhaps Elizabeth will bring something," said Charlotte, as she set a cup of milk and a five-cent loaf of bread on the table. "She was to get some sewing from the Wertley's – they may give her some cake."

"Don't!" I cried, "It vexes my pride to take such gifts yet I am so tired of potatoes and salt, and milk and water."

"And owing for the potatoes and milk," said Charlotte, grimly; "even the five dollars Elizabeth will get for playing for the Wertley's children's party ought to go in how many ways! All to the grocer, or for rent, for coal, for milk, or to get dresses dyed, or – O dear! It is after eleven; she must come soon. Ah! here she is."

Elizabeth came upstairs, tired and out of breath, with two small jars, which she set on the table, saying: "More frill and no shirt! Pickles and jam the housekeeper gave me. Good soul, she didn't know what a farce it was, that we had nothing to eat with them, that the scent of dinner in houses I passed going there tonight made me feel ill!"

We laughed, but our voices were full of tears.

"In the children's lessons, today," said Elizabeth, "we read (what I felt as they could not) about the pagan goddess of death, 'Hel' – in the realm of the Cold Storm. Hunger is her table, Starvation her knife, Delay her man, Slowness her maid, Precipice her threshold, Care her bed, burning Anguish the hangings of her room."

"Oh, don't!" I cried; "the water boils; come, we will play it is tea – but we must sweeten it with smiles, as we have no sugar."

"No one came to see the room, I suppose," said Elizabeth, as we gathered round the table, "though I answered the notice so quickly; nor anyone to take lessons."

"No," said Charlotte, "nothing has happened except that Biddy has sent us some coal and wood."

"Think of our old servant coming to own this house, and letting us the upper part – swelling round in a big fur cloak, and showing us charity! Bah!"

"Never mind," said Charlotte, "her good heart gave her grace to say the fairies sent it. We are lucky to have such a friend – when I have got word that, as someone will do the work cheaper, this is the last of my copying."

We all sighed.

"Elizabeth," said I, "I thought Mrs. Wertley was to send some sewing by you."

"Mrs. Wertley," said Elizabeth, "did not like it because I played something more than dance-music when asked to by one of her guests, and outshone her daughter. So I have lost my place as governess."

Charlotte and I groaned.

"Oh, Charlotte," said Elizabeth, "haven't you got some verses to read to us tonight?"

Charlotte searched her papers, and read:

"*Better Days*

"*What pathos sounds within the common phrase*
On careless tongues: 'They have known better days!'
As if for them were dimmed this sun's gold rays,
The dazzling miracle of winter's snow,
The festal pomp of summer's blossom show
Were seen by them through veil of sombre haze.

"*God help poor souls on whom that burden lays!*
They walk through narrow, crooked, lonely ways,
Look on their darkened life in sore amaze,
To Care and Sorrow and Regret fast bound,
To toil and moil in endless chain-gang round,
And almost view the Past as madman's craze.

"*Rare is the soul that sympathy betrays,*
As if they lose all claim to blame or praise,
Or from their poverty contagion strays.
Chafed raw by rough and seamy side of life,
They stagger, wounded, crippled, by the strife,
And often lost within the novel maze.

"*Of all the blessings that the soul portrays*
When, as the heart-sick and world-wearied prays,
We shall some time see heaven's glories blaze.
Naught can surpass the certainty of this:
That once within that sphere of perfect bliss,
Our thoughts can never turn to 'better days'!"

When Charlotte paused, Elizabeth was crying, but I said: "We *will* have good times. You must not despair. If you do not marry, I will. *I* do not mean to dress St. Catharine's hair in the next world, as the old saying has it that a maid must!" and I chanted the old prayer:

"A husband, Saint Catharine,
A handsome one, Saint Catharine,
A rich one, Saint Catharine,
A nice one, Saint Catharine,
And soon, Saint Catharine!'"

"Position before money," said Elizabeth.

"Biddy would say love before money," said Charlotte.

"No," said I, "money, money, money! Think – of our heartaches and headaches, not only the picturesque of life, but the comforts denied us, all for lack of money! I would marry the Devil if he were rich!"

"Oh, Katharine!" they cried.

"I would! I would!" said I, striking my fist on the table.

"One might be tempted," said Elizabeth to Charlotte, who nodded.

"There could be inducements," said she.

The clock struck twelve; the house shook, and the windows jarred.

"Was that a shock of earthquake?" Charlotte asked.

"Only a blast of wind," said Elizabeth.

"No," I said, "there is someone knocking at the outside door,"

"It is too late to open it," said Charlotte.

"Nonsense!" I cried. "Bright moonlight, and three of us! Let us all go. If not Fate for one of us, we can be the three Fates for him!"

They unwillingly followed me; but, at the last moment, I shrank, and it was Elizabeth who opened the door. A man who did not look quite strange to us, stood on the steps.

"Pardon me," he said, taking off his hat; "I followed you from Mrs. Wertley's, but did not start in time to overtake you. I heard you say you had a room to let. Can you excuse my coming at this untimely hour, and let me see it?"

We looked at each other. It would not do to lose a chance of a lodger. We let him in.

A true American, plain, thin, sharp-faced, alert, and confident. He wanted to avoid bad smells; he said he left his last quarters on that account. He took the room, paid a month's rent, and said he would come in the morning.

When he had gone, we took hands and danced round our table, spread with 'Duke Humphrey's dinner'.

"See what Midsummer Eve has brought us!" I cried.

At that moment the front door blew open, a wild gust of wind tore through the house, and put out the light; and, as we felt round in the dark, Charlotte said:

"There was something uncanny about that man. I am sorry he is coming."

"So am I," said Elizabeth; "but I thought I ought not to say so."

"I feel the same," I said; "but is it not as uncanny to be without money?"

And over a sputtering candle, burning blue, we all nodded at each other like so many doomed witches.

Charlotte's Diary

AUGUST 15.

IT DOES NOT seem now that less than two months ago we were in despair. Mr. Orne's taking the room, and the ease with which he helped us to work more fit for us, have been such relief. I have gone back to my pictures, and Elizabeth to her music. Katharine picked up in the street some money for which no owner could be found, that has paid half our debts.

Our handsome, dark, Spanish-looking lodger, who tells me he is a poor, 'devil-may-care' artist, went with me up on our flat roof tonight, to see a fine sunset. Strangely farsighted, more like eagle than mart, he saw things out of the range of most people's vision, and told me of ships far at sea. The great cross on Lone Mountain stood out black against scarlet clouds, while above stretched shadowy shapes as of angels.

"It reminds me," I said, "of an ecstasy of Saint Francis of Assisi, in a little chapel of Santa Croce in Milan – a cross standing up dark and strong in shade, a figure in friar's robes borne up in the gloom, as if floating on it, his arms lifted to arms of some vision he sees."

He gave one of his odd, scornful laughs. "What could the vision tell him?" he asked.

"The angels know all," I said.

"Not everything," he answered; "there are three things they do not know."

"What are they?"

"The day of the Second Advent, men's hearts, and the number of the elect. Then they have no tongues."

I thought I must try to reform this straying soul. "Don't you remember your Bible?" I asked.

"I know all about Job, Jethro, and Balaam," he answered; "they studied sorcery."

"This view changes like magic," I said; "all may be fog save where the sun rises a blood-red ball on its image in the bay, the two a huge pillar of fire, like sign and portent; or, sole rift at noon, a sheet of gold holding the shipping in black outlines; or, sky all blue, the bay looks a brook to be spanned by foot-plank, the city seems of toy-houses, the Golden Gate a mountain-hemmed lake; or the city shrunk into a patch of black mist, the bay is a great sheet of quicksilver; or, the city stretches everywhere, mountains and bay are withdrawn in vague, sad distance. It is like the views one takes in changing moods of the other world."

He seemed amused. "What do you know of the other world?" he asked.

"As much as anyone. What do you think about it?" said I.

"Nothing," he replied. "Wait till you go there yourself. All that has been fancied about it does not near the truth. People are much surprised when they die."

And he laughed low and long, as if all to himself, at some secret thought.

"Angels came in dreams in Bible-times," I said. "I once had a dream which was a great comfort to me. I thought I asked someone if we were immortal and should meet our friends. He answered, 'You ought to know by your own spirit.'"

"Has your spirit never deceived you?" asked our lodger; "does it not daily tell you wrong, for or against things you would do or think?"

I sighed to have to own how often my own thought had duped me. What strange power this man has – like a baleful star – to stir doubt in my heart! But my first distrust of him is gone; instead, he seems more like someone dear to me of old. By a fine sympathy he often seems to know before I speak what I am about to say, as if he read my mind. "If evil, there is also good—" I began.

He frowned. "There is too much light!" he cried, and we came indoors.

As I went down the stairs I looked back, saw his swarthy face in the fiery glow of the sunset, and saw for an instant a wonderful model for a picture of the Prince of Darkness.

Elizabeth's Diary

AUGUST 30.

OUR LODGER, who proves a thorough musician – though he tells me he is heir to a proud foreign title – seems like an old friend, now I am used to his odd blonde beauty. He took me tonight to hear *Faust*. It was brought out with more care than often given, the voices sweet and well-trained, the acting good; but Mr. Orne was restless, and laughed at it all; and it had not so vivid a charm for me as before, though I shuddered at the weird warnings that in the overture, with mystic awe, hint all the tragic love-tale.

"Where," I asked him, "has the music fled when the instrument is broken? It seems like a soul."

"You do not *know*," he answered, "of any hereafter for your own soul!"

"No," said I; "but neither do we know all the hidden chances for bliss or woe in our lives; that we do not *know*, does not make them less there."

"Swayed by this music," he said, "you are not the same person who left home. Self thus made and unmade each moment, one is but a drift of atoms, unlikely to meet again!"

"Is it chance, or are we clockwork?" I said, as the opera went on, and I was filled with a sense of the folly of striving against fate. "Or are we ruled by unearthly powers, as these instruments are played upon and forced to yield certain strains?"

"That is not for you to know," he said.

"Perhaps," said I, "vibrations from angels' choirs jar us like the atoms of Chladni, into our places."

"Then an infernal chorus," said he, "may cause the discord of awful crimes?"

"Yes," I said, "a spell from hell. What can the real Mephisto think of this stage copy?"

"It is as if a wild bloom tried to be a hot-house flower," he said. "How would you like a crude mockery of yourself?"

As we sat there, I could almost fancy in him a queer, flitting likeness to the Mephistopheles before us, like an image in a brook, shaken and changed by speaking to him.

While the music stirred me as wind blows a leaf, I saw so many unmoved faces in the crowd that I asked him: "Why does the effect of music vary on different persons?"

"Because," said he, "in music the unearthly touches the human. Some have no soul, no vital spark to move – like Tyndall's sensitive flame, which shrinks at a hiss, thrills at a jar, and leaps at a waltz."

"Music seems to me," I said, "as if we heard a spirit trying to take bodily shape, but failing."

"Like that Mephisto there," he said; and after we reached home he still scoffed at that singer's make-up and acting.

"Why, even his laugh," said he, "had not the true ring. This is the way he should have looked and laughed—" and he donned my cloak, with its tasseled hood above his head in grotesque shape, and gave a wild laugh, which sent cold chills over us, and made Biddy, passing along the hall, stop and cross herself.

"You have frightened Biddy," I said.

"Oh, no," he said, "it is her own soul that scares her."

Then he brought his violin, and played Tartini's 'Dream' for a goodnight – "to make you dream," he told us.

"How strange it is," I said, "that dreams – else forgotten – sometimes come back to us at the sound of music."

"If they could only be brought again and finished," said Katharine, "you might read the letter which lately came to you, Charlotte."

"What was that?" he asked, with keen interest. Charlotte read to him her verses:

"Unknown

"To me what could that note reveal
Which glimmered through my dream?
Large, white, with an unbroken seal,
From whom 't was sent no gleam.
Like planet's wheel our dreams conceal
Strange hints of Life's hid scheme.

"Was it from friend in distant star?
Or one on earth, in sleep?
Or that twin-soul whose path lies far
From waking glances sweep?'
Or sent to mar all joys that are
Where Dream-land shadows creep

"The music-score of demon-band?
Or summons to witch ball?
Or form of compact wily planned
And signed with mystic scrawl,
From fairy-land, or goblin damned,
To hold my soul in thrall?

"Did my good angel send me balm
For heart too ill at ease?
Perhaps a spray from heavenly palm,
As signal of release
Or tale of charm in that fair calm,
To cheer and give me peace?

"What were its contents, grave or glad
Reply to all I ask,
When worn and weary, baffled, mad
Despairing at Life's task,
I would have had the reason sad,
Not wear its iron mask.

*"Was it a message from the dead,
Of hope, or warning sign?
Accursed be whatever led
My soul from sleep divine!
O'er note unread in that dream fled
I often muse and pine!"*

"Do not open a letter which comes in your sleep," said Mr. Orne, plainly vexed at such nonsense; "evil spirits are as likely to be near as good ones. The world of sleep is their carnival."

Charlotte looked pale and startled. Katharine laughed.

"I do not need to dream," said I. "I have other warnings."

"What sort?" he asked, eagerly.

"Oh – a little bird tells me," I said.

"Take care," said he, as he left us; "it may be the bird of the Amazon, the 'Lost Soul'!"

Biddy Gossips

"SIT DOWN, Mrs. O'Shane; I can talk an' iron too. Did ye mind the gintleman who wint out as ye kem in? He's the strange lodger. Though he's been here since June, an' it's now the middle of September, he is, an' always will be, the strange lodger. The ladies upstairs are all greatly taken wid him, but what they can like I can't think. Him – wid his club-foot, his hair in two curls like horns, his sly, cruel eyes, wid small whites to thim, his foxy, pinted ears, an' claw-fingers!

"The first mornin' he was here, I was on the front steps, comin' from market, whin he wint out; an' the sight of him made me cross mysilf. He gave me a scowl that was heart-scaldin', and he seemed to jist melt into air like a flash, he was gone so quick – wid his flame-colored hair an' whiskers, like the Judas-beard in the garden; his hollow back, too thin to cast a shadow; an' his feet of unaven size. Sure, God's writin' is plain enough!

"It gives me a turn to hear his knock, for he'll not touch the bell. It is no work for thim to care for his room; he niver seems to have moved anythin'. They wondered why the plant died in the hangin'-basket in the hall. But I saw him brush by it one day; it was that killed it.

"Thin he nearly crazes me, makin' the wildest music on his fiddle. It's always the sly lad that takes to playin' on that, an' there's nothin' plain an' open about *him*. The three sisters are charmed wid him intoirly. But the sight I got of him one night was enough for me – warnin' for anybody. He had taken Miss Elizabeth to the theatre; an' after they kem back, he caught her opera-cloak, as it was slippin' from her shoulders to the floor, an' threw it over himsilf wid the pinted hood on his head, stickin' up like a horn. Ugh! What a divil he looked! I wondered what was in his nose thin. An' he gave a screech of a laugh that curdled my blood an' set my hair on ind. Sure, he's one of those ye ought to hate at sight; an' ye may know, if ye have much to do wid 'em, ye will come to be ready to travel many a hard mile to hear the dirt fall on their coffins.

"Even the cat there knows more than the three women; grave an' still as she is, she knows what bad spirits have power at Midsummer Eve, an' that was the night the quare man kem.

"I tell ye, I think he's sort o' bewitched the sisters. They aven think they are wid him whin I know they are not. One will be tellin' me of goin' to a concert wid him. The same afternoon another says to me she was walkin' wid him, an' the other will speak of his bein' wid her here in the house! They are not much better off than before he kem, but they think they are. Lone, worried women take odd notions. They are jist out of their heads about him, but they'll come to grief, mind ye. Mind ye, he who eats wid the Divil has need of a long spoon! Perhaps they think it's in love they are, but it's not love. It's not the feelin' I had for Patrick, which made me not care whether he had cabin an' pig, or not. Don't mind me, I have to wipe away the tears when I think of him, though his grave is far away as Ireland an' twenty-five years can make it. But whin ye have known the rale thing, ye can tell what is sham. No, they are thinkin' of what they'll git, not of the man.

"Must ye go? Wait till I open the door for ye. Stay, do ye see that tall figure, a little lame, skulkin' up the street in the moonlight? Kape on the other side of the way, an' count yer beads as ye go, an' don't look at him, for he has the evil eye. Run now, for he always moves so quick, I can think of nothin' but what I once heard the priest say in a sermon: 'And I beheld Satan like lightnin' fallin' from heaven.'"

Charlotte's Diary

SEPTEMBER 30.

TODAY Mr. Orne took me to the park to see the Victoria Regia, like a bit of a sunrise cloud. He bought me a bouquet, but the heat of his hand withered it in a moment. He is so odd – darting here and there. I was speaking of the flower of the Holy Ghost, thinking he was by me, but suddenly found him distant the whole length of the greenhouse. When we came home, he drew the great lily with one or two dashes of his pencil; but though a true copy, I thought the outline bore, too, an odd likeness to an elfin face; but he talked me out of it.

"Though Saint Cyprian saw the Devil in a flower, you need not," he said.

"You work so quickly," I replied; "it makes me think of the Devil's crucifix, painted by two strokes of his brush in the convent of the Capuchin friars at Rome. He did it for a soul bound to him; and the soul was so struck with its heartrending truth, that he made the sign of the cross, and got free."

"It is well known," he said, "the Devil would be an artist."

"Is art an evil power?" I asked.

"Doctor Donne," said he, "preached before Oliver Cromwell that the Muses were damned spirits of devils. No one can mark where the presence of evil comes and goes. It may be very near, and you not know it."

I tried to work on his portrait, but in vain. He changes so much with his moods, and the fire of his eyes is not to be copied. The girls want to see it, but I keep it screened. Today he was very restless; told me secrets of color thought to have been lost for ages; tossed over my portfolios of sketches and rhymes with mingled praise and blame. He found and read to me:

"Unfulfilled

"The night was dark and wet, in long gone age,
When Genevieve to mass with maidens went;
The gleaming torches, carried by a page
Through gusty wind and rain, were quickly spent;
She touched them, and again their ruddy glare
Shone on the pious souls who wandered there.
'No fire of this world' – thus the legend ran;

> 'T was her same force celestial that could snare
> The secret thought of man!
>
> "Upon the gilded tomb of Genevieve –
> In church of Saint Etienne du Mont, the quaint,
> With airy stair from shadowed aisle to eave –
> Behind a golden grating lies the saint.
> Forever tapers shine. Who buys one tries
> To send some earnest prayer to Paradise.
> Ah! long I watched its eager, changing flare –
> As hands raised, palm to palm, point toward the skies –
> My burning, burning prayer!
>
> "Wind-shaken, like my thought that bold aspired,
> It paused, drooped fainting, rose again, implored,
> While I, like frantic moth, all my desire
> Cast on the flame that yearningly adored.
> Around my sacred hope this aureole
> Became a steady beacon for my soul,
> And through long years of darkness and despair
> Its cheering rays athwart my care would roll,
> My glowing, glowing prayer!
>
> "At last, like smoke-wreath poising over flame,
> The shadow of my hope loomed just in view,
> But floated off, nor ever nearer came.
> Was it within my sway for joy or rue?
> Who shall define the bounds of will and fate,
> Man's choice, or hand of Providence debate?
> To lose it was to see Hell's lurid flashes,
> And Heaven is – to find there, incarnate,
> My prayer that burned to ashes!"

The strange smile that curled his lip made me in despair throw down my brush.

"There the Catholics are like the followers of Confucius," said he, "who think what is burned rises to the next world. Do you recall the Devil of human size on the outer gallery of Notre Dame in Paris? Do you think he watches the smoke of the city to know what people want? Eastern tales are nearer right that keep him in ruins and desert places."

"Like the minds he wrecks or lays waste."

He flashed upon me a glance of keen question, then bent again over the sketch-books. He found a photograph of my favorite 'Paolo and Francesca', falling, falling, forever and ever, murky shadows reaching from below to engulf them, the light of lost Paradise streaming from above, a troop of filmy forms in the background watching.

"Is it not the worst of all for each that they must both go?" I asked.

"Would not their parting be worse?" said he. "No – *that* is not hell."

With his swift pencil he sketched some woeful figures looking back – one who sees his bosom friend forget him; one who knows his foe pleased at his death; one who finds his secrets

come to the gaze of the world; one who learns that the woman for love of whom he died loves and regrets him.

"Hell," he said, "is to keep the same passions without the human frame in which to show them – to be in your old haunts and see things going against your wishes with no power to hinder; no dropping through bottomless pit, no raging flame could be worse. What would you choose for heaven?"

"To look back," I said, "and see at least one of my pictures live on. I would give my soul for that."

He clasped my hand as if to close a compact, and, as the other arm went round my waist, he said: "But your own image, mirrored in the soul that loves you, maybe more lasting."

I felt his fiery kiss upon my mouth. Bewildered, I could have believed that over his shoulder I saw the figures in his sketches begin to dance and jeer at me. I shrank back. At that moment, Katharine and Elizabeth burst in where we were, like jealous sisters in a fairy tale.

Katharine's Diary

OCTOBER 15.

I WENT with Mr. Orne to a ball last night. The girls helped me dress, and each lent of her best, but I was so dazed with the strain of trying to look gay, while dulled by vain struggle to feel well, in our old worn things, that all the hours I was gone, though I seemed to see rich robes of Flanders lace and Genoa velvet he had sent for me to wear, yet I was mindful how Elizabeth had warned me of some carefully darned lace that would not bear a touch, and Charlotte had dyed an old sash-ribbon, and painted flowers over stains, and we had all sighed over the whole.

But here I was, as if in a leaf far back in the book of my life, in full dress once more, whirling with a rich and gay escort down a long hall of dancers, the band playing the 'Lucifer' waltzes, my partner buoying me clear of the crowd. He seems to know everyone; he was nodding right and left. I would cry: "Why, do you know him?", "Intimately", he would answer. And once, as he said so, the voice of a passing dancer reached our ears, and made us smile: "The Devil is nearer a man than his coat or his shirt."

He slipped on my finger a ring set with an opal of occult power and mystic fire, like the lurid light in his eyes; and when I said, "I like 'a pearl with a soul in it'", he replied: "That is its very charm for me – the soul in it," looking at me as if he could will my very soul from me. I heard people groan that the supper was gone, but he brought me dainties in plenty, and unlike what others had found. I heard him jesting in many languages with this or that one, well known and liked by all. He told me he had just made a fortune in mining stocks. As I sipped and played with my spoon, caught the witch-gleam of my opal, felt pleased with the fine mesh of my laces, the shadow and glow of my velvet, I felt that to gain all such spendthrift wants of mine would make heaven of earth. Then the man went by who had quoted Luther. Was the Devil so near? Who was our strange lodger, who filled my mind with such wild thoughts, like an evil planet drawing forth all the bad in my nature? Then I forgot my doubts in the swift whirl of music and dance.

As we stood on our steps and he searched for his latch-key, I watched the fire of my opal, burning like a will-o'-the-wisp in the moon-lit dark.

"It has a weird life of its own!" I cried; and, fearing my sisters' eyes of wonder and envy, "Take it!" I said.

"Not without you," he answered, bending over me, and a sudden, brief kiss scorched my lips.

Then the girls, who had sat up for us, and heard the carriage, had opened the door and swept us upstairs with them.

I could have thought them jealous by the way Charlotte cried: "You look changed in some way – like a shining spirit against a dark cloud!" And Elizabeth added: "It does not matter much about your dress, after all!"

I stood before our bureau-glass. It showed me the darned lace and dyed ribbon with which they had dressed me. Had I imagined my fine things? Perhaps I had but fancied the ball, the lights, and music, and my – lover! The ring was gone.

And then the next I knew, they had undressed me and put me in bed, and Elizabeth was cooling my head with damp cloths, while Charlotte was fanning me, and I heard them murmur together, as if far off. "What did she mutter about a ring set with a spark from hell?" Elizabeth asked. And Charlotte answered: "That she was sealed to Satan!"

Elizabeth's Diary

OCTOBER 31.

THIS AFTERNOON, as I played Grégoire's fine 'Etude du Diable', I was startled to my feet by finding Mr. Orne stood close behind me to hear.

"Good, isn't it?" I asked.

"Not the right thought," said he; "listen." And he drew from his violin strains of dread meaning.

"That is more unearthly," I said; "a spirit might play so."

"And a wicked one?" he answered. "The Mussulman legend runs, that the Devil is given leave to fill his spare time with music, song, love-poetry, and dancing."

"How is it that you can surpass all others?" I asked.

"Because I have the will – the secret magic of all success."

"Teach me," I cried, "to win power, position!"

"Will you leave your sisters without farewell," he asked, "and fly with me at twelve tonight, knowing no more of where you go than that you will have rank and sway beyond your wildest dreams?"

He drew me to him; his burning lips touched mine. Then my sisters rushed in, with that new, watchful way of theirs, and he went out.

This evening, as we sat together for the last time in our safe, warm, bright room, with a rising storm stirring all round the house, I could hardly keep from telling the girls that I was going abroad, and all he had promised me. Indeed, I did hint about it, but they thought it only one of our old day-dreams, and Katharine, as if sure that hers was coming true, began to tell us how she should build her castle. Leaning proudly on the mantelpiece, she looked statuesque, as if the petrifying effect of wealth had begun.

"But how sad it is," she said, "to think that death can bear me from it all."

"My pictures," said Charlotte, "will live when I am gone."

"Position," said I, "may be prized even then, if we can look back."

"Yees can take nothin wia ye," said Biddy, who had come in unheard, "but love."

We all started, and then laughed in scorn.

"Sure, the priest was tellin' only last Sunday," said she, "how Saint Theresa could say nothing worse of the Divil than 'Poor wretch, he loves not/ Her notion of hell was that no love was there. But love is all we're sure of in heaven.'"

"Biddy, have you come to preach a sermon?" I asked.

"No, I beg yer pardon. 'Tis All Souls' Eve, and I thought maybe yees would come to vespers tonight. The music'll be fine."

For a moment we thought of going. I half rose; Katharine went a step or two toward the door; Charlotte left her seat. Was it the unfelt wind which blows us on the shoals of destiny which drove us back?

"Not now, Biddy," said I; "some other time. Tonight Charlotte is, at last, going to let us see her portrait of our lodger. Don't you want to wait and see it?"

Charlotte placed it where we could view it in the long glass, which had lights around it, "like a shrine," Biddy said, as if she did not like it.

As Charlotte unveiled it, Katharine and I cried, in surprise: "This is not *his* likeness!"

And Biddy, laughing, said: "Not a bit, not a bit like him!"

"It is not only better-looking, but it is another man," said I; "there is no Spanish knight about *him*."

"No, indeed," said Katharine; "the true type of an American I call him."

"Why no," said I; "he is a pure German blonde."

Biddy heard, half grinning, half frowning. "Oh, yees are all bewitched, an' 'tis Allhallows Eve," she said; "come to the holy vespers, do."

But we laughed and sent her off; and when she had gone Mr. Orne suddenly stood in the door, as if he had sprung through the floor, and paused, looking at his picture.

"Come and tell us," cried Katharine, "how is it that Charlotte could paint you in this way?"

"No two persons see alike," he said. "One seems to different people to have as many characters, perhaps as many aspects. How few agree when speaking of anyone!"

"But this," said Katharine, "has not your mouth; and you are neither light nor dark."

"But this," said I, "has not your chin, nor your fair hair."

"But this," said Charlotte, "has your dark curls. It is just like you, except the eyes, perhaps."

Then we all stared wildly at each other.

"But this," said Biddy, glancing in, with her bonnet on, "is All Souls' Eve, if yees would only come."

"Where?" cried Mr. Orne, in a voice of scorn. But, seeing him, she fled like lightning, and the outer door echoed like thunder after her.

He soon followed. "But not to vespers," he said, laughing.

Katharine, Charlotte, and I wrangled over the picture till Charlotte screened and put it by, and sat at her desk to rhyme; while I, at the piano, with precious minor keys, unlocked the inner gates of the realm of musing, and Katharine sat with open book on lap, but looking in the fire. Hours went by with no word between us. We did not heed when Biddy came home, nor know when Mr. Orne passed through the door, but found him with us again.

"This is a fine gale," he said. "Bodies may be housed, but think of flitting souls going out into such a night."

"Is it the wind and storm," cried Charlotte, "which set me to writing this?" And, while the winds tore round the house in a witches' dance she read to us:

"After Death

"All through the unseen realm of air I float;
The souls that, passing, mount to God, I note;
Each flashing through the void like fiery mote
By fierce wind blown.

"Death makes an anvil of our pigmy world,
And drives these sparks – these spirits upward whirled –
That glimmer on till all the dark is furled,
Before the throne!

"I would look back and linger, linger yet
What can I feel but passionate regret?
When I remember thy dear eyelids wet,
What shall atone?

"But, borne by some resistless force, I go
To learn what but immortal spirits know
Or faint and fading into darkness flow
Dread path unknown!

"The earth becomes a distant waning star.
What! is this all? A memory floating far;
My conscience for the dreaded judgment bar;
And this alone?"

In the shadowed chimney-corner Mr. Orne nearly went out of sight as she read. He seemed coming and going by the flickering fire as she paused or went on; and, at the end, I thought he had left the room; but a sudden glow of the fire showed that there he sat. Then he added some verses, while Katharine's book – *Footfalls on the Boundaries of Another World* – slid to the floor, as she bent toward pictures in the fire; Charlotte leaned on her desk, with her face in her hands; and I, drifting off in a dream-skiff, trailed my hands through a rippling tide of music.

In a few minutes he read to us:

"No dazzling ranks of angels' choirs appear,
Nor bands of wailing spirits damned are here,
A merely silent, lonely, misty sphere
Forever shown,

"Where darts that restless flame, my naked soul.
But sometimes yet at thy fond thought's control
I can return, thy faithful heart my goal,
My Love, my Own!

"Know at thy tears I tremble, almost wane,
Thy sighs revive my smoldering fire again,

The best of life, our love, may yet remain,
Eternal grown.

"But if thou canst forget, my light will pale,
When no regret of thine seeks my lost trail,
Then, only then, within dim depths I fail,
Expire, alone!"

I roused from my rapt gaze at him to find Charlotte and Katharine looking at him as intently as if they, with their sudden jealousy, fancied the lines meant for them. The winds howled and shook the house, the rain beat against the pane, Mr. Orne, uneasy, too, walked up and down the long room, and his deep, rich voice, a cordial that warmed the ear, broke forth in "King Death is a rare old fellow!" He paused after one verse before Katharine. "Even Money is powerless before him," said he.

He stopped after the next verse by Charlotte. "Yet Death may be foiled by Fame," he said.

As he came near me at another verse, he said: "On a level with all at the touch of 'his yellow hand.'"

We heard his voice die away in the distance in the ghostly old song about King Death. By the queer, subtile sway of one spirit over another, my sisters seemed to feel that parting was near. They could not have acted otherwise if either of them thought of going.

"Goodnight, girls," said Charlotte, starting, but coming back to kiss us. "Perhaps I should say goodbye. Who has seen tomorrow?'"

Soon after, Katharine rose. "Goodnight," she said, kissing me, "and goodbye – till we meet again."

I sit here alone, writing. I have listened to the vanishing sound of her footsteps; I am tempted to call them back. But it is on the stroke of twelve. The storm rages still more wildly; an awful night to be out. What a surprise is in store for my sisters! When I next see them, how strange will be our meeting!

Biddy Gossips Again

"**SURE,** an' it's kind of ye, Mrs. O'Shane, to come in this pourin' rain tonight. Give me the umbrill, an' sit ye down by the fire. Yes, it has stormed night an' day for a week – ever since Allhallows Eve, heaven save us!

"Tell ye all about it? Oh, they got worse an' worse – all three wild in love wid him, an' that jealous they didn't want one of them to be alone wid him. Now, he was all wrapped up in Miss Elizabeth, playing duets wid his witch of a fiddle, showin' her how to write music, an' talkin' of his high rank at home; then jist the same wid Miss Charlotte, teachin' her how to mix colors, an' touchin' up her pictures, an' tellin' her she was a wonder, an' folks wouldn't forget *her*, an' writin' verses wid her; an' jist as deep wid Miss Katharine, plannin' how she was to make her fortune in no time, an' always showin' off in some way how rich *he* was.

"How did I know his ways so well? Didn't I use to be goin' through the hall quite careless, an' hear it all? Ye may learn a good dale that way, by niver hurryin' yourself. Many's the time he nearly caught me, but I got into the dark corner, wid my apron over my head, quakin' as he went by. But at last he got a dog – an awful big, black crater, wid eyes like coals, an' I had to kape down here.

"I *did* talk to thim. I couldn't make thim see him as I did, try as much as I would. Ye might as well warn water not to run downhill. An' he windin' round thim like a snake, I used to think. May the holy saints kape us! Is that only the shutters knockiri'? Let us say a prayer or two. It makes me shake to think of him now.

"About the mornin' after All Souls' Eve, is it? Listen to this, thin: his sketches an' verses they thought so much of had turned to black paper! They each had his picture, they called it, but neither one looked like him, an' that mornin' they had sunk to a little heap of ashes under where they had hung! An' Miss Elizabeth's portrait of him was never as she thought she left it, nor as her sisters thought it looked, but it was like him as I saw him, only it had no eyes!

"If ye'll believe it each one showed me that night a fine necklace the strange man had given her, a secret from the others. It was good as a play to see them comin', one after the other, on the same errand. Poor dears! Bless us and save us! – don't move your chair with such a sudden noise, it makes me jump; an' *don't* kape lookin' behind ye! Miss Charlotte's was coral, all carved into little imps; Miss Elizabeth's was like great coals of fire – carbuncles, she said 'twas; an' Miss Katharine's was like little red sparks – rubies, she called them, an' said it must have cost a great deal of money. But next mornin' their bureau drawers, where they kept their fine things, held no necklaces – nothin' but a heap of dead leaves, an' dust, an' pebbles!

"No, it was only a red line round the throat each wore for a chain at daylight. Dead, then? Dead as Pharaoh!

"Yes, he was gone, an' they will not find him, either; though the police an' reporters call me a crazy old woman to doubt it, but I'm sure they'll have their trouble for their pains. Where is he? The Divil knows!"

Graveyards Full

Maxx Fidalgo

The shadows have fallen, and they wait for the day.
Inscription on Fall River's Oak Grove Cemetery gates

THE PRIEST won't do it.

Teresa has had her wife's body held at the coroner's office, cooling in a freezer, for the past two days since her suicide. It's not that she disagrees with the statement – Kira was severely obsessive compulsive and depressed. The news had been in the papers since it happened, and everyone knew. It was a suicide. Teresa was a widow at 35 and her wife had rather been dead than continue living trapped in her own mind. So of course, the priest from the big cathedral in the city won't do it.

Teresa had never stood a chance.

Father Macedo rubs his forehead and frowns. He can't be much older than her. His eyes are dark and tired, his brown skin the same shade as hers but covered in stress lines. Teresa and Kira had been coming to this church since either of them could remember. They had met in the city's cathedral. For a catholic church, it was quite liberal – but then again, they were in Massachusetts; it would be. But this was one thing that Father Macedo couldn't be liberal about. A married lesbian couple joining the parish? No problem. One of them committing suicide and the surviving partner asking for the priest to preside over her funeral? Not so much.

"I'm sorry, Teresa," he says, and she can see that he *is* sorry. "I can't. I could try to write to the bishop about it, but…" Both knew that wouldn't get either of them very far. "I'm so, so sorry. If there's anything else you need, you know I'm here for you. We all are."

I need you to set her soul to rest, Teresa thinks bitterly, but she forces a smile and takes her leave, brushing off his offer of a coffee date in the coming weeks. To be honest, she wants to lock herself in the confessional and pour out her soul to him, but she has arrangements to finish making. And besides, how could she ever look Father Macedo in the eye if he knew exactly what she was feeling? There was no anguish, no grief, only frustration that no one would help, just as no one had helped when Kira was still alive *to be* helped. Teresa had seen the suicide coming, had tried warning their family members and friends, at least the ones that were left. No one had listened, and Teresa hadn't been strong enough to do it on her own.

She misses Kira so much it feels as if she has been gutted. But Teresa has been feeling this way for at least a year now, as she watched Kira drift away from her, emotionally, mentally, and now, finally, physically.

She is leaving the cathedral, thoughts somewhere else, when she feels a hand grip her elbow. Instinct tells her to smash her fist into whoever's face it is, but she's in a church, and Teresa has always felt safer in churches than anywhere else. Pushing down her violent urge, she turns to find a deacon, judging by his robes. He is around her age, with black skin and curling hair falling into his kind, amber eyes. Teresa doesn't recognize him, but then, the church is always getting new members, of the parish *and* clergy. She looks down to her elbow and raises an eyebrow. He lets go.

"Can I help you?" she asks. There's too much to do with little time to do it in and listening to one more supposed man of God send him her sympathies is not an efficient use of that time.

"Actually, I was thinking I could help you," he responds.

"Well, I've found God, thanks. He just doesn't seem to be in the mood to help me."

The deacon looks conflicted for a moment and then says, "I heard your conversation with Father Macedo." Teresa feels anger flare in her chest and opens her mouth to snap at him, but he continues to speak. "He can't help you."

"*I know,*" she snaps, finally, because if one more man tells her she is alone one more time, she'll lose it. Teresa feels as though she has lost enough.

"But...I think I know someone who can."

* * *

"You said he's not a priest," Teresa says.

She is in her car with the deacon, Brother Landen, giving her directions. They end up in a quiet and remote part of a small town outside the city limits. Landen had only asked her to bring some of Kira's hair and hadn't given her an explanation as to why. But here she was, in a car with a strange man of God, on an eerie autumn day when the sky was grey, the ground was wet, and there was no rain. The wake had been yesterday, and Brother Landen had come to tell her that his mystery helper had accepted her case. It needed to be done before Kira went into the ground.

Whatever *it* was.

"No, he's not," Brother Landen says, pointing out a small, dirt road that led into the woods. Teresa takes the turn, feeling uneasy. She has no idea why she thought this would be a good idea, but she is desperate. If this man says he can help put her wife's soul to rest, then Teresa will go to the ends of the earth to do so. "He's..."

"He's what?"

"Something else."

"Look, I'm putting a lot of faith in you right now. You could at least tell me what the hell he's going to do and why he can do it," she says, hands gripping the steering wheel. "I have a right to know. She's my wife." Teresa stops, shakes her head. "*Was.* She *was* my wife."

"She still is," Brother Landen says in that soft, airy way that spiritual people have. "And I'm not withholding information from you to be secretive; I just don't understand how the mechanism works. But if you want a name for it, the only one I know is sin eater."

"A what now?" Teresa says, slamming the breaks to avoid hitting a wild rabbit, scampering across the road. If one could even call it that. It's dirt and gravel, with potholes full of water even though it hasn't rained in days. The murky puddles reflect the darkening sky and rings spread across their surfaces as the wind picks up. Teresa suppresses a shiver. The car is warm enough. "What the hell is a sin eater?"

"He eats the sins of those deceased. There's a ritual, a legitimate one, I promise you. And the sins of the dead become his own, so they are able to move on to eternal rest."

Teresa thinks about it. She has believed in an invisible God for all her remembered life: the big Man in the sky, with no proof. She has put belief in His virgin baby-mama, His magical demi-God son, saints who have carried out miracles that no living eyes on this earth have seen.

If she can do that for almost four decades of her life, she can do this. If it helps Kira, Teresa thinks she could do anything.

"Okay," she says slowly, continuing to drive. "Then why is he all the way out here?"

"Well, it's not exactly a Catholic ritual now is it?" Brother Landen says with a small smile. "Duarte does what he can for those in need. And he separates himself from those who would punish or stop him for succeeding where they have failed."

She considers the name. "Portuguese?"

"Mhm. Eduardo Lima. Though, he prefers Duarte," Brother Landen responds.

"I'll keep that in mind."

* * *

Brother Landen has Teresa park off the side of the road by a path leading into the woods. He leads her down the path, the wind whipping their coats around them. Teresa buttons up and shoves her hands as deep into her pockets as they'll go. It's an excuse to sneak out her phone and check for a signal. Nothing. It is a perfect setup if anyone is looking to attack her. She stares hard at the back of Brother Landen's neck. What are the odds that this is all an elaborate setup to get her out here alone and then...?

Teresa shakes her head, feeling silly. The bad weather and terrible circumstances that brought her here have gotten to her head. And the atmosphere doesn't help. As it is, she can feel the hair on the back of her neck standing up in anticipation of the coming storm.

It takes a few more minutes, but up ahead, Teresa can see a clearing. The trees part around a dilapidated house. The sky above it seems to suck it up, warping the look of the old wood and making the steeple seem to stretch on forever...

"It's a church," Teresa says, the first words from her mouth in what feels like hours. Brother Landen turns his head and nods over his shoulder, then continues up to the stairs. They too are broken, as though some giant had smashed its feet through the rotting boards. Brother Landen picks his way through them and knocks on the church door when he reaches the top. Teresa stays where she is, apprehensive now that things are finally starting to happen.

"Duarte!" Brother Landon calls as he knocks. His fist knocks dust and moths from the boards. Teresa wonders if anyone really is in there. She grips her useless phone in her pocket hard enough that the edges of her phone case dig painfully into the palms of her hands. Maybe this *had* been a ploy to get her to come out in the middle of nowhere. After all, who the hell actually lived all the way out here in a rundown church doing uncatholic rituals to help people out of the goodness of their heart?

The door opens. From the inside.

"You're late," calls a gruff voice from inside the dark doorway. From the shadows, a man appears, melting out of the blackness. He's bundled into a brown, suede bomber-jacket that has patches on the elbows and is zipped up to his throat. The knees of his jeans are ripped from age and use, and his work boots are frayed at the toes. His hair is thick and dark, and it curls at the nape of his neck. But his eyes are what catch Teresa's attention. They are wide and a murky hazel, set deep in his swarthy face. They land on her and hold her in their gaze for just a moment too long. Teresa looks away first.

"The weather is terrible, and I didn't want our guest to get lost," Brother Landen says, voice warm and bright, as though he isn't staring at a thundercloud of a man. Duarte snorts and shakes his head, plodding down the broken stairs as though they pose no danger to him or his ankles. When he comes to a halt, it's in front of Teresa and with a contemplative look on his face.

He squints at her and his gaze is almost too much before his eyes soften and he reaches out a hand. It's gloved in gray wool with the fingertips snipped off, the edges of the glove fraying around his fingers.

"Eduardo Lima. You can call me Duarte. Just, roll the 'r' in Dua*rr*te or don't say it at all," he says by way of introduction. Teresa hesitates, but she shakes his hand. He's warm.

"Teresa Higurashi."

Duarte quirks a smile. "I'm guessing you took your wife's last name?"

"What gave it away? My obviously practiced pronunciation or the fact that I look too Mexican for Higurashi to be my family name?"

"Neither," Duarte responds. "I read your wife's newspaper obituary." Teresa doesn't answer him, simply drops his hand, and stares.

"You done posturing?" Brother Landen asks, still looking fond. He begins to make his way down the steps, and Duarte walks over to him and offers a hand in support. For a moment, after Brother Landen has both feet safely on the ground, Duarte squeezes his hand a little tighter. But only for a moment. Duarte and Landen let go of each other at the same moment and make their way over to Teresa as though nothing has transpired.

"Shall we?" Duarte asks, and gestures with his head to the wooded area behind the old church. Teresa nods, still a bit confused at the earlier display of affection but wanting to get whatever this is done and over with. She follows Duarte behind the church, Brother Landen following behind her.

They walk into a cemetery. None of the graves are from after 1800, and Teresa is willing to bet that most of them date back to the first settlers of the area. Some headstones must have been pearly white at one point, though now, they are greyed with age and either spotted with lichen or else grown over with moss and brambles. None of the text can be read on any of them. Here and there they sprout from the hard ground like broken teeth in a gaping mouth. The area is large, larger than the ground the church stands on. A small portion of the cemetery is grown over with weeds, trees, and leaves, the woods slowly encroaching on the holy space. The rest of it is pruned and tidied, as far as one can tidy up the dead.

"Duarte keeps the graves and grounds in working order," Brother Landen says.

"I keep them, and they keep me," Duarte replies with a shrug, walking them through a path between the graves. "This way." He points down to the path's end, where it merges back with the creeping woods. Through the trees, Teresa can see a shack or maybe a mausoleum. Closer inspection reveals it to be the former, with a small, enclosed fire before it. Duarte has Teresa and Brother Landen sit by the fire while he disappears into the shack.

"Have you seen him do this before?" Teresa asks Brother Landen. He nods.

"Many times. I've known Duarte for a while now. Back when he tried to go to seminary school," and now, Brother Landen laughs. "It didn't work out. I don't think it would have suited him, anyway."

"Why didn't he stay?" Teresa asks.

"They kicked me out," Duarte says, coming out of the shack with a scratchy looking sack full of hand-ground flour in one hand and a bucket of supplies in the other. He dumps out the bucket, revealing baking supplies like egg, salt, and a canteen of water. Then, he sits by Teresa and begins to measure out flour, throwing it into the now-empty bucket and murmuring words over it, before adding the egg, salt, and water. The concoction looks mealy and unappetizing, more so when Duarte turns to Teresa and asks her for Kira's hair. She hands him the chunk she had cut from Kira's bangs after the wake. Half of it gets sprinkled into the flour mixture while the other half gets tossed into the fire. The smell of burning hair permeates the air as Duarte kneads his mealy dough in his hands, rolls it into a ball, and flattens it out. He places the chunky disk onto a metal plate over the fire and then sits back with a sigh.

"Why did they kick you out?" Teresa asks. Duarte scratches his nose as he wipes his hands on his pants, making Brother Landen grimace.

"I have opinions that differ from the Church's. Obviously, or I wouldn't be here." He stares into the fire. "I was different. And then, of course, they found out I was trans." Teresa bites her lip to hide her shock. Most trans people she knew didn't just out themselves so casually. Duarte was older than she was though, and probably not one for beating around the bush anymore. "My superiors thought it would be best to let me go after that. They didn't cite that as their reason though, too messy. Instead, they used sin eating against me. Said it was against the Church's practices, which…well, they're not wrong." He looks up at her with tired, dark eyes. "I'm guessing you don't care as much if you're here anyway."

"I just want her to find some peace," Teresa says. The sky is getting darker and Teresa thinks she hears thunder in the distance. Here she is, a Mexican lesbian sitting by a cemetery in the woods with a black deacon and a transgender, Portuguese heathen. She could make a bad joke about this. "That's all."

"Mmm," Duarte says, watching his small doughy loaf harden under the heat of the fire. "Don't we all?"

"How does it work?" Teresa asks, staring into the red and orange of the fire instead of at Duarte.

"The prayer I said while making the bread with her hair? It opens her soul to me, let's me see her sins. I take the greatest ones, so she can move on unencumbered."

"Isn't that cheating?" Teresa asks.

"In the sense that only a priest is supposed to be able to forgive sins? Yes, I suppose so," Brother Landen chimes in. "But sometimes, you have to wonder how they choose who to forgive and who to let suffer. Especially in cases such as these when there are rules so blatantly against those who are suffering."

"It's almost like it was done on purpose," Duarte snorts, voice heavy with sarcasm. "Imagine that. The Church, biased."

"Perish the thought," Brother Landen responds with a small grin, and Teresa feels as though she's intruding again.

"Does it really work?" Teresa asks with a small voice. She wonders if Duarte can hear her or if her voice has been snatched away by the intensifying wind.

When she looks up again, Duarte has his soft eyes on her. "It does. You'll have to put your faith in me, but then, you've been doing that with God up until now. Even He needs a break from the expectations of humanity."

"Can you prove it?" Teresa asks, wondering why all her reservations are coming up now, when she is so close to her goal.

"I can tell you her greatest mortal sin, yes," Duarte says, hunching into his coat against the gathering cold.

"How?"

"Because at that point, it'll be *my* sin."

Teresa chokes on her next breath. "What?"

"That's how sin eating works. I'm literally eating Kira's sins; that means my body, *my soul* absorbs them as though they were my own from the start," Duarte says, poking at the crusty loaf with a stick. He must decide it isn't ready because he puts the stick down and leaves the bread be.

"But...but why? Why do you do this? That sin – she—"

"I know the gist of it," Duarte says, waving her off with a hand in her direction. *But you're still going to do it*, Teresa thinks, the guilt eating away at her. This will tarnish Duarte's soul, for good. Forever. And he's still going to do it. How could she ask that of him? This is not what Kira would have wanted, Teresa thinks. But then, what *did* Kira want, if not rest?

"I can't ask you to do this," Teresa says, feeling tears well in her eyes. She wants this so bad, but she knows how wrong it is. To ask a fellow human to do something like this...

"I know," he says, and Teresa's head snaps up. "And you didn't ask. I offered. Through Landen, of course, but I still offered."

"Why?" Teresa asks, wiping her face with the backs of her hands.

"Because no one else will," Duarte answers. "My grandmother had it, and my mother inherited it. And then I came." Now he smiles a bit. But the smile slides off his face, and he checks the loaf. Almost. "The talent never went away. And after my stunt with the Church, I thought, why not? I wanted to be a priest to help people, to be a spiritual comfort to those in need. I can still do that."

"I don't think I understand," Teresa protests. "Your soul..."

"Yes, well. If the Bible is right, then I'm going to hell anyway. So, what's the problem with a few more dark marks?" He rubs his face, then looks up at the grim sky. He closes his eyes. "Someone can make it to heaven this way. Even if it's not me."

"Duarte," Teresa starts.

"I don't want people to be afraid of God, Teresa. Sometimes, by making a different path to him, I feel like I'm making that possible."

Duarte doesn't wait for her to answer him, just leans over, and slides the loaf off the pan. The burning hot bread doesn't seem to bother him; he just sets it on his lap and lets it cool off. To the side, Brother Landen is watching Duarte with wide eyes, tinged with such sadness. Teresa wants to take it all back as much as she wants him to eat that bread and set her wife free. She sits, high strung with indecision, knowing she won't stop him. If he is choosing this for himself, for whatever reasons he has, she is going to let him. God help her, but she's going to let him.

Duarte lets out a deep breath and lifts the still-steaming bread to his mouth, murmuring words that are old and too low for Teresa to hear properly. Her skin draws tight against her body and the hairs on her neck stand up in anticipation. The air feels charged, as though a lightning strike is coming, but Duarte doesn't move and neither does Brother Landen, so Teresa stays still. Shadows have fallen all around them, and Teresa can't remember if they were there moments before, but she is afraid. *Something* is there with them. *Something* is around them. There is an unmistakable inhuman energy around them, and it is not evil, but it *is* powerful. Duarte continues to murmur under his breath until suddenly his eyes flutter open and he shoves the whole loaf into his mouth without breathing. He chews and swallows faster than Teresa thought possible with bread that flat and dry. She opens eyes she hadn't realized were closed and is greeted by Duarte with bloodshot eyes and a slack-jawed face, tongue lolling out of his mouth as his chest convulses. Teresa wants to close her eyes, but she cannot look away. There is something so terrible yet so captivating about his suffering.

And suddenly, it's over. Duarte's eyes roll back into his head, and he says something she cannot understand. But the next time he opens his eyes, they're that same soft hazel, with a deep sadness and an even deeper hurt inside of them that is not his own. She knows.

She knows the truth of his actions. Kira had looked at her with those eyes for months before Teresa had walked into an empty, quiet house and had known something horrible had taken place moments before she had entered.

Duarte blinks a few times and the look is gone.

"I'm so sorry," he murmurs, rubbing his face and wiping his mouth. On the other side of the fire, Brother Landen stands. He walks over to Duarte and kneels beside him, helping him drink from a water bottle he had pulled from his robes. The palm of his hand cradles the back of Duarte's head, and Teresa looks away, hiding her own tears. "She was suffering, and she didn't know what else to do."

"I know," Teresa says, trying not to sob. She *does* know but hearing someone else say it with the same conviction is as validating as it is painful.

"I doubt you still have them, but if the pills are still in the house, toss them. I don't think she wanted them there in the first place," Duarte says, and it takes Teresa's breath away. Because she knew, objectively, that *something* had happened, that it was legitimate, and she could accept that Duarte had done something for both her and Kira in doing so. But this, the information that not even the newspapers had been allowed to print, information that Brother Landen didn't know either...*He must have seen it happen*, Teresa thinks. *As though it were happening to him.* This man had seen death for Teresa and her wife.

"Take this," Teresa says, digging around for her wallet and the money she put inside of it, specifically for this. She doesn't think the obscene amount she is about to hand over is close to being enough, but it's a start.

"I don't take payment," Duarte says, squeezing Brother Landen's shoulder before hoisting himself off the ground.

"I need to do *something*," Teresa says, aware of how desperate she sounds.

"Pray for me," Duarte says with a smile. But there's a hint of honesty behind it, of fear. "Just pray for me and my soul, Teresa." He dusts off the seat of his pants. "Trust me. By the end of all this, I'm gonna need it."

Above their heads, the sky cracks open with a flash of lightning and a clap of thunder.

"*Finally*," Duarte breathes, and turns his face up into the rain.

* * *

Teresa parks in front of the cathedral. Attached to it is a small enclave for the priests in training, the deacons, and the nuns of the parish. For a moment, she and Brother Landen sit in the car in silence, listening to the rain pattering on the windshield. Parts of her feel numb, but still other parts are just warming up and coming back to life. There is an honest sense of peace to her soul, and whatever unrest she had feared for Kira was gone now. She wonders at the price but starts to realize that she is the last person who gets to decide what Duarte does with his knowledge.

"He's going to Hell, isn't he?" she asks Brother Landen.

"Not if I can help it," Brother Landen snarls. Teresa starts in surprise. Until now, he had been so calm and quiet, collected and thoughtful. It's all still there, but there is genuine anger and determination in his eyes. "I will be ordained one day, and I will be by that man's side on his deathbed to absolve him of any and all sins he may be carrying from others. They can take my cassock after that for all I care. They won't be unable to undo the forgiveness that I would have bestowed upon him before the Lord takes him."

"You care about him," Teresa says, voice soft but not accusatory, as she feared it might sound. She puts a hand on his shoulder and squeezes. The support is all she has to offer.

"I had to choose between a life with him outside the Church but his soul being damned or a life without him but being able to absolve him. I chose the latter. He has offered to keep my heart safe in his hands and I…would love to agree. But it is that love that spurs me to continue in my religious studies so that one day I too may save him as he has saved me and countless others." He turns in his seat, eyes beseeching and searching for understanding. Something about it all reminds Teresa of Kira. She nods.

"Alright," she says, though she has no idea what she is agreeing to.

"Thank you," he responds. His face changes then, ready to take on his fellow acolytes. "Have a good night, Mrs. Higurashi. I hope to see you at mass this Sunday." Teresa nods. She has a lot to thank God for. "And in the meantime? I think we could all use a little prayer."

As Teresa pulls away, she thinks to herself that praying is the least she can do.

Luella Miller

Mary E. Wilkins Freeman

CLOSE TO the village street stood the one-story house in which Luella Miller, who had an evil name in the village, had dwelt. She had been dead for years, yet there were those in the village who, in spite of the clearer light which comes on a vantage-point from a long-past danger, half believed in the tale which they had heard from their childhood. In their hearts, although they scarcely would have owned it, was a survival of the wild horror and frenzied fear of their ancestors who had dwelt in the same age with Luella Miller. Young people even would stare with a shudder at the old house as they passed, and children never played around it as was their wont around an untenanted building. Not a window in the old Miller house was broken: the panes reflected the morning sunlight in patches of emerald and blue, and the latch of the sagging front door was never lifted, although no bolt secured it. Since Luella Miller had been carried out of it, the house had had no tenant except one friendless old soul who had no choice between that and the far-off shelter of the open sky. This old woman, who had survived her kindred and friends, lived in the house one week, then one morning no smoke came out of the chimney, and a body of neighbors, a score strong, entered and found her dead in her bed. There were dark whispers as to the cause of her death, and there were those who testified to an expression of fear so exalted that it showed forth the state of the departing soul upon the dead face. The old woman had been hale and hearty when she entered the house, and in seven days she was dead; it seemed that she had fallen a victim to some uncanny power. The minister talked in the pulpit with covert severity against the sin of superstition; still the belief prevailed. Not a soul in the village but would have chosen the almshouse rather than that dwelling. No vagrant, if he heard the tale, would seek shelter beneath that old roof, unhallowed by nearly half a century of superstitious fear.

There was only one person in the village who had actually known Luella Miller. That person was a woman well over eighty, but a marvel of vitality and unextinct youth. Straight as an arrow, with the spring of one recently let loose from the bow of life, she moved about the streets, and she always went to church, rain or shine. She had never married, and had lived alone for years in a house across the road from Luella Miller's.

This woman had none of the garrulousness of age, but never in all her life had she ever held her tongue for any will save her own, and she never spared the truth when she essayed to present it. She it was who bore testimony to the life, evil, though possibly wittingly or designedly so, of Luella Miller, and to her personal appearance. When this old woman spoke – and she had the gift of description, although her thoughts were clothed in the rude vernacular of her native village – one could seem to see Luella Miller as she had really looked. According to this woman, Lydia Anderson by name, Luella Miller had been a beauty of a type rather unusual in New England. She had been a slight, pliant sort of creature, as ready with a strong yielding to fate and as unbreakable as a willow. She had glimmering lengths of straight, fair hair, which she wore softly looped round a long, lovely face. She had blue eyes full of soft pleading, little slender, clinging hands, and a wonderful grace of motion and attitude.

"Luella Miller used to sit in a way nobody else could if they sat up and studied a week of Sundays," said Lydia Anderson, "and it was a sight to see her walk. If one of them willows over there on the edge of the brook could start up and get its roots free of the ground, and move off, it would go just the way Luella Miller used to. She had a green shot silk she used to wear, too, and a hat with green ribbon streamers, and a lace veil blowing across her face and out sideways, and a green ribbon flyin' from her waist. That was what she came out bride in when she married Erastus Miller. Her name before she was married was Hill. There was always a sight of 'l's' in her name, married or single. Erastus Miller was good lookin', too, better lookin' than Luella. Sometimes I used to think that Luella wa'n't so handsome after all. Erastus just about worshiped her. I used to know him pretty well. He lived next door to me, and we went to school together. Folks used to say he was waitin' on me, but he wa'n't. I never thought he was except once or twice when he said things that some girls might have suspected meant somethin'. That was before Luella came here to teach the district school. It was funny how she came to get it, for folks said she hadn't any education, and that one of the big girls, Lottie Henderson, used to do all the teachin' for her, while she sat back and did embroidery work on a cambric pocket-handkerchief. Lottie Henderson was a real smart girl, a splendid scholar, and she just set her eyes by Luella, as all the girls did. Lottie would have made a real smart woman, but she died when Luella had been here about a year – just faded away and died: nobody knew what ailed her. She dragged herself to that schoolhouse and helped Luella teach till the very last minute. The committee all knew how Luella didn't do much of the work herself, but they winked at it. It wa'n't long after Lottie died that Erastus married her. I always thought he hurried it up because she wa'n't fit to teach. One of the big boys used to help her after Lottie died, but he hadn't much government, and the school didn't do very well, and Luella might have had to give it up, for the committee couldn't have shut their eyes to things much longer. The boy that helped her was a real honest, innocent sort of fellow, and he was a good scholar, too. Folks said he overstudied, and that was the reason he was took crazy the year after Luella married, but I don't know. And I don't know what made Erastus Miller go into consumption of the blood the year after he was married: consumption wa'n't in his family. He just grew weaker and weaker, and went almost bent double when he tried to wait on Luella, and he spoke feeble, like an old man. He worked terrible hard till the last trying to save up a little to leave Luella. I've seen him out in the worst storms on a wood-sled – he used to cut and sell wood – and he was hunched up on top lookin' more dead than alive. Once I couldn't stand it: I went over and helped him pitch some wood on the cart – I was always strong in my arms. I wouldn't stop for all he told me to, and I guess he was glad enough for the help. That was only a week before he died. He fell on the kitchen floor while he was gettin' breakfast. He always got the breakfast and let Luella lay abed. He did all the sweepin' and the washin' and the ironin' and most of the cookin'. He couldn't bear to have Luella lift her finger, and she let him do for her. She lived like a queen for all the work she did. She didn't even do her sewin'. She said it made her shoulder ache to sew, and poor Erastus's sister Lily used to do all her sewin'. She wa'n't able to, either; she was never strong in her back, but she did it beautifully. She had to, to suit Luella, she was so dreadful particular. I never saw anythin' like the fagottin' and hemstitchin' that Lily Miller did for Luella. She made all Luella's weddin' outfit, and that green silk dress, after Maria Babbit cut it. Maria she cut it for nothin', and she did a lot more cuttin' and fittin' for nothin' for Luella, too. Lily Miller went to live with Luella after Erastus died. She gave up her home, though she was real attached to it and wa'n't a mite afraid to stay alone. She rented it and she went to live with Luella right away after the funeral."

Then this old woman, Lydia Anderson, who remembered Luella Miller, would go on to relate the story of Lily Miller. It seemed that on the removal of Lily Miller to the house of her dead brother, to live with his widow, the village people first began to talk. This Lily Miller had been hardly past her first youth, and a most robust and blooming woman, rosy-cheeked, with curls of strong, black hair overshadowing round, candid temples and bright dark eyes. It was not six months after she had taken up her residence with her sister-in-law that her rosy color faded and her pretty curves became wan hollows. White shadows began to show in the black rings of her hair, and the light died out of her eyes, her features sharpened, and there were pathetic lines at her mouth, which yet wore always an expression of utter sweetness and even happiness. She was devoted to her sister; there was no doubt that she loved her with her whole heart, and was perfectly content in her service. It was her sole anxiety lest she should die and leave her alone.

"The way Lily Miller used to talk about Luella was enough to make you mad and enough to make you cry," said Lydia Anderson. "I've been in there sometimes toward the last when she was too feeble to cook and carried her some blancmange or custard – somethin' I thought she might relish, and she'd thank me, and when I asked her how she was, say she felt better than she did yesterday, and asked me if I didn't think she looked better, dreadful pitiful, and say poor Luella had an awful time takin' care of her and doin' the work – she wa'n't strong enough to do anythin' – when all the time Luella wa'n't liftin' her finger and poor Lily didn't get any care except what the neighbors gave her, and Luella eat up everythin' that was carried in for Lily. I had it real straight that she did. Luella used to just sit and cry and do nothin'. She did act real fond of Lily, and she pined away considerable, too. There was those that thought she'd go into a decline herself. But after Lily died, her Aunt Abby Mixter came, and then Luella picked up and grew as fat and rosy as ever. But poor Aunt Abby begun to droop just the way Lily had, and I guess somebody wrote to her married daughter, Mrs. Sam Abbot, who lived in Barre, for she wrote her mother that she must leave right away and come and make her a visit, but Aunt Abby wouldn't go. I can see her now. She was a real good-lookin' woman, tall and large, with a big, square face and a high forehead that looked of itself kind of benevolent and good. She just tended out on Luella as if she had been a baby, and when her married daughter sent for her she wouldn't stir one inch. She'd always thought a lot of her daughter, too, but she said Luella needed her and her married daughter didn't. Her daughter kept writin' and writin', but it didn't do any good. Finally she came, and when she saw how bad her mother looked, she broke down and cried and all but went on her knees to have her come away. She spoke her mind out to Luella, too. She told her that she'd killed her husband and everybody that had anythin' to do with her, and she'd thank her to leave her mother alone. Luella went into hysterics, and Aunt Abby was so frightened that she called me after her daughter went. Mrs. Sam Abbot she went away fairly cryin' out loud in the buggy, the neighbors heard her, and well she might, for she never saw her mother again alive. I went in that night when Aunt Abby called for me, standin' in the door with her little green-checked shawl over her head. I can see her now. 'Do come over here, Miss Anderson,' she sung out, kind of gasping for breath. I didn't stop for anythin'. I put over as fast as I could, and when I got there, there was Luella laughin' and cryin' all together, and Aunt Abby trying to hush her, and all the time she herself was white as a sheet and shakin' so she could hardly stand. 'For the land sakes, Mrs. Mixter,' says I, 'you look worse than she does. You ain't fit to be up out of your bed.'

"'Oh, there ain't anythin' the matter with me,' says she. Then she went on talkin' to Luella. 'There, there, don't, don't, poor little lamb,' says she. 'Aunt Abby is here. She ain't goin' away and leave you. Don't, poor little lamb.'

"'Do leave her with me, Mrs. Mixter, and you get back to bed,' says I, for Aunt Abby had been layin' down considerable lately, though somehow she contrived to do the work.

"'I'm well enough,' says she. 'Don't you think she had better have the doctor, Miss Anderson?'

"'The doctor,' says I, 'I think *you* had better have the doctor. I think you need him much worse than some folks I could mention.' And I looked right straight at Luella Miller laughin' and cryin' and goin' on as if she was the center of all creation. All the time she was actin' so – seemed as if she was too sick to sense anythin' – she was keepin' a sharp lookout as to how we took it out of the corner of one eye. I see her. You could never cheat me about Luella Miller. Finally I got real mad and I run home and I got a bottle of valerian I had, and I poured some boilin' hot water on a handful of catnip, and I mixed up that catnip tea with most half a wineglass of valerian, and I went with it over to Luella's. I marched right up to Luella, a-holdin' out of that cup, all smokin'. 'Now,' says I, 'Luella Miller, 'YOU SWALLER THIS!'

"'What is – what is it, oh, what is it?' she sort of screeches out. Then she goes off a-laughin' enough to kill.

"'Poor lamb, poor little lamb,' says Aunt Abby, standin' over her, all kind of tottery, and tryin' to bathe her head with camphor.

"'YOU SWALLER THIS RIGHT DOWN,' says I. And I didn't waste any ceremony. I just took hold of Luella Miller's chin and I tipped her head back, and I caught her mouth open with laughin', and I clapped that cup to her lips, and I fairly hollered at her: 'Swaller, swaller, swaller!' and she gulped it right down. She had to, and I guess it did her good. Anyhow, she stopped cryin' and laughin' and let me put her to bed, and she went to sleep like a baby inside of half an hour. That was more than poor Aunt Abby did. She lay awake all that night and I stayed with her, though she tried not to have me; said she wa'n't sick enough for watchers. But I stayed, and I made some good cornmeal gruel and I fed her a teaspoon every little while all night long. It seemed to me as if she was jest dyin' from bein' all wore out. In the mornin' as soon as it was light I run over to the Bisbees and sent Johnny Bisbee for the doctor. I told him to tell the doctor to hurry, and he come pretty quick. Poor Aunt Abby didn't seem to know much of anythin' when he got there. You couldn't hardly tell she breathed, she was so used up. When the doctor had gone, Luella came into the room lookin' like a baby in her ruffled nightgown. I can see her now. Her eyes were as blue and her face all pink and white like a blossom, and she looked at Aunt Abby in the bed sort of innocent and surprised. 'Why,' says she, 'Aunt Abby ain't got up yet?'

"'No, she ain't,' says I, pretty short.

"'I thought I didn't smell the coffee,' says Luella.

"'Coffee,' says I. 'I guess if you have coffee this mornin' you'll make it yourself.'

"'I never made the coffee in all my life,' says she, dreadful astonished. 'Erastus always made the coffee as long as he lived, and then Lily she made it, and then Aunt Abby made it. I don't believe I *can* make the coffee, Miss Anderson.'

"'You can make it or go without, jest as you please,' says I.

"'Ain't Aunt Abby goin' to get up?' says she.

"'I guess she won't get up,' says I, 'sick as she is.' I was gettin' madder and madder. There was somethin' about that little pink-and-white thing standin' there and talkin' about coffee, when she had killed so many better folks than she was, and had jest killed another, that made me feel 'most as if I wished somebody would up and kill her before she had a chance to do any more harm.

"'Is Aunt Abby sick?' says Luella, as if she was sort of aggrieved and injured.

"'Yes,' says I, 'she's sick, and she's goin' to die, and then you'll be left alone, and you'll have to do for yourself and wait on yourself, or do without things.' I don't know but I was sort of hard, but it was the truth, and if I was any harder than Luella Miller had been I'll give up. I ain't never been sorry that I said it. Well, Luella, she up and had hysterics again at that, and I jest let her have 'em. All I did was to bundle her into the room on the other side of the entry where Aunt Abby couldn't hear her, if she wa'n't past it – I don't know but she was – and set her down hard in a chair and told her not to come back into the other room, and she minded. She had her hysterics in there till she got tired. When she found out that nobody was comin' to coddle her and do for her she stopped. At least I suppose she did. I had all I could do with poor Aunt Abby tryin' to keep the breath of life in her. The doctor had told me that she was dreadful low, and give me some very strong medicine to give to her in drops real often, and told me real particular about the nourishment. Well, I did as he told me real faithful till she wa'n't able to swaller any longer. Then I had her daughter sent for. I had begun to realize that she wouldn't last any time at all. I hadn't realized it before, though I spoke to Luella the way I did. The doctor he came, and Mrs. Sam Abbot, but when she got there it was too late; her mother was dead. Aunt Abby's daughter just give one look at her mother layin' there, then she turned sort of sharp and sudden and looked at me.

"'Where is she?' says she, and I knew she meant Luella.

"'She's out in the kitchen,' says I. 'She's too nervous to see folks die. She's afraid it will make her sick.'

"The Doctor he speaks up then. He was a young man. Old Doctor Park had died the year before, and this was a young fellow just out of college. 'Mrs. Miller is not strong,' says he, kind of severe, 'and she is quite right in not agitating herself.'

"'You are another young man; she's got her pretty claw on you,' thinks I, but I didn't say anythin' to him. I just said over to Mrs. Sam Abbot that Luella was in the kitchen, and Mrs. Sam Abbot she went out there, and I went, too, and I never heard anythin' like the way she talked to Luella Miller. I felt pretty hard to Luella myself, but this was more than I ever would have dared to say. Luella she was too scared to go into hysterics. She jest flopped. She seemed to jest shrink away to nothin' in that kitchen chair, with Mrs. Sam Abbot standin' over her and talkin' and tellin' her the truth. I guess the truth was most too much for her and no mistake, because Luella presently actually did faint away, and there wa'n't any sham about it, the way I always suspected there was about them hysterics. She fainted dead away and we had to lay her flat on the floor, and the Doctor he came runnin' out and he said somethin' about a weak heart dreadful fierce to Mrs. Sam Abbot, but she wa'n't a mite scared. She faced him jest as white as even Luella was layin' there lookin' like death and the Doctor feelin' of her pulse.

"'Weak heart,' says she, 'weak heart; weak fiddlesticks! There ain't nothin' weak about that woman. She's got strength enough to hang onto other folks till she kills 'em. Weak? It was my poor mother that was weak: this woman killed her as sure as if she had taken a knife to her.'

"But the Doctor he didn't pay much attention. He was bendin' over Luella layin' there with her yellow hair all streamin' and her pretty pink-and-white face all pale, and her blue eyes like stars gone out, and he was holdin' onto her hand and smoothin' her forehead, and tellin' me to get the brandy in Aunt Abby's room, and I was sure as I wanted to be that Luella had got somebody else to hang onto, now Aunt Abby was gone, and I thought of poor Erastus Miller, and I sort of pitied the poor young Doctor, led away by a pretty face, and I made up my mind I'd see what I could do.

"I waited till Aunt Abby had been dead and buried about a month, and the Doctor was goin' to see Luella steady and folks were beginnin' to talk; then one evenin', when I knew the Doctor had been called out of town and wouldn't be round, I went over to Luella's. I found her all dressed up in a blue muslin with white polka dots on it, and her hair curled jest as pretty, and there wa'n't a young girl in the place could compare with her. There was somethin' about Luella Miller seemed to draw the heart right out of you, but she didn't draw it out of *me*. She was settin' rocking in the chair by her sittin'-room window, and Maria Brown had gone home. Maria Brown had been in to help her, or rather to do the work, for Luella wa'n't helped when she didn't do anythin'. Maria Brown was real capable and she didn't have any ties; she wa'n't married, and lived alone, so she'd offered. I couldn't see why she should do the work any more than Luella; she wa'n't any too strong; but she seemed to think she could and Luella seemed to think so, too, so she went over and did all the work – washed, and ironed, and baked, while Luella sat and rocked. Maria didn't live long afterward. She began to fade away just the same fashion the others had. Well, she was warned, but she acted real mad when folks said anythin': said Luella was a poor, abused woman, too delicate to help herself, and they'd ought to be ashamed, and if she died helpin' them that couldn't help themselves she would – and she did.

"'I s'pose Maria has gone home,' says I to Luella, when I had gone in and sat down opposite her.

"'Yes, Maria went half an hour ago, after she had got supper and washed the dishes,' says Luella, in her pretty way.

"'I suppose she has got a lot of work to do in her own house tonight,' says I, kind of bitter, but that was all thrown away on Luella Miller. It seemed to her right that other folks that wa'n't any better able than she was herself should wait on her, and she couldn't get it through her head that anybody should think it *wa'n't* right.

"'Yes,' says Luella, real sweet and pretty, 'yes, she said she had to do her washin' tonight. She has let it go for a fortnight along of comin' over here.'

"'Why don't she stay home and do her washin' instead of comin' over here and doin' *your* work, when you are just as well able, and enough sight more so, than she is to do it?' says I.

"Then Luella she looked at me like a baby who has a rattle shook at it. She sort of laughed as innocent as you please. 'Oh, I can't do the work myself, Miss Anderson,' says she. 'I never did. Maria *has* to do it.'

"Then I spoke out: 'Has to do it I' says I. 'Has to do it!' She don't have to do it, either. Maria Brown has her own home and enough to live on. She ain't beholden to you to come over here and slave for you and kill herself.'

"Luella she jest set and stared at me for all the world like a doll-baby that was so abused that it was comin' to life.

"'Yes,' says I, 'she's killin' herself. She's goin' to die just the way Erastus did, and Lily, and your Aunt Abby. You're killin' her jest as you did them. I don't know what there is about you, but you seem to bring a curse,' says I. 'You kill everybody that is fool enough to care anythin' about you and do for you.'

"She stared at me and she was pretty pale.

"'And Maria ain't the only one you're goin' to kill,' says I. 'You're goin' to kill Doctor Malcom before you're done with him.'

"Then a red color came flamin' all over her face. 'I ain't goin' to kill him, either,' says she, and she begun to cry.

"'Yes, you *be*!' says I. Then I spoke as I had never spoke before. You see, I felt it on account of Erastus. I told her that she hadn't any business to think of another man after she'd been married to one that had died for her: that she was a dreadful woman; and she was, that's true enough, but sometimes I have wondered lately if she knew it – if she wa'n't like a baby with scissors in its hand cuttin' everybody without knowin' what it was doin'.

"Luella she kept gettin' paler and paler, and she never took her eyes off my face. There was somethin' awful about the way she looked at me and never spoke one word. After awhile I quit talkin' and I went home. I watched that night, but her lamp went out before nine o'clock, and when Doctor Malcom came drivin' past and sort of slowed up he see there wa'n't any light and he drove along. I saw her sort of shy out of meetin' the next Sunday, too, so he shouldn't go home with her, and I begun to think mebbe she did have some conscience after all. It was only a week after that that Maria Brown died – sort of sudden at the last, though everybody had seen it was comin'. Well, then there was a good deal of feelin' and pretty dark whispers. Folks said the days of witchcraft had come again, and they were pretty shy of Luella. She acted sort of offish to the Doctor and he didn't go there, and there wa'n't anybody to do anythin' for her. I don't know how she *did* get along. I wouldn't go in there and offer to help her – not because I was afraid of dyin' like the rest, but I thought she was just as well able to do her own work as I was to do it for her, and I thought it was about time that she did it and stopped killin' other folks. But it wa'n't very long before folks began to say that Luella herself was goin' into a decline jest the way her husband, and Lily, and Aunt Abby and the others had, and I saw myself that she looked pretty bad. I used to see her goin' past from the store with a bundle as if she could hardly crawl, but I remembered how Erastus used to wait and 'tend when he couldn't hardly put one foot before the other, and I didn't go out to help her.

"But at last one afternoon I saw the Doctor come drivin' up like mad with his medicine chest, and Mrs. Babbit came in after supper and said that Luella was real sick.

"'I'd offer to go in and nurse her,' says she, 'but I've got my children to consider, and mebbe it ain't true what they say, but it's queer how many folks that have done for her have died.'

"I didn't say anythin', but I considered how she had been Erastus's wife and how he had set his eyes by her, and I made up my mind to go in the next mornin', unless she was better, and see what I could do; but the next mornin' I see her at the window, and pretty soon she came steppin' out as spry as you please, and a little while afterward Mrs. Babbit came in and told me that the Doctor had got a girl from out of town, a Sarah Jones, to come there, and she said she was pretty sure that the Doctor was goin' to marry Luella.

"I saw him kiss her in the door that night myself, and I knew it was true. The woman came that afternoon, and the way she flew around was a caution. I don't believe Luella had swept since Maria died. She swept and dusted, and washed and ironed; wet clothes and dusters and carpets were flyin' over there all day, and every time Luella set her foot out when the Doctor wa'n't there there was that Sarah Jones helpin' of her up and down the steps, as if she hadn't learned to walk.

"Well, everybody knew that Luella and the Doctor were goin' to be married, but it wa'n't long before they began to talk about his lookin' so poorly, jest as they had about the others; and they talked about Sarah Jones, too.

"Well, the Doctor did die, and he wanted to be married first, so as to leave what little he had to Luella, but he died before the minister could get there, and Sarah Jones died a week afterward.

"Well, that wound up everything for Luella Miller. Not another soul in the whole town would lift a finger for her. There got to be a sort of panic. Then she began to droop in good earnest. She used to have to go to the store herself, for Mrs. Babbit was afraid to let Tommy go for her, and I've seen her goin' past and stoppin' every two or three steps to rest. Well, I stood it as long as I could, but one day I see her comin' with her arms full and stoppin' to lean against the Babbit fence, and I run out and took her bundles and carried them to her house. Then I went home and never spoke one word to her though she called after me dreadful kind of pitiful. Well, that night I was taken sick with a chill, and I was sick as I wanted to be for two weeks. Mrs. Babbit had seen me run out to help Luella and she came in and told me I was goin' to die on account of it. I didn't know whether I was or not, but I considered I had done right by Erastus's wife.

"That last two weeks Luella she had a dreadful hard time, I guess. She was pretty sick, and as near as I could make out nobody dared go near her. I don't know as she was really needin' anythin' very much, for there was enough to eat in her house and it was warm weather, and she made out to cook a little flour gruel every day, I know, but I guess she had a hard time, she that had been so petted and done for all her life.

"When I got so I could go out, I went over there one morning. Mrs. Babbit had just come in to say she hadn't seen any smoke and she didn't know but it was somebody's duty to go in, but she couldn't help thinkin' of her children, and I got right up, though I hadn't been out of the house for two weeks, and I went in there, and Luella she was layin' on the bed, and she was dyin'.

"She lasted all that day and into the night. But I sat there after the new doctor had gone away. Nobody else dared to go there. It was about midnight that I left her for a minute to run home and get some medicine I had been takin', for I begun to feel rather bad.

"It was a full moon that night, and just as I started out of my door to cross the street back to Luella's, I stopped short, for I saw something."

Lydia Anderson at this juncture always said with a certain defiance that she did not expect to be believed, and then proceeded in a hushed voice:

"I saw what I saw, and I know I saw it, and I will swear on my death bed that I saw it. I saw Luella Miller and Erastus Miller, and Lily, and Aunt Abby, and Maria, and the Doctor, and Sarah, all goin' out of her door, and all but Luella shone white in the moonlight, and they were all helpin' her along till she seemed to fairly fly in the midst of them. Then it all disappeared. I stood a minute with my heart poundin', then I went over there. I thought of goin' for Mrs. Babbit, but I thought she'd be afraid. So I went alone, though I knew what had happened. Luella was layin' real peaceful, dead on her bed."

This was the story that the old woman, Lydia Anderson, told, but the sequel was told by the people who survived her, and this is the tale which has become folklore in the village.

Lydia Anderson died when she was eighty-seven. She had continued wonderfully hale and hearty for one of her years until about two weeks before her death.

One bright moonlight evening she was sitting beside a window in her parlor when she made a sudden exclamation, and was out of the house and across the street before the neighbor who was taking care of her could stop her. She followed as fast as possible and found Lydia Anderson stretched on the ground before the door of Luella Miller's deserted house, and she was quite dead.

The next night there was a red gleam of fire athwart the moonlight and the old house of Luella Miller was burned to the ground. Nothing is now left of it except a few old cellar stones and a lilac bush, and in summer a helpless trail of morning glories among the weeds, which might be considered emblematic of Luella herself.

The Yellow Wallpaper

Charlotte Perkins Gilman

IT IS VERY SELDOM that mere ordinary people like John and myself secure ancestral halls for the summer.

A colonial mansion, a hereditary estate, I would say a haunted house, and reach the height of romantic felicity – but that would be asking too much of fate!

Still I will proudly declare that there is something queer about it.

Else, why should it be let so cheaply? And why have stood so long untenanted?

John laughs at me, of course, but one expects that in marriage.

John is practical in the extreme. He has no patience with faith, an intense horror of superstition, and he scoffs openly at any talk of things not to be felt and seen and put down in figures.

John is a physician, and *perhaps* – (I would not say it to a living soul, of course, but this is dead paper and a great relief to my mind) – *perhaps* that is one reason I do not get well faster.

You see, he does not believe I am sick!

And what can one do?

If a physician of high standing, and one's own husband, assures friends and relatives that there is really nothing the matter with one but temporary nervous depression – a slight hysterical tendency – what is one to do?

My brother is also a physician, and also of high standing, and he says the same thing.

So I take phosphates or phosphites – whichever it is, and tonics, and journeys, and air, and exercise, and am absolutely forbidden to 'work' until I am well again.

Personally, I disagree with their ideas.

Personally, I believe that congenial work, with excitement and change, would do me good.

But what is one to do?

I did write for a while in spite of them; but it *does* exhaust me a good deal – having to be so sly about it, or else meet with heavy opposition.

I sometimes fancy that in my condition if I had less opposition and more society and stimulus – but John says the very worst thing I can do is to think about my condition, and I confess it always makes me feel bad.

So I will let it alone and talk about the house.

The most beautiful place! It is quite alone, standing well back from the road, quite three miles from the village. It makes me think of English places that you read about, for there are hedges and walls and gates that lock, and lots of separate little houses for the gardeners and people.

There is a *delicious* garden! I never saw such a garden – large and shady, full of box-bordered paths, and lined with long grape-covered arbors with seats under them.

There were greenhouses, too, but they are all broken now.

There was some legal trouble, I believe, something about the heirs and co-heirs; anyhow, the place has been empty for years.

That spoils my ghostliness, I am afraid; but I don't care – there is something strange about the house – I can feel it.

I even said so to John one moonlit evening, but he said what I felt was a *draught*, and shut the window.

I get unreasonably angry with John sometimes. I'm sure I never used to be so sensitive. I think it is due to this nervous condition.

But John says if I feel so I shall neglect proper self-control; so I take pains to control myself – before him, at least – and that makes me very tired.

I don't like our room a bit. I wanted one downstairs that opened on the piazza and had roses all over the window, and such pretty old-fashioned chintz hangings! But John would not hear of it.

He said there was only one window and not room for two beds, and no near room for him if he took another.

He is very careful and loving, and hardly lets me stir without special direction.

I have a schedule prescription for each hour in the day; he takes all care from me, and so I feel basely ungrateful not to value it more.

He said we came here solely on my account, that I was to have perfect rest and all the air I could get. "Your exercise depends on your strength, my dear," said he, "and your food somewhat on your appetite; but air you can absorb all the time." So we took the nursery, at the top of the house.

It is a big, airy room, the whole floor nearly, with windows that look all ways, and air and sunshine galore. It was nursery first and then playground and gymnasium, I should judge; for the windows are barred for little children, and there are rings and things in the walls.

The paint and paper look as if a boys' school had used it. It is stripped off – the paper – in great patches all around the head of my bed, about as far as I can reach, and in a great place on the other side of the room low down. I never saw a worse paper in my life.

One of those sprawling flamboyant patterns committing every artistic sin.

It is dull enough to confuse the eye in following, pronounced enough to constantly irritate, and provoke study, and when you follow the lame, uncertain curves for a little distance they suddenly commit suicide – plunge off at outrageous angles, destroy themselves in unheard-of contradictions.

The color is repellant, almost revolting; a smoldering, unclean yellow, strangely faded by the slow-turning sunlight.

It is a dull yet lurid orange in some places, a sickly sulphur tint in others.

No wonder the children hated it! I should hate it myself if I had to live in this room long.

There comes John, and I must put this away – he hates to have me write a word.

* * *

We have been here two weeks, and I haven't felt like writing before, since that first day.

I am sitting by the window now, up in this atrocious nursery, and there is nothing to hinder my writing as much as I please, save lack of strength.

John is away all day, and even some nights when his cases are serious.

I am glad my case is not serious!

But these nervous troubles are dreadfully depressing.

John does not know how much I really suffer. He knows there is no *reason* to suffer, and that satisfies him.

Of course it is only nervousness. It does weigh on me so not to do my duty in any way!

I meant to be such a help to John, such a real rest and comfort, and here I am a comparative burden already!

Nobody would believe what an effort it is to do what little I am able – to dress and entertain, and order things.

It is fortunate Mary is so good with the baby. Such a dear baby!

And yet I *cannot* be with him, it makes me so nervous.

I suppose John never was nervous in his life. He laughs at me so about this wallpaper!

At first he meant to repaper the room, but afterwards he said that I was letting it get the better of me, and that nothing was worse for a nervous patient than to give way to such fancies.

He said that after the wallpaper was changed it would be the heavy bedstead, and then the barred windows, and then that gate at the head of the stairs, and so on.

"You know the place is doing you good," he said, "and really, dear, I don't care to renovate the house just for a three months' rental."

"Then do let us go downstairs," I said, "there are such pretty rooms there."

Then he took me in his arms and called me a blessed little goose, and said he would go down to the cellar if I wished, and have it whitewashed into the bargain.

But he is right enough about the beds and windows and things.

It is as airy and comfortable a room as anyone need wish, and, of course, I would not be so silly as to make him uncomfortable just for a whim.

I'm really getting quite fond of the big room, all but that horrid paper.

Out of one window I can see the garden, those mysterious deep-shaded arbors, the riotous old-fashioned flowers, and bushes and gnarly trees.

Out of another I get a lovely view of the bay and a little private wharf belonging to the estate. There is a beautiful shaded lane that runs down there from the house. I always fancy I see people walking in these numerous paths and arbors, but John has cautioned me not to give way to fancy in the least. He says that with my imaginative power and habit of story-making a nervous weakness like mine is sure to lead to all manner of excited fancies, and that I ought to use my will and good sense to check the tendency. So I try.

I think sometimes that if I were only well enough to write a little it would relieve the press of ideas and rest me.

But I find I get pretty tired when I try.

It is so discouraging not to have any advice and companionship about my work. When I get really well John says we will ask Cousin Henry and Julia down for a long visit; but he says he would as soon put fireworks in my pillowcase as to let me have those stimulating people about now.

I wish I could get well faster.

But I must not think about that. This paper looks to me as if it *knew* what a vicious influence it had!

There is a recurrent spot where the pattern lolls like a broken neck and two bulbous eyes stare at you upside-down.

I get positively angry with the impertinence of it and the everlastingness. Up and down and sideways they crawl, and those absurd, unblinking eyes are everywhere. There is one place where two breadths didn't match, and the eyes go all up and down the line, one a little higher than the other.

I never saw so much expression in an inanimate thing before, and we all know how much expression they have! I used to lie awake as a child and get more entertainment and terror out of blank walls and plain furniture than most children could find in a toy-store.

I remember what a kindly wink the knobs of our big old bureau used to have, and there was one chair that always seemed like a strong friend.

I used to feel that if any of the other things looked too fierce I could always hop into that chair and be safe.

The furniture in this room is no worse than inharmonious, however, for we had to bring it all from downstairs. I suppose when this was used as a playroom they had to take the nursery things out, and no wonder! I never saw such ravages as the children have made here.

The wallpaper, as I said before, is torn off in spots, and it sticketh closer than a brother – they must have had perseverance as well as hatred.

Then the floor is scratched and gouged and splintered, the plaster itself is dug out here and there, and this great heavy bed, which is all we found in the room, looks as if it had been through the wars.

But I don't mind it a bit – only the paper.

There comes John's sister. Such a dear girl as she is, and so careful of me! I must not let her find me writing.

She is a perfect and enthusiastic housekeeper, and hopes for no better profession. I verily believe she thinks it is the writing which made me sick!

But I can write when she is out, and see her a long way off from these windows.

There is one that commands the road, a lovely, shaded, winding road, and one that just looks off over the country. A lovely country, too, full of great elms and velvet meadows.

This wallpaper has a kind of sub-pattern in a different shade, a particularly irritating one, for you can only see it in certain lights, and not clearly then.

But in the places where it isn't faded, and where the sun is just so, I can see a strange, provoking, formless sort of figure, that seems to sulk about behind that silly and conspicuous front design.

There's sister on the stairs!

* * *

Well, the Fourth of July is over! The people are gone and I am tired out. John thought it might do me good to see a little company, so we just had mother and Nellie and the children down for a week.

Of course I didn't do a thing. Jennie sees to everything now.

But it tired me all the same.

John says if I don't pick up faster he shall send me to Weir Mitchell in the fall.

But I don't want to go there at all. I had a friend who was in his hands once, and she says he is just like John and my brother, only more so!

Besides, it is such an undertaking to go so far.

I don't feel as if it was worthwhile to turn my hand over for anything, and I'm getting dreadfully fretful and querulous.

I cry at nothing, and cry most of the time.

Of course I don't when John is here, or anybody else, but when I am alone.

And I am alone a good deal just now. John is kept in town very often by serious cases, and Jennie is good and lets me alone when I want her to.

So I walk a little in the garden or down that lovely lane, sit on the porch under the roses, and lie down up here a good deal.

I'm getting really fond of the room in spite of the wallpaper. Perhaps *because* of the wallpaper.

It dwells in my mind so!

I lie here on this great immovable bed – it is nailed down, I believe – and follow that pattern about by the hour. It is as good as gymnastics, I assure you. I start, we'll say, at the bottom, down in the corner over there where it has not been touched, and I determine for the thousandth time that I *will* follow that pointless pattern to some sort of a conclusion.

I know a little of the principle of design, and I know this thing was not arranged on any laws of radiation, or alternation, or repetition, or symmetry, or anything else that I ever heard of.

It is repeated, of course, by the breadths, but not otherwise.

Looked at in one way each breadth stands alone, the bloated curves and flourishes – a kind of 'debased Romanesque' with *delirium tremens* – go waddling up and down in isolated columns of fatuity.

But, on the other hand, they connect diagonally, and the sprawling outlines run off in great slanting waves of optic horror, like a lot of wallowing seaweeds in full chase.

The whole thing goes horizontally, too, at least it seems so, and I exhaust myself in trying to distinguish the order of its going in that direction.

They have used a horizontal breadth for a frieze, and that adds wonderfully to the confusion.

There is one end of the room where it is almost intact, and there, when the cross-lights fade and the low sun shines directly upon it, I can almost fancy radiation after all – the interminable grotesques seem to form around a common center and rush off in headlong plunges of equal distraction.

It makes me tired to follow it. I will take a nap, I guess.

* * *

I don't know why I should write this.

I don't want to.

I don't feel able.

And I know John would think it absurd. But I *must* say what I feel and think in some way – it is such a relief!

But the effort is getting to be greater than the relief.

Half the time now I am awfully lazy, and lie down ever so much.

John says I musn't lose my strength, and has me take codliver oil and lots of tonics and things, to say nothing of ale and wine and rare meat.

Dear John! He loves me very dearly, and hates to have me sick. I tried to have a real earnest reasonable talk with him the other day, and tell him how I wish he would let me go and make a visit to Cousin Henry and Julia.

But he said I wasn't able to go, nor able to stand it after I got there; and I did not make out a very good case for myself, for I was crying before I had finished.

It is getting to be a great effort for me to think straight. Just this nervous weakness, I suppose.

And dear John gathered me up in his arms, and just carried me upstairs and laid me on the bed, and sat by me and read to me till it tired my head.

He said I was his darling and his comfort and all he had, and that I must take care of myself for his sake, and keep well.

He says no one but myself can help me out of it, that I must use my will and self-control and not let any silly fancies run away with me.

There's one comfort, the baby is well and happy, and does not have to occupy this nursery with the horrid wallpaper.

If we had not used it that blessed child would have! What a fortunate escape! Why, I wouldn't have a child of mine, an impressionable little thing, live in such a room for worlds.

I never thought of it before, but it is lucky that John kept me here after all. I can stand it so much easier than a baby, you see.

Of course I never mention it to them anymore – I am too wise – but I keep watch of it all the same.

There are things in that paper that nobody knows but me, or ever will.

Behind that outside pattern the dim shapes get clearer every day.

It is always the same shape, only very numerous.

And it is like a woman stooping down and creeping about behind that pattern. I don't like it a bit. I wonder – I begin to think – I wish John would take me away from here!

* * *

It is so hard to talk with John about my case, because he is so wise, and because he loves me so.

But I tried it last night.

It was moonlight. The moon shines in all around, just as the sun does.

I hate to see it sometimes, it creeps so slowly, and always comes in by one window or another.

John was asleep and I hated to waken him, so I kept still and watched the moonlight on that undulating wallpaper till I felt creepy.

The faint figure behind seemed to shake the pattern, just as if she wanted to get out.

I got up softly and went to feel and see if the paper *did* move, and when I came back John was awake.

"What is it, little girl?" he said. "Don't go walking about like that – you'll get cold."

I thought it was a good time to talk, so I told him that I really was not gaining here, and that I wished he would take me away.

"Why darling!" said he, "our lease will be up in three weeks, and I can't see how to leave before. The repairs are not done at home, and I cannot possibly leave town just now. Of course if you were in any danger I could and would, but you really are better, dear, whether you can see it or not. I am a doctor, dear, and I know. You are gaining flesh and color, your appetite is better. I feel really much easier about you."

"I don't weigh a bit more," said I, "nor as much; and my appetite may be better in the evening, when you are here, but it is worse in the morning when you are away."

"Bless her little heart!" said he with a big hug; "she shall be as sick as she pleases! But now let's improve the shining hours by going to sleep, and talk about it in the morning!"

"And you won't go away?" I asked gloomily.

"Why, how can I, dear? It is only three weeks more and then we will take a nice little trip of a few days while Jennie is getting the house ready. Really, dear, you are better!"

"Better in body perhaps—" I began, and stopped short, for he sat up straight and looked at me with such a stern, reproachful look that I could not say another word.

"My darling," said he, "I beg of you, for my sake and for our child's sake, as well as for your own, that you will never for one instant let that idea enter your mind! There is nothing so dangerous, so fascinating, to a temperament like yours. It is a false and foolish fancy. Can you not trust me as a physician when I tell you so?"

So of course I said no more on that score, and we went to sleep before long. He thought I was asleep first, but I wasn't – I lay there for hours trying to decide whether that front pattern and the back pattern really did move together or separately.

On a pattern like this, by daylight, there is a lack of sequence, a defiance of law, that is a constant irritant to a normal mind.

The color is hideous enough, and unreliable enough, and infuriating enough, but the pattern is torturing.

You think you have mastered it, but just as you get well underway in following, it turns a back somersault and there you are. It slaps you in the face, knocks you down, and tramples upon you. It is like a bad dream.

The outside pattern is a florid arabesque, reminding one of a fungus. If you can imagine a toadstool in joints, an interminable string of toadstools, budding and sprouting in endless convolutions – why, that is something like it.

That is, sometimes!

There is one marked peculiarity about this paper, a thing nobody seems to notice but myself, and that is that it changes as the light changes.

When the sun shoots in through the east window – I always watch for that first long, straight ray – it changes so quickly that I never can quite believe it.

That is why I watch it always.

By moonlight – the moon shines in all night when there is a moon – I wouldn't know it was the same paper.

At night in any kind of light, in twilight, candlelight, lamplight, and worst of all by moonlight, it becomes bars! The outside pattern I mean, and the woman behind it is as plain as can be.

I didn't realize for a long time what the thing was that showed behind – that dim sub-pattern – but now I am quite sure it is a woman.

By daylight she is subdued, quiet. I fancy it is the pattern that keeps her so still. It is so puzzling. It keeps me quiet by the hour.

I lie down ever so much now. John says it is good for me, and to sleep all I can.

Indeed, he started the habit by making me lie down for an hour after each meal.

It is a very bad habit, I am convinced, for, you see, I don't sleep.

And that cultivates deceit, for I don't tell them I'm awake, – oh, no!

The fact is, I am getting a little afraid of John

He seems very queer sometimes, and even Jennie has an inexplicable look.

It strikes me occasionally, just as a scientific hypothesis, that perhaps it is the paper!

I have watched John when he did not know I was looking, and come into the room suddenly on the most innocent excuses, and I've caught him several times *looking at the paper!* And Jennie too. I caught Jennie with her hand on it once.

She didn't know I was in the room, and when I asked her in a quiet, a very quiet voice, with the most restrained manner possible, what she was doing with the paper she turned around as if she had been caught stealing, and looked quite angry – asked me why I should frighten her so!

Then she said that the paper stained everything it touched, that she had found yellow smooches on all my clothes and John's, and she wished we would be more careful!

Did not that sound innocent? But I know she was studying that pattern, and I am determined that nobody shall find it out but myself!

* * *

Life is very much more exciting now than it used to be. You see I have something more to expect, to look forward to, to watch. I really do eat better, and am more quiet than I was.

John is so pleased to see me improve! He laughed a little the other day, and said I seemed to be flourishing in spite of my wallpaper.

I turned it off with a laugh. I had no intention of telling him it was *because* of the wallpaper – he would make fun of me. He might even want to take me away.

I don't want to leave now until I have found it out. There is a week more, and I think that will be enough.

* * *

I'm feeling ever so much better! I don't sleep much at night, for it is so interesting to watch developments; but I sleep a good deal in the daytime.

In the daytime it is tiresome and perplexing.

There are always new shoots on the fungus, and new shades of yellow all over it. I cannot keep count of them, though I have tried conscientiously.

It is the strangest yellow, that wallpaper! It makes me think of all the yellow things I ever saw – not beautiful ones like buttercups, but old foul, bad yellow things.

But there is something else about that paper – the smell! I noticed it the moment we came into the room, but with so much air and sun it was not bad. Now we have had a week of fog and rain, and whether the windows are open or not, the smell is here.

It creeps all over the house.

I find it hovering in the dining room, skulking in the parlor, hiding in the hall, lying in wait for me on the stairs.

It gets into my hair.

Even when I go to ride, if I turn my head suddenly and surprise it – there is that smell!

Such a peculiar odor, too! I have spent hours in trying to analyze it, to find what it smelled like.

It is not bad – at first, and very gentle, but quite the subtlest, most enduring odor I ever met.

In this damp weather it is awful. I wake up in the night and find it hanging over me.

It used to disturb me at first. I thought seriously of burning the house – to reach the smell.

But now I am used to it. The only thing I can think of that it is like is the *color* of the paper! A yellow smell.

There is a very funny mark on this wall, low down, near the mopboard. A streak that runs round the room. It goes behind every piece of furniture, except the bed, a long, straight, even *smooch*, as if it had been rubbed over and over.

I wonder how it was done and who did it, and what they did it for. Round and round and round – round and round and round – it makes me dizzy!

* * *

I really have discovered something at last.

Through watching so much at night, when it changes so, I have finally found out.

The front pattern *does* move – and no wonder! The woman behind shakes it!

Sometimes I think there are a great many women behind, and sometimes only one, and she crawls around fast, and her crawling shakes it all over.

Then in the very bright spots she keeps still, and in the very shady spots she just takes hold of the bars and shakes them hard.

And she is all the time trying to climb through. But nobody could climb through that pattern – it strangles so; I think that is why it has so many heads.

They get through, and then the pattern strangles them off and turns them upside down, and makes their eyes white!

If those heads were covered or taken off it would not be half so bad.

* * *

I think that woman gets out in the daytime!

And I'll tell you why – privately – I've seen her!

I can see her out of every one of my windows!

It is the same woman, I know, for she is always creeping, and most women do not creep by daylight.

I see her on that long shaded lane, creeping up and down. I see her in those dark grape arbors, creeping all around the garden.

I see her on that long road under the trees, creeping along, and when a carriage comes she hides under the blackberry vines.

I don't blame her a bit. It must be very humiliating to be caught creeping by daylight!

I always lock the door when I creep by daylight. I can't do it at night, for I know John would suspect something at once.

And John is so queer now, that I don't want to irritate him. I wish he would take another room! Besides, I don't want anybody to get that woman out at night but myself.

I often wonder if I could see her out of all the windows at once.

But, turn as fast as I can, I can only see out of one at one time.

And though I always see her she *may* be able to creep faster than I can turn!

I have watched her sometimes away off in the open country, creeping as fast as a cloud shadow in a high wind.

* * *

If only that top pattern could be gotten off from the under one! I mean to try it, little by little.

I have found out another funny thing, but I shan't tell it this time! It does not do to trust people too much.

There are only two more days to get this paper off, and I believe John is beginning to notice. I don't like the look in his eyes.

And I heard him ask Jennie a lot of professional questions about me. She had a very good report to give.

She said I slept a good deal in the daytime.

John knows I don't sleep very well at night, for all I'm so quiet!

He asked me all sorts of questions, too, and pretended to be very loving and kind.

As if I couldn't see through him!

Still, I don't wonder he acts so, sleeping under this paper for three months.

It only interests me, but I feel sure John and Jennie are secretly affected by it.

* * *

Hurrah! This is the last day, but it is enough. John is to stay in town overnight, and won't be out until this evening.

Jennie wanted to sleep with me – the sly thing! But I told her I should undoubtedly rest better for a night all alone.

That was clever, for really I wasn't alone a bit! As soon as it was moonlight, and that poor thing began to crawl and shake the pattern, I got up and ran to help her.

I pulled and she shook, I shook and she pulled, and before morning we had peeled off yards of that paper.

A strip about as high as my head and half around the room.

And then when the sun came and that awful pattern began to laugh at me I declared I would finish it today!

We go away tomorrow, and they are moving all my furniture down again to leave things as they were before.

Jennie looked at the wall in amazement, but I told her merrily that I did it out of pure spite at the vicious thing.

She laughed and said she wouldn't mind doing it herself, but I must not get tired.

How she betrayed herself that time!

But I am here, and no person touches this paper but me – not *alive!*

She tried to get me out of the room – it was too patent! But I said it was so quiet and empty and clean now that I believed I would lie down again and sleep all I could; and not to wake me even for dinner – I would call when I woke.

So now she is gone, and the servants are gone, and the things are gone, and there is nothing left but that great bedstead nailed down, with the canvas mattress we found on it.

We shall sleep downstairs tonight, and take the boat home tomorrow.

I quite enjoy the room, now it is bare again.

How those children did tear about here!

This bedstead is fairly gnawed!

But I must get to work.

I have locked the door and thrown the key down into the front path.

I don't want to go out, and I don't want to have anybody come in, till John comes.

I want to astonish him.

I've got a rope up here that even Jennie did not find. If that woman does get out, and tries to get away, I can tie her!

But I forgot I could not reach far without anything to stand on!

This bed will *not* move!

I tried to lift and push it until I was lame, and then I got so angry I bit off a little piece at one corner – but it hurt my teeth.

Then I peeled off all the paper I could reach standing on the floor. It sticks horribly and the pattern just enjoys it! All those strangled heads and bulbous eyes and waddling fungus growths just shriek with derision!

I am getting angry enough to do something desperate. To jump out of the window would be admirable exercise, but the bars are too strong even to try.

Besides I wouldn't do it. Of course not. I know well enough that a step like that is improper and might be misconstrued.

I don't like to *look* out of the windows even – there are so many of those creeping women, and they creep so fast.

I wonder if they all come out of that wallpaper as I did?

But I am securely fastened now by my well-hidden rope – you don't get *me* out in the road there!

I suppose I shall have to get back behind the pattern when it comes night, and that is hard!

It is so pleasant to be out in this great room and creep around as I please!

I don't want to go outside. I won't, even if Jennie asks me to.

For outside you have to creep on the ground, and everything is green instead of yellow.

But here I can creep smoothly on the floor, and my shoulder just fits in that long smooch around the wall, so I cannot lose my way.

Why, there's John at the door!

It is no use, young man, you can't open it!

How he does call and pound!

Now he's crying for an axe.

It would be a shame to break down that beautiful door!

"John dear!" said I in the gentlest voice, "the key is down by the front steps, under a plantain leaf!"

That silenced him for a few moments.

Then he said – very quietly indeed, "Open the door, my darling!"

"I can't," said I. "The key is down by the front door under a plantain leaf!"

And then I said it again, several times, very gently and slowly, and said it so often that he had to go and see, and he got it, of course, and came in. He stopped short by the door.

"What is the matter?" he cried. "For God's sake, what are you doing!"

I kept on creeping just the same, but I looked at him over my shoulder.

"I've got out at last," said I, "in spite of you and Jane! And I've pulled off most of the paper, so you can't put me back!"

Now why should that man have fainted? But he did, and right across my path by the wall, so that I had to creep over him every time!

The Past

Ellen Glasgow

I HAD NO SOONER ENTERED the house than I knew something was wrong. Though I had never been in so splendid a place before – it was one of those big houses just off Fifth Avenue – I had a suspicion from the first that the magnificence covered a secret disturbance. I was always quick to receive impressions, and when the black iron doors swung together behind me, I felt as if I were shut inside a prison.

When I gave my name and explained that I was the new secretary, I was delivered into the charge of an elderly lady's-maid, who looked as if she had been crying. Without speaking a word, though she nodded kindly enough, she led me down the hall, and then up a flight of stairs at the back of the house to a pleasant bedroom in the third story. There was a great deal of sunshine, and the walls, which were painted a soft yellow, made the room very cheerful. It would be a comfortable place to sit in when I was not working, I thought, while the sad-faced maid stood watching me remove my wraps and hat.

"If you are not tired, Mrs. Vanderbridge would like to dictate a few letters," she said presently, and they were the first words she had spoken.

"I am not a bit tired. Will you take me to her?" One of the reasons, I knew, which had decided Mrs. Vanderbridge to engage me was the remarkable similarity of our handwriting. We were both Southerners, and though she was now famous on two continents for her beauty, I couldn't forget that she had got her early education at the little academy for young ladies in Fredericksburg. This was a bond of sympathy in my thoughts at least, and, heaven knows, I needed to remember it while I followed the maid down the narrow stairs and along the wide hall to the front of the house.

In looking back after a year, I can recall every detail of that first meeting. Though it was barely four o'clock, the electric lamps were turned on in the hall, and I can still see the mellow light that shone over the staircase and lay in pools on the old pink rugs, which were so soft and fine that I felt as if I were walking on flowers. I remember the sound of music from a room somewhere on the first floor, and the scent of lilies and hyacinths that drifted from the conservatory. I remember it all, every note of music, every whiff of fragrance; but most vividly I remember Mrs. Vanderbridge as she looked round, when the door opened, from the wood fire into which she had been gazing. Her eyes caught me first. They were so wonderful that for a moment I couldn't see anything else; then I took in slowly the dark red of her hair, the clear pallor of her skin, and the long, flowing lines of her figure in a tea-gown of blue silk. There was a white bearskin rug under her feet, and while she stood there before the wood fire, she looked as if she had absorbed the beauty and color of the house as a crystal vase absorbs the light. Only when she spoke to me, and I went nearer, did I detect the heaviness beneath her eyes and the nervous quiver of her mouth, which drooped a little at the corners. Tired and worn as she was, I never saw her afterwards – not even when she was dressed for the opera – look quite so lovely, so much like an exquisite flower, as she did on that first afternoon. When I knew her better,

I discovered that she was a changeable beauty; there were days when all the color seemed to go out of her, and she looked dull and haggard; but at her best no one I've ever seen could compare with her.

She asked me a few questions, and though she was pleasant and kind, I knew that she scarcely listened to my responses. While I sat down at the desk and dipped my pen into the ink, she flung herself on the couch before the fire with a movement which struck me as hopeless. I saw her feet tap the white fur rug, while she plucked nervously at the lace on the end of one of the gold-colored sofa pillows. For an instant the thought flashed through my mind that she had been taking something – drug of some sort – and that she was suffering now from the effects of it. Then she looked at me steadily, almost as if she were reading my thoughts, and I knew that I was wrong. Her large radiant eyes were as innocent as a child's.

She dictated a few notes – all declining invitations – and then, while I still waited pen in hand, she sat up on the couch with one of her quick movements, and said in a low voice, "I am not dining out tonight, Miss Wrenn. I am not well enough."

"I am sorry for that." It was all I could think of to say, for I did not understand why she should have told me.

"If you don't mind, I should like you to come down to dinner. There will be only Mr. Vanderbridge and myself."

"Of course I will come if you wish it." I couldn't very well refuse to do what she asked me, yet I told myself, while I answered, that if I had known she expected me to make one of the family, I should never, not even at twice the salary, have taken the place. It didn't take me a minute to go over my slender wardrobe in my mind and realize that I had nothing to wear that would look well enough.

"I can see you don't like it," she added after a moment, almost wistfully, "but it won't be often. It is only when we are dining alone."

This, I thought, was even queerer than the request – or command – for I knew from her tone, just as plainly as if she had told me in words, that she did not wish to dine alone with her husband.

"I am ready to help you in any way – in any way that I can," I replied, and I was so deeply moved by her appeal that my voice broke in spite of my effort to control it. After my lonely life I dare say I should have loved anyone who really needed me, and from the first moment that I read the appeal in Mrs. Vanderbridge's face I felt that I was willing to work my fingers to the bone for her. Nothing that she asked of me was too much when she asked it in that voice, with that look.

"I am glad you are nice," she said, and for the first time she smiled – a charming, girlish smile with a hint of archness. "We shall get on beautifully, I know, because I can talk to you. My last secretary was English, and I frightened her almost to death whenever I tried to talk to her." Then her tone grew serious. "You won't mind dining with us. Roger – Mr. Vanderbridge – is the most charming man in the world."

"Is that his picture?"

"Yes, the one in the Florentine frame. The other is my brother. Do you think we are alike?"

"Since you've told me, I notice a likeness." Already I had picked up the Florentine frame from the desk, and was eagerly searching the features of Mr. Vanderbridge. It was an arresting face, dark, thoughtful, strangely appealing, and picturesque – though this may have been due, of course, to the photographer. The more I looked at it, the more there grew upon me an uncanny feeling of familiarity; but not until the next day, while I was still trying to account for the impression that I had seen the picture before, did there flash into my mind the memory of an old portrait of a Florentine nobleman in a loan collection last winter. I can't remember the name of the painter – I am not sure that it was known – but this photograph might have been taken from the painting. There was the same imaginative sadness in both faces, the same haunting beauty of feature, and one surmised that there must be the same rich darkness of coloring. The only striking difference was that the man in the photograph looked much older than the original of the portrait, and I remembered that the lady who had engaged me was the second wife of Mr. Vanderbridge and some ten or fifteen years younger, I had heard, than her husband.

"Have you ever seen a more wonderful face?" asked Mrs. Vanderbridge. "Doesn't he look as if he might have been painted by Titian?"

"Is he really so handsome as that?"

"He is a little older and sadder, that is all. When we were married it was exactly like him." For an instant she hesitated and then broke out almost bitterly, "Isn't that a face any woman might fall in love with, a face any woman – living or dead – would not be willing to give up?"

Poor child, I could see that she was overwrought and needed someone to talk to, but it seemed queer to me that she should speak so frankly to a stranger. I wondered why anyone so rich and so beautiful should ever be unhappy – for I had been schooled by poverty to believe that money is the first essential of happiness – and yet her unhappiness was as evident as her beauty, or the luxury that enveloped her. At that instant I felt that I hated Mr. Vanderbridge, for whatever the secret tragedy of their marriage might be, I instinctively knew that the fault was not on the side of the wife. She was as sweet and winning as if she were still the reigning beauty in the academy for young ladies. I knew with a knowledge deeper than any conviction that she was not to blame, and if she wasn't to blame, then who under heaven could be at fault except her husband?

In a few minutes a friend came in to tea, and I went upstairs to my room, and unpacked the blue taffeta dress I had bought for my sister's wedding. I was still doubtfully regarding it when there was a knock at my door, and the maid with the sad face came in to bring me a pot of tea. After she had placed the tray on the table, she stood nervously twisting a napkin in her hands while she waited for me to leave my unpacking and sit down in the easy chair she had drawn up under the lamp.

"How do you think Mrs. Vanderbridge is looking?" she asked abruptly in a voice that held a breathless note of suspense. Her nervousness and the queer look in her face made me stare at her sharply. This was a house, I was beginning to feel, where everybody, from the mistress down, wanted to question me. Even the silent maid had found voice for interrogation.

"I think her the loveliest person I've ever seen," I answered after a moment's hesitation. There couldn't be any harm in telling her how much I admired her mistress.

"Yes, she is lovely – everyone thinks so – and her nature is as sweet as her face." She was becoming loquacious. "I have never had a lady who was so sweet and kind. She hasn't always been rich, and that may be the reason she never seems to grow hard and selfish, the reason she spends so much of her life thinking of other people. It's been six years now, ever since her marriage, that I've lived with her, and in all that time I've never had a cross word from her."

"One can see that. With everything she has she ought to be as happy as the day is long."

"She ought to be." Her voice dropped, and I saw her glance suspiciously at the door, which she had closed when she entered. "She ought to be, but she isn't. I have never seen anyone so unhappy as she has been of late – ever since last summer. I suppose I oughtn't to talk about it, but I've kept it to myself so long that I feel as if it was killing me. If she was my own sister, I couldn't be any fonder of her, and yet I have to see her suffer day after day, and not say a word – not even to her. She isn't the sort of lady you could speak to about a thing like that."

She broke down, and dropping on the rug at my feet, hid her face in her hands. It was plain that she was suffering acutely, and while I patted her shoulder, I thought what a wonderful mistress Mrs. Vanderbridge must be to have attached a servant to her so strongly.

"You must remember that I am a stranger in the house, that I scarcely know her, that I've never so much as laid eyes on her husband," I said warningly, for I've always avoided, as far as possible, the confidences of servants.

"But you look as if you could be trusted." The maid's nerves, as well as the mistress's, were on edge, I could see. "And she needs somebody who can help her. She needs a real friend – somebody who will stand by her no matter what happens." Again, as in the room downstairs, there flashed through my mind the suspicion that I had got into a place where people took drugs or drink – or were all out of their minds. I had heard of such houses.

"How can I help her? She won't confide in me, and even if she did, what could I do for her?"

"You can stand by and watch. You can come between her and harm – if you see it." She had risen from the floor and stood wiping her reddened eyes on the napkin. "I don't know what it is, but I know it is there. I feel it even when I can't see it."

Yes, they were all out of their minds; there couldn't be any other explanation. The whole episode was incredible. It was the kind of thing, I kept telling myself, that did not happen. Even in a book nobody could believe it.

"But her husband? He is the one who must protect her."

She gave me a blighting look. "He would if he could. He isn't to blame – you mustn't think that. He is one of the best men in the world, but he can't help her. He can't help her because he doesn't know. He doesn't see it."

A bell rang somewhere, and catching up the tea-tray, she paused just long enough to throw me a pleading word, "Stand between her and harm, if you see it."

When she had gone I locked the door after her, and turned on all the lights in the room. Was there really a tragic mystery in the house, or were they all mad, as I had first imagined? The feeling of apprehension, of vague uneasiness, which had come to me when I entered the iron doors, swept over me in a wave while I sat there in the soft glow of the shaded electric light. Something was wrong. Somebody was making that lovely woman unhappy, and who, in the name of reason, could this somebody be except her husband? Yet the maid had spoken of him as "one of the best men in the world", and it was impossible to doubt the tearful sincerity of her voice. Well, the riddle was too much for me. I gave it up at last with a sigh – dreading the hour that would call me downstairs to meet Mr. Vanderbridge. I felt in every nerve and fibre of my body that I should hate him the moment I looked at him.

But at eight o'clock, when I went reluctantly downstairs, I had a surprise. Nothing could have been kinder than the way Mr. Vanderbridge greeted me, and I could tell as soon as I met his eyes that there wasn't anything vicious or violent in his nature. He reminded me more than ever of the portrait in the loan collection, and though he was so much older than the Florentine nobleman, he had the same thoughtful look. Of course I am not an artist, but I have always tried, in my way, to be a reader of personality; and it didn't take a particularly keen observer to discern the character and intellect in Mr. Vanderbridge's face. Even now I remember it as the noblest face I have ever seen; and unless I had possessed at least a shade of penetration, I doubt if I should have detected the melancholy. For it was only when he was thinking deeply that this sadness seemed to spread like a veil over his features. At other times he was cheerful and even gay in his manner; and his rich dark eyes would light up now and then with irrepressible humor. From the way he looked at his wife I could tell that there was no lack of love or tenderness on his side any more than there was on hers. It was obvious that he was still as much in love with her as he had been before his marriage, and my immediate perception of this only deepened the mystery that enveloped them. If the fault wasn't his and wasn't hers, then who was responsible for the shadow that hung over the house?

For the shadow was there. I could feel it, vague and dark, while we talked about the war and the remote possibilities of peace in the spring. Mrs. Vanderbridge looked young and lovely in her gown of white satin with pearls on her bosom, but her violet eyes were almost black in the candlelight, and I had a curious feeling that this blackness was the color of thought. Something troubled her to despair, yet I was as positive as I could be of anything I had ever been told that she had breathed no word of this anxiety or distress to her husband. Devoted as they were, a nameless dread, fear, or apprehension divided them. It was the thing I had felt from the moment I entered the house; the thing I had heard in the tearful voice of the maid. One could scarcely call it horror, because it was too vague, too impalpable, for so vivid a name; yet, after all these quiet months, horror is the only word I can think of that in any way expresses the emotion which pervaded the house.

I had never seen so beautiful a dinner table, and I was gazing with pleasure at the damask and glass and silver – there was a silver basket of chrysanthemums, I remember, in the center of the table – when I noticed a nervous movement of Mrs. Vanderbridge's head, and saw her glance hastily towards the door and the staircase beyond. We had been talking animatedly, and as Mrs. Vanderbridge turned away, I had just made a remark to her husband, who appeared to have fallen into a sudden fit of abstraction, and was gazing thoughtfully over his soup-plate at the white and yellow chrysanthemums. It occurred to me, while I watched him, that he was probably absorbed in some financial problem, and I regretted that I had been so careless as to speak to him. To my surprise, however, he replied immediately in a natural tone, and I saw, or imagined that I saw, Mrs. Vanderbridge throw me a glance of gratitude and relief. I can't remember what we were talking about, but I recall perfectly that the conversation kept up pleasantly, without a break, until dinner was almost half over. The roast had been served, and I was in the act of helping myself to potatoes, when I became aware that Mr. Vanderbridge had again fallen into his reverie. This time he scarcely seemed to hear his wife's voice when she spoke to him, and I watched the sadness cloud his face while he continued to stare straight ahead of him with a look that was almost yearning in its intensity.

Again I saw Mrs. Vanderbridge, with her nervous gesture, glance in the direction of the hall, and to my amazement, as she did so, a woman's figure glided noiselessly over the old Persian rug at the door, and entered the dining room. I was wondering why no one spoke to her, why she spoke to no one, when I saw her sink into a chair on the other side of Mr. Vanderbridge and unfold her napkin. She was quite young, younger even than Mrs. Vanderbridge, and though she was not really beautiful, she was the most graceful creature I had ever imagined. Her dress was of gray stuff, softer and more clinging than silk, and of a peculiar misty texture and color, and her parted hair lay like twilight on either side of her forehead. She was not like anyone I had ever seen before – she appeared so much frailer, so much more elusive, as if she would vanish if you touched her. I can't describe, even months afterwards, the singular way in which she attracted and repelled me.

At first I glanced inquiringly at Mrs. Vanderbridge, hoping that she would introduce me, but she went on talking rapidly in an intense, quivering voice, without noticing the presence of her guest by so much as the lifting of her eyelashes. Mr. Vanderbridge still sat there, silent and detached, and all the time the eyes of the stranger – starry eyes with a mist over them – looked straight through me at the tapestried wall at my back. I knew she didn't see me and that it wouldn't have made the slightest difference to her if she had seen me. In spite of her grace and her girlishness I did not like her, and I felt that this aversion was not on my side alone. I do not know how I received the impression that she hated Mrs. Vanderbridge – never once had she glanced in her direction – yet I was aware, from the moment of her entrance, that she was bristling with animosity, though animosity is too strong a word for the resentful spite, like the jealous rage of a spoiled child, which gleamed now and then in her eyes. I couldn't think of her as wicked any more than I could think of a bad child as wicked. She was merely wilful and undisciplined and – I hardly know how to convey what I mean – selfish.

After her entrance the dinner dragged on heavily. Mrs. Vanderbridge still kept up her nervous chatter, but nobody listened, for I was too embarrassed to pay any attention to what she said, and Mr. Vanderbridge had never recovered from his abstraction. He was like a man in a dream, not observing a thing that happened before him, while the strange woman sat there in the candlelight with her curious look of vagueness and unreality. To my astonishment not even the servants appeared to notice her, and though she had unfolded her napkin when she sat down, she wasn't served with either the roast or the salad. Once or twice, particularly when a new course was served, I glanced at Mrs. Vanderbridge to see if she would rectify the mistake, but she kept her gaze fixed on her plate. It was just as if there were a conspiracy to ignore the presence of the stranger, though she had been, from the moment of her entrance, the dominant figure at the table. You tried to pretend she wasn't there, and yet you knew – you knew vividly that she was gazing insolently straight through you.

The dinner lasted, it seemed, for hours, and you may imagine my relief when at last Mrs. Vanderbridge rose and led the way back into the drawing room. At first I thought the stranger would follow us, but when I glanced round from the hall she was still sitting there beside Mr. Vanderbridge, who was smoking a cigar with his coffee.

"Usually he takes his coffee with me," said Mrs. Vanderbridge, "but tonight he has things to think over."

"I thought he seemed absent-minded."

"You noticed it, then?" She turned to me with her straightforward glance, "I always wonder how much strangers notice. He hasn't been well of late, and he has these spells of depression. Nerves are dreadful things, aren't they?"

I laughed. "So I've heard, but I've never been able to afford them."

"Well, they do cost a great deal, don't they?" She had a trick of ending her sentences with a question, "I hope your room is comfortable, and that you don't feel timid about being alone on that floor. If you haven't nerves, you can't get nervous, can you?"

"No, I can't get nervous." Yet while I spoke, I was conscious of a shiver deep down in me, as if my senses reacted again to the dread that permeated the atmosphere.

As soon as I could, I escaped to my room, and I was sitting there over a book, when the maid – her name was Hopkins, I had discovered – came in on the pretext of inquiring if I had everything I needed. One of the innumerable servants had already turned down my bed, so when Hopkins appeared at the door, I suspected at once that there was a hidden motive underlying her ostensible purpose.

"Mrs. Vanderbridge told me to look after you," she began. "She is afraid you will be lonely until you learn the way of things."

"No, I'm not lonely," I answered. "I've never had time to be lonely."

"I used to be like that; but time hangs heavy on my hands now. That's why I've taken to knitting." She held out a gray yarn muffler. "I had an operation a year ago, and since then Mrs. Vanderbridge has had another maid – a French one – to sit up for her at night and undress her. She is always so fearful of overtaxing us, though there isn't really enough work for two lady's maids, because she is so thoughtful that she never gives any trouble if she can help it."

"It must be nice to be rich," I said idly, as I turned a page of my book. Then I added almost before I realized what I was saying, "The other lady doesn't look as if she had so much money."

Her face turned paler if that were possible, and for a minute I thought she was going to faint. "The other lady?"

"I mean the one who came down late to dinner – the one in the gray dress. She wore no jewels, and her dress wasn't low in the neck."

"Then you saw her?" There was a curious flicker in her face as if her pallor came and went.

"We were at the table when she came in. Has Mr. Vanderbridge a secretary who lives in the house?"

"No, he hasn't a secretary except at his office. When he wants one at the house, he telephones to his office."

"I wondered why she came, for she didn't eat any dinner, and nobody spoke to her – not even Mr. Vanderbridge."

"Oh, he never speaks to her. Thank God, it hasn't come to that yet."

"Then why does she come? It must be dreadful to be treated like that, and before the servants, too. Does she come often?"

"There are months and months when she doesn't. I can always tell by the way Mrs. Vanderbridge picks up. You wouldn't know her, she is so full of life – the very picture of happiness. Then one evening she – the Other One, I mean – comes back again, just as she did tonight, just as she did last summer, and it all begins over from the beginning."

"But can't they keep her out – the Other One? Why do they let her in?"

"Mrs. Vanderbridge tries hard. She tries all she can every minute. You saw her tonight?"

"And Mr. Vanderbridge? Can't he help her?"

She shook her head with an ominous gesture. "He doesn't know."

"He doesn't know she is there? Why, she was close by him. She never took her eyes off him except when she was staring through me at the wall."

"Oh, he knows she is there, but not in that way. He doesn't know that anyone else knows."

I gave it up, and after a minute she said in an oppressed voice, "It seems strange that you should have seen her. I never have."

"But you know all about her."

"I know and I don't know. Mrs. Vanderbridge lets things drop sometimes – she gets ill and feverish very easily – but she never tells me anything outright. She isn't that sort."

"Haven't the servants told you about her – the Other One?"

At this, I thought, she seemed startled. "Oh, they don't know anything to tell. They feel that something is wrong; that is why they never stay longer than a week or two – we've had eight butlers since autumn – but they never see what it is."

She stooped to pick up the ball of yarn which had rolled under my chair. "If the time ever comes when you can stand between them, you will do it?" she asked.

"Between Mrs. Vanderbridge and the Other One?"

Her look answered me.

"You think, then, that she means harm to her?"

"I don't know. Nobody knows – but she is killing her."

The clock struck ten, and I returned to my book with a yawn, while Hopkins gathered up her work and went out, after wishing me a formal goodnight. The odd part about our secret conferences was that as soon as they were over, we began to pretend so elaborately to each other that they had never been.

"I'll tell Mrs. Vanderbridge that you are very comfortable," was the last remark Hopkins made before she sidled out of the door and left me alone with the mystery. It was one of those situations – I am obliged to repeat this over and over – that was too preposterous for me to believe in even while I was surrounded and overwhelmed by its reality. I didn't dare face what I thought, I didn't dare face even what I felt; but I went to bed shivering in a warm room, while I resolved passionately that if the chance ever came to me I would stand between Mrs. Vanderbridge and this unknown evil that threatened her.

In the morning Mrs. Vanderbridge went out shopping, and I did not see her until the evening, when she passed me on the staircase as she was going out to dinner and the opera. She was radiant in blue velvet, with diamonds in her hair and at her throat, and I wondered again how anyone so lovely could ever be troubled.

"I hope you had a pleasant day, Miss Wrenn," she said kindly. "I have been too busy to get off any letters, but tomorrow we shall begin early." Then, as if from an afterthought, she looked back and added, "There are some new novels in my sitting room. You might care to look over them."

When she had gone, I went upstairs to the sitting room and turned over the books, but I couldn't, to save my life, force an interest in printed romances, after meeting Mrs. Vanderbridge and remembering the mystery that surrounded her. I wondered if 'the Other One', as Hopkins called her, lived in the house, and I was still wondering this when the maid came in and began putting the table to rights.

"Do they dine out often?" I asked.

"They used to, but since Mr. Vanderbridge hasn't been so well, Mrs. Vanderbridge doesn't like to go without him. She only went tonight because he begged her to."

She had barely finished speaking when the door opened, and Mr. Vanderbridge came in and sat down in one of the big velvet chairs before the wood fire. He had not noticed us, for one of his moods was upon him, and I was about to slip out as noiselessly as I could when I saw that the Other One was standing in the patch of firelight on the hearthrug. I had not seen her come in, and Hopkins evidently was still unaware of her presence, for while I was watching, I saw the maid turn towards her with a fresh log for the fire. At the moment it occurred to me that Hopkins must be either blind or drunk, for without hesitating in her advance, she moved on the stranger, holding the huge hickory log out in front of her. Then, before I could utter a sound or stretch out a hand to stop her, I saw her walk straight through the gray figure and carefully place the log on the andirons.

So she isn't real, after all, she is merely a phantom, I found myself thinking, as I fled from the room, and hurried along the hall to the staircase. She is only a ghost, and nobody believes in ghosts any longer. She is something that I know doesn't exist, yet even, though she can't possibly be, I can swear that I have seen her. My nerves were so shaken by the discovery that as soon as I reached my room I sank in a heap on the rug, and it was here that Hopkins found me a little later when she came to bring me an extra blanket.

"You looked so upset I thought you might have seen something," she said. "Did anything happen while you were in the room?"

"She was there all the time – every blessed minute. You walked right through her when you put the log on the fire. Is it possible that you didn't see her?"

"No, I didn't see anything out of the way." She was plainly frightened. "Where was she standing?"

"On the hearthrug in front of Mr. Vanderbridge. To reach the fire you had to walk straight through her, for she didn't move. She didn't give way an inch."

"Oh, she never gives way. She never gives way living or dead."

This was more than human nature could stand.

"In heaven's name," I cried irritably, "who is she?"

"Don't you know?" She appeared genuinely surprised. "Why, she is the other Mrs. Vanderbridge. She died fifteen years ago, just a year after they were married, and people say a scandal was hushed up about her, which he never knew. She isn't a good sort, that's what I think of her, though they say he almost worshiped her."

"And she still has this hold on him?"

"He can't shake it off, that's what's the matter with him, and if it goes on, he will end his days in an asylum. You see, she was very young, scarcely more than a girl, and he got the idea in his head that it was marrying him that killed her. If you want to know what I think, I believe she put it there for a purpose."

"You mean—?" I was so completely at sea that I couldn't frame a rational question.

"I mean she haunts him purposely in order to drive him out of his mind. She was always that sort, jealous and exacting, the kind that clutches and strangles a man, and I've often thought, though I've no head for speculation, that we carry into the next world the traits and feelings that have got the better of us in this one. It seems to me only common sense to believe that we're obliged to work them off somewhere until we are free of them. That is the way my first lady used to talk, anyhow, and I've never found anybody that could give me a more sensible idea."

"And isn't there any way to stop it? What has Mrs. Vanderbridge done?"

"Oh, she can't do anything now. It has got beyond her, though she has had doctor after doctor, and tried everything she could think of. But, you see, she is handicapped because she can't mention it to her husband. He doesn't know that she knows."

"And she won't tell him?"

"She is the sort that would die first – just the opposite from the Other One – for she leaves him free, she never clutches and strangles. It isn't her way." For a moment she hesitated, and then added grimly – "I've wondered if you could do anything?"

"If I could? Why, I am a perfect stranger to them all."

"That's why I've been thinking it. Now, if you could corner her some day – the Other One – and tell her up and down to her face what you think of her."

The idea was so ludicrous that it made me laugh in spite of my shaken nerves. "They would fancy me out of my wits! Imagine stopping an apparition and telling it what you think of it!"

"Then you might try talking it over with Mrs. Vanderbridge. It would help her to know that you see her also."

But the next morning, when I went down to Mrs. Vanderbridge's room, I found that she was too ill to see me. At noon a trained nurse came on the case, and for a week we took our meals together in the morning-room upstairs. She appeared competent enough, but I am sure that she didn't so much as suspect that there was anything wrong in the house except the influenza which had attacked Mrs. Vanderbridge the night of the opera. Never once during that week did I catch a glimpse of the Other One, though I felt her presence whenever I left my room and passed through the hall below. I knew all the time as well as if I had seen her that she was hidden there, watching, watching—

At the end of the week Mrs. Vanderbridge sent for me to write some letters, and when I went into her room, I found her lying on the couch with a tea-table in front of her. She asked me to make the tea because she was still so weak, and I saw that she looked flushed and feverish, and that her eyes were unnaturally large and bright. I hoped she wouldn't talk to me, because people in that state are apt to talk too much and then to blame the listener; but I had hardly taken my seat at the tea-table before she said in a hoarse voice – the cold had settled on her chest:

"Miss Wrenn, I have wanted to ask you ever since the other evening – did you – did you see anything unusual at dinner? From your face when you came out I thought – I thought—"

I met this squarely. "That I might have? Yes, I did see something."

"You saw her?"

"I saw a woman come in and sit down at the table, and I wondered why no one served her. I saw her quite distinctly."

"A small woman, thin and pale, in a gray dress?"

"She was so vague and – and misty, you know what I mean, that it is hard to describe her; but I should know her again anywhere. She wore her hair parted and drawn down over her ears. It was very dark and fine – as fine as spun silk."

We were speaking in low voices, and unconsciously we had moved closer together while my idle hands left the tea things.

"Then you know," she said earnestly, "that she really comes – that I am not out of my mind – that it is not a hallucination?"

"I know that I saw her. I would swear to it. But doesn't Mr. Vanderbridge see her also?"

"Not as we see her. He thinks that she is in his mind only." Then, after an uncomfortable silence, she added suddenly, "She is really a thought, you know. She is his thought of her – but he doesn't know that she is visible to the rest of us."

"And he brings her back by thinking of her?"

She leaned nearer while a quiver passed over her features and the flush deepened in her cheeks. "That is the only way she comes back – the only way she has the power to come back – as a thought. There are months and months when she leaves us in peace because he is thinking of other things, but of late, since his illness, she has been with him almost constantly." A sob broke from her, and she buried her face in her hands. "I suppose she is always trying to come – only she is too vague – and hasn't any form that we can see except when he thinks of her as she used to look when she was alive. His thought of her is like that, hurt and tragic and revengeful. You see, he feels that he ruined her life because she died when the child was coming – a month before it would have been born."

"And if he were to see her differently, would she change? Would she cease to be revengeful if he stopped thinking her so?"

"God only knows. I've wondered and wondered how I might move her to pity."

"Then you feel that she is really there? That she exists outside of his mind?"

"How can I tell? What do any of us know of the world beyond? She exists as much as I exist to you or you to me. Isn't thought all that there is – all that we know?"

This was deeper than I could follow; but in order not to appear stupid, I murmured sympathetically,

"And does she make him unhappy when she comes?"

"She is killing him – and me. I believe that is why she does it."

"Are you sure that she could stay away? When he thinks of her isn't she obliged to come back?"

"Oh, I've asked that question over and over! In spite of his calling her so unconsciously, I believe she comes of her own will, I have always the feeling – it has never left me for an instant –

that she could appear differently if she would. I have studied her for years until I know her like a book, and though she is only an apparition, I am perfectly positive that she wills evil to us both. Don't you think he would change that if he could? Don't you think he would make her kind instead of vindictive if he had the power?"

"But if he could remember her as loving and tender?"

"I don't know. I give it up – but it is killing me."

It was killing her. As the days passed I began to realize that she had spoken the truth. I watched her bloom fade slowly and her lovely features grow pinched and thin like the features of a starved person. The harder she fought the apparition, the more I saw that the battle was a losing one, and that she was only wasting her strength. So impalpable yet so pervasive was the enemy that it was like fighting a poisonous odor. There was nothing to wrestle with, and yet there was everything. The struggle was wearing her out – was, as she had said, actually 'killing her'; but the physician who dosed her daily with drugs – there was need now of a physician – had not the faintest idea of the malady he was treating. In those dreadful days I think that even Mr. Vanderbridge hadn't a suspicion of the truth. The past was with him so constantly – he was so steeped in the memories of it – that the present was scarcely more than a dream to him. It was, you see, a reverse of the natural order of things; the thought had become more vivid to his perceptions than any object. The phantom had been victorious so far, and he was like a man recovering from the effects of a narcotic. He was only half awake, only half alive to the events through which he lived and the people who surrounded him. Oh, I realize that I am telling my story badly! – that I am slurring over the significant interludes! My mind has dealt so long with external details that I have almost forgotten the words that express invisible things. Though the phantom in the house was more real to me than the bread I ate or the floor on which I trod, I can give you no impression of the atmosphere in which we lived day after day – of the suspense, of the dread of something we could not define, of the brooding horror that seemed to lurk in the shadows of the firelight, of the feeling always, day and night, that some unseen person was watching us. How Mrs. Vanderbridge stood it without losing her reason I have never known; and even now I am not sure that she could have kept her reason if the end had not come when it did. That I accidentally brought it about is one of the things in my life I am most thankful to remember.

It was an afternoon in late winter, and I had just come up from luncheon, when Mrs. Vanderbridge asked me to empty an old desk in one of the upstairs rooms. "I am sending all the furniture in that room away," she said; "it was bought in a bad period, and I want to clear it out and make room for the lovely things we picked up in Italy. There is nothing in the desk worth saving except some old letters from Mr. Vanderbridge's mother before her marriage."

I was glad that she could think of anything so practical as furniture, and it was with relief that I followed her into the dim, rather musty room over the library, where the windows were all tightly closed. Years ago, Hopkins had once told me, the first Mrs. Vanderbridge had used this room for a while, and after her death her husband had been in the habit of shutting himself up alone here in the evenings. This, I inferred, was the secret reason why my employer was sending the furniture away. She had resolved to clear the house of every association with the past.

For a few minutes we sorted the letters in the drawers of the desk, and then, as I expected, Mrs. Vanderbridge became suddenly bored by the task she had undertaken. She was subject to these nervous reactions, and I was prepared for them even when they seized her so spasmodically. I remember that she was in the very act of glancing over an old letter when she rose impatiently, tossed it into the fire unread, and picked up a magazine she had thrown down on a chair.

"Go over them by yourself, Miss Wrenn," she said, and it was characteristic of her nature that she should assume my trustworthiness. "If anything seems worth saving you can file it – but I'd rather die than have to wade through all this."

They were mostly personal letters, and while I went on, carefully filing them, I thought how absurd it was of people to preserve so many papers that were entirely without value. Mr. Vanderbridge I had imagined to be a methodical man, and yet the disorder of the desk produced a painful effect on my systematic temperament. The drawers were filled with letters evidently unsorted, for now and then I came upon a mass of business receipts and acknowledgements crammed in among wedding invitations or letters from some elderly lady, who wrote interminable pale epistles in the finest and most feminine of Italian hands. That a man of Mr. Vanderbridge's wealth and position should have been so careless about his correspondence amazed me until I recalled the dark hints Hopkins had dropped in some of her midnight conversations. Was it possible that he had actually lost his reason for months after the death of his first wife, during that year when he had shut himself alone with her memory? The question was still in my mind when my eyes fell an the envelope in my hand, and I saw that it was addressed to Mrs. Roger Vanderbridge. So this explained, in a measure at least, the carelessness and the disorder! The desk was not his, but hers, and after her death he had used it only during those desperate months when he barely opened a letter. What he had done in those long evenings when he sat alone here it was beyond me to imagine. Was it any wonder that the brooding should have permanently unbalanced his mind?

At the end of an hour I had sorted and filed the papers, with the intention of asking Mrs. Vanderbridge if she wished me to destroy the ones that seemed to be unimportant. The letters she had instructed me to keep had not come to my hand, and I was about to give up the search for them, when, in shaking the lock of one of the drawers, the door of a secret compartment fell open, and I discovered a dark object, which crumbled and dropped apart when I touched it. Bending nearer, I saw that the crumbled mass had once been a bunch of flowers, and that a streamer of purple ribbon still held together the frail structure of wire and stems. In this drawer someone had hidden a sacred treasure, and moved by a sense of romance and adventure, I gathered the dust tenderly in tissue paper, and prepared to take it downstairs to Mrs. Vanderbridge. It was not until then that some letters tied loosely together with a silver cord caught my eye, and while I picked them up, I remember thinking that they must be the ones for which I had been looking so long. Then, as the cord broke in my grasp and I gathered the letters from the lid of the desk, a word or two flashed back at me through the torn edges of the envelopes, and I realized that they were love letters written, I surmised, some fifteen years ago, by Mr. Vanderbridge to his first wife.

"It may hurt her to see them," I thought, "but I don't dare destroy them. There is nothing I can do except give them to her."

As I left the room, carrying the letters and the ashes of the flowers, the idea of taking them to the husband instead of to the wife flashed through my mind. Then – I think it was some jealous feeling about the phantom that decided me – I quickened my steps to a run down the staircase.

"They would bring her back. He would think of her more than ever," I told myself, "so he shall never see them. He shall never see them if I can prevent it." I believe it occurred to me that Mrs. Vanderbridge would be generous enough to give them to him – she was capable of rising above her jealousy, I knew – but I determined that she shouldn't do it until I had reasoned it out with her. "If anything on earth would bring back the Other One for good; it would be his seeing these old letters," I repeated as I hastened down the hall.

Mrs. Vanderbridge was lying on the couch before the fire, and I noticed at once that she had been crying. The drawn look in her sweet face went to my heart, and I felt that I would do anything in the world to comfort her. Though she had a book in her hand, I could see that she had not been reading. The electric lamp on the table by her side was already lighted, leaving the rest of the room in shadow, for it was a gray day with a biting edge of snow in the air. It was all very charming in the soft light; but as soon as I entered I had a feeling of oppression that made me want to run out into the wind. If you have ever lived in a haunted house – a house pervaded by an unforgettable past – you will understand the sensation of melancholy that crept over me the minute the shadows began to fall. It was not in myself – of this I am sure, for I have naturally a cheerful temperament – it was in the space that surrounded us and the air we breathed.

I explained to her about the letters, and then, kneeling on the rug in front of her, I emptied the dust of the flowers into the fire. There was – though I hate to confess it – a vindictive pleasure in watching it melt into the flames; and at the moment I believe I could have burned the apparition as thankfully. The more I saw of the Other One, the more I found myself accepting Hopkins's judgment of her. Yes, her behavior, living and dead, proved that she was not 'a good sort'.

My eyes were still on the flames when a sound from Mrs. Vanderbridge – half a sigh, half a sob – made me turn quickly and look up at her.

"But this isn't his handwriting," she said in a puzzled tone. "They are love letters, and they are to her – but they are not from him." For a moment or two she was silent, and I heard the pages rustle in her hands as she turned them impatiently. "They are not from him," she repeated presently, with an exultant ring in her voice. "They are written after her marriage, but they are from another man." She was as sternly tragic as an avenging fate. "She wasn't faithful to him while she lived. She wasn't faithful to him even while he was hers—"

With a spring I had risen from my knees and was bending over her.

"Then you can save him from her. You can win him back! You have only to show him the letters, and he will believe."

"Yes, I have only to show him the letters." She was looking beyond me into the dusky shadows of the firelight, as if she saw the Other One standing there before her, "I have only to show him the letters," I knew now that she was not speaking to me, "and he will believe."

"Her power over him will be broken," I cried out. "He will think of her differently. Oh, don't you see? Can't you see? It is the only way to make him think of her differently. It is the only way to break forever the thought that draws her back to him."

"Yes, I see, it is the only way," she said slowly; and the words were still on her lips when the door opened and Mr. Vanderbridge entered.

"I came for a cup of tea," he began, and added with playful tenderness, "What is the only way?"

It was the crucial moment, I realized – it was the hour of destiny for these two – and while he sank wearily into a chair, I looked imploringly at his wife and then at the letters lying scattered loosely about her. If I had had my will I should have flung them at him with a violence which would have startled him out of his lethargy. Violence, I felt, was what he needed – violence, a storm, tears, reproaches – all the things he would never get from his wife.

For a minute or two she sat there, with the letters before her, and watched him with her thoughtful and tender gaze. I knew from her face, so lovely and yet so sad, that she was looking again at invisible things – at the soul of the man she loved, not at the body. She saw him, detached and spiritualized, and she saw also the Other One – for while we waited I became slowly aware of the apparition in the firelight – of the white face and the cloudy hair and the look of animosity and bitterness in the eyes. Never before had I been so profoundly convinced of the malignant will veiled by that thin figure. It was as if the visible form were only a spiral of gray smoke covering a sinister purpose.

"The only way," said Mrs. Vanderbridge, "is to fight fairly even when one fights evil." Her voice was like a bell, and as she spoke, she rose from the couch and stood there in her glowing beauty confronting the pale ghost of the past. There was a light about her that was almost unearthly – the light of triumph. The radiance of it blinded me for an instant. It was like a flame, clearing the atmosphere of all that was evil, of all that was poisonous and deadly. She was looking directly at the phantom, and there was no hate in her voice – there was only a great pity, a great sorrow and sweetness.

"I can't fight you that way," she said, and I knew that for the first time she had swept aside subterfuge and evasion, and was speaking straight to the presence before her. "After all, you are dead and I am living, and I cannot fight you that way. I give up everything. I give him back to you. Nothing is mine that I cannot win and keep fairly. Nothing is mine that belongs really to you."

Then, while Mr. Vanderbridge rose, with a start of fear, and came towards her, she bent quickly, and flung the letters into the fire. When he would have stooped to gather the unburned pages, her lovely flowing body curved between his hands and the flames; and so transparent, so ethereal she looked, that I saw – or imagined that I saw – the firelight shine through her. "The only way, my dear, is the right way," she said softly.

The next instant – I don't know to this day how or when it began – I was aware that the apparition had drawn nearer, and that the dread and fear, the evil purpose, were no longer a part of her. I saw her clearly for a moment – saw her as I had never seen her before – young and gentle and – yes, this is the only word for it – loving. It was just as if a curse had turned into a blessing, for, while she stood there, I had a curious sensation of being enfolded in a kind of spiritual glow and comfort – only words are useless to describe the feeling because it wasn't in the least like anything else I had ever known in my life. It was light without heat, glow without light – and yet it was none of these things. The nearest I can come to it is to call it a sense of blessedness – of blessedness that made you at peace with everything you had once hated.

Not until afterwards did I realize that it was the victory of good over evil. Not until afterwards did I discover that Mrs. Vanderbridge had triumphed over the past in the only way that she could triumph. She had won, not by resisting, but by accepting; not by violence, but by gentleness; not by grasping, but by renouncing. Oh, long, long afterwards, I knew that she had robbed the phantom of power over her by robbing it of hatred. She had changed the thought of the past, in that lay her victory.

At the moment I did not understand this. I did not understand it even when I looked again for the apparition in the firelight, and saw that it had vanished. There was nothing there – nothing except the pleasant flicker of light and shadow on the old Persian rug.

The Birthmark

Nathaniel Hawthorne

IN THE LATTER PART of the last century there lived a man of science, an eminent proficient in every branch of natural philosophy, who not long before our story opens had made experience of a spiritual affinity more attractive than any chemical one. He had left his laboratory to the care of an assistant, cleared his fine countenance from the furnace smoke, washed the stain of acids from his fingers, and persuaded a beautiful woman to become his wife. In those days when the comparatively recent discovery of electricity and other kindred mysteries of Nature seemed to open paths into the region of miracle, it was not unusual for the love of science to rival the love of woman in its depth and absorbing energy. The higher intellect, the imagination, the spirit, and even the heart might all find their congenial aliment in pursuits which, as some of their ardent votaries believed, would ascend from one step of powerful intelligence to another, until the philosopher should lay his hand on the secret of creative force and perhaps make new worlds for himself. We know not whether Aylmer possessed this degree of faith in man's ultimate control over Nature. He had devoted himself, however, too unreservedly to scientific studies ever to be weaned from them by any second passion. His love for his young wife might prove the stronger of the two; but it could only be by intertwining itself with his love of science, and uniting the strength of the latter to his own.

Such a union accordingly took place, and was attended with truly remarkable consequences and a deeply impressive moral. One day, very soon after their marriage, Aylmer sat gazing at his wife with a trouble in his countenance that grew stronger until he spoke.

"Georgiana," said he, "has it never occurred to you that the mark upon your cheek might be removed?"

"No, indeed," said she, smiling; but perceiving the seriousness of his manner, she blushed deeply. "To tell you the truth it has been so often called a charm that I was simple enough to imagine it might be so."

"Ah, upon another face perhaps it might," replied her husband; "but never on yours. No, dearest Georgiana, you came so nearly perfect from the hand of Nature that this slightest possible defect, which we hesitate whether to term a defect or a beauty, shocks me, as being the visible mark of earthly imperfection."

"Shocks you, my husband!" cried Georgiana, deeply hurt; at first reddening with momentary anger, but then bursting into tears. "Then why did you take me from my mother's side? You cannot love what shocks you!"

To explain this conversation it must be mentioned that in the center of Georgiana's left cheek there was a singular mark, deeply interwoven, as it were, with the texture and substance of her face. In the usual state of her complexion – a healthy though delicate bloom – the mark wore a tint of deeper crimson, which imperfectly defined its shape amid the surrounding rosiness. When she blushed it gradually became more indistinct, and finally vanished amid the triumphant rush of blood that bathed the whole cheek with its brilliant glow. But if any shifting motion caused her to turn pale there was the mark again, a crimson stain upon the snow, in what Aylmer sometimes deemed an almost fearful distinctness. Its shape bore not a little similarity to the human hand, though of the smallest pygmy size. Georgiana's lovers were wont to say that some fairy at her birth hour had laid her tiny hand upon the infant's cheek, and left this impress there in token of the magic endowments that were to give her such sway over all hearts. Many a desperate swain would have risked life for the privilege of pressing his lips to the mysterious hand. It must not be concealed, however, that the impression wrought by this fairy sign manual varied exceedingly, according to the difference of temperament in the beholders. Some fastidious persons – but they were exclusively of her own sex – affirmed that the bloody hand, as they chose to call it, quite destroyed the effect of Georgiana's beauty, and rendered her countenance even hideous. But it would be as reasonable to say that one of those small blue stains which sometimes occur in the purest statuary marble would convert the Eve of Powers to a monster. Masculine observers, if the birthmark did not heighten their admiration, contented themselves with wishing it away, that the world might possess one living specimen of ideal loveliness without the semblance of a flaw. After his marriage – for he thought little or nothing of the matter before – Aylmer discovered that this was the case with himself.

Had she been less beautiful – if Envy's self could have found aught else to sneer at – he might have felt his affection heightened by the prettiness of this mimic hand, now vaguely portrayed, now lost, now stealing forth again and glimmering to and fro with every pulse of emotion that throbbed within her heart; but seeing her otherwise so perfect, he found this one defect grow more and more intolerable with every moment of their united lives. It was the fatal flaw of humanity which Nature, in one shape or another, stamps ineffaceably on all her productions, either to imply that they are temporary and finite, or that their perfection must be wrought by toil and pain. The crimson hand expressed the ineludible gripe in which mortality clutches the highest and purest of earthly mold, degrading them into kindred with the lowest, and even with the very brutes, like whom their visible frames return to dust. In this manner, selecting it as the symbol of his wife's liability to sin, sorrow, decay, and death, Aylmer's sombre imagination was not long in rendering the birthmark a frightful object, causing him more trouble and horror than ever Georgiana's beauty, whether of soul or sense, had given him delight.

At all the seasons which should have been their happiest, he invariably and without intending it, nay, in spite of a purpose to the contrary, reverted to this one disastrous topic. Trifling as it at first appeared, it so connected itself with innumerable trains of thought and modes of feeling that it became the central point of all. With the morning twilight Aylmer opened his eyes upon his wife's face and recognized the symbol of imperfection; and when they sat together at the evening hearth his eyes wandered stealthily to her cheek, and beheld, flickering with the blaze of the wood fire, the spectral hand that wrote mortality where he would fain have worshiped. Georgiana soon learned to shudder at his gaze. It needed but a glance with the peculiar expression that his face often wore to change the roses of her cheek into a deathlike paleness, amid which the crimson hand was brought strongly out, like a bass-relief of ruby on the whitest marble.

Late one night when the lights were growing dim, so as hardly to betray the stain on the poor wife's cheek, she herself, for the first time, voluntarily took up the subject.

"Do you remember, my dear Aylmer," said she, with a feeble attempt at a smile, "have you any recollection of a dream last night about this odious hand?"

"None! None whatever!" replied Aylmer, starting; but then he added, in a dry, cold tone affected for the sake of concealing the real depth of his emotion, "I might well dream of it; for before I fell asleep it had taken a pretty firm hold of my fancy."

"And you did dream of it?" continued Georgiana, hastily; for she dreaded lest a gush of tears should interrupt what she had to say. "A terrible dream! I wonder that you can forget it. Is it possible to forget this one expression? – 'It is in her heart now; we must have it out!' Reflect, my husband; for by all means I would have you recall that dream."

The mind is in a sad state when Sleep, the all-involving, cannot confine her spectres within the dim region of her sway, but suffers them to break forth, affrighting this actual life with secrets that perchance belong to a deeper one. Aylmer now remembered his dream. He had fancied himself with his servant Aminadab, attempting an operation for the removal of the birthmark; but the deeper went the knife, the deeper sank the hand, until at length its tiny grasp appeared to have caught hold of Georgiana's heart; whence, however, her husband was inexorably resolved to cut or wrench it away.

When the dream had shaped itself perfectly in his memory, Aylmer sat in his wife's presence with a guilty feeling. Truth often finds its way to the mind close muffled in robes of sleep, and then speaks with uncompromising directness of matters in regard to which we practice an unconscious self-deception during our waking moments. Until now he had not been aware of the tyrannizing influence acquired by one idea over his mind, and of the lengths which he might find in his heart to go for the sake of giving himself peace.

"Aylmer," resumed Georgiana, solemnly, "I know not what may be the cost to both of us to rid me of this fatal birthmark. Perhaps its removal may cause cureless deformity; or it may be the stain goes as deep as life itself. Again: do we know that there is a possibility, on any terms, of unclasping the firm gripe of this little hand which was laid upon me before I came into the world?"

"Dearest Georgiana, I have spent much thought upon the subject," hastily interrupted Aylmer. "I am convinced of the perfect practicability of its removal."

"If there be the remotest possibility of it," continued Georgiana, "let the attempt be made at whatever risk. Danger is nothing to me; for life, while this hateful mark makes me the object of your horror and disgust – life is a burden which I would fling down with joy. Either remove this dreadful hand, or take my wretched life! You have deep science. All the world bears witness of it. You have achieved great wonders. Cannot you remove this little, little mark, which I cover with the tips of two small fingers? Is this beyond your power, for the sake of your own peace, and to save your poor wife from madness?"

"Noblest, dearest, tenderest wife," cried Aylmer, rapturously, "doubt not my power. I have already given this matter the deepest thought – thought which might almost have enlightened me to create a being less perfect than yourself. Georgiana, you have led me deeper than ever into the heart of science. I feel myself fully competent to render this dear cheek as faultless as its fellow; and then, most beloved, what will be my triumph when I shall have corrected what Nature left imperfect in her fairest work! Even Pygmalion, when his sculptured woman assumed life, felt not greater ecstasy than mine will be."

"It is resolved, then," said Georgiana, faintly smiling. "And, Aylmer, spare me not, though you should find the birthmark take refuge in my heart at last."

Her husband tenderly kissed her cheek – her right cheek – not that which bore the impress of the crimson hand.

The next day Aylmer apprised his wife of a plan that he had formed whereby he might have opportunity for the intense thought and constant watchfulness which the proposed operation would require; while Georgiana, likewise, would enjoy the perfect repose essential to its success. They were to seclude themselves in the extensive apartments occupied by Aylmer as laboratory, and where, during his toilsome youth, he had made discoveries in the elemental powers of Nature that had roused the admiration of all the learned societies in Europe. Seated calmly in this laboratory, the pale philosopher had investigated the secrets of the highest cloud region and of the profoundest mines; he had satisfied himself of the causes that kindled and kept alive the fires of the volcano; and had explained the mystery of fountains, and how it is that they gush forth, some so bright and pure, and others with such rich medicinal virtues, from the dark bosom of the earth. Here, too, at an earlier period, he had studied the wonders of the human frame, and attempted to fathom the very process by which Nature assimilates all her precious influences from earth and air, and from the spiritual world, to create and foster man, her masterpiece. The latter pursuit, however, Aylmer had long laid aside in unwilling recognition of the truth – against which all seekers sooner or later stumble – that our great creative Mother, while she amuses us with apparently working in the broadest sunshine, is yet severely careful to keep her own secrets, and, in spite of her pretended openness, shows us nothing but results. She permits us, indeed, to mar, but seldom to mend, and, like a jealous patentee, on no account to make. Now, however, Aylmer resumed these half-forgotten investigations; not, of course, with such hopes or wishes as first suggested them; but because they involved much physiological truth and lay in the path of his proposed scheme for the treatment of Georgiana.

As he led her over the threshold of the laboratory, Georgiana was cold and tremulous. Aylmer looked cheerfully into her face, with intent to reassure her, but was so startled with the intense glow of the birthmark upon the whiteness of her cheek that he could not restrain a strong convulsive shudder. His wife fainted.

"Aminadab! Aminadab!" shouted Aylmer, stamping violently on the floor.

Forthwith there issued from an inner apartment a man of low stature, but bulky frame, with shaggy hair hanging about his visage, which was grimed with the vapors of the furnace. This personage had been Aylmer's underworker during his whole scientific career, and was admirably fitted for that office by his great mechanical readiness, and the skill with which, while incapable of comprehending a single principle, he executed all the details of his master's experiments. With his vast strength, his shaggy hair, his smoky aspect, and the indescribable earthiness that incrusted him, he seemed to represent man's physical nature; while Aylmer's slender figure, and pale, intellectual face, were no less apt a type of the spiritual element.

"Throw open the door of the boudoir, Aminadab," said Aylmer, "and burn a pastil."

"Yes, master," answered Aminadab, looking intently at the lifeless form of Georgiana; and then he muttered to himself, "If she were my wife, I'd never part with that birthmark."

When Georgiana recovered consciousness she found herself breathing an atmosphere of penetrating fragrance, the gentle potency of which had recalled her from her deathlike faintness. The scene around her looked like enchantment. Aylmer had converted those smoky, dingy, sombre rooms, where he had spent his brightest years in recondite pursuits, into a series of beautiful apartments not unfit to be the secluded abode of a lovely woman. The walls were hung with gorgeous curtains, which imparted the combination of grandeur and grace that no other species of adornment can achieve; and as they fell from the ceiling to the floor, their rich and ponderous folds, concealing all angles and straight lines, appeared to shut in the scene from infinite space. For aught Georgiana knew, it might be a pavilion among the clouds. And Aylmer, excluding the sunshine, which would have interfered with his chemical processes, had supplied its place with perfumed lamps, emitting flames of various hue, but all uniting in a soft, impurpled radiance. He now knelt by his wife's side, watching her earnestly, but without alarm; for he was confident in his science, and felt that he could draw a magic circle round her within which no evil might intrude.

"Where am I? Ah, I remember," said Georgiana, faintly; and she placed her hand over her cheek to hide the terrible mark from her husband's eyes.

"Fear not, dearest!" exclaimed he. "Do not shrink from me! Believe me, Georgiana, I even rejoice in this single imperfection, since it will be such a rapture to remove it."

"Oh, spare me!" sadly replied his wife. "Pray do not look at it again. I never can forget that convulsive shudder."

In order to soothe Georgiana, and, as it were, to release her mind from the burden of actual things, Aylmer now put in practice some of the light and playful secrets which science had taught him among its profounder lore. Airy figures, absolutely bodiless ideas, and forms of unsubstantial beauty came and danced before her, imprinting their momentary footsteps on beams of light. Though she had some indistinct idea of the method of these optical phenomena, still the illusion was almost perfect enough to warrant the belief that her husband possessed sway over the spiritual world. Then again, when she felt a wish to look forth from her seclusion, immediately, as if her thoughts were answered, the procession of external existence flitted across a screen. The scenery and the figures of actual life were perfectly represented, but with that bewitching, yet indescribable difference which always makes a picture, an image, or a shadow so much more attractive than the original. When wearied of this, Aylmer bade her cast her eyes upon a vessel containing a quantity of earth. She did so, with little interest at first; but was soon startled to perceive the germ of a plant shooting upward from the soil. Then came the slender stalk; the leaves gradually unfolded themselves; and amid them was a perfect and lovely flower.

"It is magical!" cried Georgiana. "I dare not touch it."

"Nay, pluck it," answered Aylmer – "pluck it, and inhale its brief perfume while you may. The flower will wither in a few moments and leave nothing save its brown seed vessels; but thence may be perpetuated a race as ephemeral as itself."

But Georgiana had no sooner touched the flower than the whole plant suffered a blight, its leaves turning coal-black as if by the agency of fire.

"There was too powerful a stimulus," said Aylmer, thoughtfully.

To make up for this abortive experiment, he proposed to take her portrait by a scientific process of his own invention. It was to be effected by rays of light striking upon a polished plate of metal. Georgiana assented; but, on looking at the result, was affrighted to find the features of the portrait blurred and indefinable; while the minute figure of a hand appeared where the cheek should have been. Aylmer snatched the metallic plate and threw it into a jar of corrosive acid.

Soon, however, he forgot these mortifying failures. In the intervals of study and chemical experiment he came to her flushed and exhausted, but seemed invigorated by her presence, and spoke in glowing language of the resources of his art. He gave a history of the long dynasty of the alchemists, who spent so many ages in quest of the universal solvent by which the golden principle might be elicited from all things vile and base. Aylmer appeared to believe that, by the plainest scientific logic, it was altogether within the limits of possibility to discover this long-sought medium; "but," he added, "a philosopher who should go deep enough to acquire the power would attain too lofty a wisdom to stoop to the exercise of it." Not less singular were his opinions in regard to the elixir vitae. He more than intimated that it was at his option to concoct a liquid that should prolong life for years, perhaps interminably; but that it would produce a discord in Nature which all the world, and chiefly the quaffer of the immortal nostrum, would find cause to curse.

"Aylmer, are you in earnest?" asked Georgiana, looking at him with amazement and fear. "It is terrible to possess such power, or even to dream of possessing it."

"Oh, do not tremble, my love," said her husband. "I would not wrong either you or myself by working such inharmonious effects upon our lives; but I would have you consider how trifling, in comparison, is the skill requisite to remove this little hand."

At the mention of the birthmark, Georgiana, as usual, shrank as if a redhot iron had touched her cheek.

Again Aylmer applied himself to his labors. She could hear his voice in the distant furnace room giving directions to Aminadab, whose harsh, uncouth, misshapen tones were audible in response, more like the grunt or growl of a brute than human speech. After hours of absence, Aylmer reappeared and proposed that she should now examine his cabinet of chemical products and natural treasures of the earth. Among the former he showed her a small vial, in which, he remarked, was contained a gentle yet most powerful fragrance, capable of impregnating all the breezes that blow across a kingdom. They were of inestimable value, the contents of that little vial; and, as he said so, he threw some of the perfume into the air and filled the room with piercing and invigorating delight.

"And what is this?" asked Georgiana, pointing to a small crystal globe containing a gold-colored liquid. "It is so beautiful to the eye that I could imagine it the elixir of life."

"In one sense it is," replied Aylmer; "or, rather, the elixir of immortality. It is the most precious poison that ever was concocted in this world. By its aid I could apportion the lifetime of any mortal at whom you might point your finger. The strength of the dose would determine whether he were to linger out years, or drop dead in the midst of a breath. No king on his guarded throne could keep his life if I, in my private station, should deem that the welfare of millions justified me in depriving him of it."

"Why do you keep such a terrific drug?" inquired Georgiana in horror.

"Do not mistrust me, dearest," said her husband, smiling; "its virtuous potency is yet greater than its harmful one. But see! Here is a powerful cosmetic. With a few drops of this in a vase of water, freckles may be washed away as easily as the hands are cleansed. A stronger infusion would take the blood out of the cheek, and leave the rosiest beauty a pale ghost."

"Is it with this lotion that you intend to bathe my cheek?" asked Georgiana, anxiously.

"Oh, no," hastily replied her husband; "this is merely superficial. Your case demands a remedy that shall go deeper."

In his interviews with Georgiana, Aylmer generally made minute inquiries as to her sensations and whether the confinement of the rooms and the temperature of the atmosphere agreed with her. These questions had such a particular drift that Georgiana began to conjecture that she was already subjected to certain physical influences, either breathed in with the fragrant air or taken with her food. She fancied likewise, but it might be altogether fancy, that there was a stirring up of her system – a strange, indefinite sensation creeping through her veins, and tingling, half painfully, half pleasurably, at her heart. Still, whenever she dared to look into the mirror, there she beheld herself pale as a white rose and with the crimson birthmark stamped upon her cheek. Not even Aylmer now hated it so much as she.

To dispel the tedium of the hours which her husband found it necessary to devote to the processes of combination and analysis, Georgiana turned over the volumes of his scientific library. In many dark old tomes she met with chapters full of romance and poetry. They were the works of philosophers of the middle ages, such as Albertus Magnus, Cornelius Agrippa,

Paracelsus, and the famous friar who created the prophetic Brazen Head. All these antique naturalists stood in advance of their centuries, yet were imbued with some of their credulity, and therefore were believed, and perhaps imagined themselves to have acquired from the investigation of Nature a power above Nature, and from physics a sway over the spiritual world. Hardly less curious and imaginative were the early volumes of the Transactions of the Royal Society, in which the members, knowing little of the limits of natural possibility, were continually recording wonders or proposing methods whereby wonders might be wrought.

But to Georgiana the most engrossing volume was a large folio from her husband's own hand, in which he had recorded every experiment of his scientific career, its original aim, the methods adopted for its development, and its final success or failure, with the circumstances to which either event was attributable. The book, in truth, was both the history and emblem of his ardent, ambitious, imaginative, yet practical and laborious life. He handled physical details as if there were nothing beyond them; yet spiritualized them all, and redeemed himself from materialism by his strong and eager aspiration towards the infinite. In his grasp the veriest clod of earth assumed a soul. Georgiana, as she read, reverenced Aylmer and loved him more profoundly than ever, but with a less entire dependence on his judgment than heretofore. Much as he had accomplished, she could not but observe that his most splendid successes were almost invariably failures, if compared with the ideal at which he aimed. His brightest diamonds were the merest pebbles, and felt to be so by himself, in comparison with the inestimable gems which lay hidden beyond his reach. The volume, rich with achievements that had won renown for its author, was yet as melancholy a record as ever mortal hand had penned. It was the sad confession and continual exemplification of the shortcomings of the composite man, the spirit burdened with clay and working in matter, and of the despair that assails the higher nature at finding itself so miserably thwarted by the earthly part. Perhaps every man of genius in whatever sphere might recognize the image of his own experience in Aylmer's journal.

So deeply did these reflections affect Georgiana that she laid her face upon the open volume and burst into tears. In this situation she was found by her husband.

"It is dangerous to read in a sorcerer's books," said he with a smile, though his countenance was uneasy and displeased. "Georgiana, there are pages in that volume which I can scarcely glance over and keep my senses. Take heed lest it prove as detrimental to you."

"It has made me worship you more than ever," said she.

"Ah, wait for this one success," rejoined he, "then worship me if you will. I shall deem myself hardly unworthy of it. But come, I have sought you for the luxury of your voice. Sing to me, dearest."

So she poured out the liquid music of her voice to quench the thirst of his spirit. He then took his leave with a boyish exuberance of gayety, assuring her that her seclusion would endure but a little longer, and that the result was already certain. Scarcely had he departed when Georgiana felt irresistibly impelled to follow him. She had forgotten to inform Aylmer of a symptom which for two or three hours past had begun to excite her attention. It was a sensation in the fatal birthmark, not painful, but which induced a restlessness throughout her system. Hastening after her husband, she intruded for the first time into the laboratory.

The first thing that struck her eye was the furnace, that hot and feverish worker, with the intense glow of its fire, which by the quantities of soot clustered above it seemed to have been burning for ages. There was a distilling apparatus in full operation. Around the room were retorts, tubes, cylinders, crucibles, and other apparatus of chemical research. An electrical machine stood ready for immediate use. The atmosphere felt oppressively close, and was tainted with gaseous odors which had been tormented forth by the processes of science. The severe and homely simplicity of the apartment, with its naked walls and brick pavement, looked strange, accustomed as Georgiana had become to the fantastic elegance of her boudoir. But what chiefly, indeed almost solely, drew her attention, was the aspect of Aylmer himself.

He was pale as death, anxious and absorbed, and hung over the furnace as if it depended upon his utmost watchfulness whether the liquid which it was distilling should be the draught of immortal happiness or misery. How different from the sanguine and joyous mien that he had assumed for Georgiana's encouragement!

"Carefully now, Aminadab; carefully, thou human machine; carefully, thou man of clay!" muttered Aylmer, more to himself than his assistant. "Now, if there be a thought too much or too little, it is all over."

"Ho! Ho!" mumbled Aminadab. "Look, master! Look!"

Aylmer raised his eyes hastily, and at first reddened, then grew paler than ever, on beholding Georgiana. He rushed towards her and seized her arm with a gripe that left the print of his fingers upon it.

"Why do you come hither? Have you no trust in your husband?" cried he, impetuously. "Would you throw the blight of that fatal birthmark over my labors? It is not well done. Go, prying woman, go!"

"Nay, Aylmer," said Georgiana with the firmness of which she possessed no stinted endowment, "it is not you that have a right to complain. You mistrust your wife; you have concealed the anxiety with which you watch the development of this experiment. Think not so unworthily of me, my husband. Tell me all the risk we run, and fear not that I shall shrink; for my share in it is far less than your own."

"No, no, Georgiana!" said Aylmer, impatiently; "It must not be."

"I submit," replied she calmly. "And, Aylmer, I shall quaff whatever draught you bring me; but it will be on the same principle that would induce me to take a dose of poison if offered by your hand."

"My noble wife," said Aylmer, deeply moved, "I knew not the height and depth of your nature until now. Nothing shall be concealed. Know, then, that this crimson hand, superficial as it seems, has clutched its grasp into your being with a strength of which I had no previous conception. I have already administered agents powerful enough to do aught except to change your entire physical system. Only one thing remains to be tried. If that fails us we are ruined."

"Why did you hesitate to tell me this?" asked she.

"Because, Georgiana," said Aylmer, in a low voice, "there is danger."

"Danger? There is but one danger – that this horrible stigma shall be left upon my cheek!" cried Georgiana. "Remove it, remove it, whatever be the cost, or we shall both go mad!"

"Heaven knows your words are too true," said Aylmer, sadly. "And now, dearest, return to your boudoir. In a little while all will be tested."

He conducted her back and took leave of her with a solemn tenderness which spoke far more than his words how much was now at stake. After his departure Georgiana became rapt in musings. She considered the character of Aylmer, and did it completer justice than at any previous moment. Her heart exulted, while it trembled, at his honorable love – so pure and lofty that it would accept nothing less than perfection nor miserably make itself contented with an earthlier nature than he had dreamed of. She felt how much more precious was such a sentiment than that meaner kind which would have borne with the imperfection for her sake, and have been guilty of treason to holy love by degrading its perfect idea to the level of the actual; and with her whole spirit she prayed that, for a single moment, she might satisfy his highest and deepest conception. Longer than one moment she well knew it could not be; for his spirit was ever on the march, ever ascending, and each instant required something that was beyond the scope of the instant before.

The sound of her husband's footsteps aroused her. He bore a crystal goblet containing a liquor colorless as water, but bright enough to be the draught of immortality. Aylmer was pale; but it seemed rather the consequence of a highly-wrought state of mind and tension of spirit than of fear or doubt.

"The concoction of the draught has been perfect," said he, in answer to Georgiana's look. "Unless all my science have deceived me, it cannot fail."

"Save on your account, my dearest Aylmer," observed his wife, "I might wish to put off this birthmark of mortality by relinquishing mortality itself in preference to any other mode. Life is but a sad possession to those who have attained precisely the degree of moral advancement at which I stand. Were I weaker and blinder it might be happiness. Were I stronger, it might be endured hopefully. But, being what I find myself, methinks I am of all mortals the most fit to die."

"You are fit for heaven without tasting death!" replied her husband "But why do we speak of dying? The draught cannot fail. Behold its effect upon this plant."

On the window seat there stood a geranium diseased with yellow blotches, which had overspread all its leaves. Aylmer poured a small quantity of the liquid upon the soil in which it grew. In a little time, when the roots of the plant had taken up the moisture, the unsightly blotches began to be extinguished in a living verdure.

"There needed no proof," said Georgiana, quietly. "Give me the goblet. I joyfully stake all upon your word."

"Drink, then, thou lofty creature!" exclaimed Aylmer, with fervid admiration. "There is no taint of imperfection on thy spirit. Thy sensible frame, too, shall soon be all perfect."

She quaffed the liquid and returned the goblet to his hand.

"It is grateful," said she with a placid smile. "Methinks it is like water from a heavenly fountain; for it contains I know not what of unobtrusive fragrance and deliciousness. It allays a feverish thirst that had parched me for many days. Now, dearest, let me sleep. My earthly senses are closing over my spirit like the leaves around the heart of a rose at sunset."

She spoke the last words with a gentle reluctance, as if it required almost more energy than she could command to pronounce the faint and lingering syllables. Scarcely had they loitered through her lips ere she was lost in slumber. Aylmer sat by her side, watching her aspect with the emotions proper to a man the whole value of whose existence was involved in the process now to be tested. Mingled with this mood, however, was the philosophic investigation characteristic of the man of science. Not the minutest symptom escaped him. A heightened flush of the cheek, a slight irregularity of breath, a quiver of the eyelid, a hardly perceptible tremor through the frame – such were the details which, as the moments passed, he wrote down in his folio volume. Intense thought had set its stamp upon every previous page of that volume, but the thoughts of years were all concentrated upon the last.

While thus employed, he failed not to gaze often at the fatal hand, and not without a shudder. Yet once, by a strange and unaccountable impulse he pressed it with his lips. His spirit recoiled, however, in the very act, and Georgiana, out of the midst of her deep sleep, moved uneasily and murmured as if in remonstrance. Again Aylmer resumed his watch. Nor was it without avail. The crimson hand, which at first had been strongly visible upon the marble paleness of Georgiana's cheek, now grew more faintly outlined. She remained not less pale than ever; but the birthmark with every breath that came and went, lost somewhat of its former distinctness. Its presence had been awful; its departure was more awful still. Watch the stain of the rainbow fading out the sky, and you will know how that mysterious symbol passed away.

"By Heaven! It is well-nigh gone!" said Aylmer to himself, in almost irrepressible ecstasy. "I can scarcely trace it now. Success! Success! And now it is like the faintest rose color. The lightest flush of blood across her cheek would overcome it. But she is so pale!"

He drew aside the window curtain and suffered the light of natural day to fall into the room and rest upon her cheek. At the same time he heard a gross, hoarse chuckle, which he had long known as his servant Aminadab's expression of delight.

"Ah, clod! Ah, earthly mass!" cried Aylmer, laughing in a sort of frenzy, "You have served me well! Matter and spirit – earth and heaven – have both done their part in this! Laugh, thing of the senses! You have earned the right to laugh."

These exclamations broke Georgiana's sleep. She slowly unclosed her eyes and gazed into the mirror which her husband had arranged for that purpose. A faint smile flitted over her lips when she recognized how barely perceptible was now that crimson hand which had once blazed forth with such disastrous brilliancy as to scare away all their happiness. But then her eyes sought Aylmer's face with a trouble and anxiety that he could by no means account for.

"My poor Aylmer!" murmured she.

"Poor? Nay, richest, happiest, most favored!" exclaimed he. "My peerless bride, it is successful! You are perfect!"

"My poor Aylmer," she repeated, with a more than human tenderness, "you have aimed loftily; you have done nobly. Do not repent that with so high and pure a feeling, you have rejected the best the earth could offer. Aylmer, dearest Aylmer, I am dying!"

Alas! It was too true! The fatal hand had grappled with the mystery of life, and was the bond by which an angelic spirit kept itself in union with a mortal frame. As the last crimson tint of the birthmark – that sole token of human imperfection – faded from her cheek, the parting breath of the now perfect woman passed into the atmosphere, and her soul, lingering a moment near her husband, took its heavenward flight. Then a hoarse, chuckling laugh was heard again! Thus ever does the gross fatality of earth exult in its invariable triumph over the immortal essence which, in this dim sphere of half development, demands the completeness of a higher state. Yet, had Alymer reached a profounder wisdom, he need not thus have flung away the happiness which would have woven his mortal life of the selfsame texture with the celestial. The momentary circumstance was too strong for him; he failed to look beyond the shadowy scope of time, and, living once for all in eternity, to find the perfect future in the present.

The Minister's Black Veil
A Parable

Nathaniel Hawthorne

THE SEXTON stood in the porch of Milford meeting-house pulling lustily at the bell-rope. The old people of the village came stooping along the street. Children with bright faces tripped merrily beside their parents or mimicked a graver gait in the conscious dignity of their Sunday clothes. Spruce bachelors looked sidelong at the pretty maidens, and fancied that the Sabbath sunshine made them prettier than on weekdays. When the throng had mostly streamed into the porch, the sexton began to toll the bell, keeping his eye on the Reverend Mr. Hooper's door. The first glimpse of the clergyman's figure was the signal for the bell to cease its summons.

"But what has good Parson Hooper got upon his face?" cried the sexton, in astonishment.

All within hearing immediately turned about and beheld the semblance of Mr. Hooper pacing slowly his meditative way toward the meeting-house. With one accord they started, expressing more wonder than if some strange minister were coming to dust the cushions of Mr. Hooper's pulpit.

"Are you sure it is our parson?" inquired Goodman Gray of the sexton.

"Of a certainty it is good Mr. Hooper," replied the sexton. "He was to have exchanged pulpits with Parson Shute of Westbury, but Parson Shute sent to excuse himself yesterday, being to preach a funeral sermon."

The cause of so much amazement may appear sufficiently slight. Mr. Hooper, a gentlemanly person of about thirty, though still a bachelor, was dressed with due clerical neatness, as if a careful wife had starched his band and brushed the weekly dust from his Sunday's garb. There was but one thing remarkable in his appearance. Swathed about his forehead and hanging down over his face, so low as to be shaken by his breath, Mr. Hooper had on a black veil. On a nearer view it seemed to consist of two folds of crape, which entirely concealed his features except the mouth and chin, but probably did not intercept his sight further than to give a darkened aspect to all living and inanimate things. With this gloomy shade before him good Mr. Hooper walked onward at a slow and quiet pace, stooping somewhat and looking on the ground, as is customary with abstracted men, yet nodding kindly to those of his parishioners who still waited on the meeting-house steps. But so wonder-struck were they that his greeting hardly met with a return.

"I can't really feel as if good Mr. Hooper's face was behind that piece of crape," said the sexton.

"I don't like it," muttered an old woman as she hobbled into the meeting-house. "He has changed himself into something awful only by hiding his face."

"Our parson has gone mad!" cried Goodman Gray, following him across the threshold.

A rumor of some unaccountable phenomenon had preceded Mr. Hooper into the meeting-house and set all the congregation astir. Few could refrain from twisting their heads toward the door; many stood upright and turned directly about; while several little boys clambered upon the seats, and came down again with a terrible racket. There was a general bustle, a rustling of the women's gowns and shuffling of the men's feet, greatly at variance with that hushed repose which should attend the entrance of the minister. But Mr. Hooper appeared not to notice the perturbation of his people. He entered with an almost noiseless step, bent his head mildly to the pews on each side and bowed as he passed his oldest parishioner, a white-haired great-grandsire, who occupied an armchair in the center of the aisle. It was strange to observe how slowly this venerable man became conscious of something singular in the appearance of his pastor. He seemed not fully to partake of the prevailing wonder till Mr. Hooper had ascended the stairs and showed himself in the pulpit, face to face with his congregation except for the black veil. That mysterious emblem was never once withdrawn. It shook with his measured breath as he gave out the psalm, it threw its obscurity between him and the holy page as he read the Scriptures, and while he prayed the veil lay heavily on his uplifted countenance. Did he seek to hide it from the dread Being whom he was addressing?

Such was the effect of this simple piece of crape that more than one woman of delicate nerves was forced to leave the meeting-house. Yet perhaps the pale-faced congregation was almost as fearful a sight to the minister as his black veil to them.

Mr. Hooper had the reputation of a good preacher, but not an energetic one: he strove to win his people heavenward by mild, persuasive influences rather than to drive them thither by the thunders of the word. The sermon which he now delivered was marked by the same characteristics of style and manner as the general series of his pulpit oratory, but there was something either in the sentiment of the discourse itself or in the imagination of the auditors which made it greatly the most powerful effort that they had ever heard from their pastor's lips. It was tinged rather more darkly than usual with the gentle gloom of Mr. Hooper's temperament. The subject had reference to secret sin and those sad mysteries which we hide from our nearest and dearest, and would fain conceal from our own consciousness, even forgetting that the Omniscient can detect them. A subtle power was breathed into his words. Each member of the congregation, the most innocent girl and the man of hardened breast, felt as if the preacher had crept upon them behind his awful veil and discovered their hoarded iniquity of deed or thought. Many spread their clasped hands on their bosoms. There was nothing terrible in what Mr. Hooper said – at least, no violence; and yet with every tremor of his melancholy voice the hearers quaked. An unsought pathos came hand in hand with awe. So sensible were the audience of some unwonted attribute in their minister that they longed for a breath of wind to blow aside the veil, almost believing that a stranger's visage would be discovered, though the form, gesture and voice were those of Mr. Hooper.

At the close of the services the people hurried out with indecorous confusion, eager to communicate their pent-up amazement, and conscious of lighter spirits the moment they lost sight of the black veil. Some gathered in little circles, huddled closely together, with their mouths all whispering in the center; some went homeward alone, wrapped in silent meditation; some talked loudly and profaned the Sabbath-day with ostentatious laughter. A few shook their sagacious heads, intimating that they could penetrate the mystery, while one or two affirmed that there was no mystery at all, but only that Mr. Hooper's eyes were so weakened by the midnight lamp as to require a shade.

After a brief interval forth came good Mr. Hooper also, in the rear of his flock. Turning his veiled face from one group to another, he paid due reverence to the hoary heads, saluted the middle-aged with kind dignity as their friend and spiritual guide, greeted the young with mingled authority and love, and laid his hands on the little children's heads to bless them. Such was always his custom on the Sabbath-day. Strange and bewildered looks repaid him for his courtesy. None, as on former occasions, aspired to the honor of walking by their pastor's side. Old Squire Saunders – doubtless by an accidental lapse of memory – neglected to invite Mr. Hooper to his table, where the good clergyman had been wont to bless the food almost every Sunday since his settlement. He returned, therefore, to the parsonage, and at the moment of closing the door was observed to look back upon the people, all of whom had their eyes fixed upon the minister. A sad smile gleamed faintly from beneath the black veil and flickered about his mouth, glimmering as he disappeared.

"How strange," said a lady, "that a simple black veil, such as any woman might wear on her bonnet, should become such a terrible thing on Mr. Hooper's face!"

"Something must surely be amiss with Mr. Hooper's intellects," observed her husband, the physician of the village. "But the strangest part of the affair is the effect of this vagary even on a sober-minded man like myself. The black veil, though it covers only our pastor's face, throws its influence over his whole person and makes him ghost-like from head to foot. Do you not feel it so?"

"Truly do I," replied the lady; "and I would not be alone with him for the world. I wonder he is not afraid to be alone with himself."

"Men sometimes are so," said her husband.

The afternoon service was attended with similar circumstances. At its conclusion the bell tolled for the funeral of a young lady. The relatives and friends were assembled in the house and the more distant acquaintances stood about the door, speaking of the good qualities of the deceased, when their talk was interrupted by the appearance of Mr. Hooper, still covered with his black veil. It was now an appropriate emblem. The clergyman stepped into the room where the corpse was laid, and bent over the coffin to take a last farewell of his deceased parishioner. As he stooped the veil hung straight down from his forehead, so that, if her eyelids had not been closed for ever, the dead maiden might have seen his face. Could Mr. Hooper be fearful of her glance, that he so hastily caught back the black veil? A person who watched the interview between the dead and living scrupled not to affirm that at the instant when the clergyman's features were disclosed the corpse had slightly shuddered, rustling the shroud and muslin cap, though the countenance retained the composure of death. A superstitious old woman was the only witness of this prodigy.

From the coffin Mr. Hooper passed into the chamber of the mourners, and thence to the head of the staircase, to make the funeral prayer. It was a tender and heart-dissolving prayer, full of sorrow, yet so imbued with celestial hopes that the music of a heavenly harp swept by the fingers of the dead seemed faintly to be heard among the saddest accents of the minister. The people trembled, though they but darkly understood him, when he prayed that they and himself, and all of mortal race, might be ready, as he trusted this young maiden had been, for the dreadful hour that should snatch the veil from their faces. The bearers went heavily forth and the mourners followed, saddening all the street, with the dead before them and Mr. Hooper in his black veil behind.

"Why do you look back?" said one in the procession to his partner.

"I had a fancy," replied she, "that the minister and the maiden's spirit were walking hand in hand."

"And so had I at the same moment," said the other.

That night the handsomest couple in Milford village were to be joined in wedlock. Though reckoned a melancholy man, Mr. Hooper had a placid cheerfulness for such occasions which often excited a sympathetic smile where livelier merriment would have been thrown away. There was no quality of his disposition which made him more beloved than this. The company at the wedding awaited his arrival with impatience, trusting that the strange awe which had gathered over him throughout the day would now be dispelled. But such was not the result. When Mr. Hooper came, the first thing that their eyes rested on was the same horrible black veil which had added deeper gloom to the funeral and could portend nothing but evil to the wedding. Such was its immediate effect on the guests that a cloud seemed to have rolled duskily from beneath the black crape and dimmed the light of the candles. The bridal pair stood up before the minister, but the bride's cold fingers quivered in the tremulous hand of the bridegroom, and her death-like paleness caused a whisper that the maiden who had been buried a few hours before was come from her grave to be married. If ever another wedding were so dismal, it was that famous one where they tolled the wedding-knell.

After performing the ceremony Mr. Hooper raised a glass of wine to his lips, wishing happiness to the new-married couple in a strain of mild pleasantry that ought to have brightened the features of the guests like a cheerful gleam from the hearth. At that instant, catching a glimpse of his figure in the looking-glass, the black veil involved his own spirit in the horror with which it overwhelmed all others. His frame shuddered, his lips grew white, he spilt the untasted wine upon the carpet and rushed forth into the darkness, for the Earth too had on her black veil.

The next day the whole village of Milford talked of little else than Parson Hooper's black veil. That, and the mystery concealed behind it, supplied a topic for discussion between acquaintances meeting in the street and good women gossiping at their open windows. It was the first item of news that the tavernkeeper told to his guests. The children babbled of it on their way to school. One imitative little imp covered his face with an old black handkerchief, thereby so affrighting his playmates that the panic seized himself and he wellnigh lost his wits by his own waggery.

It was remarkable that, of all the busybodies and impertinent people in the parish, not one ventured to put the plain question to Mr. Hooper wherefore he did this thing. Hitherto, whenever there appeared the slightest call for such interference, he had never lacked advisers nor shown himself averse to be guided by their judgment. If he erred at all, it was by so painful a degree of self-distrust that even the mildest censure would lead him to consider an indifferent action as a crime. Yet, though so well acquainted with this amiable weakness, no individual among his parishioners chose to make the black veil a subject of friendly remonstrance. There was a feeling of dread, neither plainly confessed nor carefully concealed, which caused each to shift the responsibility upon another, till at length it was found expedient to send a deputation of the church, in order to deal with Mr. Hooper about the mystery before it should grow into a scandal. Never did an embassy so ill discharge its duties. The minister received them with friendly courtesy, but became silent after they were seated, leaving to his visitors the whole burden of introducing their important business. The topic, it might be supposed, was obvious enough. There was the black veil swathed round Mr. Hooper's forehead and concealing every feature above his placid mouth, on which, at times, they could perceive the glimmering of a melancholy smile. But that piece of crape, to their imagination, seemed to hang down before his heart, the symbol of a fearful secret between him and them. Were the veil but cast aside, they might speak freely of it, but not till then. Thus they sat a considerable time, speechless, confused and shrinking uneasily from Mr. Hooper's eye, which they felt to be fixed upon them with an invisible glance. Finally, the deputies returned abashed to their constituents, pronouncing the matter too weighty to be handled except by a council of the churches, if, indeed, it might not require a General Synod.

But there was one person in the village unappalled by the awe with which the black veil had impressed all besides herself. When the deputies returned without an explanation, or even venturing to demand one, she with the calm energy of her character determined to chase away the strange cloud that appeared to be settling round Mr. Hooper every moment more darkly than before. As his plighted wife it should be her privilege to know what the black veil concealed. At the minister's first visit, therefore, she entered upon the subject with a direct simplicity which made the task easier both for him and her. After he had seated himself she fixed her eyes steadfastly upon the veil, but could discern nothing of the dreadful gloom that had so overawed the multitude; it was but a double fold of crape hanging down from his forehead to his mouth and slightly stirring with his breath.

"No," said she, aloud, and smiling, "there is nothing terrible in this piece of crape, except that it hides a face which I am always glad to look upon. Come, good sir; let the sun shine from behind the cloud. First lay aside your black veil, then tell me why you put it on."

Mr. Hooper's smile glimmered faintly.

"There is an hour to come," said he, "when all of us shall cast aside our veils. Take it not amiss, beloved friend, if I wear this piece of crape till then."

"Your words are a mystery too," returned the young lady. "Take away the veil from them, at least."

"Elizabeth, I will," said he, "so far as my vow may suffer me. Know, then, this veil is a type and a symbol, and I am bound to wear it ever, both in light and darkness, in solitude and before the gaze of multitudes, and as with strangers, so with my familiar friends. No mortal eye will see it withdrawn. This dismal shade must separate me from the world; even you, Elizabeth, can never come behind it."

"What grievous affliction hath befallen you," she earnestly inquired, "that you should thus darken your eyes for ever?"

"If it be a sign of mourning," replied Mr. Hooper, "I, perhaps, like most other mortals, have sorrows dark enough to be typified by a black veil."

"But what if the world will not believe that it is the type of an innocent sorrow?" urged Elizabeth. "Beloved and respected as you are, there may be whispers that you hide your face under the consciousness of secret sin. For the sake of your holy office do away this scandal."

The color rose into her cheeks as she intimated the nature of the rumors that were already abroad in the village. But Mr. Hooper's mildness did not forsake him. He even smiled again – that same sad smile which always appeared like a faint glimmering of light proceeding from the obscurity beneath the veil.

"If I hide my face for sorrow, there is cause enough," he merely replied; "and if I cover it for secret sin, what mortal might not do the same?" And with this gentle but unconquerable obstinacy did he resist all her entreaties.

At length Elizabeth sat silent. For a few moments she appeared lost in thought, considering, probably, what new methods might be tried to withdraw her lover from so dark a fantasy, which, if it had no other meaning, was perhaps a symptom of mental disease. Though of a firmer character than his own, the tears rolled down her cheeks. But in an instant, as it were, a new feeling took the place of sorrow: her eyes were fixed insensibly on the black veil, when like a sudden twilight in the air its terrors fell around her. She arose and stood trembling before him.

"And do you feel it, then, at last?" said he, mournfully.

She made no reply, but covered her eyes with her hand and turned to leave the room. He rushed forward and caught her arm.

"Have patience with me, Elizabeth!" cried he, passionately. "Do not desert me though this veil must be between us here on earth. Be mine, and hereafter there shall be no veil over my face, no darkness between our souls. It is but a mortal veil; it is not for eternity. Oh, you know not how lonely I am, and how frightened to be alone behind my black veil! Do not leave me in this miserable obscurity forever."

"Lift the veil but once and look me in the face," said she.

"Never! It cannot be!" replied Mr. Hooper.

"Then farewell!" said Elizabeth.

She withdrew her arm from his grasp and slowly departed, pausing at the door to give one long, shuddering gaze that seemed almost to penetrate the mystery of the black veil. But even amid his grief Mr. Hooper smiled to think that only a material emblem had separated him from happiness, though the horrors which it shadowed forth must be drawn darkly between the fondest of lovers.

From that time no attempts were made to remove Mr. Hooper's black veil or by a direct appeal to discover the secret which it was supposed to hide. By persons who claimed a superiority to popular prejudice it was reckoned merely an eccentric whim, such as often mingles with the sober actions of men otherwise rational and tinges them all with its own semblance of insanity. But with the multitude good Mr. Hooper was irreparably a bugbear. He could not walk the street with any peace of mind, so conscious was he that the gentle and timid would turn aside to avoid him, and that others would make it a point of hardihood to throw themselves in his way. The impertinence of the latter class compelled him to give up his customary walk at sunset to the burial-ground; for when he leaned pensively over the gate, there would always be faces behind the gravestones peeping at his black veil. A fable went the rounds that the stare of the dead people drove him thence. It grieved him to the very depth of his kind heart to observe how the children fled from his approach, breaking up their merriest sports while his melancholy figure was yet afar off. Their instinctive dread caused him to feel more strongly than aught else that a preternatural horror was interwoven with the threads of the black crape. In truth, his own antipathy to the veil was known to be so great that he never willingly passed before a mirror nor stooped to drink at a still fountain lest in its peaceful bosom he should be affrighted by himself. This was what gave plausibility to the whispers that Mr. Hooper's conscience tortured him for some great crime too horrible to be entirely concealed or otherwise than so obscurely intimated. Thus from beneath the black veil there rolled a cloud into the sunshine, an ambiguity of sin or sorrow, which enveloped the poor minister, so that love or sympathy could never reach him. It was said that ghost and fiend consorted with him there. With self-shudderings and outward terrors he walked continually in its shadow, groping darkly within his own soul or gazing through a medium that saddened the whole world. Even the lawless wind, it was believed, respected his dreadful secret and never blew aside the veil. But still good Mr. Hooper sadly smiled at the pale visages of the worldly throng as he passed by.

Among all its bad influences, the black veil had the one desirable effect of making its wearer a very efficient clergyman. By the aid of his mysterious emblem – for there was no other apparent cause – he became a man of awful power over souls that were in agony for sin. His converts always regarded him with a dread peculiar to themselves, affirming, though but figuratively, that before he brought them to celestial light they had been with him behind the black veil. Its gloom, indeed, enabled him to sympathize with all dark affections. Dying sinners cried aloud for Mr. Hooper and would not yield their breath till he appeared, though ever, as he stooped to whisper consolation, they shuddered at the veiled face so near their own. Such were the terrors of the black veil even when Death had bared his visage. Strangers came long distances to attend service at his church with the mere idle purpose of gazing at his figure because it was forbidden them to behold his face. But many were made to quake ere they departed. Once, during Governor Belcher's administration, Mr. Hooper was appointed to preach the election sermon. Covered with his black veil, he stood before the chief magistrate, the council and the representatives, and wrought so deep an impression that the legislative measures of that year were characterized by all the gloom and piety of our earliest ancestral sway.

In this manner Mr. Hooper spent a long life, irreproachable in outward act, yet shrouded in dismal suspicions; kind and loving, though unloved and dimly feared; a man apart from men, shunned in their health and joy, but ever summoned to their aid in mortal anguish. As years wore on, shedding their snows above his sable veil, he acquired a name throughout the New England churches, and they called him Father Hooper. Nearly all his parishioners who were of mature age when he was settled had been borne away by many a funeral: he had one congregation in the church and a more crowded one in the churchyard; and, having wrought so late into the evening and done his work so well, it was now good Father Hooper's turn to rest.

Several persons were visible by the shaded candlelight in the death-chamber of the old clergyman. Natural connections he had none. But there was the decorously grave though unmoved physician, seeking only to mitigate the last pangs of the patient whom he could not save. There were the deacons and other eminently pious members of his church. There, also, was the Reverend Mr. Clark of Westbury, a young and zealous divine who had ridden in haste to pray by the bedside of the expiring minister. There was the nurse – no hired handmaiden of Death, but one whose calm affection had endured thus long in secrecy, in solitude, amid the chill of age, and would not perish even at the dying-hour. Who but Elizabeth! And there lay the hoary head of good Father Hooper upon the death-pillow with the black veil still swathed about his brow and reaching down over his face, so that each more difficult gasp of his faint breath caused it to stir. All through life that piece of crape had hung between him and the world; it had separated him from cheerful brotherhood and woman's love and kept him in that saddest of all prisons his own heart; and still it lay upon his face, as if to deepen the gloom of his darksome chamber and shade him from the sunshine of eternity.

For some time previous his mind had been confused, wavering doubtfully between the past and the present, and hovering forward, as it were, at intervals, into the indistinctness of the world to come. There had been feverish turns which tossed him from side to side and wore away what little strength he had. But in his most convulsive struggles and in the wildest vagaries of his intellect, when no other thought retained its sober influence, he still showed an awful solicitude lest the black veil should slip aside. Even if his bewildered soul could have forgotten, there was a faithful woman at his pillow who with averted eyes would have covered that aged face which she had last beheld in the comeliness of manhood.

At length the death-stricken old man lay quietly in the torpor of mental and bodily exhaustion, with an imperceptible pulse and breath that grew fainter and fainter except when a long, deep and irregular inspiration seemed to prelude the flight of his spirit.

The minister of Westbury approached the bedside.

"Venerable Father Hooper," said he, "the moment of your release is at hand. Are you ready for the lifting of the veil that shuts in time from eternity?"

Father Hooper at first replied merely by a feeble motion of his head; then – apprehensive, perhaps, that his meaning might be doubtful – he exerted himself to speak.

"Yea," said he, in faint accents; "my soul hath a patient weariness until that veil be lifted."

"And is it fitting," resumed the Reverend Mr. Clark, "that a man so given to prayer, of such a blameless example, holy in deed and thought, so far as mortal judgment may pronounce – is it fitting that a father in the Church should leave a shadow on his memory that may seem to blacken a life so pure? I pray you, my venerable brother, let not this thing be! Suffer us to be gladdened by your triumphant aspect as you go to your reward. Before the veil of eternity be lifted let me cast aside this black veil from your face;" and, thus speaking, the Reverend Mr. Clark bent forward to reveal the mystery of so many years.

But, exerting a sudden energy that made all the beholders stand aghast, Father Hooper snatched both his hands from beneath the bedclothes and pressed them strongly on the black veil, resolute to struggle if the minister of Westbury would contend with a dying man.

"Never!" cried the veiled clergyman. "On earth, never!"

"Dark old man," exclaimed the affrighted minister, "with what horrible crime upon your soul are you now passing to the judgment?"

Father Hooper's breath heaved: it rattled in his throat; but, with a mighty effort grasping forward with his hands, he caught hold of life and held it back till he should speak. He even raised himself in bed, and there he sat shivering with the arms of Death around him, while the black veil hung down, awful at that last moment in the gathered terrors of a lifetime. And yet the faint, sad smile so often there now seemed to glimmer from its obscurity and linger on Father Hooper's lips.

"Why do you tremble at me alone?" cried he, turning his veiled face round the circle of pale spectators. "Tremble also at each other. Have men avoided me and women shown no pity and children screamed and fled only for my black veil? What but the mystery which it obscurely typifies has made this piece of crape so awful? When the friend shows his inmost heart to his friend, the lover to his best-beloved; when man does not vainly shrink from the eye of his Creator, loathsomely treasuring up the secret of his sin – then deem me a monster for the symbol beneath which I have lived and die. I look around me, and, lo! on every visage a black veil!"

While his auditors shrank from one another in mutual affright, Father Hooper fell back upon his pillow, a veiled corpse with a faint smile lingering on the lips. Still veiled, they laid him in his coffin, and a veiled corpse they bore him to the grave. The grass of many years has sprung up and withered on that grave, the burial-stone is moss-grown, and good Mr. Hooper's face is dust; but awful is still the thought that it moldered beneath the black veil.

Old Homeplace

Joshua Hiles

THE CAR rolls over the cracked concrete of the backroads. Forest and time have almost swallowed these paths. Old arabesques of dried mud layer one atop the other, telling of yearly floods. The car does not fit. A late model hybrid, nearly soundless. It confuses the deer. Hearing nothing, they burst from the dense foliage: glorious, rampant; only to scramble and fall down the crumbling verge as the slim hatchback rolls on. Another of the seemingly endless bends in this labyrinth of forest and the driver sighs hard at what had once been a town. The car slides to a stop. He unclenches a big-knuckled hand from the wheel to swipe sweat from his brow.

"Jesus."

Flooding left the town a ramshackle ruin. A backwoods Venice sinking not into a lagoon but into the black, bottomland soil along the Missouri. Ten homes that could be called 'intact' out of generosity. Most with boarded up windows and 'No Trespassing' signs. A few wheel ruts in overgrown, muddy driveways. Maybe another thirty show every stage of decay, skeletal frames thrusting toward indifferent sky, low tumulus mounds future archeologists will find fascinating. A maniacally leaning church steeple supports a roofless chapel. The only solid-looking building is a one-story brick blockhouse on which someone had once painted 'Ashchar General Store and Post Office'.

"Ha." His exclamation is neither triumphant or happy.

He swings open the door and steps into the squelching mud. His weight sinks his steel-toes past the sole; standing brings the town hall into view. Stained marble rises from the foundation, crusted with verdant growth along a clearly marked waterline. Higher up, the stone changes to brown and red, streaked by sunbaked water rills. Everywhere not marked by nature is marked by man: paint splattered in senseless blotches, windows broken. Under the filth, sharp clean lines speak of money and someone's aspirations. Tall sweeping columns and long Jet Age swoops – relics of a mid-century flirtation with art deco – rise towards a sky now overgrown with oak and ash trees. Two steel doors hang on sagging hinges, held closed by a chain of rusted iron, and a great padlock at least fifty years old. A *thunk,* tin on stone, from behind and to the left. The man turns, one great hand dives into the open flaps of his cardigan. His eyes zero in on a young girl, rail-thin, poverty skinny. A bucket, sloshing with muddy water, rests on the ground as she regards him with wide brown eyes before looking into the bucket. He removes his hand and raises it in greeting.

"Howdy," he says, voice pleasant.

No response from the child. Her white legs are totally clean.

"It's alright darlin'. I know you're not supposed to talk to strangers. Can you run and catch your momma for me?"

The little girl squats in the mud and reaches into the bucket. Her age is indeterminate. Starvation and dirt rob her of distinctiveness. She could be six or a sickly thirteen.

"I'm looking for Virginia Titus."

The little girl raises her eyes back to him.

"You know that name?"

She slides her hand from the bucket, gripping a great, slick frog.

"Gigging frogs?" He laughs. "Not bad eating if you can catch them."

The little girl wraps the frog in both hands and holds it up to her face. Her lips part and she plants a loud kiss on its face.

"Looking for princes, then. Can you point me the right way, Your Highness?"

She stares into the frog's eyes, her mouth opens wider and she digs her teeth into the flesh around its head. The legs kick wildly, popping and crunching noises loud in the stillness. She jerks her head, ripping, and rank, sticky blood flows over her chin and drips onto the faded flowers of her dress.

"Goddamn!" The man starts towards the girl and a hand lands on his shoulder.

"What you want?" grumbled a voice behind him.

This time the man turns more slowly, hands at his side. Three men confront him, one of them has a shotgun broken and hanging over his shoulder, hand wrapped around the barrels. The other two are less obviously armed, a hatchet tucked into a belt and a long buck-knife hanging on a swatch of denim tied to a belt loop. They start, staring hard at his face. Three sets of brown eyes look into the man's own, all the exact same shade. The hatchet-man runs his hand through thinning hair of the same deep brown color as everyone else's. Other things hint too. Large ears flush with the skull, lumpy noses, thick brows shading deep set eyes, and wide generous mouths.

"Your name, mister?" The man with the knife, the oldest, asks.

"Elijah Torence."

The three armed men turn and spit.

The one with the shotgun snaps the barrel casually into place. "A Torence."

"Now, now," Elijah chides, "no way to treat a cousin."

"No family of yours."

"Your looks say different, cousin. You're Virginia Torence's children or grandchildren."

There's rage in the man's face. His dirty-nailed hand grabs the flannel of Elijah's shirt. The cardigan flaps, revealing a belt-holstered automatic. The shotgun comes up. The hatchet-man moves to clear the line of fire. Everyone freezes. A small half-smile plays on Elijah's face.

"You won't shoot me," he says. "And I won't shoot you."

"Well now, Eli," his hand tangled in Elijiah's shirt, "she goes by Virginia Titus and nevermind what the paperwork says."

"He's right mister," the shotgun is rock-steady, it's wielder's voice calm, "we've no business with Torences."

"Of course. Always best to honor local custom."

"What's your business?" The youngest, hand on hatchet, asks.

"I'm here to see my great-aunt."

That same anger. "I told you about claiming us as family. I won't say it again."

"You will or you won't," Elijah spreads his feet in the mud, "that's nothing to do with me."

"This'll go on all day, or get you shot in the next few minutes." He tightens his grip on Elijah's shirt.

"Don't threaten the fellah, Horace," the man with the shotgun orders, "hit him or get out of the way and I'll gut-shoot him."

"Let's pick another way. Take me to see Virginia Titus, please."

The men exchange looks.

"Fine," Horace lets go of Elijah's shirt. "The old lady can tell you to go to hell as well as we can."

The men back away deeper into the muddy, green boulevards of Ashchar.

"What about the girl?" Elijah squelches after them. "One of yours?"

"What girl?" the hatchet-man says over his shoulder.

Elijah turns to point. There is nothing, not even footprints or the mark of a bucket in the mud. Through the town they go, coming out of the avalanche field of houses into a broad square. There's a worn path around an overgrown center. The grass there stands higher than Elijah's shoulder, no obvious path leading into or out of it. Now and again something rustles in there. The men avoid the overgrowth, walking to its far side, and then back up towards the city hall.

"Is it dangerous to get too close?" Elijah points toward the marble stairs.

They all stop and look at him, deep-set eyes suspicious and hating.

"The structure. Is it unstable or something?"

They turn and continue their trudge. He slinks behind them, hands in pockets. To the east, the river laps against its crumbling banks, claiming a few more clumps of earth. Toward the center of the bowl of mud and ruins they lead Elijah, ending at a lovely little clapboard house. Old wood dressed in fresh green paint, muddy driveway clothed in gravel. A piece of stained glass as a door window, red and purple, winks in the sunset light.

The hatchet-man grunts. "I'm Granville."

"Pleased to meet you." Elijah smiles.

"Why you carry a gun to go visiting?"

"Why do you carry a hatchet to walk down the street?"

Nothing else is said. Their mud-laden boots ring dully on the wood of the porch, and Horace passes around an antique boot scraper.

"I'll be right here." The man with the shotgun sits in an old rocker and rests the gun across his lap.

The door swings open and an ancient woman dressed in calico steps out. Her eyes are faded brown matching the hair caught up in a loaf at the back of her neck. Her face is a mask of wrinkles, but her back is straight and her shoulders unstooped.

"What's your name boy?" she has all her teeth still.

"Elijah Torence."

"Then get off my porch."

"No."

The rocker stops creaking and the shotgun lines up with his gut. Horace is behind him and Granville to his left.

"Maybe you don't know," the woman's voice is soft, "maybe the trash that raised you didn't tell you, you're a Titus."

"No. I am not."

"Then..." She points back at the muddy street.

"My grampa, your brother, was a bootlegger. Your daddy fought in the Great War and lost a leg. Your momma was a Titus but you aren't anymore than I am."

The moment stretches. The woman cackles.

"No fear in you."

"Nothing to be scared of."

"Oh Elijah Titus," she says, "you are wrong."

* * *

The house is a warm cave. In the gloam, he sees lacy curtains and oily polished wood. A puff of wind through the open back door brings the smell of a grandmother's house to him. Roasted meat and vegetables, lemon and vinegar and coffee. Familiar as a childhood Sunday. The three brothers wait on the porch. Her cold, paper-skinned hand falls across Elijah's forearm and she leads him inside. The kitchen is lit by a glowing charcoal fire in a cast-iron stove. She throws some pine knots on it and draws an old oil lantern down from the hook on the wall.

"Power company pulled out after my third marriage," she strikes a match, "I am a Titus by the by, married my third cousin for my third marriage and had my third child by him."

Elijah looks around the room. "Third times the charm."

The lantern *shuffs* to life, showing wood-paneled walls glowing with oil. A pot bubbles on the stove, and she sets the lantern down on the table, gesturing at the kitchen chairs. He sits, facing her, and the stove. Shelves on the wall bear scores of Mason jars packed with home-canned food.

"You know about your family," she says, "I can see the knowing on you, smell it on your breath." He rests forearms on the table.

She reaches one long-nailed finger towards him and pushes it into his forehead, dimpling the flesh. "You marked."

"It's not a hard story to track down."

"It was made harder."

He waves a hand. "Old crimes."

"Your grandfather shot my brother from ambush and ran off to the big city."

"My grandfather *was* your brother and shot your cousin from ambush because he'd killed both of *your* Uncles over a drunken card game."

"Your great-granddaddy did dirt to my family after the war and stole the land."

"Your father outbid your grandfather in a land auction and offered him usage of the land and a fair shake on the crops."

"Tried to make us sharecroppers!"

"After the Depression took our wealth your grandfather refused his own daughter a decent burial because she married my great-grandfather. Her grave is hid."

"Buried her inheritance with her too." Virginia is triumphant.

His eyes flash but she is far away, counting grievances.

"Shall we go back to the Civil War? Or argue over who was first over the Cumberland?" He murmurs.

"Yes!" she shouts.

"No. It's a waste of time and not why I'm here."

"I don't care why you're here, just go."

"Out there?" Elijah thumbs back over his shoulder. "Into the town square? Into the dark?" Her shocked face freezes.

"I know more than a long list of who hurt who going back two hundred years."

"No."

"I know about the chancery and the cat and the soldiers."

"Then you're going into the bottom of a cellar-hole with your throat cut, and we're tumbling a house onto you."

"You'll slay blood family? Here in town?"

"I…" she stops. "Damn you, how?"

The door opens and her sons come tramping in.

"Getting dark, momma," Granville says. "Best he get back to his car."

"Just make up a pallet for me anywhere," Elijah smiles, "I don't even need feeding. I stopped on the road."

"The hell you say." Granville's jaw gapes open.

"Do it," Virginia says.

"Just as soon as he gives up his gun." Horace holds his hand out.

Elijah stares at him smiling.

"What's the point," Virginia says, "we can't kill him and he knows what happens if he kills us."

"Meow," Elijah claws at the air.

* * *

There is no light once the lantern is extinguished, and the three men and Virginia tramp upstairs. For a time the charcoal fire glows ghostly around the iron edges of the stove door, but soon even that is gone. Elijah lies on the rough, uneven, wooden floor. A thin double wedding ring quilt is all they admitted to having. "Not rightly used to company," Virginia said when she tossed it at his feet. Elijah stares into the ceiling, smiling a satisfied smile, and dozes off. After a dreamless sleep, he awakens to a small noise. His searching glance fastens on the near window, where a pale face floats in the black pane. He comes to his feet, drawing out the gun from where it rested under the quilt. He walks to the window and looks down into the wide brown eyes of the little girl. Her face is innocent of frog blood or expression. Just that wide, waiting stare. He sways on his feet like a drunken man and jerks himself away towards the front door. He looks back and sees her, nose pressed to glass to keep him in sight, and opens the door. He nearly trips over her, standing on the mat, toes pressed against the threshold. His hiss of indrawn breath is the only noise. Beyond the occulting branches of the trees, the constellations wheel overhead. The girl turns and hops down the stairs, skipping into the tall foliage of the town square. Her feet do not sink into or mark the mud-covered street. Elijah steps forward, eying the fescue and ryegrass as it sways in the total lack of night breeze. He hears no insects, no river, nothing. He puts his left foot on the top stair and feels his heart hammer as a voice speaks out.

"I wouldn't."

To his right, the man who carried the shotgun sits in the rocking chair unarmed, dressed in an old-fashioned night shirt and a pair of faded woolen trousers.

"Dammit," Elijah hisses at him.

"Come up off the stair."

Elijah does. "Who was that?"

"My daughter."

"You let her run around out there?"

"Don't see as it rightly matters." The man rocks once. "Cat took her five years ago."

"But, I saw her."

"I see her most nights." The man's voice becomes wistful. "Dancing round the house, coming onto the porch and peeping in windows. If I sit out she comes up and tugs at my arms, trying to get me to follow her into the tall grass."

Elijah stares at him.

"Her momma followed her out a few years ago. Ain't seen her since, but my little Becky, she comes to visit."

"Why not go after her?"

"See where the grass is waving? Right where she went in. Ain't no breeze doing that."

"Then why?"

"Fire that little popgun of yours right there."

"Your girl," Elijah protests.

"I've shot her so full of buckshot she should rattle, she doesn't mind that sort of thing now."

Elijah needs no further encouragement. He raises the pistol and fires twice into the clump of swaying grass. The scream is like the scream of a tortured child and for a moment Elijah is sure he's killed the girl until he sees the two green blobs of eyes glaring hatefully in the dark. The man raises a high-powered flashlight from beside his chair and clicks it on. The beam spears out and reveals a huge black panther. Elijah's mind stutters and a low whine issues from his throat. It crouches, ready to spring.

The rocking chair creaks as the man stands. "Best go in and not come out again till morning."

Elijah stumbles into the house. Behind him the man latches the door and looks him up and down.

"I'm Clive," he says. "Don't go out again, even if Becky should come looking for a playmate."

Clive heads upstairs, and Elijah stares at the front door for a long time, listening to the wooden porch creak under some great weight.

* * *

In the morning Clive says nothing about the night, and Elijah remains silent as well. Breakfast is a hash of sausage, potatoes and egg fried up in fat from a Pringles can. There is no attempt at conversation. Granville collects the plates and kisses his mother on the cheek before going out back to the pump to wash. Virginia leans back and sips at her coffee, already her third cup since sunrise.

"What do you want?"

"The chancery records in city hall."

Clive and Horace stare at him, and a vein rises on Virginia's temple.

"It was a court of equity," he sips at his own coffee. "Outdated and mostly merged into the law courts these days. But Pike County had one through 1945, and its seat was here."

"What's in it for you?" Horace asks, still hostile.

"For all of us," Elijah downs the rest of the cup. "The chancery didn't award damages or punish people. Writs and injunctions and orders for specific performance, that's all."

"We handled it locally," Virginia pats Clive's arm, "swapping and cutting and pasting, neighborly."

"Hiding and shaming and driving people out, I'd say."

"Watch how you talk to my Momma Torence." Clive's voice is friendly but his fingers clench white around his coffee cup.

"My family did it too," Elijah holds the cup out for a refill. "If guilt is hereditary, and that black devil-cat out there argues it is, we're all guilty."

"We don't talk about that," Horace shoves the pot across the table.

Elijah picks it up and pours. "We need to. The cat showed up after the fine people of Ashchar suckered a bunch of their border ruffian neighbors and kin into a trap, including my several times great-grandfather."

"Your people paid us back for that," Virginia's face is red, "with months of slit throats and burnt cabins and barns."

"Bodies buried out in the river mud," Elijah adds. "Lots of them."

They look away from each other, uncomfortable in agreement.

"It forever marked this town," Elijah finally says. "The cat showed up a month after and people started to disappear."

"Forever marked your family." Horace says.

"Yours too."

"I warned you about that!"

"Sit down, Horace." Clive kicks a chair to him. "What're the court records gonna do?"

"It's proof. A record of claims and counter-claims going on down the years until my grandfather shot his cousin and put an end to it by running."

Virginia sets her cup down, "It wasn't a law court, you said, it won't prove my...your grandfather is guilty."

"My great-grandfather worked on old man Titus's farm every Wednesday for 19 years ," Elijah says. "One day a week for every year of Richard Titus's life. That court order is down there."

"What's the point?" Clive asks.

"I hate that thing," Elijah hisses suddenly, his demeanor altering completely, "I hate it. It's the failure of all our blood, the shame of our families given form and substance by a vengeful god, and I will see it scrubbed from the earth."

The back door creaks open, Granville returns with a stack of dishes. "What's everybody talking about?"

"Virginia," Elijah pleads, "I don't want anything from you, I don't want the feud to go on, I don't care if you never want to see me again, but let me do this. Let me have the records. I'll take them to the State Historical Society, lay this whole thing bare, and maybe Ashchar can live again. At the very least you and yours could live out your days here, and let it die clean instead of festering on."

"You do need something or else you'd just go."

"You're right, I need to know if it's safe or can be made safe. I need to know where the records are and I need someone to open the door for me if the key still exists."

Clive blurts. "You really think this'll end the cat?"

Elijah runs his hands through his hair. "It's not like there are rules or a manual for this. I think that thing is our secrets and hates made flesh. I think it stalks us as retribution for those crimes, and to punish anyone who sheds family blood here in town."

"My granddaddy would hate the idea of laying all this out for outsiders to fawn over." Horace says.

"So would mine," Elijah agrees, "but wounds don't heal without being drained."

"It's safe enough in the day." Clive leans forward, resting gnarled hands on his knees.

"Clive!" Three voices speak as one.

"Best get going now, though." Clive stands with a grunt. "Don't do nothing stupid like walk through the town square, don't follow anything down there into dark corners, and you'll be fine."

"Clive Titus, you shut your damn mouth!" Virginia glows with rage.

"Court records are in the basement, burial and taxes upstairs. Town clerk was always a Titus. My granddaddy was the last one."

"The key," Elijah says.

"Mayor's got it." Clive digs into his trousers pocket. "Here."

He draws out a heavy key more rust than iron.

"Mayor?"

"Won the election in '63 and we never had another."

* * *

Clive follows him out onto the porch in silence. He feels Virginia, Horace, and Granville's hating eyes fixed on him from the windows. The day is hot and close. He smells the rank, green smell of the town square. He stares at it. Trying to part the entwined prairie grasses and spiderwort blossoms with his eyes before turning up the path towards the courthouse. The overgrowth shields him from view. He pauses, checking his gun, and car keys. Sweat runs down his face. He pulls the cardigan off and tosses it into the mud. Verdigris streaks the doors, he mounts the stairs and reaches for the chain. Elijah glances into the crack and for a second sees big brown eyes looking back. His hand does not shake as he grates Clive's key into the lock and draws the chain from the handles. The door sags open, revealing sunburst patterns in broken tile, rusted iron, and bronze light fixtures. He places the chain, padlock, and key in a neat pile under a tarnished brass wall lamp. There is plenty of light inside. The skylight's glass shattered long ago and crunches under his boots, its steel support ribs casting geometrical shadows over the curving reception desk. He hears a clatter to his right, where a dark hallway yawns. Doors stand open, frosted glass with names and titles worn off long ago. A child's head and shoulders are silhouetted in the nearest. He turns his back on her and walks further into the reception hall. A sign says 'Records', and points the way to a spiral staircase. Stepping into the round landing, he wipes dust from another sign and sees 'Burial Registry', with an arrow pointing up the stairs. Glancing down into the darkness he sets his feet on the stairs and begins to climb up.

* * *

Hours pass. Elijah digs through piles of moldering, rotted paper. He snaps open drawers and cabinets. His search grows more frantic. Room to room he moves, scanning the heading of each sheet and casting it away. From time to time he sees the girl watching him, always obscured. As the sunlight dims, she comes closer each time. Finally he squints at a sheet and holds it aloft. Spidery, crabbed handwriting scrawls across it in unmistakable rage and sadness. He folds it and tucks it into his shirt pocket. He picks his way back towards the stairs. It is almost dark inside and he speeds his pace. The girl is nowhere to be seen. He flies down the stairs and screams aloud when he comes face to face with Granville leaning against the doorway to the reception hall.

"Easy mister," Granville's hand is held up to him.

"Christ," Elijah rasps, "you gave me a start."

"C'mon," Granville walks away, "I don't like this place, there's still a half hour of daylight outside."

"Damn right," Elijah follows.

When they come level with that hallway, Elijah cannot keep himself from glancing down it. No girl. Granville suddenly stops, blocking Elijah's view of the yawning abyss.

"You ain't got no papers."

"What?" Elijah peers over his shoulder.

"Papers," Granville's brow is furrowed, "you got nothing."

"Oh, I've carried everything to the car already. I was having one last look around."

"I been standing on that landing since before lunchtime and you ain't come," Granville pauses. "Down." He finishes, voice flat.

"What?" Elijah shrugs.

"What was you doing upstairs? No court records up there."

"Certainly there are."

"Nope, heard Clive plain, court records in the basement, burial upstairs."

"Listen."

"You're trying to find the grave my granddaddy hid, the one for your whore of a great-grandmother that married a Torence."

"Buried with her inheritance," Elijah relaxes. "Old man Titus was a hard sumbitch who reckoned every jot and tittle of what she would've had, and buried it with her. The paper money and the coins are worth more than face value to collectors now."

"You said this was about making things better."

"So it is," Elijah reaches out and takes Granville's arm, "better for me *and* you if you like."

Granville looks a question at him.

"Come with me, help me dig it up. We'll go to Columbia together and get it appraised. I'll give you half, plenty to go 'round, wouldn't need to tell your mother."

"Not that easy," Granville shrugs away from him.

"To hell with you, our families are both idiots however you slice it. A damned black panther stalking them in the night for killing each other and they keep on doing it for decades."

"Blood answers blood."

"At least Gramps had the sense to get out."

Granville's hand flashes to his belt and Elijah suddenly remembers the hatchet. His pistol is in his grip and the shot bangs off the marble walls. Granville's dead face smiles as he slumps. The little girl is three steps behind his crumpled body, triumph written in her eyes. She begins to scream and runs at Elijah, bare feet still not touching the glass-strewn floor. He stumbles backwards toward the sunset light of the doors. He barely makes it, shouldering the heavy metal portal, it screeches as it drags back into place. He leans hard against it as something much heavier than a child slams into the other side. Finally it stops, he laughs and pumps a fist into the air, turning around. At least a hundred people fill the lanes around the overgrown town square. Some wear rough homespun cloth, red bandannas tied around their arms. Others wear overalls, or nightshirts. The sun setting behind them stretches their shadows towards him like crawling fingers cutting off his escape. Elijah sprints for a gap. They move, fast, so very fast, closing on him from all sides. He darts and backpedals, trying to find a way through. His breath wracks and his chest burns as he stumbles, mud-covered and sweating, from one side of the square to the other. He runs past the courthouse and circles through the ruined homes, only to see more people coming out of the woods. With a growl he fires again and again at the advancing crowd. Over their heads he sees Virginia leaning into Horace's chest, hands clasped to her face, weeping. Clive sits in the rocking chair, staring into the tall grass.

"Help me!" Elijah shouts.

Clive stands and takes one of Virginia's elbows, Horace takes the other. The thunk-click of the door closing and latching behind them is the loudest sound Elijah has ever heard. He hurls the useless pistol into the mass of bodies and plunges into the overgrowth. He veers right, intending only to cut the corner of the square and then run for his car. He suddenly remembers the years of flood and rainfall and the slow sinking of the town. His leg plomps almost to the shin in the muddy slope, and he's falling. His boot yanks free in the sucking goop, he rolls down and splashes into the foot of stagnant water in the center of the town. His hands scramble, catching at prairie grass, crushing spiderwort blossoms, slipping off slime-slicked bones. A heavy weight lays itself lovingly across his back. A hot breath teases the hair on his neck. He sobs as the grass in front of him parts and the little girl kneels down to look into his eyes.

"Welcome home cousin," she says as teeth dig into him.

The Devil and Tom Walker

Washington Irving

A FEW MILES from Boston in Massachusetts, there is a deep inlet, winding several miles into the interior of the country from Charles Bay, and terminating in a thickly-wooded swamp or morass. On one side of this inlet is a beautiful dark grove; on the opposite side the land rises abruptly from the water's edge into a high ridge, on which grow a few scattered oaks of great age and immense size. Under one of these gigantic trees, according to old stories, there was a great amount of treasure buried by Kidd the pirate. The inlet allowed a facility to bring the money in a boat secretly and at night to the very foot of the hill; the elevation of the place permitted a good lookout to be kept that no one was at hand; while the remarkable trees formed good landmarks by which the place might easily be found again. The old stories add, moreover, that the devil presided at the hiding of the money, and took it under his guardianship; but this, it is well known, he always does with buried treasure, particularly when it has been ill-gotten. Be that as it may, Kidd never returned to recover his wealth; being shortly after seized at Boston, sent out to England, and there hanged for a pirate.

About the year 1727, just at the time that earthquakes were prevalent in New England, and shook many tall sinners down upon their knees, there lived near this place a meagre, miserly fellow, of the name of Tom Walker. He had a wife as miserly as himself: they were so miserly that they even conspired to cheat each other. Whatever the woman could lay hands on, she hid away; a hen could not cackle but she was on the alert to secure the new-laid egg. Her husband was continually prying about to detect her secret hoards, and many and fierce were the conflicts that took place about what ought to have been common property. They lived in a forlorn-looking house that stood alone, and had an air of starvation. A few straggling savin-trees, emblems of sterility, grew near it; no smoke ever curled from its chimney; no traveler stopped at its door. A miserable horse, whose ribs were as articulate as the bars of a gridiron, stalked about a field, where a thin carpet of moss, scarcely covering the ragged beds of pudding-stone, tantalized and balked his hunger; and sometimes he would lean his head over the fence, look piteously at the passer-by, and seem to petition deliverance from this land of famine.

The house and its inmates had altogether a bad name. Tom's wife was a tall termagant, fierce of temper, loud of tongue, and strong of arm. Her voice was often heard in wordy warfare with her husband; and his face sometimes showed signs that their conflicts were not confined to words. No one ventured, however, to interfere between them. The lonely wayfarer shrunk within himself at the horrid clamor and clapper-clawing; eyed the den of discord askance; and hurried on his way, rejoicing, if a bachelor, in his celibacy.

One day that Tom Walker had been to a distant part of the neighborhood, he took what he considered a shortcut homeward, through the swamp. Like most shortcuts, it was an ill-chosen route. The swamp was thickly grown with great gloomy pines and hemlocks, some of them ninety feet high, which made it dark at noonday, and a retreat for all the owls of the neighborhood. It was full of pits and quagmires, partly covered with weeds and mosses, where the green surface often betrayed the traveler into a gulf of black, smothering mud: there were also dark and stagnant pools, the abodes of the tadpole, the bull-frog, and the water-snake; where the trunks of pines and hemlocks lay half-drowned, half-rotting, looking like alligators sleeping in the mire.

Tom had long been picking his way cautiously through this treacherous forest; stepping from tuft to tuft of rushes and roots, which afforded precarious footholds among deep sloughs; or pacing carefully, like a cat, along the prostrate trunks of trees; startled now and then by the sudden screaming of the bittern, or the quacking of a wild duck rising on the wing from some solitary pool. At length he arrived at a firm piece of ground, which ran out like a peninsula into the deep bosom of the swamp. It had been one of the strongholds of the Indians during their wars with the first colonists. Here they had thrown up a kind of fort, which they had looked upon as almost impregnable, and had used as a place of refuge for their squaws and children. Nothing remained of the old Indian fort but a few embankments, gradually sinking to the level of the surrounding earth, and already overgrown in part by oaks and other forest trees, the foliage of which formed a contrast to the dark pines and hemlocks of the swamp.

It was late in the dusk of evening when Tom Walker reached the old fort, and he paused there awhile to rest himself. Anyone but he would have felt unwilling to linger in this lonely, melancholy place, for the common people had a bad opinion of it, from the stories handed down from the time of the Indian wars; when it was asserted that the savages held incantations here, and made sacrifices to the evil spirit.

Tom Walker, however, was not a man to be troubled with any fears of the kind. He reposed himself for some time on the trunk of a fallen hemlock, listening to the boding cry of the tree-toad, and delving with his walking-staff into a mound of black mold at his feet. As he turned up the soil unconsciously, his staff struck against something hard. He raked it out of the vegetable mold, and lo! a cloven skull, with an Indian tomahawk buried deep in it, lay before him. The rust on the weapon showed the time that had elapsed since this death-blow had been given. It was a dreary memento of the fierce struggle that had taken place in this last foothold of the Indian warriors.

"Humph!" said Tom Walker, as he gave it a kick to shake the dirt from it.

"Let that skull alone!" said a gruff voice. Tom lifted up his eyes, and beheld a great black man seated directly opposite him, on the stump of a tree. He was exceedingly surprised, having neither heard nor seen anyone approach; and he was still more perplexed on observing, as well as the gathering gloom would permit, that the stranger was neither negro nor Indian. It is true he was dressed in a rude half Indian garb, and had a red belt or sash swathed round his body; but his face was neither black nor copper-color, but swarthy and dingy, and begrimed with soot, as if he had been accustomed to toil among fires and forges. He had a shock of coarse black hair, that stood out from his head in all directions, and bore an ax on his shoulder.

He scowled for a moment at Tom with a pair of great red eyes.

"What are you doing on my grounds?" said the black man, with a hoarse growling voice.

"Your grounds!" said Tom, with a sneer, "No more your grounds than mine; they belong to Deacon Peabody."

"Deacon Peabody be d—d," said the stranger, "as I flatter myself he will be, if he does not look more to his own sins and less to those of his neighbors. Look yonder, and see how Deacon Peabody is faring."

Tom looked in the direction that the stranger pointed, and beheld one of the great trees, fair and flourishing without, but rotten at the core, and saw that it had been nearly hewn through, so that the first high wind was likely to blow it down. On the bark of the tree was scored the name of Deacon Peabody, an eminent man, who had waxed wealthy by driving shrewd bargains with the Indians. He now looked around, and found most of the tall trees marked with the name of some great man of the colony, and all more or less scored by the ax. The one on which he had been seated, and which had evidently just been hewn down, bore the name of Crowninshield; and he recollected a mighty rich man of that name, who made a vulgar display of wealth, which it was whispered he had acquired by buccaneering.

"He's just ready for burning!" said the black man, with a growl of triumph. "You see I am likely to have a good stock of firewood for winter."

"But what right have you," said Tom, "to cut down Deacon Peabody's timber?"

"The right of a prior claim," said the other. "This woodland belonged to me long before one of your whitefaced race put foot upon the soil."

"And pray, who are you, if I may be so bold?" said Tom.

"Oh, I go by various names. I am the wild huntsman in some countries; the black miner in others. In this neighborhood I am known by the name of the black woodsman. I am he to whom the red men consecrated this spot, and in honor of whom they now and then roasted a white man, by way of sweet-smelling sacrifice. Since the red men have been exterminated by you white savages, I amuse myself by presiding at the persecutions of Quakers and Anabaptists; I am the great patron and prompter of slave-dealers, and the grand-master of the Salem witches."

"The upshot of all which is, that, if I mistake not," said Tom, sturdily, "you are he commonly called Old Scratch."

"The same, at your service!" replied the black man, with a half civil nod.

Such was the opening of this interview, according to the old story; though it has almost too familiar an air to be credited. One would think that to meet with such a singular personage, in this wild, lonely place, would have shaken any man's nerves; but Tom was a hard-minded fellow, not easily daunted, and he had lived so long with a termagant wife, that he did not even fear the devil.

It is said that after this commencement they had a long and earnest conversation together, as Tom returned homeward. The black man told him of great sums of money buried by Kidd the pirate, under the oak-trees on the high ridge, not far from the morass. All these were under his command, and protected by his power, so that none could find them but such as propitiated his favor. These he offered to place within Tom Walker's reach, having conceived an especial kindness for him; but they were to be had only on certain conditions. What these conditions were may be easily surmised, though Tom never disclosed them publicly. They must have been very hard, for he required time to think of them, and he was not a man to stick at trifles when money was in view. When they had reached the edge of the swamp, the stranger paused. "What proof have I that all you have been telling me is true?" said Tom.

"There's my signature," said the black man, pressing his finger on Tom's forehead. So saying, he turned off among the thickets of the swamp, and seemed, as Tom said, to go down, down, down, into the earth, until nothing but his head and shoulders could be seen, and so on, until he totally disappeared.

When Tom reached home, he found the black print of a finger burnt, as it were, into his forehead, which nothing could obliterate.

The first news his wife had to tell him was the sudden death of Absalom Crowninshield, the rich buccaneer. It was announced in the papers with the usual flourish, that 'A great man had fallen in Israel.'

Tom recollected the tree which his black friend had just hewn down, and which was ready for burning. "Let the freebooter roast," said Tom, "who cares!" He now felt convinced that all he had heard and seen was no illusion.

He was not prone to let his wife into his confidence; but as this was an uneasy secret, he willingly shared it with her. All her avarice was awakened at the mention of hidden gold, and she urged her husband to comply with the black man's terms, and secure what would make them wealthy for life. However Tom might have felt disposed to sell himself to the Devil, he was determined not to do so to oblige his wife; so he flatly refused, out of the mere spirit of contradiction. Many and bitter were the quarrels they had on the subject; but the more she talked, the more resolute was Tom not to be damned to please her.

At length she determined to drive the bargain on her own account, and if she succeeded, to keep all the gain to herself. Being of the same fearless temper as her husband, she set off for the old Indian fort towards the close of a summer's day. She was many hours absent. When she came back, she was reserved and sullen in her replies. She spoke something of a black man, whom she had met about twilight hewing at the root of a tall tree. He was sulky, however, and would not come to terms: she was to go again with a propitiatory offering, but what it was she forbore to say.

The next evening she set off again for the swamp, with her apron heavily laden. Tom waited and waited for her, but in vain; midnight came, but she did not make her appearance: morning, noon, night returned, but still she did not come. Tom now grew uneasy for her safety, especially as he found she had carried off in her apron the silver teapot and spoons, and every portable article of value. Another night elapsed, another morning came; but no wife. In a word, she was never heard of more.

What was her real fate nobody knows, in consequence of so many pretending to know. It is one of those facts which have become confounded by a variety of historians. Some asserted that she lost her way among the tangled mazes of the swamp, and sank into some pit or slough; others, more charitable, hinted that she had eloped with the household booty, and made off to some other province; while others surmised that the tempter had decoyed her into a dismal quagmire, on the top of which her hat was found lying. In confirmation of this, it was said a great black man, with an ax on his shoulder, was seen late that very evening coming out of the swamp, carrying a bundle tied in a check apron, with an air of surly triumph.

The most current and probable story, however, observes, that Tom Walker grew so anxious about the fate of his wife and his property, that he set out at length to seek them both at the Indian fort. During a long summer's afternoon he searched about the gloomy place, but no wife was to be seen. He called her name repeatedly, but she was nowhere to be heard. The bittern alone responded to his voice, as he flew screaming by; or the bullfrog croaked dolefully from a neighboring pool. At length, it is said, just in the brown hour of twilight, when the owls began to hoot, and the bats to flit about, his attention was attracted by the clamor of carrion crows hovering about a cypress-tree. He looked up, and beheld a bundle tied in a check apron, and hanging in the branches of the tree, with a great vulture perched hard by, as if keeping watch upon it. He leaped with joy; for he recognized his wife's apron, and supposed it to contain the household valuables.

"Let us get hold of the property," said he, consolingly to himself, "and we will endeavor to do without the woman."

As he scrambled up the tree, the vulture spread its wide wings, and sailed off, screaming, into the deep shadows of the forest. Tom seized the checked apron, but, woeful sight! found nothing but a heart and liver tied up in it!

Such, according to this most authentic old story, was all that was to be found of Tom's wife. She had probably attempted to deal with the black man as she had been accustomed to deal with her husband; but though a female scold is generally considered a match for the devil, yet in this instance she appears to have had the worst of it. She must have died game, however; for it is said Tom noticed many prints of cloven feet deeply stamped about the tree, and found handfuls of hair, that looked as if they had been plucked from the coarse black shock of the woodman. Tom knew his wife's prowess by experience. He shrugged his shoulders, as he looked at the signs of a fierce clapper-clawing. "Egad," said he to himself, "Old Scratch must have had a tough time of it!"

Tom consoled himself for the loss of his property, with the loss of his wife, for he was a man of fortitude. He even felt something like gratitude towards the black woodman, who, he considered, had done him a kindness. He sought, therefore, to cultivate a further acquaintance with him, but for some time without success; the old black-legs played shy, for whatever people may think, he is not always to be had for calling for: he knows how to play his cards when pretty sure of his game.

At length, it is said, when delay had whetted Tom's eagerness to the quick, and prepared him to agree to anything rather than not gain the promised treasure, he met the black man one evening in his usual woodman's dress, with his ax on his shoulder, sauntering along the swamp, and humming a tune. He affected to receive Tom's advances with great indifference, made brief replies, and went on humming his tune.

By degrees, however, Tom brought him to business, and they began to haggle about the terms on which the former was to have the pirate's treasure. There was one condition which need not be mentioned, being generally understood in all cases where the devil grants favors; but there were others about which, though of less importance, he was inflexibly obstinate. He insisted that the money found through his means should be employed in his service. He proposed, therefore, that Tom should employ it in the black traffic; that is to say, that he should fit out a slave-ship. This, however, Tom resolutely refused: he was bad enough in all conscience; but the devil himself could not tempt him to turn slave-trader.

Finding Tom so squeamish on this point, he did not insist upon it, but proposed, instead, that he should turn usurer; the devil being extremely anxious for the increase of usurers, looking upon them as his peculiar people.

To this no objections were made, for it was just to Tom's taste.

"You shall open a broker's shop in Boston next month," said the black man.

"I'll do it tomorrow, if you wish," said Tom Walker.

"You shall lend money at two per cent a month."

"Egad, I'll charge four!" replied Tom Walker.

"You shall extort bonds, foreclose mortgages, drive the merchants to bankruptcy—"

"I'll drive them to the d—l," cried Tom Walker.

"You are the usurer for my money!" said black-legs with delight. "When will you want the rhino?"

"This very night."

"Done!" said the devil.

"Done!" said Tom Walker. So they shook hands and struck a bargain.

A few days' time saw Tom Walker seated behind his desk in a counting-house in Boston.

His reputation for a ready-moneyed man, who would lend money out for a good consideration, soon spread abroad. Everybody remembers the time of Governor Belcher, when money was particularly scarce. It was a time of paper credit. The country had been deluged with government bills, the famous Land Bank had been established; there had been a rage for speculating; the people had run mad with schemes for new settlements; for building cities in the wilderness; land-jobbers went about with maps of grants, and townships, and Eldorados, lying nobody knew where, but which everybody was ready to purchase. In a word, the great speculating fever which breaks out every now and then in the country had raged to an alarming degree, and everybody was dreaming of making sudden fortunes from nothing. As usual the fever had subsided; the dream had gone off, and the imaginary fortunes with it; the patients were left in doleful plight, and the whole country resounded with the consequent cry of 'hard times'.

At this propitious time of public distress did Tom Walker set up as usurer in Boston. His door was soon thronged by customers. The needy and adventurous; the gambling speculator; the dreaming land-jobber; the thriftless tradesman; the merchant with cracked credit; in short, everyone driven to raise money by desperate means and desperate sacrifices, hurried to Tom Walker.

Thus Tom was the universal friend of the needy, and acted like a 'friend in need'; that is to say, he always exacted good pay and good security. In proportion to the distress of the applicant was the hardness of his terms. He accumulated bonds and mortgages; gradually squeezed his customers closer and closer: and sent them at length, dry as a sponge, from his door.

In this way he made money hand over hand; became a rich and mighty man, and exalted his cocked hat upon 'Change. He built himself, as usual, a vast house, out of ostentation; but left the greater part of it unfinished and unfurnished, out of parsimony. He even set up a carriage in the fullness of his vainglory, though he nearly starved the horses which drew it; and as the ungreased wheels groaned and screeched on the axle-trees, you would have thought you heard the souls of the poor debtors he was squeezing.

As Tom waxed old, however, he grew thoughtful. Having secured the good things of this world, he began to feel anxious about those of the next. He thought with regret on the bargain he had made with his black friend, and set his wits to work to cheat him out of the conditions. He became, therefore, all of a sudden, a violent church-goer. He prayed loudly and strenuously, as if heaven were to be taken by force of lungs. Indeed, one might always tell when he had sinned most during the week, by the clamor of his Sunday devotion. The quiet Christians who had been modestly and steadfastly traveling Zionward, were struck with self-reproach at seeing themselves so suddenly outstripped in their career by this new-made convert. Tom was as rigid in religious as in money matters; he was a stern supervisor and censurer of his neighbors, and seemed to think every sin entered up to their account became a credit on his own side of the page. He even talked of the expediency of reviving the persecution of Quakers and Anabaptists. In a word, Tom's zeal became as notorious as his riches.

Still, in spite of all this strenuous attention to forms, Tom had a lurking dread that the devil, after all, would have his due. That he might not be taken unawares, therefore, it is said he always carried a small Bible in his coat-pocket. He had also a great folio Bible on his counting-house desk, and would frequently be found reading it when people called on business; on such occasions he would lay his green spectacles in the book, to mark the place, while he turned round to drive some usurious bargain.

Some say that Tom grew a little crack-brained in his old days, and that, fancying his end approaching, he had his horse new shod, saddled and bridled, and buried with his feet uppermost; because he supposed that at the last day the world would be turned upside down; in which case he should find his horse standing ready for mounting, and he was determined at the worst to give his old friend a run for it. This, however, is probably a mere old wives' fable. If he really did take such a precaution, it was totally superfluous; at least so says the authentic old legend; which closes his story in the following manner.

One hot summer afternoon in the dog-days, just as a terrible black thunder-gust was coming up, Tom sat in his counting-house, in his white linen cap and India silk morning-gown. He was on the point of foreclosing a mortgage, by which he would complete the ruin of an unlucky land-speculator for whom he had professed the greatest friendship. The poor land-jobber begged him to grant a few months' indulgence. Tom had grown testy and irritated, and refused another day.

"My family will be ruined, and brought upon the parish," said the land-jobber.

"Charity begins at home," replied Tom; "I must take care of myself in these hard times."

"You have made so much money out of me," said the speculator.

Tom lost his patience and his piety. "The devil take me," said he, "if I have made a farthing!"

Just then there were three loud knocks at the street-door. He stepped out to see who was there. A black man was holding a black horse, which neighed and stamped with impatience.

"Tom, you're come for," said the black fellow, gruffly. Tom shrank back, but too late. He had left his little Bible at the bottom of his coat-pocket, and his big Bible on the desk buried under the mortgage he was about to foreclose: never was sinner taken more unawares. The black man whisked him like a child into the saddle, gave the horse the lash, and away he galloped, with Tom on his back, in the midst of the thunder-storm. The clerks stuck their pens behind their ears, and stared after him from the windows. Away went Tom Walker, dashing down the street; his white cap bobbing up and down; his morning-gown fluttering in the wind, and his steed striking fire out of the pavement at every bound. When the clerks turned to look for the black man, he had disappeared.

Tom Walker never returned to foreclose the mortgage. A countryman, who lived on the border of the swamp, reported that in the height of the thunder-gust he had heard a great clattering of hoofs and a howling along the road, and running to the window caught sight of a figure, such as I have described, on a horse that galloped like mad across the fields, over the hills, and down into the black hemlock swamp towards the old Indian fort; and that shortly after a thunder-bolt falling in that direction seemed to set the whole forest in a blaze.

The good people of Boston shook their heads and shrugged their shoulders, but had been so much accustomed to witches and goblins, and tricks of the devil, in all kinds of shapes, from the first settlement of the colony, that they were not so much horror-struck as might have been expected. Trustees were appointed to take charge of Tom's effects. There was nothing, however, to administer upon. On searching his coffers, all his bonds and mortgages were found reduced to cinders. In place of gold and silver, his iron chest was filled with chips and shavings; two skeletons lay in his stable instead of his half-starved horses, and the very next day his great house took fire and was burnt to the ground.

Such was the end of Tom Walker and his ill-gotten wealth. Let all griping money-brokers lay this story to heart. The truth of it is not to be doubted. The very hole under the oak-trees, whence he dug Kidd's money, is to be seen to this day; and the neighboring swamp and old Indian fort are often haunted in stormy nights by a figure on horseback, in morning-gown and white cap, which is doubtless the troubled spirit of the usurer. In fact, the story has resolved itself into a proverb, and is the origin of that popular saying, so prevalent throughout New England, of 'The Devil and Tom Walker'.

My Uncle in the Garden

Shirley Jackson

I HAVE ALWAYS taken presents when I go to visit my uncle Oliver and my uncle Peter: a fruit cake, certainly, and a dozen oranges, and toys, a little jumping rabbit that winds with a key for Uncle Oliver, and a chocolate bone for Uncle Peter's cat. I get on the ferry at San Francisco, stopping in the ferry building for identical boxes of candied cherries, and run at Sausalito for the train that will take me into San Rafael. Then, carrying my packages and my suitcases and my book, I must walk slowly up the long country road in the sun, waiting for Uncle Peter to catch the first sight of me, or Uncle Oliver to look up from the wicker chair on the porch and come running down to meet me. Their cottage is halfway up a steep little country hill, with flowers growing down to the road on both sides, and orchards beyond, and Uncle Oliver will be out of breath walking up with me, eyeing the packages and saying: "Peter will be pleased to see what you have brought him." Both Uncle Oliver and I know that Peter will be pleased to see what I have brought, but Uncle Oliver will carry the presents away, to be disposed of carefully and doled out slowly.

When I reach the cottage, I must stop for a moment in the road, looking at the roof low enough to touch from the garden, the roses going up the walls and leaning over the doorway, the two flat stone steps, and the orchard and the vegetable garden creeping around the sides of the house, not content with their position in the back yard, and I must stand there for a moment and then say: "Nothing has been changed since last year, Uncle Oliver; how do you and Uncle Peter stay so young, and keep your home so pretty?"

And then Uncle Oliver, twisting his hands with delight, will say, as he always does: "I never get any older; Peter ages for both of us, and for the house, too." Then I may go inside to be graciously received by Uncle Peter.

I call them my uncles only because it is so difficult to address both of them as Mr Duff; some fifty years ago, when Uncle Oliver was courting my grandmother, she is said to have declared that they would be satisfactory only as bachelor brothers who would take her future grandchildren to the zoo, and so Uncles Peter and Oliver did, and her children, too, and probably my children someday as well. Aside from the one incredible year Uncle Oliver spent married to a lady known as Mrs Duff, they have lived together, at first in a little flat in San Francisco, and finally in this rose-covered cottage, which the semi-mythical Mrs Duff planned and arranged as a suitable bower for her husband. Neither Uncle Peter nor Uncle Oliver has ever tried to work at anything; some farsighted relative left them a small mutual income, which, augmented by the presents of oranges and fruitcake that they receive from the children whom they took to the zoo, keeps them excellently, with their several cats. Uncle Peter is lean and tried; he cares for the house and watches over the garden and the three or four trees in the orchard and the one cat that is especially his own; Uncle Oliver is rounder and lazier; he does the cooking and watches the vegetable garden and the five other cats. Uncle Peter's gray cat, Sandra Williamson, is the only one distinguished by a name; the others, all white cats left in the house by Mrs Duff, operate as a unit and come and go to the name of Kitty.

"They all had names once," Uncle Oliver explains mournfully, "Mrs Duff used to call them pretty things. One was Rosebud, as I remember, and all the others were pretty things, too."

"Someday we will name them all again," Uncle Peter adds, "and I will make little leather collars for them, each with his own name around his neck on a leather collar."

The white cats will all be sitting on the front porch when I come, washing one another and playing with the sunlight. Uncle Oliver will stop and touch one or two of them on the head; "pretty little things," he will say. "Nice kitty." I do not believe that the white cats understand Uncle Oliver the way Sandra Williamson understands Uncle Peter; wherever Uncle Peter goes, Sandra Williamson will follow him, sometimes so far forgetting her dignity as to touch at a dangling shoelace. And when I come, she will be standing next to Uncle Peter in the little living room, waiting to receive me.

"Peter," Uncle Oliver will say joyously, including Sandra Williamson in his expansive loving gesture, "here is such a nice child, such a nice child, and I walked up the hill with her, and she has brought you presents."

And then Uncle Peter, who always remembers my name and will take Uncle Oliver aside later and tell him what to call me, will come forward and kiss me on the forehead while Sandra Williamson rubs against my ankles, and Uncle Oliver will pull at my sleeve and point to the packages, winking and giggling, and, with Peter on one side and Oliver on the other, and Sandra Williamson perched on the windowsill above the sofa, I will open the packages.

"Oranges," Uncle Peter will say with pleasure, and he will take one and offer it solemnly to Sandra Williamson, who will touch it with her gray paw.

"Look, Peter, what Sandra Williamson may have for her own, instead of an orange which we will eat ourselves, look at what this dear pretty child has brought Sandra Williamson," Uncle Oliver will say, with the chocolate bone. Peter must offer the bone to Sandra himself, and she will sit cheerfully with it under her paw until Uncle Peter moves to another room and requires her to bring it along.

Finally, when all of us have watched Uncle Oliver's mechanical toy move about the room, crashing into the furniture and even moving out to the front porch to startle the white cats, Uncle Oliver will gather together all the presents except Sandra Williamson's bone and an orange apiece for his and Uncle Peter's dinner, and hide them away in the back of kitchen cabinet, to be taken out at a less exciting time. Then Uncle Oliver will remove himself to the stove, and dinner, and Uncle Peter will show me his garden, Sandra Williamson following and the white cats moving about under the trees in the dusk.

I do not think that there is any possibility that Uncle Peter and Uncle Oliver and the cats and the cottage will change or go away with time. Every year, when spring has irrevocably asserted itself, I begin to wonder about Uncle Oliver and Uncle Peter, and every year I gather together the fruitcake and the oranges, the toys and the candied cherries, and take the ferry to Sausalito. They are as apt not to be there as San Rafael is apt to have moved to Florida.

Always, during the two or three days I spend with Uncle Peter and Uncle Oliver, some minor domestic crisis arrives, brought on principally by the strain of having company. One year Sandra Williamson was ill from too much company food, one year the strain of baking a chicken pie brought Uncle Oliver into a hysterical temper, and one year Uncle Peter and Uncle Oliver quarrelled. That is the visit I remember most clearly; the quarrel first made itself evident at the dinner table the evening of my arrival, and over the tomatoes, or rather the lack of them.

"Don't we always have tomatoes?" Uncle Oliver asked me angrily, indicating the table with the creamed beef on toast and the plain lettuce salad. "Don't we usually have tomatoes when you come?"

"I seem to remember that you do," I said placatingly, "but everything is so delicious…"

"We have always had tomatoes up until this year," Uncle Oliver persisted, "and we have always grown them in our own vegetable garden, too. My particular care," he added bitterly in Uncle Peter's direction.

"Possibly something got into the vines this year," I said. "They very often die off just when you expect them to be the best."

"We *would* have had tomatoes this year," Uncle Oliver said.

"I always thought the tomatoes were the least important," Uncle Peter said suddenly. "I prefer the radishes myself, and the squash."

"I notice nothing happened to the apples," Uncle Oliver said pointedly. There was a long moment of silence, and then Uncle Peter excused himself and left the table. Sandra Williamson followed him, and they went out into the garden.

"I think you hurt Uncle Peter's feelings," I said to Oliver.

"I intended to," he answered, staring at his plate. "He has been very wicked, and the tomatoes were mine by rights."

"What could he do to the tomatoes?" I was bewildered. "Surely he isn't directly responsible if the tomato vine doesn't bear tomatoes."

"Ah," said Uncle Oliver. "That is just it. Heaven only knows what the tomato vine *will* bear now. He has been consorting with the devil."

"Surely, Uncle Oliver," I began, "surely you cannot say that just because there are no tomatoes—"

"Ah," said Uncle Oliver, "but in the garden at night, in only his nightshirt, and dancing. And with Sandra Williamson dancing along behind him, the garden at night, and both of them going among the trees and over the vegetable garden. Is it any wonder," he cried out despairingly, "that the tomato vine refuses to bear tomatoes!"

"I should, in its place," I agreed, suppressing the picture of Uncle Peter dancing in his nightshirt.

"The devil has no place in San Rafael, and no business with Peter or with Sandra Williamson, and certainly no traffic with my tomatoes! Perhaps you can put a stop to it?" he asked me.

"What makes you think it's the devil?"

Uncle Oliver waved his hands. "Peter brought him to lunch one day. He smiled at me, his pointed little nose right at me, and said, 'You cook admirably, Oliver Duff,' and I said, 'I'll have no thanks from you, evil sir,' and he smiled at me still."

"Couldn't it be a neighbor?"

"It could not," Uncle Oliver said absolutely, "and I'll thank you not to suggest it."

"I'll speak to Uncle Peter," I said.

"Speak, better, to my tomato vine," Uncle Oliver said sullenly. Uncle Peter was coming in the door, followed by Sandra Williamson. He came over to Oliver and said, "It's been so long since we quarreled. What do we say to each other now?" They both looked at me.

"Uncle Oliver," I instructed, "you will say that you regret being ugly about the tomato vine, and Uncle Peter, you will say that you will make every effort to console Uncle Oliver for its loss."

"Regret ugly," Uncle Oliver muttered to Uncle Peter.

"Make every effort," Uncle Peter said. They smiled at each other.

"Now," I said, "I will go out into the garden with Uncle Peter."

Uncle Peter held the back door open for me, and we went out into the dark garden. The fruit trees were silent in the night, and the vegetable garden lay in heavy masses against the fence. Sandra Williamson preceded us down between the trees to the foot of the garden, where the grass was tall against the fence.

"Is this where he comes?" I asked Uncle Peter.

"To the other side of the fence," Uncle Peter said. "He seldom comes over. He lives in the woods on the hill."

"Are you sure it isn't a neighbor?" I said.

"Quite sure," Uncle Peter answered in surprise. "I have been consorting with the devil."

"Tell me about him."

"He comes down from the hill and stands on the other side of the fence. He came first some weeks ago, and Sandra Williamson saw him and came over to talk to him and I came over, too, and we talked to him."

"What about the tomatoes?"

Uncle Peter shrugged. "He asked me what in the garden I would give him for tribute; he said he would protect the fruit trees and the rest if I gave him something and I said he could have the tomato vine, because Oliver likes tomatoes least. He said that would do splendidly; I didn't know that Oliver would mind."

"Possibly if you talked to him," I said, "and asked him what else he would accept..."

"I had thought of giving him the apple tree," Peter said. "He will come later tonight, and I had thought of asking him then."

"Wait," I said. I ran back through the garden and into the house. Uncle Oliver was standing miserably by the sink, washing dishes.

"If you could have the tomatoes back," I said, "would you mind losing the apple tree?"

"The pretty little apples?" Uncle Oliver gasped. "Your uncle Peter likes them boiled with a little cinnamon and just a fragment of a sugar lump."

I thought. "If I were to promise to send you another fruitcake when I got back to town..." I suggested. Uncle Oliver sighed, but he dried his hands and opened the cupboard. Carefully he took out the bag with the oranges, the two boxes of candied cherries, the mechanical rabbit, and, finally, the fruitcake.

He looked up at me. "Do you suppose one orange...or perhaps two?"

"I think the fruitcake," I said.

He sighed again, and handed me the fruitcake. While he was storing the rest back in the cupboard I hurried out with the fruitcake and down through the garden to Uncle Peter. "Here," I said. "Try this." Uncle Peter brightened.

"Do you suppose it will work?" he asked. "I was thinking about the apple tree. You see, Oliver likes apples, and the white cats eat them."

"Try the fruitcake first," I said.

Uncle Oliver and I sat in the living room until very late, watching the white cats settle to sleep, and Uncle Peter stayed in the garden. When I finally went to bed I glanced out of my window and thought I saw, far down among the trees, a white shape moving and Sandra Williamson capering along behind.

The next morning I woke very early and went into the garden before Peter and Oliver were awake. There was no sign of the fruitcake near the fence, but the white cats were walking about, stretching in the morning and unafraid. When I came in to breakfast there were tomatoes on the table, ripe and red and sitting on a green place, with Uncle Oliver crowing over them.

"See, how pretty," he said. "Pretty tomatoes. A little boy brought them."

Peter came into the doorway, smiling. "He was so pleased with the fruitcake," he said. "Perhaps next time you come you will bring two?"

All during breakfast Peter and Oliver were smiling at each other, making quick little gestures of friendship. Oliver insisted on my having a tomato with my coffee, and asked if it were not the prettiest I had ever tasted, while Peter sat back and watched admiringly.

Finally, when the dishes had been cleared off, Uncle Oliver sat down beside Peter and they smiled again at each other. "Perhaps soon we will go to the city for a visit," Peter said to me. Neither of them had ever come into the city since they left it to live in San Rafael, and neither of them ever expected to come; it was enough to know that they could if they wanted to. Next to the death of Mrs Duff, it was their favorite mutual whimsy, and mention of it meant that everything was friendly again between them.

And Oliver took up the conversation from there:

"I remember so clearly the morning she died," he said to me. "Mrs Duff, in the house here, and so pleasant a morning. And all the white cats one after another going over the fence and away."

"It was over a week before they came back at all," Uncle Peter added, "and then, just over the fence one after another, with never an explanation."

"She had pretty little names for them all," Uncle Oliver said.

"They should all have little leather collars with their names on. You could name them, Oliver, and I would make each one a little leather collar with its name on." Uncle Peter stroked Sandra Williamson's head. "All with little leather collars," he said.

When I left they walked down to the bottom of the hill with me, standing to wave goodbye, with Sandra Williamson sitting behind them, while I went along down the dirt road, carrying my suitcase.

But ever since then, when I go back each spring, I take oranges, the fruitcakes, and three toys, and three boxes of candied cherries, and Oliver puts them all away, some to be given out to himself and Peter in less exciting times, and some to be doled out carefully and exactly over the back fence at the foot of the garden.

In the Domain of Doctor Baldwin

Russell James

VETERANS of what we in the South called the War of Northern Aggression reside in every city. Many former soldiers tell tales of how war is Hell. My role in the conflict was far from the front, so you might think that I'd never had such an experience. But I most certainly did.

In 1864, family connections had arranged for me a captaincy in the Confederate Quartermaster Corps, working very indirectly for General Johnston of the Army of Tennessee. My never-ending assignment was to provide the victuals to keep tens of thousands of men standing up on their feet so that later bullets could bring them down to their knees. The war created all manner of shortages, and encouraged unconscionable prices for many goods. The men could consume as fast as I could consign, so my job was never done.

I did have one shining star in my otherwise dim constellation of suppliers. Dr. Cristopher Baldwin, a surgeon retired from the service of the Confederate Army, ran a hog farm southwest of the town of Macon. While most of my suppliers had to be hounded to meet the conditions of their contracts, Dr. Baldwin never did. He delivered smoked meats on time in the agreed upon amount. And also unlike his competitors, his pork and bacon were of the finest quality. I directed it first to the officer's messes.

Normally, Dr. Baldwin would come into Macon to sign his contracts covering the next few months. Alas, infirmity had recently confined him to a wheelchair and he was unable to do so. He asked if a courier could bring the papers to him. His exemplary contributions to the Cause had merited a special commendation letter from the general, so delivering that and signing the contracts were my excuse to visit this purveyor of porcine products. Certainly having a captain arrive to recognize his patriotism would warm his heart.

I brought with me on my journey Sergeant Abner Holt. The stout man had lost the use of his left arm in the Battle of Jackson and been reassigned from the artillery to my meager command. His limp left arm did not affect his right, and he was still a crack shot with a pistol. I would be armed only with an effectively ceremonial sword, so I felt having his skill at my disposal when traveling such a distance would be a wise choice.

For our journey we requisitioned two horses and drew a pair of splendid bays that had somehow escaped the clutches of Forrest's cavalry. We set out early in the morning as the journey promised to take the better part of a day. I admit to being a garrison soldier who was neither accustomed to nor desirous of spending a night in bivouac in the woods.

We encountered our first ominous obstacle an hour into our journey: a bridge washed out across a wide and rushing river. Sergeant Holt consulted the map and found us an alternate and more circuitous route to Dr. Baldwin's farm. The delay displeased me greatly, for we would be making our return trip in the dark along the same less-travelled route.

Like sailing ships, the Georgia plantations at the time all carried names. Dr. Baldwin's property was no exception and was named Magnolia Blossom. We arrived and I was impressed. A great two story home arose a quarter mile down a driveway off the main road. Wide columns supported a balcony that stretched the structure's full length. Cotton plants covered the acreage around the house, but they were last season's crop, and had gone unharvested. Weeds now threatened to take command of the fields.

When we were partway to the house, a covered wagon of the Confederate Army arrived on the road. The mule driver wore the ragged butternut colors of a corporal in the Georgia Home Guard. The Guard had become a refuge for those of poor character who wished to avoid conscription into the fighting forces of the Confederacy. They performed guard duty over prisoners and locations so far removed from the front that they would have been just as safe, perhaps safer, being undefended. The nearest was Camp Sumter, near Andersonville, housing Northern prisoners.

Upon spying me on my fine horse in my best uniform, the guardsman's face went white. With a crack of his whip the mules pulled his wagon away from Magnolia Blossom.

"Whatever business he had here he opted not to transact," I said to Sergeant Holt.

"Home Guard," Holt said. He spit on the ground. "Probably stopping to steal something at gunpoint."

At the home's porch, we dismounted and climbed the steps. A young male slave opened the door before we knocked. He wore an immaculate white shirt and sharp black knee britches. He looked confused.

"May I help you, sir?"

His clean diction and proper grammar were as shocking to me as his tidy clothing. House slaves were always treated better than field hands, but the exigencies of war had taken their toll on that distinction at most plantations.

"Captain Chambliss. Delivering the procurement contracts for Dr. Baldwin."

"Indeed," he said. "The master expected an enlisted man, and much earlier in the day."

Dr. Baldwin rolled up to us in a wheelchair. Despite the heat of the day, a blanket covered his legs. His bone white hair hung unfashionably long against a dark suit coat, and a full snowy beard framed his frowning face.

"What's this about?" he said. "Who are you?"

"Captain Isaac Chambliss from General Johnston's Quartermaster Corps. I have your contracts. My pleasure to bring them to one who's done so much to keep our troops fed in the field."

The old man appeared far more leery than enthused. I had thought such special treatment would yield appreciation, not apprehension.

"Let's be quick about it," he said. He spun his chair around and rolled down the hallway.

Sergeant Holt scraped some mud from his boots and followed me inside. The house slave continued to watch out the door down the driveway, as if expecting someone else.

"You can attend to the rest of your duties, Henry," Dr. Baldwin said over his shoulder.

"Yes, sir." Henry said. He stepped out on the porch and closed the door behind him.

We followed the doctor back to a dining room in the rear. The open windows overlooked the rear of the plantation.

"Also a surprise for you, sir," I said, knowing the commendation would turn about his mood. I handed him the envelope from General Johnston.

Baldwin opened it and read the letter. I expected to see joy, but instead his face flushed with anger.

"Now it's a letter of thanks," Baldwin grumbled. "Where was he when the Surgeon General…"

Baldwin stopped himself, as if realizing his words were being spoken aloud. He returned the letter to his envelope.

"A problem, sir?" I asked.

"Not at all, not at all. Happy for the recognition, but not at all necessary. Just doing my part for the Cause."

Perhaps in Baldwin's previous military career he'd crossed with Johnston, who could be difficult. But even if that was so, such recognition should have buried the hatchet, not sharpened it.

"Let's get those papers signed so you can be on your way," Baldwin said.

None of this interaction was playing out as I had anticipated. The good doctor obviously did not want us here at all. I passed Baldwin the new contracts which he signed without reading. Sergeant Holt stood by the window splitting his observations between the room and the out-of-doors. Baldwin handed me back the contracts.

"Your cotton has gone unharvested," I observed.

"Some of my slaves were confiscated by the government, others ran off after rumors of an Emancipation Proclamation, as if a northern president has any power here. But enough remain to keep the hog farm running."

Sergeant Holt pointed a thumb out the open window. I stepped over and looked outside.

A wooden boardwalk stretched down the gentle slope to a massive hog pen. Hundreds of swine rooted around in muddy red Georgia clay. Behind it a bridge crossed a stream to a dilapidated barn farther back from the pen. Acres of dead cotton plants stretched beyond the pen, peppered by a few stands of lonely trees. Two slave boys tended to the pen's split rail fence.

"In difficult times," I said, "you raise some fine pigs, sir."

"Simple process. Rich Georgia clay, clean Georgia water, and good feed. I really haven't the time to discuss animal husbandry."

The wind picked up from the west. The breeze blew across the pen and rolled the horrendous stink of the army of hogs into the house. I coughed and had to turn away. Sergeant Holt choked and put a hand over his mouth.

"Slight downside to the business is the smell," Dr. Baldwin said. "Not bad when the wind is right."

Sergeant Holt grabbed my arm. "Sir, that smell ain't right," he said. "I done raised pigs all my life. Might have a dead arm, but my smelling ain't affected none. No pig pen smells like that."

"What do you mean?"

"Smells rotten. Old battlefield rotten."

As a proper son of Charleston, I had no understanding of the proper smell for a hog pen. As a Quartermaster officer, I knew not the improper smell of a battlefield. But what now fouled my olfactory senses was certainly rank. I feared some disease had broken out among the swine, which would in turn poison our men. Perhaps an explanation for why the doctor was so defensive.

"We should inspect your pen," I said.

"Now there's no call for that," Dr. Baldwin said. "You receive fine pork."

"Sir, as an officer of the Confederacy, I have the right, and duty, to inspect the farm."

The doctor looked ready to object again, but seemed to realize I was too resolute in my decision. "As you wish. Don't stick your hand in the pen. Those hogs will eat damn near anything."

I'll confess that I had no idea how to inspect a pig at all. But I guessed that Sergeant Holt did. "Follow me, Sergeant."

I left the house and trooped down the boardwalk with Sergeant Holt at my side. Dr. Baldwin followed in his wheelchair, but could not keep up. I did not assist him, though not out of malice against the infirm. His defensiveness distressed me, and I preferred to check the pigs without his observation and potential misdirection. The two slaves working the pen saw us coming, and dashed for one of the stands of trees.

At closer range, the pungent stink of the pigs became positively abhorrent. There was also a noise from the herd, a rumble of snorting and huffing that set my hair on end. This was not the squeal and snort of the individual pigs I'd seen at the back of the butcher shop. This herd emitted a deep, basso profundo din, much more akin to a threatening growl.

We stopped at the fence and looked out across a sea of swine. Dried mud had turned their backs red and the surging rounded bodies looked uncomfortably like an undulating sea of blood.

"Them pigs ain't right," Sergeant Holt said.

Indeed, even to my eye, untrained in porcine properties, there was something off about this herd. The hair on their backs stood taller, looked tougher, than any I'd seen. Incisor teeth jutted above both lips, each inches long. Tusks with slight serrations curled upwards from their mouths. And when a head broke surface above the herd, the eyes chilled my heart. They were compressed, with an inward and downward cant that harbingered evil intent.

A pig thrust its head though a space near my knees. It roared and snapped at my leg. I jumped back. A piece of cloth hung from one tusk, as if the creature had pierced it while eating. A gold-colored metal button flickered in the sun.

"Something else ain't right," Sergeant Holt yelled to override the hogs' collective growl. "Ain't no silage. Gotta feed them hogs, but ain't nothing to feed. No corn bins, no silos. And from the size of them they been eating plenty."

The sergeant did have a point. These pigs had to be prodigious consumers. A faint trail in the grass between the bridge and the sagging barn raised my curiosity.

The slave boys who'd run off stood in a stand of trees off from the hog pen. I looked uphill and Dr. Baldwin had thus far descended halfway.

"Sergeant, go question those boys before Baldwin arrives and scares them into silence," I said. "I'll check in the barn." Leaving behind the stink of the hogs was almost as important to me as solving the silage mystery.

As I approached the barn, I perceived another scent, one more familiar and more distressing, one I'd encountered among the wounded at the rear echelon hospitals. The sickening mélange of sweat, human waste, and blood.

I pulled open the barn door. Sunlight poured through to banish the darkness.

At first I thought the ground within was moving. Then my mind reassembled the image in its proper order. Emaciated men lay upon straw, packed in, head touching foot, shoulder touching shoulder. Union soldiers all by the look of their clothing, though it was so filthy it was hard to tell. Each had his arms and legs bound and a gag stuffed in his mouth. A few recognized my arrival with widened eyes and muffled cries from behind their gags. Most did not, continuing to stare with glazed expressions at the rafters of the barn, in some form of catalepsy.

A narrow path through the men reached a crude bench at the rear, tucked in the shadows beneath a window covered by cloth. A wheelchair had worn ruts in the path. I dashed back and pulled aside the cloth. Sunlight shined in and I gasped.

The unfinished counter was a makeshift operating table, similar to those I'd seen in the hospitals. Leather straps lay ready to bind a writhing patient in place. Rusting porcelain pans hung at strategic places to catch the blood. Thick, brown stains testified that there had been much of it.

A soldier near the table struggled against his gag to speak. I bent down and removed it.

"Please, sir." The man's voice was dry as winter, barely a whisper. "Send me back. Don't let him cut me up for the hogs."

The clank and creak of a wagon sounded outside the barn. The Confederate covered wagon I'd seen earlier pulled up outside the door. The Home Guard corporal dropped from the driver's seat and grabbed his rifle. His unshaven cheeks were sallow, his eyes recessed deep into dark sockets. His mouth curled into an angry snarl.

"What the hell you doing here?"

I was never one to strictly enforce military etiquette, but such disrespect from a junior enlisted man to a captain was unheard of. I straightened my tunic and started toward him.

"Corporal, what is all this? Are these men prisoners of war?"

The corporal's eyes narrowed. "They was. Then I done bought . Now they're pig slop."

I was an advocate for a strong prosecution of the war, for the killing of the enemy on the field of battle. But there was a code, a moral responsibility to those captured. One that meant this abomination could not stand.

"You can't buy and sell prisoners of war."

"Can buy and sell them Negroes outside. Yankees ain't no different, 'cept they deserve it."

"Your commander will hear of this. I order you to—"

The corporal raised his rifle and pointed it at my chest. I stopped.

"Ain't givin' no orders here. You ain't telling nobody nothin', 'cept maybe the hogs."

The sad sword upon my belt would likely snap upon impact with the guardsman, even if I could draw it before the corporal fired. I started slowly backwards. A quick glance about the barn showed that there were no other doors, nowhere to run save through a mass of wretched men. The corporal's minié ball would find me before I went two steps.

I bumped back against the table of death. I whirled around and engaged in a frantic search for a knife, a saw, some means of my own defense. There was nothing. I turned back and stared down the black end of his rifle barrel, now aimed at my head.

A shot rang out, enormously loud in the confines of the barn. A muted shout of fear came from the still-conscious men around me. I recoiled at death's certain approach.

I felt nothing.

I checked myself, and was not shot. The corporal crumpled to the ground and revealed Sergeant Holt behind him. Smoke rose from the barrel of Holt's pistol.

I nearly screamed with relief.

"You all right, sir?" Holt holstered his weapon.

"Yes, you were just in time." I waved at the human mass around us. "Union prisoners."

"And sounds like there's another delivery out in that wagon."

"We must put a stop to this." I mustered the composure to act as if the entire event hadn't completely unnerved me, and left the barn. Sergeant Holt fell in beside me.

We rounded the edge of the wagon to see Dr. Baldwin in his wheelchair on the boardwalk's end by the hog pen. He pivoted it to face us. Rage twisted his face.

His response only stoked my anger. For him to be indignant that we'd uncovered such a barbarous activity only reinforced his depravity. I marched straight to him.

"Doctor, you are under arrest," I said when we were a few feet away.

He raised a double-barreled shotgun from under his lap blanket and pointed it at us. "I don't think so."

Sergeant Holt and I stopped. I made the futile gesture of laying a hand upon the hilt of my sword, resorting to the bluff.

"Worked hard to weave all of this," he said. "Built my own operating table when the Confederacy deemed my experimental surgeries scandalous and forced me out. Made a network of Home Guardsmen to keep me supplied with patients. Built a hog pen to dispose of the remains. I'm not letting you run off and unravel that."

"This is sick beyond measure. You are an affront to our nation."

"I *serve* our nation, despite the injustice it did to me. I remove prisoners it cannot feed, I provide food to the soldiers it fields. I am a hero to the Cause."

"You are a disgrace to the Cause, and to all mankind."

"Enough of this. It's time to feed the pigs."

Sergeant Holt darted left. The movement took the old man by surprise. He jerked the shotgun in that direction. I took the opportunity and dove to the right. The shotgun boomed.

The balls whizzed by my ear as buckshot shredded the space where we'd just been standing. I landed hard upon the ground

Dr. Baldwin hadn't locked his wheelchair. The kick from the gun rocketed him in reverse. The chair slammed into the fence, snapped the top rail and laid Baldwin backwards with his shoulders over the hogs.

A roar rose from the herd. They attacked.

One hog jumped up on the left and dug its tusks into Baldwin's shoulder. Baldwin screamed. His shotgun tumbled to the ground. Bones crunched in the frail man's shoulder and blood poured from the hog's mouth. It pulled him backwards half out of his chair.

Another hog attacked from the other side. It clamped upon Baldwin's midsection. The doctor's scream reached a new, higher pitch.

The herd smelled the blood, or perhaps sensed the bloodlust of the two attackers. A guttural roar arose from the pack, and hogs swarmed in the doctor's direction.

Sergeant Holt and I rose. He drew his pistol, I my sword. Perhaps it could stop a pig.

The two hogs battled over Baldwin as he wailed heavenward in vain. They jerked him back and forth in a vicious tug of war. Then in an explosion of blood and internal organs, the old man tore asunder. The hogs pulled the halves down and off to the center of the pen. The herd converged on the site in a raucous feeding frenzy.

I jumped forward and pulled the chair from the damaged fence. Sergeant Holt and I procured a replacement rail nearby and fitted it in place to keep the hogs in the pen. As we worked, Henry appeared behind us. I realized he'd been waiting for that wagon full of prisoners when we'd arrived. Anger surged within me over his complicity. It subsided as I recognized the gratitude and relief upon his face.

"You've saved us all, stopped this madness," he said.

"Something you should have done long ago," I said.

"We slaves you fight to keep in chains? How would you treat us if we rose up, no matter the reason?"

I was forced to concur. The local's fear of independent Negroes trumped even their fear of Yankee soldiers. It was another of the many instances in my life where by class I should have risen to the defense of slavery, and by reason and temperament could not.

"I shall send a detachment from Camp Sumter to retrieve these prisoners," I said.

"First, follow me, sir," Henry said.

Henry led us back to the covered wagon. He drew back the rear cover. The men inside squinted against the light. They sat chained to the floor, all in an appalling physical condition, little better than the men in the barn.

"The camp is as much a death sentence as this place," Henry said. "Leave them here. We'll care for them."

"Can't be leavin' all them Yankee prisoners just wanderin' free," Sergeant Holt said.

"Do they look dangerous?" Henry said. He turned to me. "Atlanta has fallen to General Sherman. The end is coming. Union soldiers will be here long before any of these are ready to return to the fight."

I could not argue with the slave's logic. I knew that the war had been going badly since the twin tragedies of our losses at Gettysburg and Vicksburg. This servant said aloud what our leaders feared to even whisper.

And so I left an untold number of Yankee prisoners in the hands of slaves. By year's end they were liberated by Union forces, as were their tragic brethren in Andersonville. What happened to the hogs I do not know, except that I made certain that the Confederacy bought no more of them.

After returning from Magnolia Blossom, I checked the records on Camp Sumter near Andersonville. Tens of thousands of prisoners consigned there. The army barely sent enough rations to feed the guards. I reported this finding up the chain of command to no avail. I resigned my commission and went home to Alabama to wait out the war's inevitable end.

The war's scars are unique to each individual. Some are without a limb, some's skin carries purple trails from a surgeons' hasty work. My scars are unseen. Terrors rule my nights, relived memories of a barn full of men awaiting a gruesome death. Even in broad daylight, chills ripple down my spine at the scent of blood or the stink of a swine pen.

And I never eat pork.

The Landscape Chamber

Sarah Orne Jewett

Chapter I

I WAS TIRED of ordinary journeys, which involved either the loneliness and discomfort of fashionable hotels, or the responsibilities of a guest in busy houses. One is always doing the same things over and over; I now promised myself that I would go in search of new people and new scenes, until I was again ready to turn with delight to my familiar occupations. So I mounted my horse one morning, without any definite plan of my journey, and rode eastward, with a business-like haversack strapped behind the saddle. I only wished that the first day's well-known length of road had been already put behind me. One drawback to a woman's enjoyment of an excursion of this sort is the fact that when she is out of the saddle she is uncomfortably dressed. But I compromised matters as nearly as possible by wearing a short corduroy habit, light both in color and weight, and putting a linen blouse and belt into my pack, to replace the stiff habit-waist. The wallet on the saddle held a flat drinking-cup, a bit of chocolate, and a few hard biscuits, for provision against improbable famine. Autumn would be the best time for such a journey, if the evenings need not be so often spent in stuffy rooms, with kerosene lamps for company. This was early summer, and I had long days in which to amuse myself. For a book I took a much-beloved small copy of *The Sentimental Journey*.

After I left my own neighborhood I was looked at with curious eyes. I was now and then recognized with surprise, but oftener viewed with suspicion, as if I were a criminal escaping from justice. The keepers of the two country taverns at which I rested questioned me outright, until I gave a reassuring account of myself. Through the middle of the day I let the horse stand unsaddled in the shade, by the roadside, while I sat near, leaning against the broad trunk of a tree, and ate a bit of luncheon, or slept, or read my book, or strolled away up the shore of a brook or to the top of a hill. On the third or fourth day I left my faithful companion so long that he grew restless, and at last fearful, as petted horses will. The silence and strangeness of the place and my disappearance frightened him. When I returned, I found that the poor creature had twisted a forward shoe so badly that I could neither pull it off altogether, nor mount again. There was nothing to do but to lead him slowly to some farmhouse, where I could get assistance; so on went the saddle, and away we plodded together sadly along the dusty road. The horse looked at me with anxious eyes, and was made fretful by the difficulty of the projecting shoe. I should have provided myself with some pincers, he seemed to tell me; the foot was aching from the blows I had given it with a rough-edge stone in trying to draw the tenacious nails. It was all my fault, having left him in such a desolate place, fastened to a tree that grew against a creviced ledge of rock. We were both a little sulky at this mischance so early in the careless expedition.

The sea was near, and the salt-marshes penetrated deep into the country, like abandoned beds of rivers winding inland among the pine woods and upland pastures. The higher land separated these marshes, like a succession of low promontories trending seaward, and the road climbed and crossed over from one low valley to another. There had been no houses for some distance behind us. I knew that there was a village with a good tavern a few miles ahead; so far, indeed, that I had planned to reach it at sundown. I began to feel very tired, and the horse tossed his head more and more impatiently, resenting my anxious, dragging hold upon the rein close at his mouth. There was nobody to be seen; the hills became steeper, the unshaded strips of marshland seemed hotter, and I determined at last to wait until some traveler appeared who could give us assistance. Perhaps the blacksmith himself might be out adventuring that afternoon.

We halted by some pasture bars in the shade of an old cider-apple tree, and I threw the bridle over a leaning post in the unsteady fence; and there the horse and I waited, and looked at each other reproachfully. It was some time before I discovered a large rusty nail lying in the short grass, within reach of my hand. My pocket-knife was already broken, because I had tried to use it for a lever, and this was just what I needed. I quickly caught up the disabled hoof again, and with careful prying the tough nails loosed their hold at last, and the bent shoe dropped with a clink. The horse gave a whinny of evident relief, and seemed to respect me again, and I was ready to mount at once; in an instant life lost its depressing aspect. "Keep your feet out of clefts now!" I said joyfully, with a friendly stroke of the good creature's neck and tangled mane, and a moment afterward we were back in the stony road. Alas, the foot had been strained, and our long halt had only stiffened it. I was mounted on three feet, not four. Nothing was to be done but to go forward, step by step, to the far-away village, or to any friendly shelter this side of it.

The afternoon was waning: sometimes I rode, sometimes I walked; those three miles of marsh and hill seemed interminable. At last I saw the chimneys of a house; the horse raised his head high, and whinnied loud and long.

These chimneys were most reassuring; being high and square, they evidently belonged to a comfortable house of the last century, and my spirits rose again. The country was still abandoned by human beings. I had seen no one since noon, but the road was little used, and was undoubtedly no longer the main highway of that region. I wondered what impression I should make in such a migratory guise. The saddle and its well-stuffed haversack and my own dustiness amused me unexpectedly, and I understood for the first time that the rest and change of this solitary excursion had done me much good. I was no longer listless and uninterested, but ready for adventure of any sort. It had been a most sensible thing to go wandering alone through the country. But now the horse's ankle was swollen. I grew anxious again, and looked at the chimneys with relief. Presently I came in sight of the house.

It was disappointing, for the first view gave an impression of dreariness and neglect. The barn and straggling row of out-buildings were leaning this way and that, mossy and warped; the blinds of the once handsome house were broken; and everything gave evidence of unhindered decline from thrift and competence to poverty and ruin. A good colonial mansion, I thought, abandoned by its former owners, and tenanted now by some shiftless outcasts of society, who ask but meagre comfort, and are indifferent to the decencies of life. Full of uncertainty, I went along the approach to the barn, noticing, however, with surprise that the front yard had been carefully tended; there were some dark crimson roses in bloom, and broken lines of box which had been carefully clipped at no remote period. Nobody was in sight. I went to the side door, and gave a knock with my whip at arm's length, for the horse was eager to reach the uninviting, hungry-looking stable. Some time elapsed before my repeated summons were answered; then the door slowly opened, and a woman just this side of middle age stood before me, waiting to hear my errand. She had a pathetic look, as if she were forced by circumstances to deny all requests, however her own impulses might lead her toward generosity. I was instantly drawn toward her, in warm sympathy: the blooming garden was hers; she was very poor. I would plead my real fatigue, and ask for a night's lodging, and perhaps my holiday might also give her pleasure. But a curious hardness drew her face into forbidding angles, even as her sweet and womanly eyes watched me with surprised curiosity.

"I should be very sorry to take the horse any farther today," said I, after stating my appealing case. "I will give you as little trouble as possible." At this moment the haggard face of an elderly man peered at me over her shoulder.

"We don't keep tavern, young lady," he announced, in an unexpectedly musical, low voice, "but since your horse is—"

"I am ready to pay any price you ask," I interrupted, impatiently; and he gave me an eager look and then came to the outer step, ignoring both his daughter and me, as he touched the horse with real kindliness. "'T is a pretty creature!" he said, admiringly, and at once stooped stiffly down to examine the lifted foot. I explained the accident in detail, grateful for such intelligent sympathy, while he stroked the lamed ankle.

"There's no damage done," he assured me presently, looking up with transient self-forgetfulness. "A common liniment will do; there's a bottle in the house, but 't will cost you something," and his face clouded again.

I turned to the daughter, who gave me a strange, appealing look. Her eyes begged me entreatingly, "Give him his own way"; her firm-set mouth signified her assent to the idea that I had no right to demand favors.

"Do what you think best," I said, "at your own price. I shall be very grateful to you"; and having come to this understanding, the father and I unbuckled the saddle-girths, while the daughter stood watching us. The old man led the limping horse across the green dooryard to a weather-beaten stable, talking to him in a low tone. The creature responded by unusual docility. I even saw him, though usually so suspicious and fretful with strangers, put his head close to his leader's shoulder with most affectionate impulse. I gathered up my belongings – my needments, as somebody had called them, after Spenser's fashion, in the morning – and entered the door.

Chapter II

ALONG THE BY-WAYS and in the elder villages of New England stand many houses like this, from which life and vigor have long been ebbing, until all instincts of self-preservation seem to have departed. The commonplace, thrifty fears of increasing damage from cracks, or leaks, or falling plaster no longer give alarm; as age creeps through the human frame, pilfering the pleasures of enthusiasm and activity one by one, so it is with a decaying house. The old man's shrewd eyes alone seemed unrelated to his surroundings. What sorrow or misfortune had made him accept them? I wondered, as I stared about the once elegant room. Nothing new had been brought to it for years; the leather-bound books in the carved secretary might have belonged to his grandfather. The floor was carpetless and deeply worn; the faded paper on the walls and the very paint looked as old as he. The pinch of poverty could nowhere be much sharper than here, but the exquisite cleanness and order of the place made one ignore the thought of poverty in its common aspect, for all its offensive and repulsive qualities were absent. I sat down in a straight-backed mahogany chair, feeling much relieved, and not without gratitude for this unexpected episode. The hostess left me alone. I was glad enough to have the long day shortened a little, and to find myself in this lonely, mysterious house. I was pleased by the thought that the price of my food and lodging would be very welcome, and I grew more and more eager to know the history of my new friends. I have never been conscious of a more intense desire to make myself harmonious, or to win some degree of confidence. And when the silence of the old sitting room grew tiresome I went out to the stable, whence my host had not returned, and was quite reconciled at finding that I was looked upon by him, at least, merely as an appendage to my four-footed companion.

The old man regarded me with indifference, and went on patiently rubbing the horse's foot. I was silent after having offered to take his place and being contemptuously refused. His clothes were curiously old and worn, patched bravely, and an embroidery of careful darns. The color of them was not unlike the dusty gray of long-neglected cobwebs. There was unusual delicacy and refinement in his hands and feet, and I was sure, from the first glance at my new friends and the first sound of their voices, that they had inherited gentle blood, though such an inheritance had evidently come through more than one generation to whom had been sternly denied any approach to luxury or social advantage. I have often noticed in country villages the descendants of those clergymen who once ruled New England sternly and well, and while they may be men and women of undeveloped minds, without authority and even of humble circumstances, they yet bear the mark of authority and dignified behavior, like silver and copper coins with a guinea stamp.

I was more and more oppressed by the haunting sense of poverty, for I saw proofs everywhere that the inhabitants of the old house made no practical protest against its slow decay. The woman's share of work was performed best, as one might see by their mended clothes; but the master's domain was hopelessly untended, not only as to the rickety buildings, but in the land itself, which was growing wild bushes at its own sweet will, except for a rough patch near the house, which had been dug and planted that year. Was this brooding, sad old man discouraged by life? Did he say to himself, "Let things be; they will last my time"? I found myself watching his face with intense interest, but I did not dare to ask questions, and only stood and watched him. The sad mouth of the man might have been a den from which stinging wild words could assail a curious stranger. I was afraid of what he might say to me, yet I longed to hear him speak.

The summer day was at its close. I moved a step forward to get away from the level sunbeams which dazzled my eyes, and ventured to give some news about myself and the lonely journey that had hitherto brought me such pleasure. The listener looked up with sincere attention, which made me grow enthusiastic at once, and I described my various experiences, and especially the amusing comments which I had heard upon my mode of traveling about the country. It amazed me to think that I was within sixty miles of home and yet a foreigner. At last I asked a trivial question about some portion of the scenery, which was pleasantly answered. The old man's voice was singularly sweet and varied in tone, the exact reverse of a New Englander's voice of the usual rural quality. I was half startled at seeing my horse quickly turn his head to look at the speaker, as if with human curiosity equal to my own. I felt a thrill of vague apprehension. I was unwise enough for a moment to dread taking up my residence in this dilapidated mansion; a creeping horror, such as one feels at hearing footsteps behind one in a dark, strange place, made me foolishly uneasy, and I stood looking off across the level country through the golden light of closing day, beyond the marshes and beyond the sand dunes to the sea. What had happened to this uncanny father and daughter, that they were contented to let the chances of life slip by untouched, while their ancestral dwelling gradually made itself ready to tumble about their ears?

I could see that the horse's foot was much better already, and I watched with great sympathy the way that the compassionate, patient fingers touched and soothed the bruised joint. But I saw no sign of any other horse in the stable, save a few stiffened, dusty bits of harness hung on a high peg in the wall; and as I looked at these, and renewed my wonder that such a person should have no horse of his own, especially at such a distance from any town, the old man spoke again.

"Look up at that bit of dry skin over the harnesses," said he. "That was the pretty ear of the best mare that ever trod these roads. She leaped the stable-yard gate one day, caught her foot in a rope, and broke her neck. She was like those swallows one minute, and the next she was a heap of worthless flesh, a heavy thing to be dragged away and hidden in the earth." His voice failed him suddenly, poor old fellow; it told me that he had suffered cruel sorrows that made this loss of a pleasure almost unbearable. So far life had often brought me successes, and I had gained a habit of expecting my own enterprises to be lucky. I stood appalled before this glimpse of a defeated life and its long procession of griefs.

Presently the master of the place went into the house, and returned with a worn wooden trencher of bits of hard bread and some meal. The hungry creature in the stall whinnied eagerly, and nestled about, while our host ascended the broken stairway to the stable loft; and after waiting for some time, I heard the rustle of an armful of hay which came down into the crib. I looked that way, and was not surprised, when I noticed the faded, dusty dryness of it, to see my dainty beast sniff at it with disappointment, and look round at me inquiringly. The old man joined me, and I protested hastily against such treatment of my favorite.

"Cannot we get somebody to bring some better hay, and oats enough for a day or two, if you are unprovided?" I asked.

"The creature must not be overfed," he said, grudgingly, with a new harsh tone. "You will heat the foot, and we must keep the beast quiet. Anything will serve tonight; tomorrow he can graze all day, and keep the foot moving gently; next day, he can be shod."

"But there is danger in giving him green grass," I suggested. "This is too rich pasturage about the house; surely you know enough of horses to have learned that. He will not be fit to ride, either. If I meant to give him a month of pasture, it would be another thing. No; send somebody for at least an armful of decent hay. I will go myself. Are there houses near?"

The old man had gone into the stall, and was feeding the hungry horse from the trencher. I was startled to see him snatch back two or three bits of the bread and put them into his pocket, as if, with all his fondness for the horse and a sincere desire to make him comfortable, he nevertheless grudged the food. I became convinced that the poor soul was a miser. He certainly played the character exactly, and yet there was an appealing look in his eyes, which, joined with the tones of his voice, made me sure that he fought against his tyrannous inclinations. I wondered irreverently if I should be killed that night, after the fashion of traditional tavern robberies, for the sake of what might be found in my pocket, and sauntered toward the house. It remained to be proved whether the daughter was the victim or the upholder of her father's traits.

I had the satisfaction of finding that the daughter was just arranging a table for supper. As I passed the wide-open door of a closet, I was tempted to look in by the faint ancient odor of plum cakes and Madeira wine which escaped; but I never saw a barer closet than that, or one that looked hungrier in spite of the lingering fragrance of hospitality. It gave me a strange feeling as if there were a still subtler link with the past, and some invisible presence would have me contrast the house's former opulence with its present meagreness. When we sat at table I was not surprised to find, on a cloth that was half covered with darns and patches, some pieces of superb old English silver and delicate china. The fare was less than frugal, but was nobly eked out with a dish of field strawberries, as if kind Nature had come to the rescue. Cream there was none, nor sugar, nor even tea or butter. I had an aching sense of the poverty of the family, and curiously questioned in my own mind how far they found it possible to live without money. There was some thin, crisp corn bread, which had been baked in the morning, or whenever there had last been a fire. It was very good. Perhaps my entertainers even gathered their own salt from the tide-pools to flavor the native corn. Look where I would, I could see nothing for which money had been lately spent; here was a thing to be wondered at in this lavish America, and I pushed back my chair at last, while I was still half hungry, from a dread that there would be nothing for breakfast unless I saved it then.

The father and daughter were very agreeable, I must confess; they talked with me about my journey now, and my plans, as if they were my personal friends, and the strange meal was full of pleasure, after all. What had brought a lady and gentleman to such a pass?

After supper the daughter disappeared for a time, busy with her household cares; a little later the father went out of the stable and across the fields, before I could call to him or offer my company. He walked with a light, quick step, like an Indian, as if he were used to taking journeys on foot. I found myself uncommonly tired; the half-illness which had fettered me seemed to have returned, after the unusual anxiety and weariness of the afternoon, and I longed to go to bed and to sleep. I had been interested in much that my entertainers had said of the early history of that part of the country, and while we sat at the table I had begun to look forward to a later evening talk, but almost before daylight faded I was forced to go to bed.

My hostess led me through a handsome empty hall, of the wide and stately colonial type, to a comfortable upper room, furnished with a gloomy-looking curtained bedstead and heavy mahogany furniture of the best old fashion. It seemed as if the room had been long unused, and also as if the lower part of the house were in a much worse state of disrepair and threadbareness than this. But the two large windows stood open to the fading sky and sweet country air, and I bade my hostess goodnight cheerfully. She lingered to see if I were comfortable; it was the first time I had been alone with her. "You can see that we are not used to entertaining company," she whispered, reddening with sensitiveness, and smiling apologetically. "Father has kept everybody away for so many years that I rarely have anyone to speak to, or anything to do but to keep the poor old house clean. Father means to be kind, but he—" and she turned away, much embarrassed by my questioning look – "he has a monomania; he inherits it from my grandfather. He fears want, yet seems to have no power to provide against it. We are poor, God knows, yet we have resources; or had them once," she added, sorrowfully. "It was the horse that made him willing to let you in. He loves horses, yet he has long denied himself even that useful pleasure."

"But surely he ought to be controlled," I urged. "You must have suffered."

"I know all that you are eager to say," she replied; "but I promised my dear mother to be patient with him. It will not be long now; he is very feeble. I have a horror that this habit of parsimony has rooted itself too deeply in my own life to be shaken off. You will hear mockery enough of us among the farmers."

"You surely have friends?"

"Only at a distance," said she, sadly. "I fear that they are no longer friends. I have you," she added, turning to me quickly, in a pathetic way that made me wish to put my arms about her. "I have been longing for a friendly face. Yes, it is very hard," and she drearily went out of the door, and left me alone with the dim light of the sky outside, the gloomy shadows of the room within. I tried to fancy some clue to the weird misery of this poverty-stricken household, as I lay down; but I fell asleep very soon, and slept all night, without even a dream.

Chapter III

DAYLIGHT brought a new eagerness and a less anxious curiosity about my strange entertainers. I opened my eyes in broad sunlight. I was puzzled by the unfamiliar India-cotton hangings of the great bedstead; then I caught sight of my dusty habit and my riding-cap and whip, nearby. I instantly resolved that even if I found my horse in the restored condition there was every reason to expect, I would make this house my headquarters for as long time as its owners would keep me, or I could content myself. I would try to show some sisterly affection to the fast-aging woman who was so enslaved by her father's delusions. I had come out in search of adventure; it would be a difficult task to match my present surroundings.

I listened for the sound of footsteps or voices from below, but it was still very early, and I looked about the long-untenanted room with deliberate interest and scrutiny. As I changed my position a little, I caught sight of a curious old painting on the large oval panel above the empty fireplace. The colors were dull, the drawing was quaintly conventional, and I recognized the subject, though not immediately. The artist had pleased himself by making a study of the old house itself, and later, as I dressed, I examined it in detail.

From the costume of the figures I saw that it must have been painted more than a hundred years before. In astonishing contrast to the present condition, it appeared like a satirical show of the house's possibilities. Servants held capering steeds for gay gentlemen to mount, and ladies walked together in fine attire down the garden alleys of the picture. Once a hospitable family had kept open house behind the row of elms, and once the follies of the world and the fashions of brilliant, luxurious life had belonged to this decayed and withering household. I wondered if the miserly old man, to whose strangely sweet and compelling voice I had listened the evening before, could bear to look at this picture, and acknowledge his unlikeness to his prosperous ancestors.

It was well for me that the keeping of hens is comparatively inexpensive, for I breakfasted comfortably, and was never so heartily rejoiced at the vicinity of a chicken-coop. My proposal to stay with my new friends for a few days met with no opposition from either host or hostess; and again, as I looked in their pinched and hopeless faces, I planned some secret excuses for making a feast of my own, or a happy holiday. The fields and hills of the old picture were still unchanged, but what ebb and flow of purpose, of comfort, of social condition, had enriched and impoverished the household!

"Where did she sleep?" asked the master of the house, suddenly, with a strange, suspicious glance at his daughter.

"In the landscape chamber," the pale woman said, without lifting her eyes to his, though she grew whiter and thinner as she spoke.

I looked at him instinctively to see his eyes blaze with anger, and expected a torrent of abuse, because he was manifestly so much displeased. Nothing was said, but with a feeling of uneasiness we left the table, and I went out to the kitchen with my new friend.

"There is no reason why I should not have put you into the landscape chamber," she told me instantly. "It is a fancy of my father's. I had aired that room thoroughly in the morning, but the front guest-chambers have been closed for some time."

"Who painted the strange old picture?" I asked. "Some member of the family?" But I was answered that it was the work of a Frenchman, who was captured in war-time, and paroled under the charge of her great-grandfather.

"He must have had a gay visit," I suggested, "if he has left a faithful picture of the house as he saw it."

"The house used to be like that always," was the faint response, and the speaker hesitated, as if she considered whether we did right in discussing her family history; then she turned quickly away. "I believe we are under some miserable doom. Father will be sure to tell you so, at any rate," she added, with an effort at gaiety. "He believes that he fights against it, but I always say that he was cowardly, and accepted it," and she sighed wearily.

I looked at her with fresh surprise and conjecture. I forgot for the time this great, busy, prosaic world of which we were both a part, and I felt as if I had lost a score of years for each day's journey, and had gone backward into the past. New England holds many strange households within its borders, but there could not be another which approached this. The very air of the house oppressed me, and I strayed out into the beautiful wide fields, and found my spirits rising again at once. I turned at last to look back at the group of gray buildings in the great level landscape. They were such a small excrescence upon the fruitful earth, those roofs which covered awful stagnation and hindrance of the processes of spiritual life and growth. What power could burst the bonds, and liberate the man and woman I had left, from a mysterious tyranny?

I was bareheaded and the morning grew very hot. I went toward a group of oaks, to shelter myself in the shade, and found the ancient burying-place of the family. There were numerous graves, but none were marked except the oldest. There was a group of rude but stately stones, with fine inscriptions, yet curiously enough the latest of them bore a date soon after the beginning of the century; all the more recent graves were low and unmarked in any way. The family fortunes had waned long ago, perhaps; I might be wronging the present master of the house, though I remembered what had been said to me of some mysterious doom. I could not help thinking of my new acquaintances most intently, and was startled at the sound of footsteps. I saw the old man, muttering and bending his head until he could see nothing but the ground at his feet. He only picked up some dead branches that had fallen from the oaks, and went away toward the house again; always looking at the ground, as if he expected to find something. It came to my mind with greater distinctness that he was a miser, poor only by his own choice; and I indignantly resolved to urge the daughter to break her allegiance to him for a time, to claim her own and set herself free. But the miser had no cheerful sense of his hoards, no certainty of a munificence which was more to him than any use of it; there was a look upon his face as of a preying conscience within, a gnawing reptile of shame and guilt and evil memory. Had he sacrificed all sweet family life and natural ties to his craving for wealth? I watched the bent and hungry figure out of sight.

When I reached the house again, I went through the open door of the wide hall, and gained my landscape chamber without being seen by anyone. I was tired and dizzy with the unusual heat, and, quickly drawing the close shutters, I threw myself on the bed to rest. All the light in the room came from the shaded hall; there was absolute silence, except some far-off country sounds of birds high in the air or lowing cattle. The house itself was still as a tomb.

I went to sleep, but it was not sound sleep. I grew heavy and tired with my own weight. I heard soft footsteps coming up the stairs; someone stopped as if to listen outside the wide-open door; then the gray, shadowy figure of the old man stood just within, and his eyes peered about the room. I was behind the curtains; one had been unfastened, and hid me from his sight at first, but as he took one step forward he saw me, lying asleep. He bent over me, until I felt my hair stir with his breath, but I did not move. His presence was not frightful, strange to say; I felt as if I were only dreaming. I opened my eyes a little as he went away, apparently satisfied, to the closet door, and unlocked it, starting and looking at me anxiously as the key turned in the lock. Then he disappeared. I had a childish desire to shut him in and keep him prisoner, for reasons that were not clear to myself. Whether he only wished to satisfy himself that a concealed treasure was untouched I do not know, but presently he came out, and carefully locked the door again, and went away on tiptoe. I fancied that he lingered before the picture above the chimney-place, and wondered if his conscience pricked him as he acknowledged the contrast between past and present. Then he groaned softly, and went out. My heart began to beat very fast. I sprang up and tried to lock the door into the hall. My enthusiasm about spending a few days in this dismal place suddenly faded out, for I could not bear the thought that the weird old man was free to prowl about at his own sad will. But as I stood undecided in my doorway, a song sparrow perched on the sill of the wide hall window, and sang his heart away in a most cheerful strain. There was something so touching and appealing in the contrast that I felt a wistful clutch at my throat while I smiled, as one does when tears are coming like April showers to one's eyes. Without thinking what I did, I went back into the room, threw open the shutters again, and stood before the dingy landscape. How the horses pranced up to the door, and how fine the ladies were in their hoop-petticoats and high feathers! I imagined that the picture had been a constant rebuke to the dwellers in the house through their wasting lives and failing fortunes. In every human heart, said I, there is such a picture of the ideal life – the high possibilities and successes, the semblance of duties done and of spiritual achievements. It forever measures our incompleteness by its exact likeness to that completeness which we would not fight hard enough to win. But as I looked up at the panel, the old landscape became dim, and I knew that it was only because a cloud was hiding the sun; yet I was glad to leave the shadows of the room, and to hurry down the wide stairway.

I saw nothing of the daughter, though I searched for her, and even called her, through the house. When I reached the side door I found her father crossing the yard, and wondered if he would show any consciousness of our having so lately met. He stood still and waited for me, and my first impulse made me ask, "What did you want just now? I was not asleep when you were in my room; you frightened me."

"Do not be afraid," he answered with unexpected patience. "You must take us as you find us. It is a sad old house, but you need not be afraid; we are much more afraid of you!" and we both smiled amiably.

"But your daughter," said I; "I have been asking her to come away for a time, to visit me or take a journey. It would be much better for you both; and she needs a change and a little pleasuring. God does not mean that we shall make our lives utterly dismal." I was afraid, and did not dare to meet the old man's eyes after I had spoken so plainly.

He laughed coldly, and glanced at his mended coat-sleeve.

"What do you know about happiness? You are too young," said he. "At your age I thought I knew the world. What difference would it make if the old place here were like the gay ghost of it in our landscape chamber? The farmers would be jealous of our luxury; reverence and respect would be turned into idle curiosity. This quiet countryside would be disgraced by such a flaunting folly. No, we are very comfortable, my child and I; you must not try to disturb us," and he looked at me with a kind of piteous suspicion.

There was a large block of stone under one of the old elms, which had been placed there long ago for a mounting-block, and here we seated ourselves. As I looked at my companion, he seemed like a man unused to the broad light of day. I fancied that a prisoner, who had just ended many years of dungeon life, would wear exactly such a face. And yet it was such a lovely summer day of a joyful world, if he would only take or make it so. Alas, he matched the winter weather better. I could not bear to think of the old house in winter!

"Who is to blame?" said the old man suddenly, in a strange eager tone which startled me, and made me shrink away from him. "We are in bondage. I am a generous-hearted man, yet I can never follow my own impulses. I longed to give what I had with a lavish hand, when I was younger, but some power restrained me. I have grown old while I tried to fight it down. We are all in prison while we are left in this world – that is the truth; in prison for another man's sin." For the first time I understood that he was not altogether sane. "If there were an ancestor of mine, as I have been taught, who sold his soul for wealth, the awful price was this, and he lost the power of using it. He was greedy for gain, and now we cannot part with what we have, even for common comfort. His children and his children's children have suffered for his fault. He has lived in the hell of watching us from generation to generation; seeing our happiness spoiled, our power of usefulness wither away. Wherever he is, he knows that we are all misers because he was miserly, and stamped us with the mark of his own base spirit. He has watched his descendants shrivel up and disappear one by one, poor and ungenerous in God's world. We fight against the doom of it, but it wins at last. Thank God, there are only two of us left."

I had sprung to my feet, frightened by the old man's vehemence. I could not help saying that God meant us to be free and unconquered by any evil power; the gray, strange face looked blindly at me, and I could not speak again. This was the secret of the doom, then. I left the old man crying, while I hurried away to find the mistress of the desolate house, and appeal to her to let me send a companion for her father, who could properly care for him here, or persuade him to go away to some place where he would forget his misery among new interests and scenes. She herself must not be worn out by his malady of unreason.

But I only dashed my sympathy against the rock of her hopelessness. "I think we shall all disappear some night in a winter storm, and the world will be rid of us – father and the house and I, all three," she said, with bitter dreariness, and turned to her work again.

Early that evening, I said goodbye to my new friends, for the horse was sound, and not to be satisfied by such meagre stabling. Our host seemed sorry to let the creature go, and stood stroking him affectionately after I had mounted. "How the famous old breed holds its own!" he said wistfully. "I should like to have seen the ancestor who has stamped his likeness so unmistakably on all his descendants."

"But among human beings," I could not resist saying, "there is freedom, thank God! We can climb to our best possibilities, and outgrow our worst inheritance."

"No, no!" cried the old man bitterly. "You are young and fortunate. Forget us, if you can; we are of those who have no hope in a world of fate."

I looked back again and again, as I rode away. It was a house of shadows and strange moods, and I was glad when I had fairly left it behind me; yet I looked forward to seeing it again. I well remember the old man's clutch at the money I offered him, and the kiss and the bunch of roses that the daughter gave to me. But late that evening I was not sorry to shut myself into my prosaic room at a village hotel, rather than try to sleep again behind the faded figured curtains of the landscape chamber.

The Story of a Day

Grace King

IT IS REALLY NOT MUCH, the story; it is only the arrangement of it, as we would say of our dresses and our drawing rooms.

It began with the dawn, of course; and the skiff for our voyage, silvered with dew, waiting in the mist for us, as if it had floated down in a cloud from heaven to the bayou. When repeated, this sounds like poor poetry; but that is the way one thinks at day dawn, when the dew is yet, as it were, upon our brains, and our ideas are still half dreams, and our waking hearts, alas! as innocent as waking babies playing with their toes.

Our oars waked the waters of the bayou, as motionless as a sleeping snake under its misty covert – to continue the poetical language or thought. The ripples ran frightened and shivering into the rooty thicknesses of the sedge-grown banks, startling the little birds bathing there into darting to the nearest, highest rush-top, where, without losing their hold on their swaying, balancing perches, they burst into all sorts of incoherent songs in their excitement to divert attention from the near-hidden nests: bird mothers are so much like women mothers!

It soon became day enough for the mist to rise. The eyes that saw it ought to be able to speak to tell fittingly about it.

Not all at once, nor all together, but a thinning, a lifting, a breaking, a wearing away; a little withdrawing here, a little withdrawing there; and now a peep, and now a peep; a bride lifting her veil to her husband! Blue! White! Lilies! Blue lilies! White lilies! Blue and white lilies! And still blue and white lilies! And still! And still! Wherever the veil lifted, still and always the bride!

Not in clumps and bunches, not in spots and patches, not in banks, meadows, acres, but in – yes; for still it lifted beyond and beyond and beyond; the eye could not touch the limit of them, for the eye can touch only the limit of vision; and the lilies filled the whole sea-marsh, for that is the way spring comes to the sea-marshes.

The sedge-roots might have been unsightly along the water's edge, but there were morning-glories, all colors, all shades – oh, such morning-glories as we of the city never see! Our city morning-glories must dream of them, as we dream of angels. Only God could be so lavish! Dropping from the tall spear-heads to the water, into the water, under the water. And then, the reflection of them, in all their colors, blue, white, pink, purple, red, rose, violet!

To think of an obscure little Acadian bayou waking to flow the first thing in the morning not only through banks of new-blown morning-glories, but sown also to its depths with such reflections as must make it think itself a bayou in heaven, instead of in Paroisse St. Martin. Perhaps that is the reason the poor poets think themselves poets, on account of the beautiful things that are only reflected into their minds from what is above? Besides the reflections, there were alligators in the bayou, trying to slip away before we could see them, and watching us with their stupid, senile eyes, sometimes from under the thickest, prettiest flowery bowers; and turtles splashing into the water ahead of us; and fish (silver-sided perch), looking like reflections themselves, floating through the flower reflections, nibbling their breakfast.

Our bayou had been running through swamp only a little more solid than itself; in fact, there was no solidity but what came from the roots of grasses. Now, the banks began to get firmer, from real soil in them. We could see cattle in the distance, up to their necks in the lilies, their heads and sharp-pointed horns coming up and going down in the blue and white. Nothing makes cattle's heads appear handsomer, with the sun just rising far, far away on the other side of them. The sea-marsh cattle turned loose to pasture in the lush spring beauty – turned loose in Elysium!

But the land was only partly land yet, and the cattle still cattle to us. The rising sun made revelations, as our bayou carried us through a drove in their Elysium, or it might have always been an Elysium to us. It was not all pasturage, all enjoyment. The rising and falling feeding head was entirely different, as we could now see, from the rising and falling agonized head of the bogged – the buried alive. It is well that the lilies grow taller and thicker over the more treacherous places; but, misery! Misery! Not much of the process was concealed from us, for the cattle have to come to the bayou for water. Such a splendid black head that had just yielded breath! The wide-spreading ebony horns thrown back among the morning-glories, the mouth open from the last sigh, the glassy eyes staring straight at the beautiful blue sky above, where a ghostly moon still lingered, the velvet neck ridged with veins and muscles, the body already buried in black ooze. And such a pretty red-and-white-spotted heifer, lying on her side, opening and shutting her eyes, breathing softly in meek resignation to her horrible calamity! And, again, another one was plunging and battling in the act of realizing her doom: a fierce, furious, red cow, glaring and bellowing at the soft, yielding inexorable abysm under her, the bustards settling afar off, and her own species browsing securely just out of reach.

They understand that much, the sea-marsh cattle, to keep out of reach of the dead combatant. In the delirium of anguish, relief cannot be distinguished from attack, and rescue of the victim has been proved to mean goring of the rescuer.

The bayou turned from it at last, from our beautiful lily world about which our pleasant thoughts had ceased to flow even in bad poetry.

Our voyage was for information, which might be obtained at a certain habitation; if not there, at a second one, or surely at a third and most distant settlement.

The bayou narrowed into a canal, then widened into a bayou again, and the low, level swamp and prairie advanced into woodland and forest. Oak-trees began, our beautiful oak-trees! Great branches bent down almost to the water – quite even with high water – covered with forests of oak, parasites, lichens, and with vines that swept our heads as we passed under them, drooping now and then to trail in the water, a plaything for the fishes, and a landing-place for amphibious insects. The sun speckled the water with its flickering patterns, showering us with light and heat. We have no spring suns; our sun, even in December, is a summer one.

And so, with all its grace of curve and bend, and so – the description is longer than the voyage – we come to our first stopping-place. To the side, in front of the well-kept fertile fields, like a proud little showman, stood the little house. Its pointed shingle roof covered it like the top of a chafing-dish, reaching down to the windows, which peeped out from under it like little eyes.

A woman came out of the door to meet us. She had had time during our graceful winding approach to prepare for us. What an irrevocable vow to old maidenhood! At least twenty-five, almost a possible grandmother, according to Acadian computation, and well in the grip of advancing years. She was dressed in a stiff, dark red calico gown, with a white apron. Her black hair, smooth and glossy under a varnish of grease, was plaited high in the back, and dropped regular ringlets, six in all, over her forehead. That was the epoch when her calamity came to her, when the hair was worn in that fashion. A woman seldom alters her coiffure after a calamity of a certain nature happens to her. The figure had taken a compact rigidity, an unfaltering inflexibility, all the world away from the elasticity of matronhood; and her eyes were clear and fixed like her figure, neither falling, nor rising, nor puzzling under other eyes. Her lips, her hands, her slim feet, were conspicuously single, too, in their intent, neither reaching, nor feeling, nor running for those other lips, hands, and feet which should have doubled their single life.

That was Adorine Mérionaux, otherwise the most industrious Acadian and the best cottonade-weaver in the parish. It had been short, her story. A woman's love is still with those people her story. She was thirteen when she met him. That is the age for an Acadian girl to meet him, because, you know, the large families – the thirteen, fourteen, fifteen, twenty children – take up the years; and when one wishes to know one's great-great-grandchildren (which is the dream of the Acadian girl) one must not delay one's story.

She had one month to love him in, and in one week they were to have the wedding. The Acadians believe that marriage must come *au point*, as cooks say their sauces must be served. Standing on the bayou-bank in front of the Mérionaux, one could say "Good day" with the eyes to the Zévérin Theriots – that was the name of the parents of the young bridegroom. Looking under the branches of the oaks, one could see across the prairie – prairie and sea-marsh it was – and clearly distinguish another little red-washed house like the Mérionaux, with a painted roof hanging over the windows, and a staircase going up outside to the garret. With the sun shining in the proper direction, one might distinguish more, and with love shining like the sun in the eyes, one might see, one might see – a heart full.

It was only the eyes, however, which could make such a quick voyage to the Zévérin Theriots; a skiff had a long day's journey to reach them. The bayou sauntered along over the country like a negro on a Sunday's pleasuring, trusting to God for time, and to the devil for means.

Oh, nothing can travel quickly over a bayou! Ask anyone who has waited on a bayou-bank for a physician or a life-and-death message. Thought refuses to travel and turn and double over it; thought, like the eye, takes the shortest cut – straight over the sea-marsh; and in the spring of the year, when the lilies are in bloom, thought could not take a more heavenly way, even from beloved to beloved.

It was the week before marriage, that week when, more than one's whole life afterward, one's heart feels most longing – most – well, in fact, it was the week before marriage. From Sunday to Sunday, that was all the time to be passed. Adorine – women live through this week by the grace of God, or perhaps they would be as unreasonable as the men – Adorine could look across the prairie to the little red roof during the day, and could think across it during the night, and get up before day to look across again – longing, longing all the time. Of course one must supply all this from one's own imagination or experience.

But Adorine could sing, and she sang. One might hear, in a favorable wind, a gunshot, or the barking of a dog from one place to the other, so that singing, as to effect, was nothing more than the voicing of her looking and thinking and longing.

When one loves, it is as if everything was known of and seen by the other; not only all that passes in the head and heart, which would in all conscience be more than enough to occupy the other, but the talking, the dressing, the conduct. It was then that the back hair was braided and the front curled more and more beautifully every day, and that the calico dresses became stiffer and stiffer, and the white crochet lace collar broader and lower in the neck. At thirteen she was beautiful enough to startle one, they say, but that was nothing; she spent time and care upon these things, as if, like other women, her fate seriously depended upon them. There is no self-abnegation like that of a woman in love.

It was her singing, however, which most showed that other existence in her existence. When she sang at her spinning-wheel or her loom, or knelt battling clothes on the bank of the bayou, her lips would kiss out the words, and the tune would rise and fall and tremble, as if Zepherin were just across there, anywhere; in fact, as if every blue and white lily might hide an ear of him.

It was the time of the new moon, fortunately, when all sit up late in the country. The family would stop in their talking about the wedding to listen to her. She did not know it herself, but it – the singing – was getting louder and clearer, and, poor little thing, it told everything. And after the family went to bed they could still hear her, sitting on the bank of the bayou, or up in her window, singing and looking at the moon traveling across the lily prairie – for all its beauty and brightness no more beautiful and bright than a heart in love.

It was just past the middle of the week, a Thursday night. The moon was so bright the colors of the lilies could be seen, and the singing, so sweet, so far-reaching – it was the essence of the longing of love. Then it was that the miracle happened to her. Miracles are always happening to the Acadians. She could not sleep, she could not stay in bed. Her heart drove her to the window, and kept her there, and – among the civilized it could not take place, but here she could sing as she pleased in the middle of the night; it was nobody's affair, nobody's disturbance. "Saint Ann! Saint Joseph! Saint Mary!" She heard her song answered! She held her heart, she bent forward, she sang again. Oh, the air was full of music! It was all music! She fell on her knees; she listened, looking at the moon; and, with her face in her hands, looking at Zepherin. It was God's choir of angels, she thought, and one with a voice like Zepherin! Whenever it died away she would sing again, and again, and again –

But the sun came, and the sun is not created, like the moon, for lovers, and whatever happened in the night, there was work to be done in the day. Adorine worked like one in a trance, her face as radiant as the upturned face of a saint. They did not know what it was, or rather they thought it was love. Love is so different out there, they make all kinds of allowances for it. But, in truth, Adorine was still hearing her celestial voices or voice. If the cackling of the chickens, the whir of the spinning-wheel, or the 'bum bum' of the loom effaced it a moment, she had only to go to some still place, round her hand over her ear, and give the line of a song, and – it was Zepherin – Zepherin she heard.

She walked in a dream until night. When the moon came up she was at the window, and still it continued, so faint, so sweet, that answer to her song. Echo never did anything more exquisite, but she knew nothing of such a heathen as Echo. Human nature became exhausted. She fell asleep where she was, in the window, and dreamed as only a bride can dream of her groom. When she awoke, "Adorine! Adorine!" the beautiful angel voices called to her; "Zepherin! Zepherin!" she answered, as if she, too, were an angel, signaling another angel in heaven. It was too much. She wept, and that broke the charm. She could hear nothing more after that. All that day was despondency, dejection, tear-bedewed eyes, and tremulous lips, the commonplace reaction, as all know, of love exaltation. Adorine's family, Acadian peasants though they were, knew as much about it as anyone else, and all that anyone knows about it is that marriage is the cure-all, and the only cure-all, for love.

And Zepherin? A man could better describe his side of that week; for it, too, has mostly to be described from imagination or experience. What is inferred is that what Adorine longed and thought and looked in silence and resignation, according to woman's way, he suffered equally, but in a man's way, which is not one of silence or resignation – at least when one is a man of eighteen – the last interview, the near wedding, her beauty, his love, her house in sight, the full moon, the long, wakeful nights.

He took his pirogue; but the bayou played with his impatience, maddened his passion, bringing him so near, to meander with him again so far away. There was only a short prairie between him and ——, a prairie thick with lily-roots – one could almost walk over their heads, so close, and gleaming in the moonlight. But this is all only inference.

The pirogue was found tethered to the paddle stuck upright in the soft bank, and – Adorine's parents related the rest. Nothing else was found until the summer drought had bared the swamp.

There was a little girl in the house when we arrived – all else were in the field – a stupid, solemn, pretty child, the child of a brother. How she kept away from Adorine, and how much that testified!

It would have been too painful. The little arms around her neck, the head nestling to her bosom, sleepily pressing against it. And the little one might ask to be sung to sleep. Sung to sleep!

The little bed-chamber, with its high mattressed bed, covered with the Acadian home-spun quilt, trimmed with netting fringe, its bit of mirror over the bureau, the bottle of perfumed grease to keep the locks black and glossy, the prayer-beads and blessed palms hanging on the wall, the low, black polished spinning-wheel, the loom – the *métier d' Adorine* famed throughout the parish – the ever goodly store of cotton and yarn hanks swinging from the ceiling, and the little square, open window which looked under the mossy oak-branches to look over the prairie; and once again all blue and white lilies – they were all there, as Adorine was there; but there was more – not there.

Baby Girl

Clayton Kroh

BABY GIRL awoke to darkness, an all-over itching she couldn't scratch, and a mind full to sopping with a mother's misery. If her eyes were open or closed she couldn't know, and the impulse to blink caused no flutter of eyelids. Her arms would not move, but were as stiff as sticks.

A bittersweet nectar seeped in from above, leaching into her dried skin and brittle bones. At times it would flood in, a deluge acrid with anger, and then cease. But most times it drizzled in, oily with sorrow, slowly pooling around Baby Girl until she floated in an amniotic peace. She drank it in with every desiccated fiber until her belly bulged with it and she slept and dreamed.

* * *

The baby girl lay dying six months ago in the slouching home of Louise and Oliver Tunstall. The frail three-year-old had suffered much in her final days, confined to the rickety pinewood bed her father Oliver had built for her a year ago, back when her dark cherub legs were strong and had grown too long to fold comfortably in the crib.

Oliver and Louise made most of the things they needed; there wasn't enough money to buy more than flour and fabric, nails and planting seeds. Louise cooked their meals and sewed their clothes (she was a very good cook and seamstress), while her husband built their house and their furniture (he was not a good a carpenter).

As the baby moaned in fitful sleep, Oliver fed the roaring woodstove while Louise tried all the remedies her mother and grandmother had ever taught her. It was her mother's gift with herbs and humors that made the unguents and remedies that had restored to Louise her full womanhood, finally turning the hard and barren earth of her womb into the garden that gave them their only child – a miracle that took so much from her mother that not enough remained to sustain her to see the baby's birth. And now that miracle entrusted to Louise's care lay dying.

Louise scoured the woods for the rare mushrooms, stalked the bog to catch the pungent and glowing fairy gas, and reaped the fields for the common flax. She worked until the walls inside the house sweated into the thick air the smells of skunkweed, sassafras and mint.

"We got to pray harder, Lulu," Oliver told her. He believed prayer would heal her baby, or so he said. They didn't need no white doctor from town. But Louise knew his pride was what kept him weak, hovering about her, useless – not some pious strength. Certainly, she had no love for the white folks who so begrudged them the carving up and granting to them this parcel of land. But this was her baby girl. If a white doctor had a remedy that could save her child, then Louise would remember how to cast her eyes down in the way they used to have to, and beg, because God sure won't doing nothing. All the begging to

Him had got her were bloody knees full of splinters from the ill-planed planks of Oliver's wood floor. No, if God wouldn't give her help, then she'd go get it from the Devil.

When the baby girl's moans came no more and her breath barely steamed the reflecting glass, Louise tossed down her tattered Bible and rose. With a clenched jaw and fist, she fixed Oliver with a look sharpened for cutting and issued a command furious in its silence: *You fix this!*

Oliver scrambled toward the door. He snatched his hat from the wall, pulling loose the wooden hook in his haste. He ran the seven miles into town, stumbling now and then as the sole of his boot began to pull free of the leather to flap against his foot. When he returned with the dour-faced white doctor, his foot was bare and dusty, and in places it bled from sharp road stones. In one hand he held his worn leather upper, in the other his sole.

* * *

The ride back with the doctor in his expensive carriage had left Oliver nervously mute and clammy all over. The air inside the house stank, bitter and stale, a shock after the fresh night air. He hated that he felt shame when the old man crinkled his nose as he looked about for an acceptable place for his coat. Oliver took it from him, apologizing and tasting the coppery word "sir". He hung the fine garment across the back of a tippy chair.

Holding a crisp white handkerchief to his mouth with one hand, the doctor pulled a ruler from his bag. With curt and cursory efficiency, he pushed the child's head to the left, to the right, pried open her mouth and depressed her tongue. He straightened and then shook his head.

Oliver watched Louise's face cinch tight like a knot, while the slits of her eyes hanged him with the noose of her glare. Then her legs unwound beneath her, and her body collapsed in a pile. Oliver went to her, tried to hold her, to lift her, but she spilled and tumbled out of his arms like a burst sack of potatoes. Finally, he left her where she lay next to the baby's bed and sat in his tippy chair, tensing to keep the leg from tapping the floor in the heavy silence.

The doctor left his handkerchief and ruler on the sloping kitchen table and let himself out.

* * *

Today, Baby Girl could move her arms. Where they had once been stiff, she could now flex them. It produced a creaking sound, the first real sound her new bark ears had heard in this small dark space. What came down from Mamma caused a buzzing tickle in her head. It took root and grew, blossoming.

The time of Mamma's visit came, but then passed. Baby Girl's fascination with her own arms forgotten, she lay still in the darkness, waiting. Every moment that passed without Mamma's mourning became interminable and pricked her with frustration and anger. Baby Girl squeezed her jaw against the knot in her mouth, bit into it and began to grind.

Mamma wasn't coming. This caused a sob to rise into her throat. The pressure was excruciating as it swelled, until at last a channel opened around the knot in her mouth and her sob gurgled with spittle around the knot in her mouth.

An incredible sensation followed, an inward sucking of air through her nose that brought with it the smells of earth and wood and rot.

Then, a soft "baby girl" wafted in from above. Baby Girl quieted instantly. She drifted like sediment into the silent and cool darkness and drank in Mamma's sweet sadness.

Suddenly, an image caught like a bubble on the softening skin of her shriveled and burst into a memory and Baby Girl would marvel, her eye sockets wide like underground lakes sparkling with surprise at a spelunker's lantern. Texture; yarn knitted into a blanket, warm, her tiny fingers poking through the purls. Another memory popped fragrant with breast milk and the feel of soft brown flesh kneaded by her lips.

Next there came vinegary ones that inflamed and itched her hot skin; and then tart ones that made her pucker and gag. She convulsed, and the impulse to cry pushed to escape her but was stifled by a woody knot growing in her mouth that wedged it open into a gape.

Finally, there came heavy ones that Baby Girl grew to love the most, viscous with loss that clung to bones and filled her cavities like tar. A prickling vitality spread throughout her. She relished it. She wanted more.

A soft voice, quavering, flowed from above. "Oh baby girl," it cried. "My baby girl. Why my baby girl?" Yes, the voice was calling to her and she knew the name of the voice was Mamma.

Yes, Baby Girl dreamed upward as she suckled the knot in her mouth. *Cry, Mamma. I am so hungry.*

* * *

Louise sat beneath the magnolia, legs folded beneath her. She wrung a tatty handkerchief, antiqued to a dingy yellow, and dabbed at her eyes. Before her, two chocks of wood nailed together into a cross stuck out of the ground. Spring was swooping in warmly. The sap was rising in the big magnolia that was poised for summer lushness. But Louise took no notice of the reawakening life around her.

She murmured to herself, trying out prayer again, but still found the words bitter in her mouth like a swig of vinegar. The devil had come and gone, giving nothing but taking everything that mattered. She rested her fist on her thigh as she sent up to God the same message that always went unanswered: Why?

After a time, she spoke to the ground. "He left me, baby girl," she said. "He up and left me, says he can't stand my misery no more."

Louise shifted her weight. "How I'm gonna move on like he say I should, from my only baby, my flesh and my blood put in the ground to be forgot?"

In the distance, honeysuckle rioted at the edge of the line of trees with spring's sweet scent. Louise rubbed at her nose, sniffed. "I won't," she said. "'It's me or her, Lulu,' he says to me yesterday. What's to say to that? Today he come into my kitchen and says, 'I'm going, Lulu,' his bag in his hand, his eyes full up, but for what? 'Go on,' I told him. 'Leave me be. I won't cry no river for you.' And that was that."

Louise had been peeling potatoes that afternoon. She had watched her husband of eight years walk away into the dusty distance as she filled the metal tub at her feet with ten too many potatoes for just one.

What's done is done, she thought now and pushed herself up from the ground, leaning against the magnolia tree. She shook the tingles out of her sleeping legs. But even as she thought this and tried to wad him up in her mind and chuck him, the image of Oliver hammering together lopsided furniture and smiling proudly wouldn't crumple.

What would she do without him? She'd be fine, yes. She'd been hewn, but she'd survive. But what would Oliver do? He wasn't the strongest man, but he was solid and always tried to do right, and she'd loved him for his trying.

Louise slapped dry grass off her dress. She blew her nose and caught the sugary breeze from the honeysuckle, bright and promising. The world wanted a fight. God wanted a fight. She'd had a fight with the devil and lost. Alright then. Oliver was the last thing she had in this mean world that too often took things that weren't its to take. She'd be damned if she was going to oblige it and throw out the precious little it hadn't taken. After all, she probably was damned, so she might as well face it, fists up, and fight for the one thing she hoped wasn't yet lost.

Louise left her baby girl's grave and set off down the road toward town. She'd find Oliver and bring him home, and it didn't matter if it took all day and all night, and into the next. In the distance, thunderheads, slate gray and white-knuckled, hunched in from the west.

* * *

Baby Girl did not like this feeling. It set a fire inside her that ran the lengths of her limbs and burned up her strength. She gnashed at the knot in her mouth until her sharp new thorny teeth dug into its barky hide to a soft, moist middle. A sticky sweet sap oozed onto her leafy tongue. She hacked, gagging, and tried to sit up but couldn't. Her head was anchored by a thick magnolia root snaking in through the pine boards of her coffin and into one eye. It had wound in and around the confines of her skull, doubling back on itself, crimping and tangling and sprouting with Baby Girl's thoughts.

Baby Girl lurched but the root held. She needed something, up there, like air. A need she'd never felt seized her. She needed her mamma.

Grabbing the root, she jerked her head, twisted, and thrashed. At last, it broke and her head lolled free on her sapling neck. Immediately, she tried to sit up but gashed her head on the pine boards overhead. Sap trickled down her ligneous cheek.

The gagging eased as the sap coated her throat. Baby Girl was angry. Mamma had left her. She felt her strength ebbing already without the nourishment of Mamma's mourning. Mamma was somewhere up above, and Baby Girl would find her. She broke the coffin wood above her and began digging her way upward, pushing with an awesome strength toward the surface, like a sprouting seed.

* * *

Raindrops hit the dirt road around Louise in tiny, dusty splashes. A hard shower would be upon her soon, so she picked up her pace. Pebbles worked into her shoes and bruised her heels. Her destination was still a good four miles distant.

Oliver would be staying with his cousin, also a sharecropper, on the other side of Louvale. Oliver's cousin was the only relative who hadn't yet decamped the cruel south for the promises of Chicago and Philadelphia and the cities up north.

After the baby's funeral, ritual had kept Louise's life from falling in on itself: her hands knew the cooking of meals, the washing of laundry, and the picking of tobacco well enough to prop her up. She added a new ritual during those months, spending an hour each day in the late afternoon beneath the magnolia tree at the edge of their acre of land where her baby lay buried.

It seemed these moments were clearest to her. They alone held purpose. She had cursed Oliver, then. No doctor he had said, and she'd waited, waited for miracles, waited while her baby's skin erupted, waited until it was too late.

How she'd made him suffer since, in the thousand sharp ways that are revealed to a wounded wife. She spoke no words when they rose from bed in the mornings, nor when they lay down at night; when he touched her with a gentle hand seeking to console, she turned to wood. Dishes, tins, and cups upbraided him when she slammed them on to the nightly dinner table, and on Sundays in church he sang his hymns alone. Louise's days became mechanical, and dual-purposed: one, to grind the clock hands from one day to the next with work and duties, and two, to mill her weak-willed husband into powder. Only during that hour each day at the grave of her baby girl did her life briefly chime.

When she'd won the war against her husband, when he'd finally picked up and blown away like a spring breeze, even these moments at the grave began to fray and unwind for her. Soon, she realized she'd waged her war against the wrong foe. She felt she had lost everything when her baby girl died, but she hadn't felt true emptiness until Oliver left. Flawed though he may be, he had tried to set her on her feet, be her quiet foundation when he thought she'd needed it. She had needed it, needed him, but pain and stubbornness had tricked her into believing she was a rampart of stone.

* * *

Baby Girl broke through the surface. Rain splashed on her dirty skull. Her skin gushed into green life with each drop as she pulled herself out of the earth.

The air was invigorating, very different from the stale air underground. The breeze was damp and whistled through her openings as she breathed it in. Leaves unfurled across her body. Baby Girl sucked the knot in her mouth, and though she relished the rich, earthy taste of nectar welling from it, it did not quell her anger. Even as her body budded and bloomed, the vitality that animated her waned. She yearned for the sustenance that had brought her life.

Baby Girl made quick progress despite her ungainly movement. Her steps were loping with outward swings of legs that flexed like thick saplings. She held her arms aloft, a pose that felt proper, natural. Her upper body swayed to and fro with each step, creaking. A white magnolia blossom shivered open from her left eye, and the world around her burst into color, but Baby Girl did not notice it.

* * *

Louise heard a rustling behind her, but before she could turn, pain burst into her head. She stumbled forward and fell into the sharp gravel of the road. She tried to crawl. Blood ran down her temples and into her eyes.

She saw the thing behind her, lumbering toward her. It burbled at the mouth where sap bubbled. Somehow she understood it, not in words, because there were none, but heard it deeper inside her. *Mamma,* it said, but the word burned with a ravenous anger.

She saw it, there beneath the grime and vines – her baby girl's face, only now it was swollen in the cheeks and broken at the forehead. Its skin fluttered with fading green and yellowing leaves. Withering branches jutted from its body. A browning flower drooped from its eye.

Louise struggled to stand, but it seized her with arms that squeezed like a cider press. *Cry, mamma!* The thing opened its mouth, exposing a pulpy white knot.

Louise tried to scream, but couldn't. Her bones cracked. A bright sensation of pain and sudden numbness swept through her.

* * *

For a brief moment, a rush of delicious misery poured out of Mamma. It shot out like sunlight from between heavy clouds. Baby Girl drank it in, thirstily. She squeezed to wring out more, but it began to dim. Mamma's head tipped back. She fell limp in Baby Girl's embrace, and the invigorating flow was choked off. Baby Girl squeezed harder, felt things snapping inside Mamma, but it did not restart the flow. Baby Girl shook her and then let her drop.

Hollowness grew inside Baby Girl. The big magnolia blossom in her eye wilted, its petals curling with brown veins. She stumbled from the road into a freshly turned field. A shiny black beetle bored its way through the thin bark of her neck and dropped to the ground. More beetles began to rain from a thousand holes as they bore out of her body, and they scuttled into the fresh earth.

Baby Girl's legs bowed, grew brittle and snapped. She fell to the rich earth and quietly went to seed.

* * *

The new boots felt fine on Oliver's tired feet, but loneliness made his steps leaden as he walked back to his cousin's place. He hadn't bought a new pair of boots in years. His old ones had been falling apart on his feet. Louise, back when her belly was swoll and she glowed, had teased him that the baby would be wearing boots before he'd get himself a new pair.

What was he doing? The image of his wife's strong hands turning a potato against a rust-freckled paring knife came to his mind. The day he'd left her. He had opened his mouth to speak, but instead he'd toed the loose floorboard by the door. Then, he'd turned away and left her. What a damned fool he was.

It didn't take long for him to stuff his clothes into his cracked leather bag. He grabbed his hat and headed out the door. "Going home," he said, nodding to his cousin who stared at him from the kitchen table. His cousin nodded back with a simple, "yup."

Oliver ran down the road that led back home, rain coming down hard, his new boots pinching and sloshing in the puddles.

Oliver found Louise's body lying in the ditch along the road. He recognized her sandal lying in the road. The periwinkle print of her dress showed through the mud that covered it.

Oliver lifted her body and felt the unnatural slide of her bones within her.

He made his way back home. There he laid her gently beneath the magnolia behind the house. The ground was upturned where his daughter had been buried. Had Louise done this? He couldn't think about what had happened after he left. He should never have left her. What kind of husband had he been? She'd broke and he'd just cowered like a kicked hound. This was his fault. He'd failed her, his Lulu.

Oliver went to the house and brought back a shovel. He pushed the earth back into April's grave and packed it down.

Oliver spent the night building a coffin for his wife with the wood he took from his many attempts at carpentry around the house, the tippy chair, the loose floorboards

April's cockeyed cradle. He was a poor carpenter, he knew it. He'd been a poor father, too, and now he could add a poor husband to his list.

It was late evening the next day before he packed down the dirt of Lulu's grave. Exhausted, he rested and pulled his hat down to his heart. His wife's last words haunted him. *I won't cry no river for you.*

Oliver hid his face with his aching hands, the raw callouses rough like pine bark. The chapped and raw cracks of those hands stung when the tears ran into them. He did not notice the breeze that carried the sweet smell of the spring honeysuckle, nor the blossoms shivering above him as he poured out his sadness into the fresh earth at the base of the magnolia tree.

Viola's Second Husband

Sean Logan

I NEVER WANTED to stay overnight at my maternal grandparents' house. Not ever. It was tolerable enough in the afternoon, when my mother and I would make that long drive out to the Lakeview house. The house itself was not equipped for a young person – it was all lacquered antiques, hard woods, marble hearth, grainy portraits in gilded frames, and for the love of all that's holy, no television. But Grandpa was there, and he had enough warmth to make even that Victorian relic a reasonable place to be for a few short hours.

But I never wanted to stay overnight. If I did, I'd inevitably be expected to spend time with my grandmother. As it was on these afternoons, she and my mother would sit in the kitchen drinking coffee and speaking glumly about the sad state of cousins I'd never met, while Grandpa did his best to entertain me with stories and puzzles. Lord knew there were no toys in the house.

Despite all the hours they spent together, I never thought my mother liked her very much. She certainly never spoke badly of her in front of me, but they never looked happy to see each other. Even if it had been weeks since our last visit, when we finally arrived at the door it was a simple "hello" and maybe the faint whisper of a tight-lipped smile if someone was in especially good spirits that day. And my mother never called her 'Mom' or 'Mother' or any other variation of the word. She called her by her name, Viola.

I could hardly blame my mother for her formality; Viola was pulled so tight she'd make the Queen feel like she was slouching. She rarely had much to say to me. She'd comment on my attire, but that was for my mother's benefit. "I see you're wearing your tennis shoes today. Don't dress up on our account."

I have no doubt my mother understood my apprehensions, which is why she never expected me to stay overnight there. Except the one weekend when I was eleven. She said she had business out of town and said, apologetically, that she was not able to find another place for me to stay.

I suspect my mother had had a falling out with Viola. It had been months since we had visited, and when she pulled up to the front of the house that evening, she didn't take me to the door. "Sorry, dear. Have to run. See yourself in."

I hauled my satchel out of the back seat, feeling a bit sorry for myself, hoping she'd see my moping face and pouching lower lip and decide that this was more than any young man should have to endure. She'd bring me along on her business trip and I could stay in her hotel room with her and order room service and swim in the hotel pool. Surely, when she saw my forlorn face, that is what she would decide to do.

But, no. The moment I swung the door closed, she raced away from the curb like she was glad to be rid of me. I watched her shrink into the distance for a moment, giving her one last chance to see my sad face in the rearview mirror and come back for me. But instead she turned the corner, leaving me alone on the curb. There was no place for me to go other than inside.

As I made my way to the front steps, I noted the foliage along the walkway. It all seemed more untamed than usual. The beech hedgerow that lined the path was unmanicured, and there was ragweed intruding upon the gladioli. Dandelion was peeking through the cracks in the cement, and the coralbark maple had dumped its leaves carelessly across all and sundry. The crepuscular light gave the scene a surreal lavender glow.

As I climbed the front steps, my feet clomping on the hollow boards, I noted the curling gray paint that crackled underfoot. I don't think any of these imperfections were well out of the ordinary, but my dour mood put me in a state to notice them.

When I stepped onto the porch, the wrought iron lamp atop the stairs switched on. Knowing I was seen, I stood at the door waiting for it to open. After a moment, when this did not occur, I rapped on the loose, rattling screen. Perhaps the light switched on because it was mostly dark now, coinciding with my arrival only by chance.

The door opened at last, Viola standing in the entryway, her frizzy gray and black hair pinned up here and there, her lips pulled into a small tight smile. If this smile was meant to make me feel more welcome, it was not achieving the desired effect. She was wearing a maroon shawl over her black dress, and when I entered the house I found that it was nearly as cold inside as it was out in the crisp evening air.

"Hello, Jonathan," she said. "It's very nice to have you with us this evening."

"Thank you for letting me stay over," I said at my mother's direction.

"It is our pleasure," she said as if it was nothing of the sort.

"Who's making all that racket? Who's barging into my house at this ungodly hour?" As my grandfather, dressed in his dark gray robe and slippers, shuffled down the hall, I noticed immediately how much thinner he had become since my previous visit. I felt a sad tugging at my chest. It was as if I missed him, though he was right there.

"Hi, Grandpa," I said and rushed over to him.

He hooked an arm around my neck and pulled me in. "Get over here, you maniac." He felt terribly frail. My grandmother, by contrast, looked positively robust. She was a very thin woman, but there was fullness to her cheeks and a general sense of fortitude.

"Have you eaten?" Grandpa said. "I made one heck of a roast for dinner."

"My mom gave me dinner before we left," I said, which was not entirely true. I made myself a peanut butter sandwich earlier but I didn't have supper. I just didn't want roast.

"Very well," Viola said. "Let's get you upstairs to your room so you can get settled and ready for bed."

"Bed?" Grandpa said, incredulous. "It's only eight o'clock."

"If you would like to stay up and entertain our guest, you are more than welcome."

"I would, and I will!"

At the top of the stairs, I said goodnight to Viola and she retired to her bedroom, where she slept separately from Grandpa. He had his own room downstairs. Years earlier I had asked my mother why they didn't sleep together like Ami and Papi, or like she had with my father. She said Viola made Grandpa turn the living room downstairs into a bedroom because he snored and it interfered with her sleep.

Grandpa brought me to the other upstairs bedroom across the hall, which used to be my mother's room when she was a girl. Any trace of her childhood was long gone. It was now a study filled with esoteric books on subjects I did not recognize and in which I would have no interest if I did. Her bed was the only piece of her that remained.

I got undressed and into that small, cold bed, even though outside the bedroom window I could still see the faintest coloring of the evening sun behind the hills along the horizon. Grandpa got into bed next to me on top of the covers and read from *The Lion, the Witch and the Wardrobe*.

"Have you read this one?" he asked.

"Yes, but I'd like to hear it again."

Even though it was more than an hour before my regular bedtime, I must have been tired, because I don't even remember making it to the end of the first chapter before sleep pulled me under.

* * *

The next afternoon, while Viola was locked away in her room, Grandpa and I strolled about their lush, overgrown garden. The old white Victorian and the thick clusters of birch trees that surrounded the yard kept the garden perpetually in shadow and gave me the sense of being in a tropical jungle. Grandpa identified the flowers for me, pointing out the oleander and calla lilies and hydrangeas – all names I already knew well. I often spent weekends at the botanical gardens in the park with my mother, and I had my own small garden at home, but I didn't want to tell this to Grandpa and spoil his fun.

He knelt next to a patch of creeping thyme and rubbed the herb between his thumb and forefinger. He held his fingers to his nose. I did the same and found it smelled a bit like my mother's spaghetti. I stood, but when Grandpa tried to raise himself from his crouched position, he groaned and reached out for me.

"Give us a hand, eh?"

I grabbed his long, bony hand and helped him straighten – or at least get as straight as he was going to get.

"Grandpa," I said, "how old are you?"

He laughed at the timing of my question. "Pretty old! Can't you tell?" He put an arm around my shoulder. I don't know if he was being affectionate or just trying to steady himself. "Actually, I'm not as old as I probably look. I'm seventy-two."

"Ami is seventy-two, I think."

"I believe she is. And I bet she looks a lot younger than me, doesn't she?"

"Why is that?" I said, though I should have known better. At my age, I didn't fully grasp the sensitivity some adults had to their age. Though, honestly, I don't think Grandpa would be counted among them.

"Well," he said, "I'm sure your Ami takes good care of herself and eats all her vegetables. But aside from that, I guess some people just age faster than others."

"How long do people live?" If my handling of the subject of age was a bit indelicate, my bluntness around the subject of death of was positively graceless. But Grandpa took it in stride.

"Do you mean, how long will *I* live?" he said with a smile. "I don't know, but I'll be honest with you, because I think you're old enough and strong enough that I can tell you things honestly: I wouldn't expect it to be very many years more."

"Really?" I said. I felt a deep sadness at this, but even more I felt bewildered by the whole idea of life and death at that moment. "And what happens when you die?"

Grandpa laughed. "Boy, you don't shy away from the big subjects, do you? That's a conversation you should have with your mother. People believe all sorts of things. Many believe you go to heaven. Your Grandmother believes we can come back."

"Reincarnation, right?" I said, proud that I remembered the word.

"Well, yes, I mean, many people believe in reincarnation." He seemed somewhat flustered and ready to move on to lighter subjects. "Like I said, you should be taking this up with your mother. I think I'm ready for a nap. One of the great things about being O-L-D, a little walk around the yard is enough to make you tired."

I walked Grandpa up the back steps, then trotted back down to continue my tour of the garden, looking past the foliage to the soil beneath, hoping to uncover earthworms or banana slugs. I stuck my fingers into the cool black earth beneath the lilies. I didn't turn out any worms, but I did spy a potato bug. I followed it through the pink Gerber daisies and lost it behind a rose bush on the northern edge of the garden, near the storage shed. As I looked for the insect, I noticed that in the space between the old wooden shed and yard's outer fence, there was freshly turned soil. This was outside the garden proper, so it caught my attention and I thought this might be a good place to search for bugs.

I stuck my hands into the earth, and when I turned it over, I was startled to see small white bones emerge from the soil, along with ash and dried leaves. This caught me off guard, but it only took me a moment to decide they must have been there to fertilize the soil. They were small, thin and charred, like the bones of a cooked chicken. It must have been leftovers from supper that had been buried here for composting.

It all made perfect sense, but suddenly I felt very uncomfortable. I had the urge to turn around and look behind me, and when I did, I saw Viola looking down on me from the upstairs window to her room. She turned away. Not quickly; she certainly would not have been embarrassed about watching me. She merely seemed to be through with me as the subject of her attention.

I continued to explore the garden, but I was continually mindful of Viola's presence. Each time I glanced up at the window to her room, I only saw her in profile, probably reading one of her odd books. But still, for the duration of my time in the yard, I felt the faint heat of her eyes upon me.

* * *

My hopes for supper were not high. Somehow I doubted Viola would have pizza and sodas delivered. Nor did I expect her to produce a barbecue to grill us all some cheeseburgers. Despite the lowered expectations, I still managed to be disappointed. Last night they had nearly my least favorite meal – roast beef. Tonight they had the only thing worse – leftover roast beef.

Viola was down from her room for the first time that day, though she was still reading, sitting at the head of the dining room table, waiting to be served. She was wearing a long black dress, similar to the one she wore yesterday, only this time the shawl was a dark violet. Grandpa shuffled into the kitchen, bundled up like he was about to leave for the Iditarod, wearing a knit cap, a scarf coiled around his neck and his robe over his sweat suit. I didn't understand why they didn't keep it warmer in there. This couldn't possibly be good for Grandpa, and even though Viola didn't seem bothered by the temperature, she did have that shawl draped around her neck and shoulders.

Grandpa's nap did not seem to have done him much good. He was puffy-eyed and hunched over as he walked. He really did look much older than his seventy-two years. I did not remember my father's grandfather well, though I did remember him looking similarly aged. But he was an octogenarian at the time.

"So, how you doing, kiddo?" Grandpa said, trying to bring some energy to his tired voice. "You able to keep yourself entertained this afternoon?"

"Sure," I said. "I saw a potato bug and a squirrel and a whole bunch of birds, but I don't know what kind of birds they were."

"Well, good for you. I know it's not exactly Disneyland back there. Maybe one of these days I can set up a basketball hoop out front for the next time you come over."

"You will do no such thing," Viola said from behind her book. "The boy found a number of things in the yard to interest him." She glanced over the top of her book at me. I squirmed slightly in my seat. I wasn't sure if she was mad at me. She always seemed at least a bit disapproving.

"We'll see," Grandpa said. He coughed a wet, gurgling cough into his fist. He started to pick up the fork and carving knife.

"You *are* going to wash your hands, are you not?" Viola said.

"Of course I'm going to wash my hands," he said with mock irritation, "do you think I'm an animal?" He winked at me, gave his hands a perfunctory rinse under the faucet and returned to carving. He brought first me and then Viola a plate of gray-brown meat and small wrinkled potatoes, and a cup of tomato soup. When Viola received her plate, she closed her book and carefully set it on the footstool beside her.

As with the rest of the house, the details of the dinner table were uncomfortably askew with my usual experience. The heavy antique chairs on which we sat were too large, and the carved wood of the arms made it uncomfortable to rest my elbows upon. They were also too tall for me to scoot the chair into the table, so I had to sit at a bit of a distance. The table was set with a precision and formality that I found off-putting. Grandpa and Viola sat at opposite ends of the table and I was placed equidistant between them. Grandpa had set my plate on top of a larger plate, which in turn sat upon three levels of scratchy placemats that did not seem appropriate for catching spilled food. The silverware was also too large and heavy. The fork and spoon seemed as if they should be used for tossing a salad. I could not imagine how I was going to get that spoon in my mouth to eat my soup. I soon realized I should not have been considering this to begin with.

"That is not how you eat soup," Viola scolded. "You do not shove the spoon into your mouth like you're sucking on a lollypop. You sip from the side of your spoon." She demonstrated, lifting the side of the spoon to her lips and pouring the contents into her mouth. It was a very small and delicate gesture. I followed her example successfully, but I found it to be an intolerably slow and unsatisfying way to eat.

We ate without talking for a time. I was very aware of the sound of my knife and fork clicking against the plate. I tried to do this carefully because Viola managed to cut her meat in nearly complete silence and I assumed too loud a clack against the plate would get me another lesson in etiquette.

As we were nearing the end of our meal, Viola broke the silence. "So has your mother started dating again?" she said, without looking up from her precise carving.

"No," I said, horrified by the notion.

"She will, you know. She will get on with her life. It is perfectly natural that she will. I was married once before I met your grandfather. Did you know that?"

"You were married before Grandpa?" This was shocking news to me. How had my mother never told me?

"Yes, very briefly," she said, looking up from her plate, but not at me. "He was my college sweetheart. He was studying law and he came from a very wealthy family that owned a law practice. He was going to be very wealthy himself in the near future, which meant that I was meant to be wealthy as well. But it was certainly not the prospect of his future earnings that attracted me to him. In truth, of all things, it was his hair at first. He had the loveliest long hair. It was wavy and blond and it went past his shoulders, which was quiet uncommon in those days. I think he got away with it because he was English and being a foreigner granted him a certain indulgence for his eccentricities. For me, those unique qualities were absolutely irresistible. And, you may be surprised to know, I was considered a great beauty at the time. Together, we were the envy of everyone on campus. And shortly after graduation, we were wed. It was quite magical, really. But it didn't last. He drove his MG headlong into a rather large truck and just like that, I was a widow." Viola seemed to snap out of a reverie and finally turned to look at me. "But all of this is just to say that your mother will begin dating again one day and start the next phase of her life. I hope you'll be supportive."

I was surprised, and just a bit disturbed, by her story, and I wondered why she was telling it to me. She had not previously found it necessary to toss more than a passing remark in my direction, but here she was, spinning a heartfelt and very private tale. But then I realized, like many of the words she aimed at me, this story was not for my benefit.

I glanced over at my grandfather. His head was lowered and he was concentrating on his plate, stabbing glumly at the meat. I wanted to say something, to him or to her, to come to his defense, admonish her for being so insensitive, maybe even make a joke that would make him laugh and shrug off all the weight that made his shoulders stoop. But I didn't. I didn't dare say anything. I finished my meal in silence and went upstairs to bed. Grandpa read me another chapter and I pretended to sleep. I tried not to cry. I think I succeeded. He turned out the light when he left, and eventually I slept for real.

* * *

Something pulled me out of my dreams. It was dark and I was overwhelmingly and unreasonably afraid. I listened carefully and looked around the shadowy room with dread. I felt a cold, feverish prickling on my skin and a queasiness in my bowels. I saw and heard nothing and my heart began to slow, but something still felt out of sorts. I bolstered my courage and crawled out of bed. I hadn't brought slippers and my feet were cold on the wooden floorboards. It had been chilly in the evening, and the temperature had dropped considerably since then. I could see the silvery wisps of my breath.

I crossed the room and opened the door to the hallway. The idea of seeking comfort from Viola was absurd, but her room was right there and I was apprehensive about going downstairs. Her door was open. I stepped inside. It seemed brighter in there than it was in my room. Perhaps the moon was on her side of the sky. I saw at once that her bed was empty. I glanced around the room to make sure she was not crouched in a shadowed corner. It was the first time I had been in her room. There were shelves from floor to ceiling along two of the walls. They were filled with books and jars and small unfamiliar plants. I also noticed, up on the top shelf, a lidded ceramic jar, white with a blue floral pattern. It struck me as something that would contain someone's remains, though I don't know where I would have gotten that notion.

As I was about to leave the room, I noticed a strange energy. It was faint to be sure, but it seemed to charge the air like static electricity. When I stood still, I fancied that it pulsed and swirled around me.

I fled the room and crept reluctantly down the steep, narrow staircase. Whatever had roused me from sleep was unclear. The lights were off and there were no discernible noises other than the ticking of the grandfather clock in the living room.

At the bottom of the stairs, I turned down the hallway to the closed door to Grandpa's room. It was especially dark here, away from any windows, so even the moonlight could not get in. I turned the porcelain doorknob and opened the door. The scene before me made my heart freeze for a beat and my breath catch in my chest. It wasn't clear to me at first what I was seeing.

My grandfather was lying naked on his back, his arm hanging half off the bed, hand limp at the wrist. His head was lulled to the side in the direction of the door, so that when I opened it, he was staring directly at me. Viola was hunched over him, straddling his frail body fully clothed, still wearing her long black dress.

Without moving, without so much as blinking his heavy eyelids, he said to me feebly, "Go."

At the sound of his weak voice, Viola snapped her head in my direction, a savage look in her eyes.

I scurried back down the hall and up the stairs, back into my room and under the covers. I lay there, shivering, waiting for something terrible to happen. And I kept waiting. At some point, hours later, I heard Viola return to her room and quietly shut the door. I did not sleep. I lay under the blankets until the sun was up in the sky, and mother finally came and took me away from there. It was the last time I set foot in that house.

* * *

Grandpa died six months later. My mother said it was 'old age', which told me nothing. There was a service at a Unitarian church in Lakeview. I didn't know if he was a member of the church; the priest who spoke said many nice things about him, about his generous spirit, that he was a friend to everyone he met, but he did not seem to be speaking from his own experience.

Viola sat on the opposite side of the church from my mother and me. There was plenty of room for us to sit together; there were no more than a dozen people in attendance, a few old work colleagues and friends from the Navy.

Viola and my mother never looked at each other throughout the service. When it was over, Viola promptly stood and left without a word to anyone. While my mother stayed behind to talk to my grandfather's old friends, I followed Viola out to the parking lot. There was a man waiting by a long black car for her. He was wearing a suit and seemed to be dressed for the service, so I didn't know why he had not come in. He gave her a kiss on the cheek and opened the passenger side door for her.

I sat on the steps of the church and watched the man with the long wavy hair drive Viola away. It was the last time I ever saw her.

The Outsider

H.P. Lovecraft

UNHAPPY IS HE to whom the memories of childhood bring only fear and sadness. Wretched is he who looks back upon lone hours in vast and dismal chambers with brown hangings and maddening rows of antique books, or upon awed watches in twilight groves of grotesque, gigantic, and vine-encumbered trees that silently wave twisted branches far aloft. Such a lot the gods gave to me – to me, the dazed, the disappointed; the barren, the broken. And yet I am strangely content and cling desperately to those sere memories, when my mind momentarily threatens to reach beyond to *the other*.

I know not where I was born, save that the castle was infinitely old and infinitely horrible, full of dark passages and having high ceilings where the eye could find only cobwebs and shadows. The stones in the crumbling corridors seemed always hideously damp, and there was an accursed smell everywhere, as of the piled-up corpses of dead generations. It was never light, so that I used sometimes to light candles and gaze steadily at them for relief, nor was there any sun outdoors, since the terrible trees grew high above the topmost accessible tower. There was one black tower which reached above the trees into the unknown outer sky, but that was partly ruined and could not be ascended save by a well-nigh impossible climb up the sheer wall, stone by stone.

I must have lived years in this place, but I cannot measure the time. Beings must have cared for my needs, yet I cannot recall any person except myself, or anything alive but the noiseless rats and bats and spiders. I think that whoever nursed me must have been shockingly aged, since my first conception of a living person was that of somebody mockingly like myself, yet distorted, shriveled, and decaying like the castle. To me there was nothing grotesque in the bones and skeletons that strewed some of the stone crypts deep down among the foundations. I fantastically associated these things with everyday events, and thought them more natural than the colored pictures of living beings which I found in many of the moldy books. From such books I learned all that I know. No teacher urged or guided me, and I do not recall hearing any human voice in all those years – not even my own; for although I had read of speech, I had never thought to try to speak aloud. My aspect was a matter equally unthought of, for there were no mirrors in the castle, and I merely regarded myself by instinct as akin to the youthful figures I saw drawn and painted in the books. I felt conscious of youth because I remembered so little.

Outside, across the putrid moat and under the dark mute trees, I would often lie and dream for hours about what I read in the books; and would longingly picture myself amidst gay crowds in the sunny world beyond the endless forests. Once I tried to escape from the forest, but as I went farther from the castle the shade grew denser and the air more filled with brooding fear; so that I ran frantically back lest I lose my way in a labyrinth of nighted silence.

So through endless twilights I dreamed and waited, though I knew not what I waited for. Then in the shadowy solitude my longing for light grew so frantic that I could rest no more, and

I lifted entreating hands to the single black ruined tower that reached above the forest into the unknown outer sky. And at last I resolved to scale that tower, fall though I might; since it were better to glimpse the sky and perish, than to live without ever beholding day.

In the dank twilight I climbed the worn and aged stone stairs till I reached the level where they ceased, and thereafter clung perilously to small footholds leading upward. Ghastly and terrible was that dead, stairless cylinder of rock; black, ruined, and deserted, and sinister with startled bats whose wings made no noise. But more ghastly and terrible still was the slowness of my progress; for climb as I might, the darkness overhead grew no thinner, and a new chill as of haunted and venerable mold assailed me. I shivered as I wondered why I did not reach the light, and would have looked down had I dared. I fancied that night had come suddenly upon me, and vainly groped with one free hand for a window embrasure, that I might peer out and above, and try to judge the height I had once attained.

All at once, after an infinity of awesome, sightless crawling up that concave and desperate precipice, I felt my head touch a solid thing, and I knew I must have gained the roof, or at least some kind of floor. In the darkness I raised my free hand and tested the barrier, finding it stone and immovable. Then came a deadly circuit of the tower, clinging to whatever holds the slimy wall could give; till finally my testing hand found the barrier yielding, and I turned upward again, pushing the slab or door with my head as I used both hands in my fearful ascent. There was no light revealed above, and as my hands went higher I knew that my climb was for the nonce ended; since the slab was the trapdoor of an aperture leading to a level stone surface of greater circumference than the lower tower, no doubt the floor of some lofty and capacious observation chamber. I crawled through carefully, and tried to prevent the heavy slab from falling back into place, but failed in the latter attempt. As I lay exhausted on the stone floor I heard the eerie echoes of its fall, hoped when necessary to pry it up again.

Believing I was now at prodigious height, far above the accursed branches of the wood, I dragged myself up from the floor and fumbled about for windows, that I might look for the first time upon the sky, and the moon and stars of which I had read. But on every hand I was disappointed; since all that I found were vast shelves of marble, bearing odious oblong boxes of disturbing size. More and more I reflected, and wondered what hoary secrets might abide in this high apartment so many aeons cut off from the castle below. Then unexpectedly my hands came upon a doorway, where hung a portal of stone, rough with strange chiseling. Trying it, I found it locked; but with a supreme burst of strength I overcame all obstacles and dragged it open inward. As I did so there came to me the purest ecstasy I have ever known; for shining tranquilly through an ornate grating of iron, and down a short stone passageway of steps that ascended from the newly found doorway, was the radiant full moon, which I had never before seen save in dreams and in vague visions I dared not call memories.

Fancying now that I had attained the very pinnacle of the castle, I commenced to rush up the few steps beyond the door; but the sudden veiling of the moon by a cloud caused me to stumble, and I felt my way more slowly in the dark. It was still very dark when I reached the grating – which I tried carefully and found unlocked, but which I did not open for fear of falling from the amazing height to which I had climbed. Then the moon came out.

Most demoniacal of all shocks is that of the abysmally unexpected and grotesquely unbelievable. Nothing I had before undergone could compare in terror with what I now saw; with the bizarre marvels that sight implied. The sight itself was as simple as it was stupefying, for it was merely this: instead of a dizzying prospect of treetops seen from a lofty eminence, there stretched around me on the level through the grating nothing less than *the solid ground*, decked and diversified by marble slabs and columns, and overshadowed by an ancient stone church, whose ruined spire gleamed spectrally in the moonlight.

Half unconscious, I opened the grating and staggered out upon the white gravel path that stretched away in two directions. My mind, stunned and chaotic as it was, still held the frantic craving for light; and not even the fantastic wonder which had happened could stay my course. I neither knew nor cared whether my experience was insanity, dreaming, or magic; but was determined to gaze on brilliance and gaiety at any cost. I knew not who I was or what I was, or what my surroundings might be; though as I continued to stumble along I became conscious of a kind of fearsome latent memory that made my progress not wholly fortuitous. I passed under an arch out of that region of slabs and columns, and wandered through the open country; sometimes following the visible road, but sometimes leaving it curiously to tread across meadows where only occasional ruins bespoke the ancient presence of a forgotten road. Once I swam across a swift river where crumbling, mossy masonry told of a bridge long vanished.

Over two hours must have passed before I reached what seemed to be my goal, a venerable ivied castle in a thickly wooded park, maddeningly familiar, yet full of perplexing strangeness to me. I saw that the moat was filled in, and that some of the well-known towers were demolished, whilst new wings existed to confuse the beholder. But what I observed with chief interest and delight were the open windows – gorgeously ablaze with light and sending forth sound of the gayest revelry. Advancing to one of these I looked in and saw an oddly dressed company indeed; making merry, and speaking brightly to one another. I had never, seemingly, heard human speech before and could guess only vaguely what was said. Some of the faces seemed to hold expressions that brought up incredibly remote recollections, others were utterly alien.

I now stepped through the low window into the brilliantly lighted room, stepping as I did so from my single bright moment of hope to my blackest convulsion of despair and realisation. The nightmare was quick to come, for as I entered, there occurred immediately one of the most terrifying demonstrations I had ever conceived. Scarcely had I crossed the sill when there descended upon the whole company a sudden and unheralded fear of hideous intensity, distorting every face and evoking the most horrible screams from nearly every throat. Flight was universal, and in the clamor and panic several fell in a swoon and were dragged away by their madly fleeing companions. Many covered their eyes with their hands, and plunged blindly and awkwardly in their race to escape, overturning furniture and stumbling against the walls before they managed to reach one of the many doors.

The cries were shocking; and as I stood in the brilliant apartment alone and dazed, listening to their vanishing echoes, I trembled at the thought of what might be lurking near me unseen. At a casual inspection the room seemed deserted, but when I moved towards one of the alcoves I thought I detected a presence there – a hint of motion beyond the golden-arched doorway leading to another and somewhat similar room. As I approached the arch I began to perceive the presence more clearly; and then, with the first and last sound I ever uttered – a ghastly ululation that revolted me almost as poignantly as its noxious cause – I beheld in full, frightful vividness the inconceivable, indescribable, and unmentionable monstrosity which had by its simple appearance changed a merry company to a herd of delirious fugitives.

I cannot even hint what it was like, for it was a compound of all that is unclean, uncanny, unwelcome, abnormal, and detestable. It was the ghoulish shade of decay, antiquity, and dissolution; the putrid, dripping eidolon of unwholesome revelation, the awful baring of that which the merciful earth should always hide. God knows it was not of this world – or no longer of this world – yet to my horror I saw in its eaten-away and bone-revealing outlines a leering, abhorrent travesty on the human shape; and in its moldy, disintegrating apparel an unspeakable quality that chilled me even more.

I was almost paralyzed, but not too much so to make a feeble effort towards flight; a backward stumble which failed to break the spell in which the nameless, voiceless monster held me. My eyes bewitched by the glassy orbs which stared loathsomely into them, refused to close; though they were mercifully blurred, and showed the terrible object but indistinctly after the first shock. I tried to raise my hand to shut out the sight, yet so stunned were my nerves that my arm could not fully obey my will. The attempt, however, was enough to disturb my balance; so that I had to stagger forward several steps to avoid falling. As I did so I became suddenly and agonizingly aware of the *nearness* of the carrion thing, whose hideous hollow breathing I half fancied I could hear. Nearly mad, I found myself yet able to throw out a hand to ward off the foetid apparition which pressed so close; when in one cataclysmic second of cosmic nightmarishness and hellish accident *my fingers touched the rotting outstretched paw of the monster beneath the golden arch.*

I did not shriek, but all the fiendish ghouls that ride the nightwind shrieked for me as in that same second there crashed down upon my mind a single fleeting avalanche of soul-annihilating memory. I knew in that second all that had been; I remembered beyond the frightful castle and the trees, and recognized the altered edifice in which I now stood; I recognized, most terrible of all, the unholy abomination that stood leering before me as I withdrew my sullied fingers from its own.

But in the cosmos there is balm as well as bitterness, and that balm is nepenthe. In the supreme horror of that second I forgot what had horrified me, and the burst of black memory vanished in a chaos of echoing images. In a dream I fled from that haunted and accursed pile, and ran swiftly and silently in the moonlight. When I returned to the churchyard place of marble and went down the steps I found the stone trap-door immovable; but I was not sorry, for I had hated the antique castle and the trees. Now I ride with the mocking and friendly ghouls on the night-wind, and play by day amongst the catacombs of Nephren-Ka in the sealed and unknown valley of Hadoth by the Nile. I know that light is not for me, save that of the moon over the rock tombs of Neb, nor any gaiety save the unnamed feasts of Nitokris beneath the Great Pyramid; yet in my new wildness and freedom I almost welcome the bitterness of alienage.

For although nepenthe has calmed me, I know always that I am an outsider; a stranger in this century and among those who are still men. This I have known ever since I stretched out my fingers to the abomination within that great gilded frame; stretched out my fingers and touched *a cold and unyielding surface of polished glass.*

The Tomb

H.P. Lovecraft

'Sedibus ut saltem placidis in morte quiescam.'
Virgil

IN RELATING the circumstances which have led to my confinement within this refuge for the demented, I am aware that my present position will create a natural doubt of the authenticity of my narrative. It is an unfortunate fact that the bulk of humanity is too limited in its mental vision to weigh with patience and intelligence those isolated phenomena, seen and felt only by a psychologically sensitive few, which lie outside its common experience. Men of broader intellect know that there is no sharp distinction betwixt the real and the unreal; that all things appear as they do only by virtue of the delicate individual physical and mental media through which we are made conscious of them; but the prosaic materialism of the majority condemns as madness the flashes of super-sight which penetrate the common veil of obvious empiricism.

My name is Jervas Dudley, and from earliest childhood I have been a dreamer and a visionary. Wealthy beyond the necessity of a commercial life, and temperamentally unfitted for the formal studies and social recreations of my acquaintances, I have dwelt ever in realms apart from the visible world; spending my youth and adolescence in ancient and little-known books, and in roaming the fields and groves of the region near my ancestral home. I do not think that what I read in these books or saw in these fields and groves was exactly what other boys read and saw there; but of this I must say little, since detailed speech would but confirm those cruel slanders upon my intellect which I sometimes overhear from the whispers of the stealthy attendants around me. It is sufficient for me to relate events without analysing causes.

I have said that I dwelt apart from the visible world, but I have not said that I dwelt alone. This no human creature may do; for lacking the fellowship of the living, he inevitably draws upon the companionship of things that are not, or are no longer, living. Close by my home there lies a singular wooded hollow, in whose twilight deeps I spent most of my time; reading, thinking and dreaming. Down its moss-covered slopes my first steps of infancy were taken, and around its grotesquely gnarled oak trees my first fancies of boyhood were woven. Well did I come to know the presiding dryads of those trees, and often have I watched their wild dances in the struggling beams of waning moon – but of these things I must not now speak. I will tell only of the lone tomb in the darkest of the hillside thickets; the deserted tomb of the Hydes, an old and exalted family whose last direct descendant had been laid within its black recesses many decades before my birth.

The vault to which I refer is an ancient granite, weathered and discolored by the mists and dampness of generations. Excavated back into the hillside, the structure is visible only at the entrance. The door, a ponderous and forbidding slab of stone, hangs upon rusted iron hinges, and is fastened *ajar* in a queerly sinister way by means of heavy iron chains and padlocks, according to a gruesome fashion of half a century ago. The abode of the race whose scions are inurned had once crowned the declivity which holds the tomb, but had long since fallen victim to the flames which sprang up from a disastrous stroke of lightning. Of the midnight storm which destroyed this gloomy mansion, the older inhabitants of the region sometimes speak in hushed and uneasy voices; alluding to what they call 'divine wrath' in a manner that in later years vaguely increased the always strong fascination which I felt for the forest-darkened sepulchre. One man only had perished in the fire. When the last of the Hydes was buried in this place of shade and stillness, the sad urnful of ashes had come from a distant land; to which the family had repaired when the mansion burned down. No one remains to lay flowers before the granite portal, and few care to brave the depressing shadows which seem to linger strangely about the water-worn stones.

I shall never forget the afternoon when first I stumbled upon the half-hidden house of the dead. It was in mid-summer, when the alchemy of Nature transmutes the sylvan landscape to one vivid and almost homogeneous mass of green; when the senses are well-nigh intoxicated with the surging seas of moist verdure and the subtly indefinable odors of the soil and the vegetation. In such surroundings the mind loses its perspective; time and space become trivial and unreal, and echoes of a forgotten prehistoric past beat insistently upon the enthralled consciousness. All day I had been wandering through the mystic groves of the hollow; thinking thoughts I need not discuss, and conversing with things I need not name. In years a child of ten, I had seen and heard many wonders unknown to the throng; and was oddly aged in certain respects. When, upon forcing my way between two savage clumps of briers, I suddenly encountered the entrance of the vault, I had no knowledge of what I had discovered. The dark blocks of granite, the door so curiously ajar, and the funereal carvings above the arch, aroused in me no associations of mournful or terrible character. Of graves and tombs I knew and imagined much, but had on account of my peculiar temperament been kept from all personal contact with churchyards and cemeteries. The strange stone house on the woodland slope was to me only a source of interest and speculation; and its cold, damp interior, into which I vainly peered through the aperture so tantalisingly left, contained for me no hint of death or decay. But in that instant of curiosity was born the madly unreasoning desire which has brought me to this hell of confinement. Spurred on by a voice which must have come from the hideous soul of the forest, I resolved to enter the beckoning gloom in spite of the ponderous chains which barred my passage. In the waning light of day I alternately rattled the rusty impediments with a view to throwing wide the stone door, and essayed to squeeze my slight form through the space already provided; but neither plan met with success. At first curious, I was now frantic; and when in the thickening twilight I returned to my home, I had sworn to the hundred gods of the grove that *at any cost* I would some day force an entrance to the black chilly depths that seemed calling out to me. The physician with the iron-gray beard who comes each day to my room once told a visitor that this decision marked the beginnings of a pitiful monomania; but I will leave final judgment to my readers when they shall have learnt all.

The months following my discovery were spent in futile attempts to force the complicated padlock of the slightly open vault, and in carefully guarded inquiries regarding the nature and history of the structure. With the traditionally receptive ears of the small boy, I learned much; though an habitual secretiveness caused me to tell no one of my information or my resolve. It is perhaps worth mentioning that I was not at all surprised or terrified on learning of the nature of the vault. My rather original ideas regarding life and death had caused me to associate the cold clay with the breathing body in a vague fashion; and I felt that the great sinister family of the burned-down mansion was in some way represented within the stone space I sought to explore. Mumbled tales of the weird rites and godless revels of bygone years in the ancient hall gave to me a new and potent interest in the tomb, before whose door I would sit for hours at a time each day. Once I thrust a candle within the nearly closed entrance, but could see nothing save a flight of damp stone steps leading downward. The odor of the place repelled yet bewitched me. I felt I had known it before, in a past remote beyond all recollection; beyond even my tenancy of the body I now possess.

The year after I first beheld the tomb, I stumbled upon a worm-eaten translation of Plutarch's *Lives* in the book-filled attic of my home. Reading the life of Theseus, I was much impressed by that passage telling of the great stone beneath which the boyish hero was to find his tokens of destiny whenever he should become old enough to lift its enormous weight. This legend had the effect of dispelling my keenest impatience to enter the vault, for it made me feel that the time was not yet ripe. Later, I told myself, I should grow to a strength and ingenuity which might enable me to unfasten the heavily chained door with ease; but until then I would do better by conforming to what seemed the will of Fate.

Accordingly my watches by the dank portal became less persistent, and much of my time was spent in other though equally strange pursuits. I would sometimes rise very quietly in the night, stealing out to walk in those churchyards and places of burial from which I had been kept by my parents. What I did there I may not say, for I am not now sure of the reality of certain things; but I know that on the day after such a nocturnal ramble I would often astonish those about me with my knowledge of topics almost forgotten for many generations. It was after a night like this that I shocked the community with a queer conceit about the burial of the rich and celebrated Squire Brewster, a maker of local history who was interred in 1711, and whose slate headstone, bearing a graven skull and crossbones, was slowly crumbling to powder. In a moment of childish imagination I vowed not only that the undertaker, Goodman Simpson, had stolen the silver-buckled shoes, silken hose, and satin small-clothes of the deceased before burial; but that the Squire himself, not fully inanimate, had turned twice in his mound-covered coffin on the day of interment.

But the idea of entering the tomb never left my thoughts; being indeed stimulated by the unexpected genealogical discover that my own maternal ancestry possessed at least a slight link with the supposedly extinct family of the Hydes. Last of my paternal race, I was likewise the last of this older and more mysterious line. I began to feel that the tomb was *mine*, and to look forward with hot eagerness to the time when I might pass within that stone door and down those slimy stone steps in the dark. I now formed the habit of *listening* very intently at the slightly open portal, choosing my favorite hours of midnight stillness for the odd vigil. By the time I came of age, I had made a small clearing in the thicket before the mold-stained façade of the hillside, allowing the surrounding vegetation to encircle and overhang the space like the walls and roof of a sylvan bower. This bower was my temple, the fastened door my shrine, and here I would lie outstretched on the mossy ground, thinking strange thoughts and dreaming of strange dreams.

The night of the first revelation was a sultry one. I must have fallen asleep from fatigue, for it was with a distinct sense of awakening that I heard the *voices*. Of those tones and accents I hesitate to speak; of their *quality* I will not speak; but I may say that they presented certain uncanny differences in vocabulary, pronunciation, and mode of utterance. Every shade of New England dialect, from the uncouth syllables of the Puritan colonists to the precise rhetoric of fifty years ago, seemed represented in that shadowy colloquy, though it was only later that I noticed the fact. At the time, indeed, my attention was distracted from this matter by another phenomenon; a phenomenon so fleeting that I could not take oath upon its reality. I barely fancied that as I awoke, a *light* had been hurriedly extinguished within the sunken sepulchre. I do not think I was either astounded or panic-stricken, but I know that I was greatly and permanently *changed* that night. Upon returning home I went with much directness to a rotting chest in the attic, wherein I found the key which next day unlocked with ease the barrier I had so long stormed in vain.

It was in the soft glow of late afternoon that I first entered the vault on the abandoned slope. A spell was upon me, and my heart leaped with an exultation I can but ill describe. As I closed the door behind me and descended the dripping steps by the light of my lone candle, I seemed to know the way; and though the candle sputtered with the stifling reek of the place, I felt singularly at home in the musty, charnel-house air. Looking about me, I beheld many marble slabs bearing coffins, or the remains of coffins. Some of these were sealed and intact, but others had nearly vanished, leaving the silver handles and plates isolated amidst certain curious heaps of whitish dust. Upon one plate I read the name of Sir Geoffrey Hyde, who had come from Sussex in 1640 and died here a few years later. In a conspicuous alcove was one fairly well-preserved and untenanted casket, adorned with a single name which brought to me both a smile and a shudder. An odd impulse caused me to climb upon the broad slab, extinguish my candle, and lie down within the vacant box.

In the gray light of dawn I staggered from the vault and locked the chain of the door behind me. I was no longer a young man, though but twenty-one winters had chilled my bodily frame. Early-rising villagers who observed my homeward progress looked at me strangely, and marvelled at the signs of ribald revelry which they saw in one whose life was known to be sober and solitary. I did not appear before my parents till after a long and refreshing sleep.

Henceforward I haunted the tomb each night; seeing, hearing, and doing things I must never reveal. My speech, always susceptible to environmental influences, was the first thing to succumb to the change; and my suddenly acquired archaism of diction was soon remarked upon. Later a queer boldness and recklessness came into my demeanor, till I unconsciously grew to possess the bearing of a man of the world despite my lifelong seclusion. My formerly silent tongue waxed voluble with the easy grace of a Chesterfield or the godless cynicism of a Rochester. I displayed a peculiar erudition utterly unlike the fantastic, monkish lore over which I had pored in youth; and covered the flyleaves of my books with facile impromptu epigrams which brought up suggestions of Gay, Prior, and the sprightliest of Augustan wits and rimesters. One morning at breakfast I came close to disaster by declaiming in palpably liquorish accents an effusion of eighteenth-century Bacchanalian mirth; a bit of Georgian playfulness never recorded in a book, which ran something like this:

> *Come hither, my lads, with your tankards of ale,*
> *And drink to the present before it shall fail;*
> *Pile each on your platter a mountain of beef,*
> *For 'tis eating and drinking that bring us relief:*

So fill up your glass,
So life will soon pass;
When you're dead ye'll ne'er drink to your king or your lass!

Anacreon had a red nose, so they say;
But what's a red nose if ye're happy and gay?
Gad split me! I'd rather be red whilst I'm here,
Than white as a lily – and dead half a year!
So Betty, my miss,
Come give me kiss;
In hell there's no innkeeper's daughter like this!

Young Harry, propp'd up just as straight as he's able,
Will soon lose his wig and slip under the table;
But fill up your goblets and pass 'em around –
Better under the table than under the ground!
So revel and chaff
As ye thirstily quaff:
Under six feet of dirt 'tis less easy to laugh!

The fiend strike me blue! I'm scarce able to walk,
And damn me if I can stand upright or talk!
Here, landlord, bid Betty to summon a chair;
I'll try home for a while, for my wife is not there!
So lend me a hand;
I'm not able to stand,
But I'm gay whilst I linger on top of the land!

About this time I conceived my present fear of fire and thunderstorms. Previously indifferent to such things, I had now an unspeakable horror of them; and would retire to the innermost recesses of the house whenever the heavens threatened an electrical display. A favorite haunt of mine during the day was the ruined cellar of the mansion that had burned down, and in fancy I would picture the structure as it had been in its prime. On one occasion I startled a villager by leading him confidently to a shallow sub-cellar, of whose existence I seemed to know in spite of the fact that it had been unseen and forgotten for many generations.

At last came that which I had long feared. My parents, alarmed at the altered manner and appearance of their only son, commenced to exert over my movements a kindly espionage which threatened to result in disaster. I had told no one of my visits to the tomb, having guarded my secret purpose with religious zeal since childhood; but now I was forced to exercise care in threading the mazes of the wooded hollow, that I might throw off a possible pursuer. My key to the vault I kept suspended from a cord about my neck, its presence known only to me. I never carried out of the sepulchre any of the things I came upon whilst within its walls.

One morning as I emerged from the damp tomb and fastened the chain of the portal with none too steady hand, I beheld in an adjacent thicket the dreaded face of a watcher. Surely the end was near; for my bower was discovered, and the objective of my nocturnal journeys revealed. The man did not accost me, so I hastened home in an effort to overhear what he might report to my careworn father. Were my sojourns beyond the chained door about to be proclaimed to the world? Imagine my delighted astonishment on hearing the spy inform my parent in cautious whisper *that I had spent the night in the bower outside the tomb*; my sleep-filmed eyes fixed upon the crevice where the padlocked portal stood ajar! By what miracle had the watcher been thus deluded? I was now convinced that a supernatural agency protected me. Made bold by this heaven-sent circumstance, I began to resume perfect openness in going to the vault; confident that no one could witness my entrance. For a week I tasted to the full the joys of that charnel conviviality which I must not describe, when the *thing* happened, and I was borne away to this accursed abode of sorrow and monotony.

I should not have ventured out that night; for the taint of thunder was in the clouds, and hellish phosphorescence rose from the rank swamp at the bottom of the hollow. The call of the dead, too, was different. Instead of the hillside tomb, it was the charred cellar on the crest of the slope whose presiding daemon beckoned to me with unseen fingers. As I emerged from an intervening grove upon the plain before the ruin, I beheld in the misty moonlight a thing I had always vaguely expected. The mansion, gone for a century, once more reared its stately height to the raptured vision; every window ablaze with the splendor of many candles. Up the long drive rolled the coaches of the Boston gentry, whilst on foot came a numerous assemblage of powdered exquisites from the neighboring mansions. With this throng I mingled, though I knew I belonged with the hosts rather than the guests. Inside the hall were music, laughter, and wine on every hand. Several faces I recognized; though I should have known them better had they been shriveled or eaten away by death and decomposition. Amidst a wild and reckless throng I was the wildest and most abandoned. Gay blasphemy poured in torrents from my lips, and in my shocking sallies I heeded no law of God, Man, or Nature. Suddenly a peal of thunder, resonant even above the din of the swinish revelry, clave the very roof and laid a hush of fear upon the boisterous company. Red tongues of flame and searing gusts of heat engulfed the house; and the roysterers, struck with terror at the descent of a calamity which seemed to transcend the bounds of unguided Nature, fled shrieking into the night. I alone remained, riveted to my seat by a groveling fear which I had never felt before. And then a second horror took possession of my soul. Burnt alive to ashes, my body dispersed by the four winds, *I might never lie in the tomb of Hydes!* Was not my coffin prepared for me? Had I not a right to rest till eternity amongst the descendants of Sir Geoffrey Hyde? Aye! I would claim my heritage of death, even though my soul go seeking through the ages for another corporeal tenement to represent it on that vacant slab in the alcove of the vault. *Jervas Hyde* should never share the sad fate of Palinurus!

As the phantom of the burning house faded, I found myself screaming and struggling madly in the arms of two men, one of whom was the spy who had followed me to the tomb. Rain was pouring down in torrents, and upon the southern horizon were flashes of the lightning that had so lately passed over our heads. My father, his face lined with sorrow, stood by as I shouted my demands to be laid within the tomb; frequently admonishing my captors to treat me as gently as they could. A blackened circle on the floor of the ruined cellar told of a violent stroke from the heavens; and from this spot a group of curious villagers with lanterns were prying a small box of antique workmanship which the thunderbolt had brought to light. Ceasing my futile and now objectless writhing, I watched the spectators as they viewed the treasure-trove, and was permitted to share in their discoveries. The box, whose fastenings were broken by the stroke which had unearthed it, contained many papers and objects of value; but I had eyes for one thing alone. It was the porcelain miniature of a young man in a smartly curled bag-wig, and bore the initials 'J.H.' The face was such that as I gazed, I might well have been studying my mirror.

On the following day I was brought to this room with the barred windows, but I have been kept informed of certain things through an aged and simple-minded servitor, for whom I bore a fondness in infancy, and who like me loves the churchyard. What I have dared relate of my experiences within the vault has brought me only pitying smiles. My father, who visits me frequently, declares that at no time did I pass the chained portal, and swears that the rusted padlock had not been touched for fifty years when he examined it. He even says that all the village knew of my journeys to the tomb, and that I was often watched as I slept in the bower outside the grim façade, my half-open eyes fixed on the crevice that leads to the interior. Against these assertions I have no tangible proof to offer, since my key to the padlock was lost in the struggle on that night of horrors. The strange things of the past which I learnt during those nocturnal meetings with the dead he dismisses as the fruits of my lifelong and omnivorous browsing amongst the ancient volumes of the family library. Had it not been for my old servant Hiram, I should have by this time become quite convinced of my madness.

But Hiram, loyal to the last, has held faith in me, and has done that which impels me to make public at least a part of my story. A week ago he burst open the lock which chains the door of the tomb perpetually ajar, and descended with a lantern into the murky depths. On a slab in an alcove he found an old but empty coffin whose tarnished plate bears the single word *Jervas*. In that coffin and in that vault they have promised me I shall be buried.

The Outsiders in the Hawthorne Tomb

Madison McSweeney

ADRIAN HAWTHORNE died, and was subsequently buried, the way he spent the last months of his life – hidden away, a wealthy family's secret shame.

The Hawthornes were the last old money family in a town that had long ceased producing any new money. As with many families of their ilk, the last few generations had been unremarkable: Linus Hawthorne, a widower and the final patriarch of the line, had some dealings in real estate, but spent most of his time administering the family fortune; his daughter, a bright enough young woman, was studying to be an architect; and Adrian, his youngest, had been an aspiring artist before his untimely death. Adrian had never exhibited his art, so it is unknown what sort of talent he possessed; if he had any, it had deserted him long ago.

Adrian's last days were spent in solitude, although not peacefully. Awakened by nightmares, he would rage in the night, turning his wrath towards any unhappy servants who dared check in on him. By the spring of his final year, the staff stopped checking in. Unable to bear the mutterings of the house, Adrian spent his nights outside, wandering the woods in a state of profound disquiet.

The instant he died, screaming and raving, his sister woke up a hundred miles away, clutching her heart.

* * *

The Wednesday after Adrian's passing, the three men informally known as the town's 'death committee' gathered at a diner on Moore Street for their weekly lunch.

The committee was made up of Mort Blake, the coroner; Spencer Greevely, the mortician; and Damien O'Malley, the gravedigger. These men were not the sort one would generally expect to see socializing together. Spencer fancied himself a cosmopolitan, while Mort was firmly of the working class; Damien, the youngest of the group, was the most inscrutable, a morbidly philosophical vulgarian who confounded them both. They didn't enjoy each other's company, per se, but bonded over their similar professions, which were unsuitable for discussion in other company.

An air of suspicion and some bitterness hung over this week's proceedings. The night before, Mort had walked into the local bar and paid for a round – an unusual show of generosity for the frugal public servant. Something was amiss, and some of the crasser patrons had suggested that Mort's sudden windfall must have something to do with the unfortunate artist. Making the whole thing even odder was that the wealthy family of the deceased had refused the services of the local funeral home, opting for a quickie service and burial that was unbefitting of their status.

By lunchtime Wednesday, Spencer was still smarting from the snub. "It's not like they don't have the money!" he lamented, stirring a pinch of salt into his coffee.

The coroner raised an eyebrow. Suddenly aware of his petulance, the mortician added: "Of course, I'm not upset for myself – I just don't think it's a dignified way to honor one's departed son. Even if the boy was somewhat of a black sheep."

The mortician shrugged, taking a large bite from his tuna sandwich. "They probably don't realize how grubby a corpse looks after a few days on a slab," he remarked, crassly.

Damien laughed and Greevely cringed, craning his neck to ensure none of the other patrons had overheard. Other than the committee and the kitchen staff, the only other occupants of the restaurant were two old men from the lumber mill, both deaf as bats. The mortician settled back down and took another sip of his coffee.

"I daresay, Adrian wasn't looking too hot when he was alive," Damien added.

Both Mort and Spencer looked up from their meals. "What are you talking about?"

Damien shrugged. "I saw him a few weeks ago. He didn't look great."

"Adrian was an invalid," Spencer corrected. "He hadn't left his room in months."

"That's what old Linus is saying," Damien said, a perversion of a smirk crossing his pallid features. "I was walking through the cemetery last month around midnight…"

"And what, precisely, were you doing there at *that* hour?" Spencer interrupted, irritation in his voice.

The gravedigger glowered. "Business. Now do you want the story or not?" Spencer shut up.

Damien continued. "So, anyway, I was at the edge of the yard when I heard something crack behind me, like someone stepping on a branch. So, I turned around. And that's when I saw young Adrian Hawthorne skulking around right next to his family's mausoleum."

The men fixed their gazes to him, half-suspecting he was pulling their legs.

"Now, why would he do that?" Mort asked.

Damien shrugged. "I figured he was doing the tortured artist thing – wandering around, brooding about death and the decaying family line. I didn't know he was sick."

"Oh, come *on*," Spencer said. "The whole town knew *something* was wrong with him."

"I don't get my gossip 'til the body's cold," the gravedigger retorted. "But by then I know everything."

He glanced out the restaurant window as a cluster of dried leaves, lifted by the wind, brushed against the glass before continuing to somersault along the sidewalk. "That said, the Hawthorne kid didn't look well. He was talking to himself and staggering around like an old hunchback. Say, Mort, how old was the kid anyway?"

"Older than you," Mort replied. "Almost twenty-eight."

Damien sook his head. "Geez. What'd he die of?"

Mort picked up a spare crust of bread and began to dramatically wipe every spare glob of mayonnaise off his plate. He replied, "Long illness," without looking up.

Damien and Spencer exchanged a quizzical glance. The mortician shook another pinch of salt into his coffee cup.

"Why do you do that, anyway?" Damien asked.

"Cuts the bitterness," Spencer replied, his eyes drifting towards the coroner, who'd grown oddly quiet.

"You don't say," Damien replied, picking up a saltshaker and eying it suspiciously.

Mort remained fixed on the remains of his sandwich.

"So," Damien said, holding the shaker experimentally above his mug, "I've shared a tidbit of insensitive gossip about the dead. Someone else's turn now – Spence, we know that the

Hawthornes are giving *you* the cold shoulder, so that begs the question of what they paid Mort for."

Mort jumped, his dishes rattling as his knee flinched upwards and hit the underside of the table. The man winced. "I don't know what you're talking about."

Damien raised an eyebrow. "Don't evade us, Morty," Spencer said. "We weren't the only ones who thought it odd when you bought that round of pitchers."

"And the mirthless way you went about it," Damien chimed in. "Like it was blood money and you just wanted to get rid of it."

Mort was about to respond defensively when Spencer piped up. "Damien has a point. I was chatting with the bartender, and he said he thought he saw *guilt* in your eyes."

That last part was a bald-faced lie, but it shook Mort's resolve. His eyes fell to his crumbs. "Linus Hawthorne called me up the day after Adrian died. Wanted to meet with me." The man sighed. "He did offer me money, but it wasn't about that. He just looked so desperate that I didn't think any good could come of refusing him."

Spencer leaned forward hungrily, his voice a near-hiss. "What did he offer you?"

Mort looked into the eyes of his confidants, as if evaluating their hearts for the first time in many years of acquaintance. Damien's eyes widened with anticipation.

Then, in an agonized moan, Mort confessed, "He paid me not to examine the body."

* * *

The Hawthorne house was set on a steep hill overlooking the highway. A set of rock-cut stairs formed a steep, snaking path, more like a cliff than a walkway. The driveway was well-paved but treacherous, and as Damien forced his car up the incline, he got the impression that one would always have to go out of their way to enter or leave the property.

No wonder the Hawthornes were all batty, the gravedigger thought.

The front door was an elaborate wrought iron construction, engraved with impressions of gargoyles and other grotesque protector-spirits. He was greeted on the stoop not by a servant, but by a cat, a pure-white creature with piercing green eyes, who proceeded to weave its way between his legs, impertinently meowing for entry. He was staring confusedly at the cat when the door swung open, a grey-eyed butler on the other side.

The butler ignored Damien and swept the cat up in his arms, cooing at the animal before remembering himself and meeting the gravedigger's eyes. "Apologies. She wasn't supposed to be out."

"Good thing I showed up when I did, then," Damien replied.

The butler blinked. "She would have found her way home regardless," he replied, a hint of robotic hostility in his slate-colored eyes.

He probably thinks I expect a reward, Damien thought. *Rich bastards are always worried about that kind of thing.*

"I'm the gravedigger," Damien said, eager to alleviate the tension.

"Eloquently put," the butler said.

"There ain't a lot of eloquence in my job."

Was there a hint of alarm in the butler's expression? Or was it anger?

The man sputtered: "Well, mister—"

"Damien," the gravedigger replied.

"Mister…Damien. I can assure you that my master expects your duties to be carried out with as much professionalism and taste as possible, given the circumstances."

"Professionalism, I can do," Damien retorted. "Taste is Spence Greevley's territory."

The butler scowled. "I assume you know that the Hawthornes have chosen not to solicit the services of Mr. Greevley. It is to be a simple funeral – family only."

Will I be dumping him in the mass grave with the paupers, then? Damien thought, and bit back the urge to turn the thoughts into words. He frowned; perhaps Spencer's cattiness was starting to catch.

Instead, Damien said, "Understood. Will that be all?"

"No. My master would like to meet with you." The butler blinked, and his expression softened, as if this brief fluttering of the eyelids had waved away all but the faintest hint of irritation. "I fear we keep him waiting."

Damien extended an arm towards the hallway. "Lead the way."

The inside of the house was even grimmer and more daunting than the exterior. The hallways were cavernous and had been decorated at great expense but without much taste. The high walls were paneled in wood so dark it was almost black, ornamented by gaudy bronze sculptures of knights and nothing, hung with tall, stern paintings of dead Hawthornes and doubly dead greyhound dogs. Some long-ago patriarch who'd fancied himself a medieval lord had decorated this place a hundred years ago, and no one since had seen fit to update it.

Some houses are tombs, Damien mused; *just holding cells for successive generations of decreasingly impressive families, places where mediocre heirs shelter themselves from the elements while they wait around to join their ancestors in the crypt. The big family reunion, six feet under.*

The butler showed Damien into a large study and motioned for him to sit opposite a bulky wooden desk. The walls of this room were blocked by floor-to-ceiling bookshelves, packed with dozens of rows of ancient leather-bound tomes, unopened and unread. Above the desk, a large, greyish chandelier hung from the ceiling, emitting neither brightness nor beauty.

After a few minutes, Linus Hawthorne walked in.

Much like the house, Linus was elegantly-dressed but decrepit; as he limped around to the other side of the desk and lowered himself gingerly into his chair, the man gave Damien the impression, somehow, of being covered in dust.

"So," Linus said, fixing Damien with an intense, inscrutable stare. "You're the gravedigger."

"Yes," said Damien, taken aback by the man's bluntness. He remembered Mort's impression of the man, and found himself in agreement. Linus Hawthorne looked much more haggard than any of the rich men Damien had ever dealt with, like he'd been to the depths and clawed his way back up. It wasn't just grief; there was a manic intensity in his eyes that reminded Damien of an insane man he'd once seen preaching on a street corner.

Hawthorne spoke in a jagged, stilted tone, as if reading from a script that was painful to him, with no pleasantries to ease the transition. "My son's body is already in its casket," Linus croaked. "There will be no showing. His was not an easy death, and I don't believe he would have wanted anyone to see him in his current state."

Damien nodded, wondering idly who had been made to lift the corpse into the casket. He couldn't see Hawthorne doing it himself, but surely he hadn't assigned the grisly task to a servant?

Hawthorne was still speaking. "It is imperative that no one is to see or touch the body. The casket is not to be opened for any reason. You may have heard that the coroner received similar instructions."

Damien feigned surprise. "Did he?"

Linus narrowed his eyes. "Yes. I assume he mentioned something to you."

"I hadn't heard anything," Damien replied.

"Very good," Linus responded, not quite convinced. "Either way, I'm prepared to compensate your generously for your discretion on this matter."

Damien interrupted. "You said the body's already in the casket? In that case, I'm perfectly capable of shepherding it to the mausoleum intact – you don't need to pay me extra not to crack open the coffin and take a peak."

Hawthorne regarded him harshly. "I'm well aware, Mr. O'Malley – and you need not confirm nor deny – that it is not uncommon for medical students to contract men such as yourself to help them acquire research cadavers. I would be willing to pay double their going rate to ensure that my son does not meet this fate."

The gravedigger's hackles were up now. "That won't be necessary, Mr. Hawthorne. I don't deal with any of that."

Hawthorne looked suddenly touched. "You're an honest man," Linus replied. "I wonder – would you be willing to perform another service for me?"

Damien's veins turned to ice. "And what would that be?"

"You maintain the grounds at the cemetery, correct?"

"Correct."

"So, you patrol the property often?"

"Yes," Damien said, thinking the man was going to ask him to spruce up the plot along the mausoleum, or to take extra care of the grave of some Hawthorne familiar who hadn't warranted inclusion in the family crypt. Instead, the old man extended an arthritic hand leftward, fingering an ornately framed photo of a young woman.

"This is my daughter, Lillian. She's away at school but she'll be in town briefly for the funeral. Do you think you would recognize her if you saw her in person?"

Damien studied the photo. It was black and white, and the girl was dressed in elegant formal clothes that looked to him like period garb. Her face was pale, with a long, slender nose ending on a slight hook. That nose, as well as her wide, protruding eyes, slightly too large for her face, gave her a sort of emaciated look. Otherwise, though, she was very pretty.

"Probably," he said.

The old man nodded. "If you ever see my daughter at the gravesite, I want you to turn her away."

Damien blinked in surprise. "I'm not sure I understand."

Linus seemed annoyed. "I don't want my daughter visiting Adrian's grave. I know it's an odd request, but you'll have to take my word that I have the best of intentions. Lillian was hit very hard by Adrian's illness, and I don't think it's healthy for her to dwell on it further."

"May I ask – what illness did Adrian have?"

"A family illness," Hawthorne replied. "Nothing sensational, I'm afraid, but not very pleasant either. I'm glad Lillian was in Boston for the end of it." The old man gazed lovingly at the photo, running his finger across a gray cheek. He looked back at the gravedigger. "But enough brooding on that! Can you help me, or not?"

"I think I can," Damien said, immediately regretting his answer.

The old man's face lit up. He reached into a drawer, pulled out a stack of bills, and thrust them into the gravedigger's hand. And then he called the butler.

And thus, Damien left the Hawthorne Estate, mind whirling as he tried to make sense of what exactly he had agreed to, and wondered how much this bribe would eventually cost him.

* * *

The funeral was very small and very brief.

Lillian Hawthorne sat in the front row, closest to the casket; an elderly servant sat adjacent, between father and daughter. A handful of other servants filled the rows behind them, and some very elderly, out-of-town relatives brought up the rear.

Rites were read, followed by a few stilted eulogies, and the coffin was handed off to Damien. On his way into the mausoleum, the gravedigger locked eyes with Lillian Hawthorne, before turning to stare into the crypt.

* * *

Lillian didn't try to visit the grave the next day, or the day after that, and the gravedigger almost thought his duties had been discharged. That was fine by Damien; he didn't exactly relish the idea of turning a grieving woman away from her brother's grave.

Two days after the funeral, night fell colder and darker than it had all winter. It was such a night in which no one, save for the insane or the up-to-no-good, would leave their homes, and even the hardest of deviants would hesitate to cross the threshold of an isolated cemetery surrounded only by woods, and guarded solely by a vacant Presbyterian church.

It was on this night that Damien finally encountered Lillian, skulking around the mausoleum the way her brother had, weeks before his own death.

At first, Damien thought he was hallucinating. The woman was still dressed as she had been at the funeral, cloaked in a long black trench coat, her face masked by a wispy black veil hanging from a pillbox hat. The only deviations were her gloves and her shoes; the conservative patent leather flats she'd worn at the service had been replaced by a pair of heavy black boots, more suitable for the night and the cold.

Damien was about to walk over to the crypt and shoo her away, when she swiftly turned and darted straight towards him. His first instinct was to run, as it always was when he was being chased. Then he regained his senses and stood stock still and waited as she walked up to him, her veiled hat in hands, her face bare and stricken.

It occurred to him that his presence there, at this hour, was as anomalous as hers; thankfully, she was too concerned by her own tragedy to request an explanation.

"You're the groundskeeper here, right?" she demanded. "I'm Lillian Hawthorne."

"I know," Damien said.

If the remark struck her as odd, she didn't show it. "You handled my brother's funeral."

"In a sense," Damien replied warily, remembering the indignation of the mortician.

There was an urgency in her face, and a flash of red seemed to swell within her cheeks. "So, you saw him then? The body, I mean."

Damien shook his head. "All I did was deliver the coffin into the crypt."

Lillian's face fell. "Then who—?"

"No one I know."

At that point, silence would have been wise. Instead, the gravedigger's gossipy streak revealed itself. "The town coroner never examined the body, and your father didn't hire a mortician. I don't know who dumped your brother in the casket—" – Lillian cringed at his crass phrasing – "—but I'd guess one of your father's servants, or maybe even your father himself. He was very intent that no one see that corpse."

And Lillian slumped to the ground, her body sliding down the crypt wall and landing indelicately on the leaf-strewn, frostbitten earth. It was not a swoon; rather, her face wore an expression of defeat and resignation. Damien was wondering if he should comfort her when, just as suddenly as she had sat down, she stood up, pouncing on him like a cat.

Damien stepped back, his beady eyes meeting hers, shining abnormally bright and large in the gloom. Her index finger was extended inches away from his nose. "And you all just went along with it! Why? Why did you let him get away with it?"

Damien blinked. "Get away with—?"

And then he understood.

* * *

Damien was not easily spooked, but tonight the Hawthorne crypt spooked him. So, he took Lillian by the elbow (she was trembling, but it was adrenaline rather than fear) and escorted her to the other end of the cemetery, where they sat on the cold metal planks of a bench while Lillian recounted her family's sordid tale.

"My brother was ill, and my father thought he could handle it all on his own. Oh, he called in doctors, always from out of town. But the doctors never seemed to come to any conclusions, and if they did, my father never shared them with us. And all the while, Adrian just got worse and worse. At first, his symptoms were just a fever, and some strange dreams in the night. Dreams. But then, he started seeing things while he was awake – things no one else could see."

In the distance, an animal stepped lightly onto the chilled ground. She cocked her head in its direction, as if hearing footfalls over her shoulder, and continued, eyes still fixed somewhere in the distance.

"One day, I came home to find him pressed against the wall of one of the stables, his arms and legs outstretched and his whole body just plastered against the brick, like someone had tied him there. But there was nothing holding him. And he was screaming, 'Lilly, they've got me.' I had to pretend to cut him down with scissors before he would believe he was free."

"So, he was delirious a lot of the time," the gravedigger summarized. "He was sick. Why would that make your father kill him?"

Lillian looked at the ground. "Father was always about keeping up appearances – or keeping secrets, I should say. He never particularly cared if we were seen, just that we weren't seen doing anything that would disgrace the family. If my brother had been sick, fine. But if my brother had been insane and raving, embarrassing him in front of the neighbors and scaring away the help – well, I wouldn't rule out my father...putting him out of his misery."

Damien didn't reply. "I know it seems flimsy," she said. "But the way he handled all of this – why wouldn't he let anyone see the body?"

"Is that why you're here? You want to see the body?"

"I need to be sure," she said, lowering her eyes and raising them again. "Would you let me in, Damien?"

Damien sighed. "Would seeing him be enough for you? I mean – would it prove what you're trying to prove? I'm not a medical examiner, and I'm not sure there's a whole lot of difference between a murder and a violent illness, as far as appearances go."

Even before she replied, the gravedigger was wondering if he could somehow loop Mort in. But the coroner had been paid well enough to let the dead sleep.

Lillian's reply nullified the debate. "I'll know. He was my brother. If something's wrong, I'll be able to tell – and if I look at him and he's at peace, I'll leave with no doubts in my mind. But if I don't do this now, I'll never know, and that's enough to drive a person insane."

Damien looked at his feet, and then looked across the graveyard towards the mausoleum, looming tall and bleak over the other headstones. He exhaled, and a stream of mist escaped from his mouth. "Fine."

* * *

The marble of the Hawthorne Mausoleum glowed phosphorescent in the moonlight. A soft mist clung to the ground and congregated at the foot of the structure, like the substance of a thousand unsettled spirits. Damien wondered if he shouldn't still abandon the girl and leave this strange family to their problems.

All thoughts halted when he heard a screech from over his shoulder. Lillian gasped.

Damien spun around to see a white cat standing behind him, eyes blazing green. "You're not supposed to be out," Damien said. The cat hissed and darted off. Damien continued into the mausoleum.

As he walked down the echoing corridor, he couldn't help glancing at the older Hawthorne caskets. The coffins were all made of heavy stone or marble, and several of the older ones appeared to be affixed with ancient, rusted padlocks. Had this family always had such a morbid fear of graverobbers?

Finally, they reached Adrian's coffin, the one Damien had personally delivered to rest in permanent tranquility. It too was padlocked; a pair of bolt cutters made short work of that. Each link of the chain seemed to echo individually as it slipped to the ground, sending cold metallic pings ricocheting from wall to wall. The lid groaned as the pair lifted it up and slid it across the mouth of the casket, lowering it gingerly onto the floor. That done, they took a step back to look at the body.

Lillian screamed. All at once, Damien understood why Spencer's services had not been required.

Adrian Hawthorne's face was monstrous. By conventional definitions, it wasn't a face at all. Not even the staunchest of scientific skeptics could formulate a medical explanation for the disfigurement, and even the most skilled mortician could have never made the insectoid thing before them look remotely human.

Lillian had sensed something suspicious about her brother's death, and her mind had gravitated towards the foulest crime she could think of – the murder of a child by a parent. But even that had not come close to the awful truth of her brother's transformation.

But she had guessed one thing correctly: staining the creature's left breast was a pomegranate-sized patch of crimson, where a wooden stake had been jabbed through its heart.

Big, Bad

Lynette Mejía

I KNEW how the rest of my day was gonna go the minute I seen Big Mama standing in the doorway looking at me. She had that look she gets, the one that carries all her years of hurt and worry like a heavy pack that might break her at any minute. I'd seen it enough times to know what it meant: Mama was missing again. Deep inside me the whatever-sized piece of little girl that was left sat down and cried. She had really tried this time, she really had, but it had been months now, and even though I'd seen the shadows growing darker around her eyes; had watched them get that lean and hungry look in the last few days, that little girl still held onto the tiniest bit of hope that somehow this time she'd be able to say no for good. Big Mama standing in the doorway was the end of all that.

I ate the last bite of Krispy Korn and tilted the bowl up to drink the milk. Big Mama walked on into the room and turned off the TV. Standing there in her old pink bathrobe, I realized suddenly that she'd lost a lot of weight in the last few months, and that, without warning, she had gotten old before my eyes. She sat down across from me on the big blue vinyl chair that used to be Papa's, pulling a pack of Marlboro 100's out of her pocket and lighting one.

"You're gonna have to go look for her," she said, taking a long drag. She looked tired, even though it was only nine o'clock in the morning.

I sat up, pulling my feet out from under me.

"I know," I said. "I can be ready to go in just a few minutes." It was up to me, had been up to me for a long time now, to go and get Mama when she took off.

Holding the cigarette between her lips she reached into her pocket again, pulling out a brown plastic bottle and passing it to me.

"Make sure she takes 'em, even if she won't come home," she said.

I rolled my eyes. "It ain't like I never done this before."

She smiled, her sad eyes full of love. "I know, baby," she said, "You've had to grow up before your time. You and me and Beau are all your Mama's got in this world, though, so we have to take care of her the best we can."

I felt the tears coming and I blinked hard, rubbing the heel of my hand against my eyes. "I'm sick of it, though, Big Mama. I'm sick of tracking her down to give her medicine when she don't even care if she lives or dies. She probably wouldn't even notice if we disappeared."

"Don't talk about your Mama like that," she said. She caught me with a look that I knew meant business. "No matter what happens, blood is blood, and we take care of our own."

I stood up and put my arms around her. She had a smell that was uniquely hers, a mixture of hand-rolled cigarettes, fried chicken, and Chantilly dusting powder. Some people might think that was awful, but to me it was home, and comfort, and love. It was the smell of a million afternoons spent sitting at her knee while she cooked, of a million nights spent falling asleep in her arms while she rocked me and sang to me. I loved her way more than I loved my mother, and the only reason I did this at all was because I knew it hurt Big Mama for her only child to be wandering the streets, and I would do anything to keep Big Mama from hurting.

* * *

It was chilly outside, the middle of November, so I dressed in my one pair of jeans and the red hoodie sweatshirt Big Mama had given me for Christmas last year. In the next room I could hear Beau crying while she changed his diaper. Beau is almost two, and already he is almost more than me and Big Mama can handle. Most days I watch him when I get home from school so she can work on the sewing she takes in to help pay the bills. When Mama is here she tries to help a little bit sometimes, but Beau doesn't really know her, so he cries and she just ends up giving him candy or whatever he wants so he'll shut up. Needless to say, it don't help a whole lot.

Before I left I stuck my head in Big Mama's room. Beau's crib is in there, and we change him on her bed. His face was red from crying.

"I'm goin'," I said.

"Ok, baby," said Big Mama. "Give her a couple of pills so she'll have one for tomorrow, you hear?"

"She'll just lose it."

"Maybe not. Put it in her pocket."

"She'll lose it anyway."

She smiled another one of those sad smiles; the only kind she seemed to have left these days. "Your Mama's my baby, Emmie, same as you," she said. "You'll understand one day."

"I ain't having no babies. I already told you that."

"Yes, you did. Be home before dark, you hear?"

"Yes ma'am."

* * *

Outside the wind was blowing hard, trying its best to strip the trees of the last few leaves that were holding their ground like stubborn ticks on a dying dog. The sky overhead was gray and low, the leading edge of the next big cold front. Dark like it was, and with the wind and all, I thought it might storm, but I wasn't afraid. I like bad weather, always have. Big Mama says in another life I could have been one of those weather ladies on TV.

I started walking in the direction of town. We lived off of what everybody called the Back Roads, which sounds fancy but really was nothing but a series of old dirt tracks and pothole-ridden, long-neglected asphalt streets that used to be the way folks got between towns before U.S. Highway 165 sliced the countryside open from gullet to gut back in 1936. Now only the locals used them; we mostly left the big highway to the out-of-state people looking for swamp tours and casino buffets. You could still walk to town on the back roads, though mostly people drove. Big Mama had a car, a gold 1979 Ford LTD that Papa had bought new for her, but I wasn't old enough to drive it yet.

Within minutes my ears were numb with cold, so I pulled my red hood up over my ears and stuck my hands into the front pockets. I had no idea where to start looking for Mama, but I knew who would. It was the kind of association I normally avoided like the plague, but like Big Mama said, when it comes to blood, sometimes you don't have no choice. Sometimes you have to dance.

Sure enough, when I came to the place where the iron-red dirt farm track called PR133 crossed Gajan Road, he was there, standing square in the middle of the cross and looking awfully satisfied with himself. To a passerby who didn't know no better, he looked just like any other no-account farm hick, dressed as he was in frayed blue jeans, a red western shirt and a dusty, beat-up cowboy hat. Close up, though – that's when you'd really start to notice the differences. For one, he was a lot taller than might be considered normal, and for another, his hands hung down too low, looking for all the world like they were thumb-tacked onto those lanky, alien arms that moved in angles no regular arm would even consider.

He smiled as I got closer, the smile of somebody who just got served a big plate of barbecue ribs with all the fixin's; the smile of somebody with his napkin already tucked into his shirt. It wasn't midnight, but he didn't give a damn.

Everybody called him Catfish, but that wasn't his real name, and we all knew it. He had been walking the back roads a long, long time. Maybe forever.

"Where's Mama?" I asked when I got close enough. The wind picked up as I approached, swirling the red dust around my feet.

"Well hello to you too, Miss Ruby Emmaline Ledoux. My word, that sure ain't no way to greet a body. Didn't Big Mama teach you no better manners than that?"

I didn't have time for this shit, but the rules being what they were, I had to play his game.

I sighed and rolled my eyes. "Hello, Catfish. I hope you're feeling good this morning. I was just wondering if you might point me in the direction of my Mama."

He smiled, big and wide, and his teeth shined in the darkened air. They were sharp and pointed, arranged in rows like some land-walking shark.

"Much better," he said, crossing his arms in front of his chest. "Now. Did I hear you say you'd misplaced something?"

"My Mama," I said again. "She's not at home and she needs her medicine."

"Oh I'm sure she has plenty o' medicine, wherever she is."

I closed my eyes. It didn't pay to get upset when dealing with Catfish.

"Not that kind of medicine. The kind the doctor gave her."

"Ah," he said. "The little blue pills. The ones that keep that pan-fried brain a' hers from goin' all hizzy-tizzy. I might believe I can point you in the right direction." He licked his lips, sliding those too-big hands into his back pockets. "Course, you could probably find her yourself, given time. Only so many mudholes in this one-horse town your Mama could get lost in."

Out in the distance a dust devil twirled across the plowed-under fields, wriggling and twisting for a few seconds before dissolving away. I took a deep breath and pulled up the sleeve on my left arm.

"I'm willing to pay," I said. I pulled off my jacket and rolled up the sleeve on my shirt. Catfish leaned down real close, sniffing at the scars and half-healed cuts. His eyes narrowed as he considered what was already there.

"Looks like you about to run out of currency," he said.

"I'm alive ain't I?"

He laughed. "Barely! How much longer you think you can go on doing this, searching out that woman time and again just 'cause she's the one that squatted down long enough to spit you out? You coming up on fifteen years, girl, still young enough to take over the world if you took a mind to it. Your life ain't worth hers no matter what Big Mama done told you, and deep down you know that's true."

He was right. Every damn word he was saying was the truth. Still, I stuck out my arm.

"Do you want it or not?" I asked.

He smiled. "Of course I do," he said. He leaned over and whispered a name in my ear. I closed my eyes, felt him lick up and down my arm, taking his time with each prior wound, moving slow like he was greeting old friends.

When his teeth bit into the flesh it hurt, but it was the kind of pain that made you long for it; the kind that brought forgetting along like a gift. It wasn't a feeling of safety like the comfort of Big Mama's arms; this was the peacefulness that comes from knowing that oblivion is waiting for you somewhere, and I'd be lying if I said that a part of me didn't crave it. I sank down into the red clay, and felt it gather me into its arms. The whole thing felt like it could have taken an hour, or a day, or maybe forever, but eventually I opened my eyes, and when I did, I saw that Catfish was gone.

* * *

The walk into town shouldn't have taken more than a half hour, but the bright spot behind the clouds marking the sun's position was well into the west by the time I finally got there. I was tired, and lightheaded, but I didn't stop to rest. I'd lost too much time already.

The place Catfish had whispered to me wasn't in town exactly; instead it was all the way on the other side, off Highway 26. It was a trailer park, the winter home of a bunch of ex-cons who spent their summers dragging a few game booths and a couple of worn-out carnival rides from town to town while they cooked meth and traded pills behind walls lined with ratty stuffed bears and rows of plastic American flags. These weren't the big, shiny house trailers like the kind in the TV commercials; these were old travel trailers, Scotsmans, Airstreams and such, held together mostly with duct tape and cardboard. As I walked down the muddy driveway, an old mangy dog came up and looked at me with big, mournful eyes, but I shooed him off. A gang of filthy, half-naked toddlers hid behind rusting cars and piles of garbage. I'd come to get Mama here before, more than once as a matter of fact, and it had never been easy. Once these motherfuckers had their claws in her, it was hard to get them back out again.

I counted the trailers as I walked. When I came to the ninth one I stopped, jumping over deep ruts filled with oily water to get to the door. I knocked but no one answered.

"Mama!"

Nothing. I beat on the door some more, as hard as I could. The thing was so flimsy that my pounding caused the whole contraption to shake.

"Mama!"

Finally I heard footsteps. The door opened a crack into darkness.

"Whatthefuckyouwant?" a voice growled.

I pulled the medicine bottle out of the pocket of my hoodie. "I've come to see my Mama," I said.

"There ain't nothin' for you here," said the voice. "You need to git goin'." The door started to shut. From the darkness a glint of metal caught my eye. It was probably a knife, but by this time I didn't care. Without another word I put my shoulder to the door and shoved as hard as I could. It must have caught whoever was back there by surprise, because the door gave way easily, whipping all the way around and slapping against the paper-thin inside wall.

I stumbled in, carried by my own momentum, but managed to right myself before I fell. It took a minute for my eyes to adjust to the darkness, but once they did, I knew I was in the right place. People, or what had once been people, were lying around everywhere. Most of them were covered in blood, jerking uncontrollably, gurgling red bubbles dribbling from their lips. Some were missing limbs, and others looked like they had been downright *chewed*. I felt the sick rising up in my stomach, but I bit my lip and swallowed it back down. Whoever had opened the door was gone.

"Mama?" I started crawling around and over bodies, slipping and sliding in the gore but still pausing to inspect each one, looking for her bright blonde hair. Eventually I found her, still alive, lying on a tiny cot near the back. She looked so peaceful you might have thought she was sleeping if it wasn't for the hypodermic needle sticking out of her arm.

"Mama?" I shook her gently and her eyes fluttered open. "Emmie," she said, her voice hoarse and weak. Her eyes were dilated. Track marks and bruises ran up and down both arms.

I started pulling her up. "Come on," I said, putting my arm around her. "It's time to go home."

"Em," she said again. She grasped my neck, holding onto me like a child. I started to stand, and that's when I heard his voice behind me.

"Damn, girl," he said. "You stronger than I gave you credit for. Faster, too."

I laid Mama back down on the bed. Her breathing was shallow, a whisper in the darkness. I knew I was running out of time. I turned to face him, trembling inside when I saw how those unnaturally long arms now ended in claws.

"I'm not here to interfere in your business, Catfish," I said. "I just wanna take my Mama home."

He grinned, his lips thinning over the rows of teeth. "As do I," he said. He looked down at her on the bed. "She looks just about ready to head home, don't you think?" He took a step toward me.

"Please," I said. "I don't want no trouble. I paid you, fair and square."

He laughed, a barking sound that shook the walls and rattled my bones. "There ain't a *goddamned* thing in this life that's fair, girl. You of all people ought to know that." He stepped over another body, close enough now that I could feel his hot, stinking breath huffing on my cheek. Eyes the size of saucers grew even bigger as he approached, drinking in the darkness, wallowing in it. His jaws opened wide, wider than the world, wide enough to swallow me whole. I bent back down over Mama, whispering in her ear.

"Wake up, Mama. It's time to go."

He growled and leaped, and, as he did, I pulled the needle from Mama's arm and slammed it back over my shoulder, directly into his left eye. He screamed, the worst sound I'd ever heard or could have imagined, stumbling back, clawing at the thing with both hands. Among the blood and the bodies he fell, twisting as he went down to catch himself, hitting the floor and driving the syringe deep inside his skull. His body jerked a few times like a puppet on a kinked-up string, until finally he gasped and was still.

I sucked in a deep, shuddering breath, waiting for him to get back up, but he never did. Finally I found the courage to pull the pill bottle out of my pocket once again, opening it up and shaking out one of the pills into my hand. I managed to shake Mama awake enough to open her mouth, and I put it as far back on her tongue as I could, stroking her face and whispering to her to swallow, please swallow, just do this and we'd go home. Somewhere deep inside she must have heard me, because her eyes opened briefly and she choked it down.

I couldn't carry her and I knew it, so as the sun went down I pulled off my red hoodie and slipped it over her head, sliding her arms through the sleeves while she shivered and cried. When I'd gotten it on her I pulled her close, rocking and singing, waiting for her strength to return in the cold dark, there among the unassuming dead.

Bartleby, the Scrivener

A Story of Wall Street

Herman Melville

I AM A RATHER elderly man. The nature of my avocations for the last thirty years has brought me into more than ordinary contact with what would seem an interesting and somewhat singular set of men, of whom as yet nothing that I know of has ever been written: I mean the law-copyists or scriveners. I have known very many of them, professionally and privately, and if I pleased, could relate divers histories, at which good-natured gentlemen might smile, and sentimental souls might weep. But I waive the biographies of all other scriveners for a few passages in the life of Bartleby, who was a scrivener of the strangest I ever saw or heard of. While of other law-copyists I might write the complete life, of Bartleby nothing of that sort can be done. I believe that no materials exist for a full and satisfactory biography of this man. It is an irreparable loss to literature. Bartleby was one of those beings of whom nothing is ascertainable, except from the original sources, and in his case those are very small. What my own astonished eyes saw of Bartleby, that is all I know of him, except, indeed, one vague report which will appear in the sequel.

Ere introducing the scrivener, as he first appeared to me, it is fit I make some mention of myself, my *employees*, my business, my chambers, and general surroundings; because some such description is indispensable to an adequate understanding of the chief character about to be presented.

Imprimis: I am a man who, from his youth upwards, has been filled with a profound conviction that the easiest way of life is the best. Hence, though I belong to a profession proverbially energetic and nervous, even to turbulence, at times, yet nothing of that sort have I ever suffered to invade my peace. I am one of those unambitious lawyers who never addresses a jury, or in any way draws down public applause; but in the cool tranquility of a snug retreat, do a snug business among rich men's bonds and mortgages and title-deeds. All who know me, consider me an eminently *safe* man. The late John Jacob Astor, a personage little given to poetic enthusiasm, had no hesitation in pronouncing my first grand point to be prudence; my next, method. I do not speak it in vanity, but simply record the fact, that I was not unemployed in my profession by the late John Jacob Astor; a name which, I admit, I love to repeat, for it hath a rounded and orbicular sound to it, and rings like unto bullion. I will freely add, that I was not insensible to the late John Jacob Astor's good opinion.

Some time prior to the period at which this little history begins, my avocations had been largely increased. The good old office, now extinct in the State of New York, of a Master in Chancery, had been conferred upon me. It was not a very arduous office, but very pleasantly remunerative. I seldom lose my temper; much more seldom indulge in dangerous indignation at wrongs and outrages; but I must be permitted to be rash here and declare, that I consider the sudden and violent abrogation of the office of Master in Chancery, by the new Constitution, as a — premature act; inasmuch as I had counted upon a life-lease of the profits, whereas I only received those of a few short years. But this is by the way.

My chambers were upstairs at No.— Wall-street. At one end they looked upon the white wall of the interior of a spacious sky-light shaft, penetrating the building from top to bottom. This view might have been considered rather tame than otherwise, deficient in what landscape painters call 'life'. But if so, the view from the other end of my chambers offered, at least, a contrast, if nothing more. In that direction my windows commanded an unobstructed view of a lofty brick wall, black by age and everlasting shade; which wall required no spy-glass to bring out its lurking beauties, but for the benefit of all near-sighted spectators, was pushed up to within ten feet of my window panes. Owing to the great height of the surrounding buildings, and my chambers being on the second floor, the interval between this wall and mine not a little resembled a huge square cistern.

At the period just preceding the advent of Bartleby, I had two persons as copyists in my employment, and a promising lad as an office-boy. First, Turkey; second, Nippers; third, Ginger Nut. These may seem names, the like of which are not usually found in the Directory. In truth they were nicknames, mutually conferred upon each other by my three clerks, and were deemed expressive of their respective persons or characters. Turkey was a short, pursy Englishman of about my own age, that is, somewhere not far from sixty. In the morning, one might say, his face was of a fine florid hue, but after twelve o'clock, meridian – his dinner hour – it blazed like a grate full of Christmas coals; and continued blazing – but, as it were, with a gradual wane – till six o'clock p.m. or thereabouts, after which I saw no more of the proprietor of the face, which gaining its meridian with the sun, seemed to set with it, to rise, culminate, and decline the following day, with the like regularity and undiminished glory. There are many singular coincidences I have known in the course of my life, not the least among which was the fact, that exactly when Turkey displayed his fullest beams from his red and radiant countenance, just then, too, at that critical moment, began the daily period when I considered his business capacities as seriously disturbed for the remainder of the twenty-four hours. Not that he was absolutely idle, or averse to business then; far from it. The difficulty was, he was apt to be altogether too energetic. There was a strange, inflamed, flurried, flighty recklessness of activity about him. He would be incautious in dipping his pen into his inkstand. All his blots upon my documents, were dropped there after twelve o'clock, meridian. Indeed, not only would he be reckless and sadly given to making blots in the afternoon, but some days he went further, and was rather noisy. At such times, too, his face flamed with augmented blazonry, as if cannel coal had been heaped on anthracite. He made an unpleasant racket with his chair; spilled his sand-box; in mending his pens, impatiently split them all to pieces, and threw them on the floor in a sudden passion; stood up and leaned over his table, boxing his papers about in a most indecorous manner, very sad to behold in an elderly man like him. Nevertheless, as he was in many ways a most valuable person to me, and all the time before twelve o'clock, meridian, was the quickest, steadiest creature too, accomplishing a great deal of work in a style not easy to be matched – for these reasons, I was willing to overlook his eccentricities, though indeed, occasionally, I remonstrated with him. I did this very gently, however, because, though the civilest, nay, the blandest and most reverential of men in the morning, yet in the afternoon he was disposed, upon provocation, to be slightly rash with his tongue, in fact, insolent. Now, valuing his morning services as I did, and resolved not to lose them; yet, at the same time made uncomfortable by his inflamed ways after twelve o'clock; and being a man of peace, unwilling by my admonitions to call forth unseemly retorts from him; I took upon me, one Saturday noon (he was always worse on Saturdays), to hint to him, very kindly, that perhaps now that he was growing old, it might be well to abridge his labors; in short, he need not come to my chambers after twelve o'clock, but, dinner over, had best go home to his lodgings and rest himself till teatime. But no; he insisted upon his afternoon devotions. His countenance became intolerably fervid, as he oratorically assured me – gesticulating with a long ruler at the other end of the room – that if his services in the morning were useful, how indispensable, then, in the afternoon?

"With submission, sir," said Turkey on this occasion, "I consider myself your right-hand man. In the morning I but marshal and deploy my columns; but in the afternoon I put myself at their head, and gallantly charge the foe, thus!" – and he made a violent thrust with the ruler.

"But the blots, Turkey," intimated I.

"True – but, with submission, sir, behold these hairs! I am getting old. Surely, sir, a blot or two of a warm afternoon is not to be severely urged against gray hairs. Old age – even if it blot the page – is honorable. With submission, sir, we *both* are getting old."

This appeal to my fellow-feeling was hardly to be resisted. At all events, I saw that go he would not. So I made up my mind to let him stay, resolving, nevertheless, to see to it, that during the afternoon he had to do with my less important papers.

Nippers, the second on my list, was a whiskered, sallow, and, upon the whole, rather piratical-looking young man of about five and twenty. I always deemed him the victim of two evil powers – ambition and indigestion. The ambition was evinced by a certain impatience of the duties of a mere copyist, an unwarrantable usurpation of strictly professional affairs, such as the original drawing up of legal documents. The indigestion seemed betokened in an occasional nervous testiness and grinning irritability, causing the teeth to audibly grind together over mistakes committed in copying; unnecessary maledictions, hissed, rather than spoken, in the heat of business; and especially by a continual discontent with the height of the table where he worked. Though of a very ingenious mechanical turn, Nippers could never get this table to suit him. He put chips under it, blocks of various sorts, bits of pasteboard, and at last went so far as to attempt an exquisite adjustment by final pieces of folded blotting paper. But no invention would answer. If, for the sake of easing his back, he brought the table lid at a sharp angle well up towards his chin, and wrote there like a man using the steep roof of a Dutch house for his desk – then he declared that it stopped the circulation in his arms. If now he lowered the table to his waistbands, and stooped over it in writing, then there was a sore aching in his back. In short, the truth of the matter was, Nippers knew not what he wanted. Or, if he wanted anything, it was to be rid of a scrivener's table altogether. Among the manifestations of his diseased ambition was a fondness he had for receiving visits from certain ambiguous-looking fellows in seedy coats, whom he called his clients. Indeed I was aware that not only was he, at times, considerable of a ward-politician, but he occasionally did a little business at the Justices' courts, and was not unknown on the steps of the Tombs. I have good reason to believe, however, that one individual who called upon him at my chambers, and who, with a grand air, he insisted was his client, was no other than a dun, and the alleged title-deed, a bill. But with all his failings, and the annoyances he caused me, Nippers, like his compatriot Turkey, was a very useful man to me; wrote a neat, swift hand; and, when he chose, was not deficient in a gentlemanly sort of deportment. Added to this, he always dressed in a gentlemanly sort of way; and so, incidentally, reflected credit upon my chambers. Whereas with respect to Turkey, I had much ado to keep him from being a reproach to me. His clothes were apt to look oily and smell of eating-houses. He wore his pantaloons very loose and baggy in summer. His coats were execrable; his hat not to be handled. But while the hat was a thing of indifference to me, inasmuch as his natural civility and deference, as a dependent Englishman, always led him to doff it the moment he entered the room, yet his coat was another matter. Concerning his coats, I reasoned with him; but with no effect. The truth was, I suppose, that a man of so small an income, could not afford to sport such a lustrous face and a lustrous coat at one and the same time. As Nippers once observed, Turkey's money went chiefly for red ink. One winter day I presented Turkey with a highly-respectable looking coat of my own, a padded gray coat, of a most comfortable warmth, and which buttoned straight up from the knee to the neck. I thought Turkey would appreciate the favor, and abate his rashness and obstreperousness of afternoons. But no. I verily believe that buttoning himself up in so downy and blanket-like a coat had a pernicious effect upon him; upon the same principle that too much oats are bad for horses. In fact, precisely as a rash, restive horse is said to feel his oats, so Turkey felt his coat. It made him insolent. He was a man whom prosperity harmed.

Though concerning the self-indulgent habits of Turkey I had my own private surmises, yet touching Nippers I was well persuaded that whatever might be his faults in other respects, he was, at least, a temperate young man. But indeed, nature herself seemed to have been his vintner, and at his birth charged him so thoroughly with an irritable, brandy-like disposition, that all subsequent potations were needless. When I consider how, amid the stillness of my chambers, Nippers would sometimes impatiently rise from his seat, and stooping over his table, spread his arms wide apart, seize the whole desk, and move it, and jerk it, with a grim, grinding motion on the floor, as if the table were a perverse voluntary agent, intent on thwarting and vexing him; I plainly perceive that for Nippers, brandy and water were altogether superfluous.

It was fortunate for me that, owing to its peculiar cause – indigestion – the irritability and consequent nervousness of Nippers, were mainly observable in the morning, while in the afternoon he was comparatively mild. So that Turkey's paroxysms only coming on about twelve o'clock, I never had to do with their eccentricities at one time. Their fits relieved each other like guards. When Nippers' was on, Turkey's was off; and *vice versa*. This was a good natural arrangement under the circumstances.

Ginger Nut, the third on my list, was a lad some twelve years old. His father was a carman, ambitious of seeing his son on the bench instead of a cart, before he died. So he sent him to my office as student at law, errand boy, and cleaner and sweeper, at the rate of one dollar a week. He had a little desk to himself, but he did not use it much. Upon inspection, the drawer exhibited a great array of the shells of various sorts of nuts. Indeed, to this quick-witted youth the whole noble science of the law was contained in a nut-shell. Not the least among the employments of Ginger Nut, as well as one which he discharged with the most alacrity, was his duty as cake and apple purveyor for Turkey and Nippers. Copying law papers being proverbially dry, husky sort of business, my two scriveners were fain to moisten their mouths very often with Spitzenbergs to be had at the numerous stalls nigh the Custom House and Post Office. Also, they sent Ginger Nut very frequently for that peculiar cake – small, flat, round, and very spicy – after which he had been named by them. Of a cold morning when business was but dull, Turkey would gobble up scores of these cakes, as if they were mere wafers – indeed they sell them at the rate of six or eight for a penny – the scrape of his pen blending with the crunching of the crisp particles in his mouth. Of all the fiery afternoon blunders and flurried rashnesses of Turkey, was his once moistening a ginger-cake between his lips, and clapping it on to a mortgage for a seal. I came within an ace of dismissing him then. But he mollified me by making an oriental bow, and saying – "With submission, sir, it was generous of me to find you in stationery on my own account."

Now my original business – that of a conveyancer and title hunter, and drawer-up of recondite documents of all sorts – was considerably increased by receiving the master's office. There was now great work for scriveners. Not only must I push the clerks already with me, but I must have additional help. In answer to my advertisement, a motionless young man one morning, stood upon my office threshold, the door being open, for it was summer. I can see that figure now – pallidly neat, pitiably respectable, incurably forlorn! It was Bartleby.

After a few words touching his qualifications, I engaged him, glad to have among my corps of copyists a man of so singularly sedate an aspect, which I thought might operate beneficially upon the flighty temper of Turkey, and the fiery one of Nippers.

I should have stated before that ground glass folding-doors divided my premises into two parts, one of which was occupied by my scriveners, the other by myself. According to my humor I threw open these doors, or closed them. I resolved to assign Bartleby a corner by the folding-doors, but on my side of them, so as to have this quiet man within easy call, in case any trifling thing was to be done. I placed his desk close up to a small side-window in that part of the room, a window which originally had afforded a lateral view of certain grimy back yards and bricks, but which, owing to subsequent erections, commanded at present no view at all, though it gave some light. Within three feet of the panes was a wall, and the light came down from far above, between two lofty buildings, as from a very small opening in a dome. Still further to a satisfactory arrangement, I procured a high green folding screen, which might entirely isolate Bartleby from my sight, though not remove him from my voice. And thus, in a manner, privacy and society were conjoined.

At first Bartleby did an extraordinary quantity of writing. As if long famishing for something to copy, he seemed to gorge himself on my documents. There was no pause for digestion. He ran a day and night line, copying by sunlight and by candlelight. I should have been quite delighted with his application, had he been cheerfully industrious. But he wrote on silently, palely, mechanically.

It is, of course, an indispensable part of a scrivener's business to verify the accuracy of his copy, word by word. Where there are two or more scriveners in an office, they assist each other in this examination, one reading from the copy, the other holding the original. It is a very dull, wearisome, and lethargic affair. I can readily imagine that to some sanguine temperaments it would be altogether intolerable. For example, I cannot credit that the mettlesome poet Byron would have contentedly sat down with Bartleby to examine a law document of, say five hundred pages, closely written in a crimpy hand.

Now and then, in the haste of business, it had been my habit to assist in comparing some brief document myself, calling Turkey or Nippers for this purpose. One object I had in placing Bartleby so handy to me behind the screen, was to avail myself of his services on such trivial occasions. It was on the third day, I think, of his being with me, and before any necessity had arisen for having his own writing examined, that, being much hurried to complete a small affair I had in hand, I abruptly called to Bartleby. In my haste and natural expectancy of instant compliance, I sat with my head bent over the original on my desk, and my right hand sideways, and somewhat nervously extended with the copy, so that immediately upon emerging from his retreat, Bartleby might snatch it and proceed to business without the least delay.

In this very attitude did I sit when I called to him, rapidly stating what it was I wanted him to do – namely, to examine a small paper with me. Imagine my surprise, nay, my consternation, when without moving from his privacy, Bartleby in a singularly mild, firm voice, replied, "I would prefer not to."

I sat awhile in perfect silence, rallying my stunned faculties. Immediately it occurred to me that my ears had deceived me, or Bartleby had entirely misunderstood my meaning. I repeated my request in the clearest tone I could assume. But in quite as clear a one came the previous reply, "I would prefer not to."

"Prefer not to," echoed I, rising in high excitement, and crossing the room with a stride. "What do you mean? Are you moon-struck? I want you to help me compare this sheet here – take it," and I thrust it towards him.

"I would prefer not to," said he.

I looked at him steadfastly. His face was leanly composed; his gray eye dimly calm. Not a wrinkle of agitation rippled him. Had there been the least uneasiness, anger, impatience or impertinence in his manner; in other words, had there been anything ordinarily human about him, doubtless I should have violently dismissed him from the premises. But as it was, I should have as soon thought of turning my pale plaster-of-paris bust of Cicero out of doors. I stood gazing at him awhile, as he went on with his own writing, and then reseated myself at my desk. This is very strange, thought I. What had one best do? But my business hurried me. I concluded to forget the matter for the present, reserving it for my future leisure. So calling Nippers from the other room, the paper was speedily examined.

A few days after this, Bartleby concluded four lengthy documents, being quadruplicates of a week's testimony taken before me in my High Court of Chancery. It became necessary to examine them. It was an important suit, and great accuracy was imperative. Having all things arranged I called Turkey, Nippers and Ginger Nut from the next room, meaning to place the four copies in the hands of my four clerks, while I should read from the original. Accordingly Turkey, Nippers and Ginger Nut had taken their seats in a row, each with his document in hand, when I called to Bartleby to join this interesting group.

"Bartleby! Quick, I am waiting."

I heard a slow scrape of his chair legs on the uncarpeted floor, and soon he appeared standing at the entrance of his hermitage.

"What is wanted?" said he mildly.

"The copies, the copies," said I hurriedly. "We are going to examine them. There—" – and I held towards him the fourth quadruplicate.

"I would prefer not to," he said, and gently disappeared behind the screen.

For a few moments I was turned into a pillar of salt, standing at the head of my seated column of clerks. Recovering myself, I advanced towards the screen, and demanded the reason for such extraordinary conduct.

"*Why* do you refuse?"

"I would prefer not to."

With any other man I should have flown outright into a dreadful passion, scorned all further words, and thrust him ignominiously from my presence. But there was something about Bartleby that not only strangely disarmed me, but in a wonderful manner touched and disconcerted me. I began to reason with him.

"These are your own copies we are about to examine. It is labor-saving to you, because one examination will answer for your four papers. It is common usage. Every copyist is bound to help examine his copy. Is it not so? Will you not speak? Answer!"

"I prefer not to," he replied in a flute-like tone. It seemed to me that while I had been addressing him, he carefully revolved every statement that I made; fully comprehended the meaning; could not gainsay the irresistible conclusions; but, at the same time, some paramount consideration prevailed with him to reply as he did.

"You are decided, then, not to comply with my request – a request made according to common usage and common sense?"

He briefly gave me to understand that on that point my judgment was sound. Yes: his decision was irreversible.

It is not seldom the case that when a man is browbeaten in some unprecedented and violently unreasonable way, he begins to stagger in his own plainest faith. He begins, as it were, vaguely to surmise that, wonderful as it may be, all the justice and all the reason is on the other side. Accordingly, if any disinterested persons are present, he turns to them for some reinforcement for his own faltering mind.

"Turkey," said I, "what do you think of this? Am I not right?"

"With submission, sir," said Turkey, with his blandest tone, "I think that you are."

"Nippers," said I, "what do *you* think of it?"

"I think I should kick him out of the office."

(The reader of nice perceptions will here perceive that, it being morning, Turkey's answer is couched in polite and tranquil terms, but Nippers replies in ill-tempered ones. Or, to repeat a previous sentence, Nippers' ugly mood was on duty and Turkey's off.)

"Ginger Nut," said I, willing to enlist the smallest suffrage in my behalf, "what do you think of it?"

"I think, sir, he's a little *luny*," replied Ginger Nut with a grin.

"You hear what they say," said I, turning towards the screen, "come forth and do your duty."

But he vouchsafed no reply. I pondered a moment in sore perplexity. But once more business hurried me. I determined again to postpone the consideration of this dilemma to my future leisure. With a little trouble we made out to examine the papers without Bartleby, though at every page or two, Turkey deferentially dropped his opinion that this proceeding was quite out of the common; while Nippers, twitching in his chair with a dyspeptic nervousness, ground out between his set teeth occasional hissing maledictions against the stubborn oaf behind the screen. And for his (Nippers') part, this was the first and the last time he would do another man's business without pay.

Meanwhile Bartleby sat in his hermitage, oblivious to everything but his own peculiar business there.

Some days passed, the scrivener being employed upon another lengthy work. His late remarkable conduct led me to regard his ways narrowly. I observed that he never went to dinner; indeed that he never went anywhere. As yet I had never of my personal knowledge known him to be outside of my office. He was a perpetual sentry in the corner. At about eleven o'clock though, in the morning, I noticed that Ginger Nut would advance toward the opening in Bartleby's screen, as if silently beckoned thither by a gesture invisible to me where I sat. The boy would then leave the office jingling a few pence, and reappear with a handful of ginger-nuts which he delivered in the hermitage, receiving two of the cakes for his trouble.

He lives, then, on ginger-nuts, thought I; never eats a dinner, properly speaking; he must be a vegetarian then; but no; he never eats even vegetables, he eats nothing but ginger-nuts. My mind then ran on in reveries concerning the probable effects upon the human constitution of living entirely on ginger-nuts. Ginger-nuts are so called because they contain ginger as one of their peculiar constituents, and the final flavoring one. Now what was ginger? A hot, spicy thing. Was Bartleby hot and spicy? Not at all. Ginger, then, had no effect upon Bartleby. Probably he preferred it should have none.

Nothing so aggravates an earnest person as a passive resistance. If the individual so resisted be of a not inhumane temper, and the resisting one perfectly harmless in his passivity; then, in the better moods of the former, he will endeavor charitably to construe to his imagination what proves impossible to be solved by his judgment. Even so, for the most part, I regarded Bartleby and his ways. Poor fellow! thought I, he means no mischief; it is plain he intends no insolence; his aspect sufficiently evinces that his eccentricities are involuntary. He is useful to me. I can get along with him. If I turn him away, the chances are he will fall in with some less indulgent employer, and then he will be rudely treated, and perhaps driven forth miserably to starve. Yes. Here I can cheaply purchase a delicious self-approval. To befriend Bartleby; to humor him in his strange willfulness, will cost me little or nothing, while I lay up in my soul what will eventually prove a sweet morsel for my conscience. But this mood was not invariable with me. The passiveness of Bartleby sometimes irritated me. I felt strangely goaded on to encounter him in new opposition, to elicit some angry spark from him answerable to my own. But indeed I might as well have essayed to strike fire with my knuckles against a bit of Windsor soap. But one afternoon the evil impulse in me mastered me, and the following little scene ensued:

"Bartleby," said I, "when those papers are all copied, I will compare them with you."

"I would prefer not to."

"How? Surely you do not mean to persist in that mulish vagary?"

No answer.

I threw open the folding-doors nearby, and turning upon Turkey and Nippers, exclaimed in an excited manner –

"He says, a second time, he won't examine his papers. What do you think of it, Turkey?"

It was afternoon, be it remembered. Turkey sat glowing like a brass boiler, his bald head steaming, his hands reeling among his blotted papers.

"Think of it?" roared Turkey; "I think I'll just step behind his screen, and black his eyes for him!"

So saying, Turkey rose to his feet and threw his arms into a pugilistic position. He was hurrying away to make good his promise, when I detained him, alarmed at the effect of incautiously rousing Turkey's combativeness after dinner.

"Sit down, Turkey," said I, "and hear what Nippers has to say. What do you think of it, Nippers? Would I not be justified in immediately dismissing Bartleby?"

"Excuse me, that is for you to decide, sir. I think his conduct quite unusual, and indeed unjust, as regards Turkey and myself. But it may only be a passing whim."

"Ah," exclaimed I, "you have strangely changed your mind then – you speak very gently of him now."

"All beer," cried Turkey; "gentleness is effects of beer – Nippers and I dined together today. You see how gentle *I* am, sir. Shall I go and black his eyes?"

"You refer to Bartleby, I suppose. No, not today, Turkey," I replied; "pray, put up your fists."

I closed the doors, and again advanced towards Bartleby. I felt additional incentives tempting me to my fate. I burned to be rebelled against again. I remembered that Bartleby never left the office.

"Bartleby," said I, "Ginger Nut is away; just step round to the Post Office, won't you? (it was but a three minute walk) – and see if there is anything for me."

"I would prefer not to."

"You *will* not?"

"I *prefer* not."

I staggered to my desk, and sat there in a deep study. My blind inveteracy returned. Was there any other thing in which I could procure myself to be ignominiously repulsed by this lean, penniless wight? – my hired clerk? What added thing is there, perfectly reasonable, that he will be sure to refuse to do?

"Bartleby!"

No answer.

"Bartleby," in a louder tone.

No answer.

"Bartleby," I roared.

Like a very ghost, agreeably to the laws of magical invocation, at the third summons, he appeared at the entrance of his hermitage.

"Go to the next room, and tell Nippers to come to me."

"I prefer not to," he respectfully and slowly said, and mildly disappeared.

"Very good, Bartleby," said I, in a quiet sort of serenely severe self-possessed tone, intimating the unalterable purpose of some terrible retribution very close at hand. At the moment I half intended something of the kind. But upon the whole, as it was drawing towards my dinner-hour, I thought it best to put on my hat and walk home for the day, suffering much from perplexity and distress of mind.

Shall I acknowledge it? The conclusion of this whole business was that it soon became a fixed fact of my chambers, that a pale young scrivener, by the name of Bartleby, and a desk there; that he copied for me at the usual rate of four cents a folio (one hundred words); but he was permanently exempt from examining the work done by him, that duty being transferred to Turkey and Nippers, one of compliment doubtless to their superior acuteness; moreover, said Bartleby was never on any account to be dispatched on the most trivial errand of any sort; and that even if entreated to take upon him such a matter, it was generally understood that he would prefer not to – in other words, that he would refuse pointblank.

As days passed on, I became considerably reconciled to Bartleby. His steadiness, his freedom from all dissipation, his incessant industry (except when he chose to throw himself into a standing revery behind his screen), his great stillness, his unalterableness of demeanor under all circumstances, made him a valuable acquisition. One prime thing was this – *he was always there* – first in the morning, continually through the day, and the last at night. I had a singular confidence in his honesty. I felt my most precious papers perfectly safe in his hands. Sometimes to be sure I could not, for the very soul of me, avoid falling into sudden spasmodic passions with him. For it was exceeding difficult to bear in mind all the time those strange peculiarities, privileges, and unheard-of exemptions, forming the tacit stipulations on Bartleby's part under which he remained in my office. Now and then, in the eagerness of dispatching pressing business, I would inadvertently summon Bartleby, in a short, rapid tone, to put his finger, say, on the incipient tie of a bit of red tape with which I was about compressing some papers. Of course, from behind the screen the usual answer, "I prefer not to," was sure to come; and then, how could a human creature with the common infirmities of our nature refrain from bitterly exclaiming upon such perverseness – such unreasonableness. However, every added repulse of this sort which I received only tended to lessen the probability of my repeating the inadvertence.

Here it must be said, that according to the custom of most legal gentlemen occupying chambers in densely-populated law buildings, there were several keys to my door. One was kept by a woman residing in the attic, which person weekly scrubbed and daily swept and dusted my apartments. Another was kept by Turkey for convenience sake. The third I sometimes carried in my own pocket. The fourth I knew not who had.

Now, one Sunday morning I happened to go to Trinity Church, to hear a celebrated preacher, and finding myself rather early on the ground, I thought I would walk around to my chambers for a while. Luckily I had my key with me; but upon applying it to the lock, I found it resisted by something inserted from the inside. Quite surprised, I called out; when to my consternation a key was turned from within; and thrusting his lean visage at me, and holding the door ajar, the apparition of Bartleby appeared, in his shirt sleeves, and otherwise in a strangely tattered dishabille, saying quietly that he was sorry, but he was deeply engaged just then, and – preferred not admitting me at present. In a brief word or two, he moreover added, that perhaps I had better walk round the block two or three times, and by that time he would probably have concluded his affairs.

Now, the utterly unsurmised appearance of Bartleby, tenanting my law-chambers of a Sunday morning, with his cadaverously gentlemanly *nonchalance*, yet withal firm and self-possessed, had such a strange effect upon me, that incontinently I slunk away from my own door, and did as desired. But not without sundry twinges of impotent rebellion against the mild effrontery of this unaccountable scrivener. Indeed, it was his wonderful mildness chiefly, which not only disarmed me, but unmanned me, as it were. For I consider that one, for the time, is a sort of unmanned when he tranquilly permits his hired clerk to dictate to him, and order him away from his own premises. Furthermore, I was full of uneasiness as to what Bartleby could possibly be doing in my office in his shirt sleeves, and in an otherwise dismantled condition of a Sunday morning. Was anything amiss going on? Nay, that was out of the question. It was not to be thought of for a moment that Bartleby was an immoral person. But what could he be doing there? – copying? Nay again, whatever might be his eccentricities, Bartleby was an eminently decorous person. He would be the last man to sit down to his desk in any state approaching to nudity. Besides, it was Sunday; and there was something about Bartleby that forbade the supposition that he would by any secular occupation violate the proprieties of the day.

Nevertheless, my mind was not pacified; and full of a restless curiosity, at last I returned to the door. Without hindrance I inserted my key, opened it, and entered. Bartleby was not to be seen. I looked round anxiously, peeped behind his screen; but it was very plain that he was gone. Upon more closely examining the place, I surmised that for an indefinite period Bartleby must have ate, dressed, and slept in my office, and that too without plate, mirror, or bed. The cushioned seat of a rickety old sofa in one corner bore the faint impress of a lean, reclining form. Rolled away under his desk, I found a blanket; under the empty grate, a blacking box and brush; on a chair, a tin basin, with soap and a ragged towel; in a newspaper a few crumbs of ginger-nuts and a morsel of cheese. Yes, thought I, it is evident enough that Bartleby has been making his home here, keeping bachelor's hall all by himself. Immediately then the thought came sweeping across me, What miserable friendlessness and loneliness are here revealed! His poverty is great; but his solitude, how horrible! Think of it. Of a Sunday, Wall-street is deserted as Petra; and every night of every day it is an emptiness. This building too, which of week-days hums with industry and life, at nightfall echoes with sheer vacancy, and all through Sunday is forlorn. And here Bartleby makes his home; sole spectator of a solitude which he has seen all populous – a sort of innocent and transformed Marius brooding among the ruins of Carthage!

For the first time in my life a feeling of overpowering stinging melancholy seized me. Before, I had never experienced aught but a not-unpleasing sadness. The bond of a common humanity now drew me irresistibly to gloom. A fraternal melancholy! For both I and Bartleby were sons of Adam. I remembered the bright silks and sparkling faces I had seen that day, in gala trim, swan-like sailing down the Mississippi of Broadway; and I contrasted them with the pallid copyist, and thought to myself, Ah, happiness courts the light, so we deem the world is gay; but misery hides aloof, so we deem that misery there is none. These sad fancyings – chimeras, doubtless, of a sick and silly brain – led on to other and more special thoughts, concerning the eccentricities of Bartleby. Presentiments of strange discoveries hovered round me. The scrivener's pale form appeared to me laid out, among uncaring strangers, in its shivering winding sheet.

Suddenly I was attracted by Bartleby's closed desk, the key in open sight left in the lock.

I mean no mischief, seek the gratification of no heartless curiosity, thought I; besides, the desk is mine, and its contents too, so I will make bold to look within. Everything was methodically arranged, the papers smoothly placed. The pigeon holes were deep, and removing the files of documents, I groped into their recesses. Presently I felt something there, and dragged it out. It was an old bandanna handkerchief, heavy and knotted. I opened it, and saw it was a savings' bank.

I now recalled all the quiet mysteries which I had noted in the man. I remembered that he never spoke but to answer; that though at intervals he had considerable time to himself, yet I had never seen him reading – no, not even a newspaper; that for long periods he would stand looking out, at his pale window behind the screen, upon the dead brick wall; I was quite sure he never visited any refectory or eating house; while his pale face clearly indicated that he never drank beer like Turkey, or tea and coffee even, like other men; that he never went anywhere in particular that I could learn; never went out for a walk, unless indeed that was the case at present; that he had declined telling who he was, or whence he came, or whether he had any relatives in the world; that though so thin and pale, he never complained of ill health. And more than all, I remembered a certain unconscious air of pallid – how shall I call it? – of pallid haughtiness, say, or rather an austere reserve about him, which had positively awed me into my tame compliance with his eccentricities, when I had feared to ask him to do the slightest incidental thing for me, even though I might know, from his long-continued motionlessness, that behind his screen he must be standing in one of those dead-wall reveries of his.

Revolving all these things, and coupling them with the recently discovered fact that he made my office his constant abiding place and home, and not forgetful of his morbid moodiness; revolving all these things, a prudential feeling began to steal over me. My first emotions had been those of pure melancholy and sincerest pity; but just in proportion as the forlornness of Bartleby grew and grew to my imagination, did that same melancholy merge into fear, that pity into repulsion. So true it is, and so terrible too, that up to a certain point the thought or sight of misery enlists our best affections; but, in certain special cases, beyond that point it does not. They err who would assert that invariably this is owing to the inherent selfishness of the human heart. It rather proceeds from a certain hopelessness of remedying excessive and organic ill. To a sensitive being, pity is not seldom pain. And when at last it is perceived that such pity cannot lead to effectual succor, common sense bids the soul rid of it. What I saw that morning persuaded me that the scrivener was the victim of innate and incurable disorder. I might give alms to his body; but his body did not pain him; it was his soul that suffered, and his soul I could not reach.

I did not accomplish the purpose of going to Trinity Church that morning. Somehow, the things I had seen disqualified me for the time from church-going. I walked homeward, thinking what I would do with Bartleby. Finally, I resolved upon this – I would put certain calm questions to him the next morning, touching his history, etc., and if he declined to answer them openly and unreservedly (and I supposed he would prefer not), then to give him a twenty dollar bill over and above whatever I might owe him, and tell him his services were no longer required; but that if in any other way I could assist him, I would be happy to do so, especially if he desired to return to his native place, wherever that might be, I would willingly help to defray the expenses. Moreover, if, after reaching home, he found himself at any time in want of aid, a letter from him would be sure of a reply.

The next morning came.

"Bartleby," said I, gently calling to him behind his screen.

No reply.

"Bartleby," said I, in a still gentler tone, "come here; I am not going to ask you to do anything you would prefer not to do – I simply wish to speak to you."

Upon this he noiselessly slid into view.

"Will you tell me, Bartleby, where you were born?"

"I would prefer not to."

"Will you tell me *anything* about yourself?"

"I would prefer not to."

"But what reasonable objection can you have to speak to me? I feel friendly towards you."

He did not look at me while I spoke, but kept his glance fixed upon my bust of Cicero, which as I then sat, was directly behind me, some six inches above my head.

"What is your answer, Bartleby?" said I, after waiting a considerable time for a reply, during which his countenance remained immovable, only there was the faintest conceivable tremor of the white attenuated mouth.

"At present I prefer to give no answer," he said, and retired into his hermitage.

It was rather weak in me I confess, but his manner on this occasion nettled me. Not only did there seem to lurk in it a certain calm disdain, but his perverseness seemed ungrateful, considering the undeniable good usage and indulgence he had received from me.

Again I sat ruminating what I should do. Mortified as I was at his behavior, and resolved as I had been to dismiss him when I entered my offices, nevertheless I strangely felt something superstitious knocking at my heart, and forbidding me to carry out my purpose, and denouncing me for a villain if I dared to breathe one bitter word against this forlornest of mankind. At last, familiarly drawing my chair behind his screen, I sat down and said: "Bartleby, never mind then about revealing your history; but let me entreat you, as a friend, to comply as far as may be with the usages of this office. Say now you will help to examine papers tomorrow or next day: in short, say now that in a day or two you will begin to be a little reasonable: say so, Bartleby."

"At present I would prefer not to be a little reasonable," was his mildly cadaverous reply.

Just then the folding-doors opened, and Nippers approached. He seemed suffering from an unusually bad night's rest, induced by severer indigestion than common. He overheard those final words of Bartleby.

"*Prefer not*, eh?" gritted Nippers – "I'd *prefer* him, if I were you, sir," addressing me – "I'd *prefer* him; I'd give him preferences, the stubborn mule! What is it, sir, pray, that he *prefers* not to do now?"

Bartleby moved not a limb.

"Mr. Nippers," said I, "I'd prefer that you would withdraw for the present."

Somehow, of late I had got into the way of involuntarily using this word 'prefer' upon all sorts of not exactly suitable occasions. And I trembled to think that my contact with the scrivener had already and seriously affected me in a mental way. And what further and deeper aberration might it not yet produce? This apprehension had not been without efficacy in determining me to summary means.

As Nippers, looking very sour and sulky, was departing, Turkey blandly and deferentially approached.

"With submission, sir," said he, "yesterday I was thinking about Bartleby here, and I think that if he would but prefer to take a quart of good ale every day, it would do much towards mending him, and enabling him to assist in examining his papers."

"So you have got the word too," said I, slightly excited.

"With submission, what word, sir," asked Turkey, respectfully crowding himself into the contracted space behind the screen, and by so doing, making me jostle the scrivener. "What word, sir?"

"I would prefer to be left alone here," said Bartleby, as if offended at being mobbed in his privacy.

"*That's* the word, Turkey," said I – "that's it."

"Oh, *prefer*? Oh yes – queer word. I never use it myself. But, sir, as I was saying, if he would but prefer—"

"Turkey," interrupted I, "you will please withdraw."

"Oh certainly, sir, if you prefer that I should."

As he opened the folding-door to retire, Nippers at his desk caught a glimpse of me, and asked whether I would prefer to have a certain paper copied on blue paper or white. He did not in the least roguishly accent the word prefer. It was plain that it involuntarily rolled from his tongue. I thought to myself, surely I must get rid of a demented man, who already has in some degree turned the tongues, if not the heads of myself and clerks. But I thought it prudent not to break the dismission at once.

The next day I noticed that Bartleby did nothing but stand at his window in his dead-wall revery. Upon asking him why he did not write, he said that he had decided upon doing no more writing.

"Why, how now? What next?" exclaimed I, "Do no more writing?"

"No more."

"And what is the reason?"

"Do you not see the reason for yourself," he indifferently replied.

I looked steadfastly at him, and perceived that his eyes looked dull and glazed. Instantly it occurred to me, that his unexampled diligence in copying by his dim window for the first few weeks of his stay with me might have temporarily impaired his vision.

I was touched. I said something in condolence with him. I hinted that of course he did wisely in abstaining from writing for a while; and urged him to embrace that opportunity of taking wholesome exercise in the open air. This, however, he did not do. A few days after this, my other clerks being absent, and being in a great hurry to dispatch certain letters by the mail, I thought that, having nothing else earthly to do, Bartleby would surely be less inflexible than usual, and carry these letters to the post-office. But he blankly declined. So, much to my inconvenience, I went myself.

Still added days went by. Whether Bartleby's eyes improved or not, I could not say. To all appearance, I thought they did. But when I asked him if they did, he vouchsafed no answer. At all events, he would do no copying. At last, in reply to my urgings, he informed me that he had permanently given up copying.

"What!" exclaimed I; "Suppose your eyes should get entirely well – better than ever before – would you not copy then?"

"I have given up copying," he answered, and slid aside.

He remained as ever, a fixture in my chamber. Nay – if that were possible – he became still more of a fixture than before. What was to be done? He would do nothing in the office: why should he stay there? In plain fact, he had now become a millstone to me, not only useless as a necklace, but afflictive to bear. Yet I was sorry for him. I speak less than truth when I say that, on his own account, he occasioned me uneasiness. If he would but have named a single relative or friend, I would instantly have written, and urged their taking the poor fellow away to some convenient retreat. But he seemed alone, absolutely alone in the universe. A bit of wreck in the mid Atlantic. At length, necessities connected with my business tyrannized over all other considerations. Decently as I could, I told Bartleby that in six days' time he must unconditionally leave the office. I warned him to take measures, in the interval, for procuring some other abode. I offered to assist him in this endeavor, if he himself would but take the first step towards a removal. "And when you finally quit me, Bartleby," added I, "I shall see that you go not away entirely unprovided. Six days from this hour, remember."

At the expiration of that period, I peeped behind the screen, and lo! Bartleby was there.

I buttoned up my coat, balanced myself; advanced slowly towards him, touched his shoulder, and said, "The time has come; you must quit this place; I am sorry for you; here is money; but you must go."

"I would prefer not," he replied, with his back still towards me.

"You *must*."

He remained silent.

Now I had an unbounded confidence in this man's common honesty. He had frequently restored to me sixpences and shillings carelessly dropped upon the floor, for I am apt to be very reckless in such shirt-button affairs. The proceeding then which followed will not be deemed extraordinary.

"Bartleby," said I, "I owe you twelve dollars on account; here are thirty-two; the odd twenty are yours. – Will you take it?" and I handed the bills towards him.

But he made no motion.

"I will leave them here then," putting them under a weight on the table. Then taking my hat and cane and going to the door I tranquilly turned and added – "After you have removed your things from these offices, Bartleby, you will of course lock the door – since everyone is now gone for the day but you – and if you please, slip your key underneath the mat, so that I may have it in the morning. I shall not see you again; so goodbye to you. If hereafter in your new place of abode I can be of any service to you, do not fail to advise me by letter. Goodbye, Bartleby, and fare you well."

But he answered not a word; like the last column of some ruined temple, he remained standing mute and solitary in the middle of the otherwise deserted room.

As I walked home in a pensive mood, my vanity got the better of my pity. I could not but highly plume myself on my masterly management in getting rid of Bartleby. Masterly I call it, and such it must appear to any dispassionate thinker. The beauty of my procedure seemed to consist in its perfect quietness. There was no vulgar bullying, no bravado of any sort, no choleric hectoring, and striding to and fro across the apartment, jerking out vehement commands for Bartleby to bundle himself off with his beggarly traps. Nothing of the kind. Without loudly bidding Bartleby depart – as an inferior genius might have done – I *assumed* the ground that depart he must; and upon that assumption built all I had to say. The more I thought over my procedure, the more I was charmed with it. Nevertheless, next morning, upon awakening, I had my doubts – I had somehow slept off the fumes of vanity. One of the coolest and wisest hours a man has, is just after he awakes in the morning. My procedure seemed as sagacious as ever. – But only in theory. How it would prove in practice – there was the rub. It was truly a beautiful thought to have assumed Bartleby's departure; but, after all, that assumption was simply my own, and none of Bartleby's. The great point was, not whether I had assumed that he would quit me, but whether he would prefer so to do. He was more a man of preferences than assumptions.

After breakfast, I walked down town, arguing the probabilities *pro* and *con*. One moment I thought it would prove a miserable failure, and Bartleby would be found all alive at my office as usual; the next moment it seemed certain that I should see his chair empty. And so I kept veering about. At the corner of Broadway and Canal-street, I saw quite an excited group of people standing in earnest conversation.

"I'll take odds he doesn't," said a voice as I passed.

"Doesn't go? – Done!" said I, "Put up your money."

I was instinctively putting my hand in my pocket to produce my own, when I remembered that this was an election day. The words I had overheard bore no reference to Bartleby, but to the success or non-success of some candidate for the mayoralty. In my intent frame of mind, I had, as it were, imagined that all Broadway shared in my excitement, and were debating the same question with me. I passed on, very thankful that the uproar of the street screened my momentary absent-mindedness.

As I had intended, I was earlier than usual at my office door. I stood listening for a moment. All was still. He must be gone. I tried the knob. The door was locked. Yes, my procedure had worked to a charm; he indeed must be vanished. Yet a certain melancholy mixed with this: I was almost sorry for my brilliant success. I was fumbling under the door mat for the key, which Bartleby was to have left there for me, when accidentally my knee knocked against a panel, producing a summoning sound, and in response a voice came to me from within – "Not yet; I am occupied."

It was Bartleby.

I was thunderstruck. For an instant I stood like the man who, pipe in mouth, was killed one cloudless afternoon long ago in Virginia, by a summer lightning; at his own warm open window he was killed, and remained leaning out there upon the dreamy afternoon, till someone touched him, when he fell.

"Not gone!" I murmured at last. But again obeying that wondrous ascendancy which the inscrutable scrivener had over me, and from which ascendancy, for all my chafing, I could not completely escape, I slowly went downstairs and out into the street, and while walking round the block, considered what I should next do in this unheard-of perplexity. Turn the man out by an actual thrusting I could not; to drive him away by calling him hard names would not do; calling in the police was an unpleasant idea; and yet, permit him to enjoy his cadaverous triumph over me – this too I could not think of. What was to be done? Or, if nothing could be done, was there anything further that I could *assume* in the matter? Yes, as before I had prospectively assumed that Bartleby would depart, so now I might retrospectively assume that departed he was. In the legitimate carrying out of this assumption, I might enter my office in a great hurry, and pretending not to see Bartleby at all, walk straight against him as if he were air. Such a proceeding would in a singular degree have the appearance of a home-thrust. It was hardly possible that Bartleby could withstand such an application of the doctrine of assumptions. But upon second thoughts the success of the plan seemed rather dubious. I resolved to argue the matter over with him again.

"Bartleby," said I, entering the office, with a quietly severe expression, "I am seriously displeased. I am pained, Bartleby. I had thought better of you. I had imagined you of such a gentlemanly organization, that in any delicate dilemma a slight hint would have sufficed – in short, an assumption. But it appears I am deceived. Why," I added, unaffectedly starting, "you have not even touched that money yet," pointing to it, just where I had left it the evening previous.

He answered nothing.

"Will you, or will you not, quit me?" I now demanded in a sudden passion, advancing close to him.

"I would prefer *not* to quit you," he replied, gently emphasizing the *not*.

"What earthly right have you to stay here? Do you pay any rent? Do you pay my taxes? Or is this property yours?"

He answered nothing.

"Are you ready to go on and write now? Are your eyes recovered? Could you copy a small paper for me this morning? Or help examine a few lines? Or step round to the post-office? In a word, will you do any thing at all, to give a coloring to your refusal to depart the premises?"

He silently retired into his hermitage.

I was now in such a state of nervous resentment that I thought it but prudent to check myself at present from further demonstrations. Bartleby and I were alone. I remembered the tragedy of the unfortunate Adams and the still more unfortunate Colt in the solitary office of the latter; and how poor Colt, being dreadfully incensed by Adams, and imprudently permitting himself to get wildly excited, was at unawares hurried into his fatal act – an act which certainly no man could possibly deplore more than the actor himself. Often it had occurred to me in my ponderings upon the subject, that had that altercation taken place in the public street, or at a private residence, it would not have terminated as it did. It was the circumstance of being alone in a solitary office, upstairs, of a building entirely unhallowed by humanizing domestic associations – an uncarpeted office, doubtless, of a dusty, haggard sort of appearance – this it must have been, which greatly helped to enhance the irritable desperation of the hapless Colt.

But when this old Adam of resentment rose in me and tempted me concerning Bartleby, I grappled him and threw him. How? Why, simply by recalling the divine injunction: "A new commandment give I unto you, that ye love one another." Yes, this it was that saved me. Aside from higher considerations, charity often operates as a vastly wise and prudent principle – a great safeguard to its possessor. Men have committed murder for jealousy's sake, and anger's sake, and hatred's sake, and selfishness' sake, and spiritual pride's sake; but no man that ever I heard of, ever committed a diabolical murder for sweet charity's sake. Mere self-interest, then, if no better motive can be enlisted, should, especially with high-tempered men, prompt all beings to charity and philanthropy. At any rate, upon the occasion in question, I strove to drown my exasperated feelings towards the scrivener by benevolently construing his conduct. Poor fellow, poor fellow! thought I, he don't mean anything; and besides, he has seen hard times, and ought to be indulged.

I endeavored also immediately to occupy myself, and at the same time to comfort my despondency. I tried to fancy that in the course of the morning, at such time as might prove agreeable to him, Bartleby, of his own free accord, would emerge from his hermitage, and take up some decided line of march in the direction of the door. But no. Half-past twelve o'clock came; Turkey began to glow in the face, overturn his inkstand, and become generally obstreperous; Nippers abated down into quietude and courtesy; Ginger Nut munched his noon apple; and Bartleby remained standing at his window in one of his profoundest dead-wall reveries. Will it be credited? Ought I to acknowledge it? That afternoon I left the office without saying one further word to him.

Some days now passed, during which, at leisure intervals I looked a little into 'Edwards on the Will', and 'Priestly on Necessity'. Under the circumstances, those books induced a salutary feeling. Gradually I slid into the persuasion that these troubles of mine touching the scrivener, had been all predestinated from eternity, and Bartleby was billeted upon me for some mysterious purpose of an all-wise Providence, which it was not for a mere mortal like me to fathom. Yes, Bartleby, stay there behind your screen, thought I; I shall persecute you no more; you are harmless and noiseless as any of these old chairs; in short, I never feel so private as when I know you are here. At last I see it, I feel it; I penetrate to the predestinated purpose of my life. I am content. Others may have loftier parts to enact; but my mission in this world, Bartleby, is to furnish you with office-room for such period as you may see fit to remain.

I believe that this wise and blessed frame of mind would have continued with me, had it not been for the unsolicited and uncharitable remarks obtruded upon me by my professional friends who visited the rooms. But thus it often is, that the constant friction of illiberal minds wears out at last the best resolves of the more generous. Though to be sure, when I reflected upon it, it was not strange that people entering my office should be struck by the peculiar aspect of the unaccountable Bartleby, and so be tempted to throw out some sinister observations concerning him. Sometimes an attorney having business with me, and calling at my office and finding no one but the scrivener there, would undertake to obtain some sort of precise information from him touching my whereabouts; but without heeding his idle talk, Bartleby would remain standing immovable in the middle of the room. So after contemplating him in that position for a time, the attorney would depart, no wiser than he came.

Also, when a Reference was going on, and the room full of lawyers and witnesses and business was driving fast; some deeply occupied legal gentleman present, seeing Bartleby wholly unemployed, would request him to run round to his (the legal gentleman's) office and fetch some papers for him. Thereupon, Bartleby would tranquilly decline, and yet remain idle as before. Then the lawyer would give a great stare, and turn to me. And what could I say? At last I was made aware that all through the circle of my professional acquaintance, a whisper of wonder was running round, having reference to the strange creature I kept at my office. This worried me very much. And as the idea came upon me of his possibly turning out a long-lived man, and keep occupying my chambers, and denying my authority; and perplexing my visitors; and scandalizing my professional reputation; and casting a general gloom over the premises; keeping soul and body together to the last upon his savings (for doubtless he spent but half a dime a day), and in the end perhaps outlive me, and claim possession of my office by right of his perpetual occupancy: as all these dark anticipations crowded upon me more and more, and my friends continually intruded their relentless remarks upon the apparition in my room; a great change was wrought in me. I resolved to gather all my faculties together, and forever rid me of this intolerable incubus.

Ere revolving any complicated project, however, adapted to this end, I first simply suggested to Bartleby the propriety of his permanent departure. In a calm and serious tone, I commended the idea to his careful and mature consideration. But having taken three days to meditate upon it, he apprised me that his original determination remained the same; in short, that he still preferred to abide with me.

What shall I do? I now said to myself, buttoning up my coat to the last button. What shall I do? What ought I to do? What does conscience say I *should* do with this man, or rather ghost. Rid myself of him, I must; go, he shall. But how? You will not thrust him, the poor, pale, passive mortal – you will not thrust such a helpless creature out of your door? You will not dishonor yourself by such cruelty? No, I will not, I cannot do that. Rather would I let him live and die here, and then mason up his remains in the wall. What then will you do? For all your coaxing, he will not budge. Bribes he leaves under your own paperweight on your table; in short, it is quite plain that he prefers to cling to you.

Then something severe, something unusual must be done. What! Surely you will not have him collared by a constable, and commit his innocent pallor to the common jail? And upon what ground could you procure such a thing to be done? – A vagrant, is he? What! He a vagrant, a wanderer, who refuses to budge? It is because he will *not* be a vagrant, then, that you seek to count him *as* a vagrant. That is too absurd. No visible means of support: there I have him.

Wrong again: for indubitably he *does* support himself, and that is the only unanswerable proof that any man can show of his possessing the means so to do. No more then. Since he will not quit me, I must quit him. I will change my offices; I will move elsewhere; and give him fair notice, that if I find him on my new premises I will then proceed against him as a common trespasser.

Acting accordingly, next day I thus addressed him: "I find these chambers too far from the City Hall; the air is unwholesome. In a word, I propose to remove my offices next week, and shall no longer require your services. I tell you this now, in order that you may seek another place."

He made no reply, and nothing more was said.

On the appointed day I engaged carts and men, proceeded to my chambers, and having but little furniture, everything was removed in a few hours. Throughout, the scrivener remained standing behind the screen, which I directed to be removed the last thing. It was withdrawn; and being folded up like a huge folio, left him the motionless occupant of a naked room. I stood in the entry watching him a moment, while something from within me upbraided me.

I re-entered, with my hand in my pocket – and – and my heart in my mouth.

"Goodbye, Bartleby; I am going – goodbye, and God some way bless you; and take that," slipping something in his hand. But it dropped upon the floor, and then – strange to say – I tore myself from him whom I had so longed to be rid of.

Established in my new quarters, for a day or two I kept the door locked, and started at every footfall in the passages. When I returned to my rooms after any little absence, I would pause at the threshold for an instant, and attentively listen, ere applying my key. But these fears were needless. Bartleby never came nigh me.

I thought all was going well, when a perturbed-looking stranger visited me, inquiring whether I was the person who had recently occupied rooms at No.— Wall-street.

Full of forebodings, I replied that I was.

"Then sir," said the stranger, who proved a lawyer, "you are responsible for the man you left there. He refuses to do any copying; he refuses to do anything; he says he prefers not to; and he refuses to quit the premises."

"I am very sorry, sir," said I, with assumed tranquility, but an inward tremor, "but, really, the man you allude to is nothing to me – he is no relation or apprentice of mine, that you should hold me responsible for him."

"In mercy's name, who is he?"

"I certainly cannot inform you. I know nothing about him. Formerly I employed him as a copyist; but he has done nothing for me now for some time past."

"I shall settle him then – good morning, sir."

Several days passed, and I heard nothing more; and though I often felt a charitable prompting to call at the place and see poor Bartleby, yet a certain squeamishness of I know not what withheld me.

All is over with him, by this time, thought I at last, when through another week no further intelligence reached me. But coming to my room the day after, I found several persons waiting at my door in a high state of nervous excitement.

"That's the man – here he comes," cried the foremost one, whom I recognized as the lawyer who had previously called upon me alone.

"You must take him away, sir, at once," cried a portly person among them, advancing upon me, and whom I knew to be the landlord of No.— Wall-street. "These gentlemen, my tenants, cannot stand it any longer; Mr. B—" pointing to the lawyer, "has turned him out of his room, and he now persists in haunting the building generally, sitting upon the banisters of the stairs by day, and sleeping in the entry by night. Everybody is concerned; clients are leaving the offices; some fears are entertained of a mob; something you must do, and that without delay."

Aghast at this torrent, I fell back before it, and would fain have locked myself in my new quarters. In vain I persisted that Bartleby was nothing to me – no more than to anyone else. In vain: I was the last person known to have anything to do with him, and they held me to the terrible account. Fearful then of being exposed in the papers (as one person present obscurely threatened) I considered the matter, and at length said, that if the lawyer would give me a confidential interview with the scrivener, in his (the lawyer's) own room, I would that afternoon strive my best to rid them of the nuisance they complained of.

Going upstairs to my old haunt, there was Bartleby silently sitting upon the banister at the landing.

"What are you doing here, Bartleby?" said I.

"Sitting upon the banister," he mildly replied.

I motioned him into the lawyer's room, who then left us.

"Bartleby," said I, "are you aware that you are the cause of great tribulation to me, by persisting in occupying the entry after being dismissed from the office?"

No answer.

"Now one of two things must take place. Either you must do something, or something must be done to you. Now what sort of business would you like to engage in? Would you like to re-engage in copying for someone?"

"No; I would prefer not to make any change."

"Would you like a clerkship in a dry-goods store?"

"There is too much confinement about that. No, I would not like a clerkship; but I am not particular."

"Too much confinement," I cried, "why you keep yourself confined all the time!"

"I would prefer not to take a clerkship," he rejoined, as if to settle that little item at once.

"How would a bartender's business suit you? There is no trying of the eyesight in that."

"I would not like it at all; though, as I said before, I am not particular."

His unwonted wordiness inspirited me. I returned to the charge.

"Well then, would you like to travel through the country collecting bills for the merchants? That would improve your health."

"No, I would prefer to be doing something else."

"How then would going as a companion to Europe, to entertain some young gentleman with your conversation – how would that suit you?"

"Not at all. It does not strike me that there is anything definite about that. I like to be stationary. But I am not particular."

"Stationary you shall be then," I cried, now losing all patience, and for the first time in all my exasperating connection with him fairly flying into a passion. "If you do not go away from these premises before night, I shall feel bound – indeed I *am* bound – to – to – to quit the premises myself!" I rather absurdly concluded, knowing not with what possible threat to try to frighten his immobility into compliance. Despairing of all further efforts, I was precipitately leaving him, when a final thought occurred to me – one which had not been wholly unindulged before.

"Bartleby," said I, in the kindest tone I could assume under such exciting circumstances, "will you go home with me now – not to my office, but my dwelling – and remain there till we can conclude upon some convenient arrangement for you at our leisure? Come, let us start now, right away."

"No: at present I would prefer not to make any change at all."

I answered nothing; but effectually dodging everyone by the suddenness and rapidity of my flight, rushed from the building, ran up Wall-street towards Broadway, and jumping into the first omnibus was soon removed from pursuit. As soon as tranquility returned I distinctly perceived that I had now done all that I possibly could, both in respect to the demands of the landlord and his tenants, and with regard to my own desire and sense of duty, to benefit Bartleby, and shield him from rude persecution. I now strove to be entirely care-free and quiescent; and my conscience justified me in the attempt; though indeed it was not so successful as I could have wished. So fearful was I of being again hunted out by the incensed landlord and his exasperated tenants, that, surrendering my business to Nippers, for a few days I drove about the upper part of the town and through the suburbs, in my rockaway; crossed over to Jersey City and Hoboken, and paid fugitive visits to Manhattanville and Astoria. In fact I almost lived in my rockaway for the time.

When again I entered my office, lo, a note from the landlord lay upon the desk. I opened it with trembling hands. It informed me that the writer had sent to the police, and had Bartleby removed to the Tombs as a vagrant. Moreover, since I knew more about him than anyone else, he wished me to appear at that place, and make a suitable statement of the facts. These tidings had a conflicting effect upon me. At first I was indignant; but at last almost approved. The landlord's energetic, summary disposition had led him to adopt a procedure which I do not think I would have decided upon myself; and yet as a last resort, under such peculiar circumstances, it seemed the only plan.

As I afterwards learned, the poor scrivener, when told that he must be conducted to the Tombs, offered not the slightest obstacle, but in his pale unmoving way, silently acquiesced.

Some of the compassionate and curious bystanders joined the party; and headed by one of the constables arm in arm with Bartleby, the silent procession filed its way through all the noise, and heat, and joy of the roaring thoroughfares at noon.

The same day I received the note I went to the Tombs, or to speak more properly, the Halls of Justice. Seeking the right officer, I stated the purpose of my call, and was informed that the individual I described was indeed within. I then assured the functionary that Bartleby was a perfectly honest man, and greatly to be compassionated, however unaccountably eccentric. I narrated all I knew, and closed by suggesting the idea of letting him remain in as indulgent confinement as possible till something less harsh might be done – though indeed I hardly knew what. At all events, if nothing else could be decided upon, the alms-house must receive him. I then begged to have an interview.

Being under no disgraceful charge, and quite serene and harmless in all his ways, they had permitted him freely to wander about the prison, and especially in the inclosed grass-platted yard thereof. And so I found him there, standing all alone in the quietest of the yards, his face towards a high wall, while all around, from the narrow slits of the jail windows, I thought I saw peering out upon him the eyes of murderers and thieves.

"Bartleby!"

"I know you," he said, without looking round, "and I want nothing to say to you."

"It was not I that brought you here, Bartleby," said I, keenly pained at his implied suspicion. "And to you, this should not be so vile a place. Nothing reproachful attaches to you by being here. And see, it is not so sad a place as one might think. Look, there is the sky, and here is the grass."

"I know where I am," he replied, but would say nothing more, and so I left him.

As I entered the corridor again, a broad meat-like man, in an apron, accosted me, and jerking his thumb over his shoulder said – "Is that your friend?"

"Yes."

"Does he want to starve? If he does, let him live on the prison fare, that's all."

"Who are you?" asked I, not knowing what to make of such an unofficially speaking person in such a place.

"I am the grub-man. Such gentlemen as have friends here, hire me to provide them with something good to eat."

"Is this so?" said I, turning to the turnkey.

He said it was.

"Well then," said I, slipping some silver into the grub-man's hands (for so they called him). "I want you to give particular attention to my friend there; let him have the best dinner you can get. And you must be as polite to him as possible."

"Introduce me, will you?" said the grub-man, looking at me with an expression which seemed to say he was all impatience for an opportunity to give a specimen of his breeding.

Thinking it would prove of benefit to the scrivener, I acquiesced; and asking the grub-man his name, went up with him to Bartleby.

"Bartleby, this is Mr. Cutlets; you will find him very useful to you."

"Your sarvant, sir, your sarvant," said the grub-man, making a low salutation behind his apron. "Hope you find it pleasant here, sir; – spacious grounds – cool apartments, sir – hope you'll stay with us some time – try to make it agreeable. May Mrs. Cutlets and I have the pleasure of your company to dinner, sir, in Mrs. Cutlets' private room?"

"I prefer not to dine today," said Bartleby, turning away. "It would disagree with me; I am unused to dinners." So saying he slowly moved to the other side of the inclosure, and took up a position fronting the dead-wall.

"How's this?" said the grub-man, addressing me with a stare of astonishment. "He's odd, aint he?"

"I think he is a little deranged," said I, sadly.

"Deranged? Deranged is it? Well now, upon my word, I thought that friend of yourn was a gentleman forger; they are always pale and genteel-like, them forgers. I can't pity 'em – can't help it, sir. Did you know Monroe Edwards?" he added touchingly, and paused. Then, laying his hand pityingly on my shoulder, sighed, "He died of consumption at Sing-Sing. So you weren't acquainted with Monroe?"

"No, I was never socially acquainted with any forgers. But I cannot stop longer. Look to my friend yonder. You will not lose by it. I will see you again."

Some few days after this, I again obtained admission to the Tombs, and went through the corridors in quest of Bartleby; but without finding him.

"I saw him coming from his cell not long ago," said a turnkey, "maybe he's gone to loiter in the yards."

So I went in that direction.

"Are you looking for the silent man?" said another turnkey passing me. "Yonder he lies – sleeping in the yard there. 'Tis not twenty minutes since I saw him lie down."

The yard was entirely quiet. It was not accessible to the common prisoners. The surrounding walls, of amazing thickness, kept off all sounds behind them. The Egyptian character of the masonry weighed upon me with its gloom. But a soft imprisoned turf grew underfoot. The heart of the eternal pyramids, it seemed, wherein, by some strange magic, through the clefts, grass-seed, dropped by birds, had sprung.

Strangely huddled at the base of the wall, his knees drawn up, and lying on his side, his head touching the cold stones, I saw the wasted Bartleby. But nothing stirred. I paused; then went close up to him; stooped over, and saw that his dim eyes were open; otherwise he seemed profoundly sleeping. Something prompted me to touch him. I felt his hand, when a tingling shiver ran up my arm and down my spine to my feet.

The round face of the grub-man peered upon me now. "His dinner is ready. Won't he dine today, either? Or does he live without dining?"

"Lives without dining," said I, and closed his eyes.

"Eh! – He's asleep, aint he?"

"With kings and counselors," murmured I.

* * *

There would seem little need for proceeding further in this history. Imagination will readily supply the meager recital of poor Bartleby's interment. But ere parting with the reader, let me say, that if this little narrative has sufficiently interested him, to awaken curiosity as to who Bartleby was, and what manner of life he led prior to the present narrator's making his acquaintance, I can only reply, that in such curiosity I fully share, but am wholly unable to gratify it. Yet here I hardly know whether I should divulge one little item of rumor, which came to my ear a few months after the scrivener's decease. Upon what basis it rested, I could never ascertain; and hence, how true it is I cannot now tell. But inasmuch as this vague report has not been without certain strange suggestive interest to me, however sad, it may prove the same with some others; and so I will briefly mention it. The report was this: that Bartleby had been a subordinate clerk in the Dead Letter Office at Washington, from which he had been suddenly removed by a change in the administration. When I think over this rumor, I cannot adequately express the emotions which seize me. Dead letters! Does it not sound like dead men? Conceive a man by nature and misfortune prone to a pallid hopelessness, can any business seem more fitted to heighten it than that of continually handling these dead letters, and assorting them for the flames? For by the cart-load they are annually burned. Sometimes from out the folded paper the pale clerk takes a ring – the finger it was meant for, perhaps, molders in the grave; a bank-note sent in swiftest charity – he whom it would relieve, nor eats nor hungers anymore; pardon for those who died despairing; hope for those who died unhoping; good tidings for those who died stifled by unrelieved calamities. On errands of life, these letters speed to death.

Ah Bartleby! Ah humanity!

The Monster-Maker

W.C. Morrow

A YOUNG MAN of refined appearance, but evidently suffering great mental distress, presented himself one morning at the residence of a singular old man, who was known as a surgeon of remarkable skill. The house was a queer and primitive brick affair, entirely out-of-date, and tolerable only in the decayed part of the city in which it stood. It was large, gloomy, and dark, and had long corridors and dismal rooms; and it was absurdly large for the small family – man and wife – that occupied it. The house described, the man is portrayed – but not the woman. He could be agreeable on occasion, but, for all that, he was but animated mystery. His wife was weak, wan, reticent, evidently miserable, and possibly living a life of dread or horror – perhaps witness of repulsive things, subject of anxieties, and victim of fear and tyranny; but there is a great deal of guessing in these assumptions. He was about sixty-five years of age and she about forty. He was lean, tall, and bald, with thin, smooth-shaven face, and very keen eyes; kept always at home, and was slovenly. The man was strong, the woman weak; he dominated, she suffered.

Although he was a surgeon of rare skill, his practice was almost nothing, for it was a rare occurrence that the few who knew of his great ability were brave enough to penetrate the gloom of his house, and when they did so it was with deaf ear turned to sundry ghoulish stories that were whispered concerning him. These were, in great part, but exaggerations of his experiments in vivisection; he was devoted to the science of surgery.

The young man who presented himself on the morning just mentioned was a handsome fellow, yet of evident weak character and unhealthy temperament – sensitive, and easily exalted or depressed. A single glance convinced the surgeon that his visitor was seriously affected in mind, for there was never bolder skull-grin of melancholia, fixed and irremediable.

A stranger would not have suspected any occupancy of the house. The street door – old, warped, and blistered by the sun – was locked, and the small, faded-green window-blinds were closed. The young man rapped at the door. No answer. He rapped again. Still no sign. He examined a slip of paper, glanced at the number of the house, and then, with the impatience of a child, he furiously kicked the door. There were signs of numerous other such kicks. A response came in the shape of a shuffling footstep in the hall, a turning of the rusty key, and a sharp face that peered through a cautious opening in the door.

"Are you the doctor?" asked the young man.

"Yes, yes! Come in," briskly replied the master of the house.

The young man entered. The old surgeon closed the door and carefully locked it. "This way." he said, advancing to a rickety flight of stairs. The young man followed. The surgeon led the way up the stairs, turned into a narrow, musty-smelling corridor at the left, traversed it, rattling the loose boards under his feet, at the farther end opened a door at the right, and beckoned his visitor to enter. The young man found himself in a pleasant room, furnished in antique fashion and with hard simplicity.

"Sit down," said the old man, placing a chair so that its occupant should face a window that looked out upon a dead wall about six feet from the house. He threw open the blind, and a pale light entered. He then seated himself near his visitor and directly facing him, and with a searching look, that had all the power of a microscope, he proceeded to diagnosticate the case.

"Well?" he presently asked. The young man shifted uneasily in his seat.

"I – I have come to see you," he finally stammered, "because I'm in trouble."

"Ah!"

"Yes; you see, I – that is – I have given it up."

"Ah!" There was pity added to sympathy in the ejaculation.

"That's it. Given it up," added the visitor. He took from his pocket a role of banknotes, and with the utmost deliberation he counted them out upon his knee. "Five thousand dollars," he calmly remarked. "That is for you. It's all I have; but I presume – I imagine – no; that is not the word – assume – yes; that's the word – assume that five thousand – is it really that much? Let me count." He counted again. "That five thousand dollars is a sufficient fee for what I want you to do."

The surgeon's lips curled pityingly – perhaps disdainfully also. "What do you want me to do?" he carelessly inquired.

The young man rose, looked around with a mysterious air, approached the surgeon, and laid the money across his knee. Then he stopped and whispered two words in the surgeon's ear.

These words produced an electric effect. The old man started violently; then, springing to his feet, he caught his visitor angrily, and transfixed him with a look that was as sharp as a knife. His eyes flashed, and he opened his mouth to give utterance to some harsh imprecation, when he suddenly checked himself. The anger left his face, and only pity remained. He relinquished his grasp, picked up the scattered notes, and, offering them to the visitor, slowly said:

"I do not want your money. You are simply foolish. You think you are in trouble. Well, you do not know what trouble is. Your only trouble is that you have not a trace of manhood in your nature. You are merely insane – I shall not say pusillanimous. You should surrender yourself to the authorities, and be sent to a lunatic asylum for proper treatment."

The young man keenly felt the intended insult, and his eyes flashed dangerously.

"You old dog – you insult me thus!" he cried. "Grand airs, these, you give yourself! Virtuously indignant, old murderer, you! Don't want my money, eh? When a man comes to you himself and wants it done, you may fly into a passion and spurn his money; but let an enemy of his come and pay you, and you are only too willing. How many such jobs have you done in this miserable old hole? It is a good thing for you that the police have not run you down, and brought spade and shovel with them. Do you know what is said of you? Do you think you have kept your windows so closely shut that no sound has ever penetrated beyond them? Where do you keep your infernal implements?"

He had worked himself into a high passion. His voice was hoarse, loud, and rasping. His eyes, bloodshot, started from their sockets. His whole frame twitched, and his fingers writhed. But he was in the presence of a man infinitely his superior. Two eyes, like those of a snake, burned two holes through him. An overmastering, inflexible presence confronted one weak and passionate.

The result came.

"Sit down," commanded the stem voice of the surgeon.

It was the voice of father to child, of master to slave. The fury left the visitor, who, weak and overcome, fell upon a chair.

Meanwhile, a peculiar light had appeared in the old surgeon's face, the dawn of a strange idea; a gloomy ray, strayed from the fires of the bottomless pit; the baleful light that illumines the way of the enthusiast. The old man remained a moment in profound abstraction, gleams of eager intelligence bursting momentarily through the cloud of sombre meditation that covered his face.

Then broke the broad light of a deep, impenetrable determination. There was something sinister in it, suggesting the sacrifice of something held sacred. After a struggle, mind had vanquished conscience.

Taking a piece of paper and a pencil, the surgeon carefully wrote answers to questions which he peremptorily addressed to his visitor, such as his name, age, place of residence, occupation, and the like, and the same inquiries concerning his parents, together with other particular matters.

"Does anyone know you came to this house?" he asked.

"No."

"You swear it?"

"Yes."

"But your prolonged absence will cause alarm and lead to search."

"I have provided against that."

"How?"

"By depositing a note in the post, as I came along, announcing my intention to drown myself."

"The river will be dragged."

"What then?" asked the young man, shrugging his shoulders with careless indifference. "Rapid undercurrent, you know. A good many are never found."

There was a pause.

"Are you ready?" finally asked the surgeon.

"Perfectly." The answer was cool and determined.

The manner of the surgeon, however, showed much perturbation. The pallor that had come into his face at the moment his decision was formed became intense. A nervous tremulousness overcame his frame. Above it shone the light of enthusiasm.

"Have you a choice in the method?" he asked.

"Yes; extreme anaesthesia."

"With what agent?"

"The surest and quickest."

"Do you desire any – any subsequent disposition?"

"No; only nullification; simply a blowing out, as of a candle in the wind; a puff – then darkness, without a trace. A sense of your own safety may suggest the method. I leave it to you."

"No delivery to your friends?"

"None whatever."

Another pause.

"Did you say you are quite ready?" asked the surgeon.

"Quite ready."

"And perfectly willing?"

"Anxious."

"Then wait a moment."

With this request the old surgeon rose to his feet and stretched himself. Then with the stealthiness of a cat he opened the door and peered into the hall, listening intently. There was no sound. He softly closed the door and locked it. Then he closed the window blinds and locked them. This done, he opened a door leading into an adjoining room, which, though it had no window, was lighted by means of a small skylight. The young man watched closely. A strange change had come over him. While his determination had not one whit lessened, a look of great relief came into his face, displacing the haggard, despairing look of a half-hour before.

Melancholic then, he was ecstatic now. The opening of a second door disclosed a curious sight. In the center of the room, directly under the skylight, was an operating table, such as is used by demonstrators of anatomy. A glass case against the wall held surgical instruments of every kind. Hanging in another case were human skeletons of various sizes. In sealed jars, arranged on shelves, were monstrosities of divers kinds preserved in alcohol. There were also, among innumerable other articles scattered about the room, a manikin, a stuffed cat, a desiccated human heart, plaster casts of various parts of the body, numerous charts, and a large assortment of drugs and chemicals. There was also a lounge, which could be opened to form a couch. The surgeon opened it and moved the operating-table aside, giving its place to the lounge.

"Come in," he called to his visitor.

The young man obeyed without the least hesitation.

"Take off your coat."

He complied.

"Lie down on that lounge."

In a moment the young man was stretched at full length, eyeing the surgeon. The latter undoubtedly was suffering under great excitement, but he did not waver; his movements were sure and quick. Selecting a bottle containing a liquid, he carefully measured out a certain quantity. While doing this he asked:

"Have you ever had any irregularity of the heart?"

"No."

The answer was prompt, but it was immediately followed by a quizzical look in the speaker's face.

"I presume," he added, "you mean by your question that it might be dangerous to give me a certain drug. Under the circumstances, however, I fail to see any relevancy in your question."

This took the surgeon aback; but he hastened to explain that he did not wish to inflict unnecessary pain, and hence his question.

He placed the glass on a stand, approached his visitor, and carefully examined his pulse.

"Wonderful!" he exclaimed.

"Why?"

"It is perfectly normal."

"Because I am wholly resigned. Indeed, it has been long since I knew such happiness. It is not active, but infinitely sweet."

"You have no lingering desire to retract?"

"None whatever."

The surgeon went to the stand and returned with the draught.

"Take this." he said kindly.

The young man partially raised himself and took the glass in his hand. He did not show the vibration of a single nerve. He drank the liquid, draining the last drop. Then he returned the glass with a smile.

"Thank you," he said; "you are the noblest man that lives. May you always prosper and be happy! You are my benefactor, my liberator. Bless you, bless you! You reach down from your seat with the gods and lift me up into glorious peace and rest. I love you – I love you with all my heart!"

These words, spoken earnestly, in a musical, low voice, and accompanied with a smile of ineffable tenderness, pierced the old man's heart. A suppressed convulsion swept over him; intense anguish wrung his vitals; perspiration trickled down his face. The young man continued to smile.

"Ah, it does me good!" said he.

The surgeon, with a strong effort to control himself, sat down upon the edge of the lounge and took his visitor's wrist, counting the pulse "How long will it take?" the young man asked.

"Ten minutes. Two have passed." The voice was hoarse.

"Ah, only eight minutes more!...Delicious, delicious! I feel it coming...What was that? Ah, I understand. Music...Beautiful!...Coming, coming...Is that – that – water?...Trickling? Dripping? Doctor!"

"Well?"

"Thank you...thank you...Noble man...my savior...my bene...bene...factor...trickling... trickling...Dripping, dripping...Doctor!"

"Well?"

"Doctor!"

"Past hearing," muttered the surgeon.

"Doctor!"

"And blind."

Response was made by a firm grasp of the hand.

"Doctor!"

"And numb."

"Doctor!"

The old man watched and waited.

"Dripping...dripping."

The last drop had run. There was a sigh, and nothing more.

The surgeon laid down the hand.

"The first step," he groaned, rising to his feet; then his whole frame dilated. "The first step is the most difficult, yet the simplest. A providential delivery into my hands of that for which I have hungered for forty years. No withdrawal now! It is possible, because scientific; rational, but perilous. If I succeed – if? I shall succeed. I will succeed...And after success – what?...Yes, what? Publish the plan and the result? The gallows...So long as it shall exist...and I exist, the gallows. That much...But how account for its presence? Ah, that pinches hard! I must trust to the future."

He tore himself from the revery and started.

"I wonder if she heard or saw anything."

With that reflection he cast a glance upon the form on the lounge, and then left the room, locked the door, locked also the door of the outer room, walked down two or three corridors, penetrated to a remote part of the house, and rapped at a door. It was opened by his wife. He, by this time, had regained complete mastery over himself.

"I thought I heard someone in the house just now," he said, "but I can find no one."

"I heard nothing."

He was greatly relieved.

"I did hear someone knock at the door less than an hour ago," she resumed, "and heard you speak, I think. Did he come in?"

"No."

The woman glanced at his feet and seemed perplexed…"I am almost certain," she said, "that I heard footfalls in the house, and yet I see that you are wearing slippers."

"Oh, I had on my shoes then!"

"That explains it," said the woman, satisfied; "I think the sound you heard must have been caused by rats."

"Ah, that was it!" exclaimed the surgeon. Leaving, he closed the door, reopened it, and said, "I do not wish to be disturbed today." He said to himself, as he went down the hall, "All is clear there."

He returned to the room in which his visitor lay, and made a careful examination.

"Splendid specimen!" he softly exclaimed; "Every organ sound; every function perfect; fine, large frame; well-shaped muscles, strong and sinewy; capable of wonderful development – if given opportunity…I have no doubt it can be done. Already I have succeeded with a dog – a task less difficult than this, for in a man the cerebrum overlaps the cerebellum, which is not the case with a dog. This gives a wide range for accident, with but one opportunity in a lifetime! In the cerebrum, the intellect and the affections; in the cerebellum, the senses and the motor forces; in the medulla oblongata, control of the diaphragm. In these two latter lie all the essentials of simple existence. The cerebrum is merely an adornment; that is to say, reason and the affections are almost purely ornamental. I have already proved it. My dog, with its cerebrum removed, was idiotic, but it retained its physical senses to a certain degree."

While thus ruminating he made careful preparations. He moved the couch, replaced the operating-table under the skylight, selected a number of surgical instruments, prepared certain drug mixtures, and arranged water, towels, and all the accessories of a tedious surgical operation.

Suddenly he burst into laughter.

"Poor fool!" he exclaimed. "Paid me five thousand dollars to kill him! Didn't have the courage to snuff his own candle! Singular, singular, the queer freaks these madmen have! You thought you were dying, poor idiot! Allow me to inform you, sir, that you are as much alive at this moment as ever you were in your life. But it will be all the same to you. You shall never be more conscious than you are now; and for all practical purposes, so far as they concern you, you are dead henceforth, though you shall live. By the way, how should you feel without a head? Ha, ha, ha…But that's a sorry joke."

He lifted the unconscious form from the lounge and laid it upon the operating table.

* * *

About three years afterwards the following conversation was held between a captain of police and a detective:

"She may be insane," suggested the captain.

"I think she is."

"And yet you credit her story!"

"I do."

"Singular!"

"Not at all. I myself have learned something."

"What!"

"Much, in one sense; little, in another. You have heard those queer stories of her husband. Well, they are all nonsensical – probably with one exception. He is generally a harmless old fellow, but peculiar. He has performed some wonderful surgical operations. The people in his neighborhood are ignorant, and they fear him and wish to be rid of him; hence they tell a great many lies about him, and they come to believe their own stories. The one important thing that I have learned is that he is almost insanely enthusiastic on the subject of surgery – especially experimental surgery; and with an enthusiast there is hardly such a thing as a scruple. It is this that gives me confidence in the woman's story."

"You say she appeared to be frightened?"

"Doubly so – first, she feared that her husband would learn of her betrayal of him; second, the discovery itself had terrified her."

"But her report of this discovery is very vague," argued the captain. "He conceals everything from her. She is merely guessing."

"In part – yes; in other part – no. She heard the sounds distinctly, though she did not see clearly. Horror closed her eyes. What she thinks she saw is, I admit, preposterous; but she undoubtedly saw something extremely frightful. There are many peculiar little circumstances. He has eaten with her but few times during the last three years, and nearly always carries his food to his private rooms. She says that he either consumes an enormous quantity, throws much away, or is feeding something that eats prodigiously. He explains this to her by saying that he has animals with which he experiments. This is not true. Again, he always keeps the door to these rooms carefully locked; and not only that, but he has had the doors doubled and otherwise strengthened, and has heavily barred a window that looks from one of the rooms upon a dead wall a few feet distant."

"What does it mean?" asked the captain.

"A prison."

"For animals, perhaps."

"Certainly not."

"Why!"

"Because, in the first place, cages would have been better; in the second place, the security that he has provided is infinitely greater than that required for the confinement of ordinary animals."

"All this is easily explained: he has a violent lunatic under treatment."

"I had thought of that, but such is not the fact."

"How do you know?"

"By reasoning thus: He has always refused to treat cases of lunacy; he confines himself to surgery: the walls are not padded, for the woman has heard sharp blows upon them; no human strength, however morbid, could possibly require such resisting strength as has been provided; he would not be likely to conceal a lunatic's confinement from the woman; no lunatic could consume all the food that he provides; so extremely violent mania as these precautions indicate could not continue three years; if there is a lunatic in the case it is very probable that there should have been communication with someone outside concerning the patient, and there has been none; the woman has listened at the keyhole and has heard no human voice within: and last, we have heard the woman's vague description of what she saw."

"You have destroyed every possible theory," said the captain, deeply interested, "and have suggested nothing new."

"Unfortunately, I cannot; but the truth may be very simple, after all. The old surgeon is so peculiar that I am prepared to discover something remarkable."

"Have you suspicions?"

"I have."

"Of what?"

"A crime. The woman suspects it."

"And betrays it?"

"Certainly, because it is so horrible that her humanity revolts; so terrible that her whole nature demands of her that she hand over the criminal to the law; so frightful that she is in mortal terror; so awful that it has shaken her mind."

"What do you propose to do?" asked the captain.

"Secure evidence. I may need help."

"You shall have all the men you require. Go ahead, but be careful. You are on dangerous ground. You would be a mere plaything in the hands of that man."

Two days afterwards the detective again sought the captain.

"I have a queer document," he said, exhibiting torn fragments of paper, on which there was writing. "The woman stole it and brought it to me. She snatched a handful out of a book, getting only a part of each of a few leaves."

These fragments, which the men arranged as best they could, were (the detective explained) torn by the surgeon's wife from the first volume of a number of manuscript books which her husband had written on one subject – the very one that was the cause of her excitement. "About the time that he began a certain experiment three years ago," continued the detective, "he removed everything from the suite of two rooms containing his study and his operating room. In one of the bookcases that he removed to a room across the passage was a drawer, which he kept locked, but which he opened from time to time. As is quite common with such pieces of furniture, the lock of the drawer is a very poor one; and so the woman, while making a thorough search yesterday, found a key on her bunch that fitted this lock. She opened the drawer, drew out the bottom book of a pile (so that its mutilation would more likely escape discovery), saw that it might contain a clue, and tore out a handful of the leaves. She had barely replaced the book, locked the drawer, and made her escape when her husband appeared. He hardly ever allows her to be out of his sight when she is in that part of the house."

The fragments read as follows:

"...the motory nerves. I had hardly dared to hope for such a result, although inductive reasoning had convinced me of its possibility, my only doubt having been on the score of my lack of skill. Their operation has been only slightly impaired, and even this would not have been the case had the operation been performed in infancy, before the intellect had sought and obtained recognition as an essential part of the whole. Therefore I state, as a proved fact, that the cells of the motory nerves have inherent forces sufficient to the purposes of those nerves. But hardly so with the sensory nerves. These latter are, in fact, an offshoot of the former, evolved from them by natural (though not essential) heterogeneity, and to a certain extent are dependent on the evolution and expansion of a contemporaneous tendency, that developed into mentality, or mental function. Both of these latter tendencies, these evolvements, are merely refinements of the motory system, and not independent entities; that is to say, they are blossoms of a plant that propagates from its roots. The motory system is the first.

"...nor am I surprised that such prodigious muscular energy is developing. It promises yet to surpass the wildest dreams of human strength. I account for it thus: the powers of *assimilation had reached their full development. They had formed the habit of doing a certain amount of work. They sent their product to all parts of the system. As a result of my operation the consumption of these products was reduced fully one-half; that is to say, about one-half of the demand for them was withdrawn. But force of habit required the production to proceed. This production was strength, vitality, energy. Thus double the usual quantity of this strength, this energy, was stored in the remaining...developed a tendency that did surprise me. Nature, no longer suffering the distraction of extraneous interferences, and at the same time being cut in two (as it were), with reference to this case, did not fully adjust herself to the new situation, as does a magnet, which, when divided at the point of equilibrium, renews itself in its two fragments by investing each with opposite poles; but, on the contrary, being severed from laws that theretofore had controlled her, and possessing still that mysterious tendency to develop into something more potential and complex, she blindly (having lost her lantern) pushed her demands for material that would secure this development, and as blindly used it when it was given her. Hence this marvellous voracity, this insatiable hunger, this wonderful ravenousness; and hence also (there being nothing but the physical part to receive this vast storing of energy) this strength that is becoming almost hourly Herculean, almost daily appalling. It is becoming a serious...narrow escape today. By some means, while I was absent, it unscrewed the stopper of the silver feeding-pipe (which I have already herein termed 'the artificial mouth'), and in one of its curious antics, allowed all the chyle to escape from its stomach through the tube. Its hunger then became intense – I may say furious. I placed my hands upon it to push it into a chair, when, feeling my touch, it caught me, clasped me around the neck, and would have crushed me to death instantly had I not slipped from its powerful grasp. Thus I always had to be on my guard. I have provided the screw stopper with a spring catch, and usually docile when not hungry; slow and heavy in its movements, which are, of course, purely unconscious: any apparent excitement in movement being due to local irregularities in the blood-supply of the cerebellum, which, if I did not have it enclosed in a silver case that is immovable, I should expose and—"*

The captain looked at the detective with a puzzled air.

"I don't understand it all," said he.

"Nor I," agreed the detective. "What do you propose to do?"

"Make a raid."

"Do you want a man?"

"Three. The strongest men in your district."

"Why, the surgeon is old and weak!"

"Nevertheless, I want three strong men; and for that matter, prudence really advises me to take twenty."

* * *

At one o'clock the next morning a cautious, scratching sound might have been heard in the ceiling of the surgeon's operating-room. Shortly afterwards the skylight sash was carefully raised and laid aside. A man peered into the opening. Nothing could be heard.

"That is singular," thought the detective.

He cautiously lowered himself to the floor by a rope, and then stood for some moments listening intently. There was a dead silence. He shot the slide of a dark-lantern, and rapidly swept the room with the light. It was bare, with the exception of a strong iron staple and ring, screwed to the floor in the center of the room, with a heavy chain attached. The detective then turned his attention to the outer room; it was perfectly bare. He was deeply perplexed. Returning to the inner room, he called softly to the men to descend. While they were thus occupied he re-entered the outer room and examined the door. A glance sufficed. It was kept closed by a spring attachment, and was locked with a strong spring-lock that could be drawn from the inside.

"The bird has just flown," mused the detective. "A singular accident! The discovery and proper use of this thumb-bolt might not have happened once in fifty years, if my theory is correct." By this time the men were behind him. He noiselessly drew the spring-bolt, opened the door, and looked out into the hall. He heard a peculiar sound. It was as though a gigantic lobster was floundering and scrambling in some distant part of the old house. Accompanying this sound was a loud, whistling breathing, and frequent rasping gasps.

These sounds were heard by still another person, the surgeon's wife; for they originated very near her rooms, which were a considerable distance from her husband's. She had been sleeping lightly, tortured by fear and harassed by frightful dreams. The conspiracy into which she had recently entered, for the destruction of her husband, was a source of great anxiety. She constantly suffered from the most gloomy forebodings, and lived in an atmosphere of terror. Added to the natural horror of her situation were those countless sources of fear which a fright-shaken mind creates and then magnifies. She was, indeed, in a pitiable state, having been driven first by terror to desperation, and then to madness.

Startled thus out of fitful slumber by the noise at her door, she sprang from her bed to the floor, every terror that lurked in her acutely tense in mind and diseased imagination starting up and almost overwhelming her. The idea of flight – one of the strongest of all instincts – seized upon her, and she ran to the door, beyond all control of reason. She drew the bolt and flung the door wide open, and then fled wildly down the passage, the appalling hissing and rasping gurgle ringing in her ears apparently with a thousandfold intensity. But the passage was in absolute darkness, and she had not taken a half-dozen steps when she tripped upon an unseen object on the floor. She fell headlong upon it, encountering in it a large, soft, warm substance that writhed and squirmed, and from which came the sounds that had awakened her. Instantly realizing her situation, she uttered a shriek such as only an unnamable terror can inspire. But hardly had her cry started the echoes in the empty corridor when it was suddenly stifled. Two prodigious arms had closed upon her and crushed the life out of her.

The cry performed the office of directing the detective and his assistants, and it also aroused the old surgeon, who occupied rooms between the officers and the objects of their search. The cry of agony pierced him to the marrow, and a realization of the cause of it burst upon him with frightful force.

"It has come at last!" he gasped, springing from his bed.

Snatching from a table a dimly-burning lamp and a long knife which he had kept at hand for three years, he dashed into the corridor. The four officers had already started forward, but when they saw him emerge they halted in silence. In that moment of stillness the surgeon paused to listen. He heard the hissing sound and the clumsy floundering of a bulky, living object in the direction of his wife's apartments. It evidently was advancing towards him. A turn in the corridor shut out the view. He turned up the light, which revealed a ghastly pallor in his face.

"Wife!" he called.

There was no response. He hurriedly advanced, the four men following quietly. He turned the angle of the corridor, and ran so rapidly that by the time the officers had come in sight of him again he was twenty steps away. He ran past a huge, shapeless object, sprawling, crawling, and floundering along, and arrived at the body of his wife.

He gave one horrified glance at her face, and staggered away. Then a fury seized him.

Clutching the knife firmly, and holding the lamp aloft, he sprang toward the ungainly object in the corridor. It was then that the officers, still advancing cautiously, saw a little more clearly, though still indistinctly, the object of the surgeon's fury, and the cause of the look of unutterable anguish in his face. The hideous sight caused them to pause. They saw what appeared to be a man, yet evidently was not a man; huge, awkward, shapeless; a squirming, lurching, stumbling mass, completely naked. It raised its broad shoulders. It had no head, but instead of it a small metallic ball surmounting its massive neck.

"Devil!" exclaimed the surgeon, raising the knife.

"Hold, there!" commanded a stern voice.

The surgeon quickly raised his eyes and saw the four officers, and for a moment fear paralyzed his arm.

"The police!" he gasped.

Then, with a look of redoubled fury, he sent the knife to the hilt into the squirming mass before him. The wounded monster sprang to its feet and wildly threw its arms about, meanwhile emitting fearful sounds from a silver tube through which it breathed. The surgeon aimed another blow, but never gave it. In his blind fury he lost his caution, and was caught in an iron grasp. The struggling threw the lamp some feet toward the officers, and it fell to the floor, shattered to pieces. Simultaneously with the crash the oil took fire, and the corridor was filled with flame.

The officers could not approach. Before them was the spreading blaze, and secure behind it were two forms struggling in a fearful embrace. They heard cries and gasps, and saw the gleaming of a knife.

The wood in the house was old and dry. It took fire at once, and the flames spread with great rapidity. The four officers turned and fled, barely escaping with their lives. In an hour nothing remained of the mysterious old house and its inmates but a blackened ruin.

Gothic American

Joe Nazare

YOU OWE HIM THIS, Regan's conscience kept prodding her.

Actually, she owed him a helluva lot more, after everything Beale had done for her over the past eight months. He'd been a godsend, extending a much-needed hand when she tripped all over her Twelve Steps and was too ashamed to call her sponsor. Even now he was helping her get back on her feet, having gladly volunteered to deliver her to Omaha. "Why go Greyhound when you could cross the Midwest in the Bealemobile?" he'd offered with a cheek-dimpling grin.

So she couldn't really complain that the proposed diversion (Beale had seized upon the idea while studying the road atlas over a lunch of truck-stop greaseburgers) would lengthen their trip. Beale – whose license wasn't suspended for the next year and a half – had been the one stuck behind the wheel all morning since heading out from Indy. On top of that, he refused to accept any gas money, which Regan considered no small favor now that she'd officially joined the ranks of the unemployed. Yet even if she hadn't racked up such a debt of gratitude, she doubted she could have vetoed Beale's request. He was so clearly geeked to go sightseeing, the excitement in his eyes beaming through the rounded lenses of his glasses.

If Beale needed his Americana fix, so be it. Regan agreed to the detour off I-80 West, just sat back and let Beale steer the Ford Focus down towards Eldon. She was fine with her decision, didn't have the first reason to begin second-guessing it – at least not until they pulled into a service station located in the middle of the nowhere that was southeastern Iowa.

The place looked overdue for demolition. Protracted weathering had flayed most of the gray paint off the rickety garage door, and cracks webbed the window of the adjoining 'office' area. Scraggly patches of grass had slithered up through fissures in the pavement, as if aspiring to the same heights reached by the sallow weeds ringing the property. The matted German shepherd curled atop a bald tire alongside the station failed to render the view more scenic.

An attendant scurried out of the office, no doubt welcoming the break in the monotony. He nodded a greeting, and Beale instructed him to fill the car with regular. "Beale, why don't you let me put this on my debit card?" Regan gestured. Selling off her clunker had left her with *some* funds at least.

"Nope, I got this," Beale said. Lowering his voice to a conspiratorial whisper, he added: "This place looks like a strictly cash operation, anyway."

For the next half-minute, they sat and watched the attendant squeegee the windshield squeaky clean. Finishing before the gassing up had completed, the man stood waiting beside the lone pump – and staring right into the car at them. Just as unabashedly, he started scratching himself, like a baboon trapped in a fleabag motel room. He strummed his olive-shirted stomach, either shoulder blade, the stubbled skin of his neck.

Regan had no idea what to make of such behavior. The attendant hardly looked like some dentally-challenged grotesque who'd missed the casting call for *Deliverance*. If anything, he was vaguely handsome, in an Adrien Brody sort of way. Still, his complete lack of self-consciousness as he peered into the car unsettled her, stirred her own sense of awkwardness. Feeling the need to say something – anything – she leaned forward and called through the driver's side window: "Excuse me? Would you happen to know how long it takes to get to Eldon from here?"

"Eldon," he repeated. Even his voice was scratchy – pumice stone on sandpaper. "No more'n a twenty minute ride."

That said, he simply resumed his car-side vigil. Regan struggled to conjure further conversation, couldn't think of a damned thing to say. But then, out of nowhere, the man posed his own question: "So you folks are heading over to see the American Gothic House, yeah?"

Regan flinched as the gas nozzle clanked in curt announcement of a filled tank. Beale meantime sat eying the attendant. "What makes you say that?" he asked.

"That'll be thirty-two dollars," Mr. Itchy said flatly, and for a second Regan thought the nervy bastard was price-setting a bribe. But he proceeded to explain as he extracted and holstered the nozzle and recapped the tank. "It's a pretty easy guess. Those plates there on your car tell me you've come from a ways away." He stepped over and framed himself in Beale's window. "So unless you all just happen to have kin in Eldon, I figure you must be planning to go see the House."

Crooking his arm as he spoke, the attendant started rooting in his right ear with his long-nailed pinky. It looked to Regan like he'd buried the finger up to the second knuckle. She half-expected the worming digit to poke out the other ear, its wax-coated tip glinting in the late afternoon sun.

"Eldon ain't much of a tourist trap," the attendant continued. "Only has that one claim to fame – or maybe two, now that they built the edgacation center to go along with the House. Still, you won't see many billboards out on the main roads advertising the place. Really the only people who find their way there are the ones who've been deliberately seeking it out."

While the attendant chattered, Beale unpocketed his wallet and withdrew a twenty, ten, and five. "Here you go. Don't worry about the change." Beale extended his arm, yet appeared careful not to touch the man's hand when making the transaction.

"Thank you sir." Then, as if to repay the small tip with a verbal one, the attendant added: "Listen, I don't know it'd be wise if you folks drove ouT THERE RI—"

But Beale had started to pull away as soon as he relinquished the cash. Peering through the car's rear window, Regan watched the attendant shrug – then scratch – his shoulders.

"Beale!" she rebuked him, despite her inner relief at leaving the service station behind. "That guy was still talking. It sounded like…he wanted to warn us about something."

"Hunh?" Beale's face was a portrait of obliviousness. He contemplated the sideview mirror for a moment. "Well, I wouldn't fret about it," he told her, conveying the same nonchalance that had enabled him to saunter through his own Twelve Step program. "I got the feeling he was trying to have a little fun with us. Hicking it up for the city folk. Think about it: how else does a guy like that keep himself entertained out here?"

That's exactly what I'd rather not *think about*, Regan mentally answered. She dropped the subject, though, not wanting this to turn into one of those scenes from the Stephen King stories she used to read during lunchtime in the break room at Borders. Scenes where a husband and wife start squabbling as their road trip takes a turn for the weird. The lively imitation of such art, Regan could do without.

Besides, she and Beale weren't even a couple – just friends who'd bonded over coffee following an AA meeting they'd both attended. Sitting in Starbucks, they shed some of the anonymity, readily identifying themselves as Beale Stevens and Regan O'Connor. Nonetheless, the conversation had gravitated towards first names. Beale confided that his barmaid mother christened him after the bustling Memphis street along which she worked (and apparently played, once her shift had ended). When Regan in turn spoke of her dislike for her birth name, Beale remarked, "Could be worse, right? Your parents could've called you Goneril and made you sound like some ointment to treat an STD." They both laughed, even if Regan didn't quite get the joke.

The remembrance evoked no smile now as she peered out the passenger-side window and took in the rural landscape. While all those farmhouses and expansive fields weren't particularly disturbing, the local populace was. At one point she spotted a gaunt, straw-haired woman standing in her front yard hosing down her handful of children like a litter of mucked pigs. The kids wore only cut-off jeans, and one girl appeared stark naked, but Beale sped by too fast for Regan to determine if the scene was one of merriment or punishment. Whatever was going on, the family had been too preoccupied to notice the passing car. The same couldn't be said for most of the other Iowans glimpsed. Men riding mowers, wives taking in the wash, kids playing on jerry-rigged swings, all stopped what they were doing, as if they innately sensed the encroachment of outsiders. Squinting from afar, they tracked the movement of Beale's midnight-blue Ford. Their sober stares cued up the shrill theme music to *The Twilight Zone* in Regan's head.

"Hey, why so serious?" Beale hailed her. "Don't worry, things'll turn around for you in no time once you get settled in at your sister's."

"No, it's not that." That was the least of her concerns right now. "Beale…there's something not right here, with this whole area."

"Absolutely," he said, startling Regan with the rapid affirmation. "What isn't right is our government's utter disregard for the plight of the Midwestern farmer. Doesn't matter how many songs Mellencamp writes calling attention to the situation. But these here are good country people," Beale attempted to assure her. "They might not be as well off as folks in other parts of the U.S., but that doesn't mean *they're* off."

Maybe Beale was right. Her worry was probably needless, these people ultimately harmless. (*And who are you to judge anyhow?* a censorious voice barked inside her head.) Regan withdrew her focus into the car, and concentrated on studying the road atlas in her lap.

She verified that they were still on course as Beale piloted them south on Competine Road and then IA-16 hooking into Eldon. Beale kept insisting that they'd have little trouble locating the house once they entered the small town, and sure enough, after a few wandering turns, they found themselves on 'American Gothic Street'.

The recent construction on the left dominated the scene, easily overshadowing the metal sheds of the water works plant facing it across the parking lot's unlined slab. AMERICAN GOTHIC HOUSE CENTER, read the dark lettering on the front of the long, gabled building. A white rectangular banner alongside the entrance encouraged visitors to pose for their own photograph in front of the famous House – Costumes and Props Available Inside the Center! That all felt like a false lure now, though, since it was obvious that the place had already closed shop for the evening. The present scene created a perfect picture of desertion, looked as empty and lifeless as a long-since-harvested cornfield.

"Ahh, man!" Frowning, Beale twisted his wrist and stared at his watch as if it were somehow to blame. Seconds later, he lamented, "Well, I've got a good idea what that pump jockey was trying to tell us."

Regan didn't take much solace in Beale's deduction. Her gaze had telescoped through the windshield and locked onto the House up ahead.

She didn't know why the sight of the place vexed her. It was a quaint little home, almost chapel-like with its white exterior and Gothic trappings. Maybe, having been conditioned by countless viewings of the painting, she found it strange to behold an actual three-dimensional building here and not just a theater flat of a habitat. Or maybe it was the conspicuous absence of the familiar couple out front throwing her off. The lonesome scene certainly exposed more of the house, in particular the porch sporting a black-scaled roof and vaguely skeletal posts.

Regan thought of all the spoofs and visual echoes of the painting that she'd seen over the years. In *The Rocky Horror Picture Show*. On bags of Newman's Own pretzels. Photos of the cut-and-pasted heads of Presidential couples, who were transplanted onto the lawn of a much humbler white house. Paris Hilton and Nicole Ritchie posing like a pair of farm harlots to promote their reality-TV show. There were probably hundreds more Regan couldn't recall or wasn't even aware of. Sitting there now in Eldon, she wondered if all the attention given to the painting's human figures – whose popularity spiked with every imitation of their original pose – hadn't distracted viewers from the curious building rearing over the couple's shoulders.

Not that she could really point fingers at others for their skewed perspective. Back in her only semester at Indiana State, one of the assignments for her Freshman Comp class had called for her to draft an essay about her impressions of Grant Wood's *American Gothic*. While emphasizing the blackness of the painting, her response had focused more on the residents than the residence. Regan wrote about the slanted stare of the chicken-necked Woman (wife? daughter? *both?*), whose pale blue eyes bore the empty look of the traumatized. The serpentine coil of hair that had sprung loose further implied that all was not in order on her top floor. Also, the pattern on the Woman's apron closely matched the curtains hung in the upstairs window; perhaps that was where this female was normally locked away. (Because wasn't that what American Gothic was all about? – the horror hidden behind closed doors and shaded windows, the dark side of everyday life in Anytown, U.S.A.) Then there was the black-jacketed Man, looking glum as an undertaker. The shape of his representative pitchfork was clearly reflected in the folds of his overalls and the lines of his shirt, but also more subtly in the wrinkles entrenched in his long, thin face. This harmful farmer appeared ready to reach out and stab you right in the heart or up under the chin, not invite you in for some apple pie. His rigid posture suggested a man standing guard rather than posing for a family portrait in front of the home. That slight arch to his brows above his dead-on, bespectacled gaze seemed to challenge, to dare you to defy his claim to what he believed rightfully his.

Regan could also remember the not-quite-constructive criticism she'd received on her essay draft. Her adjunct professor's lone line of feedback had been: "I think you might be projecting too much onto Mr. Wood's painting." Regan took the remark as a jab at her outfit-matching black lipstick and pallid complexion (her Goth phase had coincided with her short-lived college career). Not that she really gave a damn about her teacher's opinion of her. The guy was a perv: he wore too much cologne to class, and Regan constantly caught him gauging the cleavage of the front-row floozies wearing too little shirt.

"—is, Regan," Beale's words yanked her out of her reverie. He pulled the car up ahead to the top end of the Center's parking lot. "The House that inspired America's most famous painting." After a few seconds of awed inspection, he killed the engine and reached for the door handle. "Well, we came this far," he said. "Might as well go have ourselves a look."

Regan gave up the sanctuary of the car only because she didn't relish being separated from Beale. She scampered around the front bumper and down a length of sidewalk that soon widened into what looked like the concrete mold of a crop circle. The designated viewing area was bracketed by a pair of park benches, as if someone might actually sit there and idle away the day.

Pulling up alongside Beale, Regan joined him in mute appraisal. They faced a sun-punished lawn, the grass brown and patchy. The sequence of flagstones leading towards the House struck Regan as less a pathway than a row of uncarved grave markers. Off to the right, a faded American flag hung limp as a dishrag atop a silver pole.

A sawhorse rested just behind a now-hard-right turn, on a jut of pavement marking the loss of a road that once crossed directly in front of the House. The same road that had delivered Grant Wood to this fateful spot all those years ago. Such redirection of traffic no doubt had been designed to distinguish, to set off the House as historic landmark. But there was also an uncanny quality to the isolation; with no neighboring homes adjacent to it, the place appeared remote, removed from civilization. Lifting her gaze to the wooded backdrop, Regan found no sign of the church steeple that had pierced the canopy of Chia-Pet-looking trees in the painting.

Finally, Regan allowed herself a close-up look at the House itself. The rectangular rear section stretching perpendicular to the famous A-frame gave the building a squatting, Sphinx-like aspect. It also brought to mind the old dog they'd seen lazing outside the service station, what now seemed a lifetime ago.

Standing atop the viewing area cupping her elbows, Regan noticed that the edifice's two downstairs windows were white-curtained, whereas the cross-paned arch on the second story had been opaqued by a pulled shade. Black and patternless, the covering gave the window the look of a yawning cave mouth.

"Supposedly," Beale broke the silence, "there's a private caretaker who resides here year-round. No visitors are allowed inside, though, because the building wouldn't stand up to the traffic." As Regan turned to ask how he knew any of this, Beale shrugged his shoulders and grinned sheepishly. "A few months back I read a book some Harvard professor wrote about the cultural history of the painting."

Regan returned her scrutiny to the House, which like its brush-stroked counterpart sat beneath a sky so blue and cloudless it looked dubious. Eventually, she ventured: "Beale, what do you think the painting was s'posed to mean?"

He puffed his cheeks and exhaled audibly before responding. "Impossible to say for sure, especially considering that Grant Wood himself made so many contradictory statements about it. He insisted he wasn't poking fun at Iowans by depicting a couple of grim-and-proper Bible-thumpers. Claimed he simply wanted the people to match the shape and spirit of the house. But he might've just said all that in self-defense: apparently, the locals were ready to grab their own pitchforks when they first found out about his painting. Farmwives would call Wood up at home and curse him out, tell him he should have his head bashed in. One woman even threatened to come over and bite off his ear. Talk about suffering for your art, right?" Beale chuckled, but then slowly shook his head. "The painting brought Wood a slew of publicity – probably more than he ever could've imagined when he starting brushing away on a piece of cheap beaver board – but I don't think it brought him much peace in his lifetime.

"But to get back to your question: what was Wood driving at? Was his painting a celebration of Midwestern uprightness? A satire of religious pretentiousness? A hint at something even more sinister? I wonder, though, if trying to fix on a single explanation misses the whole point. Maybe ambiguity is exactly what *American Gothic* forces us to reflect on – the difficulty of ever knowing for sure. In the end, that subtle, almost imperceptible split of the couple's faces into sunlit and shadowed halves might be the most telling detail of the entire painting."

Regan stared dumbstruck at Beale for several beats after he finished speaking; she'd had no idea he was so interested in this subject, that he had devoted so much thought to it. Finally, nodding back toward the Center, she mouthed a little white lie for his benefit. "Sorry we didn't get to do the whole picture thing."

"Who said we have to miss out on that?" Beale winked, then hurried around to the back of the car and unlocked the trunk. Watching him rummage through it, Regan felt her chest tighten; she waited for him to pull out some Norman Bates ensemble of matronly dress and gray wig for her to wear. Her apprehensions shamed her once she spotted what Beale held aloft.

"I didn't know you had a digital camera," she said as he stripped the device of its gray casing.

"Yeah, I'm not much of a photo person," he admitted. "I only break this old thing out on special occasions." The camera, a big and boxy model, seemed monstrous in comparison to the sleek handhelds popular these days. Leave it to Beale to be so out of sync with modern trends.

"Hope the batteries still have some life left in 'em," he said. Then, after fumbling with more buttons: "All right, looks like we're in business. So: ready for your portrait?"

Regan couldn't suppress her shudder. "No, I—"

"Oh, c'mon. I'm gonna need something to remember you by, what with you moving all the way to another state."

And all at once, Regan grasped that she was abandoning Beale, leaving her friend (who didn't seem to have many others) behind in Indianapolis. She'd promised to stay in touch with him, of course, but wasn't that what people always said in such situations?

An undeniable sense of guilt burgeoned within her. Had she ever been a true friend to Beale? Or had she just used him all along, taken advantage of the help he was always so quick to give?

Just let him have his picture, the stern words sounded in her head. As if prodded, she stood up straighter, but remained hesitant. "Um. Don't you want me to take one of you?" she offered.

"Sure. Just let me get you first." Waving his hand emphatically, Beale directed her towards the center of the concrete circle and the symbol of the Gothic arch etched there like an ancient rune. No doubt designed to help amateurs line up the shot, the marker somehow made the process of posing for pictures seem all the more ritualistic.

"Awesome," Beale serenaded Regan's grudging repositioning. With his camera turned for a vertical framing, he began sizing her up through the viewfinder. "Hey, betcha didn't know that the two people in the painting posed separately, and not even here in Eldon. The woman was Wood's sister, and the man his dentist over in Cedar Rapids."

Such trivia didn't interest Regan right now. She was too conscious of the House looming behind her. An icy sensation spread across her shoulder blades, and the hairs on the nape of her neck grew stiff as bristles. Worse, it felt like a circus elephant had just squatted down onto her bladder. Regan inhaled through clenched teeth. "Eww, Beale. I really have to pee."

"Ok, ok. We'll be quick here, I promise. Didn't we pass a coffee shop on our way through town?"

Regan doubted she could hold out that long. But before they could move on, they had to get these damn pictures out of the way. So she braced herself, stilled her pistoning right foot. She gazed at the camera, unable to force a smile.

Anxiousness perhaps sharpening her awareness, Regan caught sight of the American Gothic House perfectly framed within the exposed left lens of Beale's glasses. In that same miniature mirror Regan detected a faint rustle behind the upstairs window – the *shut* window, deterring any hint of a breeze from without. Deprived of the natural explanation for such movement, Regan jumped to a darker alternative: she imagined the shade itself growing animate in anticipation of the image-taking below.

Instant, instinctive dread flooded her. Even as the spit evaporated from her mouth, the desperate request for Beale to WAIT! rushed to her lips. But before she could blurt out the word she heard a mechanized hiss, and like a miniature star going nova, the camera dazzled her with its flash.

* * *

He sat alone in the red-leathered booth, thumbing buttons as if his HP PhotoSmart 315 were a handheld video game. Engrossed in his machinations, he didn't hear her approach, just sensed her standing over him. He turned, lowering the device.

MADELINE, as the block letters of her badge proclaimed, wore a honey mustard uniform stretched taut by a pair of saddlebagged hips. The plum-colored eye shadow smeared across her heavy lids gave her a pugilistic look – Rocky Balboa in the late rounds.

She stood brandishing a glass coffee pot. "Cup o' joe?" she asked him, sounding as if she was naming some lost tribe of Native Americans.

His focus zoomed past the waitress to the restrooms stationed about fifteen feet behind her. He deliberated, and then nudged the cup-crowned saucer towards the edge of the table. "Yeah, sure. Thanks."

When Madeline discharged the brew and trundled off, he returned to his camera. Propping his elbows upon the checkered tablecloth, he held the device up half a foot in front of his face. He activated the image LCD and filled the square-inch rear screen with the most recent photo taken, of Regan in front of the American Gothic House.

She stood staring dead ahead, her hot-pink t-shirt forming a vibrant contrast to the pale backdrop. A long crease slashed across her brow; her full lips had parted and formed a frozen oval, impending objection cut off in perpetuity. Smiling thinly, the photographer admired the short auburn hair tucked behind multiply-pierced ears. Sure, she was a bit jowly, having yet to shed all of her beer weight, but Regan really was an attractive girl. Not for the first time, he wished there could have been something more to their relationship.

But that was never going to happen, and pining just seemed silly at this point. Instead, he simply pressed the back arrow on the HP's controller and summoned another picture. Date-stamped nine months prior to today's singular snapshot, the photo presented a smiling blonde waif obviously braless beneath her faded yellow tanktop. The isosceles gable of the American Gothic House poked skyward behind her.

He didn't linger on the image. His thumb kept twitching on the controller, sending the camera leapfrogging back through time. Each photo offered a different figure in the same landmark setting.

←: A pair of mock-solemn twins, identical even to the point of their wispy goatees.

←: A pregnant black woman, absently scratching the track marks on her arms.

←: A shirtless, milky-lensed geriatric, staring blindly towards the camera.

And dozens and dozens more engraved upon the camera's memory card, men and woman and sometimes even children. Posed mostly solo, since group portraits were so much harder to arrange.

It wasn't really a jaunt down Memory Lane, considering that he couldn't recall the names or origins of most of these people (just as he'd long since forgotten his particular aliases, which he shucked like a chrysalis after each visit to Eldon). But sitting there in the coffee shop scrolling back through the recorded history of his artful endeavors, Renny had little interest in the human figures anyway. Background swallowed up foreground as he fixed on the upstairs arch inevitably centered in every photo. He stared at the occulting window and ruminated on the same old question, the one he wasn't sure he could ever stand to have answered:

What does the Boarder do with them all up there?

"Boarder" – now there was an appellation drenched in irony. The word implied legitimate, leased occupancy, such as what the house's resident caretaker had signed on for. No, Renny's unseen master qualified more as a squatter, dwelling undetected, secreted in the very woodwork of the place.

Renny couldn't say for certain (not that he would dare tell anyone) why the Boarder had settled into the iconic home, why He was so hellbent on taking in others. Was the intent to reacquaint Americans with the darkness inherent in the original painting, the gothicness that'd been washed out over the years by all the flippant posers and parodists? To force a final understanding of what had been misinterpreted and misrepresented for so long?

Nor did Renny possess a definitive explanation for why he'd been personally chosen, why the Boarder had called him to serve as...as what? National recruiter? Facilitator? Soul provider?

Sighing, Renny tried to clear his thoughts. One thing he did know was the uselessness of such musings. He'd sworn himself to duty, and that was all that mattered. Like in that old Tennyson rhyme: his task not to question why; his but to do or die.

He glanced back toward the restroom doors as he slid from the booth. But he still felt no prompting from his bladder, and since he had nothing to wash off his hands, he just paid his bill and left. Time to head back out on the road.

Renny drove off into the black-as-asphalt Iowan night a few minutes later, already plotting his next storyline, weaving his next identity. He kept at it for mile after country mile, eventually crossing up into Minnesota. Such determined fabrication, though, did not cloud his consciousness of his surroundings. Granted, his camera lay buried deep in the Ford's trunk once more, but he was always on the lookout for his next subject to capture.

In the Bleak

Wendy Nikel

MOONLIGHT glints off Coach's State Champion keyring, and when I turn the ignition, the ancient yellow beast growls to life. Its grumbling drowns out the nighttime sounds – all but the thrumming of my pulse in my ears – and the sharp scent of diesel stings my eyes. I pull the seatbelt tight across my chest, but it doesn't comfort me as it should. Not on a night like tonight, with the moon a silver dollar above us.

What was meant to be a one-time thing has shifted into something more dangerous. But we're careful. We'll keep the headlights off until we're off school grounds, we'll refill the tank from Matt's gas can, and Jessa will replace her dad's keys in the pocket of his letter jacket before he even realizes they were gone.

We're careful. It's always Steve's voice that sways me. *No one will know.*

The bus rattles across the vast parking lot, jostling the seats that stink of sweat and cologne and nostalgia for places I couldn't wait to leave. I gaze straight ahead – away from the darkened school windows that stare like empty eye sockets – until I reach the deep ditch before the highway. Here, the road's an endless strip of asphalt, drowning in a sea of corn. Here, moonlight glances off the stalks like silver. Overhead, shoes dangle by their laces from telephone lines, and far in the distance, the shadow of a barn leans a bit more each month.

There's nothing here. Nothing at all. And yet I know that, too, isn't right.

I flick the headlights – once, twice – and lean on the handle to unfold the door.

Biting wind rushes in, and with it come the others. Shadows shuffle in the ditch, avoiding the glow of parking lot spotlights. Arms, legs, and heads emerge, lean and strong and wrapped in hoodies and flannel blankets. They flock through the doors of the bus like startled blackbirds.

"That everyone?" I don't bother to count, to look too closely at their faces. I pretend not to know who they are, and they'll do the same when they see me at the post office where I work or the diner by the interstate or wherever our paths may cross.

"Everyone I know of," Steve says. He slides something across the dashboard toward me – something metal, wrapped in his football jersey.

"Don't give that to me," I say when the shape resolves itself and I realize what it is. "Where'd you get that anyway?"

"Dad's cabinet. The silver bullets are from the guys in shop class. I told them it was a joke."

"Did you ask Dad if you could use it?"

"What do you think?" Seeing I'm not taking it, he shoves it beneath the seat. "Just in case you need it, Sara."

"I'm not going to need it." Even if I did, I wouldn't use it. Not against him, or any of these kids.

I watch Steve in the darkened world of the rearview mirror's reflection as he slides into his seat and pops a soda can tab – something bright and sweet and sticky that will be a pain to clean up if it spills – but I don't say anything. It's going to be a long night, and later, when everyone else is exhausted, I'll be grateful for his overcaffeinated company.

All fall silent as we drive along, the only sound the hum of the tires on the highway, rising and falling in minor chords. There's an orange glow on the horizon from lights of a distant city, but at the junction, I turn away from it, down a road less traveled, where the billboards have faded into banners of white, half-blocked-out by overgrown trees, and the only landmark is a trio of small, wooden crosses by the side of the road that flash in the headlights as we pass them.

When we reach the gravel road that leads to Granddad's wooded property, I let Steve out to unlock the gate and secure it tightly behind us. It's the only way in, the only place at all where there's a gap in the rusty barbed-wire fences.

He hesitates on the bottom step, his eyes already turning jaundiced. His hands twitch, and he rubs the rope scars on his wrists – scars formed in the months when he tried to control this alone.

"It's getting late," he says, nodding to the others. "Maybe you ought to let us out here."

"Sit down. I'm not leaving you this close to the highway. I told you: we do this right or not at all."

Reluctantly, he retreats to his seat. The clock on the dash glows green, ticking off another minute closer to midnight. The gravel road is rocky, and branches scrape the windows. I try not to look in the mirror, though I can hear their breathing deepen, can sense them shuffling around as they shed layers of clothing that's grown too warm.

"Sara…"

"I know. I know. We're almost there."

"Sara, take it. Just in case." He presses the gun into my lap, and I try to bat it away, but I have to watch the road, and he holds it there until I give up and let it rest, so heavy, on my legs.

I pull the bus into park and fling the door open. 11:59 blinks into 12:00. Before I can give the word, they're tearing down the steps, tossing off the last bits of clothing as their limbs and ears lengthen and warp, as their hair thickens and coarsens, and their teeth form sharp fangs.

Steve is last off the bus. He turns to shut the door and I see the final glimmer of recognition fade. Saliva drips from the corner of his mouth, and my heart drops.

Our father's gun glistens in my lap.

My hand goes for the lever instead, and I yank it toward me, slamming the door on his elongated face the very same moment he lunges. One second ago my brother, now all that's out there is a beast.

The pistol falls to the floor.

Neither he nor the others stay near the bus long – not when there's acres of woods to explore, vermin to track, dominance to establish. There's a whole world that I can only watch through the windshield. Their strange new bodies run and leap and fight until, one by one, they melt into the darkness. Long after their yellow eyes disappear, I watch the tree line, kept awake by adrenaline that courses through my veins with each howl.

And yet there's beauty in the bleakness, and just being entrusted with something so primal is enough to keep me doing this, be it the sticky summer months or frozen winter. It's enough to keep me sitting here, my knees tucked up to my chest and my breath turning to white specters in the moonlight, throughout the longest hours of the night. Until slowly, one by one, they wander back – shivering in their lank and hairless forms – and scramble into their discarded clothing and mount the steps of the bus.

Steve is the last to arrive. My gaze meets his in the rearview mirror, and though every last bit of yellow is gone, there's a sorrow there, along with an apology that I neither want nor need. I kick the pistol back to him with a warning. "Next time, leave it home."

Then the engine rumbles to life, the moon creeps below the pine trees, and long, lonely shadows rush before us down the road.

In the Country

Christi Nogle

AT SUNSET everything is pink and blue-violet. The mother, Myrna, stands out on the balcony surveying the hills and follows the diagonal lines of them in zigzag down and past the treeline to the scene on the lawn. The little boy and little girl's nightdresses glow pink in the sunset, succulents at their feet all spiral-shaped, soft and pebbly, the harder white of lilies behind them and the red-green foliage of the roses behind them. Their hair, which always shimmers in the light – his yellow-gold and hers deep reddish brown – is darkened now and so their skin glows healthier rose against it. There are no shadows on their faces. The pebbles between the flower beds are flat rose-gold. The paper lanterns the children hold are brighter rose-gold.

The little boy moves like a little girl, carefully, cringing back from others' movements and from sharp or hard surfaces. His blond curls will be cut off soon now. His plain nightdress is already wrong. The girl's lace-trimmed nightdress cuts tight under the arms, and the sleeves are too short. She twirls with the lantern after her father lights it, then climbs the little ladder to hang it on a stake. Her legs are slim and darker rose.

The light falls further. The sky is a warm blue with cooler blue clouds. The blue flowers glow now, and all the whites look hard. The nightdresses appear white for a second, then grey-blue. The father joins the mother up on the balcony, holds her hand and leans into her. The little boy moves like a drowsy ghost in the yard, not chasing fireflies but shrugging when they do not come to him. He shrugs back at the parents in a flirtatious way, puts his jar on the ground.

Myrna thinks there is something a little less than ideal about the boy having been born second. There should be a little sister, later, so that the order no longer matters.

The girl is now pinching a rosebud off the bush, digging her fingernails into it, scattering damp half-formed petals over her head. She likes to pry the fetal plants from their seeds, likes to pick weeds in the heat of day. She likes to pick apart insects of all kinds but especially the fireflies. She will peel the glowing part off to wear on her finger – look, a ring!

* * *

Myrna takes a good look at her the next day while they pick weeds. She is growing too long. The legs are too long, the calves and thighs of the same diameter, like poles, and in the filthy terry shorts, the butt is too round, the back too swayed. The face is indistinct: narrow nose, small eyes behind thick glasses, small mouth with small teeth that do not show when she speaks. Only the hair is perfect, mahogany red in the sun, glowing like Myrna's own.

While they pick, the boy sits quietly in the shade on a blanket. If a bug crawls across his blanket, he will not molest it in any way. He will watch it with benign interest until it is gone and then will look forward at nothing. Soon the father comes to lie beside him. Soon they are both curled together like sleeping puppies.

* * *

In late summer, they sit on the front porch, the most wretched place to sit. The boards are bleached silver and full of splinters, their rails strung with wilted morning glories and the opportunistic Virginia creeper, which is deep green when the other plants start to fail.

The girl works on some packet of extra special summer homework, reciting her vocabulary words in a tone Myrna does not like, over and over: kaleidoscope, iridescent, phosphorescent, on and on.

"What weird words," Myrna says finally.

"This lesson is on *op*-tics," the girl says. "Do you know what pareidolia means?"

"I do not."

"It means that we see…patterns in chaos. You see faces in the wood of the porch floor."

"I don't see faces anywhere," she says, feeling oddly defensive.

"Sure, there is a face. You see something that looks like a nose, and so your mind works hard to find something you can use for eyes above the nose. It's natural."

"'Patterns in chaos.' That would come from Miss Griggs."

"It does."

"I see faces," Boyd says. They don't hear.

"It's nice you're learning so much, Cassie." Myrna stirs the ice in the bottom of her glass and steps down off the porch, having spotted a weed.

"It's nice you're learning so much," Cassie says.

"I saw a face in a towel in the bathroom," Boyd says. "It scared me, that time."

"It's *nice* you're learning so much, Cassie," Cassie says.

"It's nice *you're* learning so much, Cassie."

"It's nice you're *learn*ing so much, Cassie."

"It's nice you're learning *so* much, Cassie."

Boyd starts to cry, all at once. He is sitting there, then he pumps his arms in the air a couple of times, then his face is wet and he is hyperventilating.

"Thanks again, Cassie." Myrna picks up Boyd and takes him in the house.

Cassie leans down from the lowest porch step and draws the face/vase illusion from the teacher's handout in the dirt with a stick and it is so beautifully drawn, she thinks, that she needs to make it more permanent. She places dead green beetles where the eyes of the faces would be. She gathers pebbles and uses them to outline the silhouettes of the faces. She places the best of the struggling morning glory vines at the top of the vase, trailing down.

* * *

"The reason that you're able to find things when you go hunting for them is sort of the same reason you see faces everywhere. It's like if you're hunting for daisies, and you know what a daisy looks like, you have that picture in front of your eyes, and when there is a daisy there to fit into the picture, you will see it," Cassie says just as they enter the woods.

"Then I have a picture of a mushroom, and one of a pretty forest flower – *not* of a daisy – and one of a turtleshell, all at the same time" Myrna says, "since those are what I want to find."

"You can't. It doesn't work that way"

"It does. I can. I am a very able person," Myrna says, adjusting her gait to miss a slimy patch of wet moss.

Myrna feels good, set for a long walk. She ponders as they walk down the slope and deeper into woods: If Cassie had not known these new vocabulary words, she might have never known the concepts, or maybe she would have gone around saying "that thing, where you see things in other things" instead of pareidolia or "that thing where you see rainbows in the oil" instead of iridescence, sounding like an idiot or crazy person until she learned to stop saying anything about these things – and stop knowing them – just as Myrna had learned to shut up with her own stupid thoughts at a much earlier age than this. These boys just past the woods, devoted to farming and to church, don't have any mind for such a term. Myrna herself, to tell the truth, has no mind for it even though she once went to college and was forced to try to think that way, but she likes to think she would like to leave such options open to Cassie.

She wonders if Miss Griggs started something that would have started anyway, sooner or later. It's good, it's fine, but Cassie will go into a different class next year and will not have another teacher like her here, ever. Cassie must go to some sort of a better school. How? Where? Or maybe 'must' is too strong. She can go or not go and it will all be fine either way.

Myrna is skipping now from rock to rock, getting into a trotting rhythm as they descend. Boyd is happily skipping beside her but slips on a mossy rock, falls on his nose. A few drops of blood balance on the broccoli-textured moss, then flatten, staining the inside grey. Boyd is back to howling, holding his mother tight again. Misery is your element, she thinks, then hollers "Cassie, Cassie! Let's go." An echo comes back weak.

She walks forward a few more steps to see Cassie in a sunny patch far below, bounding from rock to rock as though weightless. She thinks very deliberately; if this is all you get Cassie, enjoy it. It is wonderful. You feel so strong. You have nothing but healthy memories. You are not troubled, Cassie. She likes to think positive things about Cassie when she can, and the positive thoughts make up a sweet story she tells to herself about herself, so they make her feel good.

* * *

Myrna tries again to go exploring. This time she leaves Cassie sleeping and fashions a sling to hold Boyd on her back. He is much too old to be carried about like this, and the father would probably not like it, but the father is off on a job and what are you going to do? "It's a secret," she tells Boyd. They walk without incident past the point they had been at the last time, twice as far, three times as far, and then they see it. Or Myrna sees it. With Boyd, who knows what he is seeing or not seeing?

It is a house facing them as they approach, an absurdly large one in the middle of the woods. There appears to be no road to it, or even a trail. The clearing is barely larger than the house itself, tall bare timber obscuring her view of much of its face though they are only a hundred feet away. She wants to say it is called a saltbox but is not sure that is right. It's been so many years since she thought about things like that. In any case, it is very tall, with three windows above and two below, with the door between them. There is a door in the doorframe but no glass in any of the windows. All of the siding and thick trim pieces are weathered wood, as weathered as the dead wood littering the ground, looking never painted and left out here to rot for what? Fifty years, more?

Myrna unties Boyd from her back to set him on his feet.

She feels elation, a 'wow' feeling through her whole body. "What a find, buddy," she says. "We couldn't have done better than this."

Boyd yawns, looks hopeful. "What did we find?"

"Stay here," she says, and approaches the house alone thinking that such houses have hazards, though what they are without any glass around she does not know. She walks around to the back, three windows above, three below. There is a lot of leaf mold and twigs and whatnot drifted up the sides, small beetles circling up out of it. No windows on either of the sides, no second door. She comes around the front to try the door. There is no knob or any mechanism for one inside the doorknob hole. She pushes and feels that the door must be nailed shut from inside. She turns to approach the window (thinking to look in, climb in?) and feels adrenaline hit her system in what feels like a second or more before she hears the shriek from Boyd.

Then there is the panicked run up the slope with Boyd in her arms, blood pumping out of a gash in his hand, such a long run that her lungs can barely keep up. There is the search for the keys in the mess of the kitchen, the drive to the little town hospital for stitches, the notice while waiting that it's noon now and they should get something on the drive home. There is the drive home with fragrant fries and messy ice cream cones and Boyd asleep with his head in her lap, bandage and fingers and face all sticky with ice cream and staining her jeans with his drool. Fine salt and grease give a pleasant texture to the steering wheel. This is not the first time he has been rushed to an emergency room and will probably not be the last, but would that every time turned out so sweetly.

Through all of this, she is feeling a muted version of the normal emotions, panic and then concern, relief at the hospital and then the warm flood of good will toward herself and Boyd on the drive home. She feels good, just a little sore in the shins. The pain in the backs and fronts of her thighs will start tomorrow, she knows. God, she has not run like that in years. But right now, she feels good.

The normal emotions and the normal concerns proceed in the order they should, but there is something else too that she would not be able to define if asked and that she is barely aware of. It is the heavy, inchoate static of dread. It has been building for some time and will announce itself as she lifts Boyd, sleeping, from the truck. It will build to a higher pitch the instant she is aware of it, and in the minute it takes to approach the door it will rise higher and higher until she wants to drop him and hold her ears instead, though of course the sound is from the inside and not the outside.

* * *

The father is home, squatting and leaning forward, hands on her knees as she sits back in an easy chair. He is talking and then screaming. She can hear it all to a point but not clearly. It is likely that he is speaking a language she does not know because she can hear him, sure, but she cannot understand.

There are people in the fields, people starting into the forest, not a lot of people. She watches from the balcony and begins to count them but then grows too tired. They have vests that glow. Their dogs are having a good time.

* * *

A man is getting a glass of water in the kitchen when she goes down there. She smiles and asks if she can make him a cup of coffee. He looks puzzled, thanks her but no. She is about to leave and then comes to the fridge, takes off the class photo.

"If you look at this before you go hunting, it will make it easier. The thing is, if you see the thing in your mind, you will have like a map of it in your mind, and then when you go hunting for it, you will know it when you see it. Cassie – actually – it was Cassie who told me that."

The man looks long at the picture, then hands it back.

"No, you take it," Myrna says. "You can study it before you go back out."

* * *

Myrna is feeling better now. She is worried, sure, but there are so many hands at work that there is nothing she needs to do, for once. She holds Boyd in her lap all day, stroking his bandage on the outside, careful not to touch the palm. She answers their questions politely when they come in.

The father comes in and takes Boyd from her, sets him on his feet. He takes her hand and leads her out to the front porch. Here are two lines like rivers made of little pebbles. He wants to know what this is. "A map?" she guesses. If it is a map, of what? A map maybe to where the girl has gone? She doesn't think so. She doesn't know.

He leads her again – by the wrist, not the hand – to the shed. There is a little craft project going on the bench, with the ice cube trays set out to hold the little items. In one there are sequins, pins, and beads. In the other, parts of insects and flowers, seeds and pebbles. He takes a translucent turtleshell smaller than a silver dollar and looks at it there in his hand. He picks out a locust husk.

"What were these for?" he asks.

"It's probably summer homework. She had so much of that."

* * *

Miss Griggs was questioned, intensely they said. There was nothing to suggest involvement, but she had taken such a heightened interest in the girl that the father was sure there must be something. There was nothing more to the story than a spark between an overeager young teacher from the city and a smart little girl, they told the parents. They did not tell the parents that they'd asked many people about the mother, too. There was nothing more to the story than that she was a little prim, maybe a little more focused on the boy than the girl, but that was natural with him being so young and so adorable and the girl being a little 'on the spectrum' or whatever.

They found a few more lines crafted in pebbles out around the property, and a few arrangements that the girl must have made but of which they could make no sense. One, a mouse with legs of other mice sewn on, was turned in to the police but never mentioned to the parents. There was debate about whether it was an inexpert piece of taxidermy or some kind of charm. A block of weathered wood with twelve rectangles scratched into it, six on two of its sides, was not thought to be related to the girl at all and was tossed into the brush by one of the searchers.

Then there was nothing to do but focus on Boyd. He needed to be watched in case there was an outsider involved. There was talk about moving, but that would be too much trouble even if it were not exactly wrong to do. And the community had been so supportive, how could they think of going away?

* * *

"They searched the house thoroughly, I guess," she says some time later. She is twenty weeks into a pregnancy that is making her feel less sad about the past. She thinks the baby will be a little girl, the kind of little sister she has always hoped would bring out the best in Boyd. He will love her and will focus on her. She will be dirty blonde like Boyd and his father.

"You were here," the father says, "but you don't remember. They searched the crawlspace. They practically took apart the shed."

"Oh yes," Myrna says. She wants to say no, the other house, the house out in the woods. She wonders what they did with it when they found it. They knocked it down, she hopes. It was a hazard though solid enough and with absolutely no glass.

At night, she becomes agitated. She resents the thought that keeps occurring: the house. I never actually opened my mouth and mentioned the house, did I? In all of that time when I was dreaming about it every night and seeing her there, fallen from the second story or hiding crouched in the corner, I never actually opened my mouth. I was dreaming of her haunting it after that. I was dreaming she had tiled every floor with mosaics of pebbles and papered the walls in leaves and the wings of insects. At first I think I thought I had already said it because I was so confused, and then when I realized I had not said it, I thought they must have found it anyway. They were so thorough. They had dogs.

* * *

"I love her already. It hurts," Boyd says one day when they are sitting up in bed with a picture book. He looks so much older in his plaid pajamas. His eyes are wet and he pulls toward Myrna, but he's not pulling in on himself the way he once would have. He embraces the belly instead. It is so big now that the navel has popped up, and he touches it with the tip of his finger. "We have to wait until she comes before we go," he says.

"What?" Myrna says, feeling repelled by him, which she does not expect. What she feels is a brief flash of loyalty to Cassie. What do you know about her? she wants to say. They have not talked about it, he and Myrna, though the father must have done some of that. It is the kind of thing that he would think to do.

"I mean the baby," he says. "We don't want the baby to fall."

She sees, then, what he means. "Yes, we have to wait."

"And while we wait, we don't have to think nothing," he says.

"Anything," she says.

"Anything at all." He smiles and turns back to the book, and they go on reading.

* * *

The baby is so strong, they can't believe her, and ravenous. The best baby in the whole world, everyone agrees. Boyd is a little man now. He helps with everything. He is so gentle. The family couldn't have done any better.

* * *

In midsummer they sit on chairs on the porch with the baby between them. She is quiet and good even in the heat, and they protect her from the sun with a pink umbrella that makes everything under it glow pink. Boyd has never seen so much pink in his life, and he tells Myrna it makes him feel safe just to see all of the pink things and the pretty clothes and stuffed animals that fill up the house now.

Dandelions grow up between the succulents now. Thistles grow up through the rosebushes, and the Virginia creeper smothers any other vine that might have once competed.

Boyd tells Myrna about what kindergarten is going to be like. There will be a teacher, and a teacher is like a mother but not as nice and not as pretty. The teacher teaches and you learn, but you play too. You play and play until you are so tired that you take a nap, and after the nap there is orange drink in a carton, chocolate milk, or white milk. There are cookies that the moms bring in, kept in a closet in the back, and the teacher picks two students each time to go and get them after nap. And you will have a best friend named Kiera Jean Jack.

"There is a green drink sometimes," Myrna says. He has generalized all the things she told him about her kindergarten. It's sweet to hear him talk so long at a stretch.

"Only sometimes," Boyd says, "and when there is I will not drink it."

"And you'll learn to read," she says.

"Maybe," he says.

* * *

She dries her hands on her apron after breakfast dishes, and Boyd takes them in his. The father took him into town last month for a real haircut. His hair looks darker and is already growing tendrils at the edges. He holds her hands and says he wants to go for a walk.

The baby in a sling on the front of her, Myrna picks her way carefully down the slope, so alert to every sensation. The forest is loud with the creek sounds and insects and birds and thick with the wet and earthy smells. The lurid green of the ferns stands against a chaotic background of old leaf litter, rocks and moss. The shafts of sun come in through small gaps in the cover, lighting up the tiny insects that move like schools of fish. She keeps her feet from stamping down on the dead wood, the moss, the occasional dark salamander moving away from her. The strong horizontals of the trunks have a louver effect, letting her see a part and then another part of the background as she passes, but not all at once. She is feeling good, feeling vigilant but not frightened.

Boyd walks ahead but not too far. He's being careful where to step. The walk is long. She stops for a time to pee and then to nurse the baby. She takes her shoes off, rubs her feet.

She and Boyd do not talk, but they glance at each other from time to time. This is a hunt and, if what they want is not in front, it may be to the side or even back a ways. Their paths become confused. The baby is awake again and fussing softly.

"Maybe we should go back," Myrna says. The diaper is alright now, but she didn't bring a second change.

"Maybe," Boyd says, but he keeps moving forward. He stops, holds his head as though he has a crushing headache, or is he covering his ears?

When he turns back around he is crying. His face is red. "No," he says. "I see something right over there."

He turns back away from Myrna and pushes forward, faster now. The woods are so thick here that they can't move straight for more than a few feet. He couldn't have seen it; there's nothing visible ahead, even now, and now they are a hundred yards further than when he said it.

Then she sees it through trees, at first nothing more than a hint of vertical line through the louvers of the trunks, gray behind gray. She sees the vertical line of rooftop begin to form and then as she begins descending, the darker shapes of windows.

Boyd is far ahead now, stopped and facing the lower left window. The dread doesn't come as she thought it would. She coos to the baby, makes her way down to Boyd calm and slow.

When she has reached him and looks at him from the side, he looks so drained that she thinks he will collapse, but he stands still. She pulls the baby to the side so that she can be close enough to peer in the window. She looks in at exactly what she expected to see, darkness and then far back in the static, a patch of rosy color and a dim glint of hair. The light barely reaches. Boyd is not tall enough to see inside. He turns away, strokes the scar on his hand.

How did you know? she thinks. I dreamed it like this, but I didn't know. They turn from the window and walk forward a few steps.

He is crying hard but does not reach for her. "I saw a face. It was hurt."

She was in here hurt but still alive, but you didn't want me to know, she thinks. So you cut yourself to pull me away from her. Or, you knew something was going to happen, so you took us away before it did. In either case the same, you wanted to let it happen.

"But there was nothing you could do," she says. It may as well be true.

"May-be," he hitches. He is starting to hyperventilate, but he sits and breathes deeply, hugs his arms around himself, calms down. His face when he looks up is serious but not upset.

"Is there something there behind you?" he says. He is squinting, tilting his head.

Myrna thinks of what it might be behind her. The house, no house but Cassie in a pile of leaves, or nothing, more trees.

"Did we find something or not?" He asks. "I can't remember. I thought we were hunting for something."

"Did we find something?" She says. "No, we didn't." She does not look back but takes his hand and starts back up toward home.

A Good Man Is Hard to Find

Flannery O'Connor

THE GRANDMOTHER didn't want to go to Florida. She wanted to visit some of her connections in east Tennessee and she was seizing at every chance to change Bailey's mind. Bailey was the son she lived with, her only boy. He was sitting on the edge of his chair at the table, bent over the orange sports section of the *Journal*. "Now look here, Bailey," she said, "see here, read this," and she stood with one hand on her thin hip and the other rattling the newspaper at his bald head. "Here this fellow that calls himself The Misfit is aloose from the Federal Pen and headed toward Florida and you read here what it says he did to these people. Just you read it. I wouldn't take my children in any direction with a criminal like that aloose in it. I couldn't answer to my conscience if I did."

Bailey didn't look up from his reading so she wheeled around then and faced the children's mother, a young woman in slacks, whose face was as broad and innocent as a cabbage and was tied around with a green head-kerchief that had two points on the top like rabbit's ears. She was sitting on the sofa, feeding the baby his apricots out of a jar. "The children have been to Florida before," the old lady said. "You all ought to take them somewhere else for a change so they would see different parts of the world and be broad. They never have been to east Tennessee."

The children's mother didn't seem to hear her but the eight-year-old boy, John Wesley, a stocky child with glasses, said, "If you don't want to go to Florida, why dontcha stay at home?" He and the little girl, June Star, were reading the funny papers on the floor.

"She wouldn't stay at home to be queen for a day," June Star said without raising her yellow head.

"Yes and what would you do if this fellow, The Misfit, caught you?" the grandmother asked.

"I'd smack his face," John Wesley said.

"She wouldn't stay at home for a million bucks," June Star said. "Afraid she'd miss something. She has to go everywhere we go."

"All right, Miss," the grandmother said. "Just remember that the next time you want me to curl your hair."

June Star said her hair was naturally curly.

The next morning the grandmother was the first one in the car, ready to go. She had her big black valise that looked like the head of a hippopotamus in one corner, and underneath it she was hiding a basket with Pitty Sing, the cat, in it. She didn't intend for the cat to be left alone in the house for three days because he would miss her too much and she was afraid he might brush against one of the gas burners and accidentally asphyxiate himself. Her son, Bailey, didn't like to arrive at a motel with a cat.

She sat in the middle of the back seat with John Wesley and June Star on either side of her. Bailey and the children's mother and the baby sat in front and they left Atlanta at eight forty-five with the mileage on the car at 55890. The grandmother wrote this down because she thought it would be interesting to say how many miles they had been when they got back. It took them twenty minutes to reach the outskirts of the city.

The old lady settled herself comfortably, removing her white cotton gloves and putting them up with her purse on the shelf in front of the back window. The children's mother still had on slacks and still had her head tied up in a green kerchief, but the grandmother had on a navy blue straw sailor hat with a bunch of white violets on the brim and a navy blue dress with a small white dot in the print. Her collars and cuffs were white organdy trimmed with lace and at her neckline she had pinned a purple spray of cloth violets containing a sachet. In case of an accident, anyone seeing her dead on the highway would know at once that she was a lady.

She said she thought it was going to be a good day for driving, neither too hot nor too cold, and she cautioned Bailey that the speed limit was fifty-five miles an hour and that the patrolmen hid themselves behind billboards and small clumps of trees and sped out after you before you had a chance to slow down. She pointed out interesting details of the scenery: Stone Mountain; the blue granite that in some places came up to both sides of the highway; the brilliant red clay banks slightly streaked with purple; and the various crops that made rows of green lace-work on the ground. The trees were full of silver-white sunlight and the meanest of them sparkled. The children were reading comic magazines and their mother had gone back to sleep.

"Let's go through Georgia fast so we won't have to look at it much," John Wesley said.

"If I were a little boy," said the grandmother, "I wouldn't talk about my native state that way. Tennessee has the mountains and Georgia has the hills."

"Tennessee is just a hillbilly dumping ground," John Wesley said, "and Georgia is a lousy state too."

"You said it," June Star said.

"In my time," said the grandmother, folding her thin veined fingers, "children were more respectful of their native states and their parents and everything else. People did right then. Oh look at the cute little pickaninny!" she said and pointed to a Negro child standing in the door of a shack. "Wouldn't that make a picture, now?" she asked and they all turned and looked at the little Negro out of the back window. He waved.

"He didn't have any britches on," June Star said.

"He probably didn't have any," the grandmother explained. "Little niggers in the country don't have things like we do. If I could paint, I'd paint that picture," she said.

The children exchanged comic books.

The grandmother offered to hold the baby and the children's mother passed him over the front seat to her. She set him on her knee and bounced him and told him about the things they were passing. She rolled her eyes and screwed up her mouth and stuck her leathery thin face into his smooth bland one. Occasionally he gave her a faraway smile. They passed a large cotton field with five or six graves fenced in the middle of it, like a small island. "Look at the graveyard!" the grandmother said, pointing it out. "That was the old family burying ground. That belonged to the plantation."

"Where's the plantation?" John Wesley asked.

"Gone With the Wind," said the grandmother. "Ha. Ha."

When the children finished all the comic books they had brought, they opened the lunch and ate it. The grandmother ate a peanut butter sandwich and an olive and would not let the children throw the box and the paper napkins out the window. When there was nothing else to do they played a game by choosing a cloud and making the other two guess what shape it suggested. John Wesley took one the shape of a cow and June Star guessed a cow and John Wesley said, no, an automobile, and June Star said he didn't play fair, and they began to slap each other over the grandmother.

The grandmother said she would tell them a story if they would keep quiet. When she told a story, she rolled her eyes and waved her head and was very dramatic. She said once when she was a maiden lady she had been courted by a Mr. Edgar Atkins Teagarden from Jasper, Georgia. She said he was a very good-looking man and a gentleman and that he brought her a watermelon every Saturday afternoon with his initials cut in it, E. A. T. Well, one Saturday, she said, Mr. Teagarden brought the watermelon and there was nobody at home and he left it on the front porch and returned in his buggy to Jasper, but she never got the watermelon, she said, because a nigger boy ate it when he saw the initials, E. A. T.! This story tickled John Wesley's funny bone and he giggled and giggled but June Star didn't think it was any good. She said she wouldn't marry a man that just brought her a watermelon on Saturday. The grandmother said she would have done well to marry Mr. Teagarden because he was a gentleman and had bought Coca-Cola stock when it first came out and that he had died only a few years ago, a very wealthy man.

They stopped at The Tower for barbecued sandwiches. The Tower was a part stucco and part wood filling station and dance hall set in a clearing outside of Timothy. A fat man named Red Sammy Butts ran it and there were signs stuck here and there on the building and for miles up and down the highway saying, TRY RED SAMMY'S FAMOUS BARBECUE. NONE LIKE FAMOUS RED SAMMY'S! RED SAM! THE FAT BOY WITH THE HAPPY LAUGH. A VETERAN! RED SAMMY'S YOUR MAN!

Red Sammy was lying on the bare ground outside The Tower with his head under a truck while a gray monkey about a foot high, chained to a small chinaberry tree, chattered nearby. The monkey sprang back into the tree and got on the highest limb as soon as he saw the children jump out of the car and run toward him.

Inside, The Tower was a long dark room with a counter at one end and tables at the other and dancing space in the middle. They all sat down at a board table next to the nickelodeon and Red Sam's wife, a tall burnt-brown woman with hair and eyes lighter than her skin, came and took their order. The children's mother put a dime in the machine and played 'The Tennessee Waltz', and the grandmother said that tune always made her want to dance. She asked Bailey if he would like to dance but he only glared at her. He didn't have a naturally sunny disposition like she did and trips made him nervous. The grandmother's brown eyes were very bright. She swayed her head from side to side and pretended she was dancing in her chair. June Star said play something she could tap to so the children's mother put in another dime and played a fast number and June Star stepped out onto the dance floor and did her tap routine.

"Ain't she cute?" Red Sam's wife said, leaning over the counter. "Would you like to come be my little girl?"

"No I certainly wouldn't," June Star said. "I wouldn't live in a broken-down place like this for a minion bucks!" and she ran back to the table.

"Ain't she cute?" the woman repeated, stretching her mouth politely.

"Arn't you ashamed?" hissed the grandmother.

Red Sam came in and told his wife to quit lounging on the counter and hurry up with these people's order. His khaki trousers reached just to his hip bones and his stomach hung over them like a sack of meal swaying under his shirt. He came over and sat down at a table nearby and let out a combination sigh and yodel. "You can't win," he said. "You can't win," and he wiped his sweating red face off with a gray handkerchief. "These days you don't know who to trust," he said. "Ain't that the truth?"

"People are certainly not nice like they used to be," said the grandmother.

"Two fellers come in here last week," Red Sammy said, "driving a Chrysler. It was a old beat-up car but it was a good one and these boys looked all right to me. Said they worked at the mill and you know I let them fellers charge the gas they bought? Now why did I do that?"

"Because you're a good man!" the grandmother said at once.

"Yes'm, I suppose so," Red Sam said as if he were struck with this answer.

His wife brought the orders, carrying the five plates all at once without a tray, two in each hand and one balanced on her arm. "It isn't a soul in this green world of God's that you can trust," she said. "And I don't count nobody out of that, not nobody," she repeated, looking at Red Sammy.

"Did you read about that criminal, The Misfit, that's escaped?" asked the grandmother.

"I wouldn't be a bit surprised if he didn't attact this place right here," said the woman. "If he hears about it being here, I wouldn't be none surprised to see him. If he hears it's two cent in the cash register, I wouldn't be at all surprised if he…"

"That'll do," Red Sam said. "Go bring these people their Co'-Colas," and the woman went off to get the rest of the order.

"A good man is hard to find," Red Sammy said. "Everything is getting terrible. I remember the day you could go off and leave your screen door unlatched. Not no more."

He and the grandmother discussed better times. The old lady said that in her opinion Europe was entirely to blame for the way things were now. She said the way Europe acted you would think we were made of money and Red Sam said it was no use talking about it, she was exactly right. The children ran outside into the white sunlight and looked at the monkey in the lacy chinaberry tree. He was busy catching fleas on himself and biting each one carefully between his teeth as if it were a delicacy.

They drove off again into the hot afternoon. The grandmother took cat naps and woke up every few minutes with her own snoring. Outside of Toombsboro she woke up and recalled an old plantation that she had visited in this neighborhood once when she was a young lady. She said the house had six white columns across the front and that there was an avenue of oaks leading up to it and two little wooden trellis arbors on either side in front where you sat down with your suitor after a stroll in the garden. She recalled exactly which road to turn off to get to it. She knew that Bailey would not be willing to lose any time looking at an old house, but the more she talked about it, the more she wanted to see it once again and find out if the little twin arbors were still standing. "There was a secret panel in this house," she said craftily, not telling the truth but wishing that she were, "and the story went that all the family silver was hidden in it when Sherman came through but it was never found…"

"Hey!" John Wesley said. "Let's go see it! We'll find it! We'll poke all the woodwork and find it! Who lives there? Where do you turn off at? Hey Pop, can't we turn off there?"

"We never have seen a house with a secret panel!" June Star shrieked. "Let's go to the house with the secret panel! Hey Pop, can't we go see the house with the secret panel!"

"It's not far from here, I know," the grandmother said. "It wouldn't take over twenty minutes."

Bailey was looking straight ahead. His jaw was as rigid as a horseshoe. "No," he said.

The children began to yell and scream that they wanted to see the house with the secret panel. John Wesley kicked the back of the front seat and June Star hung over her mother's shoulder and whined desperately into her ear that they never had any fun even on their vacation, that they could never do what *they* wanted to do. The baby began to scream and John Wesley kicked the back of the seat so hard that his father could feel the blows in his kidney.

"All right!" he shouted and drew the car to a stop at the side of the road. "Will you all shut up? Will you all just shut up for one second? If you don't shut up, we won't go anywhere."

"It would be very educational for them," the grandmother murmured.

"All right," Bailey said, "but get this: this is the only time we're going to stop for anything like this. This is the one and only time."

"The dirt road that you have to turn down is about a mile back," the grandmother directed. "I marked it when we passed."

"A dirt road," Bailey groaned.

After they had turned around and were headed toward the dirt road, the grandmother recalled other points about the house, the beautiful glass over the front doorway and the candle-lamp in the hall. John Wesley said that the secret panel was probably in the fireplace.

"You can't go inside this house," Bailey said. "You don't know who lives there."

"While you all talk to the people in front, I'll run around behind and get in a window," John Wesley suggested.

"We'll all stay in the car," his mother said. They turned onto the dirt road and the car raced roughly along in a swirl of pink dust. The grandmother recalled the times when there were no paved roads and thirty miles was a day's journey. The dirt road was hilly and there were sudden washes in it and sharp curves on dangerous embankments. All at once they would be on a hill, looking down over the blue tops of trees for miles around, then the next minute, they would be in a red depression with the dust-coated trees looking down on them.

"This place had better turn up in a minute," Bailey said, "or I'm going to turn around."

The road looked as if no one had traveled on it in months.

"It's not much farther," the grandmother said and just as she said it, a horrible thought came to her. The thought was so embarrassing that she turned red in the face and her eyes dilated and her feet jumped up, upsetting her valise in the corner. The instant the valise moved, the newspaper top she had over the basket under it rose with a snarl and Pitty Sing, the cat, sprang onto Bailey's shoulder.

The children were thrown to the floor and their mother, clutching the baby, was thrown out the door onto the ground; the old lady was thrown into the front seat. The car turned over once and landed right-side-up in a gulch off the side of the road. Bailey remained in the driver's seat with the cat – gray-striped with a broad white face and an orange nose – clinging to his neck like a caterpillar.

As soon as the children saw they could move their arms and legs, they scrambled out of the car, shouting, "We've had an ACCIDENT!" The grandmother was curled up under the dashboard, hoping she was injured so that Bailey's wrath would not come down on her all at once. The horrible thought she had had before the accident was that the house she had remembered so vividly was not in Georgia but in Tennessee.

Bailey removed the cat from his neck with both hands and flung it out the window against the side of a pine tree. Then he got out of the car and started looking for the children's mother. She was sitting against the side of the red gutted ditch, holding the screaming baby, but she only had a cut down her face and a broken shoulder. "We've had an ACCIDENT!" the children screamed in a frenzy of delight.

"But nobody's killed," June Star said with disappointment as the grandmother limped out of the car, her hat still pinned to her head but the broken front brim standing up at a jaunty angle and the violet spray hanging off the side. They all sat down in the ditch, except the children, to recover from the shock. They were all shaking.

"Maybe a car will come along," said the children's mother hoarsely.

"I believe I have injured an organ," said the grandmother, pressing her side, but no one answered her. Bailey's teeth were clattering. He had on a yellow sport shirt with bright blue parrots designed in it and his face was as yellow as the shirt. The grandmother decided that she would not mention that the house was in Tennessee.

The road was about ten feet above and they could see only the tops of the trees on the other side of it. Behind the ditch they were sitting in there were more woods, tall and dark and deep. In a few minutes they saw a car some distance away on top of a hill, coming slowly as if the occupants were watching them. The grandmother stood up and waved both arms dramatically to attract their attention. The car continued to come on slowly, disappeared around a bend and appeared again, moving even slower, on top of the hill they had gone over. It was a big black battered hearse-like automobile. There were three men in it.

It came to a stop just over them and for some minutes, the driver looked down with a steady expressionless gaze to where they were sitting, and didn't speak. Then he turned his head and muttered something to the other two and they got out. One was a fat boy in black trousers and a red sweatshirt with a silver stallion embossed on the front of it. He moved around on the right side of them and stood staring, his mouth partly open in a kind of loose grin. The other had on khaki pants and a blue striped coat and a gray hat pulled down very low, hiding most of his face. He came around slowly on the left side. Neither spoke.

The driver got out of the car and stood by the side of it, looking down at them. He was an older man than the other two. His hair was just beginning to gray and he wore silver-rimmed spectacles that gave him a scholarly look. He had a long creased face and didn't have on any shirt or undershirt. He had on blue jeans that were too tight for him and was holding a black hat and a gun. The two boys also had guns.

"We've had an ACCIDENT!" the children screamed.

The grandmother had the peculiar feeling that the bespectacled man was someone she knew. His face was as familiar to her as if she had known him all her life but she could not recall who he was. He moved away from the car and began to come down the embankment, placing his feet carefully so that he wouldn't slip. He had on tan and white shoes and no socks, and his ankles were red and thin. "Good afternoon," he said. "I see you all had you a little spill."

"We turned over twice!" said the grandmother.

"Once"," he corrected. "We seen it happen. Try their car and see will it run, Hiram," he said quietly to the boy with the gray hat.

"What you got that gun for?" John Wesley asked. "Whatcha gonna do with that gun?"

"Lady," the man said to the children's mother, "would you mind calling them children to sit down by you? Children make me nervous. I want all you all to sit down right together there where you're at."

"What are you telling US what to do for?" June Star asked.

Behind them the line of woods gaped like a dark open mouth. "Come here," said their mother.

"Look here now," Bailey began suddenly, "we're in a predicament! We're in..."

The grandmother shrieked. She scrambled to her feet and stood staring. "You're The Misfit!" she said. "I recognized you at once!"

"Yes'm," the man said, smiling slightly as if he were pleased in spite of himself to be known, "but it would have been better for all of you, lady, if you hadn't of reckernized me."

Bailey turned his head sharply and said something to his mother that shocked even the children. The old lady began to cry and The Misfit reddened.

"Lady," he said, "don't you get upset. Sometimes a man says things he don't mean. I don't reckon he meant to talk to you thataway."

"You wouldn't shoot a lady, would you?" the grandmother said and removed a clean handkerchief from her cuff and began to slap at her eyes with it.

The Misfit pointed the toe of his shoe into the ground and made a little hole and then covered it up again. "I would hate to have to," he said.

"Listen," the grandmother almost screamed, "I know you're a good man. You don't look a bit like you have common blood. I know you must come from nice people!"

"Yes mam," he said, "finest people in the world." When he smiled he showed a row of strong white teeth. "God never made a finer woman than my mother and my daddy's heart was pure gold," he said. The boy with the red sweatshirt had come around behind them and was standing with his gun at his hip. The Misfit squatted down on the ground. "Watch them children, Bobby Lee," he said. "You know they make me nervous." He looked at the six of them huddled together in front of him and he seemed to be embarrassed as if he couldn't think of anything to say. "Ain't a cloud in the sky," he remarked, looking up at it. "Don't see no sun but don't see no cloud neither."

"Yes, it's a beautiful day," said the grandmother. "Listen," she said, "you shouldn't call yourself The Misfit because I know you're a good man at heart. I can just look at you and tell."

"Hush!" Bailey yelled. "Hush! Everybody shut up and let me handle this!" He was squatting in the position of a runner about to sprint forward but he didn't move.

"I prechate that, lady," The Misfit said and drew a little circle in the ground with the butt of his gun.

"It'll take a half a hour to fix this here car," Hiram called, looking over the raised hood of it.

"Well, first you and Bobby Lee get him and that little boy to step over yonder with you," The Misfit said, pointing to Bailey and John Wesley. "The boys want to ast you something," he said to Bailey. "Would you mind stepping back in them woods there with them?"

"Listen," Bailey began, "we're in a terrible predicament! Nobody realizes what this is," and his voice cracked. His eyes were as blue and intense as the parrots in his shirt and he remained perfectly still.

The grandmother reached up to adjust her hat brim as if she were going to the woods with him but it came off in her hand. She stood staring at it and after a second she let it fall on the ground. Hiram pulled Bailey up by the arm as if he were assisting an old man. John Wesley caught hold of his father's hand and Bobby Lee followed. They went off toward the woods and just as they reached the dark edge, Bailey turned and supporting himself against a gray naked pine trunk, he shouted, "I'll be back in a minute, Mamma, wait on me!"

"Come back this instant!" his mother shrilled but they all disappeared into the woods.

"Bailey Boy!" the grandmother called in a tragic voice but she found she was looking at The Misfit squatting on the ground in front of her. "I just know you're a good man," she said desperately. "You're not a bit common!"

"Nome, I ain't a good man," The Misfit said after a second as if he had considered her statement carefully, "but I ain't the worst in the world neither. My daddy said I was a different breed of dog from my brothers and sisters. 'You know,' Daddy said, 'it's some that can live their whole life out without asking about it and it's others has to know why it is, and this boy is one of the latters. He's going to be into everything!'" He put on his black hat and looked up suddenly and then away deep into the woods as if he were embarrassed again. "I'm sorry I don't have on a shirt before you ladies," he said, hunching his shoulders slightly. "We buried our clothes that we had on when we escaped and we're just making do until we can get better. We borrowed these from some folks we met," he explained.

"That's perfectly all right," the grandmother said. "Maybe Bailey has an extra shirt in his suitcase."

"I'll look and see terrectly," The Misfit said.

"Where are they taking him?" the children's mother screamed.

"Daddy was a card himself," The Misfit said. "You couldn't put anything over on him. He never got in trouble with the Authorities though. Just had the knack of handling them."

"You could be honest too if you'd only try," said the grandmother. "Think how wonderful it would be to settle down and live a comfortable life and not have to think about somebody chasing you all the time."

The Misfit kept scratching in the ground with the butt of his gun as if he were thinking about it. "Yes'm, somebody is always after you," he murmured.

The grandmother noticed how thin his shoulder blades were just behind his hat because she was standing up looking down on him. "Do you ever pray?" she asked.

He shook his head. All she saw was the black hat wiggle between his shoulder blades. "Nome," he said.

There was a pistol shot from the woods, followed closely by another. Then silence. The old lady's head jerked around. She could hear the wind move through the treetops like a long satisfied insuck of breath. "Bailey Boy!" she called.

"I was a gospel singer for a while," The Misfit said. "I been most everything. Been in the arm service, both land and sea, at home and abroad, been twice married, been an undertaker, been with the railroads, plowed Mother Earth, been in a tornado, seen a man burnt alive onct," and he looked up at the children's mother and the little girl who were sitting close together, their faces white and their eyes glassy; "I even seen a woman flogged," he said.

"Pray, pray," the grandmother began, "pray, pray. . ."

"I never was a bad boy that I remember of," The Misfit said in an almost dreamy voice, "but somewheres along the line I done something wrong and got sent to the penitentiary. I was buried alive," and he looked up and held her attention to him by a steady stare.

"That's when you should have started to pray," she said "What did you do to get sent to the penitentiary that first time?"

"Turn to the right, it was a wall," The Misfit said, looking up again at the cloudless sky. "Turn to the left, it was a wall. Look up it was a ceiling, look down it was a floor. I forget what I done, lady. I set there and set there, trying to remember what it was I done and I ain't recalled it to this day. Oncet in a while, I would think it was coming to me, but it never come."

"Maybe they put you in by mistake," the old lady said vaguely.

"Nome," he said. "It wasn't no mistake. They had the papers on me."

"You must have stolen something," she said.

The Misfit sneered slightly. "Nobody had nothing I wanted," he said. "It was a head-doctor at the penitentiary said what I had done was kill my daddy but I known that for a lie. My daddy died in nineteen ought nineteen of the epidemic flu and I never had a thing to do with it. He was buried in the Mount Hopewell Baptist churchyard and you can go there and see for yourself."

"If you would pray," the old lady said, "Jesus would help you."

"That's right," The Misfit said.

"Well then, why don't you pray?" she asked trembling with delight suddenly.

"I don't want no hep," he said. "I'm doing all right by myself."

Bobby Lee and Hiram came ambling back from the woods. Bobby Lee was dragging a yellow shirt with bright blue parrots in it.

"Thow me that shirt, Bobby Lee," The Misfit said. The shirt came flying at him and landed on his shoulder and he put it on. The grandmother couldn't name what the shirt reminded her of. "No, lady," The Misfit said while he was buttoning it up, "I found out the crime don't matter. You can do one thing or you can do another, kill a man or take a tire off his car, because sooner or later you're going to forget what it was you done and just be punished for it."

The children's mother had begun to make heaving noises as if she couldn't get her breath. "Lady," he asked, "would you and that little girl like to step off yonder with Bobby Lee and Hiram and join your husband?"

"Yes, thank you," the mother said faintly. Her left arm dangled helplessly and she was holding the baby, who had gone to sleep, in the other. "Hep that lady up, Hiram," The Misfit said as she struggled to climb out of the ditch, "and Bobby Lee, you hold onto that little girl's hand."

"I don't want to hold hands with him," June Star said. "He reminds me of a pig."

The fat boy blushed and laughed and caught her by the arm and pulled her off into the woods after Hiram and her mother.

Alone with The Misfit, the grandmother found that she had lost her voice. There was not a cloud in the sky nor any sun. There was nothing around her but woods. She wanted to tell him that he must pray. She opened and closed her mouth several times before anything came out. Finally she found herself saying, "Jesus. Jesus," meaning, Jesus will help you, but the way she was saying it, it sounded as if she might be cursing.

"Yes'm," The Misfit said as if he agreed. "Jesus shown everything off balance. It was the same case with Him as with me except He hadn't committed any crime and they could prove I had committed one because they had the papers on me. Of course," he said, "they never shown me my papers. That's why I sign myself now. I said long ago, you get you a signature and sign everything you do and keep a copy of it. Then you'll know what you done and you can hold up the crime to the punishment and see do they match and in the end you'll have something to prove you ain't been treated right. I call myself The Misfit," he said, "because I can't make what all I done wrong fit what all I gone through in punishment."

There was a piercing scream from the woods, followed closely by a pistol report. "Does it seem right to you, lady, that one is punished a heap and another ain't punished at all?"

"Jesus!" the old lady cried. "You've got good blood! I know you wouldn't shoot a lady! I know you come from nice people! Pray! Jesus, you ought not to shoot a lady. I'll give you all the money I've got!"

"Lady," The Misfit said, looking beyond her far into the woods, "there never was a body that give the undertaker a tip."

There were two more pistol reports and the grandmother raised her head like a parched old turkey hen crying for water and called, "Bailey Boy, Bailey Boy!" as if her heart would break.

"Jesus was the only One that ever raised the dead," The Misfit continued, "and He shouldn't have done it. He shown everything off balance. If He did what He said, then it's nothing for you to do but thow away everything and follow Him, and if He didn't, then it's nothing for you to do but enjoy the few minutes you got left the best way you can – by killing somebody or burning down his house or doing some other meanness to him. No pleasure but meanness," he said and his voice had become almost a snarl.

"Maybe He didn't raise the dead," the old lady mumbled, not knowing what she was saying and feeling so dizzy that she sank down in the ditch with her legs twisted under her.

"I wasn't there so I can't say He didn't," The Misfit said. "I wisht I had of been there," he said, hitting the ground with his fist. "It ain't right I wasn't there because if I had of been there I would of known. Listen lady," he said in a high voice, "if I had of been there I would of known and I wouldn't be like I am now." His voice seemed about to crack and the grandmother's head cleared for an instant. She saw the man's face twisted close to her own as if he were going to cry and she murmured, "Why you're one of my babies. You're one of my own children!" She reached out and touched him on the shoulder. The Misfit sprang back as if a snake had bitten him and shot her three times through the chest. Then he put his gun down on the ground and took off his glasses and began to clean them.

Hiram and Bobby Lee returned from the woods and stood over the ditch, looking down at the grandmother who half sat and half lay in a puddle of blood with her legs crossed under her like a child's and her face smiling up at the cloudless sky.

Without his glasses, The Misfit's eyes were red-rimmed and pale and defenseless-looking. "Take her off and thow her where you shown the others," he said, picking up the cat that was rubbing itself against his leg.

"She was a talker, wasn't she?" Bobby Lee said, sliding down the ditch with a yodel.

"She would of been a good woman," The Misfit said, "if it had been somebody there to shoot her every minute of her life."

"Some fun!" Bobby Lee said.

"Shut up, Bobby Lee" The Misfit said. "It's no real pleasure in life."

Berenice

Edgar Allan Poe

*'Dicebant mihi sodales, si sepulchrum amicae visitarem,
curas meas aliquantulum forelevatas.'[1]*
Ebn Zaiat

MISERY is manifold. The wretchedness of earth is multiform. Overreaching the wide horizon as the rainbow, its hues are as various as the hues of that arch – as distinct too, yet as intimately blended. Overreaching the wide horizon as the rainbow! How is it that from beauty I have derived a type of unloveliness? – from the covenant of peace, a simile of sorrow? But as, in ethics, evil is a consequence of good, so, in fact, out of joy is sorrow born. Either the memory of past bliss is the anguish of today, or the agonies which are, have their origin in the ecstasies which might have been.

My baptismal name is Egaeus; that of my family I will not mention. Yet there are no towers in the land more time-honored than my gloomy, gray, hereditary halls. Our line has been called a race of visionaries; and in many striking particulars: in the character of the family mansion; in the frescos of the chief saloon; in the tapestries of the dormitories; in the chiselling of some buttresses in the armory, but more especially in the gallery of antique paintings, in the fashion of the library chamber and, lastly, in the very peculiar nature of the library's contents, there is more than sufficient evidence to warrant the belief.

The recollections of my earliest years are connected with that chamber, and with its volumes – of which latter I will say no more. Here died my mother. Herein was I born. But it is mere idleness to say that I had not lived before, that the soul has no previous existence. You deny it? Let us not argue the matter. Convinced myself, I seek not to convince. There is, however, a remembrance of aerial forms, of spiritual and meaning eyes, of sounds, musical yet sad – a remembrance which will not be excluded; a memory like a shadow: vague, variable, indefinite, unsteady; and like a shadow, too, in the impossibility of my getting rid of it while the sunlight of my reason shall exist.

In that chamber was I born. Thus awaking from the long night of what seemed, but was not, nonentity, at once into the very regions of fairy land: into a palace of imagination, into the wild dominions of monastic thought and erudition; it is not singular that I gazed around me with a startled and ardent eye, that I loitered away my boyhood in books and dissipated my youth in reverie; but it is singular that as years rolled away, and the noon of manhood found me still in the mansion of my fathers, it is wonderful what stagnation there fell upon the springs of my life – wonderful how total an inversion took place in the character of my commonest thought. The realities of the world affected me as visions, and as visions only, while the wild ideas of the land of dreams became, in turn, not the material of my everyday existence, but in very deed that existence utterly and solely in itself.

* * *

Berenice and I were cousins, and we grew up together in my paternal halls. Yet differently we grew: I, ill of health and buried in gloom; she, agile, graceful and overflowing with energy; hers, the ramble on the hillside; mine, the studies of the cloister; I, living within my own heart, and addicted, body and soul, to the most intense and painful meditation; she, roaming carelessly through life, with no thought of the shadows in her path, or the silent flight of the raven-winged hours. Berenice! I call upon her name, Berenice!, and from the gray ruins of memory a thousand tumultuous recollections are startled at the sound! Ah, vividly is her image before me now, as in the early days of her light-heartedness and joy! Oh, gorgeous yet fantastic beauty! Oh, sylph amid the shrubberies of Arnheim! Oh, Naiad among its fountains! And then, then all is mystery and terror, and a tale which should not be told. Disease, a fatal disease, fell like the simoon upon her frame; and, even while I gazed upon her, the spirit of change swept over her, pervading her mind, her habits and her character, and, in a manner the most subtle and terrible, disturbing even the identity of her person! Alas! The destroyer came and went! And the victim: where is she? I knew her not, or knew her no longer as Berenice.

Among the numerous train of maladies superinduced by that fatal and primary one which effected a revolution of so horrible a kind in the moral and physical being of my cousin, may be mentioned as the most distressing and obstinate in its nature, a species of epilepsy not unfrequently terminating in trance itself: trance very nearly resembling positive dissolution, and from which her manner of recovery was in most instances, startlingly abrupt. In the meantime my own disease – for I have been told that I should call it by no other appellation – my own disease, then, grew rapidly upon me, and assumed finally a monomaniac character of a novel and extraordinary form, hourly and momently gaining vigor, and at length obtaining over me the most incomprehensible ascendancy. This monomania, if I must so term it, consisted in a morbid irritability of those properties of the mind in metaphysical science termed the attentive. It is more than probable that I am not understood; but I fear, indeed, that it is in no manner possible to convey to the mind of the merely general reader an adequate idea of that nervous intensity of interest with which, in my case, the powers of meditation (not to speak technically) busied and buried themselves, in the contemplation of even the most ordinary objects of the universe.

To muse for long unwearied hours, with my attention riveted to some frivolous device on the margin, or in the typography of a book; to become absorbed, for the better part of a summer's day, in a quaint shadow falling aslant upon the tapestry or upon the floor; to lose myself, for an entire night, in watching the steady flame of a lamp, or the embers of a fire; to dream away whole days over the perfume of a flower; to repeat, monotonously, some common word, until the sound, by dint of frequent repetition, ceased to convey any idea whatever to the mind; to lose all sense of motion or physical existence, by means of absolute bodily quiescence long and obstinately persevered in: such were a few of the most common and least pernicious vagaries induced by a condition of the mental faculties, not, indeed, altogether unparalleled, but certainly bidding defiance to anything like analysis or explanation.

Yet let me not be misapprehended. The undue, earnest, and morbid attention thus excited by objects in their own nature frivolous, must not be confounded in character with that ruminating propensity common to all mankind, and more especially indulged in by persons of ardent imagination. It was not even, as might be at first supposed, an extreme condition, or exaggeration of such propensity, but primarily and essentially distinct and different. In the one instance, the dreamer, or enthusiast, being interested by an object usually not frivolous, imperceptibly loses sight of this object in a wilderness of deductions and suggestions issuing therefrom, until, at the conclusion of a daydream often replete with luxury, he finds the incitamentum, or first cause of his musings, entirely vanished and forgotten. In my case, the primary object was invariably frivolous, although assuming, through the medium of my distempered vision, a refracted and unreal importance. Few deductions, if any, were made; and those few pertinaciously returning in upon the original object as a center. The meditations were never pleasurable; and, at the termination of the reverie, the first cause, so far from being out of sight, had attained that supernaturally exaggerated interest which was the prevailing feature of the disease. In a word, the powers of mind more particularly exercised were, with me, as I have said before, the attentive, and are, with the daydreamer, the speculative.

My books, at this epoch, if they did not actually serve to irritate the disorder, partook, it will be perceived, largely, in their imaginative and inconsequential nature, of the characteristic qualities of the disorder itself. I well remember, among others, the treatise of the noble Italian, Coelius Secundus Curio, *De Amplitudine Beati Regni Dei*; St. Austin's great work, the 'City of God'; and Tertullian's *De Carne Christi*, in which the paradoxical sentence *'Mortuus est Dei filius; credible est quia ineptum est: et sepultus resurrexit; certum est quia impossibile est'*[2], occupied my undivided time, for many weeks of laborious and fruitless investigation.

Thus it will appear that, shaken from its balance only by trivial things, my reason bore resemblance to that ocean-crag spoken of by Ptolemy Hephestion, which steadily resisting the attacks of human violence, and the fiercer fury of the waters and the winds, trembled only to the touch of the flower called Asphodel. And although, to a careless thinker, it might appear a matter beyond doubt, that the alteration produced by her unhappy malady, in the moral condition of Berenice, would afford me many objects for the exercise of that intense and abnormal meditation whose nature I have been at some trouble in explaining, yet such was not in any degree the case. In the lucid intervals of my infirmity, her calamity, indeed, gave me pain, and, taking deeply to heart that total wreck of her fair and gentle life, I did not fall to ponder, frequently and bitterly, upon the wonder-working means by which so strange a revolution had been so suddenly brought to pass. But these reflections partook not of the idiosyncrasy of my disease, and were such as would have occurred, under similar circumstances, to the ordinary mass of mankind. True to its own character, my disorder revelled in the less important but more startling changes wrought in the physical frame of Berenice: in the singular and most appalling distortion of her personal identity.

During the brightest days of her unparalleled beauty, most surely I had never loved her. In the strange anomaly of my existence, feelings with me had never been of the heart, and my passions always were of the mind. Through the gray of the early morning, among the trellised shadows of the forest at noonday, and in the silence of my library at night, she had flitted by my eyes, and I had seen her: not as the living and breathing

Berenice, but as the Berenice of a dream; not as a being of the earth, earthy, but as the abstraction of such a being; not as a thing to admire, but to analyze; not as an object of love, but as the theme of the most abstruse although desultory speculation. And now, now I shuddered in her presence, and grew pale at her approach; yet, bitterly lamenting her fallen and desolate condition, I called to mind that she had loved me long, and, in an evil moment, I spoke to her of marriage.

And at length the period of our nuptials was approaching, when, upon an afternoon in the winter of the year, one of those unseasonably warm, calm, and misty days which are the nurse of the beautiful Halcyon[3], I sat, (and sat, as I thought, alone), in the inner apartment of the library. But, uplifting my eyes, I saw that Berenice stood before me.

Was it my own excited imagination – or the misty influence of the atmosphere, or the uncertain twilight of the chamber, or the gray draperies which fell around her figure – that caused in it so vacillating and indistinct an outline? I could not tell. She spoke no word; and I, not for worlds, could I have uttered a syllable. An icy chill ran through my frame; a sense of insufferable anxiety oppressed me; a consuming curiosity pervaded my soul; and sinking back upon the chair, I remained for some time breathless and motionless, with my eyes riveted upon her person. Alas! Its emaciation was excessive, and not one vestige of the former being lurked in any single line of the contour. My burning glances at length fell upon the face.

The forehead was high, and very pale, and singularly placid; and the once jetty hair fell partially over it, and overshadowed the hollow temples with innumerable ringlets, now of a vivid yellow, and jarring discordantly, in their fantastic character, with the reigning melancholy of the countenance. The eyes were lifeless, and lustreless, and seemingly pupil-less, and I shrank involuntarily from their glassy stare to the contemplation of the thin and shrunken lips. They parted; and in a smile of peculiar meaning, the teeth of the changed Berenice disclosed themselves slowly to my view. Would to God that I had never beheld them, or that, having done so, I had died!

* * *

The shutting of a door disturbed me, and, looking up, I found that my cousin had departed from the chamber. But from the disordered chamber of my brain, had not, alas, departed, and would not be driven away, the white and ghastly spectrum of the teeth. Not a speck on their surface, not a shade on their enamel, not an indenture in their edges, but what that period of her smile had sufficed to brand in upon my memory. I saw them now even more unequivocally than I beheld them then. The teeth! The teeth! They were here, and there, and everywhere, and visibly and palpably before me; long, narrow, and excessively white, with the pale lips writhing about them, as in the very moment of their first terrible development. Then came the full fury of my monomania, and I struggled in vain against its strange and irresistible influence. In the multiplied objects of the external world I had no thoughts but for the teeth. For these I longed with a frenzied desire. All other matters and all different interests became absorbed in their single contemplation. They, they alone were present to the mental eye, and they, in their sole individuality, became the essence of my mental life. I held them in every light. I turned them in every attitude. I surveyed their characteristics. I dwelt upon their peculiarities. I pondered upon their conformation. I mused upon the alteration in their nature. I shuddered as I assigned to them in imagination a sensitive and sentient power, and even when unassisted by the lips, a capability of moral expression. Of Mademoiselle Salle it has been well said, '*Que tous ses pas etaient des sentiments*'[4], and of Berenice I more seriously believed *que toutes ses dents etaient des idees.*[5] Des idees! Ah, here was the idiotic thought that destroyed me! Des idees! Ah. Therefore it was that I coveted them so madly! I felt that their possession could alone ever restore me to peace, in giving me back to reason.

And the evening closed in upon me thus and then the darkness came and tarried and went, and the day again dawned, and the mists of a second night were now gathering around, and still I sat motionless in that solitary room, and still I sat buried in meditation, and still the phantasma of the teeth maintained its terrible ascendancy, as, with the most vivid hideous distinctness, it floated about amid the changing lights and shadows of the chamber. At length there broke in upon my dreams a cry as of horror and dismay; and thereunto, after a pause, succeeded the sound of troubled voices, intermingled with many low moanings of sorrow or of pain. I arose from my seat, and throwing open one of the doors of the library, saw standing out in the ante-chamber a servant maiden, all in tears, who told me that Berenice was no more! She had been seized with epilepsy in the early morning, and now, at the closing in of the night, the grave was ready for its tenant, and all the preparations for the burial were completed.

* * *

I found myself sitting in the library, and again sitting there alone. It seemed that I had newly awakened from a confused and exciting dream. I knew that it was now midnight, and I was well aware, that since the setting of the sun, Berenice had been interred. But of that dreary period which intervened I had no positive, at least no definite comprehension. Yet its memory was replete with horror, horror more horrible from being vague, and terror more terrible from ambiguity. It was a fearful page in the record my existence, written all over with dim, and hideous, and unintelligible recollections. I strived to decipher them, but in vain; while ever and anon, like the spirit of a departed sound, the shrill and piercing shriek of a female voice seemed to be ringing in my ears. I had done a deed: what was it? I asked myself the question aloud, and the whispering echoes of the chamber answered me, "What was it?"

On the table beside me burned a lamp, and near it lay a little box. It was of no remarkable character, and I had seen it frequently before, for it was the property of the family physician; but how came it there, upon my table, and why did I shudder in regarding it? These things were in no manner to be accounted for, and my eyes at length dropped to the open pages of a book, and to a sentence underscored therein. The words were the singular but simple ones of the poet Ebn Zaiat: "*Dicebant mihi sodales si sepulchrum amicae visitarem, curas meas aliquantulum forelevatas.*" Why then, as I perused them, did the hairs of my head erect themselves on end, and the blood of my body become congealed within my veins?

There came a light tap at the library door, and, pale as the tenant of a tomb, a menial entered upon tiptoe. His looks were wild with terror, and he spoke to me in a voice tremulous, husky, and very low. What said he? Some broken sentences I heard. He told of a wild cry disturbing the silence of the night, of the gathering together of the household, of a search in the direction of the sound; and then his tones grew thrillingly distinct as he whispered me of a violated grave: of a disfigured body enshrouded, yet still breathing, still palpitating: still alive!

He pointed to garments: they were muddy and clotted with gore. I spoke not, and he took me gently by the hand: it was indented with the impress of human nails. He directed my attention to some object against the wall. I looked at it for some minutes: it was a spade. With a shriek I bounded to the table, and grasped the box that lay upon it. But I could not force it open; and in my tremor, it slipped from my hands, and fell heavily, and burst into pieces; and from it, with a rattling sound, there rolled out some instruments of dental surgery, intermingled with thirty-two small, white and ivory-looking substances that were scattered to and fro about the floor.

Footnotes for 'Berenice'

1. 'My companions told me I might find some little alleviation of my misery, in visiting the grave of my beloved.'
2. 'That the Son of God died is entirely believable simply because it seems so absurd that He would do so. That he rose from the dead is certain simply because it is impossible to do so.'
3. 'For as Jove, during the winter season, gives twice seven days of warmth, men have called this element and temperate time the nurse of the beautiful Halcyon.' – Simonides.
4. 'All her [ballet] steps were sentiments.'
5. 'All of her teeth were ideas.'

The Tell-Tale Heart

Edgar Allan Poe

TRUE! – Nervous – very, very dreadfully nervous I had been and am; but why will you say that I am mad? The disease had sharpened my senses – not destroyed – not dulled them. Above all was the sense of hearing acute. I heard all things in the heaven and in the earth. I heard many things in hell. How, then, am I mad? Hearken! And observe how healthily – how calmly I can tell you the whole story.

It is impossible to say how first the idea entered my brain; but once conceived, it haunted me day and night. Object there was none. Passion there was none. I loved the old man. He had never wronged me. He had never given me insult. For his gold I had no desire. I think it was his eye! Yes, it was this! He had the eye of a vulture – a pale blue eye, with a film over it. Whenever it fell upon me, my blood ran cold; and so by degrees – very gradually – I made up my mind to take the life of the old man, and thus rid myself of the eye forever.

Now this is the point. You fancy me mad. Madmen know nothing. But you should have seen me. You should have seen how wisely I proceeded – with what caution – with what foresight – with what dissimulation I went to work! I was never kinder to the old man than during the whole week before I killed him. And every night, about midnight, I turned the latch of his door and opened it – oh so gently! And then, when I had made an opening sufficient for my head, I put in a dark lantern, all closed, closed, that no light shone out, and then I thrust in my head. Oh, you would have laughed to see how cunningly I thrust it in! I moved it slowly – very, very slowly, so that I might not disturb the old man's sleep. It took me an hour to place my whole head within the opening so far that I could see him as he lay upon his bed. Ha! Would a madman have been so wise as this? And then, when my head was well in the room, I undid the lantern cautiously – oh, so cautiously – cautiously (for the hinges creaked) – I undid it just so much that a single thin ray fell upon the vulture eye. And this I did for seven long nights – every night just at midnight – but I found the eye always closed; and so it was impossible to do the work; for it was not the old man who vexed me, but his Evil Eye. And every morning, when the day broke, I went boldly into the chamber, and spoke courageously to him, calling him by name in a hearty tone, and inquiring how he has passed the night. So you see he would have been a very profound old man, indeed, to suspect that every night, just at twelve, I looked in upon him while he slept.

Upon the eighth night I was more than usually cautious in opening the door. A watch's minute hand moves more quickly than did mine. Never before that night had I felt the extent of my own powers – of my sagacity. I could scarcely contain my feelings of triumph. To think that there I was, opening the door, little by little, and he not even to dream of my secret deeds or thoughts. I fairly chuckled at the idea; and perhaps he heard me; for he moved on the bed suddenly, as if startled. Now you may think that I drew back – but no. His room was as black as pitch with the thick darkness (for the shutters were close-fastened, through fear of robbers), and so I knew that he could not see the opening of the door, and I kept pushing it on steadily, steadily.

I had my head in, and was about to open the lantern, when my thumb slipped upon the tin fastening, and the old man sprang up in bed, crying out – "Who's there?"

I kept quite still and said nothing. For a whole hour I did not move a muscle, and in the meantime I did not hear him lie down. He was still sitting up in the bed listening – just as I have done, night after night, hearkening to the death watches in the wall.

Presently I heard a slight groan, and I knew it was the groan of mortal terror. It was not a groan of pain or of grief – oh, no! – It was the low stifled sound that arises from the bottom of the soul when overcharged with awe. I knew the sound well. Many a night, just at midnight, when all the world slept, it has welled up from my own bosom, deepening, with its dreadful echo, the terrors that distracted me. I say I knew it well. I knew what the old man felt, and pitied him, although I chuckled at heart. I knew that he had been lying awake ever since the first slight noise, when he had turned in the bed. His fears had been ever since growing upon him. He had been trying to fancy them causeless, but could not. He had been saying to himself – "It is nothing but the wind in the chimney – it is only a mouse crossing the floor," or "It is merely a cricket which has made a single chirp." Yes, he had been trying to comfort himself with these suppositions: but he had found all in vain. All in vain; because Death, in approaching him had stalked with his black shadow before him, and enveloped the victim. And it was the mournful influence of the unperceived shadow that caused him to feel – although he neither saw nor heard – to feel the presence of my head within the room.

When I had waited a long time, very patiently, without hearing him lie down, I resolved to open a little – a very, very little crevice in the lantern. So I opened it – you cannot imagine how stealthily, stealthily – until, at length a simple dim ray, like the thread of the spider, shot from out the crevice and fell full upon the vulture eye.

It was open – wide, wide open – and I grew furious as I gazed upon it. I saw it with perfect distinctness – all a dull blue, with a hideous veil over it that chilled the very marrow in my bones; but I could see nothing else of the old man's face or person: for I had directed the ray as if by instinct, precisely upon the damned spot.

And have I not told you that what you mistake for madness is but over-acuteness of the sense? – Now, I say, there came to my ears a low, dull, quick sound, such as a watch makes when enveloped in cotton. I knew that sound well, too. It was the beating of the old man's heart. It increased my fury, as the beating of a drum stimulates the soldier into courage.

But even yet I refrained and kept still. I scarcely breathed. I held the lantern motionless. I tried how steadily I could maintain the ray upon the eye. Meantime the hellish tattoo of the heart increased. It grew quicker and quicker, and louder and louder every instant. The old man's terror must have been extreme! It grew louder, I say, louder every moment! – Do you mark me well I have told you that I am nervous: so I am. And now at the dead hour of the night, amid the dreadful silence of that old house, so strange a noise as this excited me to uncontrollable terror. Yet, for some minutes longer I refrained and stood still. But the beating grew louder, louder! I thought the heart must burst. And now a new anxiety seized me – the sound would be heard by a neighbor! The old man's hour had come! With a loud yell, I threw open the lantern and leaped into the room. He shrieked once – once only. In an instant I dragged him to the floor, and pulled the heavy bed over him. I then smiled gaily, to find the deed so far done. But, for many minutes, the heart beat on with a muffled sound. This, however, did not vex me; it would not be heard through the wall. At length it ceased. The old man was dead. I removed the bed and examined the corpse. Yes, he was stone, stone dead. I placed my hand upon the heart and held it there many minutes. There was no pulsation. He was stone dead. His eye would trouble me no more.

If still you think me mad, you will think so no longer when I describe the wise precautions I took for the concealment of the body. The night waned, and I worked hastily, but in silence. First of all I dismembered the corpse. I cut off the head and the arms and the legs.

I then took up three planks from the flooring of the chamber, and deposited all between the scantlings. I then replaced the boards so cleverly, so cunningly, that no human eye – not even his – could have detected anything wrong. There was nothing to wash out – no stain of any kind – no blood-spot whatever. I had been too wary for that. A tub had caught all – ha! Ha!

When I had made an end of these labors, it was four o'clock – still dark as midnight. As the bell sounded the hour, there came a knocking at the street door. I went down to open it with a light heart – for what had I now to fear? There entered three men, who introduced themselves, with perfect suavity, as officers of the police. A shriek had been heard by a neighbor during the night; suspicion of foul play had been aroused; information had been lodged at the police office, and they (the officers) had been deputed to search the premises.

I smiled – for what had I to fear? I bade the gentlemen welcome. The shriek, I said, was my own in a dream. The old man, I mentioned, was absent in the country. I took my visitors all over the house. I bade them search – search well. I led them, at length, to his chamber. I showed them his treasures, secure, undisturbed. In the enthusiasm of my confidence, I brought chairs into the room, and desired them here to rest from their fatigues, while I myself, in the wild audacity of my perfect triumph, placed my own seat upon the very spot beneath which reposed the corpse of the victim.

The officers were satisfied. My manner had convinced them. I was singularly at ease. They sat, and while I answered cheerily, they chatted of familiar things. But, ere long, I felt myself getting pale and wished them gone. My head ached, and I fancied a ringing in my ears: but still they sat and still chatted. The ringing became more distinct: – it continued and became more distinct: I talked more freely to get rid of the feeling: but it continued and gained definiteness – until, at length, I found that the noise was not within my ears.

No doubt I now grew *very* pale; – but I talked more fluently, and with a heightened voice. Yet the sound increased – and what could I do? It was a low, dull, quick sound – much such a sound as a watch makes when enveloped in cotton. I gasped for breath – and yet the officers heard it not. I talked more quickly – more vehemently; but the noise steadily increased. I arose and argued about trifles, in a high key and with violent gesticulations; but the noise steadily increased. Why would they not be gone? I paced the floor to and fro with heavy strides, as if excited to fury by the observations of the men – but the noise steadily increased. Oh God! What could I do? I foamed – I raved – I swore! I swung the chair upon which I had been sitting, and grated it upon the boards, but the noise arose over all and continually increased. It grew louder – louder – louder! And still the men chatted pleasantly, and smiled. Was it possible they heard not? Almighty God! – No, no! They heard! – They suspected! – They knew! – They were making a mockery of my horror! – This I thought, and this I think. But anything was better than this agony! Anything was more tolerable than this derision! I could bear those hypocritical smiles no longer! I felt that I must scream or die! And now – again! – Hark! Louder! Louder! Louder! Louder!

"Villains!" I shrieked, "Dissemble no more! I admit the deed! – Tear up the planks! Here, here! – It is the beating of his hideous heart!"

Baby Teeth

Lina Rather

LAURA WATCHED from the window while Mama took the salt packets they'd pocketed from a Speedway and sprinkled a circle around the house to hide them from the monster. She tore the top of each one off with her teeth and spread it as far as she could, then dropped the white paper scraps on the ground. Laura had stuffed her pockets with packets, so she knew Mama had enough to walk around the whole perimeter of the property. Not that it was much – the next mobile home sat just ten yards away.

When she came back inside, she swept her hands together to brush off the salt and sat next to Laura at the table. "Okay, honey, show me again."

Laura opened her mouth. She'd been probing the sore spots (one in front, on the bottom, and one on the top right) and now her mouth tasted tinny. Mama touched her swollen gums.

"These just fell out today?"

Laura nodded. She pointed at her top front tooth and the canine next to it, and tried to say, "These are loose, too" but with Mama's finger in her mouth it came out all garbled. Mama pinched the front tooth and her hands were shaking hard enough to wiggle it. When she touched the canine, it popped out in her hand easy-peasy. Mama stared at it.

"You said I should've lost them before." Most of her classmates started losing their teeth in first grade, and that was a whole four years ago.

Mama got up and took a cereal bowl out of the dish drainer. She pressed a Kleenex to the raw spot in Laura's jaw, puffy and red like a hangnail. They moved their folding chairs next to the sink, so Mama could make warm salt water for her to gargle. It was way after both their bedtimes. The canine went *ping* when she dropped it in the cereal bowl on the kitchen counter.

Ping went the front tooth that came out next.

Ping went the incisor from Laura's pocket that had fallen out during gym class, while she was jumping rope.

The cereal bowl was half full, a week of lost teeth. Too many teeth, Laura thought. They'd learned about the body in her last school and she knew that kids had twenty teeth, more or less. Her teacher back there was what Mama called a free spirit and she liked to say *Humanity is infinite variation so you're just the way you're supposed to be*, but Laura was pretty sure there was an upper limit on teeth.

* * *

Laura was nine-and-a-half and for her entire life it had been just her and Mama, and for her entire life they had been running from the monster. She was six before she realized that other people's mothers didn't salt a ring around the house every full moon, and that other kids were told to stay out of the street more than they were reminded to wash their hands and feet with black soap so their scent didn't track behind them. The year she was seven, they lived in Alabama. Laura loved the heat that sat around her shoulders like a baby blanket all summer and hated the humidity that made her hair go to frizz.

They left when the monster caught up to them, when the skulls of small things appeared on the doorstep and the air tasted of the monster, of deep, wet loam and burnt green branches. Mama stayed as long as she could, but Laura still missed the last week of school, the pizza party and the yearbook signing. Even after she saw the trail of footprints in rotted grass around the perimeter of the trailer they rented, she still resented missing the pizza party.

Now they lived in Indiana, right by the water. Laura was small for her age and she had no winter clothes. The other kids at school didn't understand her nowhere-accent or why she wore tennis shoes to school in the snow. Mama got a job at a call center where she sold kitchen gadgets from the TV to old women with not enough money.

Mama said all the water made it hard for the monster to find them, and that might have been true before Laura's teeth started coming out.

The day after Mama salted a circle around the house on a half-full moon, she packed Laura mashed potatoes and pot roast shredded to tiny pieces for lunch the next day because it hurt to chew with the new teeth coming in. Laura's face was different now too. She could tell the new teeth had pushed her jaw out and changed the angles of her skull.

Once she'd gone on a field trip to a natural history museum where they saw the skeleton of a kid who'd died of some disease nobody got anymore ("consumption" her memory said, or maybe "influenza"). All their adult teeth were inside their facial bones, waiting for their little teeth to fall out. That day in school, the pressure in her face nearly unbearable, Laura imagined that her whole skull was made of teeth, honeycomb bones stacked with incisors and molars and premolars instead of marrow.

She sat in the cool, dark space under the play escape at recess, in a pile of woodchips. Down here it smelled dank and earthy like the monster did, and she crawled in sometimes to remind herself to be afraid of it. Now, though, she only wanted the quiet.

Something scratched next to her. She opened her eyes to find a boy pulling himself through the same hole in the play structure she had. They were in the same class. His name was Jonas, he was ten-and-a-quarter, and he took what wasn't his. She didn't like him very much.

"What's wrong with your teeth?" he said, instead of hello. They sat at the same table and had to share the same box of crayons. She imagined now that he'd been staring at her mouth all day and blushed. "They're all pointy."

Laura ran her tongue over the sore places. He was right. She tasted blood when she scraped the tip of her tongue on the sharp, serrated edge of what should have been a molar. Carnivore teeth, she thought. Omnivores had flat molars for plants, and she had these, for biting. "Everybody's different."

He squinted at her in the dark, leaning so close she could smell his breath. Goldfish crackers and bubblegum toothpaste. Her stomach roiled. She knew she'd been right – there was a limit on human variation.

"You're like a crocodile," he said. He grabbed her arm and his face was right up in hers. "Like a dinosaur. Lizard Laura."

"Let go of me," she said, even though it wouldn't do any good. It wouldn't do any good to say *Dinosaurs and crocodiles aren't lizards* either, and if she screamed she'd have to explain to the lunch lady what had happened. She'd have to show her teeth.

"Is this why you talk funny?" Jonas's fingers dug into the soft spot under her arm. His other hand hovered by her face, almost touching. "Show them to me again."

She smashed her head against one of the beams when she tried to yank away and she couldn't breathe because all she could smell was him and the earth, all she could smell was the monsters. He grabbed her cheek and pulled up her lip with his thumb.

Laura bit him then. But she never heard him scream. All sound fled from the world when she tasted his blood. It filled her mouth – so, so much of it even though she knew it was just a little cut. Salt and iron and bitter sweat. And him. She saw straight through him, through clothing and skin and bone. She saw his memories and his future and his death.

"Jonas Wilder," she said, and did not recognize the sounds or the throat that made them. "I know all of you."

He lurched backward, tripped over himself, and tried to scramble away. But the hidey-hole was too small, and he couldn't make his arms and legs work together well enough to crawl out. And she was so big, she could pin him down if she wanted, she could eat him up if she wanted.

"You are very stupid," she said, and got to her feet, and brushed the woodchips off her jeans. "And you will never learn how to not be mean. You will die being stupid and mean. I can see the maggots crawling around in your skull."

She left him crying there. Afterwards everywhere she walked, even in class, she smelled the wet ground under the play escape, the decaying cedar. She cleaned off her shoes in the bathroom and walked around in wet socks for the rest of the day but the smell of the monster still followed her home.

* * *

That night, Mama found a turtle skull on the front step. It crunched under her flip-flop when she took out the trash. The bones were so dry that Laura heard the snap from inside. She also heard Mama fall against the side of the motor home and her gasping breath. Her nails scrabbled along the siding by Laura's room, and Laura lay flat on her bed very quietly so that she could not see out the window.

When Mama came back inside she shut the door softly and began packing. Laura heard her take the stack of boxes out from under the table and start putting the essentials inside. Toaster, silverware, Laura's Children's Illustrated Classics series and Mama's H.G. Wells fancy hardback. Their car was a pick-up truck from the 80s, but they still didn't have room to keep everything. Clothes they could get for cheap wherever they landed, so they would bring only the favorites that could fit in Laura's backpack. Furniture was too big to move.

Laura crept down the hall to the kitchen and watched from the doorway as Mama packed up the cans of soup and spam in the cupboard. "Are we leaving again?"

Mama stopped with a can of Homestyle Chicken Noodle in her hand. She leaned on the counter for a second. "Yeah. He's coming."

"It's too soon." Laura twirled her hair around her finger and gave it a sharp tug, so the pain would convince her this was real. Her hair was still damp from the shower. She'd scrubbed and scrubbed, first with a washcloth and soap and then with Mama's pumice stone so her skin bled, but she still smelled like dead grass. "We've only been here two months."

"He found us." Mama hefted the soup can like she was testing it for a weapon, then sighed and put it in the box. "We'll stay for a day or two to wrap things up here, but he's already close."

"Because of me." She hadn't told Mama about Jonas, but the teeth were enough.

"Yes."

Laura had known all her life that the monster was her daddy. She couldn't remember Mama telling her. It was just a fact. She had to have come from somewhere, everyone did. She'd never considered what he'd given her. It was only her and Mama who were family, after all.

She'd seen the monster only once. She was eight and they'd waited too long in Idaho. By the time Mama revved the truck they could hear it breathing, huffing, scratching at the ground. The soil turned red under the tires and Laura choked on air so heavy with moisture and decay that it clogged her lungs. Mama hadn't buckled in even though it was one of her rules. Laura curled up on her seat. They were going so fast and all she could think of was when an oil truck had overturned on these roads and everyone died including a bunch of animals poisoned by the petroleum.

She'd gathered all her courage up and peeked out the back window. She saw only the shadow, so big it blocked out the moon and the stars and the air around it shimmered like the world coming undone. It made her sick to look at. She'd begged Mama to go faster.

"Can he follow us better now?" She helped Mama get the shoebox full of switchblades and hunting knives out from under the sink. They'd done this all before.

"I don't know." Mama's tone said *probably*.

Laura got out another box and packed up the laundry detergent and dish soap, which they always took with them because it was expensive. They worked in silence, with only the whistle of the wind outside and the creaks and groans of the aluminum siding to keep them company.

"Did you—" Laura always thought of the monster as *it*, a force of nature, but that wasn't right. "—love him?"

Mama sat – no, fell – down into a chair. Her hands dropped to her knees and Laura saw every thin, white scar that criss-crossed her palms. The price of holding hands with things with claws. "Yes. But – you're old enough to know, right? That isn't always good.

"Sometimes it's comforting for someone to see right through you. I never could keep a secret from him. He knew me inside and out. I was never anyone but myself with him, and for long enough, that felt like freedom."

Mama took a great big breath and then let herself deflate. "Don't worry about it, baby. Everybody makes mistakes when they're young, and at least I got you out of it."

Laura was old enough to know that she only got called *baby* when Mama didn't want to talk about something.

This was the fifth town she'd lived in (that she could remember – they'd moved three times before she got old enough to notice), the fourth state, the ninth address. While other kids loved to talk about the places they'd go someday, she was terrified of atlases, nauseated at the thought of globes and geography lessons. All those faraway places she might someday have to go to evade the monster's reach. In class, sometimes she'd stare at the inflatable globe hanging from the ceiling and try to work out how long she'd have to run before she ran out of land, and if that would be far enough.

That thought depressed her, so she went back to her room and got her stuffed bunny. His name was Wallace and she'd picked him out at a Speedway when she was three. He was missing an ear now but that didn't matter. She sat him on her lap and chewed on his other ear even though she knew she was too old for it. Mama usually yelled at her about it, but today she didn't even pluck the ear from Laura's mouth.

Mama yanked packing tape across the first box and smoothed it down. "Tomorrow I'll get my last check and we'll figure out where to go. We can be gone by midnight, I bet."

Wallace's black safety eyes stared up at Laura. She'd chewed and chewed on them as a child but they'd stayed on true to their name. She fit one between her front teeth now, felt the shank sewn deep in the plush. A thread snapped. "I'm always going to be running, aren't I, for my whole entire life."

Mama's head shot up. Her lips parted, but there was too long of a pause while she thought of something to say. An unhappy smile stretched her mouth wrong. "No. He's enough of a man to die eventually."

"But for a long, long time. Until I'm as old as you even."

Mama laughed, but not like anything was funny. "Longer than that, sweetie."

That night Mama mixed up saltwater in the sink and rinsed Laura's hair with it, even though Laura was too old for being bathed. The salt got in her eyes and the crooks of her elbows and knees and her new teeth ached. When Mama held her hair at the scalp to keep her still Laura imagined how easy it would be to slip Mama's hand into her mouth. How easy to let her teeth catch on a groove of skin, the sweet taste of blood. Like the dirt here, all iron, it would taste so good. It would fill her up. Her stomach full of grilled cheese rumbled against her ribs. She could hear Mama's pulse so loud it drowned out everything else, the beat in her wrist so close to the one in Laura's temple that her skull rattled in tempo with it.

* * *

In the morning there was a map on the table. For the past few years they'd chased oil. Boom towns, new faces every other week, the sort of places that lived and died on pipeline money.

"We could go north," Mama said. "Alaska. If we go far enough, he'd have to swim. Or we could go east. Some of the houses there are built to keep out things like him, because they come from a time when people remembered to do that."

In the night, Laura had woken to hear something in the trees. One moment it sounded like wind and the next like breathing. Her hands itched deep below the skin like she was full of splinters and papercuts. She pressed them against the window and the glass steamed. For a second, there was only the cold. Then warmth, over one hand and then the other, like someone on the other side of the glass pressing back.

Her hands felt fine today. She rubbed her right thumb over her left knuckles and couldn't find a bone out of place, but anatomy class wasn't until high school. She didn't really know how many there were supposed to be. Would anyone really care if she had a few extra nubs in her wrist or a few less? "Will they let me in?"

"Who?"

"The houses. Out east."

Mama's mouth went round like she wanted to say *of course* but then she came around the table and cradled Laura's face in her hands. "We might have to file your teeth. Then they'll recognize you for what you really are."

That day at school, everyone said goodbye to Laura. The teacher said it was sad she had to leave so quick, and her grandmother must be very sick. Laura only nodded. Jonas waited behind the teacher and only came up when all the other children had lost interest in the momentary drama and drifted out of earshot.

"I'm not sorry you're leaving," he declared. The teacher's head turned slightly at his tone, reflexively. But she had too much to do to worry about every instance of children being cruel to each other. Jonas caught the motion and he put his hands on Laura's desk so she could see what he was doing with them. His voice went small, like something she might have imagined. "I don't want to be bad."

"Can you help it?" she asked. This wasn't the monster in her. She was just angry. His palms opened to her, helpless.

He shook his head. "I try."

They were supposed to be doing worksheets. Multiplication and division with fractions. Laura had yet to understand remainders as anything more than random numbers that appeared like magic at the end of example problems. But Mama said that in seventh grade she'd be allowed to use a calculator and she'd forget how to do it all anyway, so she hadn't really tried.

"Maybe it's just hard," she allowed. But she had seen his fate and she believed as all children did in inevitable endings, like in fairy tales and church sermons.

Jonas leaned against her desk and his hair fell over his face. She heard him breathing in and out, in and out, like the last breaths of one of the little creatures that the monster left on their doorstep to scare Mama and to ask her back.

She'd broken him, she realized. She hadn't meant to, but this was also inevitable. Her hands prickled and she wanted to tear up the carpet and the cinderblocks and the grass because she knew there was a long-dead squirrel right under their feet, and maybe if she gave him its picked-clean ribcage he would understand it as an apology.

But he didn't understand her silence. His right hand curled into a fist and he rapped his knuckles on her desk only once, with no sound, with every muscle in his arm tensed and ready. This she understood perfectly well.

* * *

She screamed so loud when the file hit the first tooth that Mama promised they could wait on the rest until they reached Pennsylvania. Laura didn't think it would help. They could blunt all her teeth, these and the ones she felt waiting in her gums, and it wouldn't matter.

She had a nightmare in the car of one of the houses out east locking her out. When she woke, sweating, expecting to find herself walled up in shiplap and bricks, it was dark and Mama was driving one-handed with a thirty-two ounce Styrofoam coffee cup bouncing on her knee. The wind howled and the only light in the whole world was the glow of their headlights. She tried propping her head on the seatbelt and stretching out across the backseat but the wind kept her up.

There was no moon, no stars. Mama slurped coffee and her nails tapped Morse code nonsense on the steering wheel.

The wind stuck its fingers through the cracks in the seals around the doors, the seams of the trunk. Outside the trees stooped over like old men. The car started making a sound like a blender full of ice cubes. The coffee tumbled from Mama's lap and spilled across the passenger seat.

The windows fogged up. Mama hissed something inappropriate under her breath.

One of Laura's front teeth wiggled. This one had already popped out once, but she could feel a new tooth underneath, the sharp edge cutting through.

The wind became a voice, and in it she heard her name over and over. Not *Laura*, but a different name, a name for the monster that waited in her bones and her blood.

Mama let go of the steering wheel and leaned over the dash to wipe the windshield clean with her shirtsleeve. The car swerved. Laura's head clunked against the door and she saw fireworks.

"You alright?" Mama asked, when she grabbed the wheel again. There was coffee splattered on her cheek.

"He's outside." She couldn't see the trees anymore, or the road. If there were other cars, they were lost in the darkness. Something that sounded like tree branches scraped across the roof of the car, and she knew that they were claws because she could feel her own hands changing shape.

"Just close your eyes," Mama said.

Laura did, and the tires squealed, and the whole car jerked. She imagined that they'd been swallowed up, and opened her eyes again. She saw Mama with tears on her face, staring into a black windshield.

It will always be like this, she thought. She felt something in her shift. Not because of what her body was turning into. Because she'd never had such an enormous thought in her entire life. It made her feel grown up and scared, and she thought that this was how Mama must feel all the time.

She rolled the window down.

"Laura." Mama was still pressing on the gas pedal, even though it was obvious they weren't moving, even though Laura knew there wasn't a road at all anymore. "Don't."

Her fingers left bloody prints on the door when her nails popped off one by one, but she could sense the form underneath now and the pain was better with a purpose.

Too late Mama hit the childlock. She fumbled with her seatbelt but her hands were shaking and Laura had always been fast. Her new legs would be faster when she shed this skin.

Before she left, Laura leaned over the seat and kissed Mama's head, the only part she could reach. Mama, who always tried to save her, who was always doomed to failure. It wasn't her fault that she would never understand.

"I'll be back," she said, "someday. And I won't be a bad monster, I promise. Maybe I'll eat him up, when I'm big enough."

She smiled, and Mama froze at the sight of her. But there was nothing to be done. This mouth couldn't speak Mama's language anymore. She dropped from the window and the shadow scooped her up with hands made of fur and claws, and she left all the rest of herself behind.

Bibliosmia

M. Regan

"THE TEA shall take a few moments, I'm afraid," she demurs from the library's entrance, her greeting offered with a curtsey in lieu of a hand. It is a logical substitution, considering; the customary kiss would've been quite impossible, engaged as she is in the delivery of refreshment. "Or rather, a few *minutes.*"

Polished silver gleams when borne beneath antiquated gas lamps, its details shifting and mercurial where golden light warps angles and contours, where it twists around ornate decorations. White teeth click in the smile that she has donned; bone china imitates, drawn together by delicate movements.

Spoons shiver. Startled saucers jump. A heavy tray settles upon the mahogany coffee table, and your host settles upon the vintage chaise that had been positioned behind it.

"Five minutes," she clarifies, the turn of an hourglass serving as punctuation. The piece's gilt matches the tray, matches the tea set, matches the room, matches the house, all of which had been designed mere years ago to evoke feelings of Gothic majesty; the hourglass shines like the storm that is leaving streaks on the oriel window.

Sand falls, rain falls. Both land as softly on the ears as the voice of a mourner. "Five minutes should do it. But I apologize. I'm sure you didn't expect to wait."

"It is no trouble." You are aware of the process for making tea, just as she is aware of your reasons for being in her home. Such remorse is primarily an act. But then, what in polite society isn't?

With propriety in mind, you seat yourself in an armchair adjacent to her own.

"Actually," you append, "as it happens, I require your attention for at least that much time, anyway."

The velvet growl of disturbed upholstery muffles the very small sigh that your hostess allows herself. Its breath catches the fine wisps that have escaped her coiffure.

"I did imagine so," she confesses on the tail of this exhalation. "Every meeting I've been made to endure since Father's murder has taken at least ten times that."

Murder. It is upsetting to hear the man's fate bluntly stated, particularly when there exist so many more ambiguous and eloquent turns of phrase to communicate such tragedy.

Then again, it *is* his death that has summoned you here. No point beating around the bush. You clear your throat. "I shall endeavor not to overstay my welcome."

"Indeed," your hostess murmurs, lacing thin hands. Lowering her eyes. Like everything else about her person, the young woman's gratitude is understated, uneasy.

What a miserable picture this lady paints, you think with overtures of sympathy. A lonely, homely heiress, her unfortunate demeanor worsened – albeit understandably – by her darkest clothes and a worn-through façade. At twenty she is fully grown, but in her newly orphaned state, seems quite young and frail and small again, particularly when set against the trappings of old money, older tomes.

Rain pitters pitifully against paned glass, each drop adding ellipses to the extended silence. Sinking sand susurrates, seconds piling up to sixty.

"...before," she announces, in that blunt, sudden way that uncomfortable people announce things, "I would refuse to partake in lemon tea."

Colors swirl atop the surface of steeping beverages, ochres and crimsons and ichor-gold; flavor bleeds between the perforations in matching infusers, dregs drifting, descending, coagulating like scabs peeled from a wound.

"It was the way the lemon turned the tea red," she explains, squeezing the hands that she has laced atop her thighs. "The first time I put such a teabag in hot water, I imagined...I believed I had killed something. That something had died within it. No one could convince me otherwise, that it was true and proper tea bleeding into my cup..."

If not for her own sheepish chuckles, your snort would be quite rude.

"A rather macabre thing for a child to think," you note, more comment than judgment. One should not condemn the daughter, after all, for the sins of the father. "However, given the environment of your upbringing, Miss, I cannot say that I am surprised."

"Mmm. The environment that you have come to discuss with me today, is that not so?" she muses, though in her current mood it is hardly a question at all; certainty dulls the edge of anything in her voice that may have once been accusatory. "Or you would discuss portions of it, if I recall your phone call correctly."

She does. The shadows beneath her eyes are a perfect match for those that lurk in the room's sharpest corners.

You cross one leg over the other, settling further into your seat.

"Yes, well...Over the course of his life, Miss, your father amassed an impressive collection of, ah, *unique* books," you tell your hostess, choosing each word with a mind for decency. To toss around such language as 'occult' and 'preternatural' seems unnecessary at this juncture; the rumors are bad enough without throwing fuel atop the fires. "Given the vast fortune that he spent upon this personal library, your father thought it wise to, shall we say, protect his assets."

"By which you mean that Father insured them," she deduces. Or perhaps remembers. For good or for ill, you are unaware of your hostess' familiarity with her sire's legal decisions. It matters little; regardless of what she does or does not know, a mild look of puzzlement well encapsulates her thoughts on the matter. "As my father's only child and the sole beneficiary stated in his will, I was under the impression that all that was his is now mine. Have you come to offer me a chance to renew his policy?"

That is what you thought you would be doing today, yes. Until you read the file.

"That is...that is rather the thing," you hedge, extracting from your pocket an unsealed envelope. With practiced care, you slide this envelope across the coffee table, pushing until its crisp, white corner is parallel to your hostess' knee. "The policy that your Father purchased from my company was...Well, it was as exceptional as the collection for which it was bought."

Her gaze is blank. You imagine the expression that you wore when first perusing the envelope's contents had been quite similar, and so can hardly blame her for intoning, "I fear I do not follow."

"My apologies. I must admit that I am at a bit of a loss, myself. In all my years, never have I seen such a policy as this," you confess, careful to maintain a professional manner, even whilst mentally cursing your eccentric predecessors. What had possessed them to write such a document? "But if I were to put it plainly, Miss, the insurance that your father purchased on behalf of these books – well, it seems that he bought life insurance. That is, he sought to receive payment in the event that certain tomes in his library should...die."

The homes in this village are built not from oak or pine, but instead from the wood of family trees that first took root in the wake of the Mayflower. Since its inception, this has been the quintessence of a puritanical town: driven more by whispers of blasphemy than by shouts of thanksgiving or prayer. This young woman's father, philanthropist that he was, did more for the morale of your community with his insanity than he ever did with his wealth.

You laugh, just once, in acknowledgment of irony.

Your hostess does not. She frowns.

"Books die."

The crystalline suggestion of grain on glass tinkles high, then low, then lower still. It slips away – another minute crumbling into nothingness – even as dust motes hang betwixt you and your hostess in temporal suspension.

"Books die," she says again, with the brusqueness of a school marm addressing a very thick student. "Can you not smell their corpses in this sepulcher around you?"

The phrasing alone turns your stomach; you wrinkle your nose as she arches a brow. "I detect nothing more offensive than the regular aromas of a library, Miss."

"Oxidization," she informs. The corner of your mouth tics, a spasm set off by flaring nostrils. It is a phenomenon she watches keenly, and perhaps with some amusement; to see yourself reflected in the black mirror of her pupils gives you reason to twitch again. "All those many things that a book is made of – paper, leather, fibers, ink, glue; materials that we might compare to our own skin and bones and organs – they decay over time, due to a process called oxidization. Volatile organic compounds are then released into the air, and depending on those compounds' basest components, so are different perfumes. Toluene is sweet, for example, while furfural smells of almonds."

"And here I had attributed that fragrance to our tea," you profess, glancing at the tray with a tinge of shame. Both cups have become a deep ruby color, as if to match your cheeks. "Rarely do I partake in anything fancier than that which comes from boxes labeled 'black'. I had assumed so enchanting a scent was a mark of quality."

"Enchanting, yes." Your hostess shifts, changing the lay of entwined fingers. Like gears, knuckles and rings click, one moving over the other; her lips stretch as if in result, tautening slowly into a simper. "Which, as it happens, is *exactly* why Father saw fit to insure certain items in his collection."

There is a lilt of implication that is not lost upon your ears, though it is more nuanced than those aromas suffusing the room.

"Now, do hold on," you splutter, indignant, before canting forward to insist, "Despite certain…speculations…whispered by our fellows in town, you do not honestly expect me to believe that your father was some sort of…of warlock, or devil worshiper, do you?"

You balk. She stares.

Only in this moment does it occur to you that she has not blinked once.

"On the contrary," she says, "I expect you to believe what I have told you. Nothing more, nothing less."

"What you have told me?" Your voice is no more than an echo, each syllable parroted vacantly. Then, no less bewildered, you think, *What she has told you?*

What *has* she told you? Nothing of significance, nothing of use. Merely that books are like bodies, and like bodies they die. A book here has died, and her father was murdered.

You draw in a breath, deeply and calm, only to cough it back into your hand. The longer you remain here, the stronger the air becomes, even though you notice it less. Even though it envelops you. By now, it has long-since permeated your lungs, your arteries, your brain; it does not register with your senses as it ought, despite the stench of almonds surely still being present. You can taste the sweet of decay the same way you do your own tongue.

"My Father knew exactly what he kept inside this room. A particular...body of work," your hostess murmurs, reaching out to gingerly straighten the lay of a teaspoon. Its grip shrills over engraved roses; in its bowl, her face distorts into something beautiful. "His hobbies came with certain inevitabilities. Those in mind, he took the liberty to arrange a few precautions. For instance, a policy that would insure your visit when the time was right."

Surprise jolts, electric, through your limbs. "My visit was of importance?"

"Oh, yes," she tells you, with every conceivable ounce of sincerity. Then, with equal earnestness, she tells you further, "And no."

In the convex curves of the righted hourglass, her reflection contorts again, even more beautifully. There is nothing within its upper chambers besides the ghost of her face.

"Visitors, I should say, are what were of importance," she amends, idly smoothing down her skirt. "While I would never dismiss the significance of your contribution, I would welcome anyone. Everyone. As many people as possible. The undertaker, the funerary director, estranged relatives, old friends. That death has a way of attracting flies from every conceivable cranny is of great convenience to me. To us."

Something hisses down the hollow of your spine, igniting every nerve that it encounters along the way. Ash, perhaps? The sandy grit of your own joints? Whatever it is, the tangible sensation speaks to you of incorporeal loss, like time trickling through, down, then out of your bones. Out of your body. *Out*, followed by—

You swallow. Questions catch in your gullet; fears wedge in your throat. In the crevasses of your molars, the cloying air putrefies.

Reflective, unaffected, your hostess hums, using the tips of willowy fingers to lay the hourglass upon its side. Matched saucers are set directly atop the table.

"There is one thing," she murmurs in afterthought, lifting from the painted cups an unrecognizable sludge of strained leaves. Of dead matter. "One thing that I have not yet told you, and that I would have you believe. Something about those compounds that I mentioned before. The volatile ones."

Fine porcelain is arranged with nimbleness, the cutlery with confidence. Doilies are involved. Sugar available, cream nearby. Refuse is dropped, still oozing copper fluids, upon the library floor without concern or ceremony. Its splatter reaches your shoes.

"Regarding these compounds' role in the context in previous comparisons."

There is something poetic – something poignant, something purposeful – about the abruptness of the waste's disposal. About the point that it once served. About what it was five minutes ago, and what it is now.

You think you could put it into words, but you do not want to.

You think you know what she will say, but you cannot disrupt her.

You think you should stop breathing, but that is impossible.

"Between the leather-skin and the paper-tissues, the ink-blood and the glue-humors," your hostess coos, her smile a hazy crescent behind a scented veil of smog, "those compounds could be considered the *spirit* of a book...Or of whatever was contained within its pages."

In the steady glow of the gas lamps, you watch her lift her teacup, indulging in a sip. Nothing spills besides her shadow, tenebrous and dark. Different, possibly. Different definitely, in that strange and subtle way that rain will change the view beyond a window.

With her almond eyes wide, your hostess nudges the second cup closer to your person, her visage the very epitome of sweetness.

"Please," she encourages, "Do give it a try. This flavor has always been a favorite of mine – a most invigorating lemon."

Water Witch

Rebecca Ring

THE POND was receding. Just the day before, Mabel had marked its edge with two willow twigs bound with twine, two twigs now drier than sun-parched bone. It had been a dry summer all right, but now the autumn rains had come, all night their incessant pounding at the farmhouse door, on the tin roof, in her ears. Presented with this offensive, however, the pond had been pigheaded – grown inhospitable to ducks as well as water – and had mustered an about-face.

Mabel stood where there had once been pond, on exposed pebbles webbed with desiccated moss, and stared into the diminishing yet mesmerizing topaz water. A trickery of course, a mere reflection of the vivid, cloudless October sky. Her husband Clive loved his duck pond almost as much as his precious ducks, which he fed every morning before heading out to the fields. How could he not notice?

He had commented that morning on the furrow setting up shop between her eyebrows. "You're going to get old before your time, Mabel, if you don't stop frowning like that." He bit off a large corner from his toast triangle and said, "What's eating you?"

"The pond look okay to you lately?" she'd said, to which he'd only scowled. As if she'd asked whether he wanted prunes for breakfast.

She saw it now, the worry reflected back at her from the pond like a snide remark. How could she make Clive understand what he somehow couldn't see? Mabel stared herself down in the too-luminous water. It seemed the less of it there was, the bluer it became, a blue intensified by the pond's decline, a rallying of forces before eventual annihilation, like a glacier's ultramarine cry for help or a honeybee's self-defeating sting. She looked up at the sky, now paled in comparison, then back at her own reflection. Dismayed by the scrawny woman looking back at her, she rubbed at the groove in her forehead. A bit of pond scum floated past, for a moment obliterating her image, and she turned away.

That night the rains came again, a torrential storm that pummeled the house and rattled the hinges. When she shook him, Clive mumbled, "Just listen to that rain, will you?" and went back to sawing logs. Mabel stayed awake – listening. Surely the pond would be full again by morning.

At some point sleep must have overcome her, because she woke to daylight with a start. In her dreams, the pond had become an immense funhouse mirror, throwing back a grotesque, distorted likeness of Mabel. "What do you want from me?" she'd cried. "I have nothing to give you!" and her wobbly reflection had echoed back, "Have – to give – *you.*"

She stalked out to the pond only to find that her twigs – placed yesterday one foot out in the water – had fallen over again on the shore, two feet from the edge. The pond was still shriveling – faster each day. Mabel picked up her twigs and walked them closer. She bent down to place them in the mud at the bottom and caught her own eye. It was not a friendly look.

"Where is all that water going?" she said, and the reflection of her mouth twisted as though a breeze had rippled the pond.

* * *

That night, when the rain started up, Mabel slipped out of bed and left the house. She stood in the yard, arms outstretched, and drank in the downpour as if her own body had suffered the pond's dehydration. Maybe it had. Her bones were getting brittle, and lately Clive had taken to saying he missed "the well-upholstered woman I married." Her nightgown soaked, her bare feet slapping the wet grass, she padded down to the water's edge. In the muddy glow of the barn's motion sensor light she could see the twigs were on shore again. How was that possible, in the middle of this pelting rain? She stepped into the pond for a closer look.

Fat drops spattered its surface, so thankfully she didn't have to see herself drooping and exposed in her sodden nightgown. She walked out as far as she could, the water up to her breasts now. She was already wet; what difference did it make? At the center of the pond where, until recently, Clive's prize ducks had loved to skim the surface for duckweed, the water swirled in angry gray. The barn light wasn't enough for it to show its true blue nature, she supposed. The swirl had a downward pull to it and, as she got closer, Mabel heard a sound. *Like sucking soda through a straw*, she thought, then laughed uneasily at her mind's choice of words – from a jumping rope rhyme, weren't they? She'd begun to shiver. The sound grew louder, a vacuuming, slurping, thirsty sound that drowned out the pattering raindrops. The pond was drinking its fill. So where was it putting all that water?

She took a step forward – and dropped into nothingness. Even her scream was submerged. Arms flapping, legs pedaling, her mouth breached first. She inhaled rainwater and pondwater and air until finally the rest of her bobbed up and she doggy-paddled for shore. In the dark and the wet she swam in circles, couldn't see anything, didn't know if she was headed the right direction. Was the pond really this deep? She couldn't even get a foothold. "Clive! Help!" she tried to call out, but her words were swamped by the hammering rain. He wouldn't have heard anyway, she thought hysterically as she flailed about. He'd still be sawing those old logs like there was no tomorrow, like he was building a goddamn log chateau. Then, a swell of water lifted and carried her to the edge of the pond, where it seemed to spit her out more than set her down. Mabel took big, heaving gulps of air, then lay panting and retching for a moment or two.

When she could finally breathe again, she scrabbled to her feet and scampered into the house, not daring to look back. She closed the door and leaned against it, still gasping for air, and wondered now if maybe Clive had built the pond over a sinkhole. That would be just like him, to have bought the farm without a full inspection. Or maybe he'd diverted someone's stream to fill his beloved pond, and they'd finally discovered it and cut him off. Though Clive was a dear, he could be a little shortsighted at times. She'd have to ask him about it in the morning.

But the next morning, on her way to milk the cows, the sight of Clive's ducks made her forget all about it. They quacked and paced around the edges of the pond, scratching at the denuded and unfamiliar strip of earth that now ringed it. Like aging call girls, they peered furtively at their reflections and then backed away, nearly tripping over their webbed feet. Mabel plucked a few leftover grains of feed from her apron pocket and tossed them out across the water, just to see what would happen. The ducks waddled toward the water but stopped just short of it. Not even the temptation of the floating grains would lure them in. Their renewed quacking grew plaintive and irate.

Later that afternoon, while taking the laundry off the line, Mabel saw the ducks a-flap in the cows' water trough. Clothespins between her lips, she watched as poor Bessie and Alice blinked and recoiled from the ducks' pitiful attempts to swim in their miserable eight inches of water. But instead of a chuckle, what came out of Mabel's mouth was, "Enough is enough!" She put down her clothespins and her laundry basket and stomped off to the barn.

* * *

She found it hung over a rusted nail against the back wall, her grandfather's old willow dowsing rod, a 'water witch' he used to call it. Clive said he had no truck for witchery and had refused to even touch the forked branch. "Besides," he claimed, "What do we need a dowser for? We have plenty of water."

Sure, Clive, she thought now, *so much water your pet ducks are swimming in a damn trough*. She walked to the edge of the pond as if driving a plow, one leg of the Y-shaped water witch clutched in each hand, the tail end out over the pond. "I'm going to find out where you're putting that water whether you like it or not," she bawled, and just as emphatically, the tail end of the dowser flipped back and smacked her in the forehead. She dropped it like a hot coal and rubbed at the sore spot between her eyes, trembling. "How dare you suggest this is all in my head!"

She picked up the dowser and stumbled with it back to the barn, then went off in search of Clive. Where had he been all day?

She found him planted in his recliner in front of the TV, watching the news – PBR in one hand, the other slapping the arm of his chair. "Unholy bunch of hogwash!" he barked when she came through the door.

Mabel looked at the TV, the voiceover pronouncing "—that climate change is at the root of all—" then moved in front of it, blocking Clive's view. He shifted his head from side to side, as if a tree had suddenly grown up in the middle of the living room and he was too busy to get up and walk around it.

"Clive," Mabel said, "there's something wrong with the pond. The ducks won't go anywhere near it. It practically drank me up last night. And it's shrinking – faster every day!"

Clive muted the TV and his eyes traveled upward to Mabel's, as if he'd just noticed her for the first time. "What's that you say? The pond did what to my ducks?"

"I've been trying to tell you. Something's not right with that pond. It's shrinking. I just can't figure out what it's doing with all that rain we've had." She flopped down in the padded rocker and wrung her hands in her lap. "Seems to be swallowing it or something."

Clive drew his bushy, salt-and-pepper eyebrows together and leaned forward. "Mabel, what on earth are you going on about? Can't you see I'm watching the news? Bad enough all that jimmy-crack-corn going on in the world" – he gestured at the TV – "without you coming in here yammering at me about shrinking and swallowing. Have you lost your ever-loving mind?"

Mabel stood, took his hand – not the one still gripping the PBR can, which had little dents in it now from his fingers, but the one waving in the air – and tugged on it. "Come see what your ever-loving pond has done to your ever-loving ducks." She knew how to get his attention. She pulled Clive to his feet, and he followed her out to the pond. The ducks were nowhere in sight.

They stood at the edge of the pond and looked down. Except that Mabel actually stood at the edge looking down, and Clive stood three feet back on the grass looking down. "So what exactly am I supposed to see, Mabel?"

She turned. "Get on over here, so you can see it."

"What, and get my new work boots soaking wet?"

"No, just down here to the edge." She pointed at the dirt and pebbles underfoot.

"I am on the edge." Clive scratched his head. "Literally and figuratively."

She'd never known him to use such fancy words. Too much TV, she guessed. "You're not even close. You're a mile away."

"And you're the one standing in the water in your house slippers."

Could he really not see it, or was he messing with her?

A thundering rumble followed immediately by a barnyard animal ruckus turned their heads, and what Mabel saw, Clive saw too. One side of the barn's roof had fallen in, sending Bessie and Alice, the chickens, and the entire retinue of ducks into some marriage of a stampede and a duster.

"Christ Almighty!" Clive broke into a run, right past his darling ducks, who had waddled to safety under the giant willow tree and now bobbed and huddled there in a quivering mass.

When Mabel reached the open barn door, she found Clive staring down at crumpled sheets of tin and a splintered pile of lumber. He'd turned the brim of his green John Deere hat around to the back and pulled at the five o'clock shadow of his chin. "Wood rot," was all he could say, over and over. "Wood rot," neither a question nor a statement. Not even an exclamation point in his words, just plain, tired disbelief.

Mabel came closer and touched a crumbled rafter beam. It was completely dry, but definitely rotten. "How long has this been going on?" she said.

Clive just shook his head. "It's water damage all right. Maybe all that rain we've been having. Don't know how that's possible, though. Tighter than a steel drum that tin roof."

But Mabel had a pretty good idea how it was possible. She marched out to the pond, those snooty ducks toddling along behind, and shouted, "Clive may be a simple man, but you can't fool me! I know you're up to something, and whatever it is, there's no earthly explanation for it. Just downright evil is what it is. I'm telling you to cease and desist right now! I will not—" The pond rippled into a grin, and the pit of Mabel's stomach turned to jelly. "Did you see that?" She whipped around to Clive, but he wasn't there. Only his cherished ducks, gawking up at her, heads tilting to one side or the other.

* * *

That evening over meatloaf and mashed potatoes, Clive flipped through his catalogue of roofing materials while Mabel drummed her fingers on the pockmarked surface of her grandmother's walnut dining table. "Did you at least notice the ducks?" she finally said. "You can't tell me there's anything natural about that."

Clive finished reading something and then raised his eyes slowly to look at her. "The ducks?" Her arms were crossed, her mouth tight. "Oh, you mean the way they won't go in the pond? Yeah, I noticed. Guess we better skim for algae." He went back to his catalogue.

It was no use trying to get through to him. He had an answer for everything. She stood and gathered up the dishes with more clatter than usual, but he kept right on reading, muttering to himself about galvanized steel and thirty-one-gauge corrugated panels and rot-resistant something or others. In the enameled cast iron farmhouse sink, Mabel sorted silverware to one side, Mason jar glasses to the other, ketchup-smeared plates in the middle. She snugged in the stopper, drizzled some Joy over everything, then turned the hot water spigot. Nothing came out. She tried the cold water spigot; still nothing. She banged on the old faucet, but not even a leftover drop emerged.

She smothered a curse word and stared out the window at the sullen sky, then turned around. His nose now two inches from the catalogue, Clive scribbled something with the nub of a pencil on a yellow pad.

"Why don't you put on your reading glasses?" she said and pushed them, skidding, to his end of the table. He reached for them without looking up.

Mabel opened the cellar door and flicked the switch. The bulb flared, then flashed into darkness. "Doggone it." She groped for the flashlight that hung from a nail inside the door and pressed the button. Of course, weak-kneed batteries. "There's no water coming out of the spigots," she called over her shoulder. "I'm going to check the main." Flashlight in one hand, handrail in the other, she trod step by step down the stairs. As she neared the bottom, though, her house slippers met slick and she did a little dance before falling onto her bony backside and thumping the rest of the way down. The flashlight spun away, its light murky and eerie where it lay below. Underwater.

With difficulty, she grappled for the handrail and pulled herself to her feet on the bottom step. Empty pickling jars bobbed around her shins, glistening in the flashlight's failing beam like large soap bubbles – or eyes. "Clive! Get down here!" she howled as she fished for her slippers.

Clive looked down the stairs at her like a man who'd had enough for one day. "Can't do anything about it 'til morning," he said. So Mabel stayed awake all night listening to the rain, sure they'd find water up to the top of the cellar stairs in the morning. But when the rooster crowed and they went to look, those pickle jars still floated like buoys around the bottom steps. And when she hurried out to the pond, she found her willow twigs fallen over again and the pond another two feet gone, grinning as if it hadn't swallowed all that rain.

By late afternoon they'd finished draining the basement, first with a borrowed sump pump and then with mops and buckets, and still found not an open window, a broken pipe, or even a backed-up sewer – nothing to account for the inundation.

Using a rope, Clive hoisted the next to last in a line of buckets up through the cellar's window and tipped its water with the rest into the gully. Mabel looked up at him from where she stood, mop in hand. "I'm telling you," she said, "this water is everywhere except where it's supposed to be." As Clive watched the little rivulet travel from the last bucket to the gully and on toward the pond, he took off his hat to scratch his head and mumbled about storm drains and tree roots. He was always going to come up with some excuse for what was clearly inexcusable. And in the meantime, all he'd done was feed that pond more water. More water it would guzzle and slurp and gulp and make disappear, more water that would turn up somewhere it shouldn't. She was going to have to take matters into her own hands. Mabel stumped up the cellar stairs and out to the barn for the water witch. She wasn't going to let a piece of willow branch intimidate her.

* * *

Night moved in like a skulking hound dog and thunder rumbled in the distance. Mabel rocked in her chair by the window while she stared out at the clouds. Like plump chickens, they scuttled across the sky, kicking up and pelting the dry earth with pebbles of rain. A heavenly smell wafted from the kitchen, and she lifted her nose to drink it in. She tried to focus on the almost-finished sweater in her lap, the one that would keep Clive warm under his oversized Carhartt coat this winter, but her eyes kept drifting to the window. She pictured where it would go this time, the torrential rain that was surely on its way.

It had not been so disagreeable after all, succumbing to the downward pull, the swirl of sky and the hungry gurgles. Comprehending at last, she'd gone in peace, let herself be siphoned up, swilled and swallowed, the water witch's tug leading the way. This time the pond had welcomed her as though she were a sponge, ready to be filled up. And now? Well, she felt easy in her mind for the first time in weeks. Whether he would perceive it or not, Clive would wake in the morning to find the pond brimming and satiated, its thirst quenched at last. She muttered a curse word at the stitches that had dropped off her knitting needle and as she worked to harness them again, a clap of thunder startled her and drew her eyes to the window, where rain now coursed, its veil obscuring the landscape.

The door opened and Clive came in, his face as gray and spongy as the muck she'd mopped out of the cellar. His rain slicker streamed into puddles on the floor as he bent down to take off his boots. "I can't find those ducks anywhere. Thought for sure Maisie and Annabelle'd be out there singing in the rain – like ducks do. Any idea where they might'a gone?"

She looked down at her knitting and smiled. "I'm sure they're tucked away somewhere safe. Sometimes there's even too much water for a duck to take to." She noticed the quill end of a stray green feather pinioned in the folds of her apron and whisked it into the pocket. Who could have known that ducks had so many feathers?

Clive looked at her and stood up. "Mabel, you okay? You look – I don't know – like you've filled out or something." He tilted his head. "Your eyes always been that blue?"

Mabel's topaz eyes flashed above her smile, and Clive tilted his head the other way. "Hey!" he said, "that crease in your forehead's gone, too."

Mabel reached up to touch her brow, rippling its surface a bit. She laughed. "Everything's fine, Clive. Now go wash up, I've made a stew for dinner that I know you'll just love."

Ring of Teeth

Mike Robinson

THE MAN waded in, and the swamp grew a pair of watching eyes.

For sixty years of his life, the large male alligator would remain nameless. Not that it made a great difference to him how any society of primates might refer to him in their lore and headlines. Hatched deep in the swamplands of Louisiana, he knew only the drowsy rhythm of the bayou, and the primal frequency on which he communed with his kin, informing him with a clarity of purpose rare to those of even higher cognition.

Silently, this creature soon to be dubbed 'Methuselah' cruised its steady sine wave toward the trespasser. Through the murk, he could feel the 'buzzing' of his kin, all attuned now to the same direction.

There only seemed to be one man in the water. He lacked clothing, too, which was unusual. A scent of terror clouded him, also unusual as many of those entering the Ring did so with a sense of determination.

Moving in bogwater gloom, Methuselah passed flitting schools of fish, crawfish reposing below and turtles small or softshell floating like windswept balloons among forest debris.

The man's lower half materialized, bare feet and legs standing in a plume of sand. He was stark naked. Methuselah could clearly see the man's top half, too, straight and clear and without refraction.

"Keep on, I say," said a garbled voice. Not from the man in the water, but from slightly farther away. From the bank. "I'll tell ya when you've gone far enough."

Methuselah was now only ten or so yards from the naked man, though barely visible. The other gators had appeared around him, too, mouths resting in an endless, joyless grin, eyes taking stock of the man. He might make for good nourishment, they ascertained, but he was not a threat to the Ageless. Not like others that had been through here.

"You can't *do* this," sputtered the naked man. He had moved only a few inches farther into the water. In a feebler voice he said, "It's a sin."

"Well then our sins can cancel each other out," said the other man. "Besides, I ain't gonna touch you. They will."

Generation by generation, the Protectors had learned not to indiscriminately destroy just anyone that entered the Ring. Backlashes might occur. People were vengeful creatures, and though Methuselah did not understand firearms, he loathed their resounding *crack* and the smoke they belched and, of course, most distasteful of all, the bodies of his kin they left floating in leaking ribbons of blood.

The Protectors in the Ring could not be careless. Much as their million-year evolution had allowed them, they had to discern. They had to strategize.

"Free lunch!" shouted the man from the bank. "Free *lunch*!" In a colder, more subdued voice he addressed the naked man. "We'll see how much you're worth to the Lord. Don't need no judgment beyond this life. This'll do, right? Here. The gators will decide. Right, preacher?"

Methuselah brushed by the naked man's calves. He stiffened, stomped his feet. Right now, Methuselah was by far the closest. A younger female of about forty years had settled on the bottom to watch, one arm continually clawing the sand. Like Methuselah himself, they could see the man on the bank, too: sun-beaten, stubbled face shaded by a hat, eyes undone. Torn dirty clothes hung off his frame. He was pointing a rifle at the naked man.

"You was hurtin' her," mumbled the man in the water. In a softer voice he said, "I done nothing *wrong*. I done what God told me."

Coarse laughter erupted.

Further understanding vibrated through the minds of Methuselah and his kin. While tempting for the ease of kill, this naked man was not a priority. He posed no threat. This was a thin and weak being, wholly unaccustomed to this place.

The man on the bank, however, the rifleman, had to go.

They drew lazily into formation. Methuselah submerged himself lower as the forty-year-old female rose to join two others in approaching the naked man. They cut triangles in the water. The naked man's terror ripened. Giddy amusement grew in the eyes of the rifleman, who did not notice the large alligator stealthily nearing the bank.

"Come *on*!" shouted the rifleman. His eyes were reddish, movements ill-coordinated. He had imbibed a few on the way here; Methuselah couldn't know this, of course. He sensed only the compromised motions that would render this an easy kill.

It took but a second to funnel into his limbs the power of his seventy-million-year lineage. He exploded from the water, mouth yawned wide, groan issuing from his throat, and he clamped hard on the leg of the man who had not even time yet to scream, and who had less than half a moment to cry his last before being dragged into the swampwater where his maladroit resistance met swift ends by the others who moved in and dismembered his arms and set upon his throat. Red bloomed in the bayou, punctured by knobs of hot white bone.

Methuselah took only faint notice that the naked man had scrambled back ashore and disappeared.

Once every twitch and pulse had left the body, the Protectors released their hold. Some swam off right away. Others, including Methuselah, lingered for a while, watching the lifeless hunk bob in the current. Maybe it would be food. Maybe not. All that mattered, said the chemistry of his ancestors, was that the Ageless remain unseen, and untouched.

* * *

Not even Methuselah had laid eyes on the Ageless. Nor had any of these Protectors, who patrolled year after year, decade after decade, this circular band of water surrounding the central Island – the dwelling place of that old and most crucial Being.

All told, the Ring was about three miles around, the Island a patchy quarter-mile in circumference. Only in momentary respites had any of the Protectors docked themselves on the Island, usually on a log or a rock a few yards offshore. It was understood – intuited – that the verdant fortress of foliage was not to be penetrated.

Occasionally, when draped sunning over some surface or drifting idly about the swamp, Methuselah knew flickers of confusion about that Island: a feeling, perhaps, that was the distant antecedent to wonder and curiosity. The kinds of emotion that brought men here. The emotions that, in turn, sharpened the vigilance of these Protectors.

Though the bayou was one of nature's most effective custodians, it had not swept away everything. To the keener eye (which, in this context, Methuselah certainly was not), the many gnarled crevices above and below water offered numerous mementos of those who had come here. Methuselah and his kin swam like blind royalty among the treasures rendered from those vanquished: spears and breechcloths and Choctaw beaded pouches, wide-brimmed hats and muskets and pocketwatches and old wooden boats on a well-rotted return to nature.

A fourth-generation Protector, Methuselah had no qualms about his geographical restrictions. He and his fellow males had sired dozens of offspring right here in the Ring, most of whom remained to become Protectors themselves. In the sixty years of Methuselah's life, the Ring had only seen a handful of outside genes, and the disproportionate amount of inbreeding yielded no ill-effects to any generation.

For the most part, Methuselah's daily life differed little from those of other alligators across the southeastern United States. The sun and the moon played celestial tag across the jungle-gnawed horizon, and all throughout he would swim and sunbathe and carve for himself burrows on the main bank, and snap up birds and fish and raccoons and turtles and he would mate, of course, and when winter came his appetite would wane, and he would grow far more inert, his only sign of life the heart that would beat once or twice a minute, and between which he would feel utterly whole, unmolested by thought of the minutes passing over him.

And the Island would sit there, a static beast unto itself, overgrown with tall cypress trees sobbing their Spanish moss, the large ferns like green-clawed hands in permanent conceal. Sometimes birds flew in and out of it. Thunderheads would often gather, spitting rain on the Island as any other part of the swamp.

Only once had Methuselah glimpsed what in our tongue might be referred to as "something more."

Belly recently sated, he had been idling in the shallow water of the main bank when he became aware of a buzzing vibration, much like that which he shared with the other Protectors. Yet this vibration lasted longer than normal and it was deeper, far more commanding.

Methuselah's eye membrane slid back, his pupils flicking toward the noises emanating from the Island: a loud splintering. A great roiling *splash*. Crows puffed cawing toward the sky. The trees at the Island's edge shuddered.

Then the buzzing abated, the Ring as calm as it ever was.

Except, of course, when it wasn't.

* * *

It could hardly be known to Methuselah, the consequences his actions might have in the world beyond. The naked man had managed the many-miles trek back through the bayou, stumbling back into the small town of Hammondburg where he was known as a young preacher and where, in a wheezy, enervated voice, he claimed he had just been spared 'Satanic retribution' by none other than 'the Hand and the Beasts of God'.

"My savior came in the form of the largest, oldest beast there," he proclaimed, "indeed a Methuselah among reptiles." He added later, "These alligators of the so-called 'Ring of Teeth' are of divine Providence. No harm should befall them."

The preacher's words were well-heeded. The 'Ring of Teeth' had over the years since the Louisiana Purchase acquired enough notoriety with white Americans and Frenchmen that its reptilian Protectors had seen steadily less and less intrusions. Choctaws and

Chitimachas had ceased visiting the area two generations before Methuselah hatched on its northeast bank.

Wrote the preacher: *The Ring of Teeth has long known to be a sacred, alluring and dangerous place, a harbor for what legends claim are Creation's oldest and largest and most vicious creatures. This may well be the case, as never in my days have I glimpsed such a precise mixture of savagery and elegance as when that enormous gator burst forth and salvaged my life.*

There is something undeniably special about the gators of the Ring. One senses that higher forces manipulate them, somehow. For what purpose? I cannot speculate. But having stood within the Ring, even at the behest and the gunpoint of a madman, I knew a queer sensation of absolute reverence, that I might have been facing some Lost Testament written on the wind, or feeling in me the pulse from Nature's breast not far away. I understand more personally the sacredness the natives place on that region. For our own sake, I believe it best we chart a similar course, and leave our interaction with the Ring of Teeth to mere lore.

Yet the preacher could not control the effect his reports might have on more restless seekers. Weeks after the incident, he confessed to a wealthy plantation owner his belief that the Ring waters had cured the gout in his foot, which he'd been suffering during his unfortunate excursion with the rifleman. The timely healing had allowed him a successful return through the woods.

"But I consider that it was not the water *itself*," he said. "For there is something striking about the island in its center, and I do not know what it is. I wonder..." Here the plantation owner, quite intrigued, pressed him to continue. "I wonder if it's much like an ice cube which has been put in drink: its presence seeps into that which surrounds it."

The wealthy plantation owner was one of many struck by the preacher's account, of course, but it was he who would relate the story to his children, the eldest of whom, a son, would later become a colonel in the Confederate Army.

The idea would haunt the colonel: what unknown magic might the South harbor in its wild bosom? And were the infamous gators there indeed guarding it? Though he tried to ignore the idea, dismiss his father's tale and all the other tales as rumor or native superstition, the notion of the Ring had clamped its jaws tight on his imagination. Dreams came to him.

Finally, as victory in the war began to elude the Confederates, the colonel's thoughts turned from fancy to desperation.

The preacher, meanwhile, began to suffer nerves in his later years. Headaches grew frequent, as did confusion. Memories faded – so much of his life gone, whole years stripped from him like meat from bone. In more coherent moments, the preacher considered his condition none too dissimilar from that day when he'd been forced to stand naked in the waters of the Ring of Teeth. The mouths of invisible predators had surrounded him – as they did now.

It was perhaps appropriate, then, that come the preacher's final second on Earth, his most durable memory, the one to withstand all the rising floodwaters of his illness, was that day in the Ring – it stood like an island amid the wayward currents of his mind.

* * *

Decades had passed since the incident with the naked man. Methuselah was now eighty-seven, had at last earned his informal moniker – he was truly the eldest of the Ring. No longer was he the largest, however, though his genes were responsible for his usurper: a thirty-two-year-old male nearly fifteen feet long.

In the time since, they had lost two Protectors to a small, ragged band of poachers that had come seeking hides and paws, not to mention the trophy-thrill of rending them from Ring-gators. Two Protectors had been shot dead, one strung up, but only one of the poachers had escaped. The rest had sustained Methuselah and his kin for weeks.

When the new parties came, storm clouds had formed over miles of the bayou, and it had only begun to rain. The air was humid, electric. Methuselah lay in a burrow on the southward bank. A buzzing reached him. He opened his eyes and nostrils.

With a low, rumbly growl he turned and slunk down the mud into the gray murk, joining the others now mobilized toward the men appearing on the northwest bank. He sensed fear in the men, but also determination; indeed, a worrisome determination.

"Set 'er down here," said a man.

The swamp bubbled with dozens of eyes, all watching the men spill from the woods carrying hefty gear and rifles and machetes and long canoes which they placed well up the bank. These particular men did not appear as haggard or foolhardy as previous trespassers. Methuselah sensed a formidable threat.

"I know no one, white or Negro or Injun, who's crossed the Ring," said the same man. Like the others, he had on a kind of worn blue uniform. He smelled of authority. "We may just carve out our own little corner of history down 'ere."

There were whistles, shouts. More buzzing among Methuselah and his kin. Yet more men had emerged on the eastern bank. They, too, bore a canoe. Methuselah's dull apprehension heightened.

On seamless cue, a group of Protectors splintered off, forming a new infantry now cruising toward this second party.

"...who's got the bang?..." said the man. Another promptly showed him the dynamite.

Then, yet more voices, echoing from the Southwest. A *third* group. Something in Methuselah tightened, tightened. They were being beset from multiple angles. Whoever these new men were, there were far more of them than any Protector could recall, and they possessed far more resources.

Methuselah remained facing the first party of the northwest bank. The others kept still, too, still and primed as the men sprinkled the shoreline water with raw meat. The splashes and the odors triggered his instincts, but it was a stronger, cautionary instinct that kept Methuselah and his kin in place.

Most of them, anyway.

A female of only eleven made her way toward the bank. The other Protectors started after her until they understood that it was Methuselah who now closed in on her tail. The bank was near, sloping up. Chicken-meat hung tempting but ripe with danger, the rippling image of the men arrayed and waiting beyond.

Methuselah lunged and nipped at the eleven-year-old's tail. She turned, agitated. Splashing.

It was enough commotion.

Crack – crack – crack – crack.

That ghastly noise, ripping open space as the bullets cut contrails through the water and pierced the young female. Blood bloomed. Methuselah flitted away, all others roused into action too. Buzzing of terror. Contempt. A thunderous *slam* against his hide and the blood he saw and smelled was his own.

He swam hastily toward the other side of the bank, the cries and the *crack*-booms reverberating just behind, and here he crawled ashore, concealed by overgrowth, and he slunk through the hot wet woods where the rain pelted down the leaves and rinsed some of the blood from what was luckily only a glancing shot.

"There! Now!"

Crack – crack – crack. Methuselah could see the men through the underbrush now. There were others, too, who were on foot: a nineteen-year-old male near him and two others on the opposite side of the party and narrowing in as he was.

He sprang, aiming for the first leg. His jaws locked and he could taste the coppery blood foaming and when he bit further his teeth bumped bone. The man screamed and flailed and assailed him with the butt of his musket but Methuselah held tight and then the man slipped in the rain-softened mud and Methuselah twisted with him and the cloth tore and then the flesh. Other shadows surrounded him, rifles ready and blades raised, but his kin launched from the brush and set upon them and soon those men moaned and screamed too, and there was a flash of lightning and Methuselah saw a spray of gore drenching the soil, a severed femoral artery, and there was more smoke and more *crack*-booms and fists raised with glinting metal and more screams.

From across the bayou, an explosion.

Mouth-reddened, Methuselah turned away from the chaos, finding protection in the brush. One of the Protectors, a thirty-two-year-old male, lay bullet-ridden and breathing his last. Methuselah crawled past him, adrenaline surging, delaying the sting from the assaults. All the dullest of his dull thoughts had fallen away now; he was an element, a wind-fired vessel of destruction.

Boom. The ground shook. An explosion close. Very close.

Crack. Foliage splintered. Men were chasing him. Methuselah could feel the agitated pulse of their footfalls. They breathed, yelled, laughed manic laughter.

He made it to the water, slipped in and disappeared. The water's gray-green had turned amber red. Other Protectors sliced in and out of the murk, some stringing along pale tissue in their teeth. Ragged human feet and fingers and a head with one hanging eye appeared floating like disparate ingredients before some new Genesis.

Methuselah swam toward the Island. He'd not sensed too much disturbance from the Ageless, not yet anyway. Though that could also present a concern. He had to be sure.

Once far enough out, he rose slowly to the surface, lifting only the knobs of his eyes and snout. In his field of vision he glimpsed the splashing, screaming end of his pursuers back at the bank, saw also the boat bobbing fifteen meters away, occupied by two men, one of whom paddled as the other stood poised with the rifle and swinging it every which way.

A leathery tail rose and slapped the surface. *Crack*-boom.

Methuselah dipped below once more, continued toward the Island. There was a tingling in his pores. A heightening vibration. He ignored the sensation. All drowned beneath his mounting, carnal anxiety.

"Go!" one of the men shouted. "Go go *go*, for the love of God!"

Methuselah made it ashore. He was on the Island.

So were men.

He did his best to focus on the vibration of their footfalls, to follow their scent. Somehow, noise of the storm and the battle had lessened. The rain had let up, too. Methuselah felt disoriented, being here. There was little outward difference between the trees and the growth of the Island and the rest of the bayou, but it still *felt* like a different place. A sense of impropriety weighed on Methuselah, though he could not cease in his ancestral duty.

The woods slapped at him as he moved, his limbs arching at maximum speed.

"Where *is* it? Where in God's name are we *going*?"

The men were ahead, little more than shadows stuttering through the forest. They didn't turn as much as might be expected, perhaps assuming the gators had more than enough to keep them occupied. A dreamlike state had also overcome them. To a distant degree, Methuselah felt it, too. Most of what he felt now, though, was panic. Never before had trespassers incurred so far.

Slinking through a passage in the underbrush, he emerged in a clearing ringed by bearded cypress trees, all brooding over a large dark swamp covered in duckweed. The two men had stopped at the water's edge. Both turned instantly at Methuselah's presence and fired wayward bullets, two of which struck his backside. He felt the *slam* of each one, though they slowed little of his momentum.

"*Shit!*" one of them cried.

Charging at full speed, Methuselah opened his mouth wide. He took little care of the firearms being raised at him. *Crack*-flash. Another sharp thunder-pain rang across his snout and it was terribly, piercingly painful yet it only fueled his rage.

All of what happened next, happened fast.

The ground shook. The air thickened with something other than humidity. It felt ancient, smelled ancient. The dark swampwater swelled higher and higher, like an enormous gas bubble – as if the Island were giving birth to another of itself.

The men cried out and staggered back. Methuselah stopped, spying the massive scaled ridgeline and then the enormous wave of teeth, each one the length of half his own body.

The giant mouth swept over the two men, took them cleanly in one groaning swallow as they cried out. He caught a whiff of breath – it smelled of dead ages.

He froze.

The titanic entity presented itself. It was one of his own, only bigger. *Impossibly* bigger. Take all the Protectors together and they would likely not fill the size of This – the Ageless. Its tail snapped branches on nearby trees. Its eye glowed a dull acid moon. Sheets of swamp muck waterfalling off its bulbous scales.

Methuselah just watched. How did it feed itself? What had sustained it? These were not questions that occurred to him necessarily, though he did find himself paralyzed, shamed in whatever primitive way he could be, as well as terrified that he would be devoured next.

Yet the Ageless came to rest halfway above the surface, stretched out like a reptilian mountain range. Its nostrils flared. A dyspeptic groan radiated from its throat; Methuselah could feel it quivering underfoot, and became strangely aware that the soil on which he stood – indeed, perhaps, this entire region of the Ring – took nourishment from this creature. Like its breath, the sound it made stirred something deeply atavistic but still alive.

The great pupil shifted, narrowed at Methuselah.

Finally he felt comfortable enough to move, though took only one step forward.

The Ageless was not going to destroy him. In fact, by its vocalization, and the buzzing now filling the space between them, Methuselah felt summoned. He was *supposed* to approach closer.

In moving further, he felt drained. Pain came rushing back. The firearms had taken their toll and he was bleeding and in him grew knowledge that he would not live much longer.

But the Ageless wanted to help him. The Ageless cared for him, as it did for the rest of his kin, and it would seek to protect him, as Methuselah and his ancestors had protected it.

The giant didn't move as Methuselah entered the water and swam slowly toward its side. More and more he felt peace. Rightness. Images blossomed in his mind. He intuited that the Ageless was instructing him to do something, but he wasn't sure yet what that was.

Until he reached the slick wall of flesh near its ribs, that wall pulsing slow in breath.

There was a vibration.

He was supposed to *bite* the Ageless.

This made him hesitate for a moment, but the wordless message being fed to him was constant and emphatic. And so, with the rest of his strength, Methuselah lunged forth and sank his teeth into that deific skin.

Instantly a power burst through him, voltaic and primeval, a stream of the world's First Energy. Lost eons filled spaces in him. An uptick in strength, growing. What was broken was now mending. A multitude of images marched through him. His whole lineage – not just Methuselah's, but his entire species, and all the species prior that had bled into one another and engendered yet more species – throbbed now in his veins, and with such an infusion of wisdom came a thought that was fleeting and exotic to his kind.

What sustained the Ageless, indeed, was none other than *time*. Whatever had happened before, from the last sunrise to all the histories and epochs and extinctions that had shaped the world, now rested in its belly, the small prey of seconds and minutes squirming next to the larger bulks of centuries and millennia.

Drowsily, Methuselah closed his eyes, his jaws still fastened to that massive flesh much as a suckling babe – one of nature's oldest creatures receiving, if briefly, its first taste of some higher understanding.

Botany Bay

Annie Trumbull Slosson

"I was his soul; he lived not but in me.
We were so close within each other's breast.
The rivets were not found that joined us first.
[...] We were so mixed
As meeting streams; both to ourselves were lost.
We were one man; we could not give or take
But from the same; for he was I, I he."
Dryden

HIS NAME WAS Balaam Montmorency. How its two incongruous parts came together, who gave him this name, with its union of the biblical and romantic, I never knew, and I think nobody in Stonington knew any more than I did. In fact, few, even in the village itself, had ever heard the whole of his name. He was generally called 'old Balaam' or 'old Bay', until some village wag hit upon the title – whose fitness you will recognize as my story goes on – Botany Bay, and so he was called to the end of his life.

I cannot remember when I first saw him, for, from my earliest childhood, he was a familiar and well-known object. So short of stature as almost to deserve the name of dwarf, with a shock head of tangled yellow hair, bleached almost white by the sun, a thin brown face, and the big blue eyes of a child, who that ever saw him can forget poor Botany Bay?

His business was one well known and much followed in former times, but now unknown save in the most primitive and rural of communities: he was a gatherer and vender of roots and herbs. Day after day, year by year, he roamed through wood and swamp, by stream and highway, over plain and hillside, in search of treasure. With bag on back, and basket in each hand, he came every day into the village from his rambles, bringing the sweetness, the spiciness, the tastes and smells and greenness of the forest with him. Birch, sassafras, and winter-green for the home-made root beer; pennyroyal and mint to 'take to meetin''; sweet-clover to lay in the linen-chest, or among the handkerchiefs in the bureau drawer; boneset, prince's pine, hardhack, yarrow, 'injun posy', peppermint, skull-cap, pokeroot, dock, snakeroot, wild-cherry, gold thread, and bloodroot, for medicines; dandelions and cowslips for 'greens'; pigeon-berries for red ink; bayberries for candles – all these were among his stores. He brought, too, wild plants to make beautiful the village gardens, the sweetbrier with its fragrant leaves and pink blossoms, the woodbine to trail over fence and wall, or cover the porch with its five-fingered leaves, so green in summer, so brightly crimson in autumn; the swamp honeysuckle, with its sticky flowers of pink or white, yellow and red lilies for the garden borders, blueflags, and vivid cardinal-flower. From his basket came the small, sweet huckleberries of the early season, the later and larger blueberries with their whitey bloom, the low and high blackberry, and wild raspberries, both black and red. No strawberries now, from garden or hot-bed, have the wild flavor of those small cone-shaped ones which old Bay brought us in early summer; even the puckery choke-cherries were pleasant to our young palates – and oh, how nice were the spicy checkerberries, the aromatic sassafras, sweet birch, and sarsaparilla, the wild plums, purple and yellow, the fox and frost grapes!

And how much he knew of these children of the wildwood! He could tell you of their haunts, their seasons, their habits, their virtues. He knew them, not only when in full bloom or mature fruit they were most easily recognized, but in earliest babyhood, when first their tender shoots of pale pink or delicate green pierced the cold ground, or in old age, when the dry and empty fruit swung on the leafless stems, and when even dry fruit and bare stalks were gone he found his friends underground by root or bulb, and knew them in their graves.

I have said that I cannot remember my first sight of old Balaam, still less can I recollect how from acquaintances we became friends. I have always from boyhood loved the woods and what grows in them, but whether this love drew Bay and me together, or whether his companionship first gave me that taste for the wildwood, I do not know; but friends we always were. Bay was not fond of the village boys generally, and "small blame to him", as the Irish say. The youngsters teased him unmercifully, stole his roots and herbs, called him names, played him tricks, and were generally nuisances to the poor man. So he avoided them, never sought their companion-ship, carefully concealed from them the locality of his rarest plants, and was obstinately silent when questioned as to where and how he found them. So I considered myself very fortunate to be in the old man's good graces, and to be allowed, as I was, day after day, to accompany him in his rambles, and I grew to know, better than most boys, the woods and swamps around our village, and what they held. As I look back now I can see myself, a small, flaxen-haired boy, with 'cheek of tan', trotting along by my queer little old friend, and listening eagerly to his quaint talk. Off the East Road, out to the Devil's Den, along Anguilla Brook, towards Mystic, through Flanders, to Lantern Hill, to Quiambaug Cove – all these ways we took, often walking the whole distance of many miles, but sometimes having a lift from a friendly farmer, on hay-cart or wagon. Some of the flowers we found in these rambles I have never since seen, others I have encountered in far northern or extreme southern parts of our country, and greeted with a strange thrill of memory as I thought of my boyhood and poor Botany Bay. I well remember as a red-letter day the July morning when we first found on Lantern Hill the rhododendron, with its thick, glossy, green leaves and flowers of pale rose. Bay called it 'big laurel', and told me of some far-away mountain country – very vaguely described – where he had seen this beautiful shrub growing in great profusion, "close together, an' taller'n a man." He carefully separated the petals – for he was very tender always with his flowers – and showed me that the throat, or 'swaller', as he called it, was greenish, and spotted with red; and he enjoined secrecy as to the discovery, as there were but few plants there, and "some pesky woman might want to dig 'em up for her posy-gardin." And with what wonder and admiration I first gazed upon the pink lady slipper found in a dry wood near Westerly! It seemed to me such an odd flower, with its rosy pouch or bag, and I was pleased with Bay's name for it of whippoorwill's shoes. He gathered the whole plant, giving me the flower on its slender stalk, but keeping the fibrous root among his choicest treasures as "good for narves and high strikes."

What had he among his herbs which was not 'good for' some ailment or other? And what wonderful tales he could tell of his marvellous cures! I remember many of these stories still; and so, as I go through the country, I find my botanical knowledge strongly mingled with reminiscences of the henbane and plantain poultice that cured Enoch Wilcox and "kep' off lockjaw when the crab bit his toe"; of the dandelion-tea, so beneficial for "old Mis Dewey's janders", and the Indian turnip, which, boiled in milk and "took fastin'", soothed Mary Bright's "creakin' cough".

As I do not remember when I first saw Botany Bay, so I cannot recall at what stage of our comradeship I began to define in my own young mind what made him so different from other people. He was generally regarded as insane, alluded to as 'crazy Balaam', avoided and feared by children as a dangerous lunatic. But I soon saw that he was not like other madmen. There was 'Wild Jimmy', the Scotchman, kept by his kinsfolk in an attic room in the small brown house near Windmill Point, and whose ravings, yells, and unearthly peals of laughter rang out on moonlit nights, striking terror to my soul. There was Vashti, with her tall, commanding figure, flashing black eyes, and fine features, her shrewd, scarcely incoherent talk, full of humorous incongruities. And everyone in the village knew Zaccheus, that harmless eccentric, with his unkempt hair and strangely patched, party-colored garments, who muttered to himself as he carried his baskets and brooms through the streets, or stood in the door of his caboose-house in the evening. Botany Bay was not at all like these. He was taciturn, reticent; but when he talked of his plants there was no sign of insanity, no incoherency or wandering. I do not think he could read or write; he knew nothing of any botanical systems or artificial classifying of plants, but he had a sort of system of his own, and by some curious instinct seemed to recognize kinship between certain herbs, which in later years I found were placed in one family by more scientific men – not closer observers.

Yet there was something wrong in Bay's brain. My childish mind was conscious of it but could not define it. There was a strange minor key in all his tones, a certain sadness underlying his happiest moods. When exultant over a new discovery, a long-sought flower, a deep-buried root of wondrous virtues, his child-smile of big-eyed delight would suddenly, swiftly fade, and a strange, mingled look of perplexity, fear, and melancholy take its place. By-and-by I went further in my analysis, and noticed what made his talk so odd and puzzling. This was the frequent recurrence of such expressions as 't'other', 'him', 'that 'un', and like phrases, not apparently referring to anything else in his sentences, or to anyone I knew.

"I'm awful glad to git this wild-ginger," he would say, as he dug up the aromatic root of the asarum, with its singular wine-colored flowers almost hidden under the earth; "old Square Wheeler's tryin' to swear off chewin'. It gives him spells now, an' he's had warnin's o' numb palsy. But he can't swear off on anything but wild-ginger root. He's tried cammermile an' rheubarb an' lots o' things, but he goes on hankerin' for terbacky. I'm plaguy glad to git this" – all this with a smile, or rather chuckle, of pleasure. Then a shadow would fall on the thin, wizened, brown face, and in a lower tone, with a kind of pathetic ring in it, he would say, "I wonder if *he's* found it this year, hope he has," and with a heavy sigh the spicy treasure, but with half its flavor gone, seemingly, for Bay, would be dropped into the basket. Or while cutting, in autumn, the witch-hazel twigs with their late, out-of-season, unflowerlike yellow blossoms, he would murmur: "I'd be sot up with gettin' these, to steep for Lodowick Pen'leton's lame arm, if 't wa'n't for t'other. I'm awfully 'fraid he ain't got any this fall." That I did not, for a long time, ask the meaning of these references shows me now that I recognized in them an element of mystery, something out of the common, which somehow awed and silenced me. I remember well the day when the explanation came. We had been roaming about the lower part of the village, gathering jimson-weed, the stramonium of botany and pharmacy. It grew very plentifully in waste places there, with its large whitish or pale violet funnel-shaped flowers and coarse leaves, and we soon had all we wanted. As the summer twilight came on we wandered down to the Point, near the old lighthouse, and finally seated ourselves on the rocks there, and looked out over the water. There had been one of those wonderful sunsets of crimson and gold so well known to old

Stonington, and believed by her inhabitants to be quite unknown elsewhere (old Captain Seth used to tell me it was "owin' to the salt in the air, which kinder fetched the colors out an' sot 'em"). A little sailboat in the distance – a homely thing enough when at the dock, and with the broad unfaltering light of noonday upon its scarred and dingy sides, stained and patched sail – now seemed a fairy shallop of rose and gold, and on this boat Botany Bay's blue, melancholy eyes were fixed. "*He* might be in that boat," he said at last, "might jest as well be there's anywheres; jest's likely to be, fortino"; and then as I looked up at the dreary sound in his voice I saw, to my amaze and distress, big tears on the brown face. I could not stand that. I laid my fingers on the sleeve of his ragged coat, and whispered:

"What's the matter, Bay?" I think he was glad to have me ask him. I think he had pined for a confidant; at any rate he turned quickly towards me, and in a strangely solemn, sad voice, the very tones of which I seem to hear as I recall the scene, he said:

"Aleck, did ye know there was two o' me?"

I scarcely understand now what there was in those words to frighten me so. Perhaps it was the tone and manner of the speaker, our surroundings of sea and sky, as well as the mysteriousness of the words themselves, which alarmed me, only a boy at the time; but I shivered with sudden fear.

"Don't be scaret, Aleck," he said, soothingly. "'Tain't nothin' new. I've knowed it years. Ye ain't scaret at me; an' he's jest the same."

"Who is, Bay?" I said, in a frightened whisper, my teeth almost chattering.

"Him," he answered, slowly, "t'other. That other *me*, ye know"; and gradually the story was told.

Many years before, how long Bay did not know, a sailor, temporarily in Stonington, while his ship was unloading, had told the simple herbalist a strange thing. He had said that somewhere far away there was another Botany Bay, another Balaam, in every respect the same as this one. His name, his looks, his pursuit, were all just the same. This is what Bay understood him to say. Whether the man was trying to impose upon the poor boy's credulity, whether in his broken tongue – for he was a foreigner – he only intended to say that he had seen a person who resembled the plant-vender, or again, if perchance he was superstitiously inclined and himself believed in this strange double, I know not. At any rate, Bay accepted the tale as true, and it colored all his after-life. If he was happy and exultant over some simple conquest in the plant world, his joy was at once shadowed by the thought that 't'other' was, perhaps, denied that pleasure. If troubled, if cold or hungry, or persecuted by the boys, he was jealous lest 't'other' was better off and free from these annoyances. He was always brooding over the existence of this other self, sometimes when lonesome rejoicing in the twinship which seemed to give him something all his own, a more than friend or even brother, sometimes hating the thought of this shadow of his he could not escape, oftenest of all fearing with a strange fear this weird, mysterious duplicate of himself. After my first alarm on hearing this strange story the terror subsided, and I began soothing and comforting my poor friend.

"I don't see what makes you so afraid, Bay," I said, as we still sat on the rocks and talked that night. "What is there so dreadful in a man's looking just like you?"

"'Tain't that, Aleck," he replied. "'Tain't jest that he favors me, but he *is* me, an' I'm him, an' we're both on us each other. It's dreffle, dreffle."

"But how can it be, Bay? How could it have happened?"

"Well, I didn't use to know 'bout that myself. But I've ciphered it out now, an' this's the way on it. I see Cap'n Pollard's little gal one day, Lois, you know, settin' on the stoop, cuttin' out figgers out o' paper with her ma's scissors, an' she went to cut out a man with a peaked hat on, an' all of a suddent she says: 'Why, look here, I got two on 'em stead o' one.' an' I see she'd doubled her paper 'thout knowin' it, an' so she'd got two men jest kezackly alike, peaked hat an' all. An' then in a jiffy it come over me that was how it happened with him an' me; God got the stuff doubled, you see, an' when he went to cut me out – or him, whichever 'twas he meant to make – he made two on us. I guess he didn't find it out till 'twas too late, or he wouldn't ha' let it go. Or mebbe he thought he'd throwed one away, but it – I mean him – or me – got off somehow. But 'twas a dreffle mistake, an' can't never, never be sot right."

His voice had a hopeless ring in it, and his blue eyes were misty as he looked off to sea. It was growing dark, and one by one the lights came out on Fisher's Island, Montauk Point, and farther to the westward, on the Hummocks.

"How *could* it be sot right?" he went on. "Mebbe you think if one on us died, 'twould fix it. But about his soul, how's that? When we was made double – by mistake – nobody to blame, you know – there couldn't ha' been but one soul pervided for. I was raised respectable on 'lection an' foreordination, jest's you was, Aleck, an' so I know that air soul was 'lected to heaven or 'tother place, an' whichever died fust would take that place pervided for Balaam Montm'rency's soul. Ther couldn't be two men 'lected guv nor o' Connecticut, could ther? No more could ther be two souls to the same man 'lected to one place."

"Oh, Balaam!" I cried, in dismay; "I can't follow you; I'm all mixed up."

"So 'm I, Aleck, an' so's him, dreffle mixed; that's the trouble."

From that night Bay and I were closer friends than ever. I knew his secret now, and he was glad I knew it. We often talked of 't'other', and passed hours in vain surmises and imaginings as to his fate. Although I knew the whole situation was impossible, and existed only in poor Bay's weak brain, still there was a fearful fascination for me in the subject, and I loved to dwell upon it.

"Would you like to see him, Balaam?" I asked one day.

Bay shook and brushed the earth from some fine large roots of the ginseng he had just been digging, as he said, doubtfully, "I don't hardly know. Sometimes I think I would, an' then agin I ain't so sure. To see yourself comin up to ye jest careless like, 's if 'twas somebody else, would be pretty scary, out of a lookin'-glass. But agin there's times when I want him bad; seem's if I must have him; 's if I wasn't a hull man without him, but on'y a piece o' one, half a pair o' scissors, you know, or one leg o' these trowses."

"But, Bay," I said, with a sudden thought, "it isn't any worse than twins. Don't you know Bill and Bob Hancox are twins, and they look so much alike nobody but their mother knows them apart."

"I've thought o' that," Bay replied, "but it ain't the same. They was meant to be in pairs, like pijin berries, or two-fingered grass. They've got two souls, an' there's a place for 'em both – one for Bob Hancox and one for Bill Hancox – in heaven or t'other place; I'm afraid Bill's place is the bad 'un, for he's a plaguey troublesome chap; but us, we ain't twins, we're each other, don't ye see?"

I did not see exactly, but that there was a difficulty too mighty to be explained away by my young self I realized too well. One summer's day we were walking near the 'Road meeting-house.' Bay had been gathering Indian tobacco, one of the lobelias, and discoursing upon its nature and properties. According to him, although a powerful "pison", yet when steeped and combined with certain other "yarbs" it had performed wonderful cures.

"There's 'nother kind," he said, "somethin' like this, only it's a good deal taller, an's got big spikes o' blooms, real blue, an' han'some. They call that the High Beelyer, 'cause this small little one's the Low Beelyer, ye know, an' it's good for the blood, like sas'p'rilla an' dock."

We sat down to rest on the church steps, and were silent for a time. Then Bay said: "I wish I was a perfessor; b'longed to the Church, ye know; I might get a sight o' comfort that way. But I can't be, 'tain't no use. I come pretty near it once. I was at the Baptist meetin one Sunday night, an' there was a big revival, an' Elder Swan was preachin'. I was awful stirred up, an' seem'd's if I'd foun' a way out o' all my troubles. But all on a suddent I thought o' 'tother one. I mos' know he's a heathen, for the man that told me about him he was a Portugee or Kanaka, an' mos' likely he'd seed t'other Balaam over in them parts. So I jest thought 'twould be pretty mean for me, with my privleges, born in a Christian land an' raised in Stonin'ton Borough, to take advantage of t'other poor heathen Bay just because he'd happened to be brought up 'mong id'ls an' things, an' take his chance away. So I gin it up."

I cannot describe fully all the phases of feeling through which Bay passed after I knew his story. But sure am I that after doubt, fear, repulsion, dread, sorrow, and pity, he came at last into a great and tender love for this strange other self. I do not think that he had ever before loved a human being. As far as I could find out he had no memory of father, mother, brother, or sister, and had hitherto led a friendless, lonesome life. So he had learned no expressions of endearment, no fond words, no pet names. Such had never been addressed to himself, nor had he ever used them. But he loved, in a certain fashion, his plants, and this helped him now. He grew more eccentric, odder than ever, was more by himself, and was always talking in a low tone, even when quite alone. The village folk said that he was "madder 'n a hatter", "crazier 'n a coot", but I did not think so. He was only talking to his other self, for I often heard such words as these:

"Poor Bay, poor t'other Bay, don't mind me, don't be scaret as I uster be, cause there's two o' ye. Some meddlin' loon's up an' told ye, I s'pose, an' ye feel bad; don't, now, *don't*."

Then his voice would sink almost to a whisper as he would say:

"Why, I love ye, Bay, I love ye; I love your peaked, pindlin' face, an' your yeller mussed-up hair, an' them silly blue eyes o' yourn. Ye see I know jest how ye look. I've got a bit o' lookin'-glass now, an' I carry it round an' keep lookin' in it, an' I can see us jest's plain. Don't be feard on me; I wouldn't no more hurt ye than I'd hurt the vilets or venuses-prides in the spring."

But more and more, as this strange love grew, did the poor man grieve – agonize almost – over that other's soul, and its ultimate state. His ideas of heathendom were vague, and derived principally from what he had heard at the 'Monthly Concerts' of the Baptist church, intensified by the pictures in illustrated missionary papers distributed at the same meetings. He sometimes fancied that 't'other Bay' was discussing this matter with him, and I would hear him say, as if in response to another voice:

"Yer a heathen, ye say? That ain't no matter. How could ye help bein', out there where ye b'long? Never min', poor old Bay, *I* don't care 'bout yer id'ls, an' yer throwin' babies to the crockerdiles, an' layin' down on the railroad track to let the Jockanock train run over ye, an' all that. I'd a done it, too, if 'twas the fash'n in the Borough here. That's what they sing over to Baptist meetin':

> 'The heathens in their blinders
> Bows down to wooden stuns.'

'Course they do; they don't know no better. But then, Bay, 'tain't a good thing to do, an' I wouldn't if I was you. O, Lord, I *am* you, I clean forgot. But won't ye try not to do it – can't ye swear off, Bay?"

Again and again, as the months rolled on, Balaam would talk with me of this matter, always dwelling now upon the point that there was but one place "pervided for Balaam Montm'rency's soul", and consequently but one of the two Bays could have a place at all.

"But," I ventured to ask one day, "what becomes of the other soul, Bay?"

"Why, it jest goes out."

"Out where?" I naturally asked.

"Jest where the light of a taller can'le goes when ye snuff it out, or the inside of a puff-ball when ye squeeze it, that's where. There ain't no soul no more; it's just stopped bein'."

The more the love for 't'other Bay' grew and deepened, the more the trouble and perplexity increased. How could he help this other – how could he set right this mighty difficulty?

One November day I had arranged to meet my friend just outside the village, and go out to the Baldwin Farm to dig gold-thread roots. It was late in the season, but Uncle David Doty was suffering with a sore mouth, and his supply of gold-thread – a certain cure – was nearly exhausted, and Botany Bay knew well how to find the little plant, even when snow was on the ground, by its glossy, evergreen, strawberry-like leaf, which told that under the earth were the bright yellow thread-like roots of bitter virtue. As I came to the place of meeting, Bay was waiting, and I at once saw that he was strangely excited. His thin brown face was pale, his big blue eyes wild, his lips worked nervously.

"Aleck, Aleck," he said, excitedly, as soon as I drew near, "I've had a message!"

"Who from, Bay?" I asked.

"Why, from him, from poor Bay, dear old Balaam. I thought there was suthin' comin', an' I've been thinkin' an' contrivin' what 'twould be, an' this mornin' as I was comin' down the road I see old Thankful Bateese, the Injun woman. She's a mighty cur'us creeter, an' they say she has dealins, an' she was in a field all by herself, an' she was a-walkin roun' an' roun' suthin' on the ground, an' kinder singin'. An' I lissened, an' – oh, Aleck, I heerd the words."

He stopped, and caught his breath with a half sob.

"What was it?" I asked, eagerly, sharing his excitement.

Still pale and trembling, he began chanting, in a strange, monotonous way, these rude rhymes:

> *"Ther's room for one, but ther ain't for two,*
> *Ther's no room for me if ther's room for you;*
> *If ye wanter save me, jest up an' say*
> *Ye'll gimme your chance, an' get outer the way."*

As he crooned the words, swaying his body and moving his head from side to side, I was at once reminded of the old squaw, so well known in the village, and her peculiar way of chanting some strange gibberish, quite unintelligible to any of us. It at once struck me that Bay had construed the Indian jargon in his own way, prompted by his one pervading thought.

"Are you sure she said that?" I asked. "I never could understand the words of anything she sings."

"*I* never could afore, Aleck, but I heerd this jest as plain. 'Twas Bay, t'other Bay, speakin' right through her. An' now I know what I've got ter do."

"Oh, what, Bay?" I asked, anxiously, drawing nearer to him.

"Why, don't ye see? I've got ter up an' say I'll gin him my chance, an' git outer the way," and his voice again fell into the strange chant.

"But who'll you say it to, Bay?"

His face fell, and a puzzled look came over it, as he said, hesitating and troubled:

"Why – why – to him – no, I can't reach him – oh, Aleck, what shall I do? What shall I do?" and he threw himself upon the ground in an agony of sorrow and bewilderment. At that moment I saw the old Indian woman coming along the road, and dashed after her. But I failed utterly in making her respond satisfactorily to my inquiries as to her song and what it meant. She threatened me, with alarming guttural sounds and wild gesticulations, and I ran away frightened.

I returned to my friend, and finally succeeded in persuading him to go on with me towards the farm, after our golden treasure. We talked long and earnestly as we went on through the gray November day.

"Ye see, Aleck," said Balaam at last, "it *must* be my soul that's 'lected – I was allers afraid 'twas – an' he's foun' it out, an' he sees a way out on it, if I wanter save him', he says. Wanter! Oh, Bay!" and there was such a depth of tenderness in the voice. It seemed as if all the love he might under other conditions have given to father, mother, wife, or child, had gone into this one affection.

"But, Bay," I said, full of love and pity for my friend, "I don't want you to give up to him this way. Why should you?"

Why, Aleck, I wanter; I'd love ter. I never had anybody to take keer on, or set by, or gin up ter, but him, an' I love it. I don't guess he sets so much by me; likely's not he's got folks – a fam'ly, mebbe – an' he wants me outer the way, body an' soul, both on 'em. He don't want me roun' here, or takin' his place there, an' I don't blame him a mite. But it's different with me. He's all the folks I've got, an' I'm dreffle glad ter do a little suthin' for him. I won't say that I ain't sometimes kinder felt's if I'd like ter see them places they tell about at meetin', an' Scripter speaks on. Ye ain't a religious boy, Aleck; that ain't cum yit with ye; so I can't talk much about that, an' tell you all my reas'ns, the whys an' whuffers; but anyway you'll understand how I'd like to see them plants an' things growin' there El der Peckham told about, that heals the nations, an' them trees bearin a dozen diffunt kin's o' fruits – grafted, mebbe – an' them never-witherin flowers in the hymn-book everlastin's I s'pose. But, law, 'tain't wuth talkin' about. I'd do more 'n that for him, poor chap. Jest to go out, you know, an' not to be roun' anymore; that ain't much."

In spite of myself I could not help talking as if the situation was a real one. I had lived so long with Bay in this strange story of another self that it was very real to me, and I could hardly bear the thought of this terrible sacrifice, this strange, paradoxical, unselfish self-love, this self-abnegatory immolation for another self. But I could do nothing.

We had gathered our roots, and were resting under the lee of a large boulder, when again Bay began his bewildering talk as to how he could effect this renunciation, to whom he could "up an' say" that he would gladly resign his chance for the other's sake. Suddenly, as we leaned against the rock, there came from overhead something like a cry. To this day I do not know what it was. It may have been the call of some belated bird fallen behind his migrating comrades, the scream of an eagle or hawk, but to Bay's excited brain it seemed a message from Heaven. He listened intently a moment, his pale face glowed, and he cried:

"O' course, o' course! I'd oughter knowed it. Thank the Lord, I know now."

"Oh, Bay, tell me, tell me, what is it?"

"Why, that there voice showed me how. Don't ye see that wh'ever made the mistake fust – made us double, ye know – he's the one to fix it now? He'll be glad enough to have the thing sot right an' off his mind, an' if I go an' tell him's well as I know how that I ain't goin to stan' in anyone's way – that he can count me out – why, the thing'll be squared somehow." He was in a state of trembling excitement.

"Go home, Aleck, that's a good boy," he said, hurriedly; "I want ter be by myself a spell; I'll come down bimeby."

He took up his basket, crossed the road, entered a piece of woods, and was soon out of sight among the leafless trees. I was frightened, and after a few minutes I stole after him, and went a little way into the woods. Suddenly I heard a voice, and involuntarily stopped to listen. I shall not tell you what I heard. I was not, as Botany Bay truly said, a religious boy – perhaps I am not a religious man; but there was something about what came to my ears in that gray and lonesome wood which filled me with awe then, and has ever since seemed to me a sacred, solemn thing. He was talking to someone, as man to man; he was telling that someone in homely phrase, which yet carried in it a terrible earnestness, of his willingness to give up his place here and hereafter – as he had often expressed it to me to 'stop bein'' – to have everything go on as if there had been but one Bay, and that one "t'other". He did not ask that this might be; he made no petition, offered no plea. He spoke as if only his expression of willingness was lacking to make the thing a fact, to complete the sacrifice.

Boy as I was, I felt that I was on holy ground, and stole away. I would go home, I thought, but tomorrow I would, at the risk of seeming to betray a confidence, ask advice of some older, wiser person.

As I came down into the village it grew grayer and more black, and soon there were snow-squalls, a sure sign there of increasing cold. And cold it grew, bitterly cold. As I sat in front of our blazing wood fire that evening I thought much of Bay, and longed for the morning. I should know better what to say to him now that I had thought the matter over, and if I could not convince him myself, why, I should go to Mr. Clifford, the minister. He would know what to say. The morning came clear and cold, sharply cold for that early season, and thoughts of skating and 'Lihu's Pond came first to me as I woke in my warm bed. Then I remembered Bay. As soon as I could I ran up the street and down the little lane opposite the doctor's to Bay's small brown house. He was not there; the neighbors said he had not been there since yesterday morning. I hurried to David Doty's, down the back street towards the Point, but he had not brought to the old man the promised gold thread. Thoroughly alarmed, I ran home and told my fears, and soon our team was ready, and my father and I, with faithful Elam, our 'help', were on our way to the woods where I had last seen poor Bay.

It did not take long to find him; he did not try to hide away. There he was, lying close at hand and very still. At first we thought that he was dead. Then he showed some signs of life, and we lifted him tenderly and carried him to our home. No pains were spared to resuscitate him; good Dr. Hines worked faithfully and untiringly, and by-and-by the eyelids trembled and were lifted.

There was a look of dazed wonderment at first; then a faint light flickered over the small, quaint, brown face, and the lips moved. We bent to listen. In a faint, broken whisper he said:

"Ther's room for one, but ther ain't for two. But – ther ain't – two now, Bay; you're – the one an' I'm – goin' out. I'm dreffle glad, Bay."

The big blue eyes opened with a sudden smile, like that of a little child, but withal so wise and deep, and Bay was still. The soul had 'gone out'. Had it 'stopped bein''?

The Devotee of Evil

Clark Ashton Smith

THE OLD LARCOM HOUSE was a mansion of considerable size and dignity, set among oaks and cypresses on the hill behind Auburn's Chinatown, in what had once been the aristocratic section of the village. At the time of which I write, it had been unoccupied for several years and had begun to present the signs of desolation and dilapidation which untenanted houses so soon display. The place had a tragic history and was believed to be haunted. I had never been able to procure any first-hand or precise accounts of the spectral manifestations that were accredited to it. But certainly it possessed all the necessary antecedents of a haunted house. The first owner, Judge Peter Larcom, had been murdered beneath its roof back in the seventies by a maniacal Chinese cook; one of his daughters had gone insane; and two other members of the family had died accidental deaths. None of them had prospered: their legend was one of sorrow and disaster.

Some later occupants, who had purchased the place from the one surviving son of Peter Larcom, had left under circumstances of inexplicable haste after a few months, moving permanently to San Francisco. They did not return even for the briefest visit; and beyond paying their taxes, they gave no attention whatever to the place. Everyone had grown to think of it as a sort of historic ruin, when the announcement came that it had been sold to Jean Averaud, of New Orleans.

My first meeting with Averaud was strangely significant, for it revealed to me, as years of acquaintance would not necessarily have done, the peculiar bias of his mind. Of course, I had already heard some odd rumors about him; his personality was too signal, his advent too mysterious, to escape the usual fabrication and mongering of village tales. I had been told that he was extravagantly rich, that he was a recluse of the most eccentric type, that he had made certain very singular changes in the inner structure of the old house; and last, but not least, that he lived with a beautiful mulatress who never spoke to anyone and who was believed to be his mistress as well as his housekeeper. The man himself had been described to me by some as an unusual but harmless lunatic, and by others as an all-round Mephistopheles.

I had seen him several times before our initial meeting. He was a sallow, saturnine Creole, with the marks of race in his hollow cheeks and feverish eyes. I was struck by his air of intellect, and by the fiery fixity of his gaze – the gaze of a man who is dominated by one idea to the exclusion of all else. Some medieval alchemist, who believed himself to be on the point of attaining his objective after years of unrelenting research, might have looked as he did.

I was in the Auburn library one day, when Averaud entered. I had taken a newspaper from one of the tables and was reading the details of an atrocious crime – the murder of a woman and her two infant children by the husband and father, who had locked his victims in a clothes-closet, after saturating their garments with oil. He had left the woman's apron-string caught in the shut door, with the end protruding, and had set fire to it like a fuse.

Averaud passed the table where I was reading. I looked up, and saw his glance at the headlines of the paper I held. A moment later he returned and sat down beside me, saying in a low voice:

"What interests me in a crime of that sort, is the implication of unhuman forces behind it. Could any man, on his own initiative, have conceived and executed anything so gratuitously fiendish?"

"I don't know," I replied, somewhat surprised by the question and by my interrogator. "There are terrifying depths in human nature – more abhorrent than those of the jungle."

"I agree. But how could such impulses, unknown to the most brutal progenitors of man, have been implanted in his nature, unless through some ulterior agency?"

"You believe, then, in the existence of an evil force or entity – a Satan or an Ahriman?"

"I believe in evil – how can I do otherwise when I see its manifestations everywhere? I regard it as an all-controlling power; but I do not think that the power is personal in the sense of what we know as personality. A Satan? No. What I conceive is a sort of dark vibration, the radiation of a black sun, of a center of malignant eons – a radiation that can penetrate like any other ray – and perhaps more deeply. But probably I don't make my meaning clear at all."

I protested that I understood him; but, after his burst of communicativeness, he seemed oddly disinclined to pursue the conversation. Evidently he had been prompted to address me; and no less evidently, he regretted having spoken with so much freedom. He arose; but before leaving, he said:

"I am Jean Averaud – perhaps you have heard of me. You are Philip Hastane, the novelist. I have read your books and I admire them. Come and see me sometime – we may have certain tastes in common."

Averaud's personality, the conception he had avowed, and the intense interest and value which he so obviously attached to these conceptions, made a singular impression on my mind, and I could not forget him. When, a few days later, I met him on the street and he repeated his invitation with a cordialness that was unfeignedly sincere, I could do no less than accept. I was interested, though not altogether attracted, by his bizarre, well-nigh morbid individuality, and was impelled by a desire to learn more concerning him. I sensed a mystery of no common order – a mystery with elements of the abnormal and the uncanny.

The grounds of the old Larcom place were precisely as I remembered them, though I had not found occasion to pass them for some time. They were a veritable tangle of Cherokee rose-vines, arbutus, lilac, ivy and crepe-myrtle, half overshadowed by the great cypresses and somber evergreen oaks. There was a wild, half-sinister charm about them – the charm of rampancy and ruin. Nothing had been done to put the place in order, and there were no outward repairs in the house itself, where the white paint of bygone years was being slowly replaced by mosses and lichens that flourished beneath the eternal umbrage of the trees. There were signs of decay in the roof and pillars of the front porch; and I wondered why the new owner, who was reputed to be so rich, had not already made the necessary restorations.

I raised the gargoyle-shaped knocker and let it fall with a dull, lugubrious clang. The house remained silent; and I was about to knock again, when the door opened slowly and I saw for the first time the mulatress of whom so many village rumors had reached me.

The woman was more exotic than beautiful, with fine, mournful eyes and bronze-colored features of a semi-negroid irregularity. Her figure, though, was truly perfect, with the curving lines of a lyre and the supple grace of some feline animal. When I asked for Jean Averaud, she merely smiled and made signs for me to enter. I surmised at once that she was dumb.

Waiting in the gloomy library to which she conducted me, I could not refrain from glancing at the volumes with which the shelves were congested. They were an ungodly jumble of tomes that dealt with anthropology, ancient religions, demonology, modern science, history, psychoanalysis and ethics. Interspersed with these were a few romances and volumes of poetry. Beausobre's monograph on Manichaeism was flanked with Byron and Poe; and *Les Fleurs du Mal* jostled a late treatise on chemistry.

Averaud entered, after several minutes, apologizing profusely for his delay. He said that he had been in the midst of certain labors when I came; but he did not specify the nature of these labors. He looked even more hectic and fiery-eyed than when I had seen him last. He was patently glad to see me, and eager to talk.

"You have been looking at my books," he observed immediately. "Though you might not think so at first glance, on account of their seeming diversity, I have selected them all with a single object: the study of evil in all its aspects, ancient, medieval and modern. I have traced it in the religions and demonologies of all peoples; and, more than this, in human history itself. I have found it in the inspiration of poets and romancers who have dealt with the darker impulses, emotion and acts of man. Your novels have interested me for this reason: you are aware of the baneful influences which surround us, which so often sway or actuate us. I have followed the working of these agencies even in chemical reactions, in the growth and decay of trees, flowers, minerals. I feel that the processes of physical decomposition, as well as the similar mental and moral processes, are due entirely to them.

"In brief, I have postulated a monistic evil, which is the source of all death, deterioration, imperfection, pain, sorrow, madness and disease. This evil, so feebly counteracted by the powers of good, allures and fascinates me above all things. For a long time past, my life-work has been to ascertain its true nature, and trace it to its fountain-head. I am sure that somewhere in space there is the center from which all evil emanates."

He spoke with a wild air of excitement, of morbid and semi-maniacal intensity. His obsession convinced me that he was more or less unbalanced; but there was an unholy logic in the development of his ideas; and I could not but recognize a certain disordered brilliancy and range of intellect.

Scarcely waiting for me to reply, he continued his monologue:

"I have learned that certain localities and buildings, certain arrangements of natural or artificial objects, are more favorable to the reception of evil influences than others. The laws that determine the degree of receptivity are still obscure to me; but at least I have verified the fact itself. As you know, there are houses or neighborhoods notorious for a succession of crimes or misfortunes; and there are also articles, such as certain jewels, whose possession is accompanied by disaster. Such places and things are receivers of evil…I have a theory, however, that there is always more or less interference with the direct flow of the malignant force; and that pure, absolute evil has never yet been manifested.

"By the use of some device which would create a proper field or form a receiving station, it should be possible to evoke this absolute evil. Under such conditions, I am sure that the dark vibration would become a visible and tangible thing, comparable to light or electricity." He eyed me with a gaze that was disconcertingly exigent. Then:

"I will confess that I have purchased this old mansion and its grounds mainly on account of their baleful history. The place is unusually liable to the influences of which I have spoken. I am now at work on an apparatus by means of which, when it is perfected, I hope to manifest in their essential purity the radiations of malign force."

At this moment, the mulatress entered and passed through the room on some household errand. I thought that she gave Averaud a look of maternal tenderness, watchfulness and anxiety. He, on his part seemed hardly to be aware of her presence, so engrossed was he in the strange ideas and the stranger project he had been expounding. However, when she had gone, he remarked:

"That is Fifine, the one human being who is really attached to me. She is mute, but highly intelligent and affectionate. All my people, an old Louisiana family, are long departed…and my wife is doubly dead to me." A spasm of obscure pain contracted his features, and vanished. He resumed his monologue; and at no future time did he again refer to the presumably tragic tale at which he had hinted: a tale in which, I sometimes suspect, were hidden the seeds of the strange moral and mental perversion which he was to manifest more and more.

I took my leave, after promising to return for another talk. Of course, I considered now that Averaud was a madman; but his madness was of a most uncommon and picturesque variety. It seemed significant that he should have chosen me for a confidant. All others who met him found him uncommunicative and taciturn to an extreme degree. I suppose he had felt the ordinary human need of unburdening himself to someone; and had selected me as the only person in the neighborhood who was potentially sympathetic.

I saw him several times during the month that followed. He was indeed a strange psychological study; and I encouraged him to talk without reserve – though such encouragement was hardly necessary. There was much that he told me – a strange medley of the scientific and the mystic. I assented tactfully to all that he said, but ventured to point out the possible dangers of his evocative experiments, if they should prove successful. To this, with the fervor of an alchemist or a religious devotee, he replied that it did not matter – that he was prepared to accept any and all consequences.

More than once he gave me to understand that his invention was progressing favorably. And one day he said, with abruptness:

"I will show you my mechanism, if you care to see it." I protested my eagerness to view the invention, and he led me forthwith into a room to which I had not been admitted before. The chamber was large, triangular in form, and tapestried with curtains of some sullen black fabric. It had no windows. Clearly, the internal structure of the house had been changed in making it; and all the queer village tales, emanating from carpenters who had been hired to do the work, were now explained. Exactly in the center of the room, there stood on a low tripod of brass the apparatus of which Averaud had so often spoken.

The contrivance was quite fantastic, and presented the appearance of some new, highly complicated musical instrument. I remember that there were many wires of varying thickness, stretched on a series of concave sounding-boards of some dark, unlustrous metal; and above these, there depended from three horizontal bars a number of square, circular and triangular gongs. Each of these appeared to be made of a different material; some were bright as gold, or translucent as jade; others were black and opaque as jet. A small hammer-like instrument hung opposite each gong, at the end of a silver wire.

Averaud proceeded to expound the scientific basis of his mechanism. The vibrational properties of the gongs, he said, were designed to neutralize with their sound-pitch all other cosmic vibrations than those of evil. He dwelt at much length on this extravagant theorem, developing it in a fashion oddly lucid. He ended his peroration:

"I need one more gong to complete the instrument; and this I hope to invent very soon. The triangular room, draped in black, and without windows, forms the ideal setting for my experiment. Apart from this room, I have not ventured to make any change in the house or its grounds, for fear of deranging some propitious element or collocation of elements."

More than ever, I thought that he was mad. And, though he had professed on many occasions to abhor the evil which he planned to evoke, I felt an inverted fanaticism in his attitude. In a less scientific age he would have been a devil-worshipper, a partaker in the abominations of the Black Mass; or would have given himself to the study and practice of sorcery. His was a religious soul that had failed to find good in the scheme of things; and lacking it, was impelled to make of evil itself an object of secret reverence.

"I fear that you think me insane," he observed in a sudden flash of clairvoyance. "Would you like to watch an experiment? Even though my invention is not completed, I may be able to convince you that my design is not altogether the fantasy of a disordered brain."

I consented. He turned on the lights in the dim room. Then he went to an angle of the wall and pressed a hidden spring or switch. The wires on which the tiny hammers were strung began to oscillate, till each of the hammers touched lightly its companion gong. The sound they made was dissonant and disquieting to the last degree – a diabolic percussion unlike anything I have ever heard, and exquisitely painful to the nerves. I felt as if a flood of finely broken glass was pouring into my ears.

The swinging of the hammers grew swifter and heavier; but, to my surprise, there was no corresponding increase of loudness in the sound. On the contrary, the clangor became slowly muted, till it was no more than an undertone which seemed to be coming from an immense depth or distance – an undertone still full of disquietude and torment, like the sobbing of far-off winds in hell, or the murmur of demonian fires on coasts of eternal ice.

Said Averaud at my elbow:

"To a certain extent, the combined notes of the gongs are beyond human hearing in their pitch. With the addition of the final gong, even less sound will be audible."

While I was trying to digest this difficult idea, I noticed a partial dimming of the light above the tripod and its weird apparatus. A vertical shaft of faint shadow, surrounded by a still fainter penumbra, was forming in the air. The tripod itself, and the wires, gongs and hammers, were now a trifle indistinct, as if seen through some obscuring veil. The central shaft and its penumbra seemed to widen; and looking down at the flood, where the outer adumbration, conforming to the room's outline, crept toward the walls, I saw that Averaud and myself were now within its ghostly triangle.

At the same time there surged upon me an intolerable depression, together with a multitude of sensations which I despair of conveying in language. My very sense of space was distorted and deformed as if some unknown dimension had somehow been mingled with those familiar to us. There was a feeling of dreadful and measureless descent, as if the floor were sinking beneath me into some nether pit; and I seemed to pass beyond the room in a torrent of swirling, hallucinative images, visible but invisible, felt but intangible, and more awful, more accursed than that hurricane of lost souls beheld by Dante.

Down, down, I appeared to go, in the bottomless and phantom hell that was impinging upon reality. Death, decay, malignity, madness, gathered in the air and pressed me down like Satanic incubi in that ecstatic horror of descent. I felt that there were a thousand forms, a thousand faces about me, summoned from the gulfs of perdition. And yet I saw nothing but the white face of Averaud, stamped with a frozen and abominable rapture as he fell beside me.

Like a dreamer who forces himself to awaken, he began to move away from me. I seemed to lose sight of him for a moment in the cloud of nameless, immaterial horrors that threatened to take on the further horror of substance. Then I realized that Averaud had turned off the switch, and that the oscillating hammers had ceased to beat on those infernal gongs. The double shaft of shadow faded in mid-air, the burden of terror and despair lifted from my nerves and I no longer felt the damnable hallucination of nether space and descent.

"My God!" I cried. "What was it?" Averaud's look was full of a ghastly, gloating exultation as he turned to me.

"You saw and felt it, then?" he queried – "that vague, imperfect manifestation of the perfect evil which exists somewhere in the cosmos? I shall yet call it forth in its entirety, and know the black, infinite, reverse raptures which attend its epiphany."

I recoiled from him with an involuntary shudder. All the hideous things that had swarmed upon me beneath the cacophonous beating of those accursed gongs, drew near again for an instant; and I looked with fearful vertigo into hells of perversity and corruption. I saw an inverted soul, despairing of good, which longed for the baleful ecstasies of perdition. No longer did I think him merely mad: for I knew the thing which he sought and could attain; and I remembered, with a new significance, that line of Baudelaire's poem – "The hell wherein my heart delights."

Averaud was unaware of my revulsion, in his dark rhapsody. When I turned to leave, unable to bear any longer the blasphemous atmosphere of that room, and the sense of strange depravity which emanated from its owner, he pressed me to return as soon as possible.

"I think," he exulted, "that all will be in readiness before long. I want you to be present in the hour of my triumph."

I do not know what I said, nor what excuses I made to get away from him. I longed to assure myself that a world of unblasted sunlight and undefiled air could still exist. I went out; but a shadow followed me; and execrable faces leered or mowed from the foliage as I left the cypress-shaded grounds.

For days afterward I was in a condition verging upon neurotic disorder. No one could come as close as I had been to the primal effluence of evil, and go thence unaffected. Shadowy noisome cobwebs draped themselves on all my thoughts, and presences of unlineamented fear, of shapeless horror, crouched in the half-lit corners of my mind but would never fully declare themselves. An invisible gulf, bottomless as Malebolge, seemed to yawn before me wherever I went.

Presently, though, my reason reasserted itself, and I wondered if my sensations in the black triangular room had not been wholly a matter of suggestion or auto-hypnosis. I asked myself if it were credible that a cosmic force of the sort postulated by Averaud could really exist; or, granting it existed, could be evoked by any man through the absurd intermediation of a musical device. The nervous terrors of my experience faded a little in memory; and, though a disturbing doubt still lingered, I assured myself that all I had felt was of purely subjective origin. Even then, it was with supreme reluctance, with an inward shrinking only to be overcome by violent resolve, that I returned to visit Averaud once more.

For an even longer period than usual, no one answered my knock. Then there were hurrying footsteps, and the door was opened abruptly by Fifine. I knew immediately that something was amiss, for her face wore a look of unnatural dread and anxiety, and her eyes were wide, with the whites showing blankly, as if she gazed upon horrific things. She tried to speak, and made that ghastly inarticulate sound which the mute is able to make on occasion as she plucked my sleeve and drew me after her along the somber hall to the triangular room.

The door was open; and as I approached it, I heard a low, dissonant, snarling murmur, which I recognized as the sound of the gongs. It was like the voice of all the souls in a frozen hell, uttered by lips congealing slowly toward the ultimate torture of silence. It sank and sank till it seemed to be issuing from pits below the nadir.

Fifine shrank back on the threshold, imploring me with a pitiful glance to precede her . The lights were all turned on and Averaud, clad in a strange medieval costume, in a black gown and cap such as Faustus might have worn, stood near the percussive mechanism. The hammers were all beating with a frenzied rapidity; and the sound became still lower and tenser as I approached. Averaud did not seem to see me: his eyes, abnormally dilated, and flaming with infernal luster like those of one possessed, were fixed upon something in mid-air.

Again the soul-congealing hideousness, the sense of eternal falling, of myriad harpy-like incumbent horrors, rushed upon me as I looked and saw. Vaster and stronger than before, a double column of triangular shadow had materialized and was becoming more and more distinct. It swelled, it darkened, it enveloped the gong-apparatus and towered to the ceiling. The double column grew solid and opaque as ebony; and the face of Averaud, who was standing well within the broad penumbral shadow, became dim as if seen through a film of Stygian water.

I must have gone utterly mad for a while. I remember only a teeming delirium of things too frightful to be endured by a sane mind, that peopled the infinite gulf of hell-born illusion into which I sank with the hopeless precipitancy of the damned. There was a sickness inexpressible, a vertigo of redeemless descent, a pandemonium of ghoulish phantoms that reeled and swayed about the column of malign omnipotent force which presided over all. Averaud was only one more phantom in this delirium, when with arms outstretched in his perverse adoration, he stepped toward the inner column and passed into it till he was lost to view. And Fifine was another phantom when she ran by me to the wall and turned off the switch that operated those demoniacal hammers.

As one who re-emerges from a swoon, I saw the fading of the dual pillar, till the light was no longer sullied by any tinge of that satanic radiation. And where it had been, Averaud still stood beside the baleful instrument he had designed. Erect and rigid he stood, in a strange immobility; and I felt an incredulous horror, a chill awe, as I went forward and touched him with a faltering hand. For that which I saw and touched was no longer a human being but an ebon statue, whose face and brow and fingers were black as the Faust-like raiment or the sullen curtains. Charred as by sable fire, or frozen by black cold, the features bore the eternal ecstasy and pain of Lucifer in his ultimate hell of ice. For an instant, the supreme evil which Averaud had worshipped so madly, which he had summoned from the vaults of incalculable space, had made him one with itself; and passing, it had left him petrified into an image of its own essence. The form that I touched was harder than marble; and I knew that it would endure to all time as a testimony of the infinite Medusean power that is death and corruption and darkness.

Fifine had now thrown herself at the feet of the image and was clasping its insensible knees. With her frightful muted moaning in my ears, I went forth for the last time from that chamber and from that mansion. Vainly, through delirious months and madness-ridden years, I have tried to shake off the infrangible obsession of my memories. But there is a fatal numbness in my brain as if it too had been charred and blackened a little in that moment of overpowering nearness to the dark ray of the black statue that was Jean Averaud, the impress of awful and forbidden things has been set like an everlasting seal.

Approaching Lavender

Lucy A. Snyder

RHETTA'S husband Scott teased her for bringing her sketchpad along on their honeymoon: "I thought this was supposed to be just you and me. Not you, me and your *hobby*."

She felt heat rise in her sunburned face at his *ha-ha-only-serious* tone. It wasn't a hobby, and he knew that. Or she'd thought he did. He'd never complained about her working on her art when they were dating. He'd praised her paintings and cheerfully accompanied her to gallery hops and art shows. It had even been his idea to stop to see the Van Goghs at the museum when they drove through Cincinnati.

"I wanted to get some details of the ocean and the palm trees," she replied.

He waved a cheap digital camera at her. The lens was smeared with sunscreen. "That's why we have this. Put that down and let's go get some margaritas."

* * *

A month after they returned from Cancun, he started complaining about her evenings at the studio.

"I never see you," he said. "A wife should be home with her husband. Not off someplace playing with crayons."

She paused, staring at him. He certainly *looked* like the man she'd dated: the same soulful brown eyes, the same tidy blond beard, the same scar on his cheek from when he fell off his bike as a kid. What had changed? Had *anything* changed?

"People are expecting illustrations from me. I have to work—"

He made a dismissive noise. "That's just a hobby. Your work is at the insurance company."

She wanted to slap him and shout *What is wrong with you?* but her hand stayed perfectly still at her side. "I have contracts. They're paying me. Some of them have already paid. My *work* is expected, and I need to finish it."

"It's hardly any money, though. Just pocket change. Barely anything compared to what you *could* make if you'd just apply yourself at your company."

He sounded just like his own father, who'd given him almost the same dressing-down when they'd visited for Christmas. Scott's accounting job wasn't good enough for Mr. Bershung. He demanded to know why Scott wasn't on the executive track and turned brutally scornful when Scott insisted he was happy where he was.

Her head spun. Scott was miserable after his father's lecture; why would he do this to her? She'd spent whole evenings talking about her plan to become a full-time artist. Scott nodded and said *I'm sure you'll do it*. He'd never cared about her making money. Or had he, and she didn't remember?

"I'd make more money at my art if I didn't have the tech writing job," she said. "I'd get everything done during the day and spend every evening with you—"

"No." He frowned like she'd just suggested they move to the bad side of town. "You can't quit your job. We need the money too much."

"But if I had more time to work—"

He didn't seem to hear her. "And that studio space is too expensive. It's at least as much as the cable bill."

She threw up her hands. "Why are you so focused on money? We're doing fine."

"No, we're *not* fine. We need to save for the house."

"House?" She was sure the apartment floor would give way beneath her feet at any moment. She wracked her memory. They hadn't discussed moving anywhere. "What house?"

"My parents' place." He fiddled with his Rolex impatiently. "They're getting a condo in Florida next year. Dad wants market price, 500K. It needs a lot of work, but it's structurally sound—"

"And when were we going to talk about this?" She'd been in the house only once: the previous, uncomfortable Christmas when he and his father argued about Scott's career. The huge Victorian was all dark wood, shrouded windows and heavy furniture from the 1940s. Even more oppressive was Scott's father: Mr. Bershung was a stern relic from an earlier era, and with his thick accent and ramrod-stiff bearing she imagined him as a sword-brandishing Prussian general. Very little about Rhetta appeared to please Scott's father. She got along much better with his mother, but the old lady seemed unable to do much besides mouth friendly platitudes and offer cookies. Conversation was a lost art in that home.

"What's to talk about?" Scott stared down at her. "We're married and we need a house."

It was a done deal to him, clearly. Her opinion wasn't required. She twisted her wedding ring and scanned the room, hoping to see the glint of a hidden camera or some other sign that this was just a sick prank. She recalled a recent Hollywood divorce: a month in, the actress declared the relationship a fraud. At the time, Rhetta wondered what could possibly constitute fraud in a marriage. Now she was starting to get the idea.

But she wasn't a starlet who could marshal lawyers at the snap of her fingers. And she made a commitment: 'til death did they part. She believed in her vows. There *had* to be a way to make this work.

"I think what we need," she replied, "is to see a marriage counselor."

* * *

Dr. Gates was a pleasant man in his late 50s who had high ratings on the insurance company's website. His office was outfitted in plush brown leather couches and expensive silk plants. A bright purple Siamese fighting fish drifted in a glass bowl on his desk. An oil painting of a woman about his age was on the wall behind his desk; Rhetta guessed it was Mrs. Gates. The woman in the portrait wore a pink cashmere sweater and gazed adoringly at a baby in her arms, the very picture of a perfect grandmother. Rhetta was impressed by the colors and the artist's technique; it seemed more life-like than many photos.

"This is exactly the kind of situation that leads to annulments," Dr. Gates said after they told him their stories. "But I'm confident we can get things back on the right track."

He turned toward her husband. "Scott, it seems that you entered this marriage with regimented gender role expectations that you failed to convey to your wife."

"Anything's possible," Scott replied.

The therapist seemingly ignored his skeptical tone. "It's important to make space for your wife's aspirations and most particularly her art. Make room for her whole life at your home. Fully include her in decisions that involve her. And *everything* involves her now."

Scott slumped beside her on the couch, fiddling with his watch.

"Spouses are life partners," the therapist said. "You need to help her become the best possible person she can be."

Something seemed to click behind her husband's eyes. He straightened up and smiled. "If you put it that way…of course I want her to be the best wife ever."

"Person," Dr. Gates corrected.

"Sure," replied Scott.

The therapist turned to Rhetta. "And I'd like to see you try to be a genuine partner to your husband."

"I thought I have been." She crossed her arms. "I work a job I don't enjoy for the sake of financial goals that are his and not mine."

"Now, Rhetta," the therapist admonished gently. "Everyone has to make a living. It's not Scott's fault you chose a job that doesn't suit you, is it? I respect your art – clearly you have some talent – but that, too, is a choice. And it's a choice that's causing your husband discomfort."

She felt a slow crab of panic start to scrabble in the pit of her stomach. She could no more choose to stop painting and drawing than she could choose to stop eating. Her soul would dry up.

"So the problem, in your view, is that I have choices?" she asked.

The therapist smiled irritably. "The *problem* is that you've been insensitive to your husband's need for comfort and routine. He's clearly a very traditional man. I find it hard to believe that after two years of dating you were unaware of that."

"I told you already. He hid that part of himself."

Inside, she had to agree: it did seem impossible that she hadn't seen that side of him. Scott's father was a domineering tyrant who wanted his wife to serve him coffee every day in exactly the same mug at 7am sharp, but her boyfriend had never been like that at all. The man she dated was attentive, kind, and spontaneous. His chivalrous streak seemed a little old-fashioned but was completely endearing in a world of oblivious hipsters. He held doors and pulled out chairs and bought dinner…was all that her cue that he'd suddenly turn into a clone of the old man after they married?

Dr. Gates broke her from her reverie: "Be more sensitive to his needs. If he makes space for you, will you stay home to paint?"

"Sure."

"And would it kill you to cook?" His tone was joking. *Ha-ha, only serious.*

She had to struggle to keep her hand tucked under her elbow. "I. Already. Do."

"But only sometimes, right? Takeout and frozen dinners make him feel unloved."

"It was his idea to get Chinese on Thursdays. And he could cook, too."

"Now, Rhetta. He has more job responsibilities than you do. It's only fair that you take over more household duties."

Rhetta almost asked him to do the math on how much work she did between her day job and her freelance, but she bit back that reply. Apparently her career was a choice, and his was a hero's quest. "Fine. I'll cook."

"Then it's settled." Dr. Gates smiled at her, then at Scott. "Be sure to give your father my best."

"I will," her husband replied.

* * *

Scott gave up the walk-in closet in the hallway. It was just big enough for her chair, an easel, a stand for her laptop and tablet, plus a few bins of supplies. She replaced the sallow overhead light with a bulb that emitted a natural spectrum. A room with a window would have been better, but at least she finally had her own space in the apartment. She lined the beige walls with her art and made do. It felt a little too much like a cell, and there wasn't enough air circulation to use oils without feeling woozy, but she immersed herself in pencil lines and watercolor strokes and got her commissions done on time.

But her new schedule got harder and harder to maintain. She had to be up by 6 to catch the bus to work, and when she got home she had dinner and chores. Then Scott would want her to keep him company while he watched his favorite sitcoms. Sometimes it was 9 or 10 before she was free to paint or sketch.

Sleep deprivation started taking its toll. She missed her bus a few times and was late to her job, and on a couple of embarrassing situations she fell asleep in long meetings. One day her boss called her into his office: she was on probation for three months. She'd be fired if her performance didn't improve.

She knew nothing good could come of telling Scott, but decided it would be bad for their relationship if she started keeping secrets.

"I can't have you unemployed and lounging around all day." His tone was an unpleasant echo of his father's Christmas lecturing. "We need the money for the house."

"I made $1000 on commissions just last month—" she began, but he'd already turned on his heel and marched off to the living room.

* * *

The following week, he surprised her with a wrapped box.

"I acted like a jerk, and I'm sorry," he said. "You're important to me, so I got you this."

Inside she found a new set of red-shellacked brushes and shiny tin tubes of oil paint. The mink, hog, and badger hair brushes were handmade, and the paints bore hand-inked German labels. She didn't recognize the brand. The whole set had the air of an expensive boutique.

"Wow. Thank you, honey." She blinked down at the set in pleased confusion. "They're lovely. Where did you get them?"

"A special order from Europe. My father commissioned a portrait of my mother after they married. My father keeps it in his study behind little curtains. I haven't seen it; I think he had her pose nude." He cleared his throat, clearly uncomfortable at the thought. "The artist used the same kind of brushes and paints…they're the best in the world."

"How do you know that if you haven't seen it?"

"He got another artist to paint a picture of me – I saw it a couple of weekends ago. My parents wanted to have a portrait of both of us made as a surprise wedding present, but they couldn't find a good photo of you. So they just had me painted, and then they decided they liked it so much they wanted to keep it. It's in the foyer; you'll see it at Christmas. It's amazing; the artist did me as a big-shot CEO. I look at it and I can see my future."

He paused, his eyes shining. "I know you can't paint in the closet because of the fumes, so I thought you could set your easel up in the living room."

She blinked at him. "Really?"

He smiled. "Just one condition."

The panic crab shuddered in her stomach. "What?"

"I want you to create a portrait of yourself that I'll feel proud to hang in my office. I want to show the world what a beautiful, talented wife I have. Can you do that for me?"

She was touched at his interest, and she couldn't think of a single reason to object. "Sure, honey, I can do that."

"That's my girl." He planted a kiss on her forehead.

The crab stirred again, but she didn't know why.

* * *

"What's that in your hands?" Scott squinted at the pencil sketch on her canvas.

"Brushes and pastel pencils," she replied.

"I don't like those. Why don't you put in some lavender?"

She paused. "I'm allergic to lavender."

"So? Lavender's pretty. I like it."

Portraying herself holding something she couldn't even be in the same room with violated the fundamental truth of the art, but it also didn't seem worth arguing about. She decided she'd treat her husband like any other client and give him what he wanted. This wouldn't be a self-portrait; it would be a painting of an idealized woman who happened to look a lot like her.

"All right, lavender it is."

* * *

With Scott looking over her shoulder during the sketching, the color scheme ended up with a lot more pinks and purples than she planned. She wanted to portray herself in her favorite gray sweater; he wanted her in a pale pink suit jacket and cream-colored blouse. She wanted to leave her lips natural; he asked for ruby red lipstick. Almost everything ended up being a shade or two different than she would have chosen for herself.

The next evening, she peeled off the thin foils sealing the paint tubes. The paints had an odd organic smell unlike any other oils she'd used. They had a strongly spicy odor: cloves and lemongrass, and maybe catnip? A touch of licorice or absinthe? Beneath the spice, there was a slight stench of rot. Perhaps the paint maker had used animal fats that had started to turn? But who would use an oil that could go rancid?

Rhetta squeezed paints into the wells on her palette and began to mix them. The thick colors flowed together wonderfully. There was no sign the paints had spoiled. She picked out a badger filbert brush and began work on her jacket.

The shaft of the wooden brush was surprisingly cold in her hand; she could almost imagine it was a chilled steel rod except it wasn't nearly heavy enough. As she worked, the cold seemed to seep into the bones of her hand and up into her wrist.

"Everything all right, honey?" Scott asked.

"It's…yes." She rubbed her wrist. "Is it cold in here?"

"Maybe a little; I'll go get you a wrap."

The afghan he brought down did little to keep her warm, and when she was done with her work for the evening, she felt exhausted and shuddered with chills. She knew she couldn't afford to call in sick now that she was on probation, so she took some echinacea and put herself right to bed. At least she'd made pretty good progress on the painting; all the shapes and colors were roughed in, and she could start work on the details the next night.

The next morning, she woke in a groggy panic, realizing she'd slept through her alarm. Scott was already gone. She washed up at the sink and dressed as quickly as she could, praying that the second bus would be early for a change. Every tick of the clock made her feel like an accused witch being pressed under an enormous stone by inquisitors.

The bus was slow. Traffic was harsh. She got to work twenty minutes late. Nearly in tears, she hurried up the stairs, trying to think of anything she could say to her supervisor to save her job—

"Oh, good, you're back." Her supervisor smiled at her and handed her a thick stack of printouts. "I need these proofed by 3pm."

"Yes, sir." Her hands shook as she took the papers.

He noticed her trembling. "Everything okay?"

"Yes. I…I just got startled on the stairwell."

"All right." He looked her up and down, frowning slightly at her khakis and blue polo. "Were you wearing a different outfit earlier?"

She shook her head, her mouth dry. "No, sir."

"Huh. Must have been a trick of the light."

Clutching the papers to her chest, Rhetta stepped down the aisle to her gray-walled cubicle. The keyboard tray was out and her computer was on, the screen dark. She set the papers down and unlocked her machine.

A Word document was open, and the cursor bar flashed at the end of a single line: *Finish the portrait.*

The sudden smell of lavender crept up her nostrils, and Rhetta sneezed. A single stalk of dried lavender lay on her desk. She quickly wrapped it in a plastic bag from her desk drawer and stuck the offending flowers in the trash.

The panic crab squeezed her lungs, and she couldn't seem to get her breath for a moment. Who had broken into her computer and left the lavender? And how did they know about the painting? What was going on?

Rhetta turned to the documentation contractor across the aisle and nervously waved to get his attention.

He pulled his earbuds out. "What's up?"

"Was tech support working on my computer this morning?" Rhetta asked.

"I didn't see them. But you were here before me, so I'm maybe not the person to ask."

It took Rhetta a moment to get more words out. "I…you got here *after* I did?"

"Oh, definitely." He nodded.

"When?"

"Like, I dunno…I cut it pretty close this morning! Like maybe 7:55 or something."

Rhetta thought she might faint. "Okay, thanks."

She turned back to her computer and the cryptic sentence. It didn't make sense. She *knew* she'd just gotten into the office, fifteen minutes late. Was her coworker in on some weird prank people were playing on her? What in the hell was going on?

The building anxiety turned her bowels to liquid, so she got up to go to the ladies' room. When she pushed through the door, she came face-to-face with what she first thought was a newly-installed full-length wall mirror. And then she realized it was a flesh-and-blood woman staring back at her. A woman who looked almost exactly like her, except her double had ruby-red lipstick and wore a stylish pale purple blouse and matching slacks. Her perfume smelled like lavender.

The woman's eerie face twisted into a scowl. "I told you to go finish the portrait!"

She slapped Rhetta across her cheek, hard, and when her palm connected it felt like she'd been hit with a taser. The electric shock made her vision go white, and she felt herself drop to the tiled floor.

* * *

Rhetta came awake in her chair in the living room, a chilly brush in her hand, the afghan draped across her shoulders. The portrait before her was nearly complete; all that was missing were some of the details on her face and in the lavender flowers.

"That is looking *so wonderful*, honey." Scott leaned down and kissed the top of her head. "I'm so proud of you."

"I...think I'm done for the evening." Her voice shook.

"You can finish it tomorrow."

He helped her clean her brushes, then took her upstairs and they went to bed. Once she was sure he was asleep, she crept out of bed, put on her favorite comfy warmup suit to combat the chill in her core, and went back down to the living room.

Rhetta stopped a yard from the painting and stared at it, afraid to touch it. Whatever was going on, the painting was at the center of it; she could feel it in her bones. She couldn't finish it. She had to make it go away. Cut it up. Bury it. Burn it.

"No," said a voice to her right. Her voice. The lavender double's voice.

Rhetta ducked and raised a hand to ward off another stunning blow, but the doppelganger tackled her instead. They landed on the couch, the double pressing her down into the cushions with its surprising strength. The smell of lavender was nearly overpowering; it was hard to breathe through the flowery stench. How much had the creature already drained from her?

"You'll finish it," growled the doppelganger. Its breath smelled rancid like the undertones in the paints. Rhetta felt an electric prickling where its bare flesh touched hers.

"No, I won't!"

"You're nothing but a lefthanded version of me. You'll do as I say." The doppelganger pried Rhetta's mouth open with hard fingers and pressed its lips to hers. The shock was intense but not enough to completely stupefy her.

The doppelganger's fingers stayed vises but the rest of its flesh turned to a foul gel. It started vomiting itself into the artist. The fluid was greasy and bitter with turpentine, poisonous herbs and heavy metals. Rhetta fought, to no avail; the doppelganger flowed into her, filling her throat and stomach and guts, seeping out into her veins and muscles.

Rhetta felt as though she was being worn like a tight suit. She felt her legs lift her body and walk her to the painting; she saw her hands uncover the palette and pick up the damp, cold brushes.

She shut her eyes, hoping that would confound the doppelganger. It did not. She felt the friction of the bristles on the canvas through the frigid shaft.

"It is finished," the doppelganger announced in her own voice. "And so are you."

It marched her out into the dark back yard, knelt beside a pile of autumn leaves, and stuck a finger down her throat.

This time, it was Rhetta's essence carried on the bitter purge. She found herself vomited from her own body, melting helplessly into the parched rakings.

"There." The doppelganger straightened up. It frowned down at the old warmup suit it wore, then stripped it off and unceremoniously dumped it beside the leaves. "An important man's wife would never wear something as frumpy this!"

The doppelganger strode back to the house and shut the door.

Rhetta dried up in the leaves in the moonlight, blind, voiceless, bodiless, but she could still feel everything.

A little after midnight, a wind rose, stirred the leaves, and carried her away into the forgotten places in the night.

Circumstance

Harriet Prescott Spofford

SHE HAD REMAINED, during all that day, with a sick neighbor – those eastern wilds of Maine in that epoch frequently making neighbors and miles synonymous – and so busy had she been with care and sympathy that she did not at first observe the approaching night. But finally the level rays, reddening the snow, threw their gleam upon the wall, and, hastily donning cloak and hood, she bade her friends farewell and sallied forth on her return. Home lay some three miles distant, across a copse, a meadow, and a piece of woods – the woods being a fringe on the skirts of the great forests that stretch far away into the North. That home was one of a dozen log-houses lying a few furlongs apart from each other, with their half-cleared demesnes separating them at the rear from a wilderness untrodden save by stealthy native or deadly panther tribes.

She was in a nowise exalted frame of spirit – on the contrary, rather depressed by the pain she had witnessed and the fatigue she had endured; but in certain temperaments such a condition throws open the mental pores, so to speak, and renders one receptive of every influence. Through the little copse she walked slowly, with her cloak folded about her, lingering to imbibe the sense of shelter, the sunset filtered in purple through the mist of woven spray and twig, the companionship of growth not sufficiently dense to band against her, the sweet home-feeling of a young and tender wintry wood. It was therefore just on the edge of the evening that she emerged from the place and began to cross the meadow-land. At one hand lay the forest to which her path wound; at the other the evening star hung over a tide of failing orange that slowly slipped down the earth's broad side to sadden other hemispheres with sweet regret. Walking rapidly now, and with her eyes wide open, she distinctly saw in the air before her what was not there a moment ago, a winding-sheet – cold, white, and ghastly, waved by the likeness of four wan hands – that rose with a long inflation, and fell in rigid folds, while a voice, shaping itself from the hollowness above, spectral and melancholy, sighed – "The Lord have mercy on the people! The Lord have mercy on the people!" Three times the sheet with its corpse-covering outline waved beneath the pale hands, and the voice, awful in its solemn and mysterious depth, sighed, "The Lord have mercy on the people!" Then all was gone, the place was clear again, the gray sky was obstructed by no deathly blot; she looked about her, shook her shoulders decidedly, and, pulling on her hood, went forward once more.

She might have been a little frightened by such an apparition, if she had led a life of less reality than frontier settlers are apt to lead; but dealing with hard fact does not engender a flimsy habit of mind, and this woman was too sincere and earnest in her character, and too happy in her situation, to be thrown by antagonism, merely, upon superstitious fancies and chimeras of the second-sight.

She did not even believe herself subject to a hallucination, but smiled simply, a little vexed that her thought could have framed such a glamor from the day's occurrences, and not sorry to lift the bough of the warder of the woods and enter and disappear in their somber path. If she had been imaginative, she would have hesitated at her first step into a region whose dangers were not visionary; but I suppose that the thought of a little child at home would conquer that propensity in the most habituated. So, biting a bit of spicy birch, she went along. Now and then she came to a gap where the trees had been partially felled, and here she found that the lingering twilight was explained by that peculiar and perhaps electric film which sometimes sheathes the sky in diffused light for many hours before a brilliant aurora. Suddenly, a swift shadow, like the fabulous flying dragon, writhed through the air before her, and she felt herself instantly seized and borne aloft. It was that wild beast – the most savage and serpentine and subtle and fearless of our latitudes – known by hunters as the Indian Devil, and he held her in his clutches on the broad floor of a swinging fir-bough. His long sharp claws were caught in her clothing, he worried them sagaciously a little, then, finding that ineffectual to free them, he commenced licking her bare arm with his rasping tongue and pouring over her the wide streams of his hot, fetid breath. So quick had this flashing action been that the woman had had no time for alarm; moreover, she was not of the screaming kind: but now, as she felt him endeavoring to disentangle his claws, and the horrid sense of her fate smote her, and she saw instinctively the fierce plunge of those weapons, the long strips of living flesh torn from her bones, the agony, the quivering disgust, itself a worse agony – while by her side, and holding her in his great lithe embrace, the monster crouched, his white tusks whetting and gnashing, his eyes glaring through all the darkness like balls of red fire – a shriek, that rang in every forest hollow, that startled every winter-housed thing, that stirred and woke the least needle of the tasselled pines, tore through her lips. A moment afterward, the beast left the arm, once white, now crimson, and looked up alertly.

She did not think at this instant to call upon God. She called upon her husband. It seemed to her that she had but one friend in the world; that was he; and again the cry, loud, clear, prolonged, echoed through the woods. It was not the shriek that disturbed the creature at his relish; he was not born in the woods to be scared of an owl, you know; what then? It must have been the echo, most musical, most resonant, repeated and yet repeated, dying with long sighs of sweet sound, vibrated from rock to river and back again from depth to depth of cave and cliff. Her thought flew after it; she knew, that, even if her husband heard it, he yet could not reach her in time; she saw that while the beast listened he would not gnaw – and this she *felt* directly, when the rough, sharp, and multiplied stings of his tongue retouched her arm. Again her lips opened by instinct, but the sound that issued thence came by reason. She had heard that music charmed wild beasts – just this point between life and death intensified every faculty – and when she opened her lips the third time, it was not for shrieking, but for singing.

A little thread of melody stole out, a rill of tremulous motion; it was the cradle-song with which she rocked her baby; – how could she sing that? And then she remembered the baby sleeping rosily on the long settee before the fire – the father cleaning his gun, with one foot on the green wooden rundle – the merry light from the chimney dancing out and through the room, on the rafters of the ceiling with their tassels of onions and herbs, on the log walls painted with lichens and festooned with apples, on the king's-arm slung across the shelf with the old pirate's cutlass, on the snow-pile of the bed, and on the great brass clock – dancing, too, and lingering on the baby, with his fringed-gentian eyes, his chubby fists clenched on the pillow, and his fine breezy hair fanning with the motion of his father's foot. All this struck her in one, and made a sob of her breath, and she ceased.

Immediately the long red tongue thrust forth again. Before it touched, a song sprang to her lips, a wild sea-song, such as some sailor might be singing far out on trackless blue water that night, the shrouds whistling with frost and the sheets glued in ice – a song with the wind in its burden and the spray in its chorus. The monster raised his head and flared the fiery eyeballs upon her, then fretted the imprisoned claws a moment and was quiet; only the breath like the vapor from some hell-pit still swathed her. Her voice, at first faint and fearful, gradually lost its quaver, grew under her control and subject to her modulation; it rose on long swells, it fell in subtle cadences, now and then its tones pealed out like bells from distant belfries on fresh sonorous mornings. She sung the song through, and, wondering lest his name of Indian Devil were not his true name, and if he would not detect her, she repeated it. Once or twice now, indeed, the beast stirred uneasily, turned, and made the bough sway at his movement. As she ended, he snapped his jaws together, and tore away the fettered member, curling it under him with a snarl – when she burst into the gayest reel that ever answered a fiddle-bow. How many a time she had heard her husband play it on the homely fiddle made by himself from birch and cherry-wood! How many a time she had seen it danced on the floor of their one room, to the patter of wooden clogs and the rustle of homespun petticoat! How many a time she had danced it herself! – And did she not remember once, as they joined clasps for eight-hands-round, how it had lent its gay, bright measure to her life? And here she was singing it alone, in the forest, at midnight, to a wild beast! As she sent her voice trilling up and down its quick oscillations between joy and pain, the creature who grasped her uncurled his paw and scratched the bark from the bough; she must vary the spell; and her voice spun leaping along the projecting points of tune of a horn pipe. Still singing, she felt herself twisted about with a low growl and a lifting of the red lip from the glittering teeth; she broke the hornpipe's thread, and commenced unraveling a lighter, livelier thing, an Irish jig. Up and down and round about her voice flew, the beast threw back his head so that the diabolical face fronted hers, and the torrent of his breath prepared her for his feast as the anaconda slimes his prey. Franticly she darted from tune to tune; his restless movements followed her. She tired herself with dancing and vivid national airs, growing feverish and singing spasmodically as she felt her horrid tomb yawning wider. Touching in this manner all the slogan and keen clan cries, the beast moved again, but only to lay the disengaged paw across her with heavy satisfaction. She did not dare to pause; through the clear cold air, the frosty starlight, she sang. If there were yet any tremor in the tone, it was not fear – she had learned the secret of sound at last; nor could it be chill – far too high a fever throbbed her pulses; it was nothing but the thought of the log-house and of what might be passing within it. She fancied the baby stirring in his sleep and moving his pretty lips – her husband rising and opening the door, looking out after her, and wondering at her absence. She fancied the light pouring through the chink and then shut in again with all the safety and comfort and joy, her husband taking down the fiddle and playing lightly with his head inclined, playing while she sang, while she sang for her life to an Indian Devil. Then she knew he was fumbling for and finding some shining fragment and scoring it down the yellowing hair, and unconsciously her voice forsook the wild war-tunes and drifted into the half-gay, half-melancholy 'Rosin the Bow'.

Suddenly she woke pierced with a pang, and the daggered tooth penetrating her flesh; dreaming of safety, she had ceased singing and lost it. The beast had regained the use of all his limbs, and now, standing and raising his back, bristling and foaming, with sounds that would have been like hisses but for their deep and fearful sonority, he withdrew step by step toward the trunk of the tree, still with his flaming balls upon her. She was all at once free, on one end of the bough, twenty feet from the ground. She did not measure the distance, but rose to drop herself down, careless of any death, so that it were not this. Instantly, as if he scanned her thoughts, the creature bounded forward with a yell and caught her again in his dreadful hold. It might be that he was not greatly famished; for, as she suddenly flung up her voice again, he settled himself composedly on the bough, still clasping her with invincible pressure to his rough, ravenous breast, and listening in a fascination to the sad, strange U-la-lu that now moaned forth in loud, hollow tones above him. He half closed his eyes, and sleepily reopened and shut them again.

What rending pains were close at hand! Death! And what a death! Worse than any other that is to be named! Water, be it cold or warm, that which buoys up blue ice fields, or which bathes tropical coasts with currents of balmy bliss, is yet a gentle conqueror, kisses as it kills, and draws you down gently through darkening fathoms to its heart. Death at the sword is the festival of trumpet and bugle and banner, with glory ringing out around you and distant hearts thrilling through yours. No gnawing disease can bring such hideous end as this; for that is a fiend bred of your own flesh, and this – is it a fiend, this living lump of appetites? What dread comes with the thought of perishing in flames! But fire, let it leap and hiss never so hotly, is something too remote, too alien, to inspire us with such loathly horror as a wild beast; if it have a life, that life is too utterly beyond our comprehension. Fire is not half ourselves; as it devours, arouses neither hatred nor disgust; is not to be known by the strength of our lower natures let loose; does not drip our blood into our faces from foaming chaps, nor mouth nor slaver above us with vitality. Let us be ended by fire, and we are ashes, for the winds to bear, the leaves to cover; let us be ended by wild beasts, and the base, cursed thing howls with us forever through the forest. All this she felt as she charmed him, and what force it lent to her song God knows. If her voice should fail! If the damp and cold should give her any fatal hoarseness! If all the silent powers of the forest did not conspire to help her! The dark, hollow night rose indifferently over her; the wide, cold air breathed rudely past her, lifted her wet hair and blew it down again; the great boughs swung with a ponderous strength, now and then clashed their iron lengths together and shook off a sparkle of icy spears or some long-lain weight of snow from their heavy shadows. The green depths were utterly cold and silent and stern. These beautiful haunts that all the summer were hers and rejoiced to share with her their bounty, these heavens that had yielded their largess, these stems that had thrust their blossoms in to her hands, all these friends of three moons ago forgot her now and knew her no longer.

Feeling her desolation, wild, melancholy, forsaken songs rose thereon from that frightful aerie – weeping, wailing tunes, that sob among the people from age to age, and overflow with otherwise unexpressed sadness – all rude, mournful ballads – old tearful strains, that Shakespeare heard the vagrants sing, and that rise and fall like the wind and tide – sailor-songs, to be heard only in lone mid-watches beneath the moon and stars – ghastly rhyming romances, such as that famous one of the Lady Margaret, when:

> *"She slipped on her gown of green*
> *A piece below the knee,*
> *And 'twas all a long cold winter's night*
> *A dead corse followed she."*

Still the beast lay with closed eyes, yet never relaxing his grasp. Once a half-whine of enjoyment escaped him – he fawned his fearful head upon her; once he scored her cheek with his tongue: savage caresses that hurt like wounds. How weary she was! And yet how terribly awake! How fuller and fuller of dismay grew the knowledge that she was only prolonging her anguish and playing with death! How appalling the thought that with her voice ceased her existence! Yet she could not sing forever; her throat was dry and hard; her very breath was a pain; her mouth was hotter than any desert-worn pilgrim's; – if she could but drop upon her burning tongue one atom of the ice that glittered about her! – but both of her arms were pinioned in the giant's vice. She remembered the winding-sheet, and for the first time in her life shivered with spiritual fear. Was it hers? She asked herself, as she sang, what sins she had committed, what life she had led, to find her punishment so soon and in these pangs – and then she sought eagerly for some reason why her husband was not up and abroad to find her. He failed her – her one sole hope in life; and without being aware of it, her voice forsook the songs of suffering and sorrow for old Covenanting hymns – hymns with which her mother had lulled her, which the class-leader pitched in the chimney-corners – grand and sweet Methodist hymns, brimming with melody and with all fantastic involutions of tune to suit that ecstatic worship – hymns full of the beauty of holiness, steadfast, relying, sanctified by the salvation they had lent to those in worse extremity than hers – for they had found themselves in the grasp of hell, while she was but in the jaws of death. Out of this strange music, peculiar to one character of faith, and than which there is none more beautiful in its degree nor owning a more potent sway of sound, her voice soared into the glorified chants of churches. What to her was death by cold or famine or wild beasts? "Though He slay me, yet will I trust in him," she sang. High and clear through the frore fair night, the level moonbeams splintering in the wood, the scarce glints of stars in the shadowy roof of branches, these sacred anthems rose – rose as a hope from despair, as some snowy spray of flower-bells from blackest mold.

Was she not in God's hands? Did not the world swing at his will? If this were in his great plan of providence, was it not best, and should she not accept it?

"He is the Lord our God; his judgments are in all the earth."

Oh, sublime faith of our fathers, where utter self-sacrifice alone was true love, the fragrance of whose unrequired subjection was pleasanter than that of golden censers swung in purple-vapored chancels!

Never ceasing in the rhythm of her thoughts, articulated in music as they thronged, the memory of her first communion flashed over her. Again she was in that distant place on that sweet spring morning. Again the congregation rustled out, and the few remained, and she trembled to find herself among them. How well she remembered the devout, quiet faces, too accustomed to the sacred feast to glow with their inner joy! How well the snowy linen at the altar, the silver vessels slowly and silently shifting! And as the cup approached and passed, how the sense of delicious perfume stole in and heightened the transport of her prayer, and she had seemed, looking up through the windows where the sky soared blue in constant freshness, to feel all heaven's balms dripping from the portals, and to scent the lilies of eternal peace! Perhaps another would not have felt so much ecstasy as satisfaction on that occasion; but it is a true, if a later disciple, who has said, "The Lord bestoweth his blessings there, where he findeth the vessels empty."

"And does it need the walls of a church to renew my communion?" she asked. "Does not every moment stand a temple four-square to God? And in that morning, with its buoyant sunlight, was I any dearer to the Heart of the World than now? – 'My beloved is mine, and I am his,'" she sang over and over again, with all varied inflection and profuse tune. How gently all the winter-wrapped things bent toward her then! Into what relation with her had they grown! How this common dependence was the spell of their intimacy! How at one with Nature had she become! How all the night and the silence and the forest seemed to hold its breath, and to send its soul up to God in her singing! It was no longer despondency, that singing. It was neither prayer nor petition. She had left imploring, "How long wilt thou forget me, Lord? Lighten mine eyes, lest I sleep the sleep of death! For in death there is no remembrance of thee," – with countless other such fragments of supplication. She cried rather, "Yea, though I walk through the valley of the shadow of death, I will fear no evil: for thou art with me; thy rod and thy staff, they comfort me," – and lingered, and repeated, and sang again, "I shall be satisfied, when I awake, with thy likeness."

Then she thought of the Great Deliverance, when he drew her up out of many waters, and the flashing old psalm pealed forth triumphantly:

> *"The Lord descended from above,*
> *and bow'd the heavens hie:*
> *And underneath his feet he cast*
> *the darknesse of the skie.*
> *On cherubs and on cherubins*
> *full royally he road:*
> *And on the wings of all the winds*
> *came flying all abroad."*

She forgot how recently, and with what a strange pity for her own shapeless form that was to be, she had quaintly sung:

> *"O lovely appearance of death!*
> *What sight upon earth is so fair?*
> *Not all the gay pageants that breathe*
> *Can with a dead body compare!"*

She remembered instead – "In thy presence is fullness of joy; at thy right hand there are pleasures forevermore. God will redeem my soul from the power of the grave: for he shall receive me. He will swallow up death in victory." Not once now did she say, "Lord, how long wilt thou look on; rescue my soul from their destructions, my darling from the lions," – for she knew that the young lions roar after their prey and seek their meat from God. "O Lord, thou preservest man and beast!" she said.

She had no comfort or consolation in this season, such as sustained the Christian martyrs in the amphitheatre. She was not dying for her faith; there were no palms in heaven for her to wave; but how many a time had she declared – "I had rather be a doorkeeper in the house of my God, than to dwell in the tents of wickedness!" And as the broad rays here and there broke through the dense covert of shade and lay in rivers of lustre on crystal sheathing and frozen fretting of trunk and limb and on the great spaces of refraction, they builded up visibly that house, the shining city on the hill, and singing, "Beautiful for situation, the joy of the whole earth, is Mount Zion, on the sides of the North, the city of the Great King," her vision climbed to that higher picture where the angel shows the dazzling thing, the holy Jerusalem descending out of heaven from God, with its splendid battlements and gates of pearls, and its foundations, the eleventh a jacinth, the twelfth an amethyst – with its great white throne, and the rainbow round about it, in sight like unto an emerald: "And there shall be no night there – for the Lord God giveth them light," she sang.

What whisper of dawn now rustled through the wilderness? How the night was passing! And still the beast crouched upon the bough, changing only the posture of his head, that again he might command her with those charmed eyes; – half their fire was gone; she could almost have released herself from his custody; yet, had she stirred, no one knows what malevolent instinct might have dominated anew. But of that she did not dream; long ago stripped of any expectation, she was experiencing in her divine rapture how mystically true it is that "he that dwelleth in the secret place of the Most High shall abide under the shadow of the Almighty."

Slow clarion cries now wound from the distance as the cocks caught the intelligence of day and re-echoed it faintly from farm to farm – sleepy sentinels of night, sounding the foe's invasion, and translating that dim intuition to ringing notes of warning. Still she chanted on. A remote crash of brushwood told of some other beast on his depredations, or some night-belated traveler groping his way through the narrow path. Still she chanted on. The far, faint echoes of the chanticleers died into distance, the crashing of the branches grew nearer. No wild beast that, but a man's step – a man's form in the moonlight, stalwart and strong – on one arm slept a little child, in the other hand he held his gun. Still she chanted on.

Perhaps, when her husband last looked forth, he was half ashamed to find what a fear he felt for her. He knew she would never leave the child so long but for some direst need – and yet he may have laughed at himself, as he lifted and wrapped it with awkward care, and, loading his gun and strapping on his horn, opened the door again and closed it behind him, going out and plunging into the darkness and dangers of the forest. He was more singularly alarmed than he would have been willing to acknowledge; as he had sat with his bow hovering over the strings, he had half believed to hear her voice mingling gayly with the instrument, till he paused and listened if she were not about to lift the latch and enter. As he drew nearer the heart of the forest, that intimation of melody seemed to grow more actual, to take body and breath, to come and go on long swells and ebbs of the night-breeze, to increase with tune and words, till a strange shrill singing grew ever clearer, and, as he stepped into an open space of moonbeams, far up in the branches, rocked by the wind, and singing, "How beautiful upon the mountains are the feet of him that bringeth good tidings, that publisheth peace," he saw his wife – his wife – but, great God in heaven! How? Some mad exclamation escaped him, but without diverting her. The child knew the singing voice, though never heard before in that unearthly key, and turned toward it through the veiling dreams. With a celerity almost instantaneous, it lay, in the twinkling of an eye, on the ground at the father's feet, while his gun was raised to his shoulder and leveled at the monster covering his wife with shaggy form and flaming gaze – his wife so ghastly white, so rigid, so stained with blood, her eyes so fixedly bent above, and her lips, that had indurated into the chiseled pallor of marble, parted only with that flood of solemn song.

I do not know if it were the mother-instinct that for a moment lowered her eyes – those eyes, so lately riveted on heaven, now suddenly seeing all life-long bliss possible. A thrill of joy pierced and shivered through her like a weapon, her voice trembled in its course, her glance lost its steady strength, fever-flushes chased each other over her face, yet she never once ceased chanting. She was quite aware, that, if her husband shot now, the ball must pierce her body before reaching any vital part of the beast – and yet better that death, by his hand, than the other. But this her husband also knew, and he remained motionless, just covering the creature with the sight. He dared not fire, lest some wound not mortal should break the spell exercised by her voice, and the beast, enraged with pain, should rend her in atoms; moreover, the light was too uncertain for his aim. So he waited. Now and then he examined his gun to see if the damp were injuring its charge, now and then he wiped the great drops from his forehead. Again the cocks crowed with the passing hour – the last time they were heard on that night. Cheerful home sound then, how full of safety and all comfort and rest it seemed! What sweet morning incidents of sparkling fire and sunshine, of gay household bustle, shining dresser, and cooing baby, of steaming cattle in the yard, and brimming milk-pails at the door! What pleasant voices! What laughter! What security! And here—

Now, as she sang on in the slow, endless, infinite moments, the fervent vision of God's peace was gone. Just as the grave had lost its sting, she was snatched back again into the arms of earthly hope. In vain she tried to sing, "There remaineth a rest for the people of God," – her eyes trembled on her husband's, and she could only think of him, and of the child, and of happiness that yet might be, but with what a dreadful gulf of doubt between! She shuddered now in the suspense; all calm forsook her; she was tortured with dissolving heats or frozen with icy blasts; her face contracted, growing small and pinched; her voice was hoarse and sharp – every tone cut like a knife – the notes became heavy to lift – withheld by some hostile pressure – impossible. One gasp, a convulsive effort, and there was silence – she had lost her voice.

The beast made a sluggish movement – stretched and fawned like one awaking – then, as if he would have yet more of the enchantment, stirred her slightly with his muzzle. As he did so, a sidelong hint of the man standing below with the raised gun smote him; he sprung round furiously, and, seizing his prey, was about to leap into some unknown airy den of the topmost branches now waving to the slow dawn. The late moon had rounded through the sky so that her gleam at last fell full upon the bough with fairy frosting; the wintry morning light did not yet penetrate the gloom. The woman, suspended in mid-air an instant, cast only one agonized glance beneath – but across and through it, ere the lids could fall, shot a withering sheet of flame – a rifle-crack, half-heard, was lost in the terrible yell of desperation that bounded after it and filled her ears with savage echoes, and in the wide arc of some eternal descent she was falling; – but the beast fell under her.

I think that the moment following must have been too sacred for us, and perhaps the three have no special interest again till they issue from the shadows of the wilderness upon the white hills that skirt their home. The father carries the child hushed again into slumber, the mother follows with no such feeble step as might be anticipated. It is not time for reaction – the tension not yet relaxed, the nerves still vibrant, she seems to herself like someone newly made; the night was a dream; the present stamped upon her in deep satisfaction, neither weighed nor compared with the past; if she has the careful tricks of former habit, it is as an automaton; and as they slowly climb the steep under the clear gray vault and the paling morning star, and as she stops to gather a spray of the red-rose berries or a feathery tuft of dead grasses for the chimney-piece of the log-house, or a handful of brown cones for the child's play – of these quiet, happy folk you would scarcely dream how lately they had stolen from under the banner and encampment of the great King Death. The husband proceeds a step or two in advance; the wife lingers over a singular footprint in the snow, stoops and examines it, then looks up with a hurried word. Her husband stands alone on the hill, his arms folded across the babe, his gun fallen – stands defined as a silhouette against the pallid sky. What is there in their home, lying below and yellowing in the light, to fix him with such a stare? She springs to his side. There is no home there. The log-house, the barns, the neighboring farms, the fences, are all blotted out and mingled in one smoking ruin. Desolation and death were indeed there, and beneficence and life in the forest. Tomahawk and scalping-knife, descending during that night, had left behind them only this work of their accomplished hatred and one subtle footprint in the snow.

For the rest – the world was all before them, where to choose.

The Ghost in the Cap'n Brown House

Harriet Beecher Stowe

"**NOW, SAM**, tell us certain true, is there any such things as ghosts?"

"Be there ghosts?" said Sam, immediately translating into his vernacular grammar: "Wal, now that are's jest the question, ye see."

"Well, grandma thinks there are, and Aunt Lois thinks it's all nonsense. Why, Aunt Lois don't even believe the stories in Cotton Mather's 'Magnalia'."

"Wanter know?" said Sam, with a tone of slow, languid meditation.

We were sitting on a bank of the Charles River, fishing. The soft melancholy red of evening was fading off in streaks on the glassy water, and the houses of Oldtown were beginning to loom through the gloom, solemn and ghostly. There are times and tones and moods of nature that make all the vulgar, daily real seem shadowy, vague, and supernatural, as if the outlines of this hard material present were fading into the invisible and unknown. So Oldtown, with its elmtrees, its great square white houses, its meeting-house and tavern and blacksmith's shop and mill, which at high noon seem as real and as commonplace as possible, at this hour of the evening were dreamy and solemn. They rose up blurred, indistinct, dark; here and there winking candles sent long lines of light through the shadows, and little drops of unforeseen rain rippled the sheeny dankness of the water.

"Wal, you see, boys, in them things it's jest as well to mind your granny. There's a consid'able sight o' gumption in grandmas. You look at the folks that's allus tellin' you what they don't believe – they don't believe this, and they don't believe that – and what sort o' folks is they? Why, like yer Aunt Lois, sort o' stringy and dry. There ain't no 'sorption got out o' not believin' nothin'.

"Lord a massy! We don't know nothin' 'bout them things. We hain't ben there, and can't say that there ain't no ghosts and sich; can we, now?"

We agreed to that fact, and sat a little closer to Sam in the gathering gloom.

"Tell us about the Cap'n Brown house, Sam."

"Ye didn't never go over the Cap'n Brown house?"

No, we had not that advantage.

"Wal, yer see, Cap'n Brown he made all his money to sea, in furrin parts, and then come here to Oldtown to settle down.

"Now, there ain't now knowin' 'bout these 'ere old shipmasters, where they's ben, or what they's ben a doin', or how they got their money. Ask me no questions, and I'll tell ye no lies, is 'bout the best philosophy for them. Wal, it didn't do no good to ask Cap'n Brown questions too close, 'cause you didn't git no satisfaction. Nobody rightly knew 'bout who his folks was, or where they come from, and, ef a body asked him, he used to say that the very fust he know'd 'bout himself he was a young man walkin' the streets in London.

"But, yer see, boys, he hed money, and that is about all folks wanter know when a man comes to settle down. And he bought that 'are place, and built that 'are house. He built it all sea-cap'n fashion, so's to feel as much at home as he could. The parlor was like a ship's cabin. The table and chairs was fastened down to the floor, and the closets was made with holes to set the casters and the decanters and bottles in, jest's they be at sea; and there was stanchions to hold on by; and they say that blowy nights the cap'n used to fire up pretty well with his grog, till he hed about all he could carry, and then he'd set and hold on, and hear the wind blow, and kind o' feel out to sea right there to hum. There wasn't no Mis' Cap'n Brown, and there didn't seem likely to be none. And whether there ever hed been one, nobody know'd. He hed an old black Guinea niggerwoman, named Quassia, that did his work. She was shaped pretty much like one o' these 'ere great crooknecked-squashes. She wa'n't no gret beauty, I can tell you; and she used to wear a gret red turban and a yaller short gown and red petticoat, and a gret string o' gold beads round her neck, and gret big gold hoops in her ears, made right in the middle o' Africa among the heathen there. For all she was black, she thought a heap o' herself, and was consid'able sort o' predominative over the cap'n. Lord massy! Boys, it's allus so. Get a man and a woman together – any sort woman you're a mind to, don't care who 'tis – and one way or another she gets the rule over him, and he jest has to train to her fife. Some does it one way, and some does it another; some does it by jawin', and some does it by kissin', and some does it by faculty and contrivance; but one way or another they alters does it. Old Cap'n Brown was a good stout, stocky kind o' John Bull sort o' fellow, and a good judge o' sperits, and alters kep' the best in them are cupboards o' his'n; but, fust and last, things in his house went pretty much as old Quassia said. Folks got to kind o' respectin' Quassia. She come to meetin' Sunday regular, and sot all fixed up in red and yaller and green, with glass beads and whatnot, lookin' for all the world like one o' them ugly Indian idols; but she was well-behaved as any Christian. She was a master hand at cookin'. Her bread and biscuits couldn't be beat, and no couldn't her pies, and there wa'n't no such pound-cake as she made nowhere. Wal, this 'ere story I'm a goin' to tell you was told me by Cinthy Pendleton. There ain't a more respectable gal, old or young, than Cinthy nowheres. She lives over to Sherburne now, and I hear tell she's sot up a manty-makin' business; but then she used to do tailorin' in Oldtown. She was a member o' the church, and a good Christian as ever was. Wal, ye see, Quassia she got Cinthy to come up and spend a week to the Cap'n Brown house, a doin' taitorin' and a fixin' over his close: 'twas along toward the fust o' March. Cinthy she sot by the fire in the front parlor with her goose and her press-board and her work: for there wa'n't no company callin', and the snow was drifted four feet deep right across the front door; so there wa'n't much danger o' anybody comin' in. And the cap'n he was a perlite man to wimmen; and Cinthy she liked it jest as well not to have company, 'cause the cap'n he'd make himself entertainin' teltin' on her sea-stories, and all about this adventures among the Ammonites, and Perresites, and Jebusites, and all sorts o' heathen people he'd been among. Wal, that 'are week there come on the master snow-storm. Of all the snow-storms that bed ben, that 'are was the beater; and I tell you the wind blew as if 'twas the last chance it was ever goin' to hey. Wal, it's kind o' scary like to be shet up in a lone house with all natur' a kind o' breakin' out, and goin' on so, and the snow a comin' down so thick ye can't see 'cross the street, and the wind a pipin' and a squeelin' and a rumblin' and a tumblin' fust down this chimney and then down that. I tell you, it sort o' sets a feller thinkin' o' the three great things – death, judgment, and etarnaty; and I don't care who the folks is, nor how good they be, there's times when they must be feelin' putty consid'able solemn.

"Wal, Cinthy she said she kind o' felt so along, and she bed a sort o' queer feelin' come over her as if there was somebody or somethin' round the house more'n appeared. She said she sort o' felt it in the air; but it seemed to her silly, and she tried to get over it. But two or three times, she said, when it got to be dusk, she felt somebody go by her up the stairs. The front entry wa'n't very light in the daytime, and in the storm, come five o'clock, it was so dark that all you could see was jest a gleam o' somethin', and two or three times when she started to go upstairs she see a soft white suthin' that seemed goin' up before her, and she stopped with her heart a beatin' like a trip-hammer, and she sort o' saw it go up and along the entry to the cap'n's door, and then it seemed to go right through, 'cause the door didn't open.

"Wal, Cinthy says she to old Quassia, says she, 'Is there anybody lives in this house but us?'

"'Anybody lives here?' says Quassia: 'What you mean?' says she.

"Says Cinthy, 'I thought somebody went past me on the stairs last night and tonight.'

"'Lord massy! How old Quassia did screech and laugh. 'Good Lord!' says she, 'How foolish white folks is! Somebody went past you? Was't the capt'in?'

"'No, it wa'n't the cap'n,' says she: 'it was somethin' soft and white, and moved very still; it was like somethin' in the air,' says she.

"Then Quassia she haw-hawed louder. Says she, 'It's hysterikes, Miss Cinthy; that's all it is.'

"Wal, Cinthy she was kind o' 'shamed, but for all that she couldn't help herself. Sometimes evenin's she'd be a settin' with the cap'n, and she'd think she'd hear somebody a movin' in his room overhead; and she knowed it wa'n't Quassia, 'cause Quassia was ironin' in the kitchen.

She took pains once or twice to find out that 'are.

"Wal, ye see, the cap'n's room was the gret front upper chamber over the parlor, and then right opposite to it was the gret spae chamber where Cinthy slept. It was jest as grand as could be, with a gret four-post mahogany bedstead and damask curtains brought over from England; but it was cold enough to freeze a white bear solid – the way spare chambers alters is. Then there was the entry between, run straight through the house: one side was old Quassia's room, and the other was a sort o' storeroom, where the old cap'n kep' all sorts o' traps.

"Wal, Cinthy she kep' a hevin' things happen and a seem' thins, till she didn't railly know what was in it. Once when she come into the parlor jest at sundown, she was sure she see a white figure a vanishin' out o' the door that went towards the side entry. She said it was so dusk, that all she could see was jest this white figure, and it jest went out still as a cat as she come in.

"Wal, Cinthy didn't like to speak to the cap'n about it. She was a close woman, putty prudent, Cinthy was.

"But one night, 'bout the middle o' the week, this 'ere thing kind o' come to a crisis. Cinthy said she'd ben up putty late a sewin' and a finishin' off down in the parlor; and the cap'n he sot up with her, and was consid'able cheerful and entertainin', tellin' her all about things over the Bermudys, and off to Chiny and Japan, and round the world ginerally. The storm that bed been a blowin' all the week was about as furious as ever; and the cap'n he stirred up a mess o' flip, and bed it for her hot to go to bed on. He was a good-natured critter, and alters had feelin's for lone women; and I s'pose he knew 'twas sort o' desolate for Cinthy.

"Wal, takin' the flip so right the last think afore goin' to bed, she went right off to sleep as sound as a nut, and slep' on till somewhere about mornin', when she said somethin' waked her broad awake in a minute. Her eyes flew wide open like a spring, and the storm hed gone down and the moon come out: and there, standin' right in the moonlight by her bed, was a woman jest as white as a sheet, with black hair hangin' down to her waist, and the brightest, mourn-fullest black eyes you ever see. She stood there lookin' right at Cinthy; and Cinthy thinks that was what waked her up; 'cause, you know, ef anybody stands and looks steady at folks asleep it's apt to wake 'em.

"Anyway, Cinthy said she felt jest as ef she was turnin' to stone. She couldn't move nor speak. She lay a minute, and then she shut her eyes, and begun to say her prayers; and a minute after she opened 'em, and it was gone."

Kerfol

Edith Wharton

Chapter I

"YOU OUGHT to buy it," said my host; "it's just the place for a solitary-minded devil like you. And it would be rather worthwhile to own the most romantic house in Brittany. The present people are dead broke, and it's going for a song – you ought to buy it."

It was not with the least idea of living up to the character my friend Lanrivain ascribed to me (as a matter of fact, under my unsociable exterior I have always had secret yearnings for domesticity) that I took his hint one autumn afternoon and went to Kerfol. My friend was motoring over to Quimper on business: he dropped me on the way, at a cross-road on a heath, and said: "First turn to the right and second to the left. Then straight ahead till you see an avenue. If you meet any peasants, don't ask your way. They don't understand French, and they would pretend they did and mix you up. I'll be back for you here by sunset – and don't forget the tombs in the chapel."

I followed Lanrivain's directions with the hesitation occasioned by the usual difficulty of remembering whether he had said the first turn to the right and second to the left, or the contrary. If I had met a peasant I should certainly have asked, and probably been sent astray; but I had the desert landscape to myself, and so stumbled on the right turn and walked across the heath till I came to an avenue. It was so unlike any other avenue I have ever seen that I instantly knew it must be *the* avenue. The grey-trunked trees sprang up straight to a great height and then interwove their pale-gray branches in a long tunnel through which the autumn light fell faintly. I know most trees by name, but I haven't to this day been able to decide what those trees were. They had the tall curve of elms, the tenuity of poplars, the ashen color of olives under a rainy sky; and they stretched ahead of me for half a mile or more without a break in their arch. If ever I saw an avenue that unmistakably led to something, it was the avenue at Kerfol. My heart beat a little as I began to walk down it.

Presently the trees ended and I came to a fortified gate in a long wall. Between me and the wall was an open space of grass, with other gray avenues radiating from it. Behind the wall were tall slate roofs mossed with silver, a chapel belfry, the top of a keep. A moat filled with wild shrubs and brambles surrounded the place; the drawbridge had been replaced by a stone arch, and the portcullis by an iron gate. I stood for a long time on the hither side of the moat, gazing about me, and letting the influence of the place sink in. I said to myself: "If I wait long enough, the guardian will turn up and show me the tombs—" and I rather hoped he wouldn't turn up too soon.

I sat down on a stone and lit a cigarette. As soon as I had done it, it struck me as a puerile and portentous thing to do, with that great blind house looking down at me, and all the empty avenues converging on me. It may have been the depth of the silence that made me so conscious of my gesture. The squeak of my match sounded as loud as the scraping of a brake, and I almost fancied I heard it fall when I tossed it onto the grass. But there was more than that: a sense of irrelevance, of littleness, of futile bravado, in sitting there puffing my cigarette-smoke into the face of such a past.

I knew nothing of the history of Kerfol – I was new to Brittany, and Lanrivain had never mentioned the name to me till the day before – but one couldn't as much as glance at that pile without feeling in it a long accumulation of history. What kind of history I was not prepared to guess: perhaps only that sheer weight of many associated lives and deaths which gives a majesty to all old houses. But the aspect of Kerfol suggested something more – a perspective of stern and cruel memories stretching away, like its own gray avenues, into a blur of darkness.

Certainly no house had ever more completely and finally broken with the present. As it stood there, lifting its proud roofs and gables to the sky, it might have been its own funeral monument. "Tombs in the chapel? The whole place is a tomb!" I reflected. I hoped more and more that the guardian would not come. The details of the place, however striking, would seem trivial compared with its collective impressiveness; and I wanted only to sit there and be penetrated by the weight of its silence.

"It's the very place for you!" Lanrivain had said; and I was overcome by the almost blasphemous frivolity of suggesting to any living being that Kerfol was the place for him. "Is it possible that anyone could *not* see—?" I wondered. I did not finish the thought: what I meant was undefinable. I stood up and wandered toward the gate. I was beginning to want to know more; not to *see* more – I was by now so sure it was not a question of seeing – but to feel more: feel all the place had to communicate. "But to get in one will have to rout out the keeper," I thought reluctantly, and hesitated. Finally I crossed the bridge and tried the iron gate. It yielded, and I walked through the tunnel formed by the thickness of the *chemin de ronde*. At the farther end, a wooden barricade had been laid across the entrance, and beyond it was a court enclosed in noble architecture. The main building faced me; and I now saw that one half was a mere ruined front, with gaping windows through which the wild growths of the moat and the trees of the park were visible. The rest of the house was still in its robust beauty. One end abutted on the round tower, the other on the small traceried chapel, and in an angle of the building stood a graceful well-head crowned with mossy urns. A few roses grew against the walls, and on an upper windowsill I remember noticing a pot of fuchsias.

My sense of the pressure of the invisible began to yield to my architectural interest. The building was so fine that I felt a desire to explore it for its own sake. I looked about the court, wondering in which corner the guardian lodged. Then I pushed open the barrier and went in. As I did so, a dog barred my way. He was such a remarkably beautiful little dog that for a moment he made me forget the splendid place he was defending. I was not sure of his breed at the time, but have since learned that it was Chinese, and that he was of a rare variety called the 'Sleeve-dog'. He was very small and golden brown, with large brown eyes and a ruffled throat: he looked like a large tawny chrysanthemum. I said to myself: "These little beasts always snap and scream, and somebody will be out in a minute."

The little animal stood before me, forbidding, almost menacing: there was anger in his large brown eyes. But he made no sound, he came no nearer. Instead, as I advanced, he gradually fell back, and I noticed that another dog, a vague rough brindled thing, had limped up on a lame leg. "There'll be a hubbub now," I thought; for at the same moment a third dog, a long-haired white mongrel, slipped out of a doorway and joined the others. All three stood looking at me with grave eyes; but not a sound came from them. As I advanced they continued to fall back on muffled paws, still watching me. "At a given point, they'll all charge at my ankles: it's one of the jokes that dogs who live together put up on one," I thought. I was not alarmed, for they were neither large nor formidable. But they let me wander about the court as I pleased, following me at a little distance – always the same distance – and always keeping their eyes on me. Presently I looked across at the ruined façade, and saw that in one of its empty window frames another dog stood: a white pointer with one brown ear. He was an old grave dog, much more experienced than the others; and he seemed to be observing me with a deeper intentness. "I'll hear from *him*," I said to myself; but he stood in the window frame, against the trees of the park, and continued to watch me without moving. I stared back at him for a time, to see if the sense that he was being watched would not rouse him. Half the width of the court lay between us, and we gazed at each other silently across it. But he did not stir, and at last I turned away. Behind me I found the rest of the pack, with a newcomer added: a small black greyhound with pale agate-colored eyes. He was shivering a little, and his expression was more timid than that of the others. I noticed that he kept a little behind them. And still there was not a sound.

I stood there for fully five minutes, the circle about me – waiting, as they seemed to be waiting. At last I went up to the little golden-brown dog and stooped to pat him. As I did so, I heard myself give a nervous laugh. The little dog did not start, or growl, or take his eyes from me – he simply slipped back about a yard, and then paused and continued to look at me. "Oh, hang it!" I exclaimed, and walked across the court toward the well.

As I advanced, the dogs separated and slid away into different corners of the court. I examined the urns on the well, tried a locked door or two, and looked up and down the dumb façade; then I faced about toward the chapel. When I turned I perceived that all the dogs had disappeared except the old pointer, who still watched me from the window. It was rather a relief to be rid of that cloud of witnesses; and I began to look about me for a way to the back of the house. "Perhaps there'll be somebody in the garden," I thought. I found a way across the moat, scrambled over a wall smothered in brambles, and got into the garden. A few lean hydrangeas and geraniums pined in the flowerbeds, and the ancient house looked down on them indifferently. Its garden side was plainer and severer than the other: the long granite front, with its few windows and steep roof, looked like a fortress-prison. I walked around the farther wing, went up some disjointed steps, and entered the deep twilight of a narrow and incredibly old box-walk. The walk was just wide enough for one person to slip through, and its branches met overhead. It was like the ghost of a box-walk, its lustrous green all turning to the shadowy greyness of the avenues. I walked on and on, the branches hitting me in the face and springing back with a dry rattle; and at length I came out on the grassy top of the *chemin de ronde*. I walked along it to the gate-tower, looking down into the court, which was just below me. Not a human being was in sight; and neither were the dogs. I found a flight of steps in the thickness of the wall and went down them; and when I emerged again into the court, there stood the circle of dogs, the golden-brown one a little ahead of the others, the black greyhound shivering in the rear.

"Oh, hang it – you uncomfortable beasts, you!" I exclaimed, my voice startling me with a sudden echo. The dogs stood motionless, watching me. I knew by this time that they would not try to prevent my approaching the house, and the knowledge left me free to examine them. I had a feeling that they must be horribly cowed to be so silent and inert. Yet they did not look hungry or ill-treated. Their coats were smooth and they were not thin, except the shivering greyhound. It was more as if they had lived a long time with people who never spoke to them or looked at them: as though the silence of the place had gradually benumbed their busy inquisitive natures. And this strange passivity, this almost human lassitude, seemed to me sadder than the misery of starved and beaten animals. I should have liked to rouse them for a minute, to coax them into a game or a scamper; but the longer I looked into their fixed and weary eyes the more preposterous the idea became. With the windows of that house looking down on us, how could I have imagined such a thing? The dogs knew better: *they* knew what the house would tolerate and what it would not. I even fancied that they knew what was passing through my mind, and pitied me for my frivolity. But even that feeling probably reached them through a thick fog of listlessness. I had an idea that their distance from me was as nothing to my remoteness from them. The impression they produced was that of having in common one memory so deep and dark that nothing that had happened since was worth either a growl or a wag.

"I say," I broke out abruptly, addressing myself to the dumb circle, "do you know what you look like, the whole lot of you? You look as if you'd seen a ghost – that's how you look! I wonder if there *is* a ghost here, and nobody but you left for it to appear to?" The dogs continued to gaze at me without moving...

* * *

It was dark when I saw Lanrivain's motor lamps at the crossroads – and I wasn't exactly sorry to see them. I had the sense of having escaped from the loneliest place in the whole world, and of not liking loneliness – to that degree – as much as I had imagined I should. My friend had brought his solicitor back from Quimper for the night, and seated beside a fat and affable stranger I felt no inclination to talk of Kerfol....

But that evening, when Lanrivain and the solicitor were closeted in the study, Madame de Lanrivain began to question me in the drawing room.

"Well – are you going to buy Kerfol?" she asked, tilting up her gay chin from her embroidery.

"I haven't decided yet. The fact is, I couldn't get into the house," I said, as if I had simply postponed my decision, and meant to go back for another look.

"You couldn't get in? Why, what happened? The family are mad to sell the place, and the old guardian has orders—"

"Very likely. But the old guardian wasn't there."

"What a pity! He must have gone to market. But his daughter—?"

"There was nobody about. At least I saw no one."

"How extraordinary! Literally nobody?"

"Nobody but a lot of dogs – a whole pack of them – who seemed to have the place to themselves."

Madame de Lanrivain let the embroidery slip to her knee and folded her hands on it. For several minutes she looked at me thoughtfully.

"A pack of dogs – you *saw* them?"

"Saw them? I saw nothing else!"

"How many?" She dropped her voice a little. "I've always wondered—"

I looked at her with surprise: I had supposed the place to be familiar to her. "Have you never been to Kerfol?" I asked.

"Oh, yes: often. But never on that day."

"What day?"

"I'd quite forgotten – and so had Hervé, I'm sure. If we'd remembered, we never should have sent you today – but then, after all, one doesn't half believe that sort of thing, does one?"

"What sort of thing?" I asked, involuntarily sinking my voice to the level of hers. Inwardly I was thinking: "I *knew* there was something...."

Madame de Lanrivain cleared her throat and produced a reassuring smile. "Didn't Hervé tell you the story of Kerfol? An ancestor of his was mixed up in it. You know every Breton house has its ghost-story; and some of them are rather unpleasant."

"Yes – but those dogs?"

"Well, those dogs are the ghosts of Kerfol. At least, the peasants say there's one day in the year when a lot of dogs appear there; and that day the keeper and his daughter go off to Morlaix and get drunk. The women in Brittany drink dreadfully." She stooped to match a silk; then she lifted her charming inquisitive Parisian face. "Did you *really* see a lot of dogs? There isn't one at Kerfol." she said.

Chapter II

LANRIVAIN, the next day, hunted out a shabby calf volume from the back of an upper shelf of his library.

"Yes – here it is. What does it call itself? *A History of the Assizes of the Duchy of Brittany. Quimper, 1702.* The book was written about a hundred years later than the Kerfol affair; but I believe the account is transcribed pretty literally from the judicial records. Anyhow, it's queer reading. And there's a Hervé de Lanrivain mixed up in it – not exactly *my* style, as you'll see. But then he's only a collateral. Here, take the book up to bed with you. I don't exactly remember the details; but after you've read it I'll bet anything you'll leave your light burning all night!"

I left my light burning all night, as he had predicted; but it was chiefly because, till near dawn, I was absorbed in my reading. The account of the trial of Anne de Cornault, wife of the lord of Kerfol, was long and closely printed. It was, as my friend had said, probably an almost literal transcription of what took place in the courtroom; and the trial lasted nearly a month. Besides, the type of the book was very bad…

At first I thought of translating the old record. But it is full of wearisome repetitions, and the main lines of the story are forever straying off into side issues. So I have tried to disentangle it, and give it here in a simpler form. At times, however, I have reverted to the text because no other words could have conveyed so exactly the sense of what I felt at Kerfol; and nowhere have I added anything of my own.

Chapter III

IT WAS in the year 16— that Yves de Cornault, lord of the domain of Kerfol, went to the *pardon* of Locronan to perform his religious duties. He was a rich and powerful noble, then in his sixty-second year, but hale and sturdy, a great horseman and hunter and a pious man. So all his neighbors attested. In appearance he was short and broad, with a swarthy face, legs slightly bowed from the saddle, a hanging nose and broad hands with black hairs on them. He had married young and lost his wife and son soon after, and since then had lived alone at Kerfol. Twice a year he went to Morlaix, where he had a handsome house by the river, and spent a week or ten days there; and occasionally he rode to Rennes on business. Witnesses were found to declare that during these absences he led a life different from the one he was known to lead at Kerfol, where he busied himself with his estate, attended mass daily, and found his only amusement in hunting the wild boar and water-fowl. But these rumors are not particularly relevant, and it is certain that among people of his own class in the neighborhood he passed for a stern and even austere man, observant of his religious obligations, and keeping strictly to himself. There was no talk of any familiarity with the women on his estate, though at that time the nobility were very free with their peasants. Some people said he had never looked at a woman since his wife's death; but such things are hard to prove, and the evidence on this point was not worth much.

Well, in his sixty-second year, Yves de Cornault went to the *pardon* at Locronan, and saw there a young lady of Douarnenez, who had ridden over pillion behind her father to do her duty to the saint. Her name was Anne de Barrigan, and she came of good old Breton stock, but much less great and powerful than that of Yves de Cornault; and her father had squandered his fortune at cards, and lived almost like a peasant in his little granite manor on the moors… I have said I would add nothing of my own to this bald statement of a strange case; but I must interrupt myself here to describe the young lady who rode up to the lych-gate of Locronan at the very moment when the Baron de Cornault was also dismounting there. I take my description from a faded drawing in red crayon, sober and truthful enough to be by a late pupil of the Clouets, which hangs in Lanrivain's study, and is said to be a portrait of Anne de Barrigan. It is unsigned and has no mark of identity but the initials A. B., and the date 16—, the year after her marriage. It represents a young woman with a small oval face, almost pointed, yet wide enough for a full mouth with a tender depression at the corners. The nose is small, and the eyebrows are set rather high, far apart, and as lightly pencilled as the eyebrows in a Chinese painting. The forehead is high and serious, and the hair, which one feels to be fine and thick and fair, is drawn off it and lies close like a cap. The eyes are neither large nor small, hazel probably, with a look at once shy and steady. A pair of beautiful long hands are crossed below the lady's breast…

The chaplain of Kerfol, and other witnesses, averred that when the Baron came back from Locronan he jumped from his horse, ordered another to be instantly saddled, called to a young page to come with him, and rode away that same evening to the south. His steward followed the next morning with coffers laden on a pair of pack mules. The following week Yves de Cornault rode back to Kerfol, sent for his vassals and tenants, and told them he was to be married at All Saints to Anne de Barrigan of Douarnenez. And on All Saints' Day the marriage took place.

As to the next few years, the evidence on both sides seems to show that they passed happily for the couple. No one was found to say that Yves de Cornault had been unkind to his wife, and it was plain to all that he was content with his bargain. Indeed, it was admitted by the chaplain and other witnesses for the prosecution that the young lady had a softening influence on her husband, and that he became less exacting with his tenants, less harsh to peasants and dependents, and less subject to the fits of gloomy silence which had darkened his widowhood. As to his wife, the only grievance her champions could call up in her behalf was that Kerfol was a lonely place, and that when her husband was away on business at Bennes or Morlaix – whither she was never taken – she was not allowed so much as to walk in the park unaccompanied. But no one asserted that she was unhappy, though one servant-woman said she had surprised her crying, and had heard her say that she was a woman accursed to have no child, and nothing in life to call her own. But that was a natural enough feeling in a wife attached to her husband; and certainly it must have been a great grief to Yves de Cornault that she bore no son. Yet he never made her feel her childlessness as a reproach – she admits this in her evidence – but seemed to try to make her forget it by showering gifts and favors on her. Rich though he was, he had never been openhanded; but nothing was too fine for his wife, in the way of silks or gems or linen, or whatever else she fancied. Every wandering merchant was welcome at Kerfol, and when the master was called away he never came back without bringing his wife a handsome present – something curious and particular – from Morlaix or Rennes or Quimper. One of the waiting-women gave, in cross-examination, an interesting list of one year's gifts, which I copy. From Morlaix, a carved ivory junk, with Chinamen at the oars, that a strange sailor had brought back as a votive offering for Notre Dame de la Clarté, above Ploumanac'h; from Quimper, an embroidered gown, worked by the nuns of the Assumption; from Rennes, a silver rose that opened and showed an amber Virgin with a crown of garnets; from Morlaix, again, a length of Damascus velvet shot with gold, bought of a Jew from Syria; and for Michaelmas that same year, from Rennes, a necklet or bracelet of round stones – emeralds and pearls and rubies – strung like beads on a fine gold chain. This was the present that pleased the lady best, the woman said. Later on, as it happened, it was produced at the trial, and appears to have struck the Judges and the public as a curious and valuable jewel.

The very same winter, the Baron absented himself again, this time as far as Bordeaux, and on his return he brought his wife something even odder and prettier than the bracelet. It was a winter evening when he rode up to Kerfol and, walking into the hall, found her sitting by the hearth, her chin on her hand, looking into the fire. He carried a velvet box in his hand and, setting it down, lifted the lid and let out a little golden-brown dog.

Anne de Cornault exclaimed with pleasure as the little creature bounded toward her. "Oh, it looks like a bird or a butterfly!" she cried as she picked it up; and the dog put its paws on her shoulders and looked at her with eyes 'like a Christian's'. After that she would never have it out of her sight, and petted and talked to it as if it had been a child – as indeed it was the nearest thing to a child she was to know. Yves de Cornault was much pleased with his purchase. The dog had been brought to him by a sailor from an East India merchantman, and the sailor had bought it of a pilgrim in a bazaar at Jaffa, who had stolen it from a nobleman's wife in China: a perfectly permissible thing to do, since the pilgrim was a Christian and the nobleman a heathen doomed to hell-fire.

Yves de Cornault had paid a long price for the dog, for they were beginning to be in demand at the French court, and the sailor knew he had got hold of a good thing; but Anne's pleasure was so great that, to see her laugh and play with the little animal, her husband would doubtless have given twice the sum.

* * *

So far, all the evidence is at one, and the narrative plain sailing; but now the steering becomes difficult. I will try to keep as nearly as possible to Anne's own statements; though toward the end, poor thing...

Well, to go back. The very year after the little brown dog was brought to Kerfol, Yves de Cornault, one winter night, was found dead at the head of a narrow flight of stairs leading down from his wife's rooms to a door opening on the court. It was his wife who found him and gave the alarm, so distracted, poor wretch, with fear and horror – for his blood was all over her – that at first the roused household could not make out what she was saying, and thought she had suddenly gone mad. But there, sure enough, at the top of the stairs lay her husband, stone dead, and head foremost, the blood from his wounds dripping down to the steps below him. He had been dreadfully scratched and gashed about the face and throat, as if with curious pointed weapons; and one of his legs had a deep tear in it which had cut an artery, and probably caused his death. But how did he come there, and who had murdered him?

His wife declared that she had been asleep in her bed, and hearing his cry had rushed out to find him lying on the stairs; but this was immediately questioned. In the first place, it was proved that from her room she could not have heard the struggle on the stairs, owing to the thickness of the walls and the length of the intervening passage; then it was evident that she had not been in bed and asleep, since she was dressed when she roused the house, and her bed had not been slept in. Moreover, the door at the bottom of the stairs was ajar, and it was noticed by the chaplain (an observant man) that the dress she wore was stained with blood about the knees, and that there were traces of small blood-stained hands low down on the staircase walls, so that it was conjectured that she had really been at the postern-door when her husband fell and, feeling her way up to him in the darkness on her hands and knees, had been stained by his blood dripping down on her. Of course it was argued on the other side that the blood-marks on her dress might have been caused by her kneeling down by her husband when she rushed out of her room; but there was the open door below, and the fact that the finger-marks in the staircase all pointed upward.

The accused held to her statement for the first two days, in spite of its improbability; but on the third day word was brought to her that Hervé de Lanrivain, a young nobleman of the neighborhood, had been arrested for complicity in the crime. Two or three witnesses thereupon came forward to say that it was known throughout the country that Lanrivain had formerly been on good terms with the lady of Cornault; but that he had been absent from Brittany for over a year, and people had ceased to associate their names. The witnesses who made this statement were not of a very reputable sort. One was an old herb-gatherer suspected of witchcraft, another a drunken clerk from a neighboring parish, the third a half-witted shepherd who could be made to say anything; and it was clear that the prosecution was not satisfied with its case, and would have liked to find more definite proof of Lanrivain's complicity than the statement of the herb-gatherer, who swore to having seen him climbing the wall of the park on the night of the murder. One way of patching out incomplete proofs in those days was to put some sort of pressure, moral or physical, on the accused person. It is not clear what pressure was put on Anne de Cornault; but on the third day, when she was brought in court, she 'appeared weak and wandering', and after being encouraged to collect herself and speak the truth, on her honor and the wounds of her Blessed Redeemer, she confessed that she had in fact gone down the stairs to speak with Hervé de Lanrivain (who denied everything), and had been surprised there by the sound of her husband's fall. That was better; and the prosecution rubbed its hands with satisfaction. The satisfaction increased when various dependents living at Kerfol were induced to say – with apparent sincerity – that during the year or two preceding his death their master had once more grown uncertain and irascible, and subject to the fits of brooding silence which his household had learned to dread before his second marriage. This seemed to show that things had not been going well at Kerfol; though no one could be found to say that there had been any signs of open disagreement between husband and wife.

Anne de Cornault, when questioned as to her reason for going down at night to open the door to Hervé de Lanrivain, made an answer which must have sent a smile around the court. She said it was because she was lonely and wanted to talk with the young man. Was this the only reason? she was asked; and replied: "Yes, by the Cross over your Lordships' heads." "But why at midnight?" the court asked. "Because I could see him in no other way." I can see the exchange of glances across the ermine collars under the Crucifix.

Anne de Cornault, further questioned, said that her married life had been extremely lonely: 'desolate' was the word she used. It was true that her husband seldom spoke harshly to her; but there were days when he did not speak at all. It was true that he had never struck or threatened her; but he kept her like a prisoner at Kerfol, and when he rode away to Morlaix or Quimper or Rennes he set so close a watch on her that she could not pick a flower in the garden without having a waiting-woman at her heels. "I am no Queen, to need such honors," she once said to him; and he had answered that a man who has a treasure does not leave the key in the lock when he goes out. "Then take me with you," she urged; but to this he said that towns were pernicious places, and young wives better off at their own firesides.

"But what did you want to say to Hervé de Lanrivain?" the court asked; and she answered: "To ask him to take me away."

"Ah – you confess that you went down to him with adulterous thoughts?"

"Then why did you want him to take you away?"

"Because I was afraid for my life."

"Of whom were you afraid?"

"Of my husband."

"Why were you afraid of your husband?"

"Because he had strangled my little dog."

Another smile must have passed around the courtroom: in days when any nobleman had a right to hang his peasants – and most of them exercised it – pinching a pet animal's windpipe was nothing to make a fuss about.

At this point one of the Judges, who appears to have had a certain sympathy for the accused, suggested that she should be allowed to explain herself in her own way; and she thereupon made the following statement.

The first years of her marriage had been lonely; but her husband had not been unkind to her. If she had had a child she would not have been unhappy; but the days were long, and it rained too much.

It was true that her husband, whenever he went away and left her, brought her a handsome present on his return; but this did not make up for the loneliness. At least nothing had, till he brought her the little brown dog from the East: after that she was much less unhappy. Her husband seemed pleased that she was so fond of the dog; he gave her leave to put her jeweled bracelet around its neck, and to keep it always with her.

One day she had fallen asleep in her room, with the dog at her feet, as his habit was. Her feet were bare and resting on his back. Suddenly she was waked by her husband: he stood beside her, smiling not unkindly.

"You look like my great-grandmother, Juliane de Cornault, lying in the chapel with her feet on a little dog," he said.

The analogy sent a chill through her, but she laughed and answered: "Well, when I am dead you must put me beside her, carved in marble, with my dog at my feet."

"Oho – we'll wait and see," he said, laughing also, but with his black brows close together. "The dog is the emblem of fidelity."

"And do you doubt my right to lie with mine at my feet?"

"When I'm in doubt I find out," he answered. "I am an old man," he added, "and people say I make you lead a lonely life. But I swear you shall have your monument if you earn it."

"And I swear to be faithful," she returned, "if only for the sake of having my little dog at my feet."

Not long afterward he went on business to the Quimper Assizes; and while he was away his aunt, the widow of a great nobleman of the duchy, came to spend a night at Kerfol on her way to the *pardon* of Ste. Barbe. She was a woman of piety and consequence, and much respected by Yves de Cornault, and when she proposed to Anne to go with her to Ste. Barbe no one could object, and even the chaplain declared himself in favor of the pilgrimage. So Anne set out for Ste. Barbe, and there for the first time she talked with Hervé de Lanrivain. He had come once or twice to Kerfol with his father, but she had never before exchanged a dozen words with him.

They did not talk for more than five minutes now: it was under the chestnuts, as the procession was coming out of the chapel. He said: "I pity you," and she was surprised, for she had not supposed that anyone thought her an object of pity. He added: "Call for me when you need me," and she smiled a little, but was glad afterward, and thought often of the meeting.

She confessed to having seen him three times afterward: not more. How or where she would not say – one had the impression that she feared to implicate someone. Their meetings had been rare and brief; and at the last he had told her that he was starting the next day for a foreign country, on a mission which was not without peril and might keep him for many months absent. He asked her for a remembrance, and she had none to give him but the collar about the little dog's neck. She was sorry afterward that she had given it, but he was so unhappy at going that she had not had the courage to refuse.

Her husband was away at the time. When he returned a few days later he picked up the animal to pet it, and noticed that its collar was missing. His wife told him that the dog had lost it in the undergrowth of the park, and that she and her maids had hunted a whole day for it. It was true, she explained to the court, that she had made the maids search for the necklet – they all believed the dog had lost it in the park...

Her husband made no comment, and that evening at supper he was in his usual mood, between good and bad: you could never tell which. He talked a good deal, describing what he had seen and done at Rennes; but now and then he stopped and looked hard at her, and when she went to bed she found her little dog strangled on her pillow. The little thing was dead, but still warm; she stooped to lift it, and her distress turned to horror when she discovered that it had been strangled by twisting twice round its throat the necklet she had given to Lanrivain.

The next morning at dawn she buried the dog in the garden, and hid the necklet in her breast. She said nothing to her husband, then or later, and he said nothing to her; but that day he had a peasant hanged for stealing a faggot in the park, and the next day he nearly beat to death a young horse he was breaking.

Winter set in, and the short days passed, and the long nights, one by one; and she heard nothing of Hervé de Lanrivain. It might be that her husband had killed him; or merely that he had been robbed of the necklet. Day after day by the hearth among the spinning maids, night after night alone on her bed, she wondered and trembled. Sometimes at table her husband looked across at her and smiled; and then she felt sure that Lanrivain was dead. She dared not try to get news of him, for she was sure her husband would find out if she did: she had an idea that he could find out anything. Even when a witchwoman who was a noted seer, and could show you the whole world in her crystal, came to the castle for a night's shelter, and the maids flocked to her, Anne held back.

The winter was long and black and rainy. One day, in Yves de Cornault's absence, some gypsies came to Kerfol with a troop of performing dogs. Anne bought the smallest and cleverest, a white dog with a feathery coat and one blue and one brown eye. It seemed to have been ill-treated by the gypsies, and clung to her plaintively when she took it from them. That evening her husband came back, and when she went to bed she found the dog strangled on her pillow.

After that she said to herself that she would never have another dog; but one bitter cold evening a poor lean greyhound was found whining at the castle-gate, and she took him in and forbade the maids to speak of him to her husband. She hid him in a room that no one went to, smuggled food to him from her own plate, made him a warm bed to lie on and petted him like a child.

Yves de Cornault came home, and the next day she found the greyhound strangled on her pillow. She wept in secret, but said nothing, and resolved that even if she met a dog dying of hunger she would never bring him into the castle; but one day she found a young sheepdog, a brindled puppy with good blue eyes, lying with a broken leg in the snow of the park. Yves de Cornault was at Bennes, and she brought the dog in, warmed and fed it, tied up its leg and hid it in the castle till her husband's return. The day before, she gave it to a peasant woman who lived a long way off, and paid her handsomely to care for it and say nothing; but that night she heard a whining and scratching at her door, and when she opened it the lame puppy, drenched and shivering, jumped up on her with little sobbing barks. She hid him in her bed, and the next morning was about to have him taken back to the peasant woman when she heard her husband ride into the court. She shut the dog in a chest, and went down to receive him. An hour or two later, when she returned to her room, the puppy lay strangled on her pillow...

After that she dared not make a pet of any other dog; and her loneliness became almost unendurable. Sometimes, when she crossed the court of the castle, and thought no one was looking, she stopped to pat the old pointer at the gate. But one day as she was caressing him her husband came out of the chapel; and the next day the old dog was gone...

This curious narrative was not told in one sitting of the court, or received without impatience and incredulous comment. It was plain that the Judges were surprised by its puerility, and that it did not help the accused in the eyes of the public. It was an odd tale, certainly; but what did it prove? That Yves de Cornault disliked dogs, and that his wife, to gratify her own fancy, persistently ignored this dislike. As for pleading this trivial disagreement as an excuse for her relations – whatever their nature – with her supposed accomplice, the argument was so absurd that her own lawyer manifestly regretted having let her make use of it, and tried several times to cut short her story. But she went on to the end, with a kind of hypnotized insistence, as though the scenes she evoked were so real to her that she had forgotten where she was and imagined herself to be re-living them.

At length the Judge who had previously shown a certain kindness to her said (leaning forward a little, one may suppose, from his row of dozing colleagues): "Then you would have us believe that you murdered your husband because he would not let you keep a pet dog?"

"I did not murder my husband."

"Who did, then? Hervé de Lanrivain?"

"No."

"Who then? Can you tell us?"

"Yes, I can tell you. The dogs—" At that point she was carried out of the court in a swoon.

* * *

It was evident that her lawyer tried to get her to abandon this line of defense. Possibly her explanation, whatever it was, had seemed convincing when she poured it out to him in the heat of their first private colloquy; but now that it was exposed to the cold daylight of judicial scrutiny, and the banter of the town, he was thoroughly ashamed of it, and would have sacrificed her without a scruple to save his professional reputation. But the obstinate Judge – who perhaps, after all, was more inquisitive than kindly – evidently wanted to hear the story out, and she was ordered, the next day, to continue her deposition.

She said that after the disappearance of the old watchdog nothing particular happened for a month or two. Her husband was much as usual: she did not remember any special incident. But one evening a pedlar woman came to the castle and was selling trinkets to the maids. She had no heart for trinkets, but she stood looking on while the women made their choice. And then, she did not know how, but the pedlar coaxed her into buying for herself a pear-shaped pomander with a strong scent in it – she had once seen something of the kind on a gypsy woman. She had no desire for the pomander, and did not know why she had bought it. The pedlar said that whoever wore it had the power to read the future; but she did not really believe that, or care much either. However, she bought the thing and took it up to her room, where she sat turning it about in her hand. Then the strange scent attracted her and she began to wonder what kind of spice was in the box. She opened it and found a gray bean rolled in a strip of paper; and on the paper she saw a sign she knew, and a message from Hervé de Lanrivain, saying that he was at home again and would be at the door in the court that night after the moon had set…

She burned the paper and sat down to think. It was nightfall, and her husband was at home… She had no way of warning Lanrivain, and there was nothing to do but to wait…

At this point I fancy the drowsy courtroom beginning to wake up. Even to the oldest hand on the bench there must have been a certain relish in picturing the feelings of a woman on receiving such a message at nightfall from a man living twenty miles away, to whom she had no means of sending a warning…

She was not a clever woman, I imagine; and as the first result of her cogitation she appears to have made the mistake of being, that evening, too kind to her husband. She could not ply him with wine, according to the traditional expedient, for though he drank heavily at times he had a strong head; and when he drank beyond its strength it was because he chose to, and not because a woman coaxed him. Not his wife, at any rate – she was an old story by now. As I read the case, I fancy there was no feeling for her left in him but the hatred occasioned by his supposed dishonor.

At any rate, she tried to call up her old graces; but early in the evening he complained of pains and fever, and left the hall to go up to the closet where he sometimes slept. His servant carried him a cup of hot wine, and brought back word that he was sleeping and not to be disturbed; and an hour later, when Anne lifted the tapestry and listened at his door, she heard his loud regular breathing. She thought it might be a feint, and stayed a long time barefooted in the passage, her ear to the crack; but the breathing went on too steadily and naturally to be other than that of a man in a sound sleep. She crept back to her room reassured, and stood in the window watching the moon set through the trees of the park. The sky was misty and starless, and after the moon went down the night was black as pitch. She knew the time had come, and stole along the passage, past her husband's door – where she stopped again to listen to his breathing – to the top of the stairs. There she paused a moment, and assured herself that no one was following her; then she began to go down the stairs in the darkness. They were so steep and winding that she had to go very slowly, for fear of stumbling. Her one thought was to get the door unbolted, tell Lanrivain to make his escape, and hasten back to her room. She had tried the bolt earlier in the evening, and managed to put a little grease on it; but nevertheless, when she drew it, it gave a squeak…not loud, but it made her heart stop; and the next minute, overhead, she heard a noise…

"What noise?" the prosecution interposed.

"My husband's voice calling out my name and cursing me."

"What did you hear after that?"

"A terrible scream and a fall."

"Where was Hervé de Lanrivain at this time?"

"He was standing outside in the court. I just made him out in the darkness. I told him for God's sake to go, and then I pushed the door shut."

"What did you do next?"

"I stood at the foot of the stairs and listened."

"What did you hear?"

"I heard dogs snarling and panting." (Visible discouragement of the bench, boredom of the public, and exasperation of the lawyer for the defense. Dogs again—! But the inquisitive Judge insisted.)

"What dogs?"

She bent her head and spoke so low that she had to be told to repeat her answer: "I don't know."

"How do you mean – you don't know?"

"I don't know what dogs…"

The Judge again intervened: "Try to tell us exactly what happened. How long did you remain at the foot of the stairs?"

"Only a few minutes."

"And what was going on meanwhile overhead?"

"The dogs kept on snarling and panting. Once or twice he cried out. I think he moaned once. Then he was quiet."

"Then what happened?"

"Then I heard a sound like the noise of a pack when the wolf is thrown to them – gulping and lapping."

(There was a groan of disgust and repulsion through the court, and another attempted intervention by the distracted lawyer. But the inquisitive Judge was still inquisitive.)

"And all the while you did not go up?"

"Yes – I went up then – to drive them off."

"The dogs?"

"Yes."

"Well—?"

"When I got there it was quite dark. I found my husband's flint and steel and struck a spark. I saw him lying there. He was dead."

"And the dogs?"

"The dogs were gone."

"Gone – whereto?"

"I don't know. There was no way out – and there were no dogs at Kerfol."

She straightened herself to her full height, threw her arms above her head, and fell down on the stone floor with a long scream. There was a moment of confusion in the courtroom. Someone on the bench was heard to say: "This is clearly a case for the ecclesiastical authorities" – and the prisoner's lawyer doubtless jumped at the suggestion.

After this, the trial loses itself in a maze of cross-questioning and squabbling. Every witness who was called corroborated Anne de Cornault's statement that there were no dogs at Kerfol: had been none for several months. The master of the house had taken a dislike to dogs, there was no denying it. But, on the other hand, at the inquest, there had been long and bitter discussions as to the nature of the dead man's wounds. One of the surgeons called in had spoken of marks that looked like bites. The suggestion of witchcraft was revived, and the opposing lawyers hurled tomes of necromancy at each other.

At last Anne de Cornault was brought back into court – at the instance of the same Judge – and asked if she knew where the dogs she spoke of could have come from. On the body of her Redeemer she swore that she did not. Then the Judge put his final question: "If the dogs you think you heard had been known to you, do you think you would have recognized them by their barking?"

"Yes."

"Did you recognize them?"

"Yes."

"What dogs do you take them to have been?"

"My dead dogs," she said in a whisper... She was taken out of court, not to reappear there again. There was some kind of ecclesiastical investigation, and the end of the business was that the Judges disagreed with each other, and with the ecclesiastical committee, and that Anne de Cornault was finally handed over to the keeping of her husband's family, who shut her up in the keep of Kerfol, where she is said to have died many years later, a harmless mad-woman.

So ends her story. As for that of Hervé de Lanrivain, I had only to apply to his collateral descendant for its subsequent details. The evidence against the young man being insufficient, and his family influence in the duchy considerable, he was set free, and left soon afterward for Paris. He was probably in no mood for a worldly life, and he appears to have come almost immediately under the influence of the famous M. Arnauld d'Andilly and the gentlemen of Port Royal. A year or two later he was received into their Order, and without achieving any particular distinction he followed its good and evil fortunes till his death some twenty years later. Lanrivain showed me a portrait of him by a pupil of Philippe de Champaigne: sad eyes, an impulsive mouth and a narrow brow. Poor Hervé de Lanrivain: it was a gray ending. Yet as I looked at his stiff and sallow effigy, in the dark dress of the Janséniste, I almost found myself envying his fate. After all, in the course of his life two great things had happened to him: he had loved romantically, and he must have talked with Pascal...

The Eyes

Edith Wharton

Chapter I

WE HAD BEEN put in the mood for ghosts, that evening, after an excellent dinner at our old friend Culwin's, by a tale of Fred Murchard's – the narrative of a strange personal visitation.

Seen through the haze of our cigars, and by the drowsy gleam of a coal fire, Culwin's library, with its oak walls and dark old bindings, made a good setting for such evocations; and ghostly experiences at first hand being, after Murchard's brilliant opening, the only kind acceptable to us, we proceeded to take stock of our group and tax each member for a contribution. There were eight of us, and seven contrived, in a manner more or less adequate, to fulfil the condition imposed. It surprised us all to find that we could muster such a show of supernatural impressions, for none of us, excepting Murchard himself and young Phil Frenham – whose story was the slightest of the lot – had the habit of sending our souls into the invisible. So that, on the whole, we had every reason to be proud of our seven 'exhibits', and none of us would have dreamed of expecting an eighth from our host.

Our old friend, Mr. Andrew Culwin, who had sat back in his armchair, listening and blinking through the smoke circles with the cheerful tolerance of a wise old idol, was not the kind of man likely to be favored with such contacts, though he had imagination enough to enjoy, without envying, the superior privileges of his guests. By age and by education he belonged to the stout Positivist tradition, and his habit of thought had been formed in the days of the epic struggle between physics and metaphysics. But he had been, then and always, essentially a spectator, a humorous detached observer of the immense muddled variety show of life, slipping out of his seat now and then for a brief dip into the convivialities at the back of the house, but never, as far as one knew, showing the least desire to jump on the stage and do a 'turn'.

Among his contemporaries there lingered a vague tradition of his having, at a remote period, and in a romantic clime, been wounded in a duel; but this legend no more tallied with what we younger men knew of his character than my mother's assertion that he had once been "a charming little man with nice eyes" corresponded to any possible reconstitution of his dry thwarted physiognomy.

"He never can have looked like anything but a bundle of sticks," Murchard had once said of him. "Or a phosphorescent log, rather," someone else amended; and we recognized the happiness of this description of his small squat trunk, with the red blink of the eyes in a face like mottled bark. He had always been possessed of a leisure which he had nursed and protected, instead of squandering it in vain activities. His carefully guarded hours had been devoted to the cultivation of a fine intelligence and a few judiciously chosen habits; and none of the disturbances common to human experience seemed to have crossed his sky. Nevertheless, his dispassionate survey of the universe had not raised his opinion of that costly experiment, and his study of the human race seemed to have resulted in the conclusion that all men were superfluous, and women necessary only because someone had to do the cooking. On the importance of this point his convictions were absolute, and gastronomy was the only science which he revered as dogma. It must be owned that his little dinners were a strong argument in favor of this view, besides being a reason – though not the main one – for the fidelity of his friends.

Mentally he exercised a hospitality less seductive but no less stimulating. His mind was like a forum, or some open meeting-place for the exchange of ideas: somewhat cold and draughty, but light, spacious and orderly – a kind of academic grove from which all the leaves had fallen. In this privileged area a dozen of us were wont to stretch our muscles and expand our lungs; and, as if to prolong as much as possible the tradition of what we felt to be a vanishing institution, one or two neophytes were now and then added to our band.

Young Phil Frenham was the last, and the most interesting, of these recruits, and a good example of Murchard's somewhat morbid assertion that our old friend 'liked 'em juicy'. It was indeed a fact that Culwin, for all his mental dryness, specially tasted the lyric qualities in youth. As he was far too good an Epicurean to nip the flowers of soul which he gathered for his garden, his friendship was not a disintegrating influence: on the contrary, it forced the young idea to robuster bloom. And in Phil Frenham he had a fine subject for experimentation. The boy was really intelligent, and the soundness of his nature was like the pure paste under a delicate glaze. Culwin had fished him out of a thick fog of family dullness, and pulled him up to a peak in Darien; and the adventure hadn't hurt him a bit. Indeed, the skill with which Culwin had contrived to stimulate his curiosities without robbing them of their young bloom of awe seemed to me a sufficient answer to Murchard's ogreish metaphor. There was nothing hectic in Frenham's efflorescence, and his old friend had not laid even a finger-tip on the sacred stupidities. One wanted no better proof of that than the fact that Frenham still reverenced them in Culwin.

"There's a side of him you fellows don't see. *I* believe that story about the duel!" he declared; and it was of the very essence of this belief that it should impel him – just as our little party was dispersing – to turn back to our host with the absurd demand: "And now you've got to tell us about *your* ghost!"

The outer door had closed on Murchard and the others; only Frenham and I remained; and the vigilant servant who presided over Culwin's destinies, having brought a fresh supply of soda-water, had been laconically ordered to bed.

Culwin's sociability was a night-blooming flower, and we knew that he expected the nucleus of his group to tighten around him after midnight. But Frenham's appeal seemed to disconcert him comically, and he rose from the chair in which he had just reseated himself after his farewells in the hall.

"*My* ghost? Do you suppose I'm fool enough to go to the expense of keeping one of my own, when there are so many charming ones in my friends' closets? – Take another cigar," he said, revolving toward me with a laugh.

Frenham laughed too, pulling up his slender height before the chimney-piece as he turned to face his short bristling friend.

"Oh," he said, "you'd never be content to share if you met one you really liked."

Culwin had dropped back into his armchair, his shock head embedded in its habitual hollow, his little eyes glimmering over a fresh cigar.

"Liked – *liked?* Good Lord!" he growled.

"Ah, you *have*, then!" Frenham pounced on him in the same instant, with a sidewise glance of victory at me; but Culwin cowered gnomelike among his cushions, dissembling himself in a protective cloud of smoke.

"What's the use of denying it? You've seen everything, so of course you've seen a ghost!" his young friend persisted, talking intrepidly into the cloud. "Or, if you haven't seen one, it's only because you've seen two!"

The form of the challenge seemed to strike our host. He shot his head out of the mist with a queer tortoise-like motion he sometimes had, and blinked approvingly at Frenham.

"Yes," he suddenly flung at us on a shrill jerk of laughter; "it's only because I've seen two!"

The words were so unexpected that they dropped down and down into a fathomless silence, while we continued to stare at each other over Culwin's head, and Culwin stared at his ghosts. At length Frenham, without speaking, threw himself into the chair on the other side of the hearth, and leaned forward with his listening smile...

Chapter II

"OH, OF COURSE they're not show ghosts – a collector wouldn't think anything of them...Don't let me raise your hopes...their one merit is their numerical strength: the exceptional fact of their being *two*. But, as against this, I'm bound to admit that at any moment I could probably have exorcised them both by asking my doctor for a prescription, or my oculist for a pair of spectacles. Only, as I never could make up my mind whether to go to the doctor or the oculist – whether I was afflicted by an optical or a digestive delusion – I left them to pursue their interesting double life, though at times they made mine exceedingly comfortable...

"Yes – uncomfortable; and you know how I hate to be uncomfortable! But it was part of my stupid pride, when the thing began, not to admit that I could be disturbed by the trifling matter of seeing two –

"And then I'd no reason, really, to suppose I was ill. As far as I knew I was simply bored – horribly bored. But it was part of my boredom – I remember – that I was feeling so uncommonly well, and didn't know how on earth to work off my surplus energy. I had come back from a long journey – down in South America and Mexico – and had settled down for the winter near New York, with an old aunt who had known Washington Irving and corresponded with N. P. Willis. She lived, not far from Irvington, in a damp Gothic villa, overhung by Norway spruces, and looking exactly like a memorial emblem done in hair. Her personal appearance was in keeping with this image, and her own hair – of which there was little left – might have been sacrificed to the manufacture of the emblem.

"I had just reached the end of an agitated year, with considerable arrears to make up in money and emotion; and theoretically it seemed as though my aunt's mild hospitality would be as beneficial to my nerves as to my purse. But the deuce of it was that as soon as I felt myself safe and sheltered my energy began to revive; and how was I to work it off inside of a memorial emblem? I had, at that time, the agreeable illusion that sustained intellectual effort could engage a man's whole activity; and I decided to write a great book – I forget about what. My aunt, impressed by my plan, gave up to me her Gothic library, filled with classics in black cloth and daguerrotypes of faded celebrities; and I sat down at my desk to make myself a place among their number. And to facilitate my task she lent me a cousin to copy my manuscript.

"The cousin was a nice girl, and I had an idea that a nice girl was just what I needed to restore my faith in human nature, and principally in myself. She was neither beautiful nor intelligent – poor Alice Nowell! – but it interested me to see any woman content to be so uninteresting, and I wanted to find out the secret of her content. In doing this I handled it rather rashly, and put it out of joint – oh, just for a moment! There's no fatuity in telling you this, for the poor girl had never seen anyone but cousins…

"Well, I was sorry for what I'd done, of course, and confoundedly bothered as to how I should put it straight. She was staying in the house, and one evening, after my aunt had gone to bed, she came down to the library to fetch a book she'd mislaid, like any artless heroine on the shelves behind us. She was pink-nosed and flustered, and it suddenly occurred to me that her hair, though it was fairly thick and pretty, would look exactly like my aunt's when she grew older. I was glad I had noticed this, for it made it easier for me to do what was right; and when I had found the book she hadn't lost I told her I was leaving for Europe that week.

"Europe was terribly far off in those days, and Alice knew at once what I meant. She didn't take it in the least as I'd expected – it would have been easier if she had. She held her book very tight, and turned away a moment to wind up the lamp on my desk – it had a ground glass shade with vine leaves, and glass drops around the edge, I remember. Then she came back, held out her hand, and said: 'Goodbye.' And as she said it she looked straight at me and kissed me. I had never felt anything as fresh and shy and brave as her kiss. It was worse than any reproach, and it made me ashamed to deserve a reproach from her. I said to myself: 'I'll marry her, and when my aunt dies she'll leave us this house, and I'll sit here at the desk and go on with my book; and Alice will sit over there with her embroidery and look at me as she's looking now. And life will go on like that for any number of years.' The prospect frightened me a little, but at the time it didn't frighten me as much as doing anything to hurt her; and ten minutes later she had my seal ring on my finger, and my promise that when I went abroad she should go with me.

"You'll wonder why I'm enlarging on this familiar incident. It's because the evening on which it took place was the very evening on which I first saw the queer sight I've spoken of. Being at that time an ardent believer in a necessary sequence between cause and effect I naturally tried to trace some kind of link between what had just happened to me in my aunt's library, and what was to happen a few hours later on the same night; and so the coincidence between the two events always remained in my mind.

"I went up to bed with rather a heavy heart, for I was bowed under the weight of the first good action I had ever consciously committed; and young as I was, I saw the gravity of my situation. Don't imagine from this that I had hitherto been an instrument of destruction. I had been merely a harmless young man, who had followed his bent and declined all collaboration with Providence. Now I had suddenly undertaken to promote the moral order of the world, and I felt a good deal like the trustful spectator who has given his gold watch to the conjurer, and doesn't know in what shape he'll get it back when the trick is over…Still, a glow of self-righteousness tempered my fears, and I said to myself as I undressed that when I'd got used to being good it probably wouldn't make me as nervous as it did at the start. And by the time I was in bed, and had blown out my candle, I felt that I really *was* getting used to it, and that, as far as I'd got, it was not unlike sinking down into one of my aunt's very softest wool mattresses.

"I closed my eyes on this image, and when I opened them it must have been a good deal later, for my room had grown cold, and the night was intensely still. I was waked suddenly by the feeling we all know – the feeling that there was something near me that hadn't been there when I fell asleep. I sat up and strained my eyes into the darkness. The room was pitch black, and at first I saw nothing; but gradually a vague glimmer at the foot of the bed turned into two eyes staring back at me. I couldn't see the face attached to them – on account of the darkness, I imagined – but as I looked the eyes grew more and more distinct: they gave out a light of their own.

"The sensation of being thus gazed at was far from pleasant, and you might suppose that my first impulse would have been to jump out of bed and hurl myself on the invisible figure attached to the eyes. But it wasn't – my impulse was simply to lie still...I can't say whether this was due to an immediate sense of the uncanny nature of the apparition – to the certainty that if I did jump out of bed I should hurl myself on nothing – or merely to the benumbing effect of the eyes themselves. They were the very worst eyes I've ever seen: a man's eyes – but what a man! My first thought was that he must be frightfully old. The orbits were sunk, and the thick red-lined lids hung over the eyeballs like blinds of which the cords are broken. One lid drooped a little lower than the other, with the effect of a crooked leer; and between these pulpy folds of flesh, with their scant bristle of lashes, the eyes themselves, small glassy disks with an agate-like rim about the pupils, looked like sea-pebbles in the grip of a starfish.

"But the age of the eyes was not the most unpleasant thing about them. What turned me sick was their expression of vicious security. I don't know how else to describe the fact that they seemed to belong to a man who had done a lot of harm in his life, but had always kept just inside the danger lines. They were not the eyes of a coward, but of someone much too clever to take risks; and my gorge rose at their look of base astuteness. Yet even that wasn't the worst; for as we continued to scan each other I saw in them a tinge of faint derision, and felt myself to be its object.

"At that I was seized by an impulse of rage that jerked me out of bed and pitched me straight on the unseen figure at its foot. But of course there wasn't any figure there, and my fists struck at emptiness. Ashamed and cold, I groped about for a match and lit the candles. The room looked just as usual – as I had known it would; and I crawled back to bed, and blew out the lights.

"As soon as the room was dark again the eyes reappeared; and I now applied myself to explaining them on scientific principles. At first I thought the illusion might have been caused by the glow of the last embers in the chimney; but the fireplace was on the other side of my bed, and so placed that the fire could not possibly be reflected in my toilet glass, which was the only mirror in the room. Then it occurred to me that I might have been tricked by the reflection of the embers in some polished bit of wood or metal; and though I couldn't discover any object of the sort in my line of vision, I got up again, groped my way to the hearth, and covered what was left of the fire. But as soon as I was back in bed the eyes were back at its foot.

"They were a hallucination, then: that was plain. But the fact that they were not due to any external dupery didn't make them a bit pleasanter to see. For if they were a projection of my inner consciousness, what the deuce was the matter with that organ? I had gone deeply enough into the mystery of morbid pathological states to picture the conditions under which an exploring mind might lay itself open to such a midnight admonition; but I couldn't fit it to my present case. I had never felt more normal, mentally and physically; and the only unusual fact in my situation – that of having assured the happiness of an amiable girl – did not seem of a kind to summon unclean spirits about my pillow. But there were the eyes still looking at me...

"I shut mine, and tried to evoke a vision of Alice Nowell's. They were not remarkable eyes, but they were as wholesome as fresh water, and if she had had more imagination – or longer lashes – their expression might have been interesting. As it was, they did not prove very efficacious, and in a few moments I perceived that they had mysteriously changed into the eyes at the foot of the bed. It exasperated me more to feel these glaring at me through my shut lids than to see them, and I opened my eyes again and looked straight into their hateful stare...

"And so it went on all night. I can't tell you what that night was, nor how long it lasted. Have you ever lain in bed, hopelessly wide awake, and tried to keep your eyes shut, knowing that if you opened 'em you'd see something you dreaded and loathed? It sounds easy, but it's devilish hard. Those eyes hung there and drew me. I had the *vertige de l'abîme*, and their red lids were the edge of my abyss....I had known nervous hours before: hours when I'd felt the wind of danger in my neck; but never this kind of strain. It wasn't that the eyes were so awful; they hadn't the majesty of the powers of darkness. But they had – how shall I say? – a physical effect that was the equivalent of a bad smell: their look left a smear like a snail's. And I didn't see what business they had with me, anyhow – and I stared and stared, trying to find out...

"I don't know what effect they were trying to produce; but the effect they *did* produce was that of making me pack my portmanteau and bolt to town early the next morning. I left a note for my aunt, explaining that I was ill and had gone to see my doctor; and as a matter of fact I did feel uncommonly ill – the night seemed to have pumped all the blood out of me. But when I reached town I didn't go to the doctor's. I went to a friend's rooms, and threw myself on a bed, and slept for ten heavenly hours. When I woke it was the middle of the night, and I turned cold at the thought of what might be waiting for me. I sat up, shaking, and stared into the darkness; but there wasn't a break in its blessed surface, and when I saw that the eyes were not there I dropped back into another long sleep.

"I had left no word for Alice when I fled, because I meant to go back the next morning. But the next morning I was too exhausted to stir. As the day went on the exhaustion increased, instead of wearing off like the lassitude left by an ordinary night of insomnia: the effect of the eyes seemed to be cumulative, and the thought of seeing them again grew intolerable. For two days I struggled with my dread; but on the third evening I pulled myself together and decided to go back the next morning. I felt a good deal happier as soon as I'd decided, for I knew that my abrupt disappearance, and the strangeness of my not writing, must have been very painful for poor Alice. That night I went to bed with an easy mind, and fell asleep at once; but in the middle of the night I woke, and there were the eyes...

"Well, I simply couldn't face them; and instead of going back to my aunt's I bundled a few things into a trunk and jumped onto the first steamer for England. I was so dead tired when I got on board that I crawled straight into my berth, and slept most of the way over; and I can't tell you the bliss it was to wake from those long stretches of dreamless sleep and look fearlessly into the darkness, *knowing* that I shouldn't see the eyes...

"I stayed abroad for a year, and then I stayed for another; and during that time I never had a glimpse of them. That was enough reason for prolonging my stay if I'd been on a desert island. Another was, of course, that I had perfectly come to see, on the voyage over, the folly, complete impossibility, of my marrying Alice Nowell. The fact that I had been so slow in making this discovery annoyed me, and made me want to avoid explanations. The bliss of escaping at one stroke from the eyes, and from this other embarrassment, gave my freedom an extraordinary zest; and the longer I savored it the better I liked its taste.

"The eyes had burned such a hole in my consciousness that for a long time I went on puzzling over the nature of the apparition, and wondering nervously if it would ever come back. But as time passed I lost this dread, and retained only the precision of the image. Then that faded in its turn.

"The second year found me settled in Rome, where I was planning, I believe, to write another great book – a definitive work on Etruscan influences in Italian art. At any rate, I'd found some pretext of the kind for taking a sunny apartment in the Piazza di Spagna and dabbling about indefinitely in the Forum; and there, one morning, a charming youth came to me. As he stood there in the warm light, slender and smooth and hyacinthine, he might have stepped from a ruined altar – one to Antinous, say – but he'd come instead from New York, with a letter (of all people) from Alice Nowell. The letter – the first I'd had from her since our break – was simply a line introducing her young cousin, Gilbert Noyes, and appealing to me to befriend him. It appeared, poor lad, that he 'had talent', and 'wanted to write'; and, an obdurate family having insisted that his calligraphy should take the form of double entry, Alice had intervened to win him six months' respite, during which he was to travel on a meagre pittance, and somehow prove his ultimate ability to increase it by his pen. The quaint conditions of the test struck me first: it seemed about as conclusive as a medieval 'ordeal'. Then I was touched by her having sent him to me. I had always wanted to do her some service, to justify myself in my own eyes rather than hers; and here was a beautiful embodiment of my chance.

"Well, I imagine it's safe to lay down the general principle that predestined geniuses don't, as a rule, appear before one in the spring sunshine of the Forum looking like one of its banished gods. At any rate, poor Noyes wasn't a predestined genius. But he *was* beautiful to see, and charming as a comrade too. It was only when he began to talk literature that my heart failed me. I knew all the symptoms so well – the things he had 'in him', and the things outside him that impinged! There's the real test, after all. It was always – punctually, inevitably, with the inexorableness of a mechanical law – it was *always* the wrong thing that struck him. I grew to find a certain grim fascination in deciding in advance exactly which wrong thing he'd select; and I acquired an astonishing skill at the game…

"The worst of it was that his *betise* wasn't of the too obvious sort. Ladies who met him at picnics thought him intellectual; and even at dinners he passed for clever. I, who had him under the microscope, fancied now and then that he might develop some kind of a slim talent, something that he could make 'do' and be happy on; and wasn't that, after all, what I was concerned with? He was so charming – he continued to be so charming – that he called forth all my charity in support of this argument; and for the first few months I really believed there was a chance for him…

"Those months were delightful. Noyes was constantly with me, and the more I saw of him the better I liked him. His stupidity was a natural grace – it was as beautiful, really, as his eyelashes. And he was so gay, so affectionate, and so happy with me, that telling him the truth would have been about as pleasant as slitting the throat of some artless animal. At first I used to wonder what had put into that radiant head the detestable delusion that it held a brain. Then I began to see that it was simply protective mimicry – an instinctive ruse to get away from family life and an office desk. Not that Gilbert didn't – dear lad! – believe in himself. There wasn't a trace of hypocrisy in his composition. He was sure that his 'call' was irresistible, while to me it was the saving grace of his situation that it *wasn't*, and that a little money, a little leisure, a little pleasure would have turned him into an inoffensive idler. Unluckily, however, there was no hope of money, and with the grim alternative of the office desk before him he couldn't postpone his attempt at literature. The stuff he turned out was deplorable, and I see now that I knew it from the first. Still, the absurdity of deciding a man's whole future on a first trial seemed to justify me in withholding my verdict, and perhaps even in encouraging him a little, on the ground that the human plant generally needs warmth to flower.

"At any rate, I proceeded on that principle, and carried it to the point of getting his term of probation extended. When I left Rome he went with me, and we idled away a delicious summer between Capri and Venice. I said to myself: 'If he has anything in him, it will come out now; and it *did*. He was never more enchanting and enchanted. There were moments of our pilgrimage when beauty born of murmuring sound seemed actually to pass into his face – but only to issue forth in a shallow flood of the palest ink...

"Well the time came to turn off the tap; and I knew there was no hand but mine to do it. We were back in Rome, and I had taken him to stay with me, not wanting him to be alone in his dismal *pension* when he had to face the necessity of renouncing his ambition. I hadn't, of course, relied solely on my own judgment in deciding to advise him to drop literature. I had sent his stuff to various people – editors and critics – and they had always sent it back with the same chilling lack of comment. Really there was nothing on earth to say about it –

"I confess I never felt more shabbily than I did on the day when I decided to have it out with Gilbert. It was well enough to tell myself that it was my duty to knock the poor boy's hopes into splinters – but I'd like to know what act of gratuitous cruelty hasn't been justified on that plea? I've always shrunk from usurping the functions of Providence, and when I have to exercise them I decidedly prefer that it shouldn't be on an errand of destruction. Besides, in the last issue, who was I to decide, even after a year's trial, if poor Gilbert had it in him or not?

"The more I looked at the part I'd resolved to play, the less I liked it; and I liked it still less when Gilbert sat opposite me, with his head thrown back in the lamplight, just as Phil's is now...I'd been going over his last manuscript, and he knew it, and he knew that his future hung on my verdict – we'd tacitly agreed to that. The manuscript lay between us, on my table – a novel, his first novel, if you please! – and he reached over and laid his hand on it, and looked up at me with all his life in the look.

"I stood up and cleared my throat, trying to keep my eyes away from his face and on the manuscript.

"'The fact is, my dear Gilbert,' I began –

"I saw him turn pale, but he was up and facing me in an instant.

"'Oh, look here, don't take on so, my dear fellow! I'm not so awfully cut up as all that!' His hands were on my shoulders, and he was laughing down on me from his full height, with a kind of mortally-stricken gaiety that drove the knife into my side.

"He was too beautifully brave for me to keep up any humbug about my duty. And it came over me suddenly how I should hurt others in hurting him: myself first, since sending him home meant losing him; but more particularly poor Alice Nowell, to whom I had so uneasily longed to prove my good faith and my immense desire to serve her. It really seemed like failing her twice to fail Gilbert –

"But my intuition was like one of those lightning flashes that encircle the whole horizon, and in the same instant I saw what I might be letting myself in for if I didn't tell the truth. I said to myself: 'I shall have him for life' – and I'd never yet seen anyone, man or woman, whom I was quite sure of wanting on those terms. Well, this impulse of egotism decided me. I was ashamed of it, and to get away from it I took a leap that landed me straight in Gilbert's arms.

"'The thing's all right, and you're all wrong!' I shouted up at him; and as he hugged me, and I laughed and shook in his incredulous clutch, I had for a minute the sense of self-complacency that is supposed to attend the footsteps of the just. Hang it all, making people happy *has* its charms –

"Gilbert, of course, was for celebrating his emancipation in some spectacular manner; but I sent him away alone to explode his emotions, and went to bed to sleep off mine. As I undressed I began to wonder what their after-taste would be – so many of the finest don't keep! Still, I wasn't sorry, and I meant to empty the bottle, even if it *did* turn a trifle flat.

"After I got into bed I lay for a long time smiling at the memory of his eyes – his blissful eyes... Then I fell asleep, and when I woke the room was deathly cold, and I sat up with a jerk – and there were *the other eyes*...

"It was three years since I'd seen them, but I'd thought of them so often that I fancied they could never take me unawares again. Now, with their red sneer on me, I knew that I had never really believed they would come back, and that I was as defenseless as ever against them...As before, it was the insane irrelevance of their coming that made it so horrible. What the deuce were they after, to leap out at me at such a time? I had lived more or less carelessly in the years since I'd seen them, though my worst indiscretions were not dark enough to invite the searchings of their infernal glare; but at this particular moment I was really in what might have been called a state of grace; and I can't tell you how the fact added to their horror...

"But it's not enough to say they were as bad as before: they were worse. Worse by just so much as I'd learned of life in the interval; by all the damnable implications my wider experience read into them. I saw now what I hadn't seen before: that they were eyes which had grown hideous gradually, which had built up their baseness coral-wise, bit by bit, out of a series of small turpitudes slowly accumulated through the industrious years. Yes – it came to me that what made them so bad was that they'd grown bad so slowly...

"There they hung in the darkness, their swollen lids dropped across the little watery bulbs rolling loose in the orbits, and the puff of fat flesh making a muddy shadow underneath – and as their filmy stare moved with my movements, there came over me a sense of their tacit complicity, of a deep hidden understanding between us that was worse than the first shock of their strangeness. Not that I understood them; but that they made it so clear that some day I should...Yes, that was the worst part of it, decidedly; and it was the feeling that became stronger each time they came back to me...

"For they got into the damnable habit of coming back. They reminded me of vampires with a taste for young flesh, they seemed so to gloat over the taste of a good conscience. Every night for a month they came to claim their morsel of mine: since I'd made Gilbert happy they simply wouldn't loosen their fangs. The coincidence almost made me hate him, poor lad, fortuitous as I felt it to be. I puzzled over it a good deal, but couldn't find any hint of an explanation except in the chance of his association with Alice Nowell. But then the eyes had let up on me the moment I had abandoned her, so they could hardly be the emissaries of a woman scorned, even if one could have pictured poor Alice charging such spirits to avenge her. That set me thinking, and I began to wonder if they would let up on me if I abandoned Gilbert. The temptation was insidious, and I had to stiffen myself against it; but really, dear boy! He was too charming to be sacrificed to such demons. And so, after all, I never found out what they wanted..."

Chapter III

THE FIRE CRUMBLED, sending up a flash which threw into relief the narrator's gnarled red face under its grey-black stubble. Pressed into the hollow of the dark leather armchair, it stood out an instant like an intaglio of yellowish red-veined stone, with spots of enamel for the eyes; then the fire sank and in the shaded lamplight it became once more a dim Rembrandtish blur.

Phil Frenham, sitting in a low chair on the opposite side of the hearth, one long arm propped on the table behind him, one hand supporting his thrown-back head, and his eyes steadily fixed on his old friend's face, had not moved since the tale began. He continued to maintain his silent immobility after Culwin had ceased to speak, and it was I who, with a vague sense of disappointment at the sudden drop of the story, finally asked: "But how long did you keep on seeing them?"

Culwin, so sunk into his chair that he seemed like a heap of his own empty clothes, stirred a little, as if in surprise at my question. He appeared to have half-forgotten what he had been telling us.

"How long? Oh, off and on all that winter. It was infernal. I never got used to them. I grew really ill."

Frenham shifted his attitude silently, and as he did so his elbow struck against a small mirror in a bronze frame standing on the table behind him. He turned and changed its angle slightly; then he resumed his former attitude, his dark head thrown back on his lifted palm, his eyes intent on Culwin's face. Something in his stare embarrassed me, and as if to divert attention from it I pressed on with another question:

"And you never tried sacrificing Noyes?"

"Oh, no. The fact is I didn't have to. He did it for me, poor infatuated boy!"

"Did it for you? How do you mean?"

"He wore me out – wore everybody out. He kept on pouring out his lamentable twaddle, and hawking it up and down the place till he became a thing of terror. I tried to wean him from writing – oh, ever so gently, you understand, by throwing him with agreeable people, giving him a chance to make himself felt, to come to a sense of what he *really* had to give. I'd foreseen this solution from the beginning – felt sure that, once the first ardor of authorship was quenched, he'd drop into his place as a charming parasitic thing, the kind of chronic Cherubino for whom, in old societies, there's always a seat at table, and a shelter behind the ladies' skirts. I saw him take his place as 'the poet': the poet who doesn't write. One knows the type in every drawing room. Living in that way doesn't cost much – I'd worked it all out in my mind, and felt sure that, with a little help, he could manage it for the next few years; and meanwhile he'd be sure to marry. I saw him married to a widow, rather older, with a good cook and a well-run house. And I actually had my eye on the widow...Meanwhile I did everything to facilitate the transition – lent him money to ease his conscience, introduced him to pretty women to make him forget his vows. But nothing would do him: he had but one idea in his beautiful obstinate head. He wanted the laurel and not the rose, and he kept on repeating Gautier's axiom, and battering and filing at his limp prose till he'd spread it out over Lord knows how many thousand sloppy pages. Now and then he would send a pailful to a publisher, and of course it would always come back.

"At first it didn't matter – he thought he was 'misunderstood'. He took the attitudes of genius, and whenever an opus came home he wrote another to keep it company. Then he had a reaction of despair, and accused me of deceiving him, and Lord knows what. I got angry at that, and told him it was he who had deceived himself. He'd come to me determined to write, and I'd done my best to help him. That was the extent of my offence, and I'd done it for his cousin's sake, not his.

"That seemed to strike home, and he didn't answer for a minute. Then he said: 'My time's up and my money's up. What do you think I'd better do?'

"'I think you'd better not be an ass,' I said.

"He turned red, and asked: 'What do you mean by being an ass?'

"I took a letter from my desk and held it out to him.

"'I mean refusing this offer of Mrs. Ellinger's: to be her secretary at a salary of five thousand dollars. There may be a lot more in it than that.'

"He flung out his hand with a violence that struck the letter from mine. 'Oh, I know well enough what's in it!' he said, scarlet to the roots of his hair.

"'And what's your answer, if you know?' I asked.

"He made none at the minute, but turned away slowly to the door. There, with his hand on the threshold, he stopped to ask, almost under his breath: 'Then you really think my stuff's no good?'

"I was tired and exasperated, and I laughed. I don't defend my laugh – it was in wretched taste. But I must plead in extenuation that the boy was a fool, and that I'd done my best for him – I really had.

"He went out of the room, shutting the door quietly after him. That afternoon I left for Frascati, where I'd promised to spend the Sunday with some friends. I was glad to escape from Gilbert, and by the same token, as I learned that night, I had also escaped from the eyes. I dropped into the same lethargic sleep that had come to me before when their visitations ceased; and when I woke the next morning, in my peaceful painted room above the ilexes, I felt the utter weariness and deep relief that always followed on that repairing slumber. I put in two blessed nights at Frascati, and when I got back to my rooms in Rome I found that Gilbert had gone…Oh, nothing tragic had happened – the episode never rose to *that*. He'd simply packed his manuscripts and left for America – for his family and the Wall Street desk. He left a decent little note to tell me of his decision, and behaved altogether, in the circumstances, as little like a fool as it's possible for a fool to behave…"

Chapter IV

CULWIN paused again, and again Frenham sat motionless, the dusky contour of his young head reflected in the mirror at his back.

"And what became of Noyes afterward?" I finally asked, still disquieted by a sense of incompleteness, by the need of some connecting thread between the parallel lines of the tale.

Culwin twitched his shoulders. "Oh, nothing became of him – because he became nothing. There could be no question of 'becoming' about it. He vegetated in an office, I believe, and finally got a clerkship in a consulate, and married drearily in China. I saw him once in Hong Kong, years afterward. He was fat and hadn't shaved. I was told he drank. He didn't recognize me."

"And the eyes?" I asked, after another pause which Frenham's continued silence made oppressive.

Culwin, stroking his chin, blinked at me meditatively through the shadows. "I never saw them after my last talk with Gilbert. Put two and two together if you can. For my part, I haven't found the link."

He rose stiffly, his hands in his pockets, and walked over to the table on which reviving drinks had been set out.

"You must be parched after this dry tale. Here, help yourself, my dear fellow. Here, Phil—" He turned back to the hearth.

Frenham still sat in his low chair, making no response to his host's hospitable summons. But as Culwin advanced toward him, their eyes met in a long look; after which, to my intense surprise, the young man, turning suddenly in his seat, flung his arms across the table, and dropped his face upon them.

Culwin, at the unexpected gesture, stopped short, a flush on his face.

"Phil – what the deuce? Why, have the eyes scared *you?* My dear boy – my dear fellow – I never had such a tribute to my literary ability, never!"

He broke into a chuckle at the thought, and halted on the hearth rug, his hands still in his pockets, gazing down in honest perplexity at the youth's bowed head. Then, as Frenham still made no answer, he moved a step or two nearer.

"Cheer up, my dear Phil! It's years since I've seen them – apparently I've done nothing lately bad enough to call them out of chaos. Unless my present evocation of them has made *you* see them; which would be their worst stroke yet!"

His bantering appeal quivered off into an uneasy laugh, and he moved still nearer, bending over Frenham, and laying his gouty hands on the lad's shoulders.

"Phil, my dear boy, really – what's the matter? Why don't you answer? *Have* you seen the eyes?"

Frenham's face was still pressed against his arms, and from where I stood behind Culwin I saw the latter, as if under the rebuff of this unaccountable attitude, draw back slowly from his friend. As he did so, the light of the lamp on the table fell full on his perplexed congested face, and I caught its sudden reflection in the mirror behind Frenham's head.

Culwin saw the reflection also. He paused, his face level with the mirror, as if scarcely recognizing the countenance in it as his own. But as he looked his expression gradually changed, and for an appreciable space of time he and the image in the glass confronted each other with a glare of slowly gathering hate. Then Culwin let go of Frenham's shoulders, and drew back a step, covering his eyes with his hands...

Frenham, his face still hidden, did not stir.

Amazing Patsy

Valerie B. Williams

"GRANNY, they did it again," Patsy wailed. Her light blonde hair dripped with a sticky orange liquid. Fanta.

"Come here, child." I motioned her to the farmhouse sink and dunked her head under running water, combing her hair with my fingers. "Kids were mean to me when I was your age. Your Mama too, God rest her soul."

"Why do they hate us?" Her pale blue eyes begged for an answer. At eight, she was three years older than I'd been when I heard the Story. It was time. Past time.

With a towel wrapped around her wet hair, she looked like a miniature version of her mother, Ellen. My heart ached at the memory of my daughter covering her bald head with colorful turbans, pretending that she was fine, all the while wasting away. Patsy, a wise child, played along. I delayed telling her the Story in the hope of preserving just a few more years of childhood and innocence. Enough of those years had been stolen by her mother's illness and lingering death. I'd raised Patsy since she was five years old.

We faced each other across the kitchen table, she with a mug of hot chocolate, me with a cup of coffee sweetened with a shot of Jack Daniels for courage.

"Honey, you know how I always tell you you're special?"

She smiled. "All grannies say that."

"That may well be, and I'm guilty as charged. But you really are special, just like your Mama was and like I am. All the way back to my Great Granny Maude." I covered her small hand with mine. "You're going to be the sixth Charmer in the family."

She furrowed her brow. "What *is* that? How does it work? Charmer? Will it work on them mean Wilkins sisters?"

I smiled and held up both hands. "Whoa, give me a chance to tell you! It doesn't work on people."

I took a long swallow from my mug, inhaling the sweet smell of Jack Daniels and feeling its warmth slide down my throat. My granddaughter's reaction to the Story would guide both our futures.

"One girl in each generation of our family is able to charm Bloody Cane Toads."

She shook her head. "Miss McCarthy says Bloody Cane Toads aren't real, someone made 'em up to scare kids away from Big Cypress Swamp."

"Teachers aren't as smart as they think they are. Sometimes old knowledge is the best knowledge."

Patsy looked skeptical.

"My Great Granny Maude was the first Charmer. She lived in the old homestead."

The old homestead was right on the edge of the Swamp. Nothing more than a shotgun shack, constantly-open windows served as air conditioning. Screens added by my father kept bugs out, but constant heat pressed down like a soggy blanket.

"Great Granddaddy Ralph worked the cane fields. His boss got the bright idea to bring in a new kind of Cane Toad from South America. Now, you know how big regular Cane Toads are."

"Big as Daddy's hand!" She put her fingers and thumbs together to outline how big she remembered his hands were. When Ellen had gotten sick, Patsy's Daddy had up and disappeared.

"That's right, honey." I didn't discourage her talking about her Daddy, but I didn't encourage it either.

"Well, these new toads were half again as big, and meaner. Some folks said they were part piranha. The company brought 'em in to eat the pests in the cane fields. And boy did they do the job – they ate mice, lizards, small frogs, birds, as well as the cane beetles. The new toads not only had poison in their skin, but poison glands near their mouths as well. And they had two rows of tiny pointed teeth like the edge of a serrated knife. Maybe they were part-piranha." I laughed, and Patsy laughed with me though it wasn't really funny. Nerves I guess.

I continued. "Eventually the toads ran out of food and moved on."

"Moved on?" asked Patsy. She wore a chocolate moustache from her drink. I motioned to her and she knuckled her hand across her mouth, leaving a small smear on her left cheek.

"Yes, but it took a while for the company to realize that. The toads moved at night and rested during the day, so no one saw them travel. Another difference from regular Cane Toads, besides being bigger and having a dark red belly."

"You mean a Bloody belly."

"Folks only added 'Bloody' after the first incident. Scarier."

Her eyes widened but she kept quiet.

"Great Granddaddy Ralph was the first to see a knot of 'em. That's what a group of toads is called, a knot," I added in response to her puzzled look. "It was January, so it got dark earlier. He and his partner, Billy, were walking out of the fields after their shift when they saw them. Ralph said it looked like an ocean of enormous toads covering the path, hopping over and on top of each other. The men froze twenty feet away. A small swamp deer leapt from the cypresses, landed in the middle of the knot, then let out a scream. Ralph said he'd never heard a deer scream like that. The toads latched onto the deer's belly and legs, pulling it down until it disappeared under a thrashing blanket of warty bodies. A noise like rubbing sandpaper filled the air as they pushed each other aside to feed. In minutes, the deer was nothing but bones and the toads moved away from the men into the swamp."

"Weren't they scared?" Patsy hugged herself and shivered.

"Of course they were. And they were lucky, too. The toads weren't interested in them, at least not that day."

"Was that when people started to call the toads 'Bloody?'"

"Not yet. When Ralph and Billy reported what they'd seen, the boss didn't believe them. Said they must have had some 'shine in their lunch buckets." I poured myself another coffee, with a generous dollop of Jack Daniels.

"Ralph invited Billy over for supper the next week. While Maude was cleaning up the kitchen, the men stepped into the back yard for cigars. She heard a horrible ruckus and ran to the door where she saw giant toads covering Billy to the waist, with more climbing him like he was a tree. A couple of them spattered in blood hopped off with big chunks of torn flesh in their mouths and more climbed on. Billy screamed 'Get 'em off, get 'em off!' while Ralph swatted at the toads with a shovel, knocking one off only to have two more latch on. Ralph's feet and ankles were covered with toads. He stood on one leg to shake them off the other and almost fell, finally pushing himself back up with the shovel and limping toward Billy.

Maude didn't know what to do. Then she knew exactly what to do, like she was following an order from God. She started singing."

I broke into the song she sang that night. "Amazing Grace, how sweet the sound...."

"Singing?" Patsy scrunched her face. "That wouldn't do any good."

"It was the best thing, the only thing, she could have done. The toads fell off both men, faced Maude, and sat in front of her like well-behaved schoolchildren. Still singing, she walked slowly into the cypresses with the knot following. When she returned singing the last line, 'Than when we've first begun,' there wasn't a toad in sight."

The child's mouth hung open. "What happened to Great Granddaddy Ralph and Billy?"

I shook my head. "Billy died. Great Granddaddy Ralph never worked again. The docs had to amputate his left foot to save him, and he walked with crutches the rest of his life."

"Did anyone try to hunt the toads?"

"Nobody believed the story. Then the tests came back as a match for Cane Toad poison and the bites were the right size for Bloody Cane Toads. But they still didn't believe that Maude had charmed them away, said the toads must have left on their own."

Patsy rested her chin on her hands. "So, anyone could get rid of the toads just by singing 'Amazing Grace?'"

"It's not the song, honey, it's the singer. One of the nurses got to talking about what happened and the story grew. Sure enough, some fool had to test it. Cissy Woodburn went into the Swamp on a dare from her sorority sisters. They heard her start to sing 'Amazing Grace', but when the song turned to screams they ran for their lives. Never found a trace of Cissy."

"How did Granny Maude know she had to sing?"

"It came over her, like a vision, she said. She could no sooner have stopped herself than she could have stopped a runaway train."

"Did she keep singing 'Amazing Grace' to the toads?"

"Yes. Yes, she did. She said the song had been given to her and it wasn't her place to change it. But when she taught my granny how to charm, she told her to be open to receiving her own song. And that's how it's been ever since."

"You sing 'Imagine' all the time. Is that your toad-charming song?"

I shrugged. "That's what I was given. Good thing I like it."

I'd been thrilled when I received that song – it was my favorite at the time. Although sometimes I do wish I'd been given a backup.

Patsy bounced in her chair. All the singing she'd heard from me and her Mama now made sense. "Was Mama's song 'I'll Stand By You?'"

"It was, but she didn't really like it. She kept trying new ones but had to fall back to the one she'd been given."

"I hope I get 'Hello', I'll never get sick of it." She thought for a minute, then looked up at me with a solemn expression. "But no one ever sees the Toads. Are they even alive anymore?"

"You'll see tonight."

"Tonight?" Her big grin was like the sun coming out from behind the clouds.

A less special child would have been terrified, but Patsy was excited. Since Ellen died, I'd carried out the inherited duties by myself. But Ellen hadn't been as strong a

Charmer as me, even before she got sick. Patsy reminded me of myself at her age. She would be a natural.

That night I strode into Big Cypress Swamp, hand-in-hand with my granddaughter. She screamed in terror at her first sight of the knot, while I admired the undulating ocean of grays, greens, and browns, with the occasional flash of a red belly. When a toad touched her bare foot, her screaming changed to a single held note – D. Then the note rose to a G, and the beautiful sounds of 'Amazing Grace' poured forth.

I remained silent with tears streaming, nearly breathless with pride. The knot turned its focus to Patsy as she completed her song. I'll never forget her look of complete elation. The flash of self-importance I also saw worried me, though. I'd felt the same when I first learned to Charm, and it had led to an unspeakable act.

"I wish it had been 'Hello'," she said as we walked out of the swamp.

"You should be proud to receive 'Amazing Grace'. Granny Maude must be looking out for you." I swallowed hard to rid myself of the lump in my throat.

"Don't like hymns." She kicked at the dirt, then gave me a determined look. "Granny, I want to practice, even if I don't like the song. Can we do this again tomorrow?"

After a month, I felt confident she could handle this as my partner. She insisted on going to the Swamp every night, even when she was tired from school. I agreed, but only if she kept up with her homework. As I'd suspected, the toads responded to her like she was their Mama. One night while she was still singing, I broke into my Charming song. A few toads hopped toward me, but most remained mesmerized by the strong voice coming from the small girl.

I told her about Sheriff Gainer. There'd been a Sheriff Gainer in town since Maude and Ralph's time. The job seemed as much a legacy for the Gainers as Charming toads was for us. Sheriff Gainer contacted us whenever there was a need for 'toad relocation', and thus kept both the incidents and the rumors to a minimum.

The better Patsy got at Charming toads, the more confidence she gained. She stopped coming home crying about the mean Wilkins sisters, and in fact, made friends with them. They really were nice girls when you got to know them, always called me 'ma'am'. The sisters were fascinated with Patsy and mimicked her singing, filling the house with a chorus of sweet girlish voices singing that great hymn.

When she wanted to picnic near the Swamp with her new best friends, I didn't object. Patsy had matured so much since taking on the mantle of Charmer. Besides, the toads didn't come out during the day and she could keep them all safe. The girls always returned from their outings laughing and holding hands and seemed to have a wonderful time.

Late this afternoon the three girls went off to play, as usual. Patsy returned alone and told me the sisters walked straight home since they were late for piano lessons.

"It was a great day, Granny, best ever!" With her face flushed pink and her pale blue eyes shining, she was the most beautiful little girl in the world.

She skipped into the back yard to play with her new puppy. The older dog, Silas, had slipped his leash a couple weeks ago while Patsy was walking him near the Swamp and had never come home. I was sure a gator had gotten him, and she'd been inconsolable until I brought Rufus home.

The phone rang.

"Mrs. Wilkins, how are you? No, the girls left here directly." My heart started racing as pieces fell into place. Silas had been old, and Patsy complained he was no fun anymore. I looked out the window to watch my granddaughter playing chase with Rufus like she hadn't a care in the world.

"Are you sure they didn't stop for ice cream? I see. I'll let you know if I hear anything."

I hung up the phone and leaned against the wall, fighting a dizzy spell. Memories of Patsy's Daddy flashed before me, his terrified eyes begging me to save him as a toad latched onto his tongue, cutting him off in mid-scream. After the toads covered him completely, I'd returned home to fix dinner for my daughter and granddaughter.

I walked to the back door on shaky legs and stopped to steady my breathing. Pasting on a smile, I pushed open the screen and stepped onto the porch.

"Patsy, honey. We need to talk."

The Hollow Tree

Nemma Wollenfang

IT IS QUICK. I'll give you that. You don't hesitate or draw it out. Stealth is your ally as you slip up behind me while I chop peppers in the kitchen, place your hands around my neck and…

One, quick, SNAP!

After that first searing flash of pain there is nothing. I don't feel the knife fall from my fingers. I don't feel my body slump in a graceless heap. I don't feel. Glassy eyes observe as you calmly switch off the hob, take the water off boil, and lay out a length of black plastic.

You prepared, it seems. My diligent husband, ever the pragmatist.

It is only as you drag my limp weight through the back yard that a semblance of 'me' begins to return. It comes in degrees. Like waking from deep sleep. I hear the scrape of tarp over grass, I smell the musk of damp earth, I recognize your huff of exertion with every tug. At the same time I am not a part of it, just some spectral observer, as intangible as air. Aware but unfeeling. There is nothing left *to* feel; no pulsing heart, no breath. Only dim apathy. Flesh falls away, the world expands below. Unsheathed, I rise up. Float like a balloon.

The hollow oak at the periphery of our land is where you take my body; the one at the border of the forest that is gnarled and knotted, stooped like an old crone, and ancient as time itself. It hides the evidence well; an encompassing ring of bark that conceals all you store inside from prying eyes – the mottling skin, the broken bones, shielded from the world.

From my strange new vantage I see more than I ever have. More than I ever wished to. You don't even dig down. Apparently I'm not worth the effort. All you do is cramp and stomp. I don't want to see this. My body brutalized. Then, wiping your hands, you return to our house to finish your beer.

Something snags. A hook, a thread and anchor to what lies below. And there I stay – tethered, somehow, to that lifeless cadaver. An incorporeal being with no fleshly boundaries to divide me from the air. Hazy, immobile, uncaring. Floating. All I can do is watch the stars dim overhead as the sun chases away the moon. How can one watch without the use of eyes? Those are the body's apparatus. With easy detachment, apparently. I watch as you take away a suitcase of my belongings the next day and remove my car. I watch as you call work to tell them I'm sick. I watch as time rolls by. Nothing changes. Everything continues on seamlessly. As if I was nothing more than a blip. Has my presence meant so little?

Work doesn't even quibble over my absence. Which makes me wonder…How will the plants in my lab survive? Will anyone tend them? My work area is secluded; a room at the building's rear. I always preferred it that way but now…None of the technicians will venture in there. No one will notice as they shrivel and crisp, deprived of water. My poor fern, an *Osmunda claytoniana*, in the window with the sun's full blast, will be the first to go. I spent my entire career battling my way up, fighting for my doctorate, scraping that professorship, championing the Amazon. *Desperate* to help plants, save the planet. To reach a position that would make a difference. How utterly naive. In the end, I couldn't even save myself.

Around me, the birches seem to wilt in commiseration. I always did relate better to vegetation than people. Perhaps that's why I didn't see you for what you are – parasitic, strangling ivy.

Neighbors do start to wonder after a while. I hear their whispers. And eventually some come by. "Violet's left me," you say. "Gone to her mother's." You even manage a few tears, reptilian though they are. With such heartfelt anguish, with your pain on show, none doubt your sincerity. There isn't even an investigation. What a sly, canny creature you are. Believable. Slithering your way around each query with such faultless precision…

…while all the bones of my body are picked clean of every wet slither of flesh.

People may not know what you placed in this tree but the worms do, and the beetles and the flies. Little rodents gnaw, tiny teeth chipping into bone. Crows strip away sloughing muscle, while songbirds pilfer tangles of hair to line their nests. And the creeping roots of the oak seek out and pry apart a rapidly hollowing torso to envelop the decaying heart within.

But that's okay; their embraces mean more than yours ever did. They are welcome; an acceptance of sorts, into their fold. Knowing that my matter cycles on brings a kind of peace. One that may have coaxed whatever phantom remains of me to drift away into oblivion…

If not for *her*. Alis.

She's exuberant, she's spry. Bursting with energy. Those elfin features, that pixie-cut hair, those big bright eyes. So childlike…Her appearance jars me back; seeing her smile as she clutches your arm. You lead her under the porch and into our house.

I learn a lot, listening in – about her humdrum background, her non-existent social life. Clearly, no one has ever charmed her like you have.

In some ways she's a lot like me. Only less shy.

More of my previous self stirs. I begin to…care. Care about who she is, her doe-like innocence, her lack of family. Care about why you brought her home, what it means.

From some unknown reserve, I find the strength to follow the thread back down. To watch. And wait. There's no mention of a previous wife and you don't take long to propose. You're married for three months – less than we were – before I start to notice a change. Small things, oddities *I* disregarded before – a tick in your cheek whenever she laughs, a twitch of your fingers whenever she calls you 'pookie'. Like there's an irritant beneath your skin, an itch that cannot be scratched. It builds, and eventually it overwhelms. From within the tree I have to watch that hellish night play out again, a helpless observer to the poor girl's terror, because this time she sees you coming. This time she recognizes the darkness in your eyes.

I strain towards her with fingers of air, no longer apathetic but crackling with the need to stop you! But I'm impotent in my nothingness, as weak as a newborn. Weaker, with no body. That does not stop me from trying. From pushing and pushing, goaded on by her cries.

"Please don't! Stop this!"

That's when I feel it, the faintest brush. Connecting life…Ivy vines. *Hedera helix.*

The name dances out from the remnants of my subconscious. Known, ingrained. Their tiny roots plaster the outer bark of my tree in pinprick strips. There's strength in them, in all of the surrounding foliage. A network of it. Untapped but ripe for the taking. I can feel it, touch it, *use* it…I think. Knowledge unfurls like a fern leaf, my botanical side re-emerging. I understand how they function, how they're *designed*. I remember. Every stringy fiber and flexing tuber is as familiar to me as my own hands. I stretch…edging outward. My essence fills a leaf-bud, moves in it. Can I move in the roots of the oak too? It takes effort, sheer will, but yes, I can. And I know oaks, I've studied *Quercus robur*. Their root systems spread far and wide, branching secretly in all directions, including the one that matters most. They reach all the way to our house, to her. Unfortunately, the discovery comes too late.

"I'll tell anyone who asks that we weren't a good match," you say when it's done. "That you were just someone I met on the rebound. We broke up. Perfectly understandable."

You toss her into the lake. Perhaps, on some unacknowledged level, sensing that the tree is no longer yours to trespass upon. Perhaps you don't want her within my reach – no solace for us, no companionship, even in death. Or perhaps you just like somewhere fresh.

Whatever the reason, it does not matter, because the roots of the hollow oak reach even there, burrowing, peeking through the cloudy silt of the lakebed and waving in the water. I can feel them, now I know what to feel for, tangling with the waxy greenery – the water lilies and the algae, the cattails and the pondweeds. *Nymphaea, Spirogyra, Typha, Lemna.* Every plant is linked and I experiment with my newfound extremities by winnowing down the branching lines. Slow at first, then fast. Learning them, making them my own as I go. From dry dirt rhizomes to slimy filamentous masses. Until I reach her. Beneath the cooling hunks of meat, deep inside, something still remains. She's a quivering, curled up ball of nictating energy, half burnt out. I touch her, and she knows me then, your second wife. Once the shock and the panic subside we embrace in what limited way we can. Twin souls on the lakebed.

I take her from you and make her my sister. And as we commune the fear mellows, sloughing away from her like a shed husk. The water swirls, filling her body, saturating her skin, embracing her too, as the watery flora sways and pricks at her with tiny tubers.

It is then that she understands: she is far from alone.

Mother Nature is a dark goddess who protects Her own.

* * *

You have a type. I've seen how you select us now. The third bride shares so many of our attributes: the ink-black hair, the dark eyes, the sweet smile. What you don't count on is the wit. This one has a sharp mind, and she sees straight through you, right to the raw truth.

Rose is…unexpected.

Why she married you is a mystery. Your charm perhaps? A whirlwind romance? It had to be something blinding, a moment of madness, because she's too strong-willed for you – a lawyer. Not your usual meek and subservient type. This time you chose imperfectly. Alis and I smile at your expense; our humor a brush of wind against the windows. But with the way she's starting to ask questions I can hazard a guess you won't be married much longer.

You'll be thrice the widower yet.

It happens on a Tuesday night. You approach her from behind once she's drowsy from two glasses of merlot. She fights, you don't expect that. The shock on your face is clear. For a moment we brace…When her nails tear rivulets down your cheeks Alis is certain she'll win.

Then you grab the bottle and bring it down with force.

It's a sad day when she joins our ranks.

This time, you opt for fire. Making a leafy pyre in the guise of yard-burning.

By the time the sun crests the horizon, all that remains is glittering black ash and charred bone. With a shovel, you spread that beneath the briar on the eastern lawn, the farthest spot from the oak and the lake, and after you're done you chuckle as you sniff the roses. Her namesake. Fury, not fear, bristles in those scarlet petals and needle-tipped thorns. Yet she is as powerless as we are now, deprived of all means of vengeance.

All Alis and I can do is reach out in mute consolation – the flora a tether between us all.

* * *

This time when the neighbors query, you tell them she ran off with a work colleague.

No one questions you. Blind acceptance.

I wonder how many more excuses there will be before someone takes notice.

* * *

Power is knowledge, as they say. And I share what I know with my sister-brides. Showing them with thought alone how to move, how to navigate these new forms. Within our wilderness we stretch ourselves, pushing ever further. We sway in grasses, we tangle in roots, we furl and unfurl in delicate fronds. Slowly, learning, *mastering* control.

There's a lantern by Rose's briar; its bracket is nailed to the outer brick wall. You light it now, every night. For some reason you've taken to keeping the garden illuminated at all hours – as if sight in the darkness provides a measure of assurance. Does it? Do you fear what you cannot see? Its orange glow attracts moths; seemingly innocuous, ultimately deadly. In a way it's like you. You were our flame, you drew us in. We were the poor gregarious creatures who unwittingly singed our wings in your vicious fire and fell. All the while you blaze on.

* * *

There's a fourth. Her name is Hope.

It's a cruel joke; that name. As if she has any when wed to you.

Does she know? What you did to us? Is that why this one hides inside? Why she never ventures out to our neglected grove? Perhaps not. Perhaps she's just not the outdoors type. Or perhaps you steer her away. I see you looking, thinking. There's a growing nervousness in your eyes, taking hold like roots, burrowing and anchoring deep. It started when the insects fell silent. Do you sense us? Lingering out here? Do you feel the ire entrenched in the bark of my oak? Do you feel the fury simmering beneath Rose's briar? Do you feel the cool wrath that laps the shores of Alis's lake? I think you do. I think you try to ignore it.

Madness, you tell yourself. It's madness to fear the dead.

One night I roll in close, hitchhiking on the banks of fog that crest against the bricks of our house, a mute caress against our windows. The warmth within is such a contradiction to the arctic chill outside, and the scene I see is one of domestic bliss. On the sofa, you drape your arm around her as she snuggles into your side, content to lounge before the crackling hearth while you watch TV. It's so cozy, so familiar. You did the same with me. And Alis. And Rose. I touch the glass, leaving invisible streaks in the dew. You have no idea I'm there, but that's fine, it's not you I came to see. She's perfect; all bright-eyed grace and bubbling laughter and absolutely *exquisite*. A delightful, happy creature. Innocent in the extreme.

Rain falls, making tiny tracks down the pane – the tears I can no longer cry.

Because I know…to the very depths of my being I know you'll destroy her too.

* * *

She has a brother, a twin. One who clearly cares about her.

"There's something about him that I don't like," he says as soon as he has her alone.

"You don't like any of my men, Hector," she laughs. "You never have."

"That's because they're always sleazebags," he mutters. They're on the back porch, basking in the sunset while you fetch refreshments. After checking it's safe, he whispers, "But there *is* something about him, something off. It's in the eyes…I've spoken to the neighbors. Do you know what they said? That all of his previous wives have gone *missing*."

That riles her, she grows defensive. "That's rubbish, they left him!"

"Are you sure?"

"He loves me," she says quietly.

"Come home," he begs.

Neither reaches a compromise before you return with their drinks.

* * *

None of us had any close friends or caring relations – no one to raise a red flag when we vanished. I wonder now if that was intentional, if you chose us because of it.

Hope has her brother, though. Did you know about him before you wed her? Or was he an unexpected complication? Perhaps his presence will make you more leery.

* * *

The signs start again. The tick is back, the twitches ever-present, sometimes you snap at her for the simplest of things – burning dinner, dropping the mail. The time is coming, I can feel it. We *all* can. And I think, to an extent, she does too. Even if she ignores it.

You don't venture out here anymore. Alis is certain it's because you're afraid. Perhaps you are. Within our green realm we sister-brides flourish. We coil and writhe, span every nuance of plant life. From leaf vein to new sapling to fungal spore. We stretch ourselves far and wide. The yard is ours now, our wild place. We've claimed it and encourage its growth, nurture its chaos, making our wilderness vast and bleak and forbidding. Wind and earth, rain and wood; we're a part of them as much as they are a part of us. Our connection is intangible, something that goes beyond flesh and blood and bone, to the raw essence of life and being. The bark of the oak, its roots and its leaves, are my domain now. As much as the water and reeds are a part of Alis and the ashes and briar are a part of Rose. She can even reach the lantern now, and mingle with its flame, frolicking amongst the sparks. Perhaps it was the manner of her death and disposal but the way she communes with them is almost familial.

There's a power in us three. We're different now. Changed from the meek little wives you knew us to be. With our bodies gone, we've evolved, adapted. Grown stronger; taken on new shapes and forms. Like larvae shedding the confines of cocoons to take wing. Now that Mother Earth has had Her way with us we're visceral, feral as a pack of wolves. Dark in ways even your twisted mind can't possibly comprehend.

No longer do we just have movement within the foliage, we have command.

Of our own emerald army.

Our minds are unfettered, our earthy bonds unbound. All we know we've passed to each other. Every seed of information has blossomed in our minds. And perhaps now, together, we finally have the strength to accomplish what none of us ever managed alone.

* * *

We know you now. We know you well.

So it's no surprise when you turn on her. What sets you off none of us can tell. What we do know is she escapes your clutches long enough to reach the garden.

She fumbles with her phone, fingers clumsy with fright. Eventually she must succeed because a crackly voice answers over the line. "Hello, Hope? You there?"

"Hector, he's…I need…Help me!"

The call alerts you and you find her quickly, cowering beside the briars.

With a scream she drops it and the phone clatters to the ground.

"Hope?" the voice crackles. "What's happening? Hope?!"

You snag her arm, dragging her up and…

A tornado of thorns scours your face, unleashed from the briars Rose now commands. *Rosa kordesii*, those hybrid perennials have the sharpest thorns. Now *you* feel their sting. Throwing up your arms as a shield, you let Hope go and fall back against the lantern. Again, Rose attacks. Lashing out with fingers of fire, clawing your face as she did once before. Through our connection, I can taste her glee, feel her vicious thrill. Her abject jubilance!

It doesn't last. She can't hold you. Swaying and cursing you tear away.

You stumble to the lake to douse your face in the icy water…which swells up, engulfing you. A tidal force shoves itself into your throat as pondweeds tangle about your wrists and ankles. You lurch back, spluttering and coughing, uncomprehending.

And Alis hisses as you break free of her grip too.

Perhaps you're blinded by your anger and the fresh burns and the inexplicable icy assault. Perhaps you just cannot see anything beyond your sopping wet hair. Whatever the case, your one target is her. Nothing else seems to matter.

She's like a fawn before a hunter, all doe-eyed and defenseless with her tear-streaked face. Too fragile for all this.

When you stalk her way, she bolts, seeking shelter inside the hollow oak. *My* oak.

My strong and noble *Quercus robur*.

Her legs tangle and she falls – straight into what's left of me.

One hand crunches through the brittle sternum, splintering ribs. There's little flesh left now but what remains is sticky with rot, the bones beneath stark white. Even in the gloom she knows what she sees, I can tell by the way her tiny gasps turn to whines. Frantically, she wipes her hand in the dirt, vainly trying to rid it of excess ick.

But she's safe here; better protected than out there.

Because this place is *mine*.

Half-blind you follow her. With grasping hands and rage clouding your mind, you charge headlong through the shards of grass and untamed weeds – *Urtica, Rumex, Plantago* – into the depths of my herbaceous lair. Big mistake. Huge. They're only the precursors, an intricately laid web of stationary sentinels, and I am the spider that waits at the heart of them.

Their General and Commander.

It's easy to order them to snag an ankle, it's easy to drop you down. At first you don't even notice, clawing at the dead leaves and uncontrolled grasses, too intent on reaching her. By the time you understand exactly what is happening it's too late. I already have a hold.

Then, it's only a matter of binding...

Alis and Rose winnow towards me via roots and leaves and grass-blades to add their strength too, ensuring you don't escape. When one vine snaps, two more rise to replace it.

Taraxacum, Agrostis, Trifolium, dandelion, bentgrass, clover...we call on them all. Every plant we have ever known. Our collective, deadly arsenal of whipping flora.

If we let you go it won't end. You'll travel somewhere new, start again. With new girls, new wives, new unsuspecting playthings. Another and another and another. The heinous cycle will continue. We can't let that happen. Not again. It's already gone on for too long.

Dandelions tighten, clovers constrict, nettles sting. Barbs of other thorny perennials dig into your skin, gaining purchase and drawing blood. Finally you panic and cry out.

But no one's going to help you.

In the end, it's quick. I give you that one mercy, same as you gave me. I don't hesitate or draw it out. Stealth is *my* ally now as I crawl up along you in rhizomes and creepers and curl around your hips, your torso, your neck, and...One, quick, SNAP!

Instant stillness. All fighting stops.

Your weight droops in our grasp.

But we're not through yet. We command our roots to break the soil, to crack open the earth, and in a shower of grit they rise like living hairs. Our vines and branches willow down in curling spirals to join them. And like a mannequin on strings, we winch you up.

Your fourth wife wavers before you, gaping mutely as she totters in the grass, eyes glassy and uncomprehending.

In the distance there's the roar of a car engine, the screech of wheels. A door slams.

"Hope? HOPE?!" Her twin comes running. Skidding around onto the back lawn, he sees the grisliness of it all – the agitated flames, the frothing lake, the roots and branches still leisurely winding. It takes some time, but eventually he grasps her arm. "Come away, Sis..."

They leave you there, to your fate, strung up by unforgiving ivy, with only the wind to accompany as you sway, limp and lifeless, up in the hollow tree.

You won't join us in the earth. No. You're destined for a much darker place, where oblivion would seem like a kindness.

The Little Room

Madeline Yale Wynne

"HOW WOULD it do for a smoking-room?"

"Just the very place! Only, you know, Roger, you must not think of smoking in the house. I am almost afraid that having just a plain, common man around, let alone a smoking man, will upset Aunt Hannah. She is New England – Vermont New England – boiled down."

"You leave Aunt Hannah to me; I'll find her tender side. I'm going to ask her about the old sea captain and the yellow calico."

"Not yellow calico – blue chintz."

"Well, yellow *shell* then."

"No, no! Don't mix it up so; you won't know yourself what to expect, and that's half the fun."

"Now you tell me again exactly what to expect; to tell the truth, I didn't half hear about it the other day; I was wool-gathering. It was something queer that happened when you were a child, wasn't it?"

"Something that began to happen long before that, and kept happening, and may happen again; but I hope not."

"What was it?"

"I wonder if the other people in the car can hear us?"

"I fancy not; we don't hear them – not consecutively, at least."

"Well, mother was born in Vermont, you know; she was the only child by a second marriage. Aunt Hannah and Aunt Maria are only half-aunts to me, you know."

"I hope they are half as nice as you are."

"Roger, be still; they certainly will hear us."

"Well, don't you want them to know we are married?"

"Yes, but not just married. There's all the difference in the world."

"You are afraid we look too happy!"

"No; only I want my happiness all to myself."

"Well, the little room?"

"My aunts brought mother up; they were nearly twenty years older than she. I might say Hiram and they brought her up. You see, Hiram was bound out to my grandfather when he was a boy, and when grandfather died Hiram said he 's'posed he went with the farm, 'long o' the critters,' and he has been there ever since. He was my mother's only refuge from the decorum of my aunts. They are simply workers. They make me think of the Maine woman who wanted her epitaph to be: 'She was a *hard* working woman.'"

"They must be almost beyond their working-days. How old are they?"

"Seventy, or thereabouts; but they will die standing; or, at least, on a Saturday night, after all the housework is done up. They were rather strict with mother, and I think she had a lonely childhood. The house is almost a mile away from any neighbors, and off on top of what they call Stony Hill. It is bleak enough up there, even in summer.

"When mamma was about ten years old they sent her to cousins in Brooklyn, who had children of their own, and knew more about bringing them up. She stayed there till she was married; she didn't go to Vermont in all that time, and of course hadn't seen her sisters, for they never would leave home for a day. They couldn't even be induced to go to Brooklyn to her wedding, so she and father took their wedding trip up there."

"And that's why we are going up there on our own?"

"Don't, Roger; you have no idea how loud you speak."

"You never say so except when I am going to say that one little word."

"Well, don't say it, then, or say it very, very quietly."

"Well, what was the queer thing?"

"When they got to the house, mother wanted to take father right off into the little room; she had been telling him about it, just as I am going to tell you, and she had said that of all the rooms, that one was the only one that seemed pleasant to her. She described the furniture and the books and paper and everything, and said it was on the north side, between the front and back room. Well, when they went to look for it, there was no little room there; there was only a shallow china-closet. She asked her sisters when the house had been altered and a closet made of the room that used to be there. They both said the house was exactly as it had been built – that they had never made any changes, except to tear down the old woodshed and build a smaller one.

"Father and mother laughed a good deal over it, and when anything was lost they would always say it must be in the little room, and any exaggerated statement was called 'little-roomy'. When I was a child I thought that was a regular English phrase, I heard it so often.

"Well, they talked it over, and finally they concluded that my mother had been a very imaginative sort of a child, and had read in some book about such a little room, or perhaps even dreamed it, and then had 'made believe', as children do, till she herself had really thought the room was there."

"Why, of course, that might easily happen."

"Yes, but you haven't heard the queer part yet; you wait and see if you can explain the rest as easily.

"They stayed at the farm two weeks, and then went to New York to live. When I was eight years old my father was killed in the war, and mother was broken-hearted. She never was quite strong afterwards, and that summer we decided to go up to the farm for three months.

"I was a restless sort of a child, and the journey seemed very long to me; and finally, to pass the time, mamma told me the story of the little room, and how it was all in her own imagination, and how there really was only a china-closet there.

"She told it with all the particulars; and even to me, who knew beforehand that the room wasn't there, it seemed just as real as could be. She said it was on the north side, between the front and back rooms; that it was very small, and they sometimes called it an entry. There was a door also that opened out-of-doors, and that one was painted green, and was cut in the middle like the old Dutch doors, so that it could be used for a window by opening the top part only. Directly opposite the door was a lounge or couch; it was covered with blue chintz – India chintz – some that had been brought over by an old Salem sea captain as a 'venture'. He had given it to Hannah when she was a young girl. She was sent to Salem for two years to school. Grandfather originally came from Salem."

"I thought there wasn't any room or chintz."

"*That is just it.* They had decided that mother had imagined it all, and yet you see how exactly everything was painted in her mind, for she had even remembered that Hiram had told her that Hannah could have married the sea captain if she had wanted to!

"The India cotton was the regular blue stamped chintz, with the peacock figure on it. The head and body of the bird were in profile, while the tail was full front view behind it. It had seemed to take mamma's fancy, and she drew it for me on a piece of paper as she talked. Doesn't it seem strange to you that she could have made all that up, or even dreamed it?

"At the foot of the lounge were some hanging shelves with some old books on them. All the books were leather-colored except one; that was bright red, and was called the *Ladies' Album.* It made a bright break between the other thicker books.

"On the lower shelf was a beautiful pink sea-shell, lying on a mat made of balls of red shaded worsted. This shell was greatly coveted by mother, but she was only allowed to play with it when she had been particularly good. Hiram had shown her how to hold it close to her ear and hear the roar of the sea in it.

"I know you will like Hiram, Roger; he is quite a character in his way.

"Mamma said she remembered, or *thought* she remembered, having been sick once, and she had to lie quietly for some days on the lounge; then was the time she had become so familiar with everything in the room, and she had been allowed to have the shell to play with all the time. She had had her toast brought to her in there, with make-believe tea. It was one of her pleasant memories of her childhood; it was the first time she had been of any importance to anybody, even herself.

"Right at the head of the lounge was a light-stand, as they called it, and on it was a very brightly polished brass candlestick and a brass tray, with snuffers. That is all I remember of her describing, except that there was a braided rag rug on the floor, and on the wall was a beautiful flowered paper – roses and morning-glories in a wreath on a light blue ground. The same paper was in the front room."

"And all this never existed except in her imagination?"

"She said that when she and father went up there, there wasn't any little room at all like it anywhere in the house; there was a china-closet where she had believed the room to be."

"And your aunts said there had never been any such room."

"That is what they said."

"Wasn't there any blue chintz in the house with a peacock figure?"

"Not a scrap, and Aunt Hannah said there had never been any that she could remember; and Aunt Maria just echoed her – she always does that. You see, Aunt Hannah is an up-and-down New England woman. She looks just like herself; I mean, just like her character. Her joints move up and down or backward and forward in a plain square fashion. I don't believe she ever leaned on anything in her life, or sat in an easy-chair. But Maria is different; she is rounder and softer; she hasn't any ideas of her own; she never had any. I don't believe she would think it right or becoming to have one that differed from Aunt Hannah's, so what would be the use of having any? She is an echo, that's all.

"When mamma and I got there, of course I was all excitement to see the china-closet, and I had a sort of feeling that it would be the little room after all. So I ran ahead and threw open the door, crying, "Come and see the little room.""

"And Roger," said Mrs. Grant, laying her hand in his, "there really was a little room there, exactly as mother had remembered it. There was the lounge, the peacock chintz, the green door, the shell, the morning-glory, and rose paper, *everything exactly as she had described it to me.*"

"What in the world did the sisters say about it?"

"Wait a minute and I will tell you. My mother was in the front hall still talking with Aunt Hannah. She didn't hear me at first, but I ran out there and dragged her through the front room, saying, 'The room *is* here – it is all right.'

"It seemed for a minute as if my mother would faint. She clung to me in terror. I can remember now how strained her eyes looked and how pale she was.

"I called out to Aunt Hannah and asked her when they had had the closet taken away and the little room built; for in my excitement I thought that that was what had been done.

"'That little room has always been there,' said Aunt Hannah, 'ever since the house was built.'

"'But mamma said there wasn't any little room here, only a china-closet, when she was here with papa,' said I.

"'No, there has never been any china-closet there; it has always been just as it is now,' said Aunt Hannah.

"Then mother spoke; her voice sounded weak and far off. She said, slowly, and with an effort, 'Maria, don't you remember that you told me that there had *never been any little room here?* And Hannah said so too, and then I said I must have dreamed it?'

"'No, I don't remember anything of the kind,' said Maria, without the slightest emotion. 'I don't remember you ever said anything about any china-closet. The house has never been altered; you used to play in this room when you were a child, don't you remember?'

"'I know it,' said mother, in that queer slow voice that made me feel frightened. 'Hannah, don't you remember my finding the china-closet here, with the gilt-edged china on the shelves, and then *you* said that the *china-closet* had always been here?'

"'No,' said Hannah, pleasantly but unemotionally – 'no, I don't think you ever asked me about any china-closet, and we haven't any gilt-edged china that I know of.'

"And that was the strangest thing about it. We never could make them remember that there had ever been any question about it. You would think they could remember how surprised mother had been before, unless she had imagined the whole thing. Oh, it was so queer! They were always pleasant about it, but they didn't seem to feel any interest or curiosity. It was always this answer: 'The house is just as it was built; there have never been any changes, so far as we know.'

"And my mother was in an agony of perplexity. How cold their gray eyes looked to me! There was no reading anything in them. It just seemed to break my mother down, this queer thing. Many times that summer, in the middle of the night, I have seen her get up and take a candle and creep softly downstairs. I could hear the steps creak under her weight. Then she would go through the front room and peer into the darkness, holding her thin hand between the candle and her eyes. She seemed to think the little room might vanish. Then she would come back to bed and toss about all night, or lie still and shiver; it used to frighten me.

"She grew pale and thin, and she had a little cough; then she did not like to be left alone. Sometimes she would make errands in order to send me to the little room for something – a book, or her fan, or her handkerchief; but she would never sit there or let me stay in there long, and sometimes she wouldn't let me go in there for days together. Oh, it was pitiful!"

"Well, don't talk any more about it, Margaret, if it makes you feel so," said Mr. Grant.

"Oh yes, I want you to know all about it, and there isn't much more – no more about the room.

"Mother never got well, and she died that autumn. She used often to sigh, and say, with a wan little laugh, 'There is one thing I am glad of, Margaret: your father knows now all about the little room.' I think she was afraid I distrusted her. Of course, in a child's way, I thought there was something queer about it, but I did not brood over it. I was too young then, and took it as a part of her illness. But, Roger, do you know, it really did affect me. I almost hate to go there after talking about it; I somehow feel as if it might, you know, be a china-closet again."

"That's an absurd idea."

"I know it; of course it can't be. I saw the room, and there isn't any china-closet there, and no gilt-edged china in the house, either."

And then she whispered: "But, Roger, you may hold my hand as you do now, if you will, when we go to look for the little room."

"And you won't mind Aunt Hannah's gray eyes?"

"I won't mind *anything*."

It was dusk when Mr. and Mrs. Grant went into the gate under the two old Lombardy poplars and walked up the narrow path to the door, where they were met by the two aunts.

Hannah gave Mrs. Grant a frigid but not unfriendly kiss; and Maria seemed for a moment to tremble on the verge of an emotion, but she glanced at Hannah, and then gave her greeting in exactly the same repressed and non-committal way.

Supper was waiting for them. On the table was the *gilt-edged china*. Mrs. Grant didn't notice it immediately, till she saw her husband smiling at her over his teacup; then she felt fidgety, and couldn't eat. She was nervous, and kept wondering what was behind her, whether it would be a little room or a closet.

After supper she offered to help about the dishes, but, mercy! She might as well have offered to help bring the seasons round; Maria and Hannah couldn't be helped.

So she and her husband went to find the little room, or closet, or whatever was to be there.

Aunt Maria followed them, carrying the lamp, which she set down, and then went back to the dish-washing.

Margaret looked at her husband. He kissed her, for she seemed troubled; and then, hand in hand, they opened the door. It opened into a *china-closet*. The shelves were neatly draped with scalloped paper; on them was the gilt-edged china, with the dishes missing that had been used at the supper, and which at that moment were being carefully washed and wiped by the two aunts.

Margaret's husband dropped her hand and looked at her. She was trembling a little, and turned to him for help, for some explanation, but in an instant she knew that something was wrong. A cloud had come between them – he was hurt; he was antagonized.

He paused for an appreciable instant, and then said, kindly enough, but in a voice that cut her deeply:

"I am glad this ridiculous thing is ended; don't let us speak of it again."

"Ended!" said she. "How ended?" And somehow her voice sounded to her as her mother's voice had when she stood there and questioned her sisters about the little room. She seemed to have to drag her words out. She spoke slowly: "It seems to me to have only just begun in my case. It was just so with mother when she—"

"I really wish, Margaret, you would let it drop. I don't like to hear you speak of your mother in connection with it. It—" He hesitated, for was not this their wedding day? "It doesn't seem quite the thing, quite delicate, you know, to use her name in the matter."

She saw it all now: *he didn't believe her*. She felt a chill sense of withering under his glance.

"Come," he added, "let us go out, or into the dining room, somewhere, anywhere, only drop this nonsense."

He went out; he did not take her hand now – he was vexed, baffled, hurt. Had he not given her his sympathy, his attention, his belief – and his hand? – and she was fooling him. What did it mean? – she so truthful, so free from morbidness – a thing he hated. He walked up and down under the poplars, trying to get into the mood to go and join her in the house.

Margaret heard him go out; then she turned and shook the shelves; she reached her hand behind them and tried to push the boards away; she ran out of the house on to the north side and tried to find in the darkness, with her hands, a door, or some steps leading to one. She tore her dress on the old rose trees, she fell and rose and stumbled, then she sat down on the ground and tried to think. What could she think – was she dreaming?

She went into the house and out into the kitchen, and begged Aunt Maria to tell her about the little room – what had become of it, when had they built the closet, when had they bought the gilt-edged china?

They went on washing dishes and drying them on the spotless towels with methodical exactness; and as they worked they said that there had never been any little room, so far as they knew; the china-closet had always been there, and the gilt-edged china had belonged to their mother, it had always been in the house.

"No, I don't remember that your mother ever asked about any little room," said Hannah.

"She didn't seem very well that summer, but she never asked about any changes in the house; there hadn't ever been any changes."

There it was again: not a sign of interest, curiosity, or annoyance, not a spark of memory.

She went out to Hiram. He was telling Mr. Grant about the farm. She had meant to ask him about the room, but her lips were sealed before her husband.

Months afterwards, when time had lessened the sharpness of their feelings, they learned to speculate reasonably about the phenomenon, which Mr. Grant had accepted as something not to be scoffed away, not to be treated as a poor joke, but to be put aside as something inexplicable on any ordinary theory.

Margaret alone in her heart knew that her mother's words carried a deeper significance than she had dreamed of at the time. "One thing I am glad of, your father knows now," and she wondered if Roger or she would ever know.

Five years later they were going to Europe. The packing was done; the children were lying asleep, with their traveling things ready to be slipped on for an early start.

Roger had a foreign appointment. They were not to be back in America for some years. She had meant to go up to say goodbye to her aunts; but a mother of three children intends to do a great many things that never get done. One thing she had done that very day, and as she paused for a moment between the writing of two notes that must be posted before she went to bed, she said:

"Roger, you remember Rita Lash? Well, she and Cousin Nan go up to the Adirondacks every autumn. They are clever girls, and I have entrusted to them something I want done very much."

"They are the girls to do it, then, every inch of them."

"I know it, and they are going to."

"Well?"

"Why, you see, Roger, that little room—"

"Oh—"

"Yes, I was a coward not to go myself, but I didn't find time, because I hadn't the courage."

"Oh! *That* was it, was it?"

"Yes, just that. They are going, and they will write us about it."

"Want to bet?"

"No; I only want to know."

Rita Lash and Cousin Nan planned to go to Vermont on their way to the Adirondacks. They found they would have three hours between trains, which would give them time to drive up to the Keys farm, and they could still get to the camp that night. But, at the last minute, Rita was prevented from going. Nan had to go to meet the Adirondack party, and she promised to telegraph her when she arrived at the camp. Imagine Rita's amusement when she received this message: 'Safely arrived; went to the Keys farm; it is a little room.'

Rita was amused, because she did not in the least think Nan had been there. She thought it was a hoax; but it put it into her mind to carry the joke further by really stopping herself when she went up, as she meant to do the next week.

She did stop over. She introduced herself to the two maiden ladies, who seemed familiar, as they had been described by Mrs. Grant.

They were, if not cordial, at least not disconcerted at her visit, and willingly showed her over the house. As they did not speak of any other stranger's having been to see them lately, she became confirmed in her belief that Nan had not been there.

In the north room she saw the roses and morning-glory paper on the wall, and also the door that should open into – what?

She asked if she might open it.

"Certainly," said Hannah; and Maria echoed, "Certainly,"

She opened it, and found the china-closet. She experienced a certain relief; she at least was not under any spell. Mrs. Grant left it a china-closet; she found it the same. Good.

But she tried to induce the old sisters to remember that there had at various times been certain questions relating to a confusion as to whether the closet had always been a closet. It was no use; their stony eyes gave no sign.

Then she thought of the story of the sea captain, and said, "Miss Keys, did you ever have a lounge covered with India chintz, with a figure of a peacock on it, given to you in Salem by a sea captain, who brought it from India?"

"I dun'no' as I ever did," said Hannah. That was all. She thought Maria's cheeks were a little flushed, but her eyes were like a stone wall.

She went on that night to the Adirondacks. When Nan and she were alone in their room she said, "By-the-way, Nan, what did you see at the farmhouse? And how did you like Maria and Hannah?"

Nan didn't mistrust that Rita had been there, and she began excitedly to tell her all about her visit. Rita could almost have believed Nan had been there if she hadn't known it was not so. She let her go on for some time, enjoying her enthusiasm, and the impressive way in which she described her opening the door and finding the 'little room'. Then Rita said: "Now, Nan, that is enough fibbing. I went to the farm myself on my way up yesterday, and there is *no* little room, and there *never* has been any; it is a china-closet, just as Mrs. Grant saw it last."

She was pretending to be busy unpacking her trunk, and did not look up for a moment; but as Nan did not say anything, she glanced at her over her shoulder. Nan was actually pale, and it was hard to say whether she was most angry or frightened. There was something of both in her look. And then Rita began to explain how her telegram had put her in the spirit of going up there alone. She hadn't meant to cut Nan out. She only thought—

Then Nan broke in: "It isn't that; I am sure you can't think it is that. But I went myself, and you did not go; you can't have been there, for *it is a little room!*"

Oh, what a night they had! They couldn't sleep. They talked and argued, and then kept still for a while, only to break out again, it was so absurd. They both maintained that they had been there, but both felt sure the other one was either crazy or obstinate beyond reason. They were wretched; it was perfectly ridiculous, two friends at odds over such a thing; but there it was – 'little room', 'china-closet' – 'china-closet', 'little room'.

The next morning Nan was tacking up some tarlatan at a window to keep the midges out. Rita offered to help her, as she had done for the past ten years. Nan's "No, thanks," cut her to the heart.

"Nan," said she, "come right down from that step-ladder and pack your satchel. The stage leaves in just twenty minutes. We can catch the afternoon express train, and we will go together to the farm. I am either going there or going home. You better go with me."

Nan didn't say a word. She gathered up the hammer and tacks, and was ready to start when the stage came round.

It meant for them thirty miles of staging and six hours of train, besides crossing the lake; but what of that, compared with having a lie lying round loose between them! Europe would have seemed easy to accomplish, if it would settle the question.

At the little junction in Vermont they found a farmer with a wagon full of meal-bags. They asked him if he could not take them up to the old Keys farm and bring them back in time for the return train, due in two hours.

They had planned to call it a sketching trip, so they said, "We have been there before, we are artists, and we might find some views worth taking; and we want also to make a short call upon the Misses Keys."

"Did ye calculate to paint the old *house* in the picture?"

They said it was possible they might do so. They wanted to see it, anyway.

"Waal, I guess you are too late. The *house* burnt down last night, and everything in it."

Biographies & Sources

Gertrude Atherton
The Bell in the Fog
(Originally Published in *The Bell in the Fog and Other Stories*, 1905)
Gertrude Atherton (1857–1948), who also wrote under the pseudonyms 'Frank Lin' and 'Asmodeus', was born in California. She wrote her first novel while living with her husband in the Atherton Mansion in San Francisco. Her family disapproved of her writing, which often featured independent, driven women. After her husband died at sea she moved to New York, and traveled in Europe. Her novel *Black Oxen* (1923) was made into a silent film, and her other supernatural tales include 'The Striding Place', 'The Foghorn' and 'Death and the Woman'.

Ambrose Bierce
An Occurrence at Owl Creek Bridge
(Originally Published in *The San Francisco Examiner*, 1890)
A Vine on a House
(Originally Published in *Cosmopolitan (New York)*, 1905)
Ambrose Bierce (1842–c. 1914) was born in Meigs County, Ohio. He was a famous journalist and author known for writing *The Devil's Dictionary*. After fighting in the American Civil War, Bierce used his combat experience to write stories based on the war, such as in 'An Occurrence at Owl Creek Bridge'. Following the separate deaths of his ex-wife and two of his three children he gained a sardonic view of human nature and earned the name 'Bitter Bierce'. His disappearance at the age of 71 on a trip to Mexico remains a great mystery and continues to spark speculation.

Charles Brockden Brown
Somnambulism: A Fragment
(Originally Published in *The Literary Magazine, and American Register*, 1805)
Charles Brockden Brown (1771–1810) was a significant early author who produced the first American novels to be translated into other European languages. Born to a large Quaker family, Brown was expected to become a lawyer, but instead followed a career in writing and became part of a New York group of intellectuals. His novel *Wieland, or The Transformation* (1798), is generally regarded as the first American Gothic novel, and went on to influence Mary Shelley, Edgar Allan Poe and Nathaniel Hawthorne.

Terri Bruce
Stone Baby
(First Publication)
Terri Bruce is the author of the paranormal/contemporary fantasy *Afterlife* series, which includes *Hereafter* (Afterlife #1) and *Thereafter* (Afterlife #2), and numerous short stories in various anthologies. She has been making up adventure stories for as long as she can remember. Like Anne Shirley, she prefers to make people cry rather than laugh, but is happy if she can do either. She produces strange, hard-to-classify fantasy and science fiction stories that explore the supernatural side of everyday things from beautiful Downeast ME, where she lives with her husband and several cats. Visit her on the web at www.terribruce.net.

George Washington Cable
Jean-ah Poquelin
(Originally Published in *Scribner's Monthly Magazine*, 1875)
The early Southern writer George Washington Cable (1844–1925) was a native of New Orleans, Louisiana. Born to rich slave-owners, Cable's view of society was transformed while serving in the Confederate States Army. He became a writer and journalist opposed to racial injustice. In 1885, Cable and his family moved to Massachusetts after two of his essays, promoting racial equality and denouncing the Jim Crow system, provoked rage among white Southerners. He is known for his realistic depictions of Creole life and the multicultural tensions of post-war New Orleans.

Ramsey Campbell
The Tomb-Herd
(Originally Published in *Crypt of Cthulhu* volume 6, number 1, whole number 43, edited by Robert M. Price. Copyright © 1986 by Ramsey Campbell.)
The Oxford Companion to English Literature describes Ramsey Campbell as 'Britain's most respected living horror writer'. He has been given more awards than any other writer in the field, including the Grand Master Award of the World Horror Convention, the Lifetime Achievement Award of the Horror Writers Association, the Living Legend Award of the International Horror Guild and the World Fantasy Lifetime Achievement Award. In 2015 he was made an Honorary Fellow of Liverpool John Moores University for outstanding services to literature. Among his novels available from Flame Tree Press are *Thirteen Days by Sunset Beach* and *Think Yourself Lucky*. 'The Tomb-Herd' is among his earliest Lovecraftian stories, written when he was fifteen.

Charles W. Chesnutt
Po' Sandy
(Originally Published in *The Conjure Woman*, 1899)
Charles W. Chesnutt (1858–1932) was an African-American writer, lawyer and political activist. He began to write short stories after passing the bar and establishing a successful court-reporting business. His 1887 story 'The Goophered Grapevine' was the first story to be published by an African American in *The Atlantic Monthly*, and they encouraged him to write more. As well as a biography of the abolitionist Frederick Douglass, Chesnutt produced a number of novels that highlighted the complex racial issues in Southern society.

Kate Chopin
Désirée's Baby
(Originally Published in *Vogue*, 1893)
Kate Chopin (1850–1904) was born in St. Louis, Missouri, and later managed several small plantation businesses with her husband in Louisiana. Following the deaths of her husband and mother, Chopin struggled with depression and was encouraged to write. She turned to short stories after a negative reaction to her novel *The Awakening* (1899) and its treatment of female sexuality and motherhood. Now, she is considered an early precursor of feminist Southern writers like Flannery O'Connor, Katherine Anne Porter, Eudora Welty and Tennessee Williams.

E.E.W. Christman
The Dark Presser
(First Publication)

E.E.W. Christman lives in Seattle, WA. Her work has appeared in *RASCAL Magazine*, *New Delta Review*, and Flame Tree Publishing's *Supernatural Horror* anthology. She loves all things horror. Her fiction is deeply influenced by Shirley Jackson, Ursula K. LeGuin, N.K. Jemisin, and John Carpenter movies. She has a bad habit of rewatching *In the Mouth of Madness*. She also likes staying up late at night to play spooky video games instead of sleeping. You can follow her on Twitter @mecha_liz.

Ralph Adams Cram
The Dead Valley
(Originally Published in *Black Spirits and White: A Book of Ghost Stories*, 1895)
Ralph Adams Cram (1863–1942) was born in Hampton Falls, New Hampshire, United States. He wrote a number of fiction stories and was praised by H.P. Lovecraft for his horror. In addition to his work as a writer, Cram was also one of the foremost architects of the Gothic revival in the United States. His influence helped to establish Gothic as the standard style of the period for American college and university buildings.

Stephen Crane
The Monster
(Originally Published in *Harper's Magazine*, 1898)
Poet, novelist and short story writer Stephen Crane (1871–1900) was born in Newark, New Jersey, and started writing at the age of four, becoming an important figure in American literature during his life. His writing is classified as representing naturalism and American realism. His first novel, *Maggie: A Girl on the Streets*, focused on a street prostitute and the struggles she faces. *The Red Badge of Courage* followed a young soldier trying to find reality amongst warfare. Themes throughout Crane's writing include spiritual crises and fear. He was praised by such writers as Ernest Hemingway and is thought to have influenced Modernists.

Emma Dawson
Singed Moths
(Originally Published in *The Argonaut*, before 1896)
Emma Frances Dawson (1839–1926) was an accomplished musician, translator, writer and poet. Although born in New England, she lived most of her life in San Francisco, where most of her stories were set. Ambrose Bierce spoke highly of her work, praising the strong regional identity present in her ghostly fiction. Her supernatural stories were originally published in local magazines and later collected in *An Itinerant House and Other Stories* in 1896.

Monika Elbert
Foreword: American Gothic Short Stories
Monika Elbert, Professor of English and Distinguished University Scholar at Montclair State University, N.J., has published widely on American Gothic, with essays on the Gothic tradition in various authors, such as Hawthorne, Poe, Stowe, Alcott, Spofford, Phelps, Bierce, Jewett, and Wharton. She has co-edited two books on American Gothic: with Wendy Ryden, *Haunting Realities: Naturalist Gothic and American Realism*, University of Alabama Press, 2017, and with Bridget M. Marshall, *Transnational Gothic: Literary and Social Exchanges in the Long Nineteenth Century*, Ashgate, Jan. 2013 (Reprinted by Routledge, 2014). Her edited collection *Nathaniel Hawthorne in Context* (Cambridge University Press) was published in November 2018.

Maxx Fidalgo

Graveyards Full

(First Publication)

Maxx Fidalgo is a 22-year-old queer writer from New Bedford, Massachusetts. This is his first formal publication and he is very excited about it. He enjoys writing about the point where the weird, religious, and occult meet. A New England boy through and through, the region is the backdrop for most of his stories. His influences range from Charles Fort to his Portuguese-Catholic upbringing. Previously, Maxx has published works in Whitman College's student-run magazine *Quarterlife*, including the poem 'We Had It Made' and a flash fiction piece titled 'Part Time Lover'.

Mary E. Wilkins Freeman

Luella Miller

(Originally Published in *Everybody's Magazine*, 1902)

The American author Mary Eleanor Wilkins Freeman (1852–1930) was born in Randolph, Massachusetts. Most of Freeman's works were influenced by her strict childhood, as her parents were orthodox Congregationalists and harbored strong religious views. While working as a secretary for the author Oliver Wendell Holmes, Sr., she was inspired to write herself. Supernatural topics kept catching her attention, and she began to write many short stories with a combination of supernatural and domestic realism, her most famous being 'A New England Nun'. She wrote a number of ghost tales, which were compiled into famous ghost story collections after her death.

Charlotte Perkins Gilman

The Yellow Wallpaper

(Originally Published in *The New England Magazine*, 1892)

Celebrated feminist writer Charlotte Perkins Gilman (1860–1935) was born in Hartford, Connecticut. She is perhaps best remembered as the author of the short story 'The Yellow Wallpaper', which details a woman's descent into madness after she is cooped up in a misguided attempt to restore her to health. The story was a clear indicator of Gilman's views on the restraints of women and related to her own treatment for postpartum depression. She is also notable for having written the utopian novel *Herland*, in which three men stumble across a society composed entirely of women. Gilman's writings are not only engrossing in their own right, but also continue to spark discussion about gender and society.

Ellen Glasgow

The Past

(Originally Published in *Good Housekeeping*, 1920)

The celebrated Southern writer Ellen Glasgow (1873–1945) was born in Virginia, the ninth of what would become ten children in a wealthy family. Glasgow published a number of bestselling novels over her lifetime, as well as poetry, short stories and essays on literary criticism. Her 1941 novel *In This Our Life* won the 1942 Pulitzer Prize for the Novel and was adapted into a Warner Brothers film the same year. She is known for her strong female characters and skillful depictions of the decaying Southern aristocracy.

Nathaniel Hawthorne

The Birthmark

(Originally Published in *The Pioneer*, 1843)

The Minister's Black Veil: A Parable
(Originally Published in *The Token and Atlantic Souvenir*, 1836)
The prominent American writer Nathaniel Hawthorne (1804–64) was born in Salem, Massachusetts. His most famous novel *The Scarlet Letter* helped him become established as a writer in the 1850s. Most of his works were influenced by his friends Ralph Waldo Emerson and Herman Melville, as well as by his extended financial struggles. Hawthorne's works often incorporated a dark romanticism that focused on the evil and sin of humanity. Some of his most famous works detailed supernatural presences or occurrences, as in his *The House of the Seven Gables* as well as many of his short stories.

Joshua Hiles

Old Homeplace
(First Publication)
Joshua Hiles is a life-long resident of the American Midwest. In between trying to be a writer, husband, father and all around good-guy he enjoys travel to Missouri's myriad small towns and the investigation of the mysteries contained therein. He hasn't been haunted, stalked, or even inconvenienced yet but he's holding out hope. His poetry can be found in current and past issues of Alban Lake's *Scifaikuest*. His short fiction has appeared in two Millhaven Press anthologies to date. If you'd like to read more check out *Fierce Tales: Shadow Realms* and the forthcoming *Fierce Tales: Crumbling Empires*.

Washington Irving

The Devil and Tom Walker
(Originally Published *in Tales of a Traveller*, 1824)
Washington Irving (1783–1859) was a famous American author, essayist, biographer and historian born in New York City. He was influenced by his private education and law school studies to begin writing essays for periodicals. Traveling and working all over the globe, Irving established a name for himself with his successful short stories 'Rip Van Winkle' and 'The Legend of Sleepy Hollow'. These works in particular reflected the mischievous and adventurous behavior of his childhood. Years later, Irving lived in Spain as a US Ambassador. He returned to America towards the end of life, where he wrote several successful historical and biographical works including a five-volume biography of George Washington.

Shirley Jackson

My Uncle in the Garden
Reprinted with permission from The Shirley Jackson Estate.
(Originally Published in *Just an Ordinary Day*, 1996)
Often considered 'The Queen of American Gothic', Shirley Jackson (1916–65) was born in California and settled in Vermont with her husband Stanley Edgar Hyman in 1940. Her most famous works include the short story 'The Lottery', and the novels *The Haunting of Hill House* and *We Have Always Lived in the Castle*. Her work has been adapted for the radio, TV, film and stage, and has had a profound influence on modern genre fiction. In recognition of Jackson's legacy, the 'Shirley Jackson Awards' were founded in 2007 to mark outstanding literary achievements in horror, psychological suspense, and the dark fantastic.

Russell James

In the Domain of Doctor Baldwin
(First Publication)

Russell James grew up on Long Island, New York, and spent too much time watching late-night horror. After flying helicopters with the U.S. Army, he now spins twisted tales, including horror thrillers *Dark Inspiration, Q Island*, and *The Playing Card Killer*. His Grant Coleman adventure series covers *Cavern of the Damned, Monsters in the Clouds*, and *Curse of the Viper King*. He resides in sunny Florida. His wife reads his work, rolls her eyes, and says "There is something seriously wrong with you". Visit his website at www.russellrjames.com, follow on Twitter @RRJames14, or say hello at rrj@russellrjames.com.

Sarah Orne Jewett
The Landscape Chamber
(Originally Published in *The Atlantic Monthly*, 1887)
Sarah Orne Jewett (1849–1909) was born in Maine to an old New England family and is principally remembered for her local color work. She published her first story at the age of nineteen, and wrote three novels and several short story collections. *The Country of the Pointed Firs* (1896) consisted of inter-related sketches centering around small-town life, taking the declining fishing villages on the Maine coast as inspiration for their setting.

Grace King
The Story of a Day
(Originally Published in *The Century*, 1893)
The Southern writer Grace King (1851/2–1932) was born in New Orleans, where she spent most of her life. Living in relative poverty after the Civil War, the family nevertheless kept their aristocratic status. King defended the Southern way of life, but is credited for elevating women's lives and voices, black and white, in her work. Her first story, 'Monsieur Motte', was written in response to the popularity of George Washington Cable's works, which had criticized the attitudes of Southern slave-owners.

Clayton Kroh
Baby Girl
(Originally Published in *Penumbra*, 2013)
Clayton Kroh lives in Washington state where he writes fiction and does freelance editing. He grew up in rural eastern Virginia where his Southern Gothic predilections probably find their swampy roots. His work has appeared in *Weird Tales Magazine, Flash Fiction Online, Penumbra*, as well as in multiple game titles such as *EverQuest* and *Magic: The Gathering*. He attended the Odyssey Writing Workshop 2006. Clay can be found on the web at claytonkroh.com, and on Twitter @claytonkroh.

Sean Logan
Viola's Second Husband
(Originally Published in *The New Gothic*, 2013)
Sean Logan's stories have appeared in more than thirty-five publications, including *Black Static, Supernatural Tales, Eulogies II, Twice Upon an Apocalypse* and *Dark Visions Vol. 1*. He lives in northern California with his lovely wife, a giant white Kuvasz and a pair of boy and girl twins on the way. He's currently working on a darkly comic crime novel, and when he's not reading or writing, he enjoys loud music, spicy food, bad movies and good tequila.

H.P. Lovecraft
The Outsider

(Originally Published in *Weird Tales*, 1926)
The Tomb
(Originally Published in *The Vagrant*, 1922)
Master of weird fiction Howard Phillips Lovecraft (1890–1937) was born in Providence, Rhode Island. Featuring unknown and otherworldly creatures, his stories were one of the first to mix science fiction with horror. Plagued by nightmares from an early age, he was inspired to write his dark and strange fantasy tales; the isolation he must have experienced from suffering frequent illnesses can be felt as a prominent theme in his work. Lovecraft inspired many other authors, and his most famous story 'The Call of Cthulhu' has influenced many aspects of popular culture.

Madison McSweeney

The Outsiders in the Hawthorne Tomb
(First Publication)
Madison McSweeney is a Canadian horror and fantasy author. Her short stories have appeared in publications such as *Under the Full Moon's Light, Unnerving Magazine, Women in Horror Annual Vol. 2*, and *Zombie Punks F**k Off*, and her poems have been featured in *Bywords, Cockroach Conservatory*, and *Rhythm & Bones: Dark Marrow*. Her influences include Neil Gaiman, Clive Barker, H.P. Lovecraft, and Stephen King. She lives in Ottawa, Ontario, with her family and her cat.

Lynette Mejía

Big, Bad
(First Publication)
Lynette Mejía writes science fiction, fantasy, and horror prose and poetry from the middle of a deep, dark forest in the wilds of southern Louisiana. Her work has appeared in *Daily Science Fiction, Nature: Futures*, and *Strange Horizons*, among others, and has been nominated for the Pushcart Prize, the Rhysling Award and the Million Writers Award. An avid gardener, she can often be found chatting with trees and conspiring with roses. You can find her online at www.lynettemejia.com.

Herman Melville

Bartleby, the Scrivener: A Story of Wall Street
(Originally Published in *Putnam's Magazine*, 1853)
Herman Melville (1819–91) is the author of the novel *Moby Dick*, which was a commercial failure during his lifetime but is now considered a classic. Born in New York City, Melville enjoyed some years as a successful writer following the publication of his first book *Typee* in 1896. He produced a number of travelogues and nautical works, inspired by his earlier experience as a sailor. During his later years, however, his work fell out of favor and he became largely forgotten until the 1910s and 20s saw a revival of his work.

W.C. Morrow

The Monster-Maker
(Originally Published in *The Ape, the Idiot, and Other People*, 1897)
William Chambers Morrow (1854–1923) was an American author now chiefly remembered for his short horror tales. Raised in Alabama, Morrow went on to run his father's hotel. In 1896, he moved to California and began writing stories for *The Argonaut*. His most famous tale is 'The Unconquerable Enemy', but he also wrote novels such as *Blood-Money* (1882), *A Strange Confession* (serialized in 1880–81), and *A Man; His Mark* (1900).

Joe Nazare
Gothic American
(First Publication)
Joe Nazare's fiction, poetry, and nonfiction has appeared in such places as *Pseudopod, Dark Discoveries, Clowns: The Unlikely Coulrophobia Remix, The Lovecraft eZine, The Zombie Feed – Vol. 1, Star*Line, Grievous Angel,* and *Butcher Knives & Body Counts: Essays on the Formula, Frights, & Fun of the Slasher Film.* He is also the author of the collection *Autumn Lauds: Poems for the Halloween Season.* Dispatches from the Macabre Republic, his blog devoted to American Gothic in literature and culture, is posted at joenazare.com. Joe lives somewhere in the swamps of (New) Jersey.

Wendy Nikel
In the Bleak
(First Publication)
Wendy Nikel is a speculative fiction author residing in Utah with a degree in elementary education, a fondness for road trips, and a terrible habit of forgetting where she's left her cup of tea. Her short fiction has been published by *Daily Science Fiction, Nature: Futures,* and is forthcoming from *Analog* and *Beneath Ceaseless Skies.* Her time travel novella series, beginning with *The Continuum,* is available from World Weaver Press. For more info, visit wendynikel.com.

Christi Nogle
In the Country
(Originally Appeared on the Pseudopod *Artemis Rising* Horror Podcast, 2017)
Christi Nogle's 'In the Country' originally played on the Pseudopod horror podcast with commentary from Faculty of Horror podcasters Andrea Subissati and Alexandra West. Christi's short stories have also appeared in publications such as *Lady Churchill's Rosebud Wristlet, Escape Pod, The Arcanist,* and *Automata Review* along with anthologies such as C.M Muller's *Nightscript III* and *IV* and Unnerving's *Haunted Are These Houses.* Christi is a member of the Horror Writers Association and Codex Writers' Group. She teaches college composition and lives in Boise, Idaho with her partner Jim and their dogs and cats. Follow her on Twitter @christinogle.

Flannery O'Connor
A Good Man Is Hard to Find
Reprinted by permission of Peters Fraser & Dunlop (www.petersfraserdunlop.com) on behalf of the Estate of Flannery O'Connor.
(Originally Published in *A Good Man Is Hard to Find and Other Stories,* 1955)
Flannery O'Connor (1925–64) was one of the most famous Southern Gothic writers. Born in Savannah, Georgia, O'Connor was a devout Roman Catholic, and her work often explored issues of morality. She wrote two novels in her lifetime, *Wise Blood* (1952) and *The Violent Bear It Away* (1960), but it is for her short stories that she is principally known. O'Connor died at the age of thirty-nine from Lupus, a condition she had inherited from her father.

Edgar Allan Poe
Berenice
(Originally Published in *Southern Literary Messenger,* 1835)
The Tell-Tale Heart
(Originally Published in *The Pioneer,* 1843)

The versatile writer Edgar Allan Poe (1809–1849) was born in Boston, Massachusetts. Poe was as an influential author, poet, editor and literary critic that wrote during the American Romantic Movement. Poe is generally considered the inventor of the detective fiction genre, and his works are famously filled with terror, mystery, death and hauntings. Some of his better-known works include his poems 'The Raven' and 'Annabel Lee', and the short stories 'The Tell-Tale Heart' and 'The Fall of the House of Usher'. The dark, mystifying characters of his tales have captured the public's imagination and reflect the struggling, poverty-stricken lifestyle he lived his whole life.

Lina Rather

Baby Teeth

(Originally Published in *Gamut #11*, 2017)

Lina Rather is a speculative fiction author from Michigan, now living in Washington, D.C. She wishes she could say she has a dog, but alas, she lives under the tyranny of landlords. When she isn't writing, she likes to cook, go hiking, and collect terrible 90s comic books. Her work has appeared in a variety of publications, including *Shimmer*, *Flash Fiction Online*, and *Lightspeed*. You can find more about her and her other stories on her website, linarather.wordpress.com. She also spends altogether too much time on Twitter as @LinaRather.

M. Regan

Bibliosmia

(First Publication)

M. Regan has been writing in various capacities for over a decade, with credits ranging from localization work to scholarly reviews, advice columns to short stories. In addition to pieces in a growing number of anthologies, she co-authored a collection of tech-based horror with Caitlin Marceau entitled 'Read-Only'. Deeply fascinated by the fears and maladies personified by monsters, M. Regan enjoys composing dark fiction, studying supernatural creatures, and traveling to places with rich histories of folklore. She presently lives in the Pacific Northwest.

Rebecca Ring

Water Witch

(First Publication)

Rebecca Ring was born in Colorado, came of age in Northern California, married and had children in Quebec, and recently left her teaching career in Utah to be a full-time writer. She has degrees in film and education, a couple of Emmy awards to her name, and an MFA in Writing from the Vermont College of Fine Arts. She enjoys the occasional step away from working on a novel to write short stories. Her work has appeared in *Sediments Literary-Arts Journal*, *The Ghost Story*, and the *21st Century Ghost Stories* anthology.

Mike Robinson

Ring of Teeth

(First Publication)

A writer since age six, Mike Robinson is the author of seven novels: the trilogy *The Enigma of Twilight Falls*, *The Prince of Earth*, *Dreamshores*, *The Atheist*, *Skunk Ape Semester*; and the short story collection *Too Much Dark Matter, Too Little Gray*. A native of Los Angeles, he is also a charter member of The Greater Los Angeles Writers Society, co-editor of its publication Literary Landscapes, and is an active screenwriter/producer with a supernatural mystery feature film, *Blood Corral*, debuting soon. See more at www.mike-robinsonauthor.com.

Annie Trumbull Slosson

Botany Bay

(Originally Published in *Seven Dreamers*, 1890)

Annie Trumbull Slosson (1838–1926) was an American author noted for her local color tales, many of which were published in *Harper's Bazaar* and *The Atlantic Monthly*. In her later life she became principally known for her work in entomology and botany. One of the founders of The New York Entomological Society, she wrote scientific papers and collected a vast number of insects, over one hundred of which bear her name as collector of their first specimens.

Clark Ashton Smith

The Devotee of Evil

Published with permission of CASiana Enterprises, the Literary Estate of Clark Ashton Smith.

(Originally Published in *The Double Shadow and Other Fantasies*, 1933)

Clark Ashton Smith (1893–1961) was born in Long Valley, California. He is well regarded as both a poet and a writer of horror, fantasy and science fiction stories. Along with H.P. Lovecraft and Robert E. Howard, he was a prolific contributor to the magazine *Weird Tales*. His stories are full of dark and imaginative creations, and glimpses into the worlds beyond. His unique writing style and incredible vision have led to many of his stories influencing later fantasy writers.

Lucy A. Snyder

Approaching Lavender

(Originally Published in Chiral Mad 2, 2013)

Lucy A. Snyder is the five-time Bram Stoker Award-winning author of over 100 published short stories. Her books include the forthcoming novel *The Girl with the Star-Stained Soul*, the novels *Spellbent*, *Shotgun Sorceress*, and *Switchblade Goddess*, and the collections *Garden of Eldritch Delights*, *While the Black Stars Burn*, *Soft Apocalypses*, *Chimeric Machines*, and *Installing Linux on a Dead Badger*. Her writing has appeared in publications such as *Asimov's Science Fiction*, *Apex Magazine*, *Nightmare Magazine*, *Pseudopod*, *Strange Horizons*, and *Best Horror of the Year*. She lives in Columbus, OH. Learn more at www.lucysnyder.com.

Harriet Prescott Spofford

Circumstance

(Originally Published in *The Atlantic Monthly*, 1860)

Harriet Prescott Spofford (1835–1921) was born in Maine, with the family moving to Massachusetts during her early life. From the age of seventeen she supported her family with her early published stories: her mother was an invalid and her father, one of the California Gold Rush Pioneers and a founder of Oregon City, suffered from paralysis. Spofford published over one hundred stories in the next few years, but it was her 1858 publication of 'In a Cellar' in *The Atlantic Monthly* that elevated her reputation and secured her future as a widely successful author.

Harriet Beecher Stowe

The Ghost in the Cap'n Brown House

(Originally Published in *The Atlantic Monthly*, 1870)

The American abolitionist and author Harriet Beecher Stowe (1811–96) is most known for her hugely influential 1852 novel *Uncle Tom's Cabin; or Life Among the Lowly*. She wrote short stories most of her life, but in 1850 she declared that she felt compelled to write about the problem of slavery. She began to write *Uncle Tom's Cabin*, whose impact in the run-up to the American Civil War proved Stowe to be a galvanizing force on the social issues of her day.

Edith Wharton
Kerfol
(Originally Published in *Scribner's Magazine*, 1916)
The Eyes
(Originally Published in *Scribners' Magazine*, 1910)
Edith Wharton (1862–1937), the Pulitzer Prize-winning writer of *The Age of Innocence*, was born in New York. As well as her talent as an American novelist, Wharton was also known for her short stories and designer career. Wharton was born into a controlled New York society where women were discouraged from achieving anything beyond a proper marriage. Defeating the norms, Wharton not only grew to become one of America's greatest writers, she grew to become a very self-rewarding woman. Writing numerous ghost stories and murderous tales such as 'The Lady's Maid's Bell', 'Mr. Jones' and 'Afterward', Wharton is widely known for the ghost tours that now take place at her old home, The Mount.

Valerie B. Williams
Amazing Patsy
(First Publication)
Valerie Williams is a 'military brat', grew up in many locations in the U.S. and Europe, and now lives near Charlottesville, Virginia. She got her love of writing (and of horror in particular) from her English mother. Her short horror story 'The Succession' appeared in *Skyline 2018*, the annual anthology of the Virginia Writers Club. Valerie is a member of the Horror Writers Association and worked with Stoker Award-winning author Tim Waggoner in the 2017 HWA Mentorship program. She survived the 2018 Borderlands Press Writers Boot Camp and participated in the 2018 HWA online writing group.

Nemma Wollenfang
The Hollow Tree
(First Publication)
Nemma Wollenfang is an MSc Postgraduate and prize-winning short story writer who lives in Northern England. Generally she adheres to Science Fiction – perhaps as a result of years in the laboratory cackling like a mad scientist – but she has been known to branch out. Her stories have appeared in several anthologies, including: *Dark Voices, Hidden Menagerie* and Chicken Soup for the Soul's *The Wonder of Christmas*, as well as previously in Flame Tree's Gothic Fantasy series. Two of her unpublished novels have now been shortlisted in, or won, awards.

Madeline Yale Wynne
The Little Room
(Originally Published in *Harper's Magazine*, 1895)
Madeline Yale Wynne (1847–1918) was an American artist, writer and teacher. Following her divorce in 1874, she studied painting at the Museum of Fine Arts, Boston, and pursued an interest in art. She began to write short stories in 1895, and her fiction appeared in publications like *Harper's Monthly* and *The Atlantic Monthly*. Accomplished in metalwork, woodwork, painting and weaving, she for many years worked closely with fellow craft-worker Annie Cabot Putnam in developing a strong arts and crafts scene in her community.

FLAME TREE PUBLISHING
Short Story Series
New & Classic Writing

Flame Tree's Gothic Fantasy books offer a carefully curated series of new titles, each with combinations of original and classic writing:

*Chilling Horror • Chilling Ghost • Science Fiction
Murder Mayhem • Crime & Mystery • Swords & Steam
Dystopia Utopia • Supernatural Horror • Lost Worlds
Time Travel • Heroic Fantasy • Pirates & Ghosts
Agents & Spies • Endless Apocalypse • Alien Invasion
Robots & AI • Lost Souls • Haunted House
Cosy Crime • Urban Crime*

Also, new companion titles offer rich collections of classic fiction, myths and tales in the gothic fantasy tradition:

*H.G. Wells • Lovecraft • Sherlock Holmes
Edgar Allan Poe • Bram Stoker • Mary Shelley
African Myths & Tales • Celtic Myths & Tales
Chinese Myths & Tales • Norse Myths & Tales
Greek Myths & Tales • Irish Fairy Tales
King Arthur & The Knights of the Round Table
Alice's Adventures in Wonderland • The Divine Comedy
The Wonderful Wizard of Oz • The Age of Queen Victoria • Brothers Grimm*

Available from all good bookstores, worldwide, and online at
flametreepublishing.com

See our new fiction imprint
FLAME TREE PRESS | FICTION WITHOUT FRONTIERS
New and original writing in Horror, Crime, SF and Fantasy

And join our monthly newsletter with offers and more stories:
FLAME TREE FICTION NEWSLETTER
flametreepress.com

GOTHIC FANTASY

For our books, calendars, blog
and latest special offers please see:
flametreepublishing.com